Surveying the scene, I saw that the birds filled the marsh to the shrouded distance, hundreds, perhaps thousands of them, broad wings fluttering and heads bobbing continually in between gaping their beaks to join their voices to the chorus.

They had much to sing about, for these beasts had been given a great bounty of carrion. Numerous as they were, there were more corpses than birds. They lay part-submerged in the murky bog water. Some were soldiers, their armour catching a dull gleam from the veiled sun. Others were churls, children and old folk among them. Here and there, I glimpsed the bright colours of noble garb. All had died by violence and the marsh was red with the blood leaking from their many wounds.

"This, Alwyn," Erchel told me with a shrill giggle. "This is what you made…"

A shout erupted from my throat and I lunged for him, sword rising high to cut him down. But, as is often the way in dreams, nothing came of my action. Erchel vanished and the blade met air.

"You saved her, you see."

I whirled, finding his crouched, leering form at my back. His face quivered with the same malicious enjoyment I had seen whenever he snared a living thing to torment.

"You saved the Risen Martyr," he taunted, his voice taking on a sing-song cadence. "And made a world of corpses…"

Praise for Anthony Ryan and
The Pariah

"Gritty and well-drawn, this makes a rich treat for George R. R. Martin fans." —*Publishers Weekly* (starred review)

"A gritty, heart-pounding tale of betrayal and bloody vengeance. I loved every single word."
—John Gwynne, author of *The Shadow of the Gods*

"A master storyteller." —Mark Lawrence, author of *Prince of Thorns*

"In *The Pariah*, Ryan creates a wonderfully slow burn and a protagonist who resonates in spite of—or because of—his flaws. I loved wandering with Alwyn from one scrape to the next, and I'm ready for more."
—Django Wexler, author of *Ashes of the Sun*

"*The Pariah* is Anthony Ryan at his best. A fast-paced, brutal fantasy novel with larger than life characters and a plot full of intrigue and suspense. With bloody twists and turns aplenty, this novel is destined to become a favourite of the grimdark community."
—*Grimdark Magazine*

By Anthony Ryan

THE
MARTYR

BOOK TWO OF
THE COVENANT OF STEEL

ANTHONY RYAN

orbitbooks.net

Copyright © 2022 by Anthony Ryan
Excerpt from *The Justice of Kings* copyright © 2022 by Richard Swan
Excerpt from *Engines of Empire* copyright © 2022 by R. S. Ford

Cover design by Lauren Panepinto
Cover illustration by Jaime Jones
Cover copyright © 2022 by Hachette Book Group, Inc.
Map by Anthony Ryan
Author photograph by Ellie Grace Photography

Orbit
Hachette Book Group
1290 Avenue of the Americas
New York, NY 10104
orbitbooks.net

First Edition: June 2022
Simultaneously published in Great Britain by Orbit

Orbit is an imprint of Hachette Book Group.
The Orbit name and logo are trademarks of Little, Brown Book Group Limited.

The publisher is not responsible for websites (or their content)
that are not owned by the publisher.

The Hachette Speakers Bureau provides a wide range of authors for speaking events. To find out more, go to www.hachettespeakersbureau.com or call (866) 376-6591.

Library of Congress Control Number: 2022930920

ISBNs: 9780316430807 (trade paperback), 9780316430791 (ebook)

Printed in the United States of America

LSC-C

Printing 1, 2022

Dedicated to the memory of the late Lloyd Alexander,
author of The Chronicles of Prydain, *who first threw*
open the door and invited me in

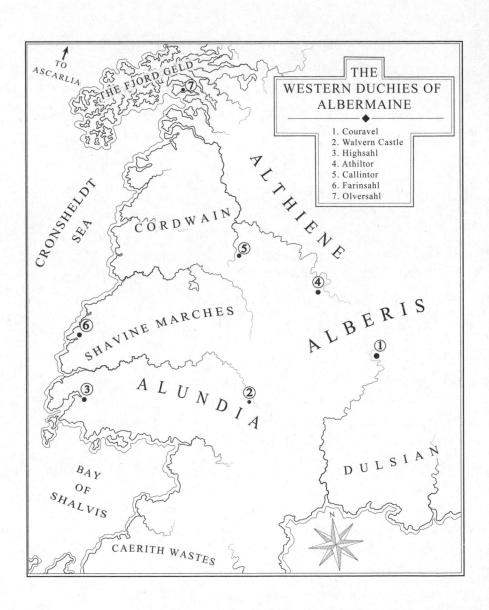

TO
ASCARLIA

THE FJORD GELD

⑦

CRONSHELDT
SEA

CORDWAIN

ALTHIENE

⑤

④

SHAVINE MARCHES

⑥

ALBERIS

①

③

ALUNDIA

②

DULSIAN

BAY
OF
SHALVIS

N

CAERITH WASTES

THE
WESTERN DUCHIES OF
ALBERMAINE
◆

1. Couravel
2. Walvern Castle
3. Highsahl
4. Athiltor
5. Callintor
6. Farinsahl
7. Olversahl

DRAMATIS PERSONAE

Alwyn Scribe – Outlaw, scribe and later Supplicant Blade in the Covenant Company

Evadine Courlain – Noble-born Captain of the Covenant Company, Communicant and later Aspirant cleric in the Covenant of Martyrs

Celynne Cohlsair – Duchess of Alundia, wife of Duke Oberharth, daughter of Duke Guhlton

Oberharth Cohlsair – Duke of Alundia

Roulgarth Cohlsair – Knight Warden of Alundia, younger brother to Duke Oberharth

Ducinda Cohlsair – Daughter to Oberharth and Celynne

Merick Albrisend – Baron of Lumenstor, nephew by marriage to Oberharth Cohlsair

Guhlton Pendroke – Duke of Althiene, father to Duchess Celynne

Erchel – Slain outlaw of vile inclinations

Shilva Sahken – Outlaw leader and friend of Deckin Scarl, The Outlaw King

King Tomas Algathinet – Monarch of Albermaine

Princess Leannor Algathinet-Keville – Sister to King Tomas

Ehlbert Bauldry – Knight of famed martial abilities, champion to King Tomas

Altheric Courlain – veteran knight of high standing, father to Evadine

Luminant Durehl Vearist – Principal Cleric of the Luminants' Council, governing body of the Covenant of Martyrs

Ascendant Arnabus – Senior Cleric in the Covenant of Martyrs and adviser to Princess Leannor

Aspirant Viera – Cleric and Senior Librarian of the Covenant Library at Athiltor

Alfric Keville – Son to Princess Leannor and the late Lord Alferd Keville

Magnis Lochlain – Pretender to the Throne of Albermaine, also known as the "True King"

Lorine Blousset (formerly Lorine D'Ambrille) – Duchess of the Shavine Marches, former lover of Deckin Scarl the Outlaw King and associate of Alwyn

Albyrn Swain – Supplicant Captain of the Covenant Company

Ofihla Barrow – Supplicant Sergeant of the Covenant Company

Delric Cleymount – Supplicant and healer of the Covenant Company

The Sack Witch – Caerith spell worker and healer, said to be of hideous appearance beneath the sackcloth mask she wears. Also known as the *Doenlisch* in the Caerith tongue

Wilhum Dornmahl – Disgraced turncoat knight formerly in service to the Pretender. Childhood friend to Evadine. Soldier in the Covenant Company

Eamond Astier – Former novice Supplicant and volunteer member of the Mounted Guard of the Covenant Company

Ayin – Soldier in the Covenant Company and page to Lady Evadine Courlain

Juhlina (known also as the Widow) – Former adherent to the Most Favoured pilgrimage sect, recruit to the Covenant Company

Fletchman – Former poacher and soldier in the Covenant Company

Tiler – Former outlaw and soldier in the Covenant Company

Aurent Vassier – Skilled artisan and builder of siege engines, in service to Princess Leannor

Liahm Woodsman – Former churl, member of the Commons Crusade and recruit to the Covenant Company

Elfons Raphine – Minor Alberis noble and commander of a free-sword company during the Alundian campaign. Later Protector Royal of Alundia

Chops – Alundian rebel and outlaw of treacherous character

Uhlla – Caerith village headwoman

Kuhlin – Caerith woodsman, Uhlla's grandson

Lilat – Caerith huntress, Uhlla's great-niece

The Eithlisch – Caerith of arcane power and importance

Estrik – Soldier in the Covenant Company, Sergeant Castellan of Walvern Castle, later the Martyr's Reach

Desmena Lehville – Rebel knight in service to the Pretender Magnis Lochlain

WHAT HAS GONE BEFORE . . .

Missive to the Luminant's Council of the Eastern Reformed Covenant of Martyrs – Archivist's note: fragment only. Date and author unknown.

Blessed Brethren of the Council,

It is with greatest excitement that I relate the following news: I have in my possession what I believe to be a genuine personal narrative penned by none other than that figure of direst legend – Alwyn Scribe himself.

I will, of course, forward a full transcript of the Scribe's account once I have completed my labours. Yet, I am able, having read the manuscript in its malign entirety, to provide a summation of its contents. I presume upon your good graces to not judge this poor scholar for merely stating the Scribe's falsehoods. Rest assured my soul remains unsullied by heresy.

It should come as scant surprise to learn that Alwyn Scribe had a wretched beginning. Born into a whorehouse, he never knew his own mother, nor his father, and claims to have been named after the whoremaster's favourite pig. Cast out at a young age, he naturally fell in with a band of miscreants bedevilling a region known as the Shavine Forest, located in one of the western coastal duchies of what was then the Kingdom of Albermaine.

The leader of this pack of villains, a self-styled Outlaw King, went by the name Deckin Scarl. I can attest to the existence of this person since many surviving ballads and tales from this region make mention of him, and his beauteous but scheming paramour Lorine D'Ambrille. According to the Scribe, Scarl was in fact the unacknowledged bastard of the local duke, a noble who had recently lost his head due to treachery against King Tomas Algathinet, Monarch of Albermaine. Scarl learned of his father's fall from a band of Fjord Geld exiles led by a learned young woman named Berrine Jurest, of whom more will be spoken later. A man of ruthless cunning but excessive ambition, Scarl hatched a plot to usurp the newly installed duke. However, the band was betrayed and ambushed by crown soldiers led by the dreaded King's Champion Sir Ehlbert Bauldry. Alwyn, as is the way with vermin, contrived to escape the subsequent massacre, murdering one of his own compatriots in the process.

Beset by a curious sense of loyalty that puts one in mind of a beaten dog's attachment to its master, Alwyn made his way to the castle where the captured Scarl had been taken, arriving just in time to watch his execution. Unable to resist an inclination towards indulgence, Alwyn then resolved to drown his grief in drink, leading to his own capture by kingsmen. A sound beating was followed by a hanging, interrupted by the intervention of one Sir Althus Levalle, Knight Commander of the Crown Company. Although Sir Althus spared Alwyn the noose, he did not spare him the pillory and many hours suffering the torments of the local churls. When the ordeal was done, Sir Althus explained to Alwyn that his mercy arose from a prior association with Deckin Scarl, for they had served together as soldiers in the Duchy Wars. So Alwyn would live, but only for as long as he could survive the notorious Pit Mines, a terrible place of underground toil that no condemned soul ever escaped.

Alwyn's facility for untruth makes itself plain in his description of his journey to the Pit Mines. He claims to have been taken there by a Caerith gaoler known as the chainsman, a man with an unnatural facility for hearing the voices of the dead. I ascribe this to the Scribe's desire to enliven his tale with fanciful nonsense, however his patent dread of this Caerith mystic does ring true. It was during this journey that Alwyn became acquainted with a young thief named Toria, forming a fractious friendship that would nevertheless endure for several years.

Upon being cast into the Pit Mines, Alwyn had the good fortune to come under the wing of one Sihlda Doisselle. Ascendant Sihlda, as you know, Blessed Brethren, has been named a Martyr by lesser branches of the Covenant. She is often cited as an exemplar of the importance of adhering to truth in the face of deceitful authority, an attitude that saw her condemned to the Pit on supposedly false charges of murder. Apparently unconcerned by her imprisonment, Sihlda went about forming her fellow inmates into a faithful congregation. The Scribe's legend is rich in allusions to the tutelage he received at the Sihlda's hands and his own account leaves no doubt that, but for her, he would never have been named Scribe. His facility for letters and scholarly skills were the fruit of her teachings and it was through her careful guidance that he formed the conclusion that the betrayal of Deckin's band had been orchestrated by Lorine D'Ambrille. It was also from Sihlda's lips that he learned another secret of gravest import, to be revealed in due course. Despite the fondness she exhibited towards him, it is my contention that had she known the nature of the creature she nurtured, she would have sunk a pickaxe into Alwyn's head the moment she met him.

It was through Sihlda's clever machinations and the tunnelling efforts of her congregation that Alwyn was able to escape the Pit Mines after four long years. He describes Sihlda's sacrifice to ensure his escape, collapsing the tunnel and killing herself and her congregation apart from a devotional brute named Brewer and the foul-mouthed but ever loyal Toria. Together, the three of them succeeded in evading their pursuers to reach the Covenant Sanctuary City of Callintor. Here Alwyn was able to persuade the local Ascendant to grant refuge in return for handing over a copy of Sihlda's Testament, a most valuable document to any cleric.

But, though now tutored and lettered, Alwyn retained the heart of a vicious outlaw. This came to the fore when he espied a former associate named Erchel. Believing Erchel, a vile creature of bestial inclinations, to have been part of Lorine's scheme, Alwyn resolved to torture to the truth from him. However, before he could do so, Erchel's dire habits led to him being gelded by a one Ayin, a sweet-natured girl of uncomplicated manners that concealed a lethal tendency towards men of violently carnal nature. Despite being innocent of Erchel's death, Alwyn was soon blamed for the murder. Fortunately, it is at this juncture that he would make the most fateful meeting of his life.

The Scroll of the Risen Martyr Evadine Courlain relates that she did indeed call at Callintor around this time. Charged with raising the first Covenant Company to contend the resurgence of the Pretender's Rebellion, Martyr Evadine sought recruits from among the gathered villainy of the Sanctuary City. Driven not by any faithful leanings but a desire to escape the noose, Alwyn and his two companions enlisted under Martyr Evadine's banner. They were also joined by the guileless Ayin to whom Alwyn exhibits a curiously protective attitude. There are numerous tales regarding the Scribe's apparently genuine bravery at the subsequent Battle of the Traitor's Field, but his own account paints a picture of reluctant if undoubtedly effective participation. He also confirms the widely held belief that he saved Martyr Evadine's life at one point.

Most of the Pretender's Horde were slaughtered in the rout, but Evadine managed to secure the person of Sir Wilhum Dornmahl, a childhood friend. Marked as a traitor, Wilhum was stripped of his titles but spared death by enlisting in the Covenant Company.

It was in the aftermath of battle that Alwyn besmirched his soul by seeking out a Caerith healer known as the Sack Witch to tend to Brewer, mortally stricken by a poison arrow. The Sack Witch was so named due to her habit of going about with a sack on her head, apparently to conceal the hideous, ravaged visage lurking beneath. Before agreeing to heal Brewer, she struck a bargain with Alwyn: in return for healing his friend he must accept from her hands a small, ancient book written in a script he couldn't decipher. Mystified by this, he agreed and Brewer lived to see the dawn. The exact nature of the brute's healing is not recorded but it is clear that Alwyn ascribes it to the Sack Witch's unearthly powers.

Here the narrative tracks with the accepted tale of Martyr Evadine, relating how the Covenant Company was sent north to the port of Olversahl in the troubled duchy of the Fjord Geld to stave off local rebellion and the encroachment of the heathen Ascarlians. While in Olversahl, Alwyn became reacquainted with Berrine Jurest, now a custodian of the famed Library of King Aeric. Persuading her to translate the book given to him by the Sack Witch, he learned it had been written in an archaic form of Caerith script and contained a near verbatim account of their prior meeting in the Shavine Woods. Before Alwyn could discover more, the Port of Olversahl was overrun by a horde of ravening Ascarlians. Martyr Evadine suffered severe wounds at the hands of a figure known as the Tielwald but was saved by Alwyn and Wilhum. The survivors of the Covenant Company sailed away in captured Ascarlian ships while Olversahl and its famed library were consumed by heathen flames.

Arriving in the port city of Farinsahl, Martyr Evadine lay near death for days until Alwyn and Captain Swain of the Covenant Company conspired to damn their souls with a plan to heal her: Alwyn would seek out the Sack Witch and prevail upon her to heal their beloved commander. Upon venturing forth to seek out the Sack Witch, Alwyn found himself swiftly captured by the chainsman. Convinced by his imaginary spirits that Alwyn would one day orchestrate his demise, the chainsman had been plotting his death for years. Bound to a tree, Alwyn could only suffer the chainsman's torments and await his end. At this point Lorine D'Ambrille, now risen to Duchess of the Shavine Marches, appeared and revealed that she conspired with the Chainsman in Alwyn's capture. She further stated that she was innocent of betraying Deckin, that crime being the work of a man named Todman, long since dead by her hand. To illustrate the truth of her words, she killed the Chainsman, saving Alwyn but also punishing him for his incautious tongue by leaving him tied to a tree.

Alwyn was saved from eventual starvation by the appearance of the Sack Witch. Freeing Alwyn, she took back the book she had given him, along with Berrine's instructions on how to translate it. She also revealed that the face beneath the sack she wore to be far from ravaged. Together, they returned to Farinsahl where, and it pains my faithful heart to relate these words, Alwyn Scribe claims to have partaken in an arcane rite that saved the Lady Evadine from imminent death. Her resurrection at the hands of the Seraphile was, he attests, merely a delusion born of delirium. He further compounds this blasphemy by alluding to some form of carnal attraction between himself and the Risen Martyr. I hope you see now, Blessed Brethren, the grave need to keep this narrative from all but the most devout eyes.

The account is surprisingly concordant with scripture in its subsequent description of Martyr Evadine's famous address to the Faithful of Farinsahl, and the nefarious conspiracy that saw her ambushed and kidnapped by rogue servants of the Crown fearful of her ascendancy. Alwyn adds certain illuminating details, such as the death of Brewer at the hands of Martyr Evadine's kidnappers. It was also at this point that Alwyn severed his alliance with Toria who opted to flee the impending crisis on board a smuggler's vessel. Alwyn claims his refusal to accompany her arose from some form of arcane bond with the Risen Martyr. Given his character, I am more inclined to ascribe it to a villain's nose for a potentially lucrative gamble.

Whatever his motives, Alwyn accompanied the Covenant Company to Castle Ambris where Martyr Evadine had been subjected to a farce trial conducted by an obscure cleric named Arnabus. Condemned to death on spurious charges of treason and blasphemy, the Risen Martyr faced the noose until Alwyn, clad in armour borrowed from Wilhum Dornmahl, forced his way through the crowd to assert the right to contest the verdict by combat. This aspect of Martyr Evadine's story is too well attested by other sources to be denied – Alwyn Scribe did indeed fight a duel with Knight Commander Sir Althus Levalle that day, winning great acclaim thanks to his success in holding his own against a renowned veteran knight, at least for a time. It was during this duel that Alwyn revealed the secret entrusted to him by Ascendant Sihlda Doiselle, the secret that had seen her condemned to the Pit Mines: King Tomas of Albermaine was in truth the bastard son of his champion with no right to sit the throne.

Beaten down by the enraged Knight Commander, Alwyn was saved from the killing stroke by the Risen Martyr. Having leapt clear of the scaffold, Martyr Evadine struck down Sir Althus with a stolen sword, whereupon a combined force of Covenant soldiery and faithful churls launched an attack upon the Crown Company. Martyr Evadine and her followers spirited a near-dead Alwyn away in the ensuing chaos, carrying him back to the woods where he had spent his misbegotten youth. Martyr and outlaw were now united in rebellion, but could such a union ever last?

PART I

I have heard it asked, though only ever in whispers: "Ascendant, was the Scourge real? Did the Seraphile truly bring fire and destruction down upon the earth to cleanse it of the Malecite? Can it be believed that thousands perished and great cities fell in this tumult of fiery salvation?"

My answer, though many will condemn me for it, has always been thus: "Does it matter?"

From *The Testament of Ascendant Sihlda Doisselle*,
as recorded by Sir Alwyn Scribe

CHAPTER ONE

I found Erchel waiting for me in the dream. Of all the many dead souls littering my memory, it chose him. Not sweet, light-fingered Gerthe. Not Deckin, the fearsome, mad but occasionally wise Outlaw King. Not even faith-addled, tiresome Hostler who I had left murdered in my wake one snowbound night years ago. No, it was Erchel who greeted me with a leering grin, stained teeth dark in the bleached white of his face, fresh blood dripping from the rent and ragged fabric of his crotch. Despite his grin, I could tell he wasn't pleased to see me, but then castration was sure to have a souring effect on even the kindliest soul, not that he had ever been kindly in life.

"Come to see, have you, Alwyn?" he asked, head dipping and swaying on his scrawny neck. It lengthened and twisted like a snake as he spoke, his voice that of a desperate beggar rather than a gelded sadist with a grievance. "Come to see what you made, eh?"

His hands, longer and spindlier of finger than I recalled, scratched and jabbed at the plate armour of the vambrace covering my forearm, leaving red stains on the metal.

"A knight now, eh?" he hissed in gleeful realisation, head bobbing on his elongated neck. "Risen high have you? Higher than poor Erchel ever could. High enough to spare some coin for an old friend."

"I'm not a knight," I told him, jerking my arm free of his touch which stung despite the armour. "And we were never friends."

"Don't be a tight-fist to poor old Erchel." He crouched in a peevish sulk, long-fingered hand clutching at the bloody mess between his legs. "He's got no tackle, remember? You let that little bitch slice it off."

"Didn't let her do anything," I reminded him. "Though I can't claim that I would've stopped her."

He clenched his teeth, emitting a sound that was a grotesque melange of laugh and hiss. "She'll get what's coming," he assured me, teeth chattering as something dark and wet coiled in the shadowed recess of his mouth. "You'll see to that."

Possessed of a sudden rage, I reached for my sword, drawing it free to find that Erchel had already moved beyond the reach of my blade. "Come, come," he said, beckoning. "Don't you want to see what you made?"

A gust of wind sent a pall of fog across the tufted grass surrounding us, rendering Erchel into a crouch-backed shadow. Soft ground squelched beneath my boots as I pursued him, drawn by curiosity as much as the desire to hack him down, a pleasure that had been denied me in the waking world. It was apparent we were in a marsh, but not one I recognised. The fog was thick all around, obscuring any land-marks save the uneven, twisted shades of rocky tors rising from the bogs; silent, unmoving monsters in the gloom. Wherever we were, it was a place I didn't know.

I soon lost sight of Erchel in the haze and spent a brief interval wandering the marsh in aimless hunting until the faint cry of some unseen beast drew me on like a beacon. It was an unfamiliar call that mixed a grating hiss with a guttural roar, growing in volume and joined by others to form a discordant chorus. The source became clear when the wind once again dispelled the fog to reveal a large bird perched on a half-sunken corpse. I had never seen its like before, as big as an eagle but lacking any kind of majesty. Like Erchel's dream-self, the bird's head bobbed on an elongated neck, bright, bulbous eyes regarding me with baleful hunger above a gore-flecked beak that resembled a barbed cleaver. The beak parted as the bird let out another ugly cry, the sound mirrored by many throats.

"They're called vultures, so I'm told," Erchel informed me, eyes agleam as he enjoyed the sight of my horrified disgust.

Surveying the scene, I saw that the birds filled the marsh to the shrouded distance, hundreds, perhaps thousands of them, broad wings fluttering and heads bobbing continually in between gaping their beaks to join their voices to the chorus. They had much to sing about, for these beasts had been given a great bounty of carrion. Numerous as they were, there were more corpses than birds. They lay part-submerged in the murky bog water. Some were soldiers, their armour catching a dull gleam from the veiled sun. Others were churls, children and old folk among them. Here and there, I glimpsed the bright colours of noble garb. All had died by violence and the marsh was red with the blood leaking from their many wounds.

"This, Alwyn," Erchel told me with a shrill giggle. "This is what you made . . ."

A shout erupted from my throat and I lunged for him, sword rising high to cut him down. But, as is often the way in dreams, nothing came of my action. Erchel vanished and the blade met air.

"You saved her, you see."

I whirled, finding his crouched, leering form at my back. His face quivered with the same malicious enjoyment I had seen whenever he snared a living thing to torment.

"You saved the Risen Martyr," he taunted, his voice taking on a sing-song cadence. "And made a world of corpses . . ."

I raised the sword level with my chest, both hands on the handle, intending to skewer this leering wretch through one of his bright, unblinking eyes. Once again, he slipped into nothingness when I thrust, only to cast more taunts at my back.

"What did you think you had accomplished?" he asked, his tone a parody of genuine curiosity. He stood in the water alongside the vulture, now busily worrying at the corpse it perched upon. "Did you really imagine keeping her in this world would make it better?"

"Shut up!" I grated, advancing towards him.

"Did you learn nothing from Ascendant Sihlda?" Erchel enquired, overlong neck raising his head to an unnatural height, eyebrow arched in judgemental enquiry. "How shamed she would be to look upon you now . . ."

An inchoate roar of fury escaped me as I charged towards him, sword angled for a swipe that would sever his head from that snake neck. Instead, I found myself plunging into the marsh water, the weight of my armour dragging me beneath the surface. Panic flared and I thrashed, casting the sword away to claw for the surface. When I tasted air again, I found Erchel floating above, the vulture perched on his shoulder. Above him the sky grew dark as the other birds took flight, forming a dense, circling mass.

"My friends won't finish you right away," Erchel promised me in grave assurance before adding with a broadening grin, "Not until I've had the pleasure of watching them bite your balls off. I wonder if you'll scream as loud as I did."

Letting out a squawk, the huge bird on his shoulder flared its wings then leapt for me, long claws extending to clamp onto my head, pushing me down into the marsh once more. It kept hold as I sank, talons shredding the steel vambrace like paper, beak tearing into the skin beneath, tugging at the flesh, tugging, tugging . . .

"Alwyn!"

My hand lashed out to snare the beak tearing into the meat of my forearm, instead closing on the smoothness of a human wrist. A startled yelp banished the dream, the swirl of red water fading to reveal Ayin's frowning face. I stared into her bemused eyes for a second, feeling the caress of winter's chill, senses flooded by the familiar sounds and scents of a camp at sunrise.

"Dreaming again?" Ayin asked with a pointed glance at my hand still enclosing her wrist.

"Sorry," I mumbled, releasing my grip. I shifted on the collection of furs and sundry fabric that formed my bed, sitting up to run a hand through tousled hair. My head was filled with the throbbing ache that had greeted me ever since waking to full consciousness two weeks before, the legacy of Sir Althus Levalle, slain and unlamented

Knight Commander of the Crown Company. Whatever the many criticisms I could voice regarding his character, the strength of his arm could never be doubted.

"I don't dream any more," Ayin told me. "Not since the captain blessed me."

"That's . . . good," I replied, looking about for the small green bottle that was rarely far from my reach these days.

"You should get her to bless you too," Ayin went on. "Then you won't dream either. What did you dream about?"

A man you cut the balls from not so long ago. I caged the snapped response before it could reach my lips. Irritating though she could be, Ayin didn't deserve such a harsh reminder of her former nature. Although, given what I had seen her do to that Ascendant in Farinsahl following Evadine's abduction, I was no longer sure she had been fully cured of her prior tendencies.

"Did you ever hear tell of a vulture?" I asked instead.

"No." She blinked blank eyes and shrugged. "What is it?"

"A big, ugly bird that eats corpses, apparently."

I let out a thin sigh of relief as I found the green bottle nestling beneath the rolled blanket that served as my pillow. Supplicant Delric called the bottle's contents his "deceiving elixir" on account of its ability to banish pains without applying any curative effect. Deceiver or not, I was continually grateful for the speed with which the bitter, oily concoction would dispel the throb in my head. Delric's face had been the first I saw upon waking from my prolonged, beating-induced slumber, finding his features arranged in a disconcerting aspect of surprise. He had spent some time carefully prodding my head with his deft fingers, grunting now and then as they traced over the various ridges and bumps, one being of particular interest.

"Did that bastard crack my skull?" I had enquired as his fingers lingered.

"Yes," he told me with brisk honesty. "Seems to be healing, though." With that he had handed me the green bottle with instructions that I return to him every day for more head prodding. Also, I was to seek him out immediately should my nose or ears start bleeding.

"Lessons," Ayin said, shifting her satchel from her shoulder to her lap. "I've got some new ink, parchment too."

I grimaced and swallowed another drop from the bottle before replacing the stopper. Delric had warned that overuse would make me a slave of this stuff if I wasn't careful, although it was a daily struggle to resist the urge to gulp down as much as my tongue could bear.

"From where?" I asked, returning the bottle to its place beneath my pillow.

"Those folk from Ambriside brought more supplies this morning. Another bunch've recruits too. I did a count." She reached into her satchel to retrieve a scrap of parchment inscribed with some laboured tally marks. "That makes one thousand, one hundred and eighty-two."

Not yet an army, I thought. *But in a month or two, it could be.* The notion raised uncomfortable questions regarding the inevitable reaction of Duke Elbyn and, more importantly, King Tomas to the prospect of a great many ardent followers of the Risen Martyr gathering in the Shavine Woods. In truth, I found myself surprised each day when our scouts failed to report any incursion by Crown or ducal soldiery.

"Lessons," Ayin said again, poking my shoulder with insistent emphasis. Successive days spent tutoring her in letters and numeracy revealed her to be a student of perhaps overly keen attentiveness. Many churls looked upon reading and writing as some form of arcane art, known only to clerics or the better educated nobles. At first, Ayin had been little different, regarding the characters I had her copy out with a frown of suspicious bafflement. However, this had swiftly given way to delighted comprehension once she grasped the basic idea that these abstract scratchings represented component sounds which could be fused into words. Her hand remained clumsy and her letters uneven, but her reading was already remarkable in its fluency, lacking the prolonged laboured vowels and stumbles that had been such a feature of my early lessons.

"We haven't finished the first revelation of Martyr Stevanos," she reminded me, extracting a scroll from her satchel. In teaching her,

I had adopted Ascendant Sihlda's practice of reciting principal Covenant scripture and having her write it down, correcting her spelling and grammar in the process. "We just got to the bit where he resisted the lustful temptations of that Malecite whore Denisha."

Ayin unfurled the scroll with features brightened by anticipation, making me ponder the bizarre bundle of contradictions she represented. In many ways she remained a guileless child, as innocent and trusting as any infant obliged to navigate the swirl of confusion that is this world. But she was also a multiple murderer who exhibited scant guilt for her crimes. Her devotion to Evadine, our Anointed Captain and Risen Martyr, was as fierce as ever and she displayed a zeal for the more lurid elements of Covenant lore I found troubling, especially in the aftermath of my dream.

"I think we'll try something different today," I said, reaching for my boots.

We emerged from the notch between two ancient stone blocks where I made my shelter, finding the sun bright and sky clear above the matrix of bare branches. Although I had no memory of it, I had directed our fleeing company to this spot during my delirious interval following Evadine's rescue beneath the walls of Castle Ambris. However, it was clear that, while its many pre-Scourge ruins made a perfect hideout for a band of outlaws, it had already been outgrown by the burgeoning throng of Evadine's followers. Trees had been felled to create makeshift huts for the company soldiers and our new recruits, most of whom were suffering the attentions of Sergeant Swain and the other Supplicant Blades this morning.

"Stand straight, I said!" Swain barked at one lanky churl as he vainly attempted to shuffle into place in the first rank of a ragged cohort. "Don't you know what straight is, you dung-brained piss-streak?"

From the fellow's gaping, wide-eyed response, I did in fact doubt that the concept of straightness had ever been taught to him.

"Martyrs preserve us," Swain muttered, snatching the lanky fellow's pike from his grip. "This," he said, holding the weapon vertically, "is straight. So is this." Levelling the pike, he shoved the shaft hard into the gaping churl's chest, sending him sprawling into the row behind along with those standing to either side. "Fail to stand straight in a battle line and you'll suffer worse than a chilled arse," Swain told him. "Get up!"

I could see other troops receiving similarly harsh treatment, spread out among the sparse clearings in this stretch of the deep forest. The recruits were a mixed bag, callow youths with no knowledge of arms mingled with veterans or those who had at least once marched with the ducal levies. They were almost all churls rather than townsfolk, imbued with a deep if poorly expressed desire to follow the Risen Martyr. A few clerics had also appeared in recent days, young novices for the most part who hadn't yet been confirmed as Supplicants. Much as the increasing number of churls stirred worries over the reaction of the king, the arrival of deserters from the orthodox faith would surely inflame rather than diminish the Covenant hierarchy's disapproval of one they still refused to acknowledge as a Risen Martyr.

I guided Ayin away from the shouts and curses of soldiers in training, leading her from the ruins to a shallow stream. Frost dusted its banks and the moss-covered stones jutting from its current. I gathered my cloak and perched on a boulder near a bend in the stream's course, waiting in silence until Ayin prodded my arm again.

"What are we . . . ?"

"Wait," I told her, eyes on the middle of the stream where a large rock rose from the water. The bird appeared soon after, fluttering down to perch on the stone and poke its small beak into the moss in search of mites.

"What do you see?" I asked Ayin.

"A bird on a stone," she said, squinting in bafflement.

"What manner of bird?"

"A redbreast." Her squint faded a little as her perennial liking for animals asserted itself. "It's pretty."

"Yes." I nodded to her satchel. "Write it down."

"Write what down?"

"What you see. The bird, the stone, the stream. Write it all down."

This was another of Sihlda's lessons, albeit one I had been obliged to rely on my memory to accomplish, since there were so few scenes of any variety in the Pit Mines worthy of description.

Ayin duly reached into her satchel for her quill, ink, parchment and the flat wooden board she used as a desk. The sight of the crudely carved thing summoned a pang for my marvellous, foldable writing desk which I had lost in the chaos of Olversahl's sacking at the hands of the Ascarlians.

Doubt lingered on Ayin's face as she removed the stopper from the ink pot, asking, "What for?"

"Merely recreating the words of others will not truly teach you how to write," I told her. "Real skill comes with understanding."

Squinting again, she settled herself beside me, carefully placing the ink pot so it wouldn't topple before dipping her quill and beginning to write. As was our custom, I corrected her mistakes as she worked, sometimes guiding her hand to form the characters. Her lettering remained a clumsy, jagged scrawl but in recent days had begun to acquire a basic legibility. Today she was more hesitant than usual, the quill faltering on the parchment much as mine had when Sihlda first set me to this lesson. Rote learning was always easier, but, if she was ever to become a true scribe, Ayin would need to craft her own words.

"The redbreast sits on the rock," she read after a few moments' toil, a prideful smile on her lips. While she still seemed a child to my eyes, when she smiled I was reminded she was in fact now a young woman, and a comely one at that. I found it dispiriting and distracting in equal measure.

"Good," I said. "Keep going. Describe the bird, describe the rock. And not just what you see. What sound does the stream make? What does the air smell of?"

I watched her quill scratch away for a time but my mind soon began to wander back to the dream. I wanted to think that the sight of previously unseen birds feasting on corpses was just the product of a mind subjected to recent trauma. Who knew what effects a cracked skull might have on the brain within? However, the birds had seemed more real, more detailed in their form than seemed possible for mere figments of a distressed imagination. Also, Erchel's words possessed a grating note of truth that set them apart from the nonsensical utterances of those we encounter in our nightly sojourns. *You saved the Risen Martyr, and made a world of corpses . . .*

I shivered, drawing my cloak tight and becoming aware of the tune Ayin hummed as she worked. Her voice was a pleasant, naturally melodious thing, her humming occasionally giving way to short verses. Usually, these were nonsense ditties formed with scant allusion to anything save rhyme, but today her song possessed a modicum of sense.

"*So goodbye to you all, my sisters, my brothers,*" she sang, the tune novel but pleasingly sombre. "*Goodbye to you all, my brethren of steel . .* "

"What's that?" I asked, causing her to glance up from the parchment.

"Just a tune," she said, shrugging. "I sing when I work."

"Did you make it up?"

"I make up all my songs. Always have since I was young. Ma liked it when I sang for her." Her expression clouded a little. "She'd be less angry when I sang so I did it a lot."

I gestured to the parchment. "Write it down, the one you were just singing."

She gave a doubtful frown. "I don't know how to letter all the words."

"I'll show you."

Her hand was even more hesitant than usual at first, but soon grew in confidence and clarity as she warmed to her task, singing the verses as she wrote them. "*For here do we come to the eve of our battle, and here do I know that my fate will be sealed . . .*"

"That's all of it?" I asked a while later when she had filled the entire sheet with verse.

"All I've thought up, anyway."

"What do you call it? A good song needs a title."

"'The Battle Song', 'cause I started singing bits of it after the Traitors' Field."

"That's a little obvious." I took the quill and parchment from her and added a title to the top of the verse, putting flourishes to the letters for good measure.

"'The Warrior's Fate,'" Ayin read, pursing her lips in muted disdain.

"It's poetic," I said, a tint of annoyance to my voice, which she seemed to find amusing.

"If you say so."

Frowning at her impish smile, I pondered the wisdom of a rebuke, but quickly forgot it as the sound of a voice calling my name drifted through the trees. A young man soon appeared, face flushed as he hurried towards us, tripping over a root and nearly falling flat on his face. Like many of the former Supplicant noviciates to flock to Evadine's banner, Eamond Astier was a child of town rather than country. These keen but often sheltered youngsters tended to traverse their new forest home with a clumsiness born as much from fear as unfamiliarity.

"Master Scribe," he said, the greeting emerging in a breathless gasp from reddened features. I swallowed a weary sigh when he gave an accompanying bow. Despite my lack of rank, many of the newcomers tended to honour me this way and I had given up telling them to stop. "The Anointed Lady requests your presence."

There was an urgency to his voice, also a small tremor that betrayed some measure of fear. Eamond was only a year or two shy of my own age, yet his smooth, beardless face appeared very young as he straightened. His eyes had the rapid blink of the uninitiated confronting the prospect of battle.

"Trouble?" I asked, handing the parchment back to Ayin.

"Scouts reported in from the east," he said, eyes flicking to Ayin before returning to me. I was impressed that he still managed to find himself distracted by a pretty face despite his fear. However, my amusement vanished as he went on, "They've come, Master Alwyn. The king's soldiers."

"And you're sure they're all kingsmen?"

From the way Fletchman nodded in servile confirmation I deduced this was the first time he had been directly addressed by the Anointed

Lady. He was clearly a stout fellow of some experience, a poacher judging by his rough but hardy garb and the ash bow he carried, yet he squirmed under the gaze of the Risen Martyr Evadine Courlain like a bashful child.

"How many?" Swain asked.

"I counted a hundred, Supplicant Sergeant," Fletchman replied. "Could be just a vanguard, o'course. We thought it best to bring word rather than linger. They're camped at Shriver's Orchard, 'bout eight miles east of here."

"Camped?" I asked, frowning in surprise.

"That they are, Master Scribe," the poacher told me, his tone less respectful but markedly more comfortable. Outlaws tend to recognise their own. "Thought it strange, myself. No ranging for tracks nor scouting for trails. And they haven't brought any hunters or hounds. Just a hundred mounted men under three banners."

"Three banners," Evadine repeated. Her voice was soft but I detected a note of dismay in her next words. "Please describe them."

"The tallest is the king's banner, my lady. Two big gold cats. The second was a rose, black on a white flag. The third was just a pennant striped in red and blue."

I saw Evadine and Wilhum exchange a glance at the description of the second banner, it being one they knew very well. I knew it too, having seen it in the aftermath of the Battle of the Traitors' Field, the day the legend of the Anointed Lady truly began. Also the day her childhood friend and turncoat noble Wilhum Dornmahl had been delivered into her hands by a knight bearing a shield adorned with a black rose on a white background.

"A blue and red pennant is the flag of truce," Evadine told Fletchman. She smiled and reached out to clasp his hand, the fellow immediately sinking to one knee at her touch. "Please don't, good sir," she told him. "Only princes require such formality. Rise with my thanks for your fine deed this day. Go now and rest."

"A truce, then," Wilhum said after the scout had retreated, head still bowed despite Evadine's instruction. "Clever of King Tomas to send him of all his knights."

"Clever," Evadine agreed before a flicker of annoyance passed over her brow. "Or cruel."

"A hundred kingsmen is a decent force," Swain said. "But one we can deal with, if need be."

"If that's all there is," I pointed out. I settled a careful gaze on Evadine before adding, "If it's a trap, it's well baited."

"You imagine I am about to ride blindly into this camp, Master Scribe?" Evadine asked, arching an eyebrow.

"I imagine the king, or his advisers, knew to send the one knight you would be sure to spare. But, if they came without hounds, it's a good sign. It might mean they actually want to talk."

"We left a great many dead kingsmen at Castle Ambris," Wilhum said. "Along with their knight commander, slain while enforcing the laws of both Crown and Covenant. That's a weight not easily balanced."

"For a rebel lord or a common outlaw, perhaps," I returned, eyes still on Evadine. "But not a Risen Martyr."

Evadine folded her arms and lowered her head. She was clad in the simple cotton trews and shirt she wore when shorn of her armour, with a bearskin cloak draped about her shoulders to ward against the cold. Her face was pale, as always, but by now I knew it well enough to discern an additional pitch of fatigue; the slightly drawn mouth and pink tinge to her eyes indicated a sleepless night, or at least a troubled sleep. It made me wonder if she too suffered a nightmare and, if so, had she also seen vultures?

Finally, I saw the hardening of her mouth that told of a decision, another sign I had learned to read and mark well. Her decisions could mean life or death for all of us. "Pick a hundred soldiers," she told Swain. "The best we have. At midday, we march to meet my father."

CHAPTER TWO

Upon seeing our party emerge from the treeline, Sir Altheric Courlain strode clear of the picket line surrounding the encamped kingsmen. The place was well chosen for defence. Shriver's Orchard was a long-disused farmstead comprising a cluster of tumbled buildings atop a low rise in the heart of a small clearing. The advantage of raised ground was augmented by a series of partly fallen stone walls, creating a useful barrier sure to impede an attacker's charge. It also afforded a certain surety against unwanted visitors. Outlaws tended to shun the place due to tales of Shriver's Shade, the lingering, malicious spirit of the long-dead orchard keeper who had murdered his family decades before. The story went that, having strangled them all due to an unspecified form of mania, he hung their bodies from the branches of his apple trees in the belief that they would grow back into life. When they failed to do so he expired under the weight of his guilt. As an unredeemed soul denied passage through the Divine Portals, he was condemned to wander his stead in eternal torment. Many had claimed to have seen him over the years, although I never had. The trees remained, unpruned, twisted versions of their prior selves, but if any bodies had ever adorned their branches, they were gone now.

Sir Altheric wore a fine leather jerkin in place of his armour and his only weapon was the longsword at his belt. He also carried the blue and red striped pennant as he strode forth, coming to a halt some twenty paces from the picket line to plant the flag in the earth. A man of impressive size and evident strength, it was an easy matter for him to sink the flagstaff deep enough to stay upright when he released his grip. That done, he stepped back and, in a pointed gesture, unbuckled his sword belt and tossed the weapon on the ground.

"You shouldn't go alone," Wilhum advised Evadine as she also removed her sword and handed it to him. "The spot he's chosen is too close to their line for my liking."

"I have every confidence in my father's attachment to honour," she told him. "Should any kingsmen sally forth to capture me, he'll kill them himself. However, I agree it would be best if another were present to hear what he has to say." She raised a hand as Wilhum began to remove his sword belt. "I mean no offence, Wil, but you know he has detested you ever since our broken betrothal, and you were never best disposed towards him either. I believe I shall require a more objective witness."

She turned to me with raised brows, gesturing at the waiting knight and pennant. "If you would do me the honour, Master Alwyn."

As we ascended the slope, Sergeant Swain barked orders at our hundred-strong escort, all Covenant Company veterans who had fought at both the Traitors' Field and Olversahl. He arranged them in a tight formation at the edge of the trees, ready to be sent forward at a rapid march should need arise. Sir Altheric adopted a pose that mirrored his daughter's: arms crossed and features set in appraisal, albeit considerably more stern of character. As might be expected, much of his attention was focused on Evadine, but he also deigned to afford me a long glance as we came to a halt a half-dozen paces from the pennant. I had only seen him fully armoured before and found his face very much an older, masculine version of Evadine's: high cheekbones and pale skin, his dark hair longer and beard thicker than was typical for knights. The inky tresses tumbled in the wind, shot through with streaks of silver, as his eyes tracked over my face before slipping back to Evadine.

"Father," she said, bowing low. I also bowed, dropping to one knee as was expected of a churl when greeting a noble. Sir Altheric, however, felt no compulsion to reply in kind.

"You're thinner," he told Evadine as she straightened, his voice, like his face, a gruff echo of hers. "Been eating grubs and nuts have you?"

"Rest assured I eat well enough, Father," Evadine replied. Glancing at my still-crouching form, a flicker of irritation passed over her face before she gestured for me to rise. "I present—" she began only for Sir Altheric to cut her off.

"The scribe who fought the knight commander." His eyes tracked across the misaligned planes of my face, the product of an outlaw's life and the more recent attentions of Sir Althus Levalle. "I heard it was quite a spectacle. Every churl from here to Couravel is gabbling about it. The outlaw who nearly humbled a knight, one of great renown no less." A faint smile passed across his lips. "But only nearly."

I saw a test in his bearing, an invitation to voice either defiance or the knuckled forehead and averted eyes of the cowed commoner. I decided to show him neither. "Quite so, my lord," I responded in affable agreement. "I fought him and he would surely have killed me if your daughter hadn't sunk her sword into his skull." I should have stopped there, but it has never been my way to resist the chance to bait those who set themselves above me. "A fate I consider to be far more merciful than he deserved."

Sir Altheric's eyes narrowed, but in restrained humour rather than offence. "A point I'll not argue over, to be sure," he grunted, then returned his full attention to Evadine. "I'll forgo useless formality or empty words." He nodded to the pennant fluttering above. "You know what this means, I assume?"

"The king has sent you to parley on his behalf," Evadine said. "Which would indicate you have terms to relate. May I hazard a guess as to their nature?"

The knight's features darkened then, his muted humour of a moment before replaced by the rigidity and twitch of burgeoning but habitual anger. I divined this to be a man well accustomed to being enraged by his daughter. "If you must," he muttered.

"My company is to disband," Evadine said. "All who follow me are to give up their arms and return to their homes on promise of amnesty. I am required to swear fealty to King Tomas and retire to a cloistered shrine where I will live out my days in silent supplication beseeching the Martyrs for forgiveness." She offered him a bland smile. "Do I have it right, Father?"

His anger diminished a good deal then, softening into a regretful grimace. Also, I saw much in the way his eyes failed to blink as they regarded his daughter, surely the most wayward offspring his noble line had ever produced. This man's love for his child may have been sorely tested, but never had it faded.

"Right," he told her in a sigh, "and wrong." He paused to stiffen his back before speaking on in the clipped tones of one reciting a memorised missive. "King Tomas wishes it known that the unfortunate events at Castle Ambris were undertaken without his knowledge or consent. He has issued no decree against the person of Lady Evadine Courlain nor voiced any condemnation of her actions. He has, however, called upon Duke Elbyn of the Shavine Marches to answer for his unsanctioned proclamations in the king's name and unlawful abduction of the Anointed Lady, a valiant and greatly valued sword who has performed unmatched service in His Majesty's cause. Those others of noble rank found to have partaken in this crime will also face royal sanction. Lady Evadine is cordially invited to attend the king in Couravel where she will receive due honour for her service in the Fjord Geld. His Majesty also looks forward to receiving her sincere expression of loyalty and ardent disavowal of any and all treason, either in word or deed."

His eyes flicked to me as he spoke the last few words. I had wondered if the statement I spat at Sir Althus, delivered in the heat and tumult of single combat, had been missed by the mass of onlookers. *Tomas Algathinet is a bastard with no more right to sit the throne than I.* Ascendant Sihlda's secret, set down in her testament and entrusted to me, now it appeared, given wing. I wondered how far it had flown and how many, having heard it, believed its truth, including the king himself. Given that he continued to sit the throne, it was plain the man either didn't credit the tale of his own bastardy or simply didn't care that he was not the son of King Mathis but of his famed champion.

I watched Evadine digest her father's words in silence, face lowered in sombre contemplation. Before her capture at Farinsahl she had been filled with zeal for her impending crusade, fired by her vision of deliverance at the hands of a Seraphile made flesh. Her apparently divine healing was but the first step towards restoring the people of this land to the unpolluted truth of the Covenant of Martyrs, a divine confirmation of the rightness of her life's mission to prevent the resurgence of the Malecite and the coming of the Second Scourge. But during our weeks in the forest since the carnage at Castle Ambris, I had been witness to a more introspective Evadine. She gave few sermons these days despite the continual flow of recruits to her banner, spending her days wandering the periphery of the camp and offering only bland affirmations to the awed folk who greeted her. The little time I spent in her presence left me worried over the tiredness I saw in her face, and the doubtful cast that made her gaze wander and voice soft.

Sir Altheric watched her for a time before stepping closer, causing me to tense in response. I had also left my sword in Wilhum's care but, never one to trust to the strictures of custom, secreted a knife in my boot. However, the knight's bearing lacked all aggression as he moved to his daughter, reaching out to clasp her hand. When he spoke his voice was low but coloured by sincere entreaty.

"You have been afforded an avenue of escape, Evadine. I beg you to take it."

She closed her eyes then, jaw tensing and lips drawing tight. I divined that she hadn't felt the touch of her father's hand for a very long time, in either kindness or anger. I knew a little of Sir Altheric's care for his only child from the correspondence I had penned on behalf of her would-be suitor, the late dullard Sir Eldurm Gulatte. His bitter asides regarding Evadine's father conveyed a sense of a fiercely protective man bent on denying his daughter any chance at love, regardless of the worthiness of the prospective husband. I also knew that Evadine's pursuit of the knightly arts and her decision to accept clerical rank in the Covenant had sundered her from this man's house, thereby removing all chance of inheritance. For a man of such noble lineage and esteem the disgrace and disrespect must have been hard to bear, and yet still he had come, although whether it was to save her or the kingdom I couldn't tell. Bastard or not, King Tomas held the throne. With the Pretender defeated, or at least subdued, Tomas had no more rivals, save an inconveniently Risen Martyr unjustly tried and condemned in his name.

I pondered the notion of voicing a warning lest her father's solicitation gain purchase on Evadine's heart. There was much to consider in this offer, much to bargain over in fact. If Tomas was willing to condemn Duke Elbyn and the slain Sir Althus in this way, it bespoke a deep need for this crisis to be resolved. Such need created opportunities of a kind that sprang readily to my mind but not so to Evadine's. Also, I had paid careful heed to Sir Altheric's words and found a good deal of meaning in some of the blander phrases. However, no warning proved necessary for when Evadine opened her eyes, they flashed with an angry animation rather than the doubtful fatigue of recent weeks.

"Tell me, Father," she said, "do you still think me a liar? Or, what was it? Stricken by the madness common to her sex when womanhood blossoms?" Sir Altheric's features hardened and he removed his hand, stepping back as she continued. "You recall the first time I told you of my visions, don't you? How I sobbed and pleaded for you to make them go away?"

The knight's face flushed dark, a faint glimmer of shame showing in his eyes. "I'll not claim to have been a faultless man, in fatherhood or anything else. But I did try to help you."

"Yes." A humourless laugh escaped her lips. "With all manner of healers ready to pour foul concoctions down my throat to leave me retching or screaming in pain. Then came a Caerith mummer to wave charms over my body and cast her stinking potions at me as I begged the Martyrs to guard my soul against her heathen nonsense. And when none of it worked, there was a perverted Supplicant willing to whip the madness from me. Now there was a man who enjoyed his work. All of this inflicted upon a thirteen-year-old girl who had committed the crime of telling her father the truth."

She fell silent, her anger fading as quickly as it rose. Father and daughter stared at each other for the space of a single heartbeat before Sir Altheric lowered his gaze while Evadine's lingered. "Master Alwyn," she said, not looking at me. "What answer do you consider appropriate to the king's most generous offer?"

The unexpectedness of such a bluntly asked question might have shown on my face but for the fact that the throb had once again decided to flare into aggravating life. So, instead of a surprised frown the sudden pulse of pain brought a deep crease to my brows and slight hunch to my shoulders.

"Would it be remiss of me, my lord," I began, rubbing a hand over my forehead, which did nothing to banish the throb, "if I were to indulge in some brief conjecture?"

Sir Altheric apparently took my distracted air as a sign of accustomed authority afforded me by the Anointed Lady, for he replied in a neutral murmur, lacking the disdain I expected. "Indulge in whatever you like, Master Scribe."

"The king states that he regards Lady Evadine as a valued sword," I said. "He also alludes to treason, in both word and deed. Would I be wrong in concluding that this kingdom's travails did not end on the Traitors' Field?"

The noble gave a nod of grudging accedence, shifting his focus back to his daughter. "King Tomas has need of all loyal subjects," he said. "Especially those of proven battle-skill."

"Another war to fight, then," Evadine replied, features becoming yet grimmer. "That's the price of my pardon?"

"I do not profess to know the king's mind. All I am permitted to say is that trouble brews in the south. The terms of your service are a matter between you and the Crown."

"I note you make ample mention of the king, my lord," I said, concluding he had no more to impart on the subject of a fresh war. "But you say little of the Covenant. What, may I enquire, is the opinion of senior clergy on this matter?"

"The king," Sir Altheric said, turning to me with a cold stare, "is at liberty to make his own laws and offer his own beneficence as he sees fit, without clerical advice."

"Lady Evadine is an ordained Aspirant in the Covenant of Martyrs," I pointed out. "And a Risen Martyr herself. And yet it was one of the Covenant's own, a certain Ascendant Arnabus, who oversaw the criminal farce that was her trial. King Tomas's largesse and wisdom are greatly appreciated, I assure you. However, the security of Lady Evadine, which is the principal concern of all who follow her, can only be fully guaranteed by a concordance between Crown and Covenant regarding her future in this realm."

The knight shook his head in curt irritation. "I cannot speak for the Covenant."

"No." I inclined my head in agreement. "They will have to speak for themselves." I paused and turned to Evadine, finding she had finally stopped glaring at her father. Raising my eyebrow in an unspoken question I received a terse nod in response. Ever since her healing at the hands of the Sack Witch, our interactions had featured a facility for wordless understanding. She had just given leave for me to negotiate on her behalf.

"Which is why," I said, turning back to Sir Altheric, "acceptance of King Tomas's terms will not be given here, or in Couravel, but in Athiltor, most holy of cities, where the Luminants' Council will also avow their agreement with this arrangement and their recognition of the Anointed Lady as a Risen Martyr. To ensure the council's understanding of the esteem Lady Evadine currently enjoys among the commons, she will travel there with her full company and any who care to join it along the way."

"You intend to march on Athiltor with an army of churls?" Sir Altheric's tone betrayed a note of appalled consternation but, I noted, still held a modicum of respect. This was a man who appreciated the workings of a tactical mind.

"We intend to adhere to the king's desire for a peaceful end to this unfortunate business," I replied. "When the Risen Martyr makes entry to the holiest place in Albermaine, cheered by thousands and greeted by the king himself, all will know how well he favours her. Nor would any but a fool contend that he might ever wish to do her harm."

Sir Altheric sighed and stooped to retrieve his sword from the frosted grass. "Does this man speak for you?" he asked Evadine, fastening his belt.

"He has my trust," she replied, "because he earned it, Father. You have given us the king's terms and you have heard mine. Tomorrow you will depart this forest and convey them to the king and the Luminants' Council. Within the month they will find me at Athiltor, with my full company."

She nodded to me and we turned to go, although her stride faltered when Sir Altheric called after us.

"You know your mother would have wept to see this?"

Evadine came to a halt and I caught angry tears welling in her eyes as she turned back to him. Her retort was hoarse but loud enough to reach his ears. "You made her weep far more than I ever could. Now, get you hence, my lord."

CHAPTER THREE

"Alundia," Wilhum said with a forbidding grimace. "That's where the king wants us. I'd wager all my coin on it, if I had any."

We rode some fifty paces ahead of the column, scouting the road and its verges for threats. The Covenant Company had emerged from the Shavine Woods three days before to follow the King's Road east. In just that time, our number had swollen by another two hundred ardent souls as word of the Anointed Lady's march spread from hamlet to village to town. My gratification at their presence would have been of a higher pitch had more than a handful possessed the wit to bring some supplies to sustain them on the march. Most also neglected to bring any form of weapon. I have often observed that a surfeit of faith will walk hand in hand with a dearth of common sense.

"You've been there?" I asked, tugging my mount's reins as he became distracted by a juniper bush. Jarik was an amenable beast for a warhorse, one of several captured from the Crown Company at Castle Ambris, but thought mainly with his stomach. I didn't yet possess Wilhum's effortless way with horses so keeping a constantly hungry animal on track required a diligent hand on the reins.

"Sadly, yes." Wilhum's grimace took on a sour remembrance. "It's pretty in places, but terribly dry and dusty in others. Can't fault the quality of their brandy, though. It's certainly more appealing than the people. If you thought Fjord Gelders were a fractious lot, next to Alundians they appear positively agreeable. There's an old saying: if you want to start a fight, put an Alundian in a room with a mirror."

"So they're fond of feuding?"

"That they are, though not as fond as they are of finding reasons to fight their fellow duchies, and the Covenant is usually at the heart of any grievance."

I recalled what Toria had told me of the southern form of Covenant belief, how it differed from orthodox practice in ways that had seemed petty to me but not to her. Thoughts of Toria brought a familiar pang and a fond inner wince as I imagined what her foul tongue would have made of this venture. *Marching a bunch of deluded fucks off to get fucking killed on the steps of the greatest shrine in Albermaine. Maybe someone'll paint a fucking picture one day: the* Massacre of the Stupid.

The smile that played over my lips faded quickly as I realised that Toria would never have lingered long enough to pass such a judgement. Even if she hadn't taken ship in Farinsahl and gone in search of our much-dreamt-of treasure, I knew she would never have consented to join this march, especially not if Alundia proved to be our ultimate destination.

"Another rebellion, then?" I suggested. "I would've thought even a fractious folk would be tired of war by now."

"Really?" Wilhum's lips formed a sardonic grin as he gave a pointed glance over his shoulder at the long column snaking its way along the road. "Do they look tired to you? We've close to seven hundred now, all willing to fight and die because they believe a woman rose from the dead to tell them what a disappointment they are to the Seraphile."

I didn't like the bitter, recriminatory edge to his voice, or the worrying thoughts it raised. "You still haven't told her, have you?" I asked, keeping my voice low even though there were no ears close enough to hear. Wilhum's adherence to the Covenant was far from profound. It was love for his only living friend that kept him at

Evadine's side, a love that I knew made our shared betrayal and silence harder to bear with each passing day.

"Do you really think she would tolerate either of us in this company if I had?" He snorted a derisive laugh. "The Risen Martyr learns she isn't anything of the sort, in fact owes her life to the arcane machinations of a Caerith witch. We'd be lucky not to find ourselves hanging from the nearest tree."

Although I doubted Evadine's reaction would involve murder, neither did I relish the prospect of her discovering this unpalatable truth. Her mood had improved since the parley with Sir Altheric. She resumed the nightly sermons that had been such a feature when the company was young and we marched towards the Traitors' Field. This time she preached to an even more rapt audience. I could tell it fed her heart to be listened to by so attentive a congregation and was loath for anything to sour her mood. However, the course she had set us upon was far from certain and who could say what mood would claim her if it should prove calamitous?

"This could still be a trap," I said. "No king likes to be humbled and I suspect the Covenant would greatly prefer that its martyrs stay dead."

Wilhum smiled one of his winning smiles, albeit with a cynical twist to the lips. "For all your wit, you're missing a fundamental truth, my scribbling friend." He turned in the saddle, nodding to Evadine's tall form at the head of the column. She always wore her armour on the march and it never failed to gleam, no matter how overcast the sky. "Ever since her . . . restoration, in any way that matters she *is* the Covenant. Although—" the smile became a frown as he shifted to regard the road ahead "—whether those miserable old pinchfarts on the council realise it is yet to be seen."

By the time the tall spire of the Shrine to Martyr Athil rose above the horizon our number had grown to close to five thousand souls. It could well have been more had Evadine not been compelled to forbid others from joining our ranks. The villages and towns we passed through were generous in the provisions they gave to the

Anointed Lady's host, overly generous in fact since it was apparent some were leaving themselves with scant provision to see them through the winter. There are things the rational mind can never fully comprehend, or at least my rational mind. In this case I couldn't fathom why already beggared people would give over what little they had to a passing noblewoman just because they happened to believe she had risen from death.

"Devotion is inherently nonsensical," Wilhum quipped when I voiced the strangeness of it all. We sat atop our mounts on a hill overlooking a hamlet in the rolling hills of the southern Shavine borderlands. Below Evadine stood conversing with the village's elder churl. Their words were unheard but I knew she was politely refusing the piled sacks of grain and sundry victuals he had offered, down on his knees and forehead scraping the ground as he did so. I suspected Wilhum's opinion stemmed more from noble prejudice towards the lower orders rather than insight. He was a clever man in many respects, but also lazy of mind. Sihlda would have found him a frustrating, perhaps hopeless, student.

"The faithful worship. It's what they do," Wilhum added with a yawn. "The Ascarlians swear oaths to their gods. The Caerith wave their charms about and sing their cants. Covenanters grovel before Martyrs, risen or dead. You look for reason where there is none."

"It's a trade," Ayin said.

She sat nearby, quill busy on her parchment as she recorded the scene below. She had taken to riding with us most days, bouncing along on the back of her small pony, writing at every pause in the march. That moment in the forest when she composed her song appeared to have kindled a desire to concoct lyrical descriptions of everything she could, to the extent that she frequently ran out of parchment and was in constant search of more.

"A trade?" Wilhum enquired, his tone indulgent. "How so, my dear?"

"She gave so they give." Ayin's tongue poked between her lips, quill scratching away. "She won more of the Seraphile's grace than anyone ever has, except perhaps Martyr Athil. By giving to her, these folk gain just a little bit of that grace for themselves."

"Oh, the wisdom of children," Wilhum sighed, although to my ears Ayin had come far closer to the truth than he.

Despite Evadine's injunction, the number of those following in her wake continued to swell, those denied recruitment to the Covenant Company simply trailing after and garnering what alms they could from well-meaning churls. Even with so much generosity it was inevitable that some went hungry on the march. The Anointed Lady's progress to Athiltor, an event destined to become a celebrated feature of her legend, was marked by more than a few bodies littering the roadside. They were mostly the old or the sick, foolishly come in search of some manner of healing at the hands of the Risen Martyr. Their plight pained Evadine greatly and several times she ordered a halt so that these stumbling ardents could be afforded some measure of care, although she was strict in denying them her supposed healing touch.

"It is not given to me to heal the body," she informed her nightly congregation more than once. "It is to your souls that I offer salvation."

Sergeant Swain and the other Supplicant Blades continued to train our recruits on the march while I spent most nights under Wilhum's tutelage in knightly combat. He opined that my duel with Sir Althus had honed my sword skills far better than a year of teaching ever could, even though it was plain that he still outmatched me, especially when mounted. Still, as we neared our journey's end I began to feel truly comfortable in my armour. The blue enamelled plate I had worn that fateful day at Castle Ambris had, of course, been returned to Wilhum, but the men-at-arms and kingsmen who had also fallen on that field provided ample pickings with which to craft a replacement. Consequently, the suit I wore had a motley, mismatched appearance. The vambrace on my right forearm was black enamelled steel richly decorated in brass while its opposite was a dented if sturdy amalgamation of iron and leather. My breastplate was especially ill favoured in appearance, featuring numerous scratches and scorch marks that refused to yield to copious scrubbing. So ugly was it, I had only consented to wear the thing at Wilhum's insistence.

"Looks like shit, I know," he told me, hefting the linked pieces of steel over my quilted jerkin. "But it's the best-made piece of plate I've seen for a good long while. Could stop a windlass crossbow bolt with this."

My helm at least had the appearance of quality. It was a standard great helm, resembling an upturned, fancied bucket augmented by a hinged visor that could be easily raised or lowered. This was always a useful feature as the heat of exertion while I sparred with Wilhum could become unbearable in short order. The helm's frame was formed of brass and the iron plates lacquered in dark blue with some pleasing gold-leaf filigree.

"You look like a jackanapes done up like a knight," Ayin said, always happy to provide a blunt view. She let out a rare laugh at my peeved scowl. "Sir Alwyn Jackanapes," she went on. "That's what they'll call you."

Whatever the discordance of my appearance, my first bout of sparring left me with no doubt about the suit's efficacy. Blows that would previously have left me winded and bruised now felt more like hard shoves. Despite its weight, this collection of discarded plate was also remarkably flexible, allowing a rapid scramble to my feet whenever Wilhum succeeded in knocking me on my arse.

"It's because it's not all on your back," he explained, "but carried by the whole body. Also, the better crafted armour is always lighter. This suit will serve you well, Master Scribe."

The principal feature of the great Shrine to Martyr Athil was its spire, a great granite spike rising near a hundred feet high. The many buttresses that kept it upright gave it a jagged, almost sinister appearance shared by the broad bulk of its main hall. Even when viewed from a mile distant the shrine resembled the carcass of some monstrous beast that had somehow come to rest amid a sprawl of far less impressive buildings, its dark flanks wreathed in the accumulated smoke of many chimneys.

Like the far smaller conurbation of Callintor, the sanctuary city I had been forced to forsake to join the company after Erchel's demise, Athiltor was a city fully governed by the Covenant of Martyrs. The list of strictures under which its population were obliged to live was long and harsh enough to dissuade all but the most ardently faithful from lingering within its bounds. It was also unusual in lacking a wall or accompanying castle. In all the troubled history of these duchies, only Athiltor had escaped the depredations of siege or storm for none but the vilest heretic would dream of making war within sight of this holiest of shrines.

"Well," Wilhum said, nodding to the large encampment east of the city. "He came."

We had gathered at Evadine's side atop a grassy slope affording a clear view of the city. She shielded her eyes against the sun to squint at the encampment where a tall banner rose above the tents. It was too distant to make out the sigil, even though the size of the camp made it plain King Tomas had, in fact, consented to come to Athiltor to greet the Risen Martyr.

"How many do you reckon, Scribe?" Sergeant Swain asked. Still not my most enthusiastic admirer, these days he at least deigned to acknowledge my facility for numbers.

"Three full companies, is my guess," I said. "Plus attendants and a coterie of his most loyal knights. Two thousand at most."

"Then we have the advantage," Wilhum observed. "Should it come to it."

"It will not," Evadine stated. Lowering her hand, she turned to regard us all. In addition to Wilhum, Swain and myself, Ayin was also present along with Supplicant Blade Ofihla, the five souls she trusted most. "Whatever should occur here, there will be no fighting," she told us. "If I am seized upon entering the city, you will do nothing. If I am brought before the king and the council in chains to face trial, you will do nothing. If they hang me and desecrate my corpse in the main square—" her eyes moved to meet each of ours in turn, voice hard and precise with authority "—you will do nothing. This realm will not descend into war on my account. I will have your word on it."

"We can swear all the oaths you demand, my lady," I said, knowing none of the others would speak the truth at this juncture. Even so, I knew she needed to hear it. "Should any harm come to you, there will be no holding *them*." I gestured over my shoulder at the mass of followers crowding the shallow valley to our rear. "However," I went on quickly as her face darkened, "I believe the king and his court will be as aware of this as I am. There will be no attempt to seize you for trial. The danger that lies here resides in words not blades. We must have the greatest care over the terms we settle upon, for therein lies the trap and the chains of the future."

At Evadine's insistence only Wilhum and I were permitted to escort her to the shrine. Swain was left to take charge of the company, drawn up in tidy ranks on the road skirting Athiltor's western fringes. I had joined with Swain in arguing for a larger retinue but she wouldn't hear of it. "I do not come to seize this place," she said, "and will give no succour to those who would claim otherwise."

I took some heart from the impression of strength and military order conveyed by the Covenant Company. Swain had marshalled them into a well-drilled force equal in number to the king's escort. I knew only the hard core of veterans would be capable of matching the Crown Company if this day descended into a pitched battle, but neither would the others turn tail and run. I also knew that, despite the oaths we had sworn to Evadine, should she be harmed in any way Swain would lead this force into the heart of the holy city to retrieve her, regardless of the price in blood or dishonour.

The mob of ardent, untrained followers was a different matter, however, and no amount of Evadine's preaching could have prevented them from following her into the city. Overnight their number had increased yet further as we camped within sight of Athiltor, Evadine having acceded to my suggestion that a pause for rest would be in order. A good portion of these fresh and eager souls came from surrounding villages but, to my surprise, most hailed from the city. Lay adherents and plainly attired churls indentured to Covenant service thronged the shallow valley below our camp. They milled about in an untidy swirl, many silent, others loudly reciting scripture, some clustering together to sing Martyr-inspired hymns. However, whenever Evadine emerged from her tent, they would fall into collective, reverential quietude. The hush would linger until, inevitably, some inflamed soul shouted out an acclamation whereupon the rest would erupt into adulation. Watching them all as the hour grew late, I felt any doubts as to the outcome of this meeting slip away. These people had ensured Evadine's survival better than I, Wilhum and the whole company ever could.

The morning dawned with an unpleasant chill and a pale overcast sky. A flurry of snow accompanied our progress along the last mile of road where we parted from the company and entered the city proper. The inclement weather, however, did nothing to cool the ardour of the crowd trailing along after the Anointed Lady, nor that of the many townsfolk who thronged the streets to greet her.

"The Seraphile have blessed you, my lady!" a matronly woman called out from an upper-storey window, tears streaming down her cheeks, a wailing infant clutched to her ample bosom.

"You will save us all, Anointed One!" a thin man in a lay adherent's robe cried, hands raised and eyes wide in adoration. He stumbled into my path in his ardour, reaching to touch a hand to Evadine's armoured foot. Seeing how his fingers latched onto her stirrup, I kicked Jarik forward, the warhorse's shoulder sending the fellow sprawling back into the crowd. The mass of people, yelling, screaming and waving, soon became so dense Wilhum and I were forced to place ourselves directly alongside Evadine's mount to maintain progress.

Fortunately, a more orderly sight greeted us as we neared the shrine. Here, dozens of black-robed Covenant custodians lined the streets leading to the main square, linking arms to form a cordon and allow for an uninterrupted journey. I saw several adoring faces among these servants of the faith, but most were rigid in their lack of expression and a few wore dark, disapproving scowls. Whereas the majority of the city's populace were fervent in their acclaim of the Anointed Lady, apparently such sentiments were not universally shared by those only one step up in the Covenant hierarchy. It didn't bode well for the reception we were likely to receive from senior clergy.

The city's main square occupied a half-acre of cobbled ground leading to the broad steps of the Shrine to Martyr Athil. Today it was ringed with a line of fully armoured kingsmen standing with halberds crossed. They weren't shy in using the staves of their weapons to discourage the crowd from surging after the Risen Martyr as her party passed through their line, but the shoving and occasional blows did little to stem the crowd's enthusiasm. Glancing to my right, I saw an elderly man at the forefront of the throng madly waving both arms, face rapt with zealous wonder and uncaring of the blood trickling from the fresh cut to his forehead.

Devotion is inherently nonsensical, I thought in echo of Wilhum's words as I turned my eyes from the crowd to the shrine and the brightly coloured array of nobles awaiting Evadine's arrival. It was clear some thought had been put into the arrangement of King Tomas's court at this most auspicious moment. Courtiers and senior servants occupied the lowest tier while knights and retainers of the Algathinet family stood in the middle. Standing higher still were those of the royal household, a short parade of finely attired nobles with one very tall exception. Sir Ehlbert Bauldry towered over those around him, long red cloak trailing in the stiff, snow-rich breeze. Like Evadine, his armour contrived to gleam despite the lack of sun. My previous glimpses of the King's Champion had been brief, denying me the chance to see his features. I found them blunter and lacking the heroic handsomeness I imagined. His nose was crooked and the bones of his face made stark beneath skin possessed of the mottled look that came from overlapping scars exposed to the chill. Invincible he may have been, but it was still jarring to note that even mighty Sir Ehlbert was not immune to injury.

Standing to the champion's right and occupying the spot closest to the king was a young woman in a dark velvet cloak that matched the lustrous hair cascading over her shoulders. She wore a thin golden band on her head, a signal of status rather than officially required courtly etiquette, but nevertheless ensuring all present were reminded of her royal blood. This, I knew, must be Princess Leannor, elder sister to the king and mother to the bored-looking lad of ten years fidgeting at her side. The boy's irked frown and shifting feet made a notable contrast to his mother's stern-faced rigidity. She stared at

Evadine in hard, concentrated focus, her features lacking any of the condescension or forced civility worn by the other members of the court. Also, her hand, laden with several bejewelled rings, was clutched to her son's shoulder with a fierce grip.

Standing highest of all, of course, was the king himself. Tomas had chosen not to wear armour this day, opting instead for a golden-hued cloak and a white doublet emblazoned with the two rearing leopards that were the sigil of his house. I saw also that no sword hung at his belt. He stood watching Evadine's approach with grave, regal authority, or at least a decent facsimile of such. When he delivered his barely heard exhortation before battle was joined at the Traitors' Field, I had noted how the king was only an inch or so shorter than his champion. Now his tallness, combined with the set of his features, made the truth of his parentage seem starkly, even comically obvious.

A man who isn't truly a king stands ready to greet a woman who isn't truly a Martyr, I mused, wondering if all noteworthy moments in history might in fact comprise a grand, mendacious pantomime. The notion brought a smile to my lips, one I was quick to quell for, despite its absurdity, the outcome of this day would have far from humorous consequences.

Occupying the flat expanse of tiled granite beneath the shrine's cavernous doorway stood the assembled Luminants of the Covenant of Martyrs. I found it significant that the full number of the council was present this day, a dozen men and women of middling or advanced years clad in robes of plain grey cotton. The Covenant was a faith that extended far beyond Albermaine and only five members of this council hailed from the realm's duchies. I knew from Sihlda's teachings that the full council typically convened only once a decade given the time required to gather them all, yet they were gathered now. This could only mean that those Luminants from the more far-flung corners of Covenant-dom had begun their journeys before this meeting had been agreed. Clearly, the appearance of a Risen Martyr, recognised or not, had given the faith's most senior clergy a great deal to discuss.

Reining her mount to a halt at the base of the steps, Evadine climbed free of the saddle, Wilhum and I following suit. A hushed expectation settled on the massed onlookers as she handed her reins to me. "Stay here," she told us with a tight smile. Turning, she paused before setting foot upon the first step, adding in a quiet voice, "And remember your oaths to me."

None of the various artistic renderings of the event that followed have come close to capturing its truth, the mood and the character varying greatly. The colours are either too garish or the poses too dramatic. Depending on the artist's prejudice, Tomas is depicted either as a pinch-faced, suspicious tyrant forced to a hated act or a boyishly handsome but witless buffoon. The Luminants look on with expressions that are appalled or stoic. However, Evadine herself is, of course, invariably presented as an idealised perfection of sanctified beauty. It's also a particular point of irritation that, while many of these artists were happy to include Wilhum, few felt the need to include me even though all the trustworthy accounts attest to my presence. Therefore, the serious student of history should always look to the written word for truth as all artists are liars, also frequently drunkards in my experience.

However, the principal error to be found in depictions of the Risen Martyr Evadine Courlain's meeting with King Tomas Algathinet is the failure to capture the mood. Watching her climb those steps, all eyes locked on her tall, armoured form, the sense of a world in balance weighed heavily on any with the slightest modicum of wit. The fate of an entire realm, if not a faith that encompassed millions, rested upon this one moment.

Evadine came to a halt one step below King Tomas whereupon, moving with unhurried surety, she unbuckled her sword belt and sank to one knee. Gripping the sword by the scabbard in both hands, she raised it up and bowed her head. When she spoke her voice once again betrayed the facility to carrying far and wide, even though she didn't shout, her tone instead one of firm, unwavering sincerity.

"Your Majesty, my sword is yours."

CHAPTER FOUR

E vadine's humble submission on the steps of the shrine was met with a roar of ear-straining volume from the massed faithful. I felt the king displayed creditable good sense in not immediately reaching out to rest his hand on Evadine's proffered sword. Instead, he took a moment to form his lips into a smile of grave acceptance, showing no sign of having heard the wild jubilation filling the air.

"Your sword is as precious to me as your soul, my lady," he said, although only those nearby could hear him above the tumult. The sight of his royal hand resting on Evadine's scabbard sent the crowd into a yet higher pitch of celebration.

"Come," King Tomas said, stepping back with a sweep of his cloak and gesturing towards the shrine's entrance. "Let us join in supplication to the Seraphile's grace and the Martyrs' example."

Although Evadine hadn't gestured for us to follow, Wilhum and I were quick to scale the steps and move to her side as she strode into the shadowed interior. The air was musty with incense and the cavernous space shafted by multi-hued light streaming through tall, stained glass windows. My eyes darted about in search of a possible ambush, but all I saw were Supplicants and sundry other clerics and lay folk. The Luminants failed to offer a greeting, formal or otherwise, instead trooping off towards the gloomy recesses beyond the many pillars lining the shrine's central chapel, their overlapping footsteps echoing loud.

"Before supplications can begin," the king said, affording Evadine a gracious bow, "we have been invited to partake of the Luminants' wisdom. If you would care to join me, my lady." He stepped closer, voice lowered in wry solicitation. "Truth be told, I doubt I could endure their company alone."

The crowd's cheers could still be heard in the high vaulted chamber where the Luminants convened their council. They all sat at a semi-circular table, positioned to either side of the king, who occupied the central position. His sister, denied a place at the table, sat to his rear. I was to discover later that no king, of Albermaine or any other realm, had ever sat at this table before. That he had done so today was obviously intended to signal the unity of Crown and Covenant, at least in relation to its unforeseen and surely unwanted Risen Martyr.

Only one of the Luminants addressed us that day, a man I found to my surprise I knew, albeit only by name and reputation. The last word I had heard of Durehl Vearist came from a drover outside the walls to Castle Ambris several years before. Then it had been Ascendant Durehl, most senior cleric of the Shavine Marches, who had heard the testament of old Duke Rouphon in the moments before Sir Ehlbert took his head. It appeared he had risen high since and, judging by the fellow's tone and bearing during this meeting, his ascendency to the rank of Luminant hadn't been due to any diplomatic skills.

"Stories regarding your . . . martyrdom abound, Aspirant," he told Evadine as she stood before this faithful assemblage. A sturdy man who exuded a sense of vitality despite his years, Luminant Durehl regarded her with broad, blunt features set in a steady gaze utterly lacking the awe or even fear I had seen in other clerics. "Perhaps," he went on, "you would be good enough to provide a full, unembellished account."

"Certainly," Evadine replied, her own tone one of placidity. "I was wounded in battle when the Ascarlians stormed the port of Olversahl.

My beloved comrades—" she gave a brief glance of muted affection at Wilhum and I "—bravely fought to rescue me and convey me back to Farinsahl. I lay close to death for some time, enduring recurring bouts of delirium. In the midst of my suffering I felt my heart stop, whereupon I was visited by one of the Seraphile who restored me to health."

When told to a congregation of rapt and ardent followers, with the benefit of more colourful phrasing, this story invariably summoned a round of gasps and moist-eyed whispers. Here, it provoked only the exchange of guarded glances and a good deal of discomfited shifting.

"Long has it been known," Durehl said, "that the Seraphile do not visit this earthly plain. Their grace is communicated via the example of the Martyrs, those who have transcended mortal concerns to earn the Seraphile's favour and guidance. It is through the Martyrs' example alone that they allow us to partake of their divine message."

"I would contend, Luminant," Evadine replied with equanimity, "that such a thing is not so much *known* as *believed*. A subtle but important distinction. For centuries it was believed that the Seraphile do not descend to the earthly plain, but only because it has never happened before. Also, I can say without fear of contradiction, that there is nothing in Covenant scripture to avow that such a thing is impossible."

Durehl's face darkened at this but the king interjected before the Luminant could speak on. "Did the Seraphile speak to you, my lady?" he asked in a tone of genuine curiosity rather than the barely concealed doubt of the cleric at his side.

"She did, Your Majesty," Evadine confirmed with a warm smile. "And what wondrous things she said."

"She?" Durehl cut in, thick brows bunching in a disapproving scowl. "The Seraphile are beyond such mundanities as gender."

"Another thing believed rather than known, Luminant," Evadine replied before pointedly turning back to the king. "She spoke to me of love, Your Majesty. The love of the divine for the mortal. A love that had compelled her to restore me and convey the message of that love to all who will listen. She spoke of how our endless discontent pains the Seraphile, how the darkness we allow to steal over our hearts endangers the world entire. For in surrendering to our base jealousies and grievances we give succour to the Malecite and bring the Second Scourge ever closer, and it is already perilously close."

"And was there anyone else present to hear this divine wisdom?" Durehl enquired. "A witness to this vision?"

"Her words were for me alone." Evadine turned and gestured to me. "However, this most faithful soldier was present when I was restored to health. He can attest to the truth of my rising."

"Really?" Durehl's voice lost the marginal restraint he had adopted when addressing Evadine, taking on a harsher edge when he settled his scowl upon me. "And this would be the scribe we've heard so much about, I presume?"

At Evadine's nod, I stepped forwards and bowed, bobbing my head at the Luminant but sinking to one knee when I shifted to face the king. "Alwyn Scribe, Your Majesty, Your Luminance. At your service."

"Rise," Durehl snapped. "I like to see a man's face when I ask him a question." I found a humourless ghost of a smile on his lips as I regained my feet. "You're the one who escaped the Pit Mines," he said. "An outlaw and cut-throat who once ran with the notorious brigand Deckin Scarl. Is that not so?"

"Quite true, Your Luminance," I replied. That this council would have sought out all intelligence on Evadine and her companions came as no surprise. It was jarring to find myself the focus of their attention, but I had never been one to find my tongue cowed by a hostile audience.

"My crimes are many," I went on. "I'll not deny a single one. Nor will I deny the faith I felt blossom in my soul the day the Anointed Lady came to speak in Callintor, for that day was my salvation."

"Really?" Durehl's brows twitched in a flicker of amusement. "So your salvation didn't come in the Pits where, I'm reliably informed, you were taught letters by the condemned murderess Sihlda Doisselle."

"Ascendant Sihlda was no murderess." I managed to keep my retort below a shout, but a good deal of heat still coloured my words. "Luminance," I added in a more respectful tone, letting my eyes stray towards the king. "The tale of her unlawful imprisonment is long, but one I'm happy to relate in full, if it please you."

The king's features took on a puzzled frown at my words but, seeing his sister shift in agitation, I could tell this barb had hit close to the mark. Princess Leannor coughed, just a small sound but it echoed loud in the high, vaulted ceiling of this chamber. King Tomas, it seemed to me, heard it very clearly.

"Perhaps, Your Luminance," he said, favouring Durehl with a smile, "we could confine ourselves to more immediate matters."

Durehl's scowl was joined by a grimace of frustration as he continued to stare at me, voicing a gruff demand. "You were witness to this woman's resurrection?"

"I was, Luminance."

"Tell us what you saw. Tell us *all* that you saw."

I allowed a momentary pause, forming my features into an expression that mingled reverence with mystification. "We took turns to sit with the captain, Lady Evadine, as she lay . . . dying," I said. "The healers in Farinsahl, and our own Supplicant Delric, had done all they could and we knew it wouldn't be long before she made her journey through the Portals. None of us wanted her to be alone, you see, at the end, even though her mind appeared lost to the world. It happened just after dawn, when I had nearly succumbed to sleep. Rousing myself, I looked upon Lady Evadine's face and beheld it to be . . . changed." I faltered, putting a distant cast to my eyes and shaking my head in apparent wonder. "The pains that wracked her, that made her a wasted shadow of her former self, they were gone and I looked upon a woman as hale and healthy as any could be. Then, she opened her eyes. So bright, so . . . alive." I let out a laugh that combined chagrin with awe. "I'm shamed to say that I fainted then, such was my shock. When I came to, the Anointed Lady stood over me." I laughed again. "I recall she asked if I was drunk."

The king was gracious enough to let out a chuckle at this, while the Luminants all continued to stare in stone-faced silence.

"But you," Luminant Durehl said, "saw no Seraphile with your own eyes?"

"Saw? No, Luminant. But I did . . . feel them. I recall a great inner warmth, and a lightening of my soul which had been burdened by the terrible sights I witnessed in Olversahl. I can't account for it, nor explain it. But I know something entered that room that night, something far beyond my humble comprehension, except its boundless compassion. That I understood in full."

By rights, voicing such outrageous lies in this of all places should have brought a stumble to my tongue, or at least a stutter or two. Curiously, despite the lofty status of all present, save myself and Wilhum, and the fact that I stood in the heart of the holiest site in Covenant-dom, these untruths had flowed from my mouth with ease. I ascribed my lack of hesitancy to the fact that I had been lying to save my skin for as long as I could remember, ever since the day I told the whoremaster his prize pig had taken that apple, not I. That lie, sadly for the state of my buttocks, hadn't worked. I've little doubt that the lies I told the king and the Luminants that day met with any greater success in convincing those present of my sincerity. Fortunately, both I and they understood that what they believed in this moment mattered no more than a dog's turd. What mattered was proof. I had nothing to attest to the truth of my words, save Evadine's testimony, but neither had these exalted clerics any proof that I was lying to their disbelieving faces.

This mutually understood but unspoken truth was given greater emphasis by a fresh upsurge of cheering from the crowd beyond the shrine's walls. For a few seconds it sounded as if every voice in the city was raised in adulatory song. I saw Luminant Durehl's face twitch as he fought to contain a spasm of anger. I had little doubt then, and certainly have felt none since, that, if not for the horde of believers massed outside, the Luminants' Council would have lost no time in condemning Evadine as a heretical deceiver. It would have been their great delight, and relief, to have strung her from a gallows in the main square, with my lying carcass dangling alongside. But that course was denied them, even though their prolonged silence indicated a marked reluctance to say so. The king, however, felt no such reticence.

"How blessed we are to hear this tale, my lady," he said, lowering his head in humble acknowledgement. "If the scholars of a later age are to remark upon my reign, I feel it is this day that will stand highest in the chronicles. Come." He got to his feet, much to the evident surprise of the Luminants. "These esteemed persons will wish to spend time formulating the edict confirming their recognition of your status as a Risen Martyr." He extended a hand to Evadine. "We will leave them to their labour. Will you consent to walk with me? I've a yen to see the shrine gardens, a place I've not set eyes on since I was a boy."

King Tomas led Evadine from one flower bed to another, making polite and inconsequential conversation, for what felt like an interminable age, before his true purpose became apparent. Princess Leannor accompanied us in this aimless tour of the shrine's extensive gardens. She walked behind the king and Evadine with a steady, even stride while Wilhum and I were required to trail along at a decent remove. My eyes roved the gardens in wary vigilance for even now I harboured suspicions regarding our hosts' intentions. But, besides the gardeners tending the neat rows of bushes and blossoms, the only figure of interest was the tall form of Sir Ehlbert Bauldry. For reasons unknown he didn't walk at the king's side, instead choosing to watch from a distance, keeping to the shadowed cloisters that ringed the gardens. I knew this man's presence made the need for assassins somewhat redundant, having little doubt he could defeat both myself and Wilhum without great difficulty should the need arise. As we walked, I caught a few hard glances from the princess in the champion's direction, but whether these were in admonition or warning I couldn't tell.

"Blast this leg," the king said, pausing beside a rectangular hedge, the interior of which was filled with rose bushes, the thorny branches bare in the midwinter chill. He ran a hand over his upper thigh and I realised he had been moving with a slight limp. "One of the Pretender's turncoats gave me a mighty whack with his mace on the Traitors' Field. Gets worse in cold weather."

"I have heard many stories of your bravery that day, Your Majesty," Evadine said.

"Though not so many as yours, eh?" The king's words were accompanied by a smile that was both rueful and warm. "You actually crossed swords with the great liar himself, did you not?"

"Only briefly, Majesty. The press of battle shifted and we were pushed apart. Apparently he fled shortly after."

"Yes." King Tomas sighed, resuming his slow stride along the gravel path. "Leannor has collected all manner of lurid tales about his escape. Supposedly, at one point he hid in the stomach of some rotting beast to evade my knights." He glanced over his shoulder at his sister. "Was it a bull, dear sister? I forget."

"A shire horse, dear brother," the princess said. These were the first words I had heard from her lips and found them carefully flat. She kept her hands within the bell-shaped cuffs of her emerald-green robe and maintained a stiff posture that told me she viewed this odd meeting with as much wariness as I.

"A shire horse, yes," the king repeated. "Would that he had stayed mired in those guts and rotted to nothing. I'm told by trustworthy sources he's currently grubbing about in a cave somewhere in the Althiene mountains. I've been hectoring poor Duke Guhlton to send more troops to root the dastard out, but the clan country was ever a difficult place to search. Still, the Pretender is as broken as a man can be. No horde, no more than a handful of followers. He is, in truth, a pretender no more, and the least of our current trials, for this realm is beset by many."

As he spoke, the king's words had lost their initial flippancy to assume a weightier tone, one that required a response when he lapsed into expectant silence. Never short of perception, Evadine was quick to fill the void.

"Today I swore my sword to your service, Majesty," she said. "Command me and I will contest any threat to this realm."

"Your sword, yes," the king said, nodding and pursing his lips. "But what of your company? If company is truly the correct term for a host so large."

"My company and my sword are as one, Majesty. Please have no doubt of it."

The king glanced again at his sister, silently this time. I saw a faintly smug satisfaction in his raised brows before he returned his attention to Evadine.

"Doubts?" he said, laughing and clapping a hand to her pauldron. "Please know, my lady, I never entertained any doubts regarding your loyalty, regardless of the calumny whispered against you. You may not recall, but we did play together as children, just once. It was a fine summer day in the palace grounds in Couravel. You were throwing a ball around with some beefy lad and another who was half his size. I'm afraid I can't recall either of their names. In any case, there was some manner of disagreement and the big lad pushed you over and you bloodied your knee rather badly. I expected you to cry but instead you scraped up a handful of gravel, threw it in his eyes then kicked him square in the balls."

He gave a nostalgic laugh, one Evadine failed to match, summoning only a pained smile. "Sir Eldurm Gulatte, Majesty," she said.

The king's mirth faded and he raised an eyebrow. "Mmm?"

"The beefy lad," Evadine said. "His name was Sir Eldurm Gulatte, until recently Lord Warden of Your Majesty's Pit Mines. He drowned in the river during the pursuit after the Traitors' Field."

"Oh, of course." King Tomas's features took on a sorrowful cast. "I recall being told of his fate. A sad story, to be sure. But sad stories abound in times of war and I find it is a king's duty to ensure such tales are few in number. I would contend it is also, and please correct me if I err, the duty of a Risen Martyr, for is peace not the eternal promise of the Seraphile's grace?"

These days there are many folk who will tell you King Tomas Algathinet was a guileless fool, a fey poltroon elevated far above his abilities and therefore doomed to ultimate failure. In that moment, however, I knew him to be among the cleverest and most cunning souls I ever encountered. Failure was, of course, to be his lot in life, but given the tribulations he faced the fact that he survived so long should be regarded as a triumph of sorts. It is not only through fear or loyalty that kings keep their thrones, but through the craft of weaving alliances and securing debts. Today he had orchestrated a debt in so readily accepting Evadine's status as a Risen Martyr, obliging the reluctant old hypocrites of the Luminants' Council to do the same. Now we came to the matter of payment.

"Peace is ever to be cherished, Majesty," Evadine said.

"Yes," the king sighed, "and yet what should be a simple thing is always so very difficult. You would think those who had seen war, and who in this kingdom has not, would wish to avoid its terrors at all costs. But, as one conflict dies another is kindled, this time in Alundia."

My eyes slid to meet Wilhum's, finding his eyebrow raised and mouth quirking in restrained self-congratulation.

"Alundia, Majesty?" Evadine asked.

"I'm afraid so." Tomas clasped both hands behind his back, the affable artifice of moments before replaced by a more serious aspect. "Duke Oberharth grows less temperate with each passing year. As a youth he troubled my grandfather no end, and my father even more so. It was I who brokered his marriage to the most fair Lady Celynne, daughter of Duke Guhlton of Althiene, possessed of a considerable dowry and the sweetest soul in all the realm. It was not purely a political matter, for the lady herself had been quite besotted with Oberharth for some time. I had hoped her nature would cool his temper, make him more amenable to just taxes and toleration of orthodox Covenanters within his duchy. Unfortunately, while age mellows others it appears to have soured the Duke of Alundia, despite the efforts of the loving wife he doesn't deserve. There have been . . . incidents of late."

Evadine's face took on a sudden focus, eyes narrowing as she mirrored the king's sober demeanour. "Incidents, Majesty?"

"Massacres, in point of fact," Princess Leannor interjected before her brother could respond. "Orthodox shrines put to the torch and their congregations hacked down as they fled the flames. A month ago, the streets of Highsahl ran red with the blood of true-faith adherents, slain when they gathered for the feast day of Martyr Ihlander. We only received word of this outrage a week ago. True-faithers have been fleeing across the borders into Alberis and the Shavine Marches, all bearing tales of murder and persecution."

"Duke Oberharth has ordered this?" Evadine asked.

"He says not," King Tomas replied. "His missives are as terse as ever, but he is firm in disavowing these outrages. However, as is the way with kings, and . . ." he smiled tightly and nodded to his sister ". . . princesses, we have other sources of information that cast doubt on his innocence."

"Information that would be borne out in trial?"

"Not as such, but I find it credible nonetheless. The Duke of Alundia may be intemperate, but neither is he dim-witted. While we hear tales of ducal gold passed in shadowy corners to fund wicked deeds and the spreading of false rumours, proving such a thing in a fair trial would be nigh-on impossible. A formal accusation would also provide Oberharth with the pretence he needs to declare his duchy sundered from the realm. I feel we need a more demonstrative, but also suitably restrained, course of action."

The king halted again and straightened, addressing Evadine in formal terms. "Lady Evadine Courlain, as one who has sworn her sword to my service, I give you this charge: march your company to Walvern Castle and hold it in my name."

I saw Wilhum stiffen then scowl in warning at Evadine, apparently hoping she would look his way. The name Walvern Castle meant nothing to me, but evidently it meant a great deal to him. However, Evadine's gaze was fully captured by the king in that moment. I have often wondered how very different everything that follows in this narrative would have been if she had paused then, just for the barest fraction of a second needed to catch a glimpse of Wilhum's cautionary glare. But here we were at the crux of the matter, the price she had known the king would demand, one she had already resolved herself to pay and spare the realm the agonies of civil strife. Also, I couldn't help but admire Tomas's cleverness in presenting her with so compelling a task. While Evadine Courlain was destined to transform the Covenant of Martyrs, it should always be remembered that her radicalism began and ended with her claim to martyrdom. In all other respects she was as orthodox and traditional in her beliefs as the most aged and hidebound cleric.

So, instead of indulging in a pause for reflection or seeking guidance from her trusted companions, for the second time that day Evadine promptly sank to one knee and lowered her head. "As you command, Your Majesty."

"Excellent," the king said, resting his hand on her head in acknowledgement before stepping back. "Rise, my lady, and be about your king's business."

"If I may, Majesty," Evadine said, getting to her feet. "A march of such length will require that the company be reordered and provisioned. Many are without proper weapons and few have been trained . . ."

She trailed off as Princess Leannor stepped forward to present her with a scroll. It bore a large wax seal and fine ribbon of gold silk. "The King's Writ is given unto you," the princess told her. "It commands all subjects of this realm to provide such assistance as you require to fulfil your mission. Any and all goods will be given free of charge. Any merchant or vendor who refuses will be subject to a warrant of execution. As for reordering—" the princess exchanged a brief glance with her brother "—His Majesty will be happy to permit a delay of one week to properly constitute your forces. In regards to training, I'm told soldiers can be trained on the march, can they not?"

"They can, Your Majesty," Evadine told her, forcing a smile as she clutched the sealed scroll. I knew she understood its worth as well as I. Words on paper, even those penned by a king, can never substitute for hard coin. She had just committed her company to marching on a hostile duchy with no war chest and parlous supplies. The strength of her congregation's devotion was about to be sorely tested.

"Very well, then," the king said, turning and resuming his walk, this time towards the shrine. "Rest assured you will not be unsupported. Walvern Castle has long been abandoned so the taking of it requires no bloodshed. While you hold it, I shall be gathering a host. Paid soldiers this time. No more benighted, fearful churls forced into line for me. Learned the folly of that fighting the Pretender. Once my host is fully gathered, I shall march it towards Duke Oberharth's north-eastern border which, on the basis of prior experience, should suffice to compel him to swear a renewed oath of loyalty and take proper measures to curtail the chaos in his duchy. I doubt the duke will be so foolish as to attack you in the meantime, but he's a devious fellow so expect all manner of mischief. If the Seraphile grace us with fortune, it could well be that this crisis can be resolved without war. Wouldn't that be refreshing?"

"It would, Majesty," Evadine replied. "However, it strikes me that averting one crisis will only invite another. The dark deeds besetting Alundia all stem from one cause: the adoption of a perverted, heretic form of Covenant belief, a heresy that has been allowed to persist for far too long. To prevent a recurrence of this evil I would propose a more permanent solution."

"I see." I saw Tomas and Princess Leannor share another glance. Their expressions remained neutral but the stiffness of the princess's bearing bespoke a stern warning. "And what would that be?"

"Instead of merely menacing the Alundian border, march across it," Evadine said. "And bring missionaries as well as soldiers. The corrupting unorthodoxy of Alundia must be extinguished. For a tree to flourish, its diseased limbs must be cut away."

"You would have me launch a crusade?" the king asked. "With all the fire and slaughter that would bring?"

"Fire and slaughter need not be the fruits of a crusade, not if we march in the name of salvation. In their grace and beneficence the Seraphile have gifted me a voice, one that those previously deaf to the Covenant's truth can hear. Were I given leave to do so, I could make all Alundia hear it and, having opened their hearts, they will soon cast off their heresy."

The fact that King Tomas was no fool was amply demonstrated in the part-bemused, part-alarmed expression that flickered across his face. I wondered if, until that moment, he and his sister had entertained the false assumption that in Evadine they would be dealing with a soul as steeped in cynical machination as they. Now he found himself confronting the uncomfortable reality of her devotion. This was a woman who believed her own legend.

"Clearly, we are of similar mind when it comes to the . . . danger presented by Alundian heresy," Tomas said, smiling, his tone cautious. "But you will understand a king's reluctance to make war upon his own subjects. And war will be the result should I do as you ask, my lady. Make no mistake of that. I don't doubt your gifts, but you cannot convert an entire duchy in an instant, and only that could prevent the fire and slaughter I'm sure we both dread. No." He set his hand upon her armoured shoulder once more, his touch a good deal firmer this time. "To Walvern Castle you will go, and there you will raise my standard high upon its mighty walls. As for now—" he kept his hand on her pauldron, steering her back towards the shrine "—I believe we've given our clerical friends ample time to phrase their edict of recognition. I, for one, shall greatly enjoy hearing it proclaimed from the steps of the shrine with you at my side."

CHAPTER FIVE

"The place is a bloody ruin, Evie!"

Wilhum's temper was ever an even thing, placid at most times, weary at others and rarely flaring to anger. However, that evening it burned hot indeed, his handsome features reddened and mouth set in a harsh grimace as he stabbed a finger at the map spread out on the table before us. "The king talks of mighty walls but you'd be hard pressed to find one without a breach. Walvern Castle has been taken more times than the cheapest whore in the Couravel slums."

"Wil," Evadine chided with a wince, causing the former knight to sigh and step back, arms crossed and face lowered.

Evadine had called Wilhum, Swain and myself to attend her rooms. They were located in a cluster of unedifying buildings at the furthest extremity of the substantial acreage occupied by the Shrine to Martyr Athil. These were the storerooms and barracks of gardeners and sundry servants, many of whom had been swept up in the frenzy of enforced military service when King Tomas marched through Athiltor on his way to confront the Pretender. A large portion of these unfortunates had failed to return, leaving their former domiciles empty. Although hardly luxurious, these stone halls with their stoves and well-maintained roofs were greatly preferable to sleeping in tents on frosted ground.

The bulk of Evadine's followers lingered outside the city in a make-shift camp. Their excited celebrations following the Luminants' proclamation of recognition, issued in voluminous if uninflected tones by Luminant Durehl, apparently made the congregants immune to the worsening weather. Before convening this meeting, Evadine had toured the camp and given a sermon that was notable for its lack of triumph. She acknowledged their devotion with humble gratitude before stoking it with some allusions to Covenant lore, raising up an outpouring of jubilant cheering. When the tumult eventually subsided the newly confirmed Risen Martyr, in a carefully phrased proclamation of her own – crafted with my help, I should add – told them all to go home.

"We have done great things together," she said, arms held wide as if to embrace them, "and know that by your actions we have done much to avert the Second Scourge. Now I must ask you to do more: I must ask that you return to your homes, to your families. There will be other tasks set before us in time, but this one is done. I beseech you, my dearest friends, go home and await my word."

The response had been more cheers, albeit with an undertone of confused, even aggrieved, muttering. Only the most fit and able had been accepted into the ranks of the company proper and these discards now faced a future without their beloved Anointed Lady. Whether Evadine's words would have the desired effect was yet to be seen, however I had little doubt that, come the morn, the camp of ardent souls would barely have shrunk at all.

"What's so bad about this place?" I asked Wilhum, watching his darkened visage play over the map. "Besides the state of its walls."

The map had been sourced from the Covenant archives and was therefore considerably more accurate than the often fanciful renderings of the royal cartographers. The Covenant was assiduous in its records, as befits a body that owned more than half the land in all the realm. This chart included Crown possessions such as Walvern Castle, but its main purpose was to illustrate the Covenant holdings in the border regions between Alundia, the Shavine Marches and Alberis, all clearly marked and properly scaled. It also displayed the principal pilgrim routes tracking between various shrines, trails that often aligned with the better-maintained roads as well as revealing paths unknown to those unfamiliar with the region.

"It's a stronghold that should never have been built," Wilhum replied, pointing to the location of Walvern Castle. It was represented by a fortress-shaped pictogram below which a helpful scribe had added the word "Abandoned." It sat within the bend of a river some ten miles south-west of the junction between the three duchies, therefore inside Alundian territory.

"King Tomas's great-grandfather felt the need to have a castle controlling this stretch of the border," Wilhum went on, "but his builders chose the worst possible site. The hill it sits on and the Crowhawl River curving around three flanks offer an illusion of security." His finger traced over the various landmarks. "But an illusion it remains. The Crowhawl is in full spate only one month of the year and the rest of the time can be easily forded in several places. Also the hills to the south and the east are tall enough to obscure the approach of an enemy host until they're almost within arrow shot of the walls. They also provide ideal platforms for siege engines. The last time it was taken the Duke of Alundia didn't even bother storming the place. He simply had his engines pound three different breaches in the walls and waited for the defenders to surrender, which they were wise to do shortly after. That was nigh a hundred years ago and no monarch of Albermaine has been so unwise as to garrison it since."

"Breaches can be repaired," Evadine said, "and mounted patrols can cover the approaches."

"Mounted patrols?" Wilhum gave a mirthless laugh. "Besides the scribe and I there are barely a dozen churls in this company who know how to ride."

"Then find more or teach those willing to learn. Teach them mounted combat too, since I feel we will have need of soldiers with such skills."

"That will require months." Wilhum jerked his head at me. "I've only just managed to get this one to sit properly in the saddle at full gallop."

"Then he will be able to help with your lessons. Make no mistake, Wil." Evadine fixed him with an unwavering stare. "We have been given this castle to hold and hold it we will, whatever the circumstances." She held his gaze for a moment longer until he consented to provide a tight-lipped nod. "Supplicant Captain Swain," she said, turning to the recently elevated former sergeant. "How goes it with our newest recruits?"

Swain took a moment to reply, rubbing a hand over the stubble-covered, scarred dome of his head, clearly making an effort not to look too long at the map. I divined that he had no more liking for this mission than Wilhum, but as ever possessed a more circumspect tongue in Evadine's presence. "They're keen enough, my lady," he said. "Clumsy, slow-witted and barely capable of forming a line, but keen."

"You only have one week before we march, so work them hard," Evadine instructed. "Harder even than you worked Master Scribe and his fellows from Callintor. Also, make it clear that any who wish to leave can do so without fear of punishment or shame. I think it best we winnow out the less hardy souls before setting off."

She glanced at the map, allowing her gaze to linger only for a moment before gesturing to me to furl it. "Keep it close," she told me. "And study it well. Especially the pilgrim trails."

"I shall, my lady," I assured her, taking the map.

She sighed and ran a tired hand through her hair, smothering a yawn. "Best if we go over the accounts and logs while I still have strength to keep my eyes open. Wil, Captain, get yourselves some rest. In the morning have the company arranged in full kit for inspection. Those with the most slovenly appearance will be dismissed. We may as well start the winnowing right away."

After Wilhum and Swain knuckled their foreheads and departed the room, Evadine settled into a chair by the stove, wrapping a cloak about her shoulders and gesturing for me to sit opposite. "I think you'll find Ayin's hand has improved considerably," I said, proffering the leather-bound tome of the company log. "Her letters become richer in flourishes by the day."

"That wasn't quite how I remember it," she said, not taking the book, elaborating at my puzzled look. "The tale you told the council. As I recall, when I awoke after the Seraphile healed me, you were already lying senseless on the floor. I don't recall you fainting."

"A little colour always enhances a story." Seeing the insistent doubt on her face, I shrugged and added, "There were many liars in that room today. I've little doubt I was the least of them."

She blinked and glanced at the ledger I continued to hold out. "I'm sure it's all in order," she said with a smile. "You know I didn't ask you to tarry so we could pore over dates and figures, Alwyn."

My face tensed in reluctance as I set the ledger on my knees, fingers tapping the binding as I sought to concoct the right response. This was how it had been since my waking in the forest, our time alone marked by an abrupt divestment of formality and desire for honest counsel.

"Just tell me your thoughts," she said, noting my hesitation. "As unvarnished and distasteful as they may be."

"This is a snare," I said. "A royal snare, in fact. I can think of only one reason why the king would send you off to garrison a castle that can't be held. He's hoping Oberharth, or whatever gang of heretic fanatics is running rampant in his duchy, will do what he can't. I'd also hazard a guess that he managed to persuade the Luminants to issue their proclamation on the promise that their new Risen Martyr won't remain risen for too long."

"They hate me," Evadine conceded in a sad murmur. "That I see clearly. It is . . . dispiriting that those who have given their lives to Covenant service should act with such pettiness when presented with inarguable proof of their faith."

I was unable to contain a short, bitter laugh. "Since when was the Covenant about faith?"

This brought a stern frown of admonition to her brow, prompting me to add, "You asked for my unvarnished thoughts. Here they are, as guided by the peerless insight of Ascendant Sihlda Doisselle, possibly the last truly faithful soul to hold senior clerical rank. Sihlda taught me that the Covenant may have begun as a concordance of believers driven together by persecution, but it persists as a bastion of wealth and power. This—" I held up the scrolled map she had entrusted to me "—is but a fraction of the Covenant's holdings. Through their strictures, their land and their wealth, they control the lives of millions and compel the obeisance of kings. All of this was built on faith in the Martyrs' example, and the genius of it lies in that word. A martyr, by definition, is dead. They are legends, heroes, figures of myth who do not linger to gainsay the words clerics preach in their name. The Covenant knows well how to deal with a dead Martyr. It knows nothing about dealing with a living one. Therein lies their fear, and their hate."

"Then what would you have me do? Refuse the king? Rescind the oath I swore to him, with all the chaos that would entail?"

"No. This snare is too well made to slip, and I've no more desire to see this realm consumed by strife than you do. But it's a long road to Alundia and who knows what we'll find when we get there. I'm no longer an outlaw, but I retain an outlaw's insight. If the duchy has truly descended into chaos, then we face danger, but also opportunity. They sent you off to face death in Olversahl, remember? You confounded them then. I've no doubt you'll confound them again. As for this tumbledown castle, you promised to hold it in the king's name. Who's to say in what manner? Ten soldiers are still a royal garrison as long as they raise the king's banner above the walls. That done, the company will be free to march where you ordain."

"Assuming we can provision them for the march."

"The King's Writ may be just paper but it will surely have its uses. If it please you, my lady, I suggest you leave provision of supplies in my hands."

Her eyes narrowed a little. For all her regard for me, the inescapable truth of my past loomed large enough to raise doubt over placing such trust in a man burdened by so many crimes. "I will expect, Master Scribe, not to find your purse growing any fatter in the course of our march."

I inclined my head with a rueful grin. "If you knew me better, my lady, you would entertain no worries on that score. I've never owned a purse that held coin long enough to grow fat."

"Very well. But ensure proper recording of all transactions, and don't doubt that I'll check your numbers."

"I would expect nothing less." I rose and knuckled my forehead, drawing an annoyed grimace for she disliked my displays of formal respect. "By your leave, my lady," I said, moving to the door.

"It's not a snare, Alwyn," she said, causing my hand to pause on the latch.

"No?" I asked, turning back to find her staring into the flames of the iron stove.

"You see a snare, I see a door," she said. "A . . . portal, you might say. And through that portal those denied the truth of the Covenant will be drawn, willingly or not. The king has provided me a gift, albeit unknowingly. The greatest gift in fact." Her voice faded and she huddled in her cloak. Since her healing I had noticed that, while she exhibited only vital energy during the day, when night fell and sleep loomed, she felt the chill worse than most. "In Alundia," she murmured. "That's where it begins, Alwyn. The crusade that will save us all."

The next day I spent the morning assisting Wilhum in his tutelage of those recruits appointed to serve as the Anointed Lady's Mounted Guard, a grandiose and ill-fitting title given our charges. There was a score of them, thirteen men and seven women. Most were young and shy of their twentieth summer, with two brawny exceptions. Brickman, befitting his name, had been a travelling artisan, his years of journeying giving him a familiarity with horses. Although more skilled as a drover than a rider, he had no difficulty staying in the saddle and had a calming way with the beasts that was highly welcome.

Estrik was of much the same broad, thick-armed stature as Brickman, but with none of the placidity. A soldier since boyhood, he had learned to ride as a man-at-arms to some minor lord in the Cordwain. As would be expected of one steeped in the soldier's life, there was a hardness to this man, his words clipped and his heavy features marked by scars. His mix of faith and brutality reminded me of Brewer, but without my slain friend's capacity for words. Never a good speaker in public, in private Brewer could at least articulate his thoughts with impressive clarity. I doubted Estrik had ever actually felt the need to explain his faith out loud, even to himself, but that didn't mean it wasn't deeply felt. One of the first to appear at our camp in the Shavine Woods, he walked over a hundred miles to find us upon hearing the tale of the Risen Martyr. Estrik had sunk to both knees before Evadine to offer his service in a strained, choked whisper. When she accepted him, he wept.

My ability with the sword was sufficiently developed to teach the basics of the craft to the less experienced recruits, but I felt my other, un-knightly skills were more useful. "There are several veins that will bleed an enemy dry in just a few seconds," I told my assembled pupils, keeping a firm hand on the chin of former Supplicant novice Eamond. I had instructed him to come at me with a sheathed dagger, a task he performed with the clumsiness I expected, enabling me to take the dagger away and force him to his knees in short order.

"But finding them in the heat and fury of a fight isn't easy, so always make it simple. First, a stunning blow to keep him quiet for a moment or two." I jabbed the dagger's pommel against Eamond's temple, not as hard as I would have had this been a real fight, but still enough to leave him dazed. "Then the cut." I set the dagger's sheathed blade to the flesh beneath Eamond's left ear. "Don't slice," I said, the unfortunate novice choking as I pressed the dagger hard. "Cut and go deep. When you feel the blood on your hand, draw it thus." I dragged the dagger across Eamond's throat, the sheath leaving a red mark on his skin. "Yank his head back to make sure the flow is thick. A slow count of three and he's done."

My knee thudded into Eamond's back sending him flat. He uttered a sharp grunt as his cheek connected painfully with the frost-hard ground. I let him pant for a moment before prodding his arse with the toe of my boot. "Let's be up and at it, soldier. I've six more ways to kill you before the midday meal."

To his credit, Eamond proved to be no whiner, nor did he shirk the bruises and exertion of his lessons. Like the rest of these recruits to the Mounted Guard, the ardency of his devotion caused him to view pain as a price worth paying to serve the Anointed Lady. He was a quick student too, heeding my instruction without need for repetition. That being said, his life before the company had evidently been lacking in violence or danger, always the best teachers in my experience.

"Too slow," I told him, sidestepping his thrust and delivering a blow to his upper thigh with the flat of my wooden blade. We had switched to swords after an hour with the dagger, whereupon the lack of martial skills among this lot became starkly apparent. "And don't attack my blade, attack me."

As with the dagger, Eamond had been quick to learn the proper grip on the sword's handle and he copied the basic strokes and parries well. However, when it came to the fight, he resembled a child stumbling through a dance step, all jerky and hesitant.

"Never actually been in a fight, have you?" I asked, blocking a laggardly overhead swipe before shoving him away.

"To be truthful, Master Scribe," he said, palming sweat from his eye, "no, I haven't."

"There's something to be said for having folk try to kill you before your balls have even dropped." I flicked my wooden sword at his head in a feint then slashed it across his shins. "Sharpens a fellow for the trials of life, don't you think?"

"An . . ." he winced, hobbling back a few paces ". . . insightful observation, I'm sure."

"Then I'm glad we're in agreement." I paused, tossing my ash blade aside and drawing the dagger from my belt. Eamond's eyes widened as I strode towards him but, once again to his credit, he failed to flee. "Land a blow," I told him, "or I'll cut you."

"Master Scri—?" he began, only to jerk back in pained alarm as my dagger lanced out to leave a small nick under his eye.

"That's just a tickle," I said, crouching and circling, dagger poised. "The next won't be."

I thrust without further delay, striking at his face again. As is the way when real danger looms, Eamond's reaction was swift, dodging to the side and his sword swinging up to deflect the dagger. I found it impressive, as was the fact that he still hadn't run.

"Land a blow," I told him again, this time dipping low to aim the dagger's edge at his midriff. Eamond scrambled back, just too slow to avoid the slash that left a rent in his jerkin. He thrust his sword at my head, straight and true, but once again too slow. I jerked my head aside to avoid it and swept the dagger across Eamond's upper arm, slicing through the wool of his shirt and leaving a shallow cut on the skin beneath. I find that pain has unpredictable effects on people. Many will cower from it while others will be rendered into shocked immobility. Some, like Eamond, will respond with anger and new-found strength and speed.

His wooden sword birthed a loud crack as it connected with my skull, sending a blaze of stars across my eyes and summoning the throb. It had been absent since that morning, drowned by a hefty dose of Delric's marvellous elixir. Thanks to Eamond's blow, it returned in full, with an additional dose of agony to teach me the folly of underestimating an opponent.

"Master Scribe?"

I blinked, the stars fading from my gaze to reveal Eamond regarding me with a worried frown. It said much for his good sense that he had retreated beyond the reach of my dagger. Behind him the other recruits had all abandoned their sparring to spectate upon my embarrassment.

I smothered a groan and resisted the urge to rub at my head, forcing a smile instead. "That was well done," I told Eamond, sliding the dagger back into its sheath. Raising my voice, I called out to the others. "That's enough for now. Get some food inside you then report to Sergeant Dornmahl for horse work. See if you lot can manage a trot without falling on your arse."

They duly trooped off, save for Eamond, hesitating with the worry lingering on his face. "Are you sure you're all right?" he asked.

The snarling rebuke rising to my lips never reached them for Ayin chose that moment to interject. "Whacked him a good one there," she congratulated Eamond, appearing at my side, all smiles and girlish bouncing. It was her habit to watch the Mounted Guards at training, her quill ever busy on her parchment as she recorded our capering with increasingly deft phrasing. She offered a comical pout in reply to my scowl before giggling and looping her arm through mine. "Come on. It's time to eat. They've a new cook from the shrine kitchens. She's not as good as me, but not bad either. I hear there's pie."

"Go on without me," I said, blinking as the throb pulsed through my head, making me wonder if it might be possible for a man's skull to burst from within. "Got business elsewhere."

"Oh well." She squeezed my arm and scampered off. Despite my pains, I caught the way Eamond's eyes tracked her, lingering on the calves revealed by her raised robe as she ran.

"Oi!" I said, snapping my fingers in front of his eyes.

"I . . . meant no offence, Master Scribe," Eamond stuttered. "I would never . . ."

"Good. Keep it that way." Seeing the pitch of his abashed contrition, I softened my tone and looked closer at the cut on his arm. "No stitches needed. Bathe it in vinegar and wrap it in clean cotton. If it starts to pus up, take yourself off to Supplicant Delric." I slapped a hand to his shoulder as I walked away. "Steering clear of Ayin is good for your health. Not every pretty thing should be touched. Go and eat. If anyone asks after me, I'll be at the library."

CHAPTER SIX

I drank the rest of Delric's physic as I made my way to the Covenant Library, wincing at the taste and the doleful prospect of having to wheedle more from the reluctant healer's clutches that evening. I resolved to find an apothecary before returning to the shrine, just in case Delric proved unpersuadable. The prospect of trying to sleep without something to banish the throb was a frightening one.

I knew from Sihlda that the Covenant Library of Athiltor held the largest collection of original scripture and scholarship in all of Albermaine, an archive even larger than the tragically lost Library of King Aeric in Olversahl. It was therefore a surprise to find the building itself markedly less impressive than its destroyed northern cousin. It was clearly of older construction than the shrine, its uneven walls formed of round stone and mortar rather than finely measured and elegantly buttressed granite. In truth, it resembled a very large cattle shed more than a renowned place of learning. However, my lack of awe evaporated upon stepping through the large oaken doors to behold the treasure within.

While the exterior of this building held little in the way of impressive construction, the interior was a marked contrast. The shelves occupied three tiers, the lowest dug deep into vaults below ground level and accessed via a number of spiral wooden stairwells. The shelves of the middle tier sat upon thick beamed platforms connected by walkways while the stacks of the upper tier jutted up through a matrix of rafters. Berobed librarians toiled on each tier, checking inventory or porting armfuls of books and scrolls hither and yon. Deep in the recesses of the lowest tier, I glimpsed the slanted desks and bowed backs of scribes at work in a scriptorium. For any scribe or soul with a love of words, this was an irresistibly enticing place where one could spend a lifetime reading and never come close to exhausting the supply of fresh material.

"The scribe who fought the knight, eh?" Aspirant Viera asked. I had been conveyed to her presence after presenting myself to the custodians at the door. Clearly wary but unwilling to face the uncertain outcome that might arise from refusing me entry, they had been swift in offloading my troublesome person to the senior librarian. She was a tall, thin woman with a good few years behind her, although her overall impression of strident vitality made it hard to guess her true age. She had been engaged in perusing an ancient illuminated tome, peering at a garish illustration through a pair of lenses set into a frame. However, as she lowered the lenses and turned her hard, penetrating gaze upon me I doubted that her faculties were in any way dimmed by age. She scanned me from head to toe with quick, perceptive eyes, only briefly lingering on my face before shifting to the longsword at my belt. However, her scrutiny lingered longest on the bundle of scrolls protruding from the satchel slung over my shoulder.

"Am I supposed to be impressed?" she added, arching an eyebrow.

"Certainly not," I said, liking her instantly. "But, I entertained the hope that you might be grateful."

Her mouth curved a little but she quelled the smile before it broadened. "For what, pray tell?"

"The fruits of my recent labour." I stepped forward to set my satchel on her desk, undoing the straps to extract the topmost scroll. "A first-hand account of the Covenant Company's role in the Battle of the Traitors' Field," I said, holding it out to her.

Aspirant Viera refused to reach for the scroll right away, instead indulging in a doubtful snort and partaking of a sip of tea before consenting to take it. The ten pages of quality parchment it contained had been set down during my first days of full sensibility back in the forest. The penmanship was therefore not my best, but, conceited though it may sound, even my worst work will usually outshine the hand of most other scribes. I watched the Aspirant's eyes widen a little, although she was quick to return her features to a neutral scowl as she leafed through the pages.

"Your own hand?" she asked after a thorough and, I suspected, deliberately prolonged examination.

"It is. As are these." I placed the other scrolls alongside the first, naming each in turn. "'A True Account of the Fall of Olversahl to the Heathen Ascarlians'. Here we have 'The Collected Sermons of the Risen Martyr Evadine Courlain'. Also, this is a verbatim transcription of 'The Anointed Lady's Address to the Congregants of Farinsahl on the day of her Rising'." I smiled as the Aspirant's face lost its scowl. "I was there for all of it, you see."

Her hands, ink stained as I knew they would be, played over the scrolls with an anticipatory twitch. She coughed before asking her question, "What do you want?"

"I want only what all servants of the Covenant want, to further the faith in all respects. Take these, with my humble thanks for even considering them worthy of inclusion in this most vaunted archive. I would, however, and only if it please you, consider it an honour if I were to be permitted just a brief few hours in the library, perhaps with the benefit of expert assistance."

Her eyebrow arched once more. "Looking for something?"

"Merely to expand my knowledge so as to better assist the Anointed Lady in her holy mission."

"I see. And what particular portion of your knowledge requires expansion?"

"The Duchy of Alundia," I said, pausing then adding with a casual offhandedness which I'm certain this woman saw through with ease, "and the Caerith. Our mission will put us in proximity to the Wastes, so it would probably behove me to learn what I can of their ways."

*

Aspirant Viera took the role of my assistant upon herself, I supposed as a means of preventing any mischief on my part. It was obvious that she knew a good deal of my tale and the prospect of allowing so learned a thief into her domain stirred an understandable caution. Books are valuable, after all. However, she did appear to warm to her task when it became apparent that my interest was not a mask for some nefarious scheme.

"The schism between the orthodox and Alundian form of Covenant belief occurred some three centuries ago," she explained, "the outcome of the brief but impactful career of a previously unremarkable cleric named Korbil. He's considered a Martyr by the Alundians but not, of course, by the true faith. It was Korbil who first avowed the heresy that the formalities and rituals adopted by the Covenant had become a barrier between the Seraphile's grace and the mortal realm. The very notion of clerics became anathema to him, so much so that he tore off his Supplicant's robe and went about naked for a full year to atone for the perfidy of having worn it. He was also fond of whipping himself outside shrines during supplications, loudly proclaiming the evil he believed to be occurring within."

"A madman, then?" I said, recalling Hostler's often manic zeal.

"He didn't think so, but yes, obviously. However, even the mad can gain a following." Viera leafed through the pages of a thick, decades old tome before coming to a full-page illustration. "'The Massacre of the Faithful,'" she said, turning the book about to display the image. It was a block-printed etching in faded ink, the lines crudely formed and the presentation archaic in its rendering of human form. However, it did benefit from a certain gruesome clarity in its depiction of many slain and dismembered bodies littering the foreground. In the background, flames rose above a cityscape, the swirling lines coalescing into the glowering face of a man, the words 'The False Martyr Korbil Did Foul Deeds Upon This Day' inscribed about his head in uneven, poorly spaced lettering.

"Korbil's followers fell upon a congregation gathered for supplications at the Shrine to Martyr Elliana, on her feast day no less," Viera told me. "They killed them all, supposedly employing a range of inventively sadistic methods, although the contemporary accounts differ on this point. What is clear is that a vile outrage occurred in the principal Covenant shrine in the capital of Alundia, after which Korbil and his cult set fire to the shrine and much of the city. It was the fire that accounted for most of the deaths, over a thousand people by some accounts. King Arthin the First was not long in marching an army into Alundia to exact revenge, a crusade that, of course, claimed far more souls than those lost to Korbil's derangements. When the king caught him, he decreed five days of torture before the false martyr was finally granted the mercy of death. If he hadn't been mad before, he certainly was by the time the headsman's axe fell.

"But the king didn't stop there. The Duke of Alundia was judged to have aided the heretics, stripped of all titles and exiled to the Caerith Wastes, flogged into the mountains never to be seen again, his heirs rendered beggars and his lands forfeit to the Crown. Arthin then ranged across the duchy, passing judgement on those deemed heretics, often on the flimsiest evidence. Several scholars have opined that the king was in fact engaged in a grand theft, for those judged as traitors were often landowners and Arthin was a monarch ever in need of funds to fight his wars and settle the many debts they incurred. The Alundians call it the Great Harrowing, and the stain of it lingers long in their memory. Your Anointed Lady should not expect a warm welcome, young man."

"The council have ordained that Martyr Evadine belongs to the Covenant entire," I reminded her, keeping my tone light but also insistent. "Therefore she is also *your* Anointed Lady, Aspirant." I smiled at her frown before reaching for another book. "This is the most recent guide to pilgrim trails in the duchy?"

"Yes," Viera said, a new chill to her voice, which brought a pang of regret to my chest; I felt she had been starting to like me. "There are eighteen shrines within the borders of Alundia. All have been desecrated and rebuilt several times over the years, and vandalism is a constant worry for the true-faith clerics who serve them. It is a brave pilgrim indeed who walks the trails of Alundia. The unorthodox have no truck with the whole notion of pilgrimage, considering abasement before relics to be another blasphemous ritual."

"But the trails themselves are maintained in good order?"

"Where they follow the roads, I assume. Those that track to the lesser shrines are harder to walk, often hard to find. That guide will provide all the necessary pointers, however."

I smoothed a hand over the guide's leather binding. It was a substantial volume, but not too weighty. "Is this the only copy?"

"No." It took her a moment but Aspirant Viera managed to summon an empty smile. "Take it, and be sure to convey the compliments of the Covenant Library to the Anointed Lady."

"I shall." I consigned the book to my satchel before turning an expectant eye on Viera. "Now, the Caerith."

"We have several books on the subject. But I warn you they tend to be somewhat fanciful in nature. Ulfin's *Travels in the Wastes* is the most often read, but many scholars have pointed out its numerous inconsistencies and absurdities."

"Absurdities?"

"Oh." Viera paused to utter a small, dismissive laugh. "References to Caerith superstitions and such. Descriptions, typically lurid, of impossible things. Ulfin was a disgraced scribe who eked a living penning doggerel for an audience of gullible nobles and the less discerning scholar. Hardly a trustworthy source."

"Nevertheless, I'll take a copy of his travels, assuming you can spare it. However, I was hoping you might possess some works in the Caerith language. I know they have books of their own. Where better to seek them out than here?"

Viera's gaze narrowed again, this time in puzzled concern rather than disapproval. "We have a small collection," she said, voice cautious. "Rarely viewed since there are none who can translate them. Yet today, not one but two servants of the Covenant come to request sight of them."

"Two?" I asked, my interest piquing. "Who was the other?"

"See for yourself." She stepped back, gesturing to one of the descending spiral stairwells. "He's still here and has been for several hours."

*

The Aspirant declined to accompany me to the lower tier of the library, claiming pressing business in the upper stacks. However, I detected a notable wariness in her expression as she glanced at the maze of shelves below that told me her reluctance may not be entirely due to disdain for my company.

"You will find the Caerith texts towards the rear of the building," she advised before moving away. She surprised me by pausing and turning back, a grudging regard showing in her voice when she said, "If you should feel compelled to pen an account of your adventures in the south, I do hope you will think of us upon your return."

"I shall, Aspirant." I bowed with grave and genuine respect. "Assuming I am spared to write them."

Upon descending the winding stairs, I at first found the shelves busy with minor clerics engaged in the myriad chores of maintaining a well-used archive. However, these industrious functionaries became notably less evident as I made my way into the darker recesses of this level, the reason soon becoming apparent.

I heard him before I saw him, the voice grimly familiar even though it spoke words I couldn't comprehend. "*Vearath uhla zeiten elthiela Caihr?*" the voice asked, soft-spoken but carrying easily in the quiet, dry air. I could not translate the words but still I knew the language. This question was posed in Caerith, in a voice I knew I would hear again one day. I just hadn't expected that day to be so soon.

Rounding a corner, I found him holding an open book in one hand and a small oil lamp in the other. Bared flames were, of course, forbidden here and only lamps of limited dimensions permitted. As a consequence, Aspirant Arnabus's face was mostly lost to shadow, not that this prevented me from recognising him. Nor, apparently, did my featureless silhouette prevent him from discerning my identity.

"Master Alwyn Scribe," he said, a smile of apparently genuine pleasure spreading over his face. "What a delight to see you again, and to find you so well recovered."

I said nothing, continuing to stand in silent regard, my fist suddenly tight on the handle of my sword.

"I had feared Sir Althus's last few blows might have proven fatal," he went on, lowering the book and stepping closer until the glow of his lantern touched my face. His eyes scanned my features in careful appraisal. "How gratified I am to find such fears misplaced."

"Step back from me," I instructed, my own voice a raspy, thin grate, although he evidently heard the promise it held for he duly inclined his head and retreated. Despite his wise caution, I detected no overt fear in his bearing. As the principal orchestrator of Evadine's farce trial and attempted execution, he must have known how much pleasure it would have given me to hack him down there and then and yet he acted as if I were merely a scholarly acquaintance he had happened upon in this place of learning.

"Come to gather knowledge for your southward march, have you?" he asked with affable but not especial interest. "Very wise. Though, I confess finding you among this parlous bundle of heathen scribblings is surprising. I would have thought a thorough delving into Alundian history more fruitful."

I was tempted to once again offer no response, simply stand and stare until he left. But the Caerith words he had spoken compelled me to speak. "What is that?" I said, nodding to the book in his hand.

"Oh, this?" He closed the book with a snap, casually slotting it back into a gap on the shelf to his left. "Page after page of meaningless scrawl in the heathen tongue. Setting eyes upon such things may sully my soul, I know, but I think the Martyrs will forgive a small indulgence born of curiosity, don't you?"

"You were reading from it," I said, feeling my head begin to throb once more. I had noticed how it tended to do so whenever something stirred me to anger.

"Was I?" Arnabus's brows creased in puzzlement. "I don't imagine why I would, or could for that matter."

"You were." I moved closer to him, letting the lantern light reveal my features and knowing he would see the grim intent they held. "What did it mean?"

"I couldn't say." His face, still lacking even the smallest modicum of fear, formed another smile. "Perhaps you misheard."

At this juncture, my younger self would probably have slammed this man's head into the hard oakwood corner of the nearest shelf, forced him to his knees and then pressed a dagger to his neck. We would then have engaged in a brief and one-sided conversation on the subject of good and sound hearing. Master Alwyn Scribe, trusted lieutenant to the Anointed Lady, was, of course, above such things, at least for now.

"I intend to kill you," I told him, attempting a smile that, thanks to the throb, emerged as more of a strained grimace. "You should know that. For what you did at Castle Ambris and—" I bared my teeth, knowing it would create a feral spectacle in this secluded, shadowed place "—because there is something about you that stirs my hatred, good sir. You lie too easily and I see the delight it gives you. And you are cruel. There's a pleasure in cruelty, to be sure, but it's one all decent souls should struggle against. I suspect you are no more capable of forgoing a sadistic act than a drunk is his next drink. I have found it best not to leave one such as you living if I can avoid it."

"Oh." A faintly pained frown passed across Arnabus's thin features, rendered a yellow half-mask in the lamplight. "That's a shame, I suppose. I had hoped we might proceed on a more amicable basis."

"I find it hard to imagine any basis upon which we might proceed, or where we might ever proceed to."

"Ah, but we already are, my young friend. We have been for some time, in fact, although I'll confess I didn't know it until you strode free of the mob at Castle Ambris. Ah, surprise." He smiled fondly, shaking his head. "Such a rare delight."

"Is there a purpose to these riddles? Or are you hoping that conjuring a mystery might compel me to spare you?"

"Oh, I know there is nothing I can say that will achieve that, although I would advise against indulging in certainty. Some outcomes are unavoidable, that is true, others as ephemeral as dust, easily cast into nothingness by the smallest miscalculation or just blind chance. Take your survival, for example. I fully expected Sir Althus to kill you, in short order too. And yet the world tilted, just a little, and so here you stand while the knight commander lies dead. Oh well." He sighed and shifted his head to an expectant angle, splaying his free hand in invitation. "Here I stand, Alwyn Scribe. I bear no arms, nor the skill to wield them if I did. Draw your sword and strike me down, if that is your wish."

"You know full well that killing an Aspirant in this place will mean my death, regardless of the Anointed Lady's favour." I moved closer, leaning forward so that our faces nearly touched. "But all wise outlaws learn patience. I survived two wars and make no doubt I'll survive a third, ensuring the great victory of a Risen Martyr in the process. Imagine her glory when she returns from Alundia. Imagine her power. I think you already have, as has the king and his sister. Rest assured, Aspirant, I am equal to whatever schemes you hatch. But please hatch away, for in doing so you will give me the evidence I'll need to hang you."

Arnabus pursed his lips, brows drawn and head moving in a faint nod, the face of a man humouring an idiot in fact. He still exhibited no sign of fear, which caused the throb to flare to a yet greater pitch. But it was what he said next that summoned sufficient anger to strip away my control.

"Where has all our wisdom gone?"

"What?" I demanded, teeth gritted in pain and anger.

"*Vearath uhla zeiten elthiela Caihr*," he said. "The Caerith passage you heard me speak. That's its meaning, or a reasonable translation in any case. The full quotation goes: 'Where has all our wisdom gone? Our life? Our beauty? Oh, what the Fall didst steal from us.' Beautifully sad, don't you think? But Caerith is a language rich in sorrow. Take another word, for instance: '*Doenlisch*.'" His gaze was suddenly lacking all humour or artifice, eyes gleaming with hungry perception in the lamplight. "Have you heard this word before, Master Scribe? Would you like to know what it means?"

Doenlisch. Yes, I had heard it before. First on the road when I watched the chainsman murder Raith, the Caerith charm worker whose supposed skills had failed to warn Deckin of his doom, thereby landing us both in the caged cart. The chainsman, another Caerith, cursed with the ability to hear the voices of the dead, had spoken several words of his native tongue that day. However, even then I had discerned one to hold far more significance than the others: *Doenlisch*.

The same word he hissed at me years later in the moments before his death in the forest near Farinsahl, his voice and face filled with as much fear as it was loathing. As a consequence, I knew who the *Doenlisch* was, but not the meaning of the name borne by the woman most commonly referred to as the Sack Witch.

"Tell me," I grated, hand lashing out to grasp Arnabus's neck, pushing him against the shelves. He grunted as my grip tightened, but still his expression betrayed no fear. Instead, from the way his body twisted and his skin flushed hot in my grasp, I felt sure he was in fact drawing pleasure from this assault.

"Gladly," he said, voice constrained but smoothly agreeable, "although the meaning changes with the inflection . . . "

His voice dwindled as I exerted more pressure, spurred on by a fresh upsurge of pain from the throb. "No more fucking riddles. Tell me."

"Fated," he rasped, smiling again, "or 'The Fated' to be formal about it. Some, however, would translate the word as 'cursed' or 'doomed' depending on the context."

"How do you know this?"

This time he merely smiled, continuing to do so even as my hand increased the pressure.

"I know of only one soul who could translate Caerith," I said, squeezing harder, "and they are very far away—"

"Am I interrupting something?"

My head snapped towards the new voice, one that held a note of amusement as well as stern admonition. Princess Leannor stood in a shaft of sunlight beyond the edge of the shelves, hands concealed within the bell-shaped cuffs of her satin robe. It was red instead of the green she had worn the day before, the gold-thread embroidery tracing over the bodice and sleeves catching a flicker as she stooped to peer closer.

"Should I return later?" she asked, mouth curving as she smothered a laugh. "When you are both . . . finished, perhaps?"

In that moment the throb grew so bad that, even if I had ignored her presence, I wouldn't have had the strength to keep hold of Arnabus. Stifling a grunt, I removed my hand and stepped away from him, dropping to one knee.

"Your Majesty," I said.

The princess inclined her head at me in response before turning her eye on Arnabus. "We were discussing linguistics, Majesty," he said, also bending the knee. "It seems Master Alwyn and I share many interests."

I sensed some manner of rebuke in the hardness of her gaze then, also a certain suppressed repugnance in the curl of her lips. She might have given voice to it but for another interruption.

"I found it, Mother!" the boy said, appearing at her side, one hand clutching at her skirts as he brandished a small book in the other. "And it has pictures. The Aspirant says I can keep it."

"The Aspirant is too kind," the princess said, taking the book to examine the binding. "*Auriel's Fables*," she said, glancing at the two kneeling men before her. "The copy we have at the palace is old and incomplete. Also—" she handed the book back to her son with an indulgent smile "—lacking in pictures."

She straightened, posture and voice assuming a regal authority as she cast her eye on Arnabus once more. "I shouldn't wish to detain you further, Ascendant."

Another undeserving soul raised high, I thought, noting for the first time that Arnabus's robe was now that of an Ascendant rather than an Aspirant. I swallowed a peeved groan at the realisation, knowing it made him far harder to kill.

Arnabus rose to his feet, pausing to regard me with an expression that was a picture of amiable equanimity. "I greatly look forward to resuming our discussion, Master Scribe. In the meantime, please accept my blessing on your mission to Alundia." He bowed to the princess, keeping his back bent as he edged around her before disappearing from sight.

"Master Alwyn," Princess Leannor said, gesturing for me to rise. "Would it be an imposition to ask you to escort myself and my son to the king's encampment? I have guards, of course, but their conversation is immensely tedious."

The throb had abated a little, but still lingered with irksome insistence. I had no desire to suffer this woman's company for one moment longer. I knew a clever and intrigue-driven soul when I saw one and playing her games with wits dulled by pain was an unappetising prospect. But she was a princess, and I little more than a churl, albeit one with an important mistress.

"Of course, Majesty," I said, pressing a knuckle to my lowered head.

"Horrid little weasel, isn't he?"

The snows of recent days had faded, leaving behind a cloudless sky and an aggravatingly bright sun that did nothing to alleviate the throb or sharpen my perception. I squinted at Princess Leannor in confusion for a moment, distracted by her son, who scampered about constantly as we made our way along the main thoroughfare of Athiltor. The king's encampment lay outside the city bounds but this was not a large conurbation and the distance was short enough for a member of the royal family to be seen walking rather than riding.

"Ascendant Arnabus, I mean," she added in response to my confused squint.

"My acquaintance with the man is meagre, Majesty," I replied, opting for a neutral course.

"Really? I was under the impression it was to him you proclaimed your challenge when you saved the Anointed Lady from the gallows. And the conversation I interrupted appeared to be of a . . . familiar nature."

Another ache from the throb momentarily overthrew my caution, causing me to rub a hand across my brow and mutter, "Weasel is too kind a word for that wretch."

The princess laughed, the sound surprising me with its unconcealed and honest humour. "In that we agree," she said before adding in a decidedly less amused tone, "but even wretches have their uses. Sadly, Arnabus has many and therefore enjoys the king's protection. I trust that's understood."

My caution still failed to rise as the throb pulsed unabated through my head, allowing words to slip from my lips it would have been best to keep caged. "And is orchestrating unlawful murder in the king's name one of his uses?"

No laughter this time, just a shrewd narrowing of her eyes. "I doubt you will believe me when I say neither I nor my brother had any hand in what occurred at Castle Ambris, but nonetheless it remains the truth. The late Knight Commander Althus and certain other parties conceived of their lack-brained plot with no instruction or encouragement from the Crown. You have now met myself and the king, Master Scribe, and I feel sure a man of your perception would know we would never act with such gauche stupidity."

This I found it hard to argue. The king was no fool and, despite only a short time in her company, I had a full appreciation of this woman's brand of cunning.

"Certain other parties," I said, jaw clenching against the pain in my head as I fought to wring what knowledge I could from this encounter. "Duke Elbyn and Ascendant Arnabus, I think you mean. The knight commander earned death for his crime but the duke and the cleric have not. If justice is to have meaning, should it not be evenly applied?"

"And where would it stop? Duke Elbyn and Arnabus were not alone on that platform the day they proclaimed the Anointed Lady's execution. Many of the senior clerics and most powerful nobles of the Shavine Marches were there too. Do you have any notion of the consequences that would arise from executing them all?"

"I do, Majesty. And I have an equally clear notion of the consequences if Martyr Evadine were to discover her . . . accommodation with your brother to be unwise."

I expected anger from her, but she laughed again. Not the genuine peal of amusement from moments before, but a snort of satisfied curiosity. "Your voice is still rough in places, but your words are fine. The product of Ascendant Sihlda's teachings, no doubt. Yes," she added at my sharpened gaze, "I know the story. An outlaw cast into the Pit Mines only to emerge years later transformed by the tutelage of a condemned cleric."

"All true, Majesty," I assured her, putting a bland smile on my lips. "Ascendant Sihlda told me *many* things."

Princess Leannor came to a halt, obliging me to do the same as she turned to face me. "I feel we've bandied words long enough," she said. "You called my brother a bastard, Master Scribe, as many witnesses to the Anointed Lady's salvation have attested. Such speech is treason."

"Not if such speech is true," I returned. "Only under the reign of a tyrant should it be a crime to speak the truth, wouldn't you agree, Majesty?" I attempted another smile but the throb chose this inopportune moment to flare to its worst pitch yet, causing me to stagger a little, nausea roiling in my gut. I was unable to stifle a groan this time and the pain was such that it stripped away my last vestige of restraint. "Still, treason is treason, as you say. Have your guards seize me and fetch a rope, if it please you. I'll even forgo the right to a trial."

Princess Leannor's shrewd eyes searched my tensed, quivering features. "You are unwell."

"Sir Althus had a very strong arm," I hissed, teeth clenching. "If this keeps on for much longer, mayhap you won't need that rope."

She shook her head. "That won't do, Master Scribe. Lady Evadine's mission to Alundia is of grave import. She cannot fail and I feel her chances of success would be increased with you at her side. I will send the king's physician to attend you tonight."

"Despite my apparent treason?"

"As Arnabus enjoys protection because of his uses, so shall you. But know that my brother is not so tolerant as I of these things. I believe Ascendant Sihlda gave testament before she died, did she not?"

"She did. Copies were made."

"Anyone can scribble ink on a page, Master Scribe. However, for your sake, I urge you to burn those copies. Their existence will not prolong your life. In fact they may well shorten it."

Her son came trotting back as I matched stares with his mother, the boy tugging at her sleeve in annoyed insistence. "Mother, I'm hungry, and I want to read my book."

His tugging stopped when his mother fixed him with a stern frown. "What have I told you about rudeness, Alfric?"

The boy's face took on a sullen pout of reluctant compliance, feet shifting in a discomfited fidget. "Don't interrupt when Mother is talking to people," he said in a toneless mutter. "No matter how low their station."

"That's right," the princess said. "What do rude people do when their rudeness is pointed out?"

Lord Alfric shot me a glance, one I was surprised to find lacking the resentment I expected. Instead he appeared mostly embarrassed, even a little guilty. "My apologies, good sir," he said.

Perhaps it was the boy's lack of animus, or just some minor twitch in the workings of my brain, but the throb left off its torments then. The pain and the anger quickly faded to a dull ache and I bowed low to the little noble. "No offence was suffered, my lord," I told him. As I straightened, I nodded to the book in his hand. "*Auriel's Fables* are a fine collection, but a lad of your age might want to seek out the *Epic of Sir Maltern Legille*. That one has flying lions and fire-breathing serpents, plus all manner of battles and quests."

Lord Alfric's face lit up as he turned excited eyes upon the princess. "Do we have it, Mother?"

"I'm sure it's lurking about the palace library somewhere," she said, casting a reproachful eye at me, "in all its blood-spattered glory. I recall all the nightmares it gave me when I was about your age."

"I won't get nightmares," the boy insisted, tugging at her sleeve again. "Please, Mother!"

"We'll see." She ran an indulgent hand through his hair. "Now, say goodbye to the Master Scribe. Your uncle is no doubt awaiting our presence at table."

After the lad had made his farewells and scampered off, the princess lingered to accept my parting bow. "The physician will arrive at the shrine by nightfall," she told me. "Please heed his instructions closely."

"I shall, Majesty, with all due gratitude."

She turned and gathered up her skirts. "And have a care in Alundia," she advised, striding off with a straight-backed and elegant stride. "In time, I suspect you will find the Pit Mines were a less treacherous place."

CHAPTER SEVEN

Although I had studied many maps, it was only during the journey south from Athiltor that I gained a true appreciation for the size of the wider realm and the comparative smallness of the duchy of my birth. The Shavine Marches was mostly woodland which had seemed endless to my once childish eyes; now I realised it was but one diminutive corner of a far larger dominion. The middle and southern regions of the Duchy of Alberis are characterised by a great swathe of farmland, a hedge-bordered patchwork stretching over plain and shallow valley as far as one can see. Yet, as the Covenant Company marched past acre after acre of cultivated fields frosted by winter, I gained a true understanding of why this duchy stood highest among the lands comprising Albermaine. It was from these fields that true wealth arose. A lord may gain the throne through force of arms, but without wealth he could never hope to hold it. Tomas was a king, but he was also Duke of Alberis and thereby second only to the Covenant in the wealth of his holdings. The realisation made me ponder the utter folly of the Pretender's failed ambition. Ultimately, how could any usurper hope to overturn such riches?

"You're looking all thoughtful again," Ayin observed, gazing up at me from the back of her pony. We were at the front of the column as usual, the Mounted Guard spread out along the road ahead to ward against threats. We expected no trouble this deep in the king's domain but it was good practice. Also, every day inevitably brought some faithful loon keen to cast themselves at the Anointed Lady's feet and it was best to bar their progress before they could trouble her notice. The least delusional were permitted to linger until nightfall to hear Evadine's sermon, some even afforded the honour of a brief moment in her presence. Come the morning they were sent on their way since she had issued a strict edict that further recruitment was now forbidden.

"Haven't done that for a while," Ayin added with a quizzical squint. "Is your head better?"

"Somewhat," I said. In truth, the medicinal concoction handed over by the sour-faced royal physician was markedly more effective than Delric's physic.

"Two drops in clean boiled water in the mornings," the fellow told me, slapping the bottle into my hand. "Two before sleeping. Don't partake of liquor after taking it or you might never wake up."

From the pinched disdain on his face I divined this was a man who saw ministering to churls as beneath his dignity. The fact that he had been unable to refuse this task said much for Princess Leannor's authority. Still, he clearly knew his business, spending a long interval examining the lumps misshaping my skull and asking curt but pointed questions about my symptoms.

"The skull was evidently cracked by a heavy blow or two," he told me. "Not an uncommon injury among knights or soldiers. The bones have healed but in doing so they created a protrusion both within and without the skull, hence the ache. It will be with you all your days. As you age the pain will worsen and may even kill you. One of the many reasons why there are so few old knights about." His tone was blandly factual and lacking any sympathy. It should have angered me but instead I found myself grateful for the unvarnished honesty of his verdict.

"So I'll need more of this," I said, holding up the bottle.

"You will." He handed me a small piece of folded parchment. "The ingredients are listed here and can be mixed by any decent physician or apothecary."

"Would some form of . . . surgery cure it?" I asked as he began packing away his accoutrements. "I've read of such things . . ."

"Surgeons are butchers and charlatans," he said sniffily. "Certainly best avoided in your case, unless you want to spend what years you have left as a gibbering simpleton. The brain does not respond well to poking or scraping. I suggest you accommodate yourself to your circumstances and make the best of it." He hefted his satchel and moved to the door to my chamber where he paused to add in a grudging voice, "If the pain becomes unbearable, five drops of that will ensure a painless end. Good day."

We camped that night on a rise amid the first stretch of forest I had seen for days. Although it covered little more than a few acres, the sight of trees stirred an unexpected nostalgia for the Shavine Woods, made all the sharper by what lay beyond. The patchwork of fields was less well ordered here, the hedgerows fewer in number creating a series of broad featureless plains.

"Best get used to it," Wilhum advised, regarding the landscape with doleful familiarity. "The southlands are mostly scrub where they're not mountains or craggy valleys. Be grateful we're not marching in summer else we'd be choking on dust for days to come."

After assisting Wilhum in training the Mounted Company and overseeing Ayin's entries in the company log, I settled by the campfire to continue my examination of Ulfin's *Travels in the Wastes*. I found the disgraced scribe to possess an inelegant but entertaining pen, his descriptions mercifully brief and lacking pretension. He also exhibited a refreshing honesty, particularly in regards to his own failings. His description of his disgrace and exile from Couravel was rich in allusions to a weakness for whores, dice and intoxicants, none of which appeared to arouse in him the slightest guilt or shame. However, this was clearly the work of an aged soul for it was also shot through with the sombre tone of an old man with much to regret. Ulfin was fulsome in describing the many debts, both personal and financial, that beset his later years. However, I was surprised to find that chief among his regrets was the fact that he could never return to the Caerith Wastes.

Such beauty is there, he wrote. *Such wonder. All I was told of the Caerith proved to be lies, yet the truth I wished to tell of them has been met with either scorn or indifference. 'Wastes' we call their land, and there is truth in that, for once they were great and what made them so has long fallen into ruin. But in its place they have built something new, something better, yet formed of the heart and the soul rather than mere stone.*

"What's that?" Ayin asked, striding out of the gloom with Eamond at her side. The former novice lowered his head in response to the hardness of my stare and quickly went to his own bedroll, busying himself with cleaning his gear. "Who's Ulfin?" Ayin persisted, planting herself on her bedroll, legs crossed beneath her as she peered at the spine of the book.

"He appears to have been a man of considerable insight," I told her. "Much of it apparently ignored."

"Can I read it when you're done?" Ayin's appetite for reading had grown considerably once the skill had become embedded in her brain, proving as unquenchable as her passion for song. She would scour the camp at night seeking to trade what little coin or trinkets she had for books, usually without success for there were few other readers in our number. Lacking better alternatives, she had resorted to poring over the stack of ledgers that comprised the company logs, taking irksome delight in ferreting out my occasional accounting errors.

"If you like," I said, brow furrowing as the throb began its nightly torment and the words before my eyes grew fuzzy. Sighing, I set the book aside and reached for the bottle containing my medicine.

"You take too much of that," Ayin told me with a disapproving scowl. "Wilhum said as much to the Lady."

My eyes slid to where Wilhum sat running a cloth over the scabbard of his longsword, careful to avoid my gaze. "Did he now?"

"Yes." Ayin tilted her face to look down her nose at me in what I assumed to be an attempt at mimicking Evadine's air of authority. "You should throw it away and follow the Martyrs' example. They knew the value of suffering."

"And I know the value of a decent night's sleep." I took a pointed gulp from the bottle, replacing the stopper and consigning it to the pocket of my trews. Once a notion took root in Ayin's head it was hard to dislodge and I wouldn't have put it past her to steal the physic while I lay sleeping.

"She spoke of suffering tonight," Ayin went on, her tone taking on an insistent edge when I settled down, turning on to my side and pulling my blanket over my head. "As you would know if you'd been there to hear it."

The urge to snap at her to be quiet rose then faded from my breast. The effects of the physic, I assumed, for its ability to banish pain also invariably calmed my moods. "What did she say?" I asked.

There was a short silence that I knew indicated a sulk. It reminded me once again that I was speaking to a young woman in many ways still tethered to childhood. "She said it's inevitable," Ayin muttered finally. "That no life can be lived without suffering, therefore we should welcome it as a teacher."

"Wise and valuable words, as always." My voice dulled to a whisper as I spoke, for sleep was never long in coming once the medicine went down. I drifted away to the sound of Ayin's murmured answer.

"Mother was my teacher. She taught me a lot . . ."

One of the benefits of the royal physician's concoction was its ability to bar the slumbering mind from dreams, at least mostly. It was both my misfortune and my luck that it failed to do so that night and, of course, it was Erchel I found waiting for me.

"Where've you been?" he asked in a not particularly interested tone. I found him crouched at the edge of a well in a subterranean vault, one I found, after some investigation, to be a place I recognised.

"You remember," Erchel muttered, tossing a stone into the well. "Though you never had the balls to get this close, as I recall."

"Neither did you," I shot back, the memory of this place stirring childish pique, for this had been one of our boyhood haunts. "Dared you a whole shek and still you wouldn't look into the well," I added, my gaze busily scouring the many shadows of this vault. It was subtly different to my memories, the ceiling lower and the well broader, its depths hidden beneath a veil of impenetrable gloom.

"The ghosts of the Dire Keep don't like to be disturbed," Erchel reminded me with a leer. "That's what they used to tell us, remember? But we couldn't keep away, could we? What perverse creatures children are."

The Dire Keep was an old ruin located in the north-easterly portion of the Shavine Forest, torn down many years ago due to some forgotten noble feud. Whenever Deckin's band ventured into this region the whelps would inevitably be drawn to the place, lured by the terrible but irresistible chance that we might catch sight of one of the ghosts said to still haunt the place, especially the well. I had been truthful in my taunt, for Erchel had been too afraid to peer into it when the time came. Now, however, he reached into the lightless orifice with an unhesitant hand.

"They've got company these days," he said, arm swishing about in the blackness, "those old ghosts." He grunted and wrenched free a bone, torn from the meat of a thigh judging by its length. "Cousin Rachil," he said, turning it this way and that as if he possessed the ability to recognise the gristle and sinew that dangled from it. "Never liked her much. She used to torment me when we were pups. Showed her my cock once and she laughed, called me 'Thimble Knob' from that day forth." With that, he tossed the bone back into the well. "Should've been me who got to kill the bitch."

He turned to me and I found myself struck by the change in his features. Before, he had been a distended, deformed version of his living self. Now he appeared more human, if still inarguably dead. His skin had sagged and taken on a grey hue, darkening to near black around his eyes. Also, there was no trace of a grin on his lips, just the curling sneer of one enduring unwanted company.

"Lorine had the bodies dumped in there," he said, flicking a hand at the well. As he did so I noted that his nails were a greenish yellow, protruding like stunted, misshapen barbs from the receding flesh of his fingers. "It happened only a stone's throw from here, y'see, Alwyn. This was where she massacred my kin."

"Or gave them the justice they deserved." I smiled at the hard glare he turned upon me. "Depending on how you choose to view the matter."

"She wasn't discerning, y'know. Had her husband's band of bastards kill every one they could lay hands on, even those who'd had no part in what occurred at Moss Mill."

"But not you."

The fierceness faded from Erchel's dead features and he returned his gaze to the well. "Had the good sense to drop and lay still, didn't I? Then the good fortune for my cousins to fall dead on top of me. I lay there while the slaughter went on. I could taste their blood, Alwyn. My own kin's blood . . . " He trailed off into miserable silence for a time, contemplating the void of the well's depths.

I looked around as the silence stretched, finding the shadows between the pillars of the vault far darker than was natural, as if they were a barrier between us and some great void beyond.

"There's nothing outside this," Erchel told me in a doleful grunt. "It changes from time to time. Things past, things to come, but always a scene of death I can't escape. This is my world, now. This is what she shackled me to."

"She?" I started towards him, then stopped at the unpleasant stench emerging from the well.

Erchel's eyes slid towards me, a knowing smile playing over his lips. "The chainsman was not the only one cursed to hear the voices of the dead." Seeing the fearful bafflement on my face, his smile blossomed to a laugh. "Do you really think you're merely dreaming me, Alwyn?"

My fear rose, fed by a sick and burgeoning sense of realisation. These nightly visits had always felt too real, too detailed, and the Erchel I met in them far more insightful in death than he had been in life. "What are you?" I demanded, starting towards him. "Who was this *she* you speak of?"

Erchel's laugh faded into a scornful sigh. "You know who she is," he said, shaking his head. "As for what I am, well, a fool must have a guard dog if he's to survive his own foolishness."

I lurched across the last yard separating us, hand lashing out to grab at his throat, but of course it found no purchase. As my flailing fingers passed through him, an icy chill spread up my arm, its frozen grip so violent that it forced me to a shuddering halt.

"Wake up, you stupid bastard," Erchel instructed. "Someone's here to kill you."

The chill remained as I started awake, breath misting the air, my hand reaching for the longsword at my side. I shifted into a low crouch, heart hammering and eyes searching the surrounding gloom for threats. I saw nothing, only Ayin huddled in her usual contented slumber a yard to my right. Wilhum also slept on undisturbed on the far side of our extinguished fire.

Just a lie told me by a dream, I thought. However, I kept hold of my sword and sought to calm the thudding pulse in my chest as I continued to survey the camp. My eyes tracked over Eamond's blanketed form, then the other members of the Mounted Guard, before coming to rest on the only one upright. Brickman had drawn the second watch and sat with his shoulder propped against the gnarled trunk of an old oak, the handle of his sword jutting above his cloaked form. By rights he should have been standing, but there were few sentries who wouldn't sit for a while in between touring the fringes of the camp. My eyes began to track away from him but stopped, a frown creasing my brow as I noticed that there was no vapour rising from Brickman's form. Not even the barest sign of a breath.

Quick glances to either side revealed nothing, the shadows betwixt the trees as blank and anonymous as ever. *Skilled, whoever they are*, I muttered inwardly in aggrieved admiration. *That doesn't bode well.*

Slipping from my blankets, I crept to Ayin's side. Not so foolish as to risk a hand in her proximity, I jabbed the tip of my scabbard against her shoulder, soft at first then harder when she failed to wake. As expected, her knife flashed out the moment she woke, eyes wide and face blank.

"It's me!" I hissed at her, staring into her empty eyes until reason returned.

"What . . ." she began, face bunching in the annoyed grimace of one dragged from sleep.

"Shh!" I jerked my head at Brickman's unmoving, breathless silhouette. "Trouble. Rouse Wilhum and Eamond. Keep low and stay quiet."

Ayin's gaze snapped to Brickman then back at me, the grimace fading from her features. Nodding, she crept from her coverings and began to crawl towards Wilhum. Keeping low, I inched my way towards the nearest tree, searching the gloom for the danger I knew to be close yet couldn't see. I felt a strong urge to approach Brickman, check to see if he was truly dead, but outlaw's instinct warned me against such folly. In my youth, I had seen guards lured to their deaths by fallen comrades. Instead, I kept sweeping my eyes across the camp, looking for anything out of place but seeing only slumbering soldiers and the thin grey wisps rising from faded campfires.

I almost missed the warning thanks to Eamond's startled yelp as Ayin nudged him awake. The noise was quickly smothered by her hand, just in time to allow my ears to detect the creak of a tree branch above my head. All branches creak in the wind, but the old yew I crouched beneath had thick limbs which would only protest in a gale or under the weight of something large.

Pushing myself away from the trunk, I heard the swish of something fast and narrow slashing close to my head. My sword came free of its scabbard with the swiftness born of instinct and many hours' practice, the blade flashing up to slice into a dark form plummeting from the branches. I felt the blade bite deep, then the hot rush of spilt blood upon my hands and forearms, before the body fell to the ground with a hard thud. I took in the sight of a slim figure clad all in ash-black cotton, twitching and still clutching a long knife. Panicked, agony-filled eyes stared at me from behind a plain wooden mask. At such moments it is easy to become transfixed by the sight of death, its grim fascination capable of spelling doom for the less experienced.

Tearing my gaze away, I sank into a crouch once more just as a fast-moving hornet buzzed the air above my head. A hard thwack of metal finding wood and I saw a crossbow bolt juddering in the yew trunk. Whirling, I spied the crossbow bearer a dozen paces off. They were part-concealed by the narrow trunk of a pine, hands moving with rapid precision as they rewound their weapon. It was smaller than most crossbows, easy to loose with one hand and also much swifter to reload. I charged towards the assassin with a yell, seeing little need for silence now. I covered the distance quickly, legs given speed by fear, which is always the most potent stimulant. Still the crossbow bearer had contrived to redraw the string and slot the bolt into place before I could cover the last yard. Fortunately, they hadn't noticed Ayin moving to their rear while I charged their front.

She fell on the assassin with a catlike screech, knife rising and falling in rapid jabs, blood spurting in torrents as she drove the blade repeatedly into the meat of neck and shoulder. The crossbow bearer collapsed almost immediately, indicating Ayin had found a major vein with one of her initial thrusts. Undeterred, she continued to assault the body despite its lack of animation and I knew better than to interrupt her frenzy.

"Company up!" I shouted with all the volume I could muster, voice echoing loud through the forest. "We are attacked! Look to the Lady!"

The pickets were the first to respond, taking up the cry of alarm and kicking their comrades awake, the whole company rousing in the space of seconds. A fresh tumult to my right drew my gaze to the sight of Wilhum parrying the thrust of an assassin armed with some sort of short-bladed falchion. Steel rang as Wilhum's longsword clashed with the assassin's blade, driving it aside to leave him open for a lateral slash across the chest. The sword cut through flesh to smash ribs, leaving the assassin a broken thing, wheezing out its last few breaths in a cloud of red spittle.

Beyond Wilhum, I saw Eamond rolling on the ground in a desperate struggle with another black-clad figure. The novice tore and bit at his opponent with undaunted energy, although it was clear his opponent outmatched him in skill. Driving a headbutt into Eamond's nose, he pinned him with a hand to the throat, rearing up with dagger raised to finish the job. Wilhum's sword flashed again, dagger and hand tumbling away into the gloom and the assassin left writhing on the ground, blood gouting from the stump of his wrist.

"Alive!" I shouted, sprinting towards them. "Keep the bastard alive!"

Wilhum quickly stamped a foot on the assassin's wrist, holding it down and staunching the flow of blood. "Get his other arm!" he snapped at Eamond. The novice gaped at him for a second before hurrying to comply, the hesitation just too long. Snatching a second smaller dagger from his belt, the assassin drove it into his own neck. I fancied there must have been poison on the blade for the man was dead by the time I reached the scene.

"Shit!" I cursed, driving a kick into the dead man's side in frustration, an act I instantly regretted for I had forgotten I wore no boots. I swore again as my toes crumpled against something hard and unyielding, obliging me to spend a few seconds hopping about in profanity-laden fury.

"Sovereigns," Wilhum said with a grin after rummaging in the corpse's clothes and emerging with a purse. He spilled the contents on its owner's unmoving chest, silver coins tumbling free amid a thick wad of fibrous cotton to mask the chink. "*Crown* sovereigns," Wilhum added with careful emphasis as he poked a finger through the riches.

I looked around at the torches now blazing throughout the camp, bobbing through the trees and shouts echoing as soldiers ran about, the light flickering on dozens of bared blades. However, there were no sounds of combat. "Best check on her," I grunted at Wilhum as I hobbled towards my bedroll. "I'll be along when I've put on my fucking boots."

"Anyone recognise this filth?" Swain's question had been addressed to all present, but his eyes lingered most on me. The assassins' bodies lay in a row, masks removed and garb thoroughly searched. One woman and three men, each with a fat purse of silver crown sovereigns. The rising sun added a golden tint to the frost-speckled trees but did nothing to banish the ugly, grey-white pallor that coloured each slack, empty face.

"I am not acquainted with every cut-throat in Albermaine," I told Swain. I had, in truth, closely scrutinised each face in the hopes of triggering a memory, without result. They had a good number of scars between them, a couple bearing tattoos that told of a seafaring past, but nothing that clearly indicated name, allegiance or origin. In addition to the unlucky Brickman, this quartet of murderers had slain another three sentries before my fortunate waking had interrupted their progress.

Fortunate? a taunting inner voice enquired, summoning memories of Erchel's sagging, resentful face. *Wake up . . . someone's here to kill you.*

"I'd guess this one's Dulsian," Swain said, his foot nudging the woman's body. "Sun-bronzed skin and the way she's braided her hair tells of the Dulsian coast, and that duchy's the only place I've seen a weapon like this." He reached for the crossbow Ayin held, stopping when she enfolded it tightly in her arms and stepped back.

"It's mine," she said. "I won it."

"Spoils of war, Captain," I told Swain and he wisely didn't press the matter.

"Four unnamed assassins sent to kill you, my lady," he said, turning to Evadine. "And paid silver crown sovereigns for the task. That's all we can say with any surety."

Evadine regarded the corpses with a studious frown, hands clasped behind her back as was often the case when she lost herself in thought. Finally, she looked at me, one eyebrow raised.

"It's clumsy," I said, knowing I was probably voicing a conclusion she had already reached. "The king and his sister are not."

"The sovereigns are a blind, then?" Wilhum asked. "Intended to divert blame."

"Why else carry them?" I said. "No professional cut-throat would do so unless ordered to it."

"So, they were expected to fail."

"Or lose at least one of their number." I shrugged. "But we should assume that their intent was sincere and the coins merely insurance against failure. Someone doesn't want the Anointed Lady leading this company into Alundia. I'd say the list of suspects is, therefore, quite long."

"Duke Oberharth surely sits at the top," Wilhum said. "He must have heard we're on our way by now, and I've never heard anyone accuse him of being overly clever. This—" he jerked his chin at the bodies "—is the kind of scheme dreamt up by an arrogant fool who thinks he's cunning."

Evadine spent another moment in silent contemplation before looking to Swain. "The soldiers we lost. Did any have families?"

"I'll need to enquire, my lady," Swain said.

"Brickman's wife died years ago," Wilhum said. "But he did have a daughter in northern Alberis. She'll take some finding, though."

"Half the sovereigns will go to her and any other family of the slain we can identify, in due course," Evadine said. "The funds will be held in trust until they can be found. The rest will go to the company coffers. It would be nice to actually pay for our victuals for a time. Consign the dead to the earth and I'll say the words before we begin the day's march."

She settled a steady, intent gaze on each of us as she spoke on, "I was never so foolish as to think all our enemies vanquished and it is clear we must have the greatest care from now on. Care requires circumspection as well as vigilance. Henceforth, no word of this is to be spoken. Make sure all those under your charge understand. On the instruction of the Anointed Lady, this never happened."

CHAPTER EIGHT

"Not quite an army," Wilhum said, shading his eyes against the low winter sun to view the force drawn up on the opposite bank. "But not exactly not an army either. If that makes sense."

"It doesn't," I assured him.

The Covenant Company had arrived at the ford across the Crowhawl River late in the morning of our eighteenth day on the march. Arrayed on the far side of the shallow but busy waters stood what I estimated to be two hundred mounted knights and men-at-arms, plus close to a thousand foot. From the numerous glints of sunlight rising from their ranks I judged these to be well-armed and -armoured infantry rather than pressed churls, no doubt leavened with a good many crossbowmen. In short, it was precisely not what one wished to find when attempting to ford a river.

"I doubt they would pitch so fine a tent if their intent was hostile," Evadine said, pointing out the large canvas structure rising from the centre of their ranks. A banner fluttered from a tall pole rising from the tent's conical roof: a rearing black bear on a sky-blue background.

"The banner of the Duke of Alundia," Wilhum said. "And I see no truce flag beside it."

"A truce would indicate we are already at war." Evadine took a firmer hold of her reins causing Ulstan, her tall russet-coated charger, to shift in anticipation. "And we are not. Let us see what our welcomers have to say. Master Scribe, you will accompany me. Sergeant Dornmahl, array the Mounted Guard in as tidily as you can but keep them in place. Tell Captain Swain to draw the company up in parade order, no battle formations."

Wilhum's reluctance was plain as he cast a dubious eye over the Alundian ranks. "The duke is not known for his welcoming nature, Evie," he said. "At least let me bring the guard across . . ."

"There'll be no fighting, Wil," she cut in, kicking her charger into motion. "The day is just too fine for blood."

She gave him a final smile of reassurance before spurring to a trot, Ulstan churning the river white. Evadine made a typically impressive figure as she traversed the ford, straight-backed and dark hair streaming, the raised water catching a rainbow from the sun which gleamed bright on her armour. Naturally, my own progress was far less impressive since guiding a horse through a fast-flowing river was not a skill Wilhum had seen fit to teach me. Also, Jarik possessed none of Ulstan's innate nobility and sure-footedness, huffing and stumbling his way through the water in a manner that came close to tipping me into the current more than once. Consequently, Evadine had already reined Ulstan to a halt on the far bank and begun conversing with a dismounted Alundian knight by the time Jarik struggled free of the water.

" . . . such things are custom here, my lady," the knight was saying as I halted Jarik a few paces from Evadine's side. "Visiting nobles present themselves to the duke or duchess, not the other way around."

The knight spoke with a clipped hardness to his voice that marked him as a man striving for a note of civility he clearly didn't feel. He was a well-built fellow in fine armour. His breastplate and pauldrons were inlaid with silver, tracing across the plate to form a motif that replicated the bear adorning the banner fluttering above our heads. He held his helm at his side, I assumed to convey a less hostile welcome, although the glower he failed to keep from his black-bearded face told another story. As he spoke his eyes flicked from Evadine to me, lingering a moment in careful appraisal before shifting back to his principal object.

"How fortunate then," he went on, gesturing to the fine tent at his back, "that Duchess Celynne has, in her kind condescension, journeyed far to offer you the chance do so without the inconvenience of travelling all the way to Highsahl."

"Fortunate and kind indeed, Lord Roulgarth," Evadine replied with smooth affability, inclining her head. "I assume the duke himself is engaged elsewhere?"

"My brother's duties are many. I'm sure you understand." Lord Roulgarth's smile broadened as his eyes grew harder. He gestured towards the tent again, this time with more insistence. "If you would allow me to escort you to the duchess's presence, my lady."

"Of course, my lord." Evadine dismounted, nodding at me to do the same. "May I also present Master Alwyn Scribe? He bears missives from the king regarding our mission."

The knight's eyes settled on me once more, just for a moment. "Yes, I've heard of him," he said before standing aside with a bow. "Shall we?"

The tent's interior was carpeted in velvet and furnished with numerous cushions, the air warmed by a brazier of glowing coals. It was also a chaos of five small children and what appeared to be a greater number of wolfhound puppies. Giggles and yapping filled the air as the tots and pups cavorted among the cushions, a slender blonde woman in blue and white silks standing serenely amid the carnage. A bright, seemingly genuine smile spread over her face at the sight of Evadine as she came forward, extending her arms.

"My lady," she said, clasping Evadine's hands before enfolding her in an embrace. She lacked Evadine's height and her arms didn't quite meet as they wrapped around the Anointed Lady's armoured torso. "How wonderful to see you again." Studying the blonde woman's happy, open visage, I concluded that if this was an act, this lady's facility for artifice would put Lorine to shame.

"Duchess," Evadine began, sinking to one knee only for the blonde woman to wave a hand.

"Don't trouble yourself with all that silliness," she said. "And call me Celynne, as you used to when we were at court. Unless you've forgotten your old playmate."

"Of course not." A smile appeared on Evadine's lips, one that mirrored some of the warmth on display although a creditable caution lingered in her eyes. "We bring royal missives . . . " she went on, gesturing to me.

"Oh, I'm sure you do." Duchess Celynne rolled her eyes in dismissal. "All that can wait. Come!" She took Evadine's hand again, drawing her into the swirl of dogs and infants. "It's time you met my darlings."

It transpired that the duchess had a tendency to produce multiple siblings; the boys were triplets and the two older girls twins. They all had the same golden locks and bright blue eyes as their mother. They made a great fuss of Evadine, whom the duchess insisted they call "Auntie". The girls were particularly fascinated by her hair, tracing small fingers through the long dark tresses while the triplets crawled over her armour, poking at the varied plates in fascination.

"No gold," one of the boys observed. "Father's armour has gold bits on it. Uncle's only has silver." He paused to poke his tongue out at Lord Roulgarth. The knight responded by angling his head and forming his features into a grimace of mock rage that sent the lad squealing in delighted terror. Roulgarth and I stood throughout it all, our stoic observance interrupted now and then by curious pups, both human and dog.

"Stop that, Lutcher," one of the girls said, tugging away a wolfhound pup in the act of cocking a leg over my foot. "Naughty, Lutcher." She gazed up at me with a small, serious face. "He's mine," she said. "Mother said I get to name him and take care of him. Do you have wolfhounds in your castle?"

"I have no castle, my lady," I said, sinking to my haunches to meet her eye. "Nor any hounds to put in it, if I did. I've been chased by a few, though." I ran a hand over Lutcher's pelt, the pup responding by nibbling at my fingers with his small teeth. "He'll grow to be very big in time."

A puzzled line appeared in the girl's brow. "Why were they chasing you?"

"Because he's an outlaw, Ducinda," Lord Roulgarth said, moving to pat a gauntleted hand to the girl's head, although his gaze lingered on me. "A man guilty of many terrible crimes, so they say. Run along now."

The girl duly scampered off and I straightened, trying to resist the urge to return the challenge plain in the Alundian's stare. As ever, I failed. "May I compliment you on your armourer, my lord," I said, nodding to his breastplate. "I've rarely seen finer work. So well maintained too, nary a scratch on it. I assume you had it repaired after the Traitors' Field. Oh . . . " I trailed off, giving a laugh of apologetic embarrassment. "Forgive my poor memory. You weren't actually there, were you?"

To my annoyance, I was greeted by the dispiriting sight of a barb failing to find its mark, for Lord Roulgarth just grunted a laugh. "No," he said, "went boar hunting instead. Thought it a better use of my time. Haven't been north for some years now, truth be told. Last occasion was for the Grand Tourney to mark King Tomas's twenty-second birthday. By happenstance, it was Sir Althus Levalle I faced in the sword that year. I beat him, quite handily, as I recall." He bared his teeth in a smile, speaking on with a soft but very precise intonation, "All on my own."

"So, you have missives for me, Master Scribe," the duchess called to me, providing a welcome reason to remove myself from the unwise temptations offered by Lord Roulgarth's company.

"My lady," I said, navigating a shifting barrier of pup and child to take a knee before her. The letters bearing the royal seal I carried were in fact addressed to her husband. However, I deduced from Evadine's acceptance of this meeting that this was not a time to insist on formalities.

Duchess Celynne and Evadine were perched on cushions, drinking the tea a servant had provided in a silver urn and small cups. The cup sat well in the duchess's hand, adding to the overall impression of dainty delicacy, while Evadine appeared almost comical sipping the beverage in full armour with little Ducinda curled contentedly in her lap.

"Walvern Castle?" the duchess asked after perusing the first letter. I saw some suppressed amusement on her face as she exchanged a short glance with her brother-in-law. "That's where Tomas has sent you?"

"It is, my lady," Evadine confirmed.

"Then I hope you brought some masons with you. It's a terribly draughty place, especially in winter." The duchess smothered a laugh before reaching for the second letter, her amusement fading quickly as she read the opening lines. This time the look she shared with Roulgarth was far longer and much graver. "Are you aware of the contents of this missive, Lady Evadine?" she asked.

"Royal correspondence is not for my eyes, my lady," Evadine replied. Although the duchess's bearing barely altered, the air in the tent took on a decided chill. Ducinda began to squirm in Evadine's lap and the other children's play quieted with a suddenness that told me they were well attuned to reading their mother's shifting moods.

"Time for your lessons, my dears," Duchess Celynne said, clapping her hands. A servant duly appeared to usher the children from the tent along with the yipping pups. Before scampering off to join the others, Ducinda paused to press herself to Evadine's breastplate.

"Bye bye, Auntie," she said, waving as the servant led her out. "Bye bye, Master Outlaw . . . "

"The king sends us a list of names, my lord," Celynne said, rising from her cushions to hand the letter to Roulgarth. "A list of Alundian names, all of whom he demands be arrested and conveyed to Walvern Castle for the Anointed Lady's judgement."

In the north, nobles were scarcely more likely than churls to be lettered. Here in Alundia things appeared to be different for the knight read the king's letter with rapid, if increasingly glowering ease. "There are over a hundred names here," he said. "Many are nobles of good standing or great import in this duchy. King Tomas lays all manner of foul deeds at their door, yet I know without doubt there are people on this list who have never raised a hand to anyone."

Now it was mine and Evadine's turn to exchange a weighty glance. Here then was the spike in King Tomas's trap, and, in accordance

with my estimation of him, it was far from clumsy. Simply marching
the Covenant Company across the border to occupy a derelict castle
wasn't enough. Evadine had been given a mission sure to rouse the
great and the good of this land to certain anger and potential rebellion. It should have occurred to me to read the royal missives before
now, since it wasn't a particularly hard thing to reseal a letter, nor to
burn it and pen a more suitable replacement. Yet, this simple subterfuge hadn't entered my thoughts. *You take too much of that*, Ayin had
said of my medicine and perhaps she had it right.

I saw only a brief grimace of consternation pass over Evadine's
brow before she got to her feet, speaking with an impressive surety.
"My oath is given to the king," she said. "And I am honoured by his
trust in me. As I have my command to follow, Duchess, your husband
has his. Today we have talked of pleasant things, of children and the
delights they bring. Of tea, of the vineyards to the south that produce
such fine brandy. We have not talked of murder, or massacre, or the
vile persecution suffered by those who follow the true faith. That is
the principal concern of both Crown and Covenant, and that is why
I am here."

"The Risen Martyr speaks," Roulgarth said, his voice pitched just
short of a growl. "Do not imagine your fantastical nonsense will bring
you any converts here. In Alundia the dead do not rise . . . "

"Brother!" the duchess said, her voice a hard snap. Roulgarth's jaw
bunched as he swallowed his words and I took careful note of the
way his hand tightened on his sword.

"Clearly," Celynne went on, her composure a match for Evadine's,
"you have given us much to ponder and it is not within the gift of a
mere duchess to agree to these terms. That will be for my husband
to decide. I will convey this missive to him with utmost urgency. Feel
at liberty to make your way to Walvern Castle and await his response."

It would have been within Evadine's rights to point out that such
permission was not required, since she had been sent here under a
royal command. Luckily, her pragmatism compelled her to reply with
a bow and a moderated tone. "I shall look forward to receiving swift
word of the duke's compliance with a royal edict, my lady. Rest assured

that any who stand before me to receive judgement shall be afforded a full hearing and no innocent soul will suffer unjust punishment. You have my word as an Ascendant of the Covenant of Martyrs and a Risen Martyr."

My hand inched towards my own sword as Roulgarth gave a visible shudder, jaw clenching as he bit down on a tirade. I felt sure the word "heresy" would feature prominently in whatever he wished to say. Fortunately, the restraining hand his sister-in-law rested on his gauntlet proved sufficient to keep a lid on his outrage.

"Evadine . . . " she said, before trailing off into a regretful sigh. "This is not the north," she went on after a short, sorrowful pause. "The Covenant as you understand it does not prevail here. You cannot force belief upon unwilling souls, however much you try. You think you are here to protect the faithful? No, you are here because the king demanded double the taxes of last year to make good his debts from the Pretender's War. My husband refused and now Tomas sends you to torment us, to your peril. Why do you serve those who would have killed you, and still would had they the chance? I beg you, as a friend, go back to the north, for there your true enemies lie."

"Those who persecute the Covenant are my true enemy," Evadine replied. "Wherever they may be found." She bowed again. "By your leave, Duchess."

"What did you make of Lord Roulgarth?"

We had waded our horses halfway across the ford when she asked her question, keeping our mounts at a steady plod. Clearly, she wished for the kind of counsel better kept between us than voiced in front of Wilhum and Swain.

"Arrogant certainly," I said. "Bragged about defeating Sir Althus at a tourney some years ago."

"He wasn't bragging. I was there, and it was handily done." I felt her gaze upon me as I frowned. "I'd prefer you forget any unwise inclinations towards that man, Alwyn. You've grown skilled, to be sure, but he is of a different order. In any case, it's not his sword I want you to match, but his wits. From what I could gather from Lady

Celynne, Duke Oberharth leaves military matters in his brother's hands, and I judge him to be no fool. If there's a battle to fight here, he'll be the captain we face."

"We've survived cunning captains before. That Ascarlian bastard Gruinskard, for one."

"Survival is not victory, and, henceforth, only victory will suffice for the Anointed Lady." I detected no self-regard in her tone, just an honest appreciation of her mission. "We must prevail here, Alwyn, whatever the foes set against us. I know how to fight a battle, but I've seen enough of war to know that most battles are won before the first clash of blades. To triumph here requires a plan and for that I have you."

"Swain is more a soldier than I'll ever be. It wasn't so long ago I was just an outlaw churl running from the Pit Mines."

"Captain Swain is as fine a soldier as I will ever meet, and a sound tactician. But, Martyrs bless him, his mind lacks . . . scope. Sadly, having met Lord Roulgarth, I don't think the same can be said of him. His wits are sharp and his mind far from limited."

I recalled the Alundian knight's outrage when Evadine referred to herself as a Risen Martyr, something I now understood to have been a calculated prod at his beliefs. "Wits can be addled by fanaticism," I said. "Or at least, placing excessive stock in one's faith." I thought back to my researches in the Covenant Library. "Unorthodox doctrine holds that the Covenant achieved a state of perfection with the death of the one they call Martyr Korbil. Therefore, in their eyes there can be no new Martyrs, Risen or otherwise. I'd hazard Lord Roulgarth and his ilk see you as anathema to all they believe. Something I suspect you already knew, my lady."

Evadine responded to my raised eyebrow with a faint smile. "Suspected," she said. "Not knew. It stood to reason he would follow the unorthodox creed, but I didn't know his attachment to it would be so fierce. Something we can employ to our advantage, perhaps?"

"Perhaps. Ultimately, however, achieving victory here will depend on the state of our stronghold."

CHAPTER NINE

"By the Martyrs' many arses," Wilhum said with a despairing sigh, "what a shit-pile."

At first glance Walvern Castle was certainly an uninspiring sight. I knew little of the finer points of castle construction but trusted to Wilhum's judgement of this one as archaic. It consisted of an outer wall zigzagging a roughly rectangular course around a courtyard of dilapidated buildings and a taller inner wall. Rising within this second barrier was a high, conical mound covered in tall grass atop which a squat round tower rose to a height of perhaps fifty feet. We had reined to a halt alongside Evadine on a ridge a quarter-mile from the castle, and even at this distance the breaches in the outer wall were clearly visible. Unlike all the castles of my prior experience, this one lacked a nearby village or settlement. In fact, the surrounding country was mostly empty save for the carts carrying goods along the road to the northern border. The company had passed through a number of hamlets after fording the Crowhawl, finding ourselves greeted by stern-faced churls, more than a few of whom felt no compunction over spitting on the ground as we marched by. They appeared to occupy a prosperous land; all seemed well fed and content except when confronted by northern interlopers.

"Alundia doesn't have churls," Wilhum explained when I commented on the haleness of the locals. "Not as we do. Commoners pay rent to their lord but aren't bound to him, so are free to take themselves off if they like. Also, once they've paid their tithes, any crops left over are theirs to sell. A farmer's more likely to get all they can from their land if there's profit to be had."

It was odd that a region so reputedly arid should be so heavily cultivated. We passed through many miles of rolling hills terraced with vines and fruit trees, the branches bare in winter but sure to blossom come spring. This fecundity, however, faded into rocky, steep-sided hills bare of vegetation as we drew nearer to Walvern Castle.

"Built slap in the middle of land that produces nothing to sustain it." Wilhum sniffed, wrapping his cloak about him as he stared miserably at the castle. "Another reason for its repeated failure."

"Thanks to the Master Scribe," Evadine said, "we have provisions enough to last the whole company through winter."

It was true that we had crossed into Alundia with a long baggage train of carts laden with salted meats, grain and preserves. These riches were the result of various bargains struck with merchants during the march south. I had been careful in seeking out those with reputations for honest devotion to the Covenant, pious types who could be counted on to make gratis contributions to the Anointed Lady's holy mission. This had involved persuading Evadine to conduct personal sermons and blessings for a number of houses, farms and mills, a task she suffered through with admirable forbearance. Faith, however, only stretches so far and even a pious merchant would never willingly see themselves out of pocket. Accumulating sufficient goods to sustain the company for months had required much liberal waving about of the King's Writ buttressed by a judicious dipping into our supply of recently acquired sovereigns. The Anointed Lady's sworn oath that all debts would be settled come the following summer also worked well to fill our carts. Despite it all, I disliked the prospect of sitting in this place at the end of such a long and fragile line of supply or, more importantly, reinforcements.

"The small folk'll carry off worked stone every chance they get,"

Estrik the veteran Cordwainer explained. Rarely a verbose soul, he had something to say when it came to castles. The place proved even less impressive upon closer inspection; the gaps in the outer wall were wide and the ground bare of fallen rubble which might have made for easy repairs. "Were we to look closer at the houses we passed a-ways back, it's certain you'd find more than a few outsize bricks in those walls. Given how bare the ground is, they probably carted off all the useful stuff years ago."

"You know masonry then, Trooper Estrik?" Wilhum asked him.

"Some, my lord." Estrik began to knuckle his forehead in ingrained servility then stopped himself. Apparently a life of soldiering made some habits hard to break. "Sergeant, I mean to say." He coughed before speaking on. "My father was a mason. Worked castles all over the Cordwain and Althiene, he did. Would have taught me the whole trade had he not fallen in the Duchy Wars."

"Can these be repaired?" I asked him, gesturing to the breaches.

"Everything that falls can be built again, Master Scribe." Estrik's blunt features took on a dubious frown as he scanned the walls. "Just a matter of having the stone and the labour to do it. Plenty of stone in these hills, for sure, but quarrying it and getting it here would be no easy matter. I'd suggest using timber to fill these holes but there's scant trees to be had nearby." He pondered a moment longer, stroking stubby fingers over his scarred chin. "Could try a shortening, I s'pose."

"Shortening?" Wilhum asked.

"Take stone from the top of the wall," Estrik replied. "Use that to make safe the breaches. Means your outer wall won't be so much of a barrier but, having lived through a siege or two, I'd say some wall is better than none."

One thing that did meet with Estrik's approval was the deep defensive ditch that traced around the outer wall. "Clever," he mused as we halted at the part-rotted drawbridge spanning the gap between the ditch's edge and the broad arch of the main gate. "Adds another dozen feet to the height an attacker would have to scale and it's too wide to be easily bridged with ladders or towers."

"Someone knew what they were doing, at least," Wilhum commented before turning to Evadine. "My lady, it appears we have a fine castellan in Trooper Estrik. I propose he be made sergeant and placed in charge of works."

"An excellent suggestion," Evadine said, favouring Estrik with a smile. "Congratulations, Sergeant Castellan."

As ever when finding himself the focus of her attention, Estrik lost his resemblance to an oversized bulldog, instead transforming into a discomfited, bashful child. For a moment I wondered if the man had been struck dumb. He sat in the saddle with his eyes lowered and skin flushing a mottled shade of pink. Finally, he darted a glance at Evadine and stuttered out a reply. "Never . . . never been raised to a sergeant before, my lady. No captain ever thought me worthy."

"The foolishness of your previous captains is not my concern, Sergeant." Evadine gave a brisk nod to the weathered, cracked walls before us. "Your first task is to make a thorough inspection of this place and report to me with a plan of works. I'll hear your initial thoughts after tonight's sermon. As for now . . ." She cast a doubtful eye over the frayed and splintered timbers of the drawbridge. "I ask that you find a way to get us inside without undue danger."

Fortunately, I had acquired two cartfuls of decent timber during the march south, purchased on the insistent advice of Captain Swain. "Even if we don't need it for building," he had said, "a company always needs firewood." I had also anticipated the need for tools, buying a load of picks, axes, hammers and sundry other implements. Consequently, we had the materials on hand for a new drawbridge and the tools with which to build it. Estrik proved an efficient overseer, recruiting the small number of carpenters among our ranks and setting them to the task within the space of a few hours. Until it was complete, however, the company had to camp outside the walls. Evadine ordered sentries posted on the surrounding slopes and sent Wilhum off with the Mounted Guard to patrol the approaches until nightfall. We used the hours before sunset to tour the castle, risking the old drawbridge to gain entry. Ayin took it upon herself to precede us, lightly skipping between the less degraded planks to show the way.

We found the main courtyard a weed-encrusted shambles of old wood, shattered tiles and fallen stone. As Estrik had predicted, the stone was mostly loose rubble with little value for building. "It's still good for throwing," Evadine said when I voiced my thoughts. "Even a small stone can crack a skull if dropped from a decent height. We'll have it all gathered up and placed around the battlements."

"I'd guess this was the barracks." I kicked an aged roof beam lying amid a carpet of overgrown tiles and bricks. "I'm no mason, but I doubt there's any chance of rebuilding this."

"We have tents," Evadine said. "They'll have to suffice until we can garner more materials." She looked up at the tower atop the tall grassy mound beyond the second wall. "This looks reasonably intact."

Her estimation proved correct after we climbed the steep, winding steps to the tower. Although the thick iron-braced door that once guarded its main entrance had fallen into rusted ruin, the rest of the structure lacked the damage seen elsewhere. The door was flanked by two bastions rising to half the tower's height, their inner walls rich in arrow slits overlooking the entrance. The interior of the ground level consisted of a broad circular chamber, the centre of which was occupied by a raised dais. A few smaller rooms lined the wall behind the dais, each one featuring a fireplace which marked them as living quarters. A large trapdoor, intact despite its age, sat in the centre of the chamber, revealing a set of descending steps when drawn up. We lacked a torch to enable an inspection of the gloomy vaults below, but the pebble I kicked into the void produced a long echo.

"Ample space for storage," Evadine commented.

"And prisoners," I added. "Never saw a castle that lacked a dungeon."

I heaved the trapdoor back into place then strode to the dais. "Here the lord of this place once sat," I said. It would have been nice to find a tall-backed, lordly chair to perch upon, but instead there was only dust. "According to the chronicles, the last northern noble to sit here never even got to properly hold court before the Alundians arrived to bash down his walls."

"It's awful cold," Ayin griped, grimacing as she hugged her slender form. "Shall I build a fire, my lady?"

"Please do, Ayin," Evadine told her, gesturing to the rooms at the rear of the chamber. "Pick one out for me, and for yourself. Make sure the chimneys are clear before lighting anything, though," she added as Ayin hurried off.

I went to the foot of the stairs tracing along the curved interior of the tower, a spiral of dusty steps ascending into the gloomy upper levels. The ceiling of the ground level was some twenty feet high and mostly shadowed, but as my gaze rose, I made out a surprising sight.

"Martyrs," I said to Evadine, pointing to the ceiling. Looking up, she gave a soft exclamation of delight as she beheld the painting that covered it from end to end. It was formed of a circle of portraits arranged around a blazing sun. All of the principal Martyrs were depicted, rendered with a vibrancy and clarity far beyond the stilted images found in illuminated manuscripts. These appeared to be real people caught in mid-action. The portrait of Martyr Stevanos was particularly striking, a tall, vibrant figure with flowing grey hair and beard. The scene was a well-known tale from the opening pages of his scroll, the first Martyr standing frozen in the act of placing himself between a captured enemy soldier and the mob that intended to stone him to death.

"Have you ever seen the like?" I asked Evadine.

"Some murals in Couravel have similar detail," she said. "But I've seen nothing so . . ."

"Alive?" I suggested as she fumbled for the words.

"Yes, alive . . . real. Nor can I place the artist's hand. Surely one capable of this must be known to history."

"There's probably a signature somewhere among it all." I squinted, eyes flicking from one shadowed Martyr to another. "I'll search for it when we get some light in here. Though we'll need to be careful if we want to preserve it. Soot and oil-smoke will stain the paint and dim the colours. I'd guess it's survived so well because the tower has been empty for years."

"This is a sign, Alwyn." Evadine's voice took on a reverent hush. When she turned to regard me I saw the same disconcerting certainty that had shone so bright after her waking in Farinsahl. "This is where we are supposed to be. This is where our task begins in earnest."

I replied only with a short nod, quickly turning to mount the steps. Usually, words flowed easily between us but when her ardency came to the fore I found my tongue knotted by uncertainty and the weight of the lie we had told her. "Here's hoping these are intact," I said, trying to distract her, without success.

"I haven't told the others yet," she said, following as I began the ascent, "but I was blessed by another vision."

I hesitated before responding, disliking talk of her visions even more than her occasional lapses into faithful diatribes. "A vision?" I ventured when the expectant silence grew long. We climbed through the second tier, featureless apart from the arrow slits in the walls. The sight of them reminded me to make a full inventory of the company's crossbow bolts. According to Swain, we would expect to run through our quarrels in short order if this castle came under siege and increasing the stocks would not be easy in so remote a place.

"Yes," Evadine said, her voice riven with a dismaying level of enthused conviction. "It was the night after that ugly business with the cut-throats, which cannot be coincidental. That the Seraphile would send me a vision at such a time is surely another sign of the rightness of our course."

"Surely," I muttered.

"They showed me wonders, Alwyn," Evadine continued, apparently deaf to my sour tone. "As you know, typically my visions hold mostly horrors, the raging terror of the Second Scourge. But this . . . " She fell silent, the echo of her footfalls halting. I turned to find her staring up at me, unwavering eyes catching the dim light from the arrow slits although her face was lost to shadow. "They showed me a world of peace. A world where all our struggles are done. A world where . . ." She faltered, her hand reaching out to me, trembling then withdrawing. The twin beads lighting her eyes flickered as she blinked and looked away. "I think I was blessed with a vision of our reward," she said, voice a whisper now. "And not the paradise that awaits us beyond the Divine Portals, but in this life. And what a reward it will be. All we need do is triumph here."

That's all? The caustic, doubt-laden question stopped short of my lips. I felt a terrible yet implacable temptation to unleash the truth upon her then, finally reveal the unvarnished reality of her impossible resurrection. Even now, I couldn't discern if her visions were truly the product of divine intervention or the conjurings of a fractured mind. I had seen much in this world to lend credence to both conclusions. I did know that all my instincts cried out against this part of her, this unwavering belief in her own insight.

Despite the chill, sweat began to bead my brow as the need to gabble out the truth spurred my heart into a panicked gallop. Whatever her reaction, at least it would put a stop to these endless delusions, perhaps even set her upon a path to a healing of sorts, if she didn't kill me for it. Gritting my teeth, I clenched my heart against the lure of honesty, turning and resuming my climb.

"Then let's hope the roof of this place is still in order," I said, hoping she missed the strain in my voice. "Or we won't be triumphing over anything."

Fortunately, the roof proved to be as sound as the rest of the tower. It was a good two dozen paces wide, enough for a whole troop of crossbowmen, and ringed with sturdy and tall crenellations to provide cover. It also boasted an unusual feature in the shape of a round plinth a yard high.

"I assume this is where the beacon fire stood," I said, hopping up on to the plinth and turning to survey the Crowhawl River, rendered a great arc of grey water by an overcast sky. "My researches told of a smaller, timber-built outpost on the far side of the river. The intention was that the beacon would be lit when the castle came under siege. Those in the outpost would then light their own beacon. Apparently, there was a relay all the way to Couravel capable of bringing the warning to the king within a day."

"No longer," Evadine said, stepping up to join me on the plinth. "Although, with King Tomas marching his new army towards the border, he shouldn't be hard to find if need arises."

"Assuming he does in fact march his army anywhere."

"So little trust in our king, Alwyn?" I heard a rare sardonic note in her voice, one that told me my faith in Tomas was of a similar order to hers.

"That . . . " I paused to suppress the profanity before speaking on " . . . letter. Judging by everything I've learned about this duchy, I can't think of anything more certain to rouse their nobles to arms. It's clear to me we have been sent here to start a war. What is less clear is if the king intends to finish it before it finishes us." I settled my gaze on the far bank, spying a low hill where presumably the second beacon once stood. "I suggest a contingency."

Evadine gave a doubtful frown "You mean to rebuild the beacons? Even if we could accomplish such a mammoth task, I see little point in calling for the king's aid if it is his object that we perish here."

"Not his aid, and not all the beacons. Just the one on the far bank. I suspect it's all we'll need when the time comes."

Chapter Ten

The following weeks saw me scouting the surrounding hill country with Wilhum and the Mounted Guard while Evadine oversaw the reconstitution of the castle. Each day the place rang with tools and the varied chorus of many souls hard at work. Although newly appointed Sergeant Castellan Estrik proved an able hand, Evadine had opted to remain in place to encourage the company to greater efforts. There was no telling how long an interval Lord Roulgarth would allow before his inevitable visit, so it was imperative that the labour be done as quickly as possible. Upon returning from our daily patrols, I was able to gauge progress on the breaches, finding the outer wall descending in height while the breaches gradually filled with untidy but sturdy stonework.

Our scouting missions had a twofold objective: firstly, to ward against any spying or sabotage, and secondly to enable me to seek out the more obscure pilgrim trails on my personal map. Establishing a network of hidden or forgotten tracks through this country would be very useful in the event of trouble. Sadly, most of those we were able to seek out had been long neglected and offered no better footing than any rock-strewn hillside. The path to the Shrine to Martyr Lowanthel, however, proved to be a notable exception.

The trail traced a wayward course through the hills west of the castle, traversing over twelve miles of gulley and slope but remaining in a useable state all the way. It had also been constructed with enough breadth to allow the passage of cattle, making it a viable route for packhorses or mules. When our enemies arrived they would be certain to cut the road to the border, and this trail might well serve as an alternative line of supply or route for reinforcements. The company was diminished in size thanks to the need to send three soldiers off to the northern bank of the Crowhawl to await our beacon fire. They were chosen partially for their riding skills but mostly for the ardency of their belief in the Anointed Lady, since their mission, should it become necessary, would require passionate oratory. I had entertained the notion of making Eamond a member of this party but his riding was still too poor and his manner too bashful, although in recent days he had displayed the irksome trait of offering unasked-for information.

"Did you know, Master Scribe," he began as we led our mounts along a narrow stretch of trail, "Martyr Lowanthel is the only figure in Covenant history known to have been killed by the Caerith."

I hadn't, in fact, known this, and would have responded with a terse, uninterested grunt but for mention of the Caerith. "They didn't like what he had to say, I assume," I said. "Not all hearts are open to the Seraphile's grace."

"The story goes that it wasn't his preaching that they objected to," Eamond replied, panting a little as we began to ascend the eastern slope of a particularly deep gulley, "but his thievery."

"A Martyred thief?" I gave a small laugh, my interest piquing further. "Tell me more."

"Well, apparently Lowanthel did venture into the Wastes fully intending to preach the Martyrs' example but found himself ignored at every turn. He related part of his tale before his unfortunate end, describing a heathen rite of some sort, one that involved the use of certain artefacts, including a strange bone he found especially interesting."

"A bone. That's what he stole?"

"So the tale would have it. Lowanthel was insistent that he took the bone, some malformed thing once part of a beast lost to history, to prevent further performance of the rites he had seen, claiming they conjured all manner of unnatural foulness. This may well be the truth, for he kept the thing at his side for the next ten years. The Caerith, however, appear to have long memories and an unforgiving nature. Those who found Lowanthel's body avowed that he must have taken a very long time to die. Of the bone there was, of course, no sign. Alundians still have a saying: 'Kill the Caerith, but never steal from them.'"

I laughed again then stopped as a gust of wind brought a familiar scent to my nostrils: *smoke*. Looking up the slope, I saw Fletchman halted at the crest, peering at what lay beyond with his bow unslung. The former poacher was not a member of the Mounted Guard for he detested riding, however his scouting skills made him an invaluable addition to our patrols. Up ahead, Wilhum handed his reins to a trooper and held up a closed fist in the sign to stay put before inclining his head at me.

"Finally, something to see," he said, starting up the slope.

We found the poacher peering at a distant column of smoke rising from the summit of a low ridge to the north-east, his gaze dark. "Brush fire?" Wilhum asked him, receiving a firm shake of the head in response.

"Not in winter, my lord." Like many in the company, Fletchman had stopped correcting himself when addressing Wilhum. Some habits were simply too ingrained to shake. "And I can taste oil on the wind, born of a big blaze, else it wouldn't have carried so far."

"A farm?" Wilhum wondered. "Village perhaps?"

"The shrine," I said, tugging the folded map from my jerkin. It was the product of my own quill, copied from a larger chart in the Covenant Library. "I'd put it just where the smoke rises." I pointed out the spot marked with a circle. "Five miles off, give or take."

"Closer to four, Master Scribe," Fletchman said, pressing a knuckle to his forehead. "Begging your pardon."

"Don't do that," I told him before turning back to Wilhum. "Shrines don't just burst into flames in midwinter. There's heretic mischief afoot. No telling how many we'll face."

"Establishing the strength of the enemy is partly our mission." Wilhum rose, surveying the ground between this rise and the ridge. "It's not so broken we can't ride at a decent pelt." He favoured Fletchman with a smile. "It appears you'll get to do some hunting today, good sir."

"Never stalked a heretic before, my lord." Fletchman grinned and hefted his bow. "But reckon they'll track just like any other beast."

The shrine was still ablaze when we reined in, my gaze tracking over the dozen or so corpses lying among the smoking and torn tents pitched nearby. The shrine was an old building of age-dry timbers that burned with fierce rapidity. It was plainly beyond salvation, the fire having already consumed the spire and most of the nave. Wilhum barked out a series of orders, sending half the troop into a loose perimeter around the site and setting Fletchman to work scouring the ground for tracks. Dismounting, I joined Wilhum in an inspection of the bodies. We counted eighteen in all, mostly folk in their middling years with a few youthful exceptions and all clad in pilgrims' garb.

"The tales of persecution weren't lies, at least," I muttered, staring down at the body of a man with a grey-black beard. His balding pate had been split open with what I assumed to be multiple blows from an axe. The blood was thick but not yet fully dried.

"Most cut down quickly," Wilhum said, voice clipped and face dark with more than just soot from the acrid pall drifting across the scene. "Looks like they took their time with some though." He nodded to the corpse of a young woman. Her mostly naked body was a splayed and broken thing, covered in blood and the tatters of her robe. I recognised Wilhum's expression from our sojourn into the Fjord Geld, the same grim desire for retribution that had consumed him when we found that wool merchant the Ascarlians had tormented to death. I knew this meant we wouldn't make it back to the castle for supper, but felt no urge to dissuade him. I was no stranger to scenes of death and thievery, for sometimes one accompanied the other. In this case, slaughter and pain had been the sole object of whoever had committed this crime. Even in the outlaw-infested forest of my youth, such a thing required a reckoning.

We found Fletchman inspecting a patch of churned earth on the southern slope of the rise. "I reckon somewheres betwixt thirty and forty of the bastards, my lord," he advised Wilhum. "Mixed bag, too. Some riding, some walking. And . . . " he scraped the sole of his boot over a long divot in the soil " . . . a captive or two, if I'm not mistaken. These are drag marks."

"Could be they were carrying off their own wounded," I suggested.

"They had no wounded," Wilhum said, jerking his head at the ruined camp. "These people were unarmed." He turned back to Fletchman. "Which way?"

The poacher pointed the tip of his bow-stave towards a line of hills to the south-west. "Not moving fast neither," he added, a hunger in his eyes that told of a hunter keen to get after his prey.

"There's a vineyard in that direction," I said. "It's the only decent-sized settlement anywhere near here but it's at least two days' march distant." I gave Wilhum a tight, humourless smile. "They'll have to camp overnight and, given their laggardly pace, it appears they're not expecting trouble."

Our quarry's ignorance of any danger stood starkly displayed when we found them encamped beside a stream snaking through a shallow valley ten miles from the shrine. Several fires glowed bright amid their tents and there was no picket line, nor any sentries posted on the surrounding slopes. From our vantage point atop a hillock a few hundred paces distant, we could hear voices raised in the discordant manner of drunken song.

"Not soldiers, whoever they are," I observed, raising an eyebrow at Wilhum. There was a tenseness to his bearing and rigidity to his features I didn't like, putting me in mind of a fighting dog straining at its leash. "Better to wait until full dark," I added. "I'll take our best dagger hands, pick off those on the fringes, fire the tents—"

"Subtlety is not required here, Master Scribe," he cut in. "There's still enough light for a charge and the ground is reasonably flat. It'll be sound tactics to cut off their retreat, however. Take Master Fletchman and four others, those good with a crossbow, and circle round to the north. They're likely to flee away from the stream." He rose to descend the lee of the hill, adding over his shoulder, "Spare their leader if you manage to pick them out. Otherwise I see no need for mercy."

An hour later I crouched alongside Eamond, Fletchman and three others a hundred paces from the northern flank of the camp. We had left our horses at the hillock, moving in a wide arc around the cluster of singing fools to take up position in a low depression. Eamond clutched his crossbow with unsteady hands, his face the pale, wide-eyed mask it had been since we found the shrine. He was a fair hand with the crossbow but far from expert and I had chosen him for this task to spare him the charge into the camp. I had little doubt he would have dutifully galloped along with the others, but ominous thoughts rose when I considered the prospects for his survival of the tumult that would surely follow. Like many a soul lured to war by visions of glory, Eamond was finding the truth of it a bitter morsel to swallow.

"Aim low," I reminded him, an oft-told lesson at the butts. "The bow will jerk up a little when you loose the lock."

He nodded, pale features sweaty despite the chill evening air, forcing a grin when I delivered a soft punch to his shoulder. "It'll be over in a trice," I told him by way of reassurance. "Bunch've drunken cowards is all we face here."

I glanced at Fletchman, finding him setting a broad-head arrow to the stave of his bow. He had another two shafts tucked into a strap on his arm. Before we'd left the castle, I had watched him play a smoking taper over the steel arrowheads to mask their gleam. Fletchman, I knew, required no advice on where to aim.

"Who did you run with?" I asked him in a murmur.

"Was never keen on running with no one but m'self," he replied. "'Cept when need arose and the pay was good. Did some work for Shilva Sahken on occasion." I watched him still his lips in a manner that told me the work he had done hadn't entailed stalking deer.

"She's still alive?" I asked, wise enough not to push at an unwelcome topic.

"Last I heard. Not so keen on ranging the woods these days, though. Makes her coin from the smuggling trade, those that once ran that business all having met with unfortunate ends some years back." He spoke with the offhand, gossipy tone outlaws tend to adopt when making light of betrayal and murder.

"Haven't seen nor heard tell of her since Moss Mill," I commented, adding inwardly, *Deckin would've been glad she made it out.*

"Bad business that," Fletchman grunted. His eyes slid towards me in careful scrutiny. "Heard tell it was the Moss Mill Massacre that set you on the path to devotion, Master Scribe."

I swallowed a caustic laugh. "You heard tell wrong. The path the mill set me on led to the Pits."

"So it's true?" The interest in his eyes deepened a notch. "You escaped the Pit Mines?"

"Me and two others. Well, there was a fourth but he didn't last long." I didn't like to ponder the escape from the Pits too much, it inevitably raising memories of Sihlda's sacrifice, Brewer who now lay dead in a grave in Farinsahl, and Toria, who was Martyrs knew where. I have often reflected upon the notion that the worst thing about having true friends is the missing of them when they're gone.

"Ran all the way to Callintor," I went on, forcing a brisk tone to my whisper. "And that's where I met the Anointed Lady, although we just called her Captain in those days."

"Her words turned your heart, then?"

"You could say that." I felt it best not to enlighten Fletchman to the fact that I had only volunteered for the Covenant Company to escape the noose a certain Ascendant wanted to put around my neck. Devoted souls prefer simple tales, shorn of the awkward complexities and nuance that characterise a truthful story.

"I was there, y'know." Fletchman shifted a little closer. "At Castle Ambris when you stepped forward to fight for the Lady. To see one of us do such a thing . . . " He shook his head, stirring my unease with the unblinking fervour in his eyes. "That's when I knew there must be truth in her words. Truth that could turn an outlaw into a knight."

"I'm not a knight." I spoke with a strained smile, avoiding his gaze. "And the knight I fought damn near killed me."

"But you fought him," Fletchman insisted. "And fought him well. I could see his fear; we all could. That was the day the churls learned nobles bleed as they do. I liked seeing him bleed, Master Scribe. I'm hoping that in time we'll see more noble swine bleed, Martyrs willing."

I coughed, looking towards the camp in the hopes of hearing their drunken revels replaced by shouts of alarm. "No love for nobles, eh?"

"They hung my boy and my brother." Fletchman's voice was just a thin hiss now, but still I heard the hate in it clear as day. "The duke's men caught 'em skinning a deer they shot to feed a starving family. They hung 'em slow, lit a fire under their feet so they could laugh at their dancing legs." I heard the stave of his bow creak under his tightening grip. "I found the scum that did it, those that had survived war and sickness. Took me years but I found 'em and with this bow I took vengeance. Would've sunk an arrow into the duke himself if he hadn't placed his head on the block with his treachery. I stood and watched when he died, hoping I would feel . . . done, finished. But it was an empty thing. When his head rolled on the planks there was nothing in my heart. So I roved the woods, hunted when I was hungry, killed when I needed coin, my heart empty all the while. But that changed the day you stepped from that crowd."

The fading sun cast a deep shadow over Fletchman's face under the broad felt cap he wore, but I could make out his smile. "We'll settle with this murdering scum," he said. "And all the other heretics in this duchy. But I think we both know, the real battle lies in the north, with the nobles and their lickspittle servants. I've more devotion in my shit than they share betwixt them . . ."

Fortunately, I was spared Fletchman's further insight by an upsurge of shouting from the camp. The drunken singing abruptly switched to a yet more discordant chorus of alarm and panic shot through by the drumbeat of galloping hooves. Dust blossomed to add to the campfire smoke, obscuring much of what came next. I could see horses wheeling in the haze, the tumult of alarm giving way to screams and the occasional clash of metal. In only a few moments there was markedly more screaming and much less clashing. The first runners came into view shortly after. As Wilhum had predicted they pelted across the frosty ground towards us, keeping well clear of the stream. I counted at least a dozen, which was dismaying. I took heart from their cowardice, however. Running so soon bespoke men with no stomach for a fight.

"Pick your marks," I said, raising my own weapon. Like the others carried by the Mounted Guard, it was a stirrup crossbow favoured for the speed with which it could be reloaded. "Loose at twenty yards," I added, training the crossbow on a fellow in the centre of the fast-approaching group. I held off until the silhouette of my chosen target grew beyond the width of the iron bracket at the fore of the crossbow. Eamond was a little quicker in loosing his bolt, although not so much as to amount to a display of indiscipline. I resisted the impulse to track the flight of his dart and made sure of my own shot. The lock rattled and the crossbow jerked as the bolt flew free, the silhouette of the running man dropping to the ground a heartbeat later.

Fletchman's ash bow thrummed as I hurried to reload the crossbow. The poacher's arrows flew fast and, as I found when I raised my weapon once more, very true indeed. There were only five runners before us now, quickly reduced to four when Fletchman loosed again, a figure jerking and spinning to the ground with a shaft jutting from his neck. His companions saw the danger now, three of them skidding to a halt and turning to sprint in varying directions. One, however, kept charging straight at us. A large, bull-like man, all hulking shoulders and brutish, snarling features, he roared as he closed with us. I saw with dismay that he already had a crossbow bolt jutting from his chest and one of Fletchman's arrows in his thigh, neither of which appeared to slow him one bit. Even more disconcerting was the woodman's axe he carried.

Cursing, I slotted another bolt onto the stock, raised the crossbow and loosed the bolt at the charging giant's head. I hoped to catch him in the eye or at least cause enough pain for him to abandon his charge.

Sadly, he ducked as I loosed, the bolt catching him a glancing blow across the cheek and slicing through his ear before spinning away. The brute bellowed in pain and fury, axe raised high, now only a few paces off. I cast my crossbow aside and drew my sword, backing away then nimbly stepping aside as the axe came down, crunching into frosted earth an inch from my foot. I slashed a cut to the Alundian's neck, the blade biting deep but failing to sever a vein of sufficient import, for he swung his axe again with undaunted energy. I swayed back, the axe blade whistling close to my nose, then thrust at the fellow's chest, gripping the sword handle with both hands and putting all my weight behind the blade.

The brute's mouth gaped wide and I had the chance to look directly into eyes wide and blank with shock, before a spray of blood erupted from his mouth to blind me. Swearing in disgust, I jerked away, leaving the sword embedded in the Alundian's chest. Wiping the gore from my eyes, I heard the multiple snap of my comrades' crossbows all loosing at once accompanied by the softer thrum of Fletchman's bowstring. When I looked again I was stunned to find the Alundian still standing. Bolts pierced his torso front and back and another of Fletchman's arrows jutted from his neck, and yet still he stood. His face was now a contrast to the roaring challenge from moments before, the heavy features slack and uncomprehending. His thick, bloodied lips twisted, a red cloud blossoming as he tried to speak. The words, naturally, were garbled, but with some effort I was able to make them out.

"Heretic . . . scum . . ."

"Not us, you murdering filth," Fletchman told him, striding forwards and drawing the long-bladed hunting knife from his belt. He slashed it across the Alundian's neck, unleashing a torrent of blood that finally saw the man consent to fall. "The heresy is yours," Fletchman added, casting his spit on the shuddering corpse. "And may the Seraphile curse your pestilent soul."

"This is their leader?" I cast a doubtful eye over the bound, kneeling figure cowering near the hooves of Wilhum's horse. The captive made a marked contrast to the hulking fanatic from whose carcass it had taken me several minutes' effort to pull free my sword. Spindle-limbed and short, he huddled low in his bonds, staring about with the bright, mostly unblinking eyes of a terrified soul.

"He led this mob of villains, all right," said a woman in ragged pilgrim's garb. She stood regarding the captive with a hard, unwavering gaze. Grime and speckles of dried blood covered her face, but I gained an impression of youthful vitality despite the bruises revealed by her tattered robe. "It was him giving all the orders at the shrine," she went on, my ear discerning a Cordwain accent. She moved closer to the hunched prisoner, staring into his unblinking eyes. "It was him who told them to cut my daughter's throat, make me watch when her blood spilt forth." She bore no weapon but the bound man shrank from her as if she stood poised with a sharp knife. From the repeated clenching of her hands, I suspected he had more to fear from her nails. Her arms were red to the elbow, indicating she had already been allowed some leeway with the Alundian wounded.

Their camp was a ransacked, corpse-littered ruin. Some had fought, others ran, while most had just milled around in panic until being cut down. In the aftermath, Wilhum happened upon this woman pounding an iron skillet to the sundered skull of one of her captors. The spindly man had been discovered hiding under a collapsed tent, seemingly rendered mute by terror.

"He will face the Anointed Lady's judgement, Mistress Juhlina," Wilhum told the Cordwainer. "You have my assurance on that."

I had expected to find no Alundians alive after his charge, but it appeared the aftermath of victory had mellowed Wilhum's vengeful urges. There were another five captives sitting bound nearby. Most maintained a prudent silence but one sobbed piteously, a bloody bandage tied across his eyes. Glancing again at Mistress Juhlina, the sole survivor of the massacre at the shrine with her bloody arms and clenching hands, told me that her retributive desires were far from sated. Apparently, she had been forced to witness the slaughter of her husband and younger brother along with fellow congregants from their parish in the Cordwain. The other captive, a girl of no more than fourteen summers, hadn't survived the trek from the shrine.

"The Anointed Lady?" The woman's face momentarily lost its hardness, her voice taking on a hushed reverence as she looked up at Wilhum. "*She* is here?"

"She is. As warden of Walvern Castle it is within her gift to dispense justice."

"You hear that, filth?" Mistress Juhlina's features took on a predatory leer as she stooped to address the spindly man once more. "I was going to rip your eyes out like I did your friend. Now I think I'll leave you to the Risen Martyr."

Mention of the Risen Martyr finally pierced the man's mute blankness and he drew back from her, a groan of mingled disgust and despair emerging from his lips.

"That's right," Juhlina taunted, leaning closer. "She'll tear your soul away before she puts your carcass to the flame . . ."

"You're injured," I said, moving to her side, gently but firmly placing myself between her and the captive. I gestured to the cut on her forehead. "Master Fletchman over there will be happy to stitch that for you before we set off."

She blinked at me, the calmness of my tone seeming to cause distress rather than reassurance. The weight of what she had suffered descended then and she sagged, emitting the first sob I had heard from her. "Don't worry," I said, beckoning Fletchman over to take her away. "He'll see you right. No steadier hand when it comes to stitches."

With the vengeful woman removed, I crouched at the captive leader's side, greeting him with a smile. "Don't mistake me, you shit-eater," I told him. "You're dead, and if I have my way it won't be quick. But that's up to the Lady. However, there's a good few miles betwixt here and the castle." I gave a meaningful glance at the now stooped and weeping form of Mistress Juhlina as Fletchman led her off. "And I fancy that's a woman who'll recover her vicious impulses soon enough. If you entertain any hopes of looking upon the Portals with your eyes intact, best answer my questions, eh?"

He gaped at me for a moment then swallowed, giving a slow nod.

"Good," I said, jerking my head at the other captives. "You and this lot, where are you from?"

He swallowed again before answering, apple bobbing in his scrawny throat. "Luhlstor," he said, his voice a croaking rasp.

"Luhlstor," I repeated, frowning as I searched my memory for the name. "That's what? A good thirty miles from here. Come a long way to do murder, haven't you?"

He hunched over, shuddering and retching. I thought he might be about to vomit, as is often the case with cowards facing inescapable death, but realised he was attempting to force out his reply. "Not . . . m-murder." he managed finally, meeting my eye with the first glimmer of defiance. "C-cleansing."

"Cleansing, eh?" I pursed my lips, shifting closer. "So, your mission is to cleanse this land of the hated true-faithers, is it?"

"Not . . . truth." He shuddered again before speaking on. "Lies. Heresy that besmirches this land, divides us from the Seraphile. T-too long has the duke allowed your pilgrims to defile us with their false shrines."

"Fine words. I'm guessing they're not your own. Where did you learn them?"

He lowered his head again, setting his mouth in a hard line that failed to open when I delivered a cuff to his head. "Who told you all this bilge?" No answer, another cuff. "Was it Lord Roulgarth? Did he set you to this?"

He raised his head a fraction and I saw a sneer play over his lips. "Roulgarth Cohlsair and his entire family are dogs," he hissed. "Slaves to the Algathinets. Our duke sullies himself with a northern whore and abases himself before your false Covenant."

Sighing, I moved back from him, looking up at Wilhum. "Fanatic scum, to be sure," I said. "But, I fancy, not quite cause for war."

Wilhum grimaced and tugged on the rope he held, hauling the prisoner to his feet. "War is here, heretic!" the Alundian snarled at me, stumbling as Wilhum dragged him away. "This is but the first ember of a fire that will consume you all!"

"Perhaps," I told him with an agreeable nod. "But you won't be there to see it, will you?"

CHAPTER ELEVEN

Upon our return to the castle, Evadine ordered no more injury be done to the captives. Instead she had them confined to the basement dungeon beneath the tower. As was custom, she sent the Mounted Guard forth to proclaim the impending trial of outlaws on charges of murder and desecration of Covenant property. Both Wilhum and I had counselled her against this, arguing it was sure to rouse the locals to anger if not outright violence. Also, word was sure to spread to the entire duchy that the Risen Martyr from the north intended to hang Alundians, adding more heat to an already simmering pot.

"Yes," she agreed with a reflective crease to her brow. "I certainly hope so."

Curiously, she ordered that our captives be well cared for, their wounds tended and proper food provided. It became her daily habit to spend long intervals in communion with these fanatics. At first she would speak to them individually, then, as days became weeks, have their cells unlocked so they could be gathered together. My curiosity inevitably drew me to investigate, spending several evenings lurking in the stairwell to listen to the voices echoing below. To my surprise, I heard no sermonising from Evadine, no hectoring or condemnation of their foul deeds. Instead, she questioned them, and it was not an interrogation. She asked about their faith, her questions posed in a tone of honest curiosity rather than scornful disdain. Equally surprising was that they answered her in much the same manner.

"It was with Korbil that perfection was achieved, my lady," their spindle-limbed leader told her. It transpired that he was a tanner who had forsaken his workshop in Luhlstor to embark upon his fateful crusade. "He saw the corruption of the Covenant, the lies that masked a great truth."

"And what is that truth, Ethrich?" Evadine asked him.

"That the Martyrs' example was the door to the Seraphile's grace. But that door has been open for centuries. It requires no more blood to keep it open. Nor does it require clerics to guard it. They are toll-takers demanding riches for a gift that is ours by right."

"But did not Martyr Stevanos himself say that ensuring passage through the Portals requires the labour of many lifetimes?"

"Labour, yes. But not blood. The orthodox Covenant has become a cult of death."

Although not particularly devout, my anger rose at the sheer hypocrisy of a man such as this condemning others for anything. I felt a strong urge to descend these steps and deliver a sound kicking while demanding, "And what manner of cult do you follow?" However, knowing Evadine would take a decidedly dim view of it, I held off. As the days went by, the tone of these gatherings changed, Evadine speaking more while the captives spoke less, instead listening with increasingly rapt attention. I had seen before how she could weave a snare around the hearts of others with words alone, but usually it was done via her sermons. Here she had been more subtle, through either calculation or the instinct of those who possess such gifts.

"I will not lie to you, brothers," I heard her tell them during the last such gathering, her words greeted by a now typically hushed expectation. They waited upon her every word, as faithful a congregation as she ever had. "In many ways your disdain for the Covenant matches my own, even though I sit here as a confirmed Aspirant. You think I do not see their corruption? You think I have not looked into the very eyes of those venal clerics who sit upon the Luminants' Council and beheld only the pettiness and envy of those hungry for naught but gold and power? Of course I have. Nor are my hands any cleaner than yours, for I have fought in service to what I know now to have been folly. So I cannot judge you, for that duty lies with the Seraphile."

I heard a sob echo from below, a scrape of bare feet on stone as the captives squirmed in discomfort. Ethrich spoke then, his voice small and tremulous. "Will they . . . they allow us through the Portals, my lady? Or are our souls too blackened?"

"No soul is so blackened it cannot be cleansed by the Seraphile's grace," Evadine told him. "But such cleansing only comes with sincere contrition. When you stand before them, there can be no lie in your heart, no facile justification for your sins. I ask that you be strong, brother. When the time comes, and it comes soon, you must speak your heart with no lie upon your lips. All who hear your voice must know it as truth. Can you do this?"

Another sob, joined by several others. Seized by a sudden chilly clench to my gut, I rose and turned away. I couldn't escape the sense of witnessing a wrong. These men deserved no mercy, I knew that, but the way she had moulded them into subservient acceptance of their fate chafed upon me. Perhaps it was my outlaw sensibilities, the innate fear and detestation of capture and the fate that awaited the condemned. But I knew it to strike deeper than that. Evadine spoke of the Covenant's lies, but the web she had spun about these deluded wretches had been crafted from untruth, even if she didn't know it.

"We can, my lady!" I heard Ethrich assure her with tearful fierceness as I climbed the steps, keen to get clear of his echoing, plaintive sobbing. "May the Seraphile hear my plea and grant me mercy . . ."

Emerging into the sunlight, I drew in a deep breath. The throb was its usual muted but persistent self thanks to my daily doses of the physician's elixir, but my quickened pulse had given it an irksome edge. Seeking distraction, I surveyed the outer keep below the mound, allowing myself a small measure of satisfaction at what I beheld. The new drawbridge was complete and the gaps in the walls nearly filled.

The company continued to sleep under canvas in the courtyard but we possessed enough spare timber to begin construction on a barracks and stables. The outer wall had an uneven appearance now. The many derricks, ropes and pulleys, and the ragged appearance of the battlements atop the outer wall, made for a ramshackle impression but I still felt it an improvement on the near ruin that had greeted us weeks before. Sergeant Castellan Estrik seemed gruffly pleased with the progress, although the occasional frown I saw on Swain's scarred brow gave me pause.

I found him putting a troop through their paces atop the battlement facing the river. Fighting from a wall required a different drill than the standard three-rank formation employed in open field, one the captain had lost no time in teaching his soldiers. Their days had become a taxing routine of labour followed by drill, with an occasional foot patrol beyond the walls. This, I assumed, was mostly done for the sake of morale, since the Mounted Guard were our main surety against an attack.

"Lower your head!" Swain snapped in his grating rasp, delivering a hard tap from the butt of his mace to the helm of a halberdier crouching behind one of the crenellations. "Bolts fly up as well as down. You!" Swain's gaze shifted to a soldier I recognised as one of the pikemen from Supplicant Blade Ofihla's troop. Pikes were of little use in castle fighting so these taller-than-most soldiers had been issued a variety of axes and maces. "What do we do when a ladder hits the wall?"

"Let through the first one up and leave them to the dagger men," the fellow replied with wise alacrity, "so those following come up faster. When the ladder's filled from top to bottom, tip the oil over them and throw over the torches."

"And if there's no more oil?" Swain demanded.

"Kill the second one up the ladder then throw his body down on the others. Push the ladder away when it's clear."

Swain grunted in grudging satisfaction. "Very well. Supplicant Ofihla, run them up the stairs twice more, then they can eat."

Ofihla duly snapped out her command and the troop descended to the courtyard. They moved with a swift orderliness that put me in shameful mind of the clumsy, often farcical stumbling of myself and the other recruits from Callintor, albeit with one exception. Mistress Juhlina didn't move with the same unconscious precision of the others, but her face bore a determined cast. She carried a hatchet with two daggers in her belt and even from here I could discern her desire to put them to use. Now scrubbed clean with her cuts stitched and bruises faded I would have called her comely, but the dark hunger in her face banished all carnal notions. Her fellow soldiers had taken to referring to her as simply "the Widow", a title she accepted without complaint.

"She volunteered right away," Swain said, noting the direction of my gaze. "Lady Evadine offered to have her escorted over the border but she wouldn't hear of it." His lips formed a rare smile, albeit a very thin one. "I don't normally approve of hate-filled soldiers. Makes for ill discipline. But my sense of things is we'll have need of her hate before long."

Knowing Swain to be a fellow upon whom careful allusions were wasted, I decided upon a question of bland directness. "Can we hold this place?"

His reply was prompt and equally unvarnished. "Depends on how many they bring against us." I caught a faint satisfaction pass over his features as he saw my annoyance, but the expression faded as he cast his gaze towards the tallest of the hills rising to the south. "And the strength of their engines," he added, his tone considerably more sombre.

I knew this particular hill had been the site of the mighty trebuchet that had tumbled Walvern Castle's walls so many years before. It sat just over two hundred paces from the walls, beyond the reach of our crossbows, and I had no doubt Lord Roulgarth would be quick to spot its tactical value.

"Could something be done?" I asked. "Some means of preventing…" My voice dwindled in the face of Swain's disparaging scowl.

"A hill cannot be brought down, Master Scribe. Nor do we have the numbers or the materials to fortify it." He took a breath, straightening and wiping the doubt from his face. "We must trust to Lady

Evadine's judgement and remember that time will be our ally. Engines or no, taking this castle will be a protracted business. We are well supplied and besiegers can suffer more than the besieged, especially in winter." He paused, his eyes slipping towards the tower. "She is . . . questioning the prisoners again?"

"If you prefer to call it that." I concealed a grin as his face tensed in discomfort. I had come to understand that Swain's devotion to Evadine was much like a dog's attachment to a beloved master. His obedience was absolute but he would never truly understand her. Not that I could claim to either.

"Thinking she should've used that by now?" I nodded to the wooden structure rising from the wall on the opposite side of the courtyard, a simple but sturdy contrivance of two beams, one vertical supporting one horizontal. Evadine had ordered it raised the day we returned with the prisoners, yet the noose that dangled from the upper beam remained empty.

"I'm sure she has her reasons." Swain's voice was curt and he coughed. "No scribing to do?"

I let the grin flourish as I knuckled my forehead and turned to the stairs. "By your leave, Captain."

The alarm rose just as I set foot on the courtyard cobbles, a hearty shout from the sentry atop the gatehouse. "Patrol returning!" he called out, hands cupping his mouth as he directed the cry towards Swain. "At the gallop!"

"Fetch her!" Swain shouted to me but I was already running for the tower. Around me the captain's barked orders had the entire company downing tools and gathering weapons before hurrying to their positions. If the Mounted Guard were returning at the gallop, the reason was clear: Lord Roulgarth had finally consented to honour us with a visit.

"How many?" Evadine asked Wilhum as we joined him atop the gatehouse. The company stood in ranks along the battlements. Pots of oils were suspended over blazing fires alongside barrels of crossbow bolts and stacked crates filled with loose masonry.

"I counted a thousand horse and three times as many foot in the vanguard," Wilhum replied. "Trained and well armed by the look of them, with more than twice as many following. All on foot and not so well armed, but they were marching in decent order."

"That'll be the Sworn Companies," I said. "In Alundia all men of fighting age are required to swear an oath of service to the duke. Only he can call the commons to arms. Knights might own the land but the small folk are beholden to the duke. They gather together a few times a year for training and have acquitted themselves well in every war to beset this land."

"So, close on ten thousand," Evadine mused, peering at the frosted gravel track tracing across the few hundred paces of flat ground separating Walvern Castle from the hills to the east. "Strange then," she added, her eyebrows lifting in surprise, "that I count only one."

The rider emerged from behind the narrow gulley carrying no banner and lacking any escort. He kept his mount to a steady walk so it wasn't until he drew within arrow shot of the walls that Lord Roulgarth's features became clear. He reined to a halt some fifty paces from the raised drawbridge, casting a placid gaze over it and the recently repaired walls before raising it to fix on Evadine.

"Your hospitality is lacking, my lady!" he called out to her, extending a hand at the drawbridge. "Have you no welcome for a weary traveller?"

"Welcome you are, my lord," Evadine called back. "Your army is not."

Roulgarth raised his arms, inclining his head at the empty ground behind. "I come without hostile intent, as you can see."

"A hidden blade is still a blade." Evadine's voice hardened as she added, "State your business or be on your way, my lord. I am ever wearied by pointless conversation."

Roulgarth's gauntleted hands closed into fists as he lowered his arms, the hardness of his tone matching Evadine's. "It is reported to me that subjects of this duchy currently reside in your custody. Furthermore, it is stated by credible witnesses that these captives were taken after a bloody and unwarranted massacre committed by soldiers of your company."

"Your first statement is correct," Evadine told him. "Your second is a lie. The captives in my custody are guilty of murder, rape and wanton sacrilege."

"I am appointed lord constable of this duchy, my lady." The knight's features took on a glower as he spoke, one I judged to arise from genuine anger rather than artifice. It was clear to me that Lord Roulgarth was not here to make empty gestures to salve his pride. "It is my duty to determine the guilt and punishment of my brother's subjects, not yours."

"I bear a King's Writ that is firm in stating the contrary." Evadine's armour shifted as she shrugged, her own features possessed of bland dismissal I felt sure to be an attempt to stoke the Alundian's anger. "Perhaps your time would be better spent in penning a letter thanking the king for sparing you additional labour."

Roulgarth lowered his head, shoulders hunching in the manner of a man forcing restraint upon himself. "I'll not bandy words or discuss legalities with you further," he said, baring his teeth as he fought to keep the snarl from his voice. "There are Alundians in your clutches and I demand they be brought forth. Should you fail to do so the consequences will be for you and your company to bear, and I promise they will be dire."

I expected Evadine to voice another infuriating rejoinder, but instead she adopted a thoughtful air, pursing her lips and nodding after a moment's apparent consideration. "As you wish, my lord. Captain Swain, have the prisoners brought forth. Also, ask Mistress Juhlina to join us."

When last I saw him Ethrich had been a defeated if defiant wretch, fighting through his fear to voice his declamations. However, the man who climbed the steps to stand at the scaffold moved with a straight-backed, uncowed surety. A decent diet had left him healthy, his beard neatly trimmed, his wiry frame clad in a clean tunic and trews. The other captives possessed much the same bearing, and, like their leader, their attention was fixed entirely on Evadine rather than the noble who had come to secure their release.

"Ethrich Tanner," Roulgarth said, his voice laden with disdainful recognition. "I guessed it might be you. I'd have hung you myself years ago if your neighbours hadn't lied on your behalf."

Ethrich spared the knight only a short, disinterested glance before returning his full focus to Evadine. "Is . . ." he began, throat working as he pushed the words from his mouth. "Is it time, then, my lady?" Strangely, I heard no fear in this question. Instead, the man's tone was one of keen, near-desperate anticipation.

"It is, brother," Evadine said, smiling as she reached out to clasp his shoulder. "How I wish we could have spoken longer for I learned so much from you. But that is selfish of me."

"Lady Evadine!" Roulgarth called out, his voice a mix of impatience and reluctant conciliation. "Have that villain and the others brought down. In recognition of your role in bringing them to justice, I will grant you the boon of making testimony at their trial."

Evadine paid him no more heed than had Ethrich. Giving a final squeeze to his shoulder, she stepped back, turning and nodding to Juhlina. "As you were promised, mistress," Evadine told her. The Widow responded with a grave nod before stepping to the gallows, her face like stone as she unfurled the noose from the beam.

"Lady Evadine!" Lord Roulgarth called again, this time receiving not even a glance in reply.

"Master Ethrich Tanner of Luhlstor," Evadine said while Juhlina looped the noose over the captive's head and drew it tight. "You stand charged with murder, rape and desecration of the Shrine to Martyr Lowanthel. After proper investigation I find these charges to be true and pronounce upon you sentence of death in accordance with the powers vested in me by Good King Tomas Algathinet and the laws of the Covenant of Martyrs." She paused, allowing Ethrich time to shudder through his last bout of fear before he mastered himself. I saw how the Widow stared at the back of his head, features still rigid, eyes unblinking.

"Do you have testament to make before sentence is carried out?" Evadine asked Ethrich when his trembling faded.

"I do, my lady." The noose about his neck flexed as he swallowed then shifted to stare down at Lord Roulgarth. "I claim no defence nor justification. Thanks to the divine insight of the Anointed Lady I see now that my crimes were born of lies taught me by heretics. I lived an apostate to the true faith but I will die its servant and can only trust to the boundless compassion of the Seraphile that I may find a place beyond the Portals. If not, I accept my fate for my crimes were many and . . ." he paused to swallow again, glancing over his shoulder at the Widow ". . . nor will I deny those I have wronged their just retribution."

As he spoke I made a careful study not of him, but of Roulgarth. The knight's features betrayed both puzzlement and mounting anger, more of the former than the latter. I knew there were times when my own face had been a mirror of his now, the face of a soul confronting something that should not be, something unnatural and yet real. In the space of a few weeks Evadine had converted a heretical fanatic into a true-faith ardent, one willing to die for his new-found beliefs. Whatever might transpire from here on, Roulgarth would know he faced an opponent the like of which he had never encountered before.

As Ethrich fell silent, I saw a spasm of emotion pass across Evadine's features, a tightening of the brow and lowering of the eyes that told of genuine grief. But it was gone in an instant and I doubted any other present knew her expressions well enough to have caught it. "May the Seraphile see your heart, brother," she said, then gave a wordless nod to the Widow.

Mistress Juhlina clearly felt no final twinges of sympathy, her previously stony visage forming a grimace of feral satisfaction as she pressed both hands into Ethrich's back and shoved him clear of the wall. He let out a sharp gasp as he fell, a sound smothered by the loud crack of his neck breaking an instant later. The subsequent silence was thick, broken only by the creak of the rope as the tanner's body swayed. When his swaying slowed, Evadine consented to turn her attention back to Lord Roulgarth.

"I recall recently placing a list in your hands, my lord," she called down to him. "Please report on your progress in filling it."

"Your list was burnt the instant you left that tent!" Roulgarth spat back. "I consider it my dishonour to have even touched it!"

"A great pity." Evadine sighed then gestured to the soldiers flanking the gallows to draw up Ethrich's body. "It appears you leave me no choice but to fulfil the king's command by my own agency. When I am done here I shall journey to Highsahl to arrest the miscreants myself. You are welcome to act as my escort if you wish."

Roulgarth let out a laugh then, the sound full of as much despair as it was dismissal. "You will not be journeying anywhere, my lady. I can assure you of that."

"Do you intend to raise your hand against a Crown agent, sir?" Evadine put a hand to her breastplate in apparent shock. "Do you dare to speak treason to me?"

"I am sworn to protect this duchy from all enemies, whatever pieces of parchment they carry." Roulgarth's features were pale now but a hard resolve shone in his eyes, the face of a man taking the first step on a perilous road, one from which he couldn't turn. "And you have made yourself our enemy this day, Lady Evadine. Remember that I came here peacefully."

"And I enjoin you to depart so." Evadine gave a shallow bow then turned to the soldiers guarding the remaining captives. "Bring them up and let us be about our just business."

"This woman is mad!" Roulgarth exploded, raising his voice to a raging shout, tracking his gaze across the walls and the soldiers who stared at him in stern regard. "Can't you see that? She has led you all to your doom!"

Had he been addressing hired men-at-arms or pressed churls his words might have found purchase on fearful souls sent far from home to fight a war they cared nothing about. But this was the Covenant Company and they answered to but one voice. An angry murmur rippled along the battlements, building quickly into shouts of defiance until Evadine barked an order for silence.

"I will ride for Highsahl soon, my lord," Evadine informed him as she moved to the second prisoner, cupping his smiling, contented face with her hand before the Widow put the noose about his neck. "For your own sake, I implore you not to impede my journey."

Lord Roulgarth Cohlsair said no more that day, although there are accounts that put a great many more words in his mouth at this juncture. Scholars of Alundian sympathies flatter him with a lengthy speech that blends the eloquent with the heroic to pleasingly dramatic effect. Those with other allegiances paint him as a raging braggart who rode about before the castle gate for an hour or more, calling out all manner of profanity-laden threats. But the truth is the Lord Constable of Alundia spared one more glance at Evadine before settling his gaze on me. Before turning to ride away, not deigning to witness the execution of another of his countrymen, I saw his lips form a smile. I might have expected a challenge in that smile, some measure of grim satisfaction at my impending end. Instead I saw something worse: pity. Lord Roulgarth fully expected to take my life in the very near future, and apparently he wasn't even looking forward to it.

Wheeling his warhorse about, he kicked his spurs and galloped away. By nightfall, long after the Widow had shoved the last of the captives from the wall, a long line of glimmering campfires flickered atop the surrounding hills. They formed a glittering crescent that swept around the castle from one stretch of riverbank to another a half-mile south. And so was Walvern Castle besieged.

CHAPTER TWELVE

I t is a curious facet of life under siege that, for much of it, nothing of particular interest happens. For the next four days the Alundians busied themselves establishing their hilltop camps, easily made out against the rising and setting sun. A few mounted men-at-arms galloped about on the plain for a short interval around midday, never coming close enough to draw a bolt from our crossbows. Lord Roulgarth did not consent to reappear and dispatched no emissaries to demand our surrender, something Swain found both encouraging and ominous when we gathered atop the tower for counsel on the morn of the fifth day.

"He had a choice between a swift attack the first night or a prolonged investment of the castle," the captain said. "He chose the latter, where I would have opted for the former. It's always best to snuff out a fortified enemy as soon as you can, especially when you're expecting trouble elsewhere."

"Meaning Roulgarth's content to bide his time because Alundia's borders remain unmenaced," I said, addressing my words to Swain but keeping my eyes on Evadine.

"Possibly," Swain admitted. "Or, having had a close look at the castle and the state of our repairs, decided his chances of a quick victory were poor. At the very least, he would have known that storming these walls will exact a heavy price."

"So, he'll either try to starve us out or . . ." I trailed off, giving a pointed glance at the closest hilltop. So far, the Alundians had confined themselves to putting a company of infantry atop it, the summit remaining free of the raised poles and pulleys that would tell of an engine under construction.

"Engines take time, sound timber, and skilled hands to craft," Wilhum said. "Perhaps the lord constable lacks them at present."

"We should assume he won't remain lacking for long," I said. I searched Evadine's face for some indication of her thinking but saw only the reflective sombreness that had coloured her mood since the hangings. "We should light the beacon, my lady," I stated which brought a quizzical frown to her brow.

"Why we would do that, Master Scribe?"

"We are besieged." I strove to keep the heat from my voice. Our mutual understanding had indeed grown since her healing but that didn't mean she had lost her facility for infuriatingly cryptic responses to reasonable suggestions. "Our enemy remains quiescent but that will surely not last much longer. There is no shame in calling for aid when it's needed."

"Quite true." She inclined her head in agreement. "And I will feel no shame in doing so when the time comes. As for now, good sirs—" she favoured us all with a smile before moving to the stairwell "—continue about your duties and maintain an appropriate state of alertness."

One week of inactivity became two, then three, the days passing in a routine of drills, meals and watches, the mood tense at first but soon taking on a tedious mundanity. I spent my time taking my turn in improving the sword and dagger skills of the Mounted Company, continuing my tutelage of Ayin and completing my reading of Ulfin's *Travels*. It was clear the long-dead scribe had been a fellow of inventive imagination as well as creditable honesty, if irksomely verbose at times. Only about a third of the account actually concerned his travels in the Caerith Wastes, the first two-thirds being taken up with the many misadventures, both financial and romantic, that led him to such a desperate course.

And lo, I read, *it was with this harlot's betrayal that I found myself at my most impoverished pass. Ah, sweet Effiah, so fair of face and form, masking the ugly greed in her heart. To leave a poor scribe who had only ever shown her kindness with naught but a cold hearth and an empty purse. With my last few sheks did I seek to quell my sorrow with good strong ale and it was in the drinking house that I met a fellow of hearty disposition with a tale of riches to be found in the Wastes.*

Ulfin went on to describe how this hearty fellow recruited him into a band of similarly impoverished souls intent on crossing the mountains into the Wastes on promise of treasure. Ulfin is vague on the precise nature of this treasure, something I ascribe to either embarrassment stemming from the fact of its non-existence or a desire to prevent others seeking it out. Real or not, his narrative is stark in detailing the abject failure of this expedition. The band's ebullient leader expired from cold on a mountainside barely a month into the journey. Others deserted shortly after leaving only Ulfin and two companions to continue the quest. Ulfin provides a frustrating lack of explanation as to the fate of these companions, confining himself to *"the terrible acts to which men are driven by hunger"*. What is clear is that he emerged from the mountains and into the Caerith Wastes alone and near dead from starvation.

And so to my certain end did I expect to fall when my legs finally failed me. I found the drift into which I plummeted an endless welcoming blanket, bringing a sleep sounder than I had ever known. But, thanks to providence and the kindly instincts of youth, this sleep was mercifully brief. My rousing was a harsh thing, full of shouting and slapping, both delivered by a child no less.

It transpired that Ulfin had been dragged from the snowdrift by a Caerith boy he guessed to be about ten years old who hauled this strange, near-dead newcomer to a nearby settlement. It is here that Ulfin's tale becomes particularly confused, due mostly to the fact that he appears to have spent some considerable time suffering through a delirium. When he is returned to his full senses he finds himself among a people speaking a language he can't understand, most of whom regard him with either indifference, disdain or outright hostility.

On several occasions their hulking chieftain sought to sunder my skull with his oddly shaped axe, each time being dissuaded from murder by the boy who saved me from the drift. Espetha! the boy would cry as he interposed himself betwixt victim and villain. Espetha! Such a blessed word for a blessed concept, for it surely saved my life.

According to Ulfin, *Espetha* relates to a custom among the Caerith regarding the treatment of outsiders. The scribe's understanding of their language remained limited despite the months he spent in their company, but he eventually gleaned sufficient understanding to attempt a translation. The word has no direct equivalent in Albermainish but Ulfin translates it as "with open hand". Apparently, by long-standing custom, one who enters Caerith lands "with open hand", to wit: bearing no weapon and exhibiting no desire to do harm, cannot themselves be harmed.

"*Espetha*," I repeated softly, resting the book on my chest. I searched my memories of the chainsman, Raith and the Sack Witch, but could recall no instance of them using this word. The pronunciation was therefore, like much concerning the Caerith, a mystery.

My pondering was interrupted by the clatter and boom of a slamming door followed by the echo of boots upon the steps. Ayin, Wilhum and I had taken up residence in the tower's second storey, while the Mounted Company bedded down in the main chamber below to keep close guard on Evadine. Wilhum stirred from slumber and shifted on his bunk at the rising drumbeat of hurrying feet and I closed my book with a soft curse. Battle, I assumed, was finally upon us. However, when Eamond appeared at the top of the stairs, features pale and eyes bright with panic, he had more surprising tidings.

"Master Scribe, my lord," he said "The lady . . . You have to come."

"What is it?" Wilhum asked in a groan, swinging his legs clear of the bunk and reaching for his sword. His lumpen fatigue vanished instantly upon hearing Eamond's next words.

"She's riding forth." In response to our astonished stares, he added, "Now."

"What are you about, Evie?" Wilhum demanded, forgetting all formality as he hurried towards Evadine across the courtyard. She sat atop Ulstan in full armour, the air loud with the rattle of chains as the drawbridge was lowered before her.

"Keeping my word, Wil," she replied. "I told Lord Roulgarth I would be riding to Highsahl and yet I have sat behind these walls for weeks. I feel dishonoured by my indolence."

"For Martyrs' sake!" Wilhum reached out to grasp Ulstan's bridle but Evadine had already spurred the stallion forward.

"Stay here!" she called over her shoulder as the warhorse thundered across the drawbridge. "And don't worry for me!"

"Mounted Guard to horse!" Wilhum called out, running for the stables. "Alwyn!" he shouted as I continued to stare after Evadine's retreating form. The light from the torches lining the walls flickered briefly on her armour before the darkness swallowed horse and rider, their progress marked only by the steady rhythm of Ulstan's hooves.

"She needs blood," I murmured, turning when Wilhum's hand fell on my shoulder.

"We have to get after her," he said.

"No," I replied. "She'll be back very soon. We need to rouse all hands and man the walls."

Wilhum squinted at me in bemused exasperation, leaning closer and lowering his voice a notch. "Have you gone as mad as her?" I had long suspected Wilhum to harbour only a marginal belief in Evadine's divine gifts and now saw even that to be absent from his soul. He loved her as fiercely as any brother loved a sister, of that I had no doubt, but it was a despairing love for one he considered detached from the world. He stayed not for faith, but to preserve her life.

"Roulgarth is attempting to wait us out," I said, my voice as quiet as his. "He knows Tomas will not be marching to our aid. So the lord constable is content to sit out there all winter until our supplies are gone. With no lives lost save a few fanatics, he expects Evadine to eventually surrender and go home, giving him a bloodless victory to claim and no open conflict with the Crown. Blood," I repeated. "That's what she needs to turn this farce into a war. She'll be back as soon as she's got it."

I tugged my shoulder free of his grip, turning to the soldiers stationed at the drawbridge windlass. "Be ready to raise it with all speed when the Lady returns," I said before casting about for Captain Swain, finding him atop the gatehouse battlement, his features just as bemused as Wilhum's. "Captain!" I snapped, capturing his attention. "We need to rouse this company for battle. Double the crossbows on the east-facing wall."

He blinked then set his face in the familiar mask of command, striding off to bark out a succession of orders that had sergeants and troopers hurrying to comply. "We should arm ourselves as best we can while time allows," I told Wilhum, turning to run for the tower. "Station the Guard in the courtyard," I added as he fell in alongside, "so they can be shifted to reinforce the most threatened parts of the wall."

"I don't recall," he panted as we ran up the steps to the tower, "the Anointed Lady putting you in charge in her absence, Master Scribe."

I gave a very hollow laugh. "Feel free to usurp me at any time, my lord."

"What's happening?" Ayin asked with a yawn upon our return to the second storey.

"The Alundians are coming," I told her, deciding a little obfuscation was best as there would be no dissuading Ayin from running off in pursuit of Evadine, clothed or no. "Get dressed. Take your crossbow and guard the infirmary. Help Supplicant Delric as needed. But," I added, heaving my breastplate on to my chest, "help me with this first."

"Scattering sand on shit and blood all night," she grumbled, casting her blankets aside. "I get all the best jobs."

With Ayin's assistance I managed to don most of my armour by the time a fresh clamour came echoing up from the lower keep. "Lady Evadine returns!"

I followed Wilhum, always swifter in armouring himself than I, down the hill while still strapping a vambrace to my right arm. He went to stand with the Mounted Guard, arrayed on foot in the centre of the courtyard, and I ran to join Swain atop the gatehouse. Evadine was already in view, guiding Ulstan towards the drawbridge at a steady, unhurried canter. I noted, however, that her sword was drawn and held out to the side. As she came closer I made out the stain covering the blade, rendered black in the shifting torchlight. Also, rising from the gloom beyond her, came the discordant tumult of many folk at the run, angry folk judging by the increasingly discernible shouts and curses that chased the Anointed Lady all the way to the drawbridge.

In accordance with my orders, the soldiers at the windlass began to heave it the moment her stallion's hooves clattered onto the courtyard cobbles. I watched her flick the blood from her sword before climbing down from the saddle. When she looked up to meet my eye, I saw no triumph in her expression, just grim satisfaction. "The road was closed," she said simply.

"Crossbows up!" Swain barked. I turned back to see the first Alundians come charging out of the darkness. A few dozen at first, pelting towards the castle with undaunted speed. I saw no ladders or grapples in their hands, only weapons, sword and axe blades flickering as they came on.

"Go back!" I shouted to them, hands cupped around my mouth. "You will die here! Go—"

My words were smothered by Swain's command to loose and the subsequent multiple snap of crossbow cords and rattling locks. The captain had been typically assiduous in following his orders, gathering over two score crossbowmen on the east-facing wall, more than enough to cast out a volley that felled every Alundian in sight. However, more came sprinting out of the darkness while the bowmen hurried to recharge their weapons. Fletchman used his ash bow to bring down two more Alundians before they reached the ditch below the walls.

The folly of surrendering to rage in war was soon displayed in stark terms as the swelling throng spread out below us. The burgeoning cluster howled and thrashed without any means of scaling the wall before them or avoiding the torrent of rocks and oil Swain ordered be cast on to their heads. Shouts of anger soon became screams of agony, counterpointed by a steady snap and thrum as the cross-bowmen resumed their work. In compliance with their training, they grouped themselves into threes to maintain a constant rain of bolts, one leaning out to shoot into the flailing mass below while two others worked to reload the bows.

The murderous labour continued for several long minutes before a chorus of pealing trumpets came echoing out of the gloom beyond the reach of our torches. The steady supply of fresh victims slowed then stopped, the charging figures halting and slipping back into the shadow after a few moments of angry dithering. As the death toll in the ditch mounted, the screams abated, allowing those still alive to hear the trumpets. Most of the survivors were quick to answer what I knew must be a command to abort this hopeless attack, scrambling clear of the ditch and running away. A few lingered to achieve their pointless deaths, taken by bolts, oil or falling rocks as they made vain efforts to climb the wall. One espe-cially large man pounded his axe against the base of the wall, working with furious industry despite the crossbow bolts jutting from both shoulders. He kept on until Fletchman sank an arrow deep into his neck. The big man tottered about for a time, the axe slipping from his grasp, raising his face to cast a final hate-filled glance at the northerners staring down at him from the wall above. When he consented to fall, his death appeared to provide the excuse his comrades needed to finally abandon their assault.

"Save your bolts!" Swain instructed as the crossbowmen trained their weapons on the fleeing Alundians, about thirty climbing from the ditch to bolt into the gloom. "We'll need all we have before long."

Peering down at the carnage below, I counted over twenty bodies littering the ditch. Smoke rose from the still-burning oil, tainting the air with the acrid stench of scorched cloth and flesh. Some bodies continued to twitch and a couple were attempting to crawl up the sides, their piteous desperate sobs mingling with the fainter groans of the dying. I knew there could be no chance of lowering the draw-bridge to provide them succour, so all who remained were likely to perish by morning. Evadine had her blood now and the farce was over. From this moment on we were truly at war.

There were no further assaults that night. It appeared that, having re-exerted control of his forces, Lord Roulgarth was not so foolish as to waste more lives in fruitless charges. Evadine had ordered half the company to stand down at first light, retiring to the tower and leaving me to oversee the morning watch in concert with Sergeant Castellan Estrik. With the dawn came a solitary Alundian knight bearing a truce pennant and a request to gather up the Alundian bodies and wounded in the ditch. The emissary was a curt, pinch-faced young noble in fine armour who clearly felt himself dishonoured by his duty.

"Lord Roulgarth lacked the balls to come begging himself, I see," I observed with a cheerful barb at his dignity.

"Shut your filthy mouth, churl!" the youth shot back, upturned face reddening in fury. "I come not to exchange insults with foul-tongued churls," he continued, "but for fair treatment of those fallen in battle. Or is your false martyr cruel as well as deceitful?"

"Mind your tongue, lordling!" Estrik advised in a growl, one echoed by the soldiers. Crossbows rose to aim bolts at the young knight who to his credit refused to cower.

"All right," I called out, raising my hands and gesturing to the crossbowmen to lower their weapons. "You know the Lady's orders, truce flags are to be respected." I turned back to the knight, eyebrows raised in expectation of the introduction that had so far not been forthcoming. "Now then, Lord . . . ?"

"Merick Albrisend," he said, voice clipped with reluctant necessity, "Baron of Lumenstor. And you are?"

"Alwyn Scribe." I bowed. "Baron of nowhere. At your service." Seeing his eyes narrow in recognition, I indulged in a short moment of reflection on the strangeness of possessing a name I never expected to be known beyond the borders of the Shavine Forest. "Your request is granted," I told him. "The Risen Martyr gives until midday to remove your comrades. Please ensure that any who come forth from your ranks do so without weapons. I would also enjoin you to advise them to be silent in their labour. Any insults, especially towards our Lady, will not be tolerated."

Lord Merick gave a brief nod of assent before favouring me with a final challenging scowl. "I'll look for you when we tear down these walls," he promised, wheeling his mount to gallop away. As agreed, the Alundian dead and wounded were carted away before the sun reached its apex. The plain stood empty save for the departing carts while campfire smoke shrouded the hilltops beyond.

"I must confess, my lady," Swain said, "I felt sure they'd come at us again as soon as they could. Angry soldiers are gold, an advantage not to be squandered."

"Lord Roulgarth waits," Evadine mused, a faintly annoyed frown on her brow as she scanned the hills. "But what for eludes me."

"Whatever it is, it won't be good," I put in with a pointed glance at the tower where the piled timber of the beacon still sat, dry and unlit under a tarpaulin.

"Good or bad, we wait also," Evadine said. "As he does."

At first, it appeared Lord Roulgarth had decided to give his reply that very night. Once the sky had grown fully dark and a thick gusting of snow swept across the river to see us all shivering in our cloaks, a volley of fire arrows came sailing out of the dark to arc over the south-facing wall. Most fell harmlessly onto the cobbles to be quickly extinguished by kicked snow or tossed water buckets, but one found a haystack in the makeshift stables. The horses were roused to considerable panic and one soldier suffered a broken leg from a flailing hoof before the blaze was quelled. The volley ended as soon as it began, the ground beyond the wall remaining bare of attackers.

"A sop to his angered army, perhaps?" I suggested to Swain as we crouched at a crenellation to peer into the gloom.

"Perhaps," the captain agreed, the wrinkles on his scarred head bunching as a chorus of shouts came echoing from the direction where the wall faced the river. "Or, more likely, a diversion."

Hurrying across the courtyard, we scaled the steps to find the two soldiers from Ofihla's troop lying dead with arrows jutting from their necks, another three wounded in the shoulder or face. Crossbowmen were bobbing up from cover to loose bolts into the gloom below the wall, the air thick with angry curses.

"See anything?" I asked a bowman as he readied his weapon for another shot. He blinked at me, brows sweaty despite the chill, replying with a shake of his head. "Then stop wasting bolts," I told him, repeating the same instruction to his comrades.

"Bodkin," Fletchman said, holding up a bloodied arrow he plucked from one victim's neck. The arrowhead was narrow with a pyramidal point and small thornlike barbs halfway along its length. "A warhead, not a huntsman's shaft. Aimed true from a good thirty yards out, and in the dark." Fletchman gave me a sober glance. "Looks like there's some in their ranks who know their business, Master Scribe. This is expert's work."

"Are Alundians known for their archery skills?" I asked Swain.

"No more than elsewhere in this realm," he replied. "Like duchies in the north, they favour the crossbow for war." He nodded to the arrow in Fletchman's grip. "If there's master archers in their ranks, I'd wager they're hired hands. Remember the arrow storm we faced at the Traitors' Field? Rumour has it that was the work of two thousand Vergundian plainsmen. With the Pretender's cause lost, could be they went looking for another paymaster."

I endeavoured to keep the wince from my features for fear of unnerving the other soldiers. I still harboured ugly memories of the iron rain on that dread field and had no desire to suffer it again.

"Vergundians," Fletchman said, pursing his lips as he continued his examination of the arrow. "Heard of 'em, but never seen one. Way I hear it, they use a curve-tip hornbow."

Meagre as it was, the former poacher's knowledge of Vergundians was greater than mine. Sihlda's lessons on the world beyond the borders of Albermaine had been fulsome only in so far as it pertained to the Martyrs. The varied clans that ranged the plains of Vergundia had never been converted to the Covenant and so lay mostly outside her tutelage. However, I did recall a vague allusion to "warlike heathens lost in an endless whirl of strife from which they can be lured by promise of gold".

"Two thousand of the buggers?" I asked Swain, receiving a shrug in response.

"They surely lost a lot in the rout. Who's to say how many lived to sell themselves to the lord constable?"

"Could they be what he's been waiting for?"

"I doubt it. Archers alone can't take a castle." He gritted his teeth and let out a sigh as another chorus of shouts erupted from the north-facing wall. "But they can make life a misery for those behind its walls."

The archers continued to assail us throughout the night, claiming the lives of eight soldiers and wounding a dozen more. Swain was quick to order all sentries to cover, permitted only one short glance over the wall every so often. Sadly, our foes were a wily lot and responded by eschewing volleys for prowling the shadows beyond the reach of our torches, waiting and watching for targets. The Vergundians, for none doubted it was those skilful heathens we faced, made it their business to torment us in this fashion for the next three nights. Their success in claiming lives waned after the first attack, their arrows missing more than they hit. However, the constancy of the danger made for watches fraught with the kind of fear to which even ardent souls can become prone. It's not too difficult a task to fire up a faithful heart with rousing words at the cusp of battle, but maintaining courage when faced with the lurking promise of a fatal arrow from the shadows was another matter.

Evadine was prudent in ordering no response to what was in effect more a nuisance than a true threat to our position. Her attitude changed on the fourth night when one young recruit, a former apprentice potter from Alberis, lost his reason after an arrow narrowly missed skewering him through the eye. Instead of thanking the Seraphile for his deliverance and resolving to keep a lowered head in future, the youth sprang atop the wall, shouting defiance into the darkness.

"Heathen bastards!" he shouted, pawing at his chest. "You think to kill me? I carry the protection of the Anointed Lady . . ." Predictably, his statement was instantly corrected by the trio of arrows arriving simultaneously to take him in the belly, chest and neck.

"This can't be permitted to continue," Evadine said, voice heavy as she smoothed her palm over the slain youth's eyes, closing his lids forever. "Sergeant Dornmahl," she said, tone brisk as she straightened and turned to Wilhum. "Tomorrow night, you will muster the Mounted Guard. It's time we sallied forth."

CHAPTER THIRTEEN

Of course, Evadine could not be persuaded to leave leading the sally to Wilhum. When Swain began a hesitant suggestion that she do so she responded with a stern narrowing of her gaze that sufficed to still the captain's tongue. No further protests were raised when she climbed onto Ulstan's back at the head of the Mounted Guard. Wilhum was mounted to her right and I sat atop Jarik to her rear. The warhorse shifted beneath me with increasing agitation, well-attuned senses warning of impending combat and stoking his excitement. I held his reins loosely in my right hand, the folly of keeping them taut having been drilled into me via many hours of Wilhum's lessons. In my left hand I held a length of rope attached to a bundle of bound kindling mixed with hay and liberally spattered with lamp oil and tar. All of the Guard bore identical bundles, causing me to ponder that tonight would be a severe test of their mostly new-won riding skills. Their mounts might be bred for war but all beasts will shy from flame and keeping control of them in the chaos of what was about to unfold would be a far from easy task.

On our flank stood two full troops of company soldiers in standard three-rank order under Swain's command. I took some measure of heart in surveying the rigid discipline of their formation. Whatever my doubts regarding the abilities of the Mounted Guard, these soldiers, veterans all, would not break this night.

"Near midnight, wouldn't you say?" Evadine asked Wilhum as we continued to loiter. Silence reigned elsewhere in the castle, the Anointed Lady having issued strict orders that the usual routine was to be followed. It wouldn't do to give our foes some clue as to our intentions.

"Near as makes no difference," Wilhum replied, looking up to scan the starlit sky. The snows of recent days were mercifully absent now, leaving a clear view of the half moon shining amid a blanket of glittering constellations. As ever when enduring the nausea of a pre-battle interval, I took no pleasure in the heavenly spectacle. It is a common misconception that repeated exposure to battle will inure the soul to its terrors. In fact, I have found the opposite to be true: the more I tasted of battle, the more sickening I found it. I knew my less experienced comrades would look upon my blank features as the composed indifference of a hardened veteran, but it was in fact the carefully arranged mask of a man unable to quell an imagination rich in coming horrors.

"Shouldn't be much longer," Wilhum went on. It was true that the Vergundians would usually loose their first arrows when the sky grew darkest, but they were laggardly this night. As the moments wore on, I entertained the hope that the keen-eyed bastards might have opted for a respite, perhaps in observance of some heathen rite or other. Sadly, the now familiar whistle and tink of an arrowhead finding stone banished such illusions.

"Remember," Evadine said, straightening in the saddle. "Two full circuits of the walls. The first tight, the second wide. Strike hard and don't spare or this will all be for naught." She looked over her shoulder to meet my eye, a smile of encouragement playing over her lips. She had suggested I stay behind and take command of the walls, but, for all my fears, at that juncture I could no more have done that than stick a dagger in my own guts.

"Torches!" Evadine said, hefting her oil- and tar-soaked bundle, the rest of the Guard doing the same. A dozen torch-bearing soldiers hurried along the outside of our narrow column, touching flame to each bundle. As expected, Jarik grew markedly more restive as the fires took hold, tossing his head and casting a wide eye at me.

"Easy," I told him, holding the bundle out to the side as far as I could. "Not long now, old boy."

When all the bundles were lit, Evadine called out command to the soldiers manning the drawbridge windlass. To ensure surprise, instead of lowering the great wood and iron door via the windlass, they simply pulled the pins from the chains holding it upright. It duly toppled forwards to bridge the ditch, slamming down in a cloud of powdered snow. Kicking her heels into Ulstan's flanks, Evadine spurred him to a gallop and thundered through the gate, the rest of us following close behind.

In order to sow maximum confusion in the enemy, the Guard split in two as soon as it cleared the drawbridge. Wilhum led half to the right while myself and the others followed Evadine as she veered left. I watched her whirl the flaming bundle she held before launching it out into the darkness, sailing high and trailing sparks like a comet before plunging down. By sheer good fortune it happened to land near an archer, the fellow standing fully revealed in the glow, a naked target for the crossbowmen now lining the castle walls. Before he fell, pierced several times by a salvo of bolts, I gained the impression of a stocky figure in furs wearing a spiked helm. The weapon that fell from his grip matched Fletchman's description, a double-curved stave very different from the simpler wooden arc of Albermainish bows.

I waited until we had rounded the castle's northern shoulder before casting out my own bundle, the Guard having been instructed to ensure they were liberally placed so as to illuminate as much of the surrounding ground as possible. I allowed myself the momentary distraction of watching the fiery ball arc down and bounce along the snowy earth then hunched low as something whipped the air above my head. My eyes caught the flicker of more shafts streaking betwixt myself and Evadine's galloping form. Above us the air was filled by the thrum of crossbow bolts, the competing projectiles criss-crossing in the night as defenders and revealed archers embarked upon a duel.

Off to the right, I saw another fur-clad figure fall, his body tumbling into a flaming bundle in an explosion of embers. Another sprinted from the dark directly into Jarik's path. I had time to take in the Vergundian's pale, panicked features before the warhorse's hooves trampled him into the earth.

I followed Evadine along the castle's western flank, around the southern shoulder then out into the broad plain to the east. She headed deep into the gloom beyond the line of flaming bundles. As expected, the archers had retreated from the light, putting themselves beyond the reach of the crossbows on the walls but not our swords. The confusion wrought by our sally had evidently been considerable for, had they realised the depth of their peril, they would surely have run for the Alundian lines rather than tarrying on flat ground devoid of cover. Ahead, I saw the flash of Evadine's sword, painted yellow in the flickering firelight, followed by the scream of a mortally wounded man. An archer appeared on my left, half in shadow, his bow raised and arrow trained on Evadine's fading silhouette. Drawing my own sword, I swung it in an overhead slash as I passed the Vergundian, the blade thudding into his helm and sending him to a sprawl, either dead or senseless.

I spurred on, glancing back at the castle to see the two infantry troops under Swain already formed up to create a bisected semicircle around the lowered drawbridge. They would be our protection when the Mounted Guard completed its second circuit of the castle, although much depended on how quickly the bulk of the Alundian forces reacted to this attack. The air was even busier with the whistle of unseen arrows now, some Vergundians evidently fully awoken to their plight, although others continued to stumble into my path. I cut down one more and sent another spinning away when Jarik's shoulder collided with his back. Darting a second glance at the castle to gauge my position, I saw that I was now far beyond the eastern wall and jerked the reins to alter Jarik's course. I caught glimpses of other galloping shadows pelting past the still-burning bundles, but none I thought to be Evadine.

For the most part my next ride around the castle proved to be uneventful. The Vergundians had wisely retreated beyond bowshot of the walls. I counted a dozen bodies lying in the islands of light created by the flaming bundles, no doubt with more littering the shadowed ground. Whether this would suffice to discourage their nightly visits was yet to be seen, but I felt it a decent reward for what amounted to only a few moments' work. In war, it is usually folly to indulge in the illusion of success, especially before the mission is fully complete, and so it proved when I once again guided Jarik around the castle's southern flank.

The drawbridge was barely a hundred paces off and the cordon of Covenant troops appeared unmolested. I was in the midst of letting out a relieved sigh when from behind I heard the thud and tumble of a horse falling while at full gallop. Twisting in the saddle, I beheld the sight of a Guard struggling free of a thrashing horse. The beast was stricken by two arrows jutting from its flailing neck, foam flying from its maw as it whinnied in shrill distress. The rider should have run for the drawbridge, but instead he paused to recover his fallen sword. He was close enough to a burning bundle for me to make out Eamond's face. I watched him duck as an arrow flicked past his head, then raise his sword to contest the pair of Vergundians who came charging out of the dark, falchions in hand and faces riven with the hungry leer unique to those intent on retribution.

As I had discovered to my detriment before, when afflicted by the urgency of combat, the soldier's ingrained instinct for aiding a comrade will often overcome sensible urges towards self-preservation. Still, I gave voice to some choice profanity as I wheeled about and charged towards the scene. Eamond displayed the fruits of his many lessons by fending off the Vergundians' first assault, ducking one swiping falchion and parrying the other. His riposte, however, was clumsy, a broad, two-handed sweep of his sword that met only air. Fortunately, it did distract the vengeful plainsmen long enough for me to close the distance and skewer the tallest of the two through the back with a sword thrust. These archers appeared to favour quilted jerkins over armour and the blade made easy passage through the fellow's torso.

His comrade recoiled in shock from the sight of his countryman sinking to his knees, collapsing into a gurgling heap as I jerked my blade free. The blank, staring horror on the surviving plainsman's youthful features made me wonder if he had just witnessed the death of a kinsman. A brother, perhaps? His father even? I would never find out for Eamond hacked the gaping lad down with a series of blows that displayed what I would soon understand as his typical state in battle: ferocious but inexpert.

"Leave that!" I barked as he continued to hack at the Vergundian's corpse. Eamond straightened, breath steaming as he panted, beset by the exhaustion that often descends in the aftermath of fury. I sheathed my sword and trotted Jarik closer, extending a hand and jerking my head at the warhorse's back. "Get on."

It was as Eamond hurried to clasp my proffered hand that the Alundian knight came charging from the darkness, warhorse at full pelt and lance levelled at my chest. Had it not been for the dwindling fire of the nearby bundle I wouldn't have seen him until the lance had already pierced my breastplate. Luckily, I had just enough time to haul Jarik's reins and send him into an untidy sidestep, the lance point glancing off my pauldron before the two horses collided with shuddering force. Eamond let out a yell as Jarik's wayward rump sent him flying. I reacted with instinctive aggression. Jarik reared in bruised alarm, and I dragged my sword free of its scabbard, putting all my strength into a downward slash as he descended. I aimed the strike at the visored helm of the attacking knight, but he was a quick fellow, rearing back in the saddle so the sword missed him, but not his charger's neck. Hot blood spattered my face as the blade bit deep, the Alundian mount screaming and stumbling clear. The knight wisely slipped from the saddle before his horse collapsed. Still, he was close enough for me to have hacked him down if Jarik, distressed beyond control by the scent of horse blood and the shock of the recent collision, hadn't decided to rear again. His movement was so sudden in its violence that I couldn't keep purchase on his back. Tumbling clear, I landed hard on unyielding, frosted earth, my armour scraping and squealing in protest as I was dragged along for a few yards until I recovered enough wit to let go of the reins.

"Bastard," I groaned, catching a glimpse of Jarik's flailing hooves disappearing into the dark. My attention was instantly diverted to the metallic crunch and clink of the Alundian knight struggling to his feet a dozen paces away.

Forcing air into winded lungs, I dug the tip of my sword into the hard ground and used it to lever myself upright. I managed to get to one knee before the knight came for me, moving with an enviable swiftness, a stud-headed mace raised high in both hands. It was an impetuous move, one I sensed to be born of youth rather than experience, for it was easily countered. I rolled clear of the descending mace at the last instant, and gripping my sword like a quarterstaff, one hand on the blade and the other the handle, I swung the pommel at the Alundian's visor. It was a stroke I had successfully delivered during the duel with Sir Althus, but now it failed to land. The knight jerked his head back before the pommel could find the hinge, although the blow succeeded in stunning him for the interval I required to move closer and kick his legs from under him.

A resolute fellow, he continued to assail me from the ground, swinging the mace at my unhelmed head with worrisome speed if not accuracy. I ended his resistance by evading a swing then trapping his arm with my own, planting a foot on his breastplate and pulling hard until I heard the muffled crunch of an arm bone wrenched clear of its socket. After that, a hard swipe of the sword to the Alundian's helm was enough to leave him stunned and sagging on the ground.

I stood over him for a few breaths, chest heaving as I surveyed the surrounding ground. My eyes found no more enemies but my ears told a different tale, detecting the steady crump of many booted feet at the march and the shouts of captains and sergeants readying troops for battle. It was time to run and I would have done so if my gaze hadn't alighted on the fine gold filigree engraved into the Alundian's helm. In addition to its pleasing aesthetics, it was also very well made, showing few dents despite the battering it had received. In short, it was a far nicer and better helm than my own. Although no longer a thief, some habits will forever ensnare our souls and it was inevitable that I would expend precious seconds in removing the helm from its owner's head.

"Villain," the young knight gasped through bloodied lips as the helm came free. He regarded me with eyes that were equal parts bleary and enraged, his voice summoning recognition more than his besmirched features. "Pillager! You have no honour, Scribe."

"This is war, my lord Baron," I told him. "Not a tourney. And you owe me a horse." I rose, hefting his helm. "This'll do as recompense."

Lord Merick Albrisend, Baron of Lumenstor, stared up at me with the face of a man expectant of death but steadfast in his refusal to beg. I found it stirred as much envy as admiration. At his age I would have begged, flailed about and clasped my hands together in desperate entreaty, gabbling out all manner of promises. Granted, I would probably have also reached for a dagger as soon as my foolishly merciful assailant's back was turned, but still, I would have begged.

"Heretic!" Eamond loomed out of the dark, sword raised high, blade reversed to stab down at the young lord's exposed face. I deflected the descending steel with my own, sweeping Eamond's sword aside and fixing his bruised and deranged eyes with a commanding glare.

"Enough for tonight," I said, jerking my head to the castle.

"The Lady said not to spare," Eamond grated, rare defiance showing in his glower.

"And I'll account for my actions to her, as you are accountable to me." I continued to match his stare until he grimaced in frustration and turned away, stomping off towards the drawbridge. I paused to regard Lord Merick, face still set in a stern grimace of judgement lacking any sign of gratitude. Sighing, I tossed the fine helm back to him, reasoning that it would have looked comically out of place among my motley armour.

"Please convey my warmest regards to Lord Roulgarth," I told him before turning to run for the drawbridge. I snapped at Eamond to hurry and we covered the distance to the cordon of Covenant troops in short order, coming perilously close to being assailed by a crossbow-bearing soldier who mistook us for Alundians.

"Easy now," Ofihla said, pushing the raised bow aside. As I drew closer, I saw that the weapon was held by the Widow, her features as hard and hungry as ever. Apparently, hanging Ethrich Tanner and the other fanatics hadn't sated her lust for revenge.

"How many did you kill?" she asked eagerly as Eamond and I passed through the ranks.

At first I intended to ignore her, but the blankness of her eyes and the sympathetic wince I saw on Ofihla's broad features told me we had another madwoman in our ranks. My time with Ayin had taught me the value of such souls, as well as the wisdom of keeping on their good side.

"There's plenty left, mistress," I told her, forcing a grin. "Be assured of that. The Lady and his lordship?" I asked, turning to Ofihla.

"Already through the gate," she told me, her brow furrowing as the rhythmic tramp of approaching soldiers arrayed in close formation grew louder. "As we should be."

Needing no further urging, I shoved Eamond's shoulder and we hurried across the drawbridge. The Alundian assault came only minutes later, a ragged, piecemeal affair, launched in haste when whoever had command of their forces sensed they were about to be denied their quarry. Several dozen Alundians, marked as Sworn Men rather than men-at-arms by their light armour and varied weapons, charged out of the shadows in a hopeless attempt to seize the drawbridge before it could be raised. Most were cut down by a hail of crossbow bolts from the gatehouse before they even reached the troops on the ground. A brief, one-sided fight ensued, the Sworn Men making little impression on the Covenant ranks. Most were speared by pikes before they even got to land a blow.

When the fracas abated, Swain barked out the orders that had the ranks re-forming into two neat columns, the soldiers trooping into the castle at a measured run. Once the last boot had cleared the drawbridge the soldiers at the windlass replaced the pins and began feverish efforts to raise it. A trio of Alundian knights, possessed of more courage than sense, charged forwards to try and achieve the castle interior before the bridge was raised. Two fell almost instantly to our crossbows while the third suffered several hits before leaping his charger onto the slanted span of the drawbridge.

Horse and rider slid down the slope and into the courtyard, the drawbridge rising behind them, where the knight expended his remaining moments of life fruitlessly slashing his sword at nearby soldiers. Seeing the blood trickling down the flanks of his horse from the dozen or more bolts punched through his armour, I shouted to leave him be. I was surprised by the authority I enjoyed by this juncture, for the Covenant soldiers duly retreated, clearing a circle in which the dying Alundian continued to wave his sword about until loss of blood eventually saw him topple from the saddle. He lay on the cobbles, gasping and coughing out his last until finally lying still. His helm, I noted, lacked the elaborate ornamentation of Lord Merick's, but was still a finely crafted thing with a conical visor offering better protection than my own. Also, his horse appeared to have suffered no injury at all.

"Leave him be," I instructed as soldiers began to gather around the body. "His helm and his horse are mine. You sods can have the rest."

Three members of the Mounted Guard failed to return from the sortie, and two had straggled in with serious wounds to be placed in the care of Supplicant Delric. The affair evidently unnerved our Vergundian tormentors for, while their harassment didn't end, their night-time visits became less frequent. Also, they tended to launch their arrows at the limits of the range offered by their hornbows, making them much less accurate. I half expected the sally to have roused a more aggressive posture in our besiegers, but the ring of campfires dotting the hills remained unchanged and days passed with no ladder-bearing formations appearing on the plain. Also, the summit of the irksomely close, flat-topped hill continued to lack any sign of siege engines.

I resumed my routine of tutoring Ayin, updating the company books and sparring with Eamond and the other Guards. Also, when possible, I spent time with my new horse. He was a more impressive beast than Jarik in many ways, his coat mostly white save for the ash-grey fetlocks that made me name him Blackfoot. As I grew to gauge his moods, I felt Snob would have been a better title for he was ever a haughty creature. Some might think it absurd to ascribe the ability to gauge human status to a horse, but I remain convinced of Blackfoot's innate prejudice towards those of churlish origins.

"Here you are," I said one morning, holding a handful of oats close to his muzzle and receiving a snort in response. He exhibited additional disdain via a raising of the head and aversion of the eye. It was only when I placed a feed bag on the stable floor and stepped back that he consented to eat. My suspicions were confirmed when later I saw him happily munch a nut from Wilhum's palm. Still, Blackfoot did consent for me to saddle, mount and trot him around the courtyard every few days. Whether he would prove so amenable during battle was another matter.

"Come on," I muttered on the morning of the sixth day since the sortie, holding a carrot up to his lips. Few horses can resist a carrot, but it seemed Blackfoot was determined to be counted among their number. "Eat, you stuck-up swine," I insisted, trying to push the treat into his unyielding mouth, to no avail.

I had resorted to eating the carrot myself, pointedly munching my way through it while Blackfoot averted his gaze in studied indifference, when the clamour of a raised alarm sounded from outside. The company preferred drums over bugles and they began to sound now with the urgent, double beat that summoned all ranks to order. "Oh, do what you want," I told Blackfoot, tossing the half-eaten carrot into his stall. "It's a fair bet you'll have a new rider soon, in any case."

Seeing the company pennant rising to flutter below the royal standard on the tower, I hurried up the hill. Evadine, Wilhum and Swain were already atop the tower when I got there, faces all turned towards the eastern plain. "At least now we know what Lord Roulgarth was waiting for," Evadine said.

One glance at the host assembling on the plain sufficed to inform me that this force was far larger than the number we had previously ascribed to the lord constable. It is never easy to arrive at a true count when surveying an opposing army, for the mind tends towards exaggeration at such times. Spread out before me was a chequerboard array of impressive martial power: men-at-arms in neat ranks, Sworn Men in orderly but not so tidy columns, knots of loosely grouped archers and knights riding the flanks. In the centre of it all sat a smaller contingent of mounted nobles beneath a fluttering banner: the black bear of the Duke of Alundia himself.

"Ten thousand, perhaps?" Wilhum suggested.

"More," Swain grunted, his tone edged by a poorly concealed bitterness as he added, "Got nothing better to do elsewhere."

I couldn't fault his reasoning. Lord Roulgarth hadn't mounted an assault on our walls or constructed any engines for the simple reason there had been no need; his brother was coming with the full might of the mustered Alundian army. That the duke had been content to march his entire force to our door made it clear that no royal host had appeared to menace his borders. The Covenant Company was entirely alone in this enterprise.

"What's that?" I said as my eyes picked out what at first I took to be a wagon train moving to the rear of the Alundian host. As it drew near, I discerned it was in fact just one long wagon, an ingenious contraption of many wheels drawn by a team of twelve draught horses. The wagon carried something that was both bulky and long, its nature concealed by sheets of canvas, although Wilhum was quick to recognise what lay beneath.

"So, we'll face an engine after all," he said with forced humour. "Just not the kind we were expecting."

Companies parted ranks to allow the long wagon to make its way to the centre of the host, the drovers bringing the horses to a halt alongside the ducal party. Carters hurried to remove the canvas sheets, revealing the long, thick trunk of a recently felled and very old pine, suspended by chains from a timber frame. Fixed to its head was an iron contrivance that resembled a ram's head crowned by overlarge horns. I doubted our drawbridge, for all the soundness of its construction, would survive a single blow from this thing, and neither would the walls.

With the ram fully revealed, a large man in brightly shining armour took hold of the ducal banner and rode forward. The army let out a chorus of acclaim as the knight reined his mount to a halt before their first rank. They fell to hushed and expectant silence as he raised a hand and paused to survey their ranks. He gave no speeches, uttered no words of exhortation or encouragement, instead thrusting the banner into the air three times, the host calling out in unison with each thrust: "For freedom! For the faith! For Alundia!"

The assault began as soon as Oberharth Cohlsair, Duke of Alundia, lowered his banner and wheeled his horse about to face the castle. The visor of his helm was raised but I couldn't make out much of his features due to the distance and the distraction of his army girding itself for battle. My impression was of a bearded, stern-faced man, staring in unblinking challenge at the tower where the Anointed Lady stood. He continued to sit as his army streamed around him, ladders raised above their heads and voices repeating the same strident call: "For freedom! For the faith! For Alundia!"

"My lady," I said turning to Evadine, finding her features an infuriatingly bland mask that lacked any particular concern. I gritted my teeth against unwise profanity and confined myself to a polite if clipped request. "I should like your permission, if you would be so kind, to finally light the beacon."

Chapter Fourteen

One of the more peculiar observations afforded by a life rich in the experience of war is that, when confronted by the imminence of their own death, people will often say the most mundane things.

"Oh, shit it all," were the words that spilled from the lips of the Sworn Man on the ladder just before my sword descended to cleave his skull open. No final declamations of defiance. No crying out the name of his love or entreaties to the Seraphile to accept his soul. The words this unfortunate would carry through the Divine Portals and into the Eternal Realm consisted of, "Oh, shit it all." His expression just before the blade bit home was equally lacking in profundity: a small raising of the eyebrows and faint grimace to the lips. It was the face of a man who had lost a minor wager rather than his entire future. But lose it he did and nor did my arm falter as I delivered the blow. Battle is an exercise in survival rather than glory, and the desire to cling to life will strip all hesitation from a killing stroke.

My inarticulate victim slipped from the ladder like a bundle of rags, dislodging two men climbing below. All three landed in the ditch. One of the fallers quickly crawled out and hurried to take shelter behind the array of wooden panels the Alundians had advanced to ward against our crossbows. The other was not so fortunate, taking a crossbow bolt in the back and sliding down to join the man with the sundered skull amid the growing carpet of bodies littering the base of the ditch.

"Have a care, Scribe," Swain warned, grabbing my pauldron and dragging me back into the shelter of a crenellation, the air near my head snapping from the passage of an Vergundian arrow.

I gave a nod of thanks and rested my back against the wall, feeling the ache of strained muscles and the weight of my armour. Siege fighting, I had discovered, had more in common with routine labour than the brief but dreadful frenzy of open battle. Combat came in repeated bursts whenever an Alundian contingent managed to rest four or five ladders against the wall at an angle that both spanned the ditch and allowed passage to the battlements. Vergundian archers and Alundian crossbowmen would then rise from the cover of their moveable wooden walls to assail the defenders while their comrades, so far always Sworn Men, climbed the ladders.

Each assault lasted an hour or more, the Alundians attacking two widely separated sections of battlement simultaneously. Despite a full day of fighting, not one Alundian had succeeded in gaining the battlement for more than a step or two before falling victim to Swain's deadly tactics. Their ladders would inevitably be thrown back or set aflame before the attack petered out and the surviving Sworn Men retreated to their lines in varied states of panic or defiance. It all struck me as a bloody and pointless exercise, especially since their commander had a very large ram sitting unused on the plain. Swain's more experienced eye, however, saw wisdom in the duke's apparent folly.

"He wears us down and bloods his men into the bargain," he sniffed during a lull when the hour grew late. He wiped the sweaty grime from his forehead and risked an appraising squint past the crenellation's edge. "And he has the numbers to do it. We lost twenty soldiers today, another half-dozen wounded. He lost perhaps a hundred all told. But he can afford the butcher's bill. We can't. The more he weakens us, the less able we'll be to contest the breaches when he brings his monstrous novelty to pound our walls. Assuming he's divined a way to span the ditch, which I don't doubt he has."

"Ruthless and clever," I observed, taking a hefty gulp of water from a goatskin. "Never a good combination."

My gaze drifted to the top of the tower where a tall column of smoke rose into the dimming sky. Ayin had been given the task of tending to the beacon, keeping the blaze fed with a stock of firewood. Once it was gone the beacon would be allowed to dwindle and we were obliged to trust to hope that the party on the far bank of the river had seen the signal. I tried to resist the lure of grim arithmetic but my mind was ever drawn to calculation. In comparing the number of days we might expect to sustain ourselves in this castle to the time required for our messengers to complete their task, I arrived at a dolefully inevitable conclusion.

"Oh," I sighed, finding wisdom in a dead man's mundanity as a fresh tumult of drums and shouts sounded from the west-facing wall, "shit on it."

Duke Oberharth allowed us no respite that night, launching three more attacks while his archers took full advantage of their proximity to the castle to resume their harassment with zealous vigour. Showing even a portion of yourself to the enemy became a perilous enterprise, although some of our soldiers amused themselves by holding up empty helms to lure the Vergundians into wasting their shafts. For the most part they seemed happy to play along, casting forth a torrent of insults in their strange, guttural tongue, apparently heedless of the arrows they wasted. I took scant comfort from the dozens of arrows we collected. Although they could be loosed back by Fletchman and our small number of bowmen, or shortened and repurposed as crossbow bolts, if our foes were willing to waste their arrows, they surely had plenty more.

Morning brought another party bearing a truce pennant to our door in what I was beginning to understand as one of the ritualistic features of siege warfare. However, instead of a curt young noble this time a party of Sworn Men appeared on foot to request leave to gather their dead.

"Custom requires parley take place between nobles of equal or similar rank," Wilhum called down to the five men standing beneath the gatehouse battlement. "Treating with you is beneath our Lady's dignity. Go back to your lines and fetch a noble."

The group shifted in trepidation but, to their credit, refused to flee. "Our nobles won't come," the stocky man carrying the truce pennant called back. "Said exchanging words with your Lady besmirches their honour, or somesuch. We had to beg the duke for leave to come ourselves."

"Then blame him when you have to fight amid the stench of your comrades' rot." Wilhum waved a dismissive hand. "Now begone or loiter there and find yourselves feathered."

Although his companions retreated a few steps in alarm, the stocky man's feet remained firmly planted to the earth. "My brother lies in that ditch, you bastard!" he shouted, casting a finger at the base of the wall. "Would you deny a man the decency of burying his kin? Is your heathen bitch so cruel?"

These ill-chosen words inevitably had every crossbowman atop the gatehouse raising their weapon. The resolute fellow's death would surely have followed if Evadine hadn't called out an order to hold. "What is this?" she asked, climbing the steps to the battlement. She had fought all through the previous day and much of the night. It was only with grudging agreement to my insistent pestering that she retired to the tower for rest. Her brow had a troubled crease to it this morning and, judging by the hollowness of her eyes, I doubted she had slept at all. *Or*, I added inwardly, feeling a pang of nervous suspicion, *she had another vision.*

"Ill-mannered commoners come begging for their dead kin," Wilhum told her. "Not a noble among them."

Evadine spared him a dull glance before moving to the wall to survey the truce party below. They stiffened at the sight of her, some having no doubt glimpsed her during the fighting the day before. Evadine in battle was always a troubling if fascinating sight and she had been especially energetic in repelling their assaults, rushing from one threatened part of the wall to the other. Often her mere presence sufficed to spur the defenders to greater efforts, rallying and hurling the attackers back before she had even been obliged to wield her sword.

As the Alundians stared up at her, she regarded them in expectant silence until the stocky man coughed and called out again, "We ask only for basic decency for the fallen. As is custom in war."

"Decency?" Evadine asked him. "What decency have you shown for the innocent pilgrims persecuted in this duchy?"

The stocky man exchanged wary glances with his fellows, his heavy features hard with reluctance as he called his reply. "We had no part of that. We are simple soldiers called to service in accordance with oaths freely given."

"An oath given to faithless liars unworthy of their title has no merit!" Evadine's voice had all the sharpness of a blade, her anger plain in the hard line of her mouth and deepening hue of her normally pale skin. I saw her lips twitch as more words rose before being caged behind clenched teeth. I wasn't sure what order would come from those lips next, but if she had commanded oil be tipped over the Alundian corpses and set alight, I wouldn't have found it a surprise.

"I came to this land not for war but for justice," she told the Sworn Men when some of the anger had leached from her bearing. "Know that your lives are as precious to me and to the Seraphile as all others. It grieves me that you waste them in service to the underserving. I grant you the span of two hours to retrieve your dead. When you bury them, I implore you to reflect upon my words and ask yourselves if a duke who will not dare face me in either battle or parley is worthy of your sacrifice. If you should speak to him, tell him I am willing to settle this matter in personal combat for I will gladly trade my life to save so many. Would your duke do the same?"

Duke Oberharth's answer came as soon as the last Alundian corpse had been dragged away, and it was not in the form of an emissary agreeing to her challenge. Instead of the dispersed assaults of the previous day, he sent three full companies of Sworn Men against the castle's southern flank. It was a well-chosen spot, for the wall was shortest here, meaning we could concentrate only limited numbers to defend against a force at least fifteen hundred strong. A dozen ladders were raised to the battlements while the contingents of archers and crossbowmen put up a veritable blizzard of bolts and arrows to cover the climbers.

At first Swain's standard drill worked just as well as before. The leading Alundians were allowed through only to be swiftly dispatched and tossed over the wall, their comrades waiting their turn suffering a hail of rocks and showers of flaming oil. However, the keen-eyed Vergundians put their hornbows to impressive use, exacting a heavy toll among those defenders obliged to show themselves between the crenellations amid the frenzy of combat. Neither did many of the Alundians who achieved the walls die easy. They had clearly been chosen for their size and aggression, some plainly buttressed with copious drink if not some form of drug.

"Orthodox filth!" one wild-eyed brute screamed as he hauled himself atop the wall. He appeared heedless of the crossbow bolts protruding from his shoulder and leg as he laid about with a short-staved warhammer, yelling out incoherent expressions of bloodlust all the while. I watched him crush the helm of a halberdier and shatter a dagger man's leg before Swain swung his mace to spill the deranged brute's brains onto the stones. Unfortunately, the Alundian's frenzy had created sufficient space for his comrades to reach the battlement unmolested. Swain met them head on, his mace trailing blood and bone as it rose and fell. Still, his efforts were akin to trying to keep eels in a sundered barrel, the increasing mass of Alundians forcing him and the nearby Covenant soldiers back several paces.

Lending my blade to Swain's efforts would surely have enhanced my standing a good deal, but I knew it would also be a pointless waste of effort. Casting around with a desperate gaze, I happened upon a cask of lamp oil. "Help me with that," I snapped at two nearby crossbowmen, crouching to heft the barrel and drag it towards the burgeoning melee. As we did so, I saw Swain borne down by weight of numbers, still swinging his mace as a rush of Alundians sent him onto his back.

Seeing the attackers swarm him, I was seized by indecision. Rushing to his aid would mean abandoning my ploy, while continuing with it would surely doom him. Fortunately, my dithering proved moot when a lightly armoured figure sprang past me to hurl itself into the midst of the Sworn Men, hatchet blurring as it severed fingers and split faces. The press around Swain's prone form thinned, the Alundians retreating a step until one caught the figure's wrist, halting the hatchet an inch from his face. As he levelled a dagger at his assailant's neck the figure writhed with feral energy, head rearing back to reveal the snarling face of the Widow, teeth bared and mouth gaping. Lunging forward, she bit into her opponent's cheek, head worrying like a terrier. The man screamed and fell under the ferocity of the assault, repeatedly stabbing with his dagger which failed to penetrate the Widow's mail.

"Throw it as soon as I get them clear," I told the two crossbowmen, setting the barrel down and drawing my sword. "And be ready with a torch."

As the Widow continued to tear at the Alundian, one of his comrades lunged at her, sword raised to slash at her head. I hacked my own blade into his face before he could deliver the blow, sending him sprawling into the press of Sworn Men. Gripping my sword in both hands, I swung it to and fro, driving them back the yard or two I needed to crouch and haul the Widow off her victim. She was still biting as I hauled her away, gristle stretching from between her teeth as she tore off a piece of the man's face. I pivoted, tossing her behind me, then grabbed hold of Swain's boot. The captain was insensible, blood streaming from his nose and eyes half closed. His head juddered on the flagstones as I dragged him from the melee, shouting, "Throw it! Throw it now!"

The two crossbowmen duly heaved the cask with creditable energy, dousing the press of Alundians in a thick cascade of oil then tossing a torch into their midst. The oil caught immediately, air whooshing as the flames engulfed the Sworn Men, birthing an instant pall of smoke rich in the stench of burning hair and skin. Burning men screamed and milled about on the battlement, some rolling on the floor in an effort to extinguish the flames, others tumbling from the walls or stumbling blindly over the edge of the walkway to tumble into the courtyard.

"Push them over!" I called to a quartet of halberdiers I glimpsed on the far side of the thickening smoke. By way of further instruction, I began to slash at the knot of flaming figures, herding them towards the gap between two crenellations. The halberdiers soon lent their weapons to the task and we succeeded in casting the Alundians down onto the heads of their comrades below. A few survived the fall and continued to writhe about in the already corpse-filled ditch, screaming their agonies to shocked countrymen who suddenly appeared seized by immobility. The ladder that had borne these fire-wreathed men to the top of the wall remained intact, marred only by a few speckles of flame, but none of the Alundians below seemed inclined to climb it. The other ladders propped against the wall to either side were also now bare of attackers.

"Cowards!" one of the halberdiers called down to the Alundians. "Just like your duke who's afeared to face our Lady! Cowards!"

The cry was swiftly taken up by all the soldiers on the south-facing wall, shouted out with cruel amusement as well as righteous fury. "Cowards! Cowards! Cowards!"

Peering through the foul-smelling smoke, I saw a number of archers scurrying about below and divined this lull was about to end. "Dislodge those ladders!" I instructed, moving along the battlement and shoving sense into these taunting fools. "Then get to cover, lest you want an arrow through the eye!"

Once again, the level of authority I now enjoyed surprised me, for every soldier in sight soon forgot their taunts and hurried to comply. I thanked the two crossbowmen for their swiftness with the oil then set them to work dousing the lingering flames and heaving the remaining bodies over the wall. I found the Widow standing in blank-eyed vigilance beside Swain. The captain was slumped against the wall with only partial focus returned to his gaze. The Widow's features lacked all emotion, her jaw working as she chewed something.

"Spit that out," I ordered upon realising the nature of her meal. The Widow opened her mouth and allowed the half-eaten lump of flesh to tumble out, her face still mostly blank. "Help me with him,"

I told her, grunting as I draped one of Swain's arms across my shoulder and began to haul him upright. Judging by his lolling head and slurred speech, I assumed the captain must have suffered a hefty knock to the head as well as a badly broken nose.

"Needed here . . ." he mumbled, swaying on unsteady legs.

"You're needed in the infirmary," I told him before turning to the Widow, squinting at the deep cut marring her forehead. "So are you. Take the captain to Supplicant Delric." I let Swain's arm slip from my shoulder and gestured to her cut. "Get that stitched while you're there."

She gave a wordless nod and began to help Swain towards the steps. As she did so, I noticed the remains of her hatchet still dangled from a strap about her wrist. The blade had been dislodged in the fury of her assault, leaving just a splintered club.

"Wait," I said, stooping to retrieve the short-staved warhammer from the limp grip of the brute Swain had brained. "Use this from now on. Looks sturdy enough to last a while."

Some measure of animation returned to her face as she accepted the weapon, turning it about and gazing at the gleam of the blade's edge with brightening eyes. *The mad have their uses*, I reminded myself, fighting down a spasm of guilt. Even if she survived this siege, I knew this to be a woman dead in all respects save for the desire to inflict further violence.

"Get some rest before you return," I added in hollow consideration as widow and captain limped down the stairs.

No further assaults came, the Alundians retreating from the south-facing wall by dusk and the Vergundian archers resuming their vexations once full dark had descended. By now, every soldier in the company had acquired an aggrieved respect for our tormentors' skills, moving about with habitual caution and wariness that denied the Vergundians more victims. Consequently, they returned to their tactic of launching random volleys of fire arrows over the walls in the hope of setting light to something of importance. However, Wilhum had the Guard standing ready with water buckets and any resultant fires were swiftly extinguished.

With my watch ended, I hoped to retire to my bedroll in the tower, intending to sleep for as many hours as Duke Oberharth allowed me before launching another attack. However, I found Evadine waiting for me in the main chamber. She sat by the fire on a tall-backed chair one of our carpenters had crafted for her from some spare timber. When she beckoned to me I was obliged to rest my weary arse on the spindly stool opposite, the legs of my perch scraping stone when I started in surprise as Evadine's next words.

"You're captain now, Alwyn." She gave me a thin, sympathetic smile. "Congratulations."

I stared at her in bafflement, gut roiling thanks to the particular brand of fear that arises from unwanted responsibility. "Swain . . . ?" I began only for her cut me off.

"He lives but Supplicant Delric tells me his injury requires that he remain drugged and abed for the time being."

"But, Wilhum, Sergeant Ofihla . . ."

"Wilhum has charge of the Guard, a task to which he is best suited. He also doesn't enjoy the trust of the company the way you do. Sergeant Ofihla is as fine and brave a soldier as I will ever meet, but her . . . tactical acumen is limited. Yours, as you demonstrated today, is not."

I began to formulate additional arguments, intending to fully elucidate my many flaws as both a soldier and a human being. However, Evadine's tight, resolved smile told me it would all be fruitless. She shared a candour with me not enjoyed with any other member of this company – even Wilhum, whom she had known since childhood – but that didn't make us equals. In truth, who could ever claim equal status with one such as her? She had made me captain, and it was not an honour to be refused.

Letting out a sigh, I spent a short moment in contemplation of the fire. Brief fantasies of somehow slipping over the walls and escaping into the Alundian wilds played through my mind. I would make for the coast and get myself aboard a ship, go in search of Toria and claim my share of Lachlan's hoard, assuming she actually found it. It was all nonsense, of course – there was no avenue of escape from this castle and, despite my absurd imaginings, even if there had been, in my core I knew wouldn't have taken it. My fate was bound with Evadine's and had been ever since the Sack Witch stole life from me to heal her. There was no sundering our bond now.

"As captain, my lady," I began, turning back to her, "I appoint the widow Juhlina as your personal guardian. I also enjoin you not to engage in further combat unless required by dire necessity. If you fall, so does this castle and every soul within its walls."

"I will not fall here, Alwyn. I think you know that. Still—" she inclined her head in accedence "—far be it from me to gainsay my captain. I will refrain from battle until such time as our foes breach the walls. Any other orders?"

Talk of breaching the walls brought a doleful but inevitable conclusion, one that needed to be faced. "Unless Duke Oberharth proves himself foolish enough to accept your challenge, his next move is obvious: he'll bring that monster ram of his against the walls. Judging by what Castellan Estrik tells me, pounding a breach will be a bloody and protracted task for the enemy but not one we can prevent. We'll need to prepare to withdraw to the tower. I suggest we keep half the crossbowmen on the outer wall with orders to ration their use of bolts. The other half will be stationed in the tower to cover our retreat. The wall around the mound will also have to be strengthened and provisioned and all supplies will be shifted from the courtyard to the tower basement."

"Spoken like a true captain." Evadine's smile broadened as she spoke. However, I discerned a lingering shadow in her eyes, the same sombre preoccupation I had seen when the Sworn Men came to beg for their dead. My facility for reading her moods led me towards an uncomfortable sense that our current predicament was in some manner trivial, a distraction from far larger concerns.

"You had another vision," I said. "Didn't you?"

Her smile slipped away and it was her turn to regard the fire. "Yes," she murmured, a rueful grimace twisting her features for a second. "After the last vision they sent me, I had . . . deluded myself that the Seraphile might spare me further sight of the Second Scourge, and the road I must travel to avert it. But, though their compassion is boundless, I have learned that the tasks they demand of those they favour are many, and not easily borne." Her eyes flicked towards me, hardening with a familiar certainty. "You have to understand, Alwyn, that what is happening here has to happen. The blood we shed and the hurts we suffer now are sacrifices demanded by the Seraphile on the road to salvation."

She reached out a hand and I took it, finding her grip fierce. "I am glad, my good friend," she said, "that I have you to walk it with me, it being so very long and its trials so numerous." I saw her throat constrict and tears glimmer in her eyes before she released me.

"Go now and rest, Captain," she said, reclining in her chair and drawing her cloak about her. "You will need it on the morrow. Our easy days are now all behind us, though I know they will come again."

CHAPTER FIFTEEN

When heard from inside the wall, the impact of the ram's great iron head sounded very much like thunder, the roar that accompanied the hammer blows of an unseen monster. Powdered stone hissed, stacked boulders creaked and rattled, but the repaired breach survived the first pounding.

"You're a credit to the builder's art, Sergeant," I told Castellan Estrik, clapping him on the shoulder as another blow from the ram failed to tumble the wall. Once the target of the device the company referred to as "Old Iron Head" had become clear, Estrik had counselled tearing down our few makeshift buildings and buttressing the repaired breach with the timber. Watching the wood and stone resist another blow, I was glad I had listened to his advice. However, I found the patent relief on Estrik's face less than comforting. Clearly, he had half expected his handiwork to fall at the ram's first kiss.

Two full troops were arranged around this threatened section of wall in a three-rank arc, the dismounted Guard positioned behind ready to rush forwards and plug any gaps in their line should the need arise. Positioned directly in front of the repaired breach was an overlapping tangle of spiked obstacles fashioned from what little surplus timber remained and sundry captured weapons. The Alundians who came streaming through the breach would have to push it aside to advance, enduring a hail of bolts from the crossbowmen positioned to either side on the battlement above. I was quite proud of my trap, though, like Estrik, relieved that it wasn't about to be sprung.

It had taken Duke Oberharth a full five days to get his ram to the walls. The first day saw most of his strength arrayed before the east-facing wall to the left of the gatehouse where the largest of the repaired breaches created an ugly but sturdy interruption in the stonework. A dozen or more moveable timber shields, providing cover to the front and topside, were methodically advanced to the edge of the ditch whereupon parties of Sworn Men rushed forwards in relays to cast hefty boulders into the gap. This piling of rubble appeared inconsequential at first; then its growing height made its intended use obvious.

"The bastards are crafting a bridge, Captain," Estrik told me, ducking as an arrow whipped the air above his head. "One we can't burn."

"But we can burn the builders," I pointed out.

Throughout the next day a torrent of oil and fire arrows rained down on the Sworn Men as they went about their perilous toil, claiming at least a dozen lives in spectacularly unpleasant fashion. Thereafter their efforts became sporadic, small groups darting from cover to hurl their stones into the ditch while the Vergundians sought to keep our heads down. Duke Oberharth, or whichever Alundian noble had charge of this task, evidently took a dim view of such caution and ordered the wooden shield wall be advanced to within a few yards of the ditch.

The following day provided much grim amusement for the company as we went about lighting their shields on fire, claiming yet more lives. However, our enemy plainly had a plentiful supply of wood for they replaced their shields with irksome speed. It wasn't long before our oil stocks grew low and I was forced to order the rest conserved. An added frustration arrived in the form of a prolonged snowfall driven by harsh easterly winds. Consequently, our crossbowmen were obliged to peer into an ice-flecked gale whenever they tried to mark their targets, giving the labouring Alundians a far easier time of it as they busily went about filling in the ditch. By the time the snows abated, Walvern Castle was liberally blanketed in the stuff and the Alundians' unburnable bridge complete.

Before joining the soldiers in the courtyard I had stood atop the tower roof alongside Evadine as we watched Old Iron Head's ponderous but inevitable approach. The great ram was pushed rather than pulled towards the walls, a thick mass of Alundians lending their strength to a framework at the rear of the elongated cart that carried it. Much of its mass was encased in a wooden box liberally covered by sheepskins. Thanks to Estrik, who had anticipated this tactic, I knew the skins would have been liberally soaked in water, creating a shield against any effort we might make to burn the ram.

"Water won't quench an oil fire, Captain," the castellan told me. "But it will stop it spreading."

"We could sally forth," Evadine commented as the ram drew ever closer to the ditch. "Charge out and burn the monster's wheels out from under it." The faint grin on her lips made it clear this suicidal suggestion was not to be taken seriously. Her capacity for humour, and general absence of concern for our circumstances, made me wonder as to the content of her vision. Clearly it had shown her much to worry about, but the outcome of this siege did not appear to be part of whatever calamity awaited us.

If what she's seeing is even real, I reminded myself.

It required another dozen blows from Old Iron Head before the wall suffered any appreciable damage, the first boulders tumbling loose and grit falling in increasingly thick streams from between shifting stone. A dozen more blows and the timber beams buttressing the barrier began to bow then splinter. However, it was only when the whole edifice started to tumble that a pounding of drums sounded from the south-western corner of the outer wall. Turning, I saw Ofihla raising an arm before pointing to the flat ground beyond the walls. The meaning was clear and not unexpected. The Alundians had been almost certain to launch a diversionary effort while they assaulted the breach. I had given Ofihla command of the battlements, placing the company's entire strength at her disposal save for the force I had assembled to contest the breach. With the two troops, the Guard and the crossbowmen it amounted to at most three hundred soldiers, a paltry sum to contest the bulk of an entire army, but I put a good deal of stock in Estrik's pronouncement on the Alundians' chances.

"They're impatient, Captain," was the sergeant castellan's judgement. "Attacking just one breach when they should've crafted at least two more. They have the advantage of numbers to be sure, but that don't count for much when only five men can attack side by side at once. I don't envy the poor sods who volunteer for their Fool's Gambit."

The Fool's Gambit, I learned, was the common term in siegecraft for the party of soldiers who would, due to unwise notions of personal glory or promise of rich reward, volunteer to be first into the breach during an attack. As events were to prove that day, it is a very apt name.

Another boom, an explosion of dust as the beams gave way and the repaired gap in the walls became a breach once more. Old Iron Head showed himself for an instant, the dented, scratched and misshapen mass of iron appearing through the descending pall of powdered stone before retreating to leave a tense silence in his wake.

"Form hedge!" I shouted, the three ranks enclosing the breach responding by adopting the standard defensive formation with swift, uniform precision. Pikemen took one step forward, levelling their long spears while the halberdiers behind brought their own weapons to readiness. To their rear the dagger men drew their hatchets and knives, shoulders hunching in habituated anticipation of combat. I had chosen these troops for their experience, all veterans who had stayed with the Anointed Lady throughout her many travails. Every one of them would stand here and die rather than retreat without orders.

I watched the dust fade from the breach as the silence stretched, continuing for so long that I began to wonder if this whole enterprise had in fact been the diversion and the attack on the south wall was the main effort. My suspicion increased upon hearing Ofihla bark out a series of orders to my rear, her words soon smothered by the familiar clamour of a castle wall coming under attack.

Seeing a couple of the dagger men glance over their shoulders, I buttressed my own conviction with a harsh command. "Eyes front!" I snapped before adding some inner reassurance: *They didn't go to all this trouble to bash a hole in our wall just to leave it empty.*

Grim confirmation was not long in coming, taking the form of a thick hail of arrows arcing over the wall to plummet into the courtyard. "Steady!" I called out as the shafts rained down. All the soldiers in the courtyard were well armoured in mail and plate, each wearing a sturdy helm. Consequently, the arrow storm, while unnerving, did little damage. An arrow tipped by a bodkin and launched from close range had a fair chance of punching through mail and a slim chance of penetrating well-made plate. Loosed from a distance at a high arc against well-protected troops, it would only score a fatal hit through blind luck. The company soldiers flinched as steel-heads glanced off their helms and armour, only three actually suffering injury. One pikeman took an arrow through a bare patch on his wrist, and two dagger men were sent hopping to the infirmary with shafts jutting from the topside of their boots. Otherwise, the first Alundians to come charging into the breach found themselves confronted by three neatly arranged lines of veteran infantry, but only for the brief instant it took our crossbowmen to scythe them down.

The Alundian Fool's Gambit numbered about fifty in all, a mix of ducal men-at-arms and Sworn Men, hurling themselves forwards with much shouting. They barely came within arm's reach of our steel-thorn barrier before the crossbows began their deadly barrage. Loosed at a near vertical angle from windlass crossbows into targets barely a dozen feet below, the bolts had little difficulty piercing the armour of the men-at-arms or the lighter mail and quilted jerkins of the Sworn Men. The first volley killed those in front, forcing those behind to slow whereupon they became even easier targets. After the initial decimating volley, our crossbowmen worked with practised efficiency, one man in three shooting while the others reloaded. Within the space of no more than five minutes, the entire Fool's Gambit lay dead or stricken in the breach. None had even managed to set foot upon the courtyard cobbles.

The second assault came quick on the heels of the first, meaning the crossbowmen on the battlement were unable to repeat the first slaughter, although they did exact a heavy toll before the first Alundians struggled free of the breach.

Steady!" I called out again as the company soldiers stirred in anticipation. "Hold and wait for the order."

I continued to keep them in place as the number of attackers held up before our makeshift barricade began to swell. The first to encounter the obstacles tried to climb over them, most falling victim to the steady hail of bolts from above. Others contrived to half clamber over before the increasing press of bodies behind impeded their efforts. I watched at least three men impaled on the steel thorns by the crush, faces turned crimson in agonised rage or despair. It was only when the heavy timbers of the barrier began to scrape over the courtyard cobbles, forced back by the weight of the struggling throng, that I ordered the troops forwards.

"Advance in order!" I barked, the crescent-shaped formation responding with swift and disciplined efficiency. The steady tread of their boots made a rhythmic contrast to the confused tumult of the Alundians, whose yells of frustration or exhortation turned to screams as the pikemen brought their lances to shoulder height, driving them forwards as the distance closed. In accordance with prior orders, the formation halted six feet from the barrier, allowing the pikemen to thrust their weapons into the seething mass of enemies with impunity. Within moments a dozen bodies were slumped on or between the spikes of the barrier. Wounded Alundians bobbed and swayed in the roiling mass of their fellows, bleached faces white with shock, most unable to even raise a hand to staunch their bleeding wounds.

While the pikemen stabbed away with the eager abandon of soldiers taken by the bloodlust of battle, the crossbowmen above continued to assail the Alundians choking the breach. As the struggle wore on and their supply of bolts thinned, they switched tactics, heaving pots of steaming pitch to the edge of the breach. I had learned by now that lamp oil was a more versatile aid to defending a castle, since it could be cast onto an enemy in its cool state before being lit by a thrown torch or fire arrow. Pitch was more cumbersome, requiring a good hour of heating before taking on the required attributes. Also, our supplies were limited so Swain had so far refrained from using it. Seeing its effects, I found myself beset by the paradoxical sensation of simultaneously wishing we had more of the stuff and a deep desire to never see it employed again.

Although not unused to the screams of burning men, I found the particularly shrill and panicked sound that rose as the steaming black torrent met the close-packed throng uniquely unnerving. Burning pitch will stick to exposed flesh, searing its way through skin and muscle while adhering to desperate hands trying to scrape it off. Also, it produced enough heat to bake a man in his armour even if it failed to find his flesh.

Faced with the unrelenting, thrusting hedge of pikes and the deadly black rain from above, the Alundian assault swiftly collapsed. To the rear of the press, screaming, pitch-covered men fled the breach in increasing numbers while those marching forwards slowed their pace and eventually came to a halt. Those who had made it as far as the barrier continued the struggle for a time, swiping their swords and halberds at the stabbing lance points without much effect. One scrawny fellow, a Sworn Man, bare of armour save a loose mail shirt, contrived to scramble under the barrier and fight his way past the thicket of pikes. He hurled himself forwards, screaming and slashing with a falchion before one of the halberdiers in the second rank buried a blade in his unprotected skull. He was the only Alundian to set foot in the courtyard that day.

"Standard formation!" I called out when the final few stalwarts had been speared and the last attacker fled from the breach. The pikemen duly raised their weapons and the three ranks retired to their prior positions. Apart from those wounded by the Vergundian arrow storm, we hadn't suffered a single casualty. It was a different story on the south-western battlement where Sergeant Ofihla had been obliged to bring all our spare strength to bear to prevent the Alundians swarming over the wall. When the reckoning was done, Ayin would strike fifty-two names from the company roster that evening. But still, we had held and the Alundians had failed. As is the way with soldiers, it wasn't long before the company gave voice to its triumph, the castle soon reverberating with cheers, discordant at first but soon taking on a familiar, rhythmic refrain.

"Cowards!" The cry echoed out from the walls, repeated over and over. "Cowards! Cowards!" The chant was augmented by numerous ribald insults and taunts, most focused on one particular subject.

"Tell your duke to come fight our Lady!" one of the crossbowmen called down to the retreating Alundians, laughing as he ducked an arrow. "Send him to die so you daft fuckers don't have to!"

I let the shouting continue until it eventually began to dwindle, knowing it would succour the company just as well as any meal. As the shouts died away, the sound was supplanted by the mingled groans and occasional screams from the Alundians piled in the ditch. Through the lingering smoke I could see bodies shifting, some attempting to crawl away, most just beset by the twitches and jerks that assail the body as life departs it.

"I'll raise the truce pennant," Wilhum said, starting towards the corner of the courtyard where our few banners were propped. "Let them come and clean up the mess."

"No," I said, voice soft but firm.

He paused, squinting at me in surprise. "Custom of battle dictates—" he began, brow creasing in annoyance when I broke in.

"Custom won't stop them slaughtering every soul in this castle if they take it. A corpse fills a breach just as well as stone, and the sight of their dead will surely slow the charge of any who come next. Let them lie where they are, Sergeant. No more truces."

I couldn't tell if it was disgust or wounded pride that caused Wilhum's expression to shift from annoyance to anger. His mouth became a hard line and face rigid as he raised a knuckle to his forehead, his tone taking on an acidic edge as he said, "As you command, *Captain.*"

Meeting his gaze, my memory flicked through the many examples I had garnered of leaders dealing with defiant subordinates. Depending on his mood, Deckin would either have beaten Wilhum bloody or simply snapped his neck. Sihlda would have let him stew for a while before soothing his inner hurts with a quietly spoken aphorism or two. Swain would have barked an order to shut his mouth and called for a flogging if he didn't. Whatever course I chose, I knew the principal lesson of this moment lay in simply recognising that things had changed between this man and I. Evadine's reasoning in promoting me over him was sound, but that didn't alter the fact that an outlaw churl now held sway over a noble, disinherited and disgraced though he may be. Time would tell if the friendship we had formed in Evadine's shadow survived this change, but it remained a profound one.

Blinking, I jerked my head at the south-western wall where Ofihla's soldiers were reorganising after the chaos of the fight on the battlements. "Take the Guard and help carry the wounded to Supplicant Delric. I doubt the duke will try again today but be ready to come at the run if he does."

Wilhum's face lost some of its stiffness as he gave a nod, this time not knuckling his forehead as he turned and snapped out orders to the Guard. I turned back to the troops still standing in ranks in the courtyard, trying not to let my eye be drawn by the plaintive cries arising from the breach.

"Third rank fall out!" I ordered. "Gather up all these arrows then get yourselves a meal. The rest of you can eat when they return. Sit if you like, but remain in formation."

As I predicted, the day wore on without another attempt to carry the breach. A party of Sworn Men bearing a truce pennant were driven off with some carefully aimed arrows from Fletchman's bow. The ugly chorus from the piled Alundian wounded continued for several hours, finally fading away with nightfall. Suspecting that the duke might mount an attack under cover of darkness, I had the company fall out in successive troops to eat and grab what sleep they could while daylight remained. Come midnight, I mustered their full number but the Alundians failed to come again, although the night was rich in the tread of marching boots and turning of cartwheels. Duke Oberharth had evidently decided to rearrange his forces and only the dawn would reveal his intentions.

I spent much of the night atop the tower after a brief, fitful sleep in the chamber below. I knew some form of dream had assailed me, but the manner of it slipped away upon waking. *Perhaps Erchel brought me another warning*, I thought, rubbing my head as the throb made its presence felt. It had abated in recent days, or perhaps I had failed to notice it due to the unending tasks that come with a captaincy. Now it clamped its hard fingers to my skull and squeezed with sadistic insistence. I had hoped to husband my stocks of the pain-banishing elixir but the throb was so overpowering that I was forced to gulp down a dangerously copious mouthful before climbing the steps to the roof.

The sun rose to a clear sky that morning, casting its rays over a patchwork of Alundian contingents drawn up in a vast circle around the castle entire. They appeared to be evenly spread, leaving me unable to gauge where the next attack would be concentrated. However, I took note of the fact that all the men-at-arms were now positioned opposite the breach. I had nurtured some hope that the duke would forsake further attacks for repositioning Old Iron Head to bash another breach into the outer wall. A second gap in our defences would render us incapable of holding the lower keep but would also have bought valuable time. Duke Oberharth, for reasons unknown, appeared unwilling to expend one more day engaged in this enterprise than he had to. Soon his entire host would attack the walls at once, forcing us to defend the battlements while his best troops forced their way through the breach.

"We'll lose the outer wall today," I told Evadine when I sent Ayin to fetch her to the tower roof. "I see no way of avoiding it. I'll tell Delric to shift the wounded to the tower vaults along with the remaining supplies."

She gave only a vague nod in response and I saw that her gaze was fixed not on the surrounding host but the far bank of the Crowhawl River. I had also spent many a pensive hour staring in that direction, finding only a frustratingly empty landscape, but following her line of sight I found myself blinking in surprise.

"Is that . . . ?" I began, leaning on the balustrade surrounding the rooftop and squinting at the faint orange smudge on the north bank.

"A beacon," Evadine said. "We have a reply, Alwyn."

"But what does it mean?" I peered hard at the distant fire, hoping to make out some other signal. A waving flag, perhaps, or the considerably more welcome sight of a great many soldiers on the march. Instead there was just the lonely beacon flickering in the morning haze. "Is help coming or are they warning us that we're on our own?"

Evadine's only reply was a placid smile before she moved to the stairwell. "I should armour myself. I believe this day will require me to lend my sword to our defence. Unless you have any objections, of course, good Captain."

CHAPTER SIXTEEN

Duke Roulgarth allowed barely an hour of daylight to pass before launching his assault. A single trumpet pealed out from the site of the ducal banner, the call swiftly echoed by others as the strident signal swept around Walvern Castle. In response, every cohort in the besieging host started forward at the run.

Viewing the onslaught from atop the gatehouse, I noted that the Alundian nobles had not been spared this trial, counting several dozen armoured knights among the ladder-bearing commoners. At first, things went badly for our attackers. The Alundians had forsaken their movable shields this morn in preference for simply running full pelt towards our walls. Consequently, many fell to the blizzard of bolts and captured arrows loosed by our crossbowmen and archers before they could carry their ladders to the ditch. When the ladders rose there began the now routine business of killing those first up before casting them away. A steady cascade of bodies tumbled into the ditch as ladder after ladder was cast down, those milling about awaiting their turn subjected to a rain of missiles. The contest wore on for near an hour, during which our foes failed to gain purchase on any section of the wall. We were stretched thin, it was true, but so were they and only so many men can climb a ladder at once.

Despite our success and the fearful toll we exacted, I allowed myself no illusions. With the walls subjected to sustained if unsuccessful assault, Duke Oberharth had yet to send his best troops against the breach. Faced with the need to defend the whole length of the outer wall, I had been compelled to leave only a small contingent of crossbowmen on the battlement overlooking the breach. Armed with all our remaining pitch and a copious supply of boulders as well as bolts, I knew they would inflict a great deal of damage, but it wouldn't be the wholesale carnage of the previous day.

I remained atop the gatehouse for much of the struggle, risking occasional glances at the contingent of ducal men-at-arms standing in neat ranks opposite the breach. The Vergundian archers and Alundian crossbowmen were dispersed but still aggravatingly keen-eyed and I was obliged to duck several times. My brief surveillance revealed that the duke had raised his banner just to the rear of his men-at-arms, which I assumed meant he had opted to share their dangers today. Apparently the taunts flung at our foes had reached his ears and chafed his pride. Although unwilling to demean himself by consenting to face Evadine in single combat, it appeared he was prepared to risk his person in a perilous charge instead. It was an act of remarkable courage, worthy of my keenest admiration but not my mercy.

Making a crouched progress along the battlement, I sought out the sergeant in charge of the crossbowmen at the breach. "The duke himself will be among them when they charge," I told him. "A big, hearty fellow in fine armour. Be sure to kill the bastard."

The sergeant, a former Callintor sanctuary seeker named Prader, had a villainous aspect, narrow of face with small eyes and unusually pointed teeth which he revealed in a half-grin. "Got a reward for us if we do, Captain?" he asked.

"The Lady's blessing," I said then inched closer, lowering my voice, "and a silver sovereign for whoever brings him down."

Hearing a fresh blaring of trumpets from the other side of the wall, I clasped a hand to Prader's mail-covered shoulder, adding, "That noble-arse dies and this is all over. Remember that." The sergeant's grin broadened and he knuckled his forehead as I turned and hurried towards the stairs.

"Stand to!" I called out upon reaching the courtyard, the two troops arrayed there snapping to attention. "Here they come, and they've brought their duke with them. Let's give him a fine welcome, eh?"

I allowed a brief chorus of laughter before marshalling them into the same crescent formation as the day before, then moved to Wilhum's side. "This won't be like yesterday," I told him, obliged to half shout above the surrounding din of battle. "We'll hold for a time, kill a good many, but sooner rather than later we'll have to withdraw to the tower." I gestured to Evadine, standing with the Widow beside the roped off corral that now served as the stables. "When the order comes, the Guard's task is to get her to the tower, whatever it takes. Drag her there if you have to."

Wilhum glanced in Evadine's direction and began to nod, then stopped, his eyes widening. "Not again," he breathed.

Turning, I saw Evadine leading Ulstan from the stable, the charger already saddled and girded for battle with a thick studded quilt that covered him from neck to rump. By the time Wilhum and I had rushed to her side she had climbed onto the stallion's back and walked him towards the drawbridge.

"My lady—" I began, stepping into Ulstan's path.

"Worry not, Captain," she cut in, fastening the buckle on her helm. "Rest assured I know what I'm about."

"The duke," I stuttered, finding it suddenly very difficult to parse coherent sentences amid my utter confusion and rising fear. "The breach . . ."

"Alwyn," she said, regarding me with exasperated impatience. "You trusted me enough to follow me here. Trust me when I say that I shall shortly ride through this gate and bring the Duke of Alundia to well-deserved justice." She tightened the buckle on her helm and took hold of her reins, favouring Wilhum and I with a smile. "It would be my great honour if you would both accompany me."

Shifting her gaze to the soldiers manning the drawbridge, she called out a strident command: "Loose the chains! Lower the bridge!"

"Belay that!" Wilhum shouted, casting a hand at the soldiers at the windlass before rounding on Evadine. "Evie, this is insanity . . ."

He continued to rail at her while she ignored him, keeping her sight fixed on the soldiers at the drawbridge. They shifted in confusion, looking from her to me. "Captain?" the burly fellow who had charge of the windlass asked, riven with a fear that I saw mirrored on the faces of every soldier witnessing this moment. I knew they were asking the same question I was: *Is the Anointed Lady intent on a second martyrdom?* However, it was the serene, placid certainty on Evadine's face that captured me, the same demeanour she had displayed before the Traitors' Field rather than the doom-laden sombreness before the calamity at Olversahl. She did not expect to die today.

"You heard the Lady's order," I snapped at the burly soldier, moving out of Ulstan's way. "Loose the chains."

Wilhum's cry of protest was swallowed by the rattle and boom of the drawbridge's descent. Evadine paused to favour me with a warm smile before kicking her heels and sending Ulstan into a gallop. She pelted through the gate, the charger's hooves thundering on the drawbridge timbers before finding the hard ground beyond whereupon she wheeled to her left and disappeared from view. The Widow sprinted after her without hesitation, leaving me to regard Wilhum's appalled, enraged countenance. His anger was of such a pitch it came as a surprise when, instead of attempting to strike me down, he set his features into a hard mask and ran off to mount his own horse, calling the Guard to do the same.

"Form line of march!" I called out, running back to the troops in the courtyard. "Five abreast. Halberdiers to the front. Pikemen second, dagger men third. Shift your arse!" I added, aiming a kick at a hesitant pikeman, one of many gaping in immobile confusion. This proved sufficient to get them moving, the narrow column forming up before the breach in short order. I moved to its head, drawing my sword and raising myself up to peer over the mound of dead still littering its base. The Alundian men-at-arms were shifting their own formation in response to an unseen threat, although it was easy to guess its nature. Glancing towards the drawbridge, I saw Wilhum leading the Guard through the gate at the gallop. I guessed it would take them less than a minute to reach the Alundians and the melee already erupting on their flank.

"Once we're through, halberdiers will follow me and advance towards the ducal banner!" I shouted to the assembled column. "Pikes and daggers split left and right and have at their flanks!" I was never fond of speech making or exhortations, finding such performance somewhat embarrassing, even at times like this, but the necessities of the moment demanded something. To this day I remain uncertain as to the origin of my next words, since they sprang from my lips without pause for reflection. Had I known just how often I would hear them in the days ahead or in what circumstances, I would surely have said nothing.

"We live for the Lady!" I called out, raising my sword above my head. "We fight for the Lady! We die for the Lady!"

The soldiers' response was immediate and so precise in echoing my words that one would be forgiven for assuming they had rehearsed it for days. "We live for the Lady! We fight for the Lady! We die for the Lady!"

Upon turning and charging into the breach, I was obliged to scale the Alundian dead. I gave silent thanks for the clamour of combat for it smothered the sound of cracking bones and squelching flesh as my steel-shot feet sank into the foul-smelling carpet. Once clear of it, I navigated the uneven causeway of piled stone spanning the ditch, arriving in the midst of a dozen or more Alundian men-at-arms. Their attention was captured by the unfolding spectacle to their rear. I couldn't fully make her out through the swaying thicket of lances, catching only glimpses of Evadine's mounted form, Ulstan rearing and lashing out with his hooves as his rider hacked away at the barrier of armoured soldiery. As I watched, the Mounted Guard charged in to add their weight to the assault. As the clang and clatter of battle sounded even louder, the strident, rallying call of a trumpet rose from the direction of the black bear banner in the centre of the Alundian ranks. The men-at-arms around me hefted their halberds and hurried to answer the call. They would have been better served in sparing a glance to their rear.

The first one I felled had no warning of impending death, which I like to think of as a mercy. My sword point slipped into the gap between the base of his helm and backplate, stabbing deep enough to sever the spine before I drew it clear. His neighbour at least had time to turn and behold my swinging blade before it caught him full in his unvisored face. I brought down one more before the company halberdiers joined the fray, wreaking swift havoc among the disordered Alundian ranks.

"To the banner!" I called out, pointing my sword to the black bear flag still swaying above the chaos. "Forwards!"

I spared a glance to either side to confirm the pike and dagger men had followed orders, grunting in satisfaction at the sight of them spreading out to assail the Alundians on both flanks. Then the tide of battle carried me into the heart of the melee and all sense of order vanished. As at the Traitors' Field, I found time became a malleable substance in the thick of a fight. Some horrors, such as an Alundian man-at-arms taking a halberd point in his gaping mouth while another speared him through the neck, unfolded in the blink of an eye. Others played out in prolonged detail. The death of a knight, compelled like his fellow nobles to fight among the foot-bound churls this day, was particularly excruciating. He managed barely a single blow with his mace before a quartet of halberds spitted him, each delivered by soldiers well tutored in finding gaps in armour. The ranks of the knight's comrades tightened behind him, creating a wall that bore him up as the halberdiers pressed forwards. Still, the knight lived, raised above the melee to flail about as blood erupted from his visor in a slow fountain.

The struggle seemed to wear on for an hour or more, but Prader, who watched the whole episode from the walls, later assured me it lasted no more than perhaps ten full minutes. Finally, having forced a gap in this tightly formed rank of professional soldiers, I stumbled clear of the fight in time to witness the duke's fate. I saw Evadine hacking and trampling her way through the rear of the Alundian formation. I saw the duke and a surrounding retinue of knights take to horse, and I saw them ignore the still-open avenue of escape to the east in favour of charging headlong at the Anointed Lady.

It was done in an instant. The duke and the Lady went straight at each other and, when they met, she killed him with just one blow. It may have been my tendency towards dramatic imaginings, but I think I heard the sound of her sword striking his helm, clear as any bell. I could tell he was dead before he slipped the saddle, his neck being at such a curious angle.

News of the duke's demise spread through the Alundians to either side of me with a speed unique to the battlefield. For soldiers in combat, an instinct for gauging abrupt changes in fortune can mean the difference between death and survival. Backward glances revealed the sudden absence of the ducal banner and those Alundians still contesting the breach started to waver, a chorus of despairing cries erupting throughout their ranks. Seeing a dozen or more turn their heads and take the first faltering backward step, I called out fresh exhortations to the company, forcing more strength into my arms as I hacked at the men to my left and right.

Routs tend to happen quickly. The primal instinct for survival will dispel the artifice of courage or hunger for glory when it becomes apparent the day is lost. So it proved now. There was no blaring trumpet to sound the Alundian retreat, yet they all appeared to abandon the fight at the same instant. The man-at-arms I had been attempting to pummel to the ground dropped his halberd, then turned and began to claw his way through the crush to his rear. To either side of him, his comrades followed his example and within seconds the entire Alundian line had evaporated. A few stout-hearted fellows attempted to stand only to be quickly hacked down as the company soldiers advanced. The ground in front of the breach soon became empty of fighters, a scattered mass of Alundians fleeing towards the eastern hills to leave behind a sprawl of corpses, save for a small cluster of knights. They numbered six in all, each one dismounted, pointing their weapons at Evadine and the Guard as they closed in. I could see a large, inert figure lying amid the Alundian knights and knew instinctively who the slain man must be.

"Hold!" I shouted upon seeing a number of company soldiers charge off in pursuit of the runners. "Re-form ranks! Standard formation!" Once marshalled, I had them spread out to join the Guard in enveloping the cluster of knights.

"Yield," Evadine called to them, trotting Ulstan forwards, her sword sheathed and hand raised. Every inch of both horse and rider appeared to be spattered with dirt or blood, but her sincere compassion still shone through the grime on Evadine's face. "There is no more need for death this day. I beseech you, yield and know peace."

"Away with you, heretic whore!" a hulking Alundian knight shouted back. He wore no helm and his bearded, heavy features were mottled in a curious mix of fury and anguish as he ranted on. "Insult us not with your lies! We know the blackness of your heart!"

I had expected to find Lord Roulgarth among this band of stalwarts but assumed he must have been given command of the assault on the walls. Looking around, I saw the fighting atop the battlements had faded, Alundians gathering in thick clusters at the base of their ladders, all eyes turned towards this scene. I knew it wouldn't be long before they were harried into battle order, while the drawbridge remained lowered and the breach undefended.

"We can't tarry here," I said, hurrying to Evadine's side, adding "my lady", in harsh spoken emphasis when she continued to regard the recalcitrant nobles.

The bearded brute had also noticed the danger, snarling out a laughing sob of eager anticipation. "You see, whore?" he screamed, pointing at the gathering horde of Alundians. "See the doom you have earned by this foul murder!"

"Your duke met his end in fair combat on field of battle," Evadine called back but her words were smothered by the cries of the Alundian nobles. Profane curses mixed with wordless shouts of defiance as they waved their weapons in keen invitation; men hungry for death.

"Kill them or spare them!" I hissed at Evadine, moving closer and reaching up to grasp her gauntleted hand. "But do it now."

She looked down at me with a face drawn in sorrow. "I hoped it would be different, Alwyn," she said, voice soft. "Sometimes I can change it, or others change it for me. As you did in Olversahl." She sighed and looked away, turning her sight not to the Alundian knights but the open plain beyond. "But it seems there's no changing it today."

Following her gaze, I at first saw only the part-frosted, sparse grass of the plain and the hills beyond. Then my eyes detected a flicker of colour in the dip between two hills, quickly joined by several more. *Banners*, I realised and felt no doubt as to their origin. The entire martial might of Alundia was already gathered here to crush the heretical interloper who called herself a Risen Martyr. What approached could not be an Alundian host.

The thunder of many horses at the gallop sent a sustained tremor through the ground as the distant banners grew yet more numerous. The leading knights came into view seconds later, at least five hundred in the vanguard, led by a familiar tall figure riding beneath a banner bearing a red flame.

"Yield!" Evadine cried to the Alundian knights, voice rich in hopeless entreaty. "Please! I beg you!"

But there was no saving nobles so lost to notions of honour. Apparently the prospect of living with the stain of having failed to save their lord from the blade of a false martyr was unthinkable. Taking up his sword, the bearded brute, whose name I still haven't learned after years of inquiry, let out a guttural yell of challenge and hurled himself towards Evadine. His countrymen followed close behind, the small party covering only a dozen paces before Wilhum barked out a command and the Guard spurred forward. The slaughter was brief but thorough, Wilhum dispatching the bearded knight with a single slash of his sword while the others were cut down or trampled.

I turned away from the sight, finding I had seen my fill of death this day, yet it was far from done. Off to our right, Sir Ehlbert Bauldry led his vanguard in a charge towards the south wall, wreaking predictable havoc among the mass of still disorganised Alundians. A larger contingent flying the banners of the Crown Company swept towards the castle's northern flank with similar effect. A survey of the plain revealed a broad line of infantry advancing in disciplined order while, to their right, a far less cohesive mass came on at the run. As they drew closer, I discerned them as a mob lacking all discipline, their weapons consisting mostly of axes, pitchforks or crude lances fashioned from sharpened tree branches. They appeared to be equal parts men and women, varying in age, yet even the oldsters among them came on at a fair lick. Riding at their head were the two members of the Guard we had sent to watch for the beacon, the success of their mission given stark evidence in the sheer number of churls who had answered the Anointed Lady's call.

As they streamed past, yelling devotional exhortations or the wordless cries of folk subsumed into the madness of battle, I guessed their number to exceed at least eight thousand. Seeing their emaciation and quality of their besmirched cloth, I knew these to be the lowest order of churls. The displaced, the beggared, the orphaned, these were the people who came to save the Anointed Lady that day. The many stories since spun about this Common Crusade, as it came to be known, fail to register the fact that it would surely have been slaughtered to the last had it hurled itself at the Alundian host without the accompaniment of a royal army. Those who promote the Risen Martyr's legend would have it that the commoners alone triumphed over the remaining Alundians, putting Lord Roulgarth to flight with only a few hundred horsemen to his name.

In truth, these devotional churls suffered greatly that day. I saw dozens brought down by Vergundian bowmen before they even reached the re-formed lines of the Sworn Men who proceeded to reap an even greater harvest. It must be said, however, that the Common Crusade deserves credit for occupying most of the Alundians' attention while the main body of royal infantry arrived. Fully engaged with a mob of fanatics, the Sworn Men were unable to shift their line to meet the charge the Crown Company foot drove into their flank and rear. Ducal levies soon charged in to put the outcome beyond doubt.

Less than an hour after the death of Duke Oberharth, his army lay slain or in full flight towards the eastern hills. In the aftermath, those churls not killed or maimed came in search of the object of their devotion. Evadine had ordered me to muster the full company on the plain before leading them against what remained of the Alundian right. In the event the enemy line disintegrated before we even reached it, leaving us standing amid the detritus, corpses and wounded that litter the battlefield at the terminus of combat. The Traitors' Field had failed to inure me to such sights and a rising nausea built in my gut to accompany the resurgent throb of my head. My discomfort was made worse by the growing crowd of churls, many clutching wounds or with faces showing recent scars. I saw a few crawling towards the Anointed Lady despite grievous injury.

Evadine, however, greeted them all with the same bright smile and welcoming demeanour she adopted when delivering a sermon. Sitting tall in the saddle she raised her arms as the churls clustered around in a thickening mass, all sinking to their knees as one when she began to speak.

"Today you have blessed me," she told them. "Today you have drunk deep of the Seraphile's grace, for was there ever a finer mirror of the Martyrs' courage?"

I found myself retreating from the sight, snapping out orders to see to our wounded before turning and stomping off towards the castle, intent on gulping down as much of the pain-banishing elixir as I could stomach. With any luck, several hours of senseless oblivion would follow. Finding my path blocked by a large, armoured figure, I gave an annoyed grunt and shoved hard at the obstacle. It was like pushing a granite wall, one that let out a good-hearted chuckle as I balled a gauntleted fist and prepared to do more than shove.

"Not had enough fighting for one day, eh?" a deep, rich voice asked.

My eyes tracked over a brass motif in the shape of a flame before ascending to behold a face I had only ever seen at a distance before now. Sir Ehlbert Bauldry wore his dark hair cropped short on the sides and nape, as was common with knights, his face clean shaven and absent of any scars. It was a tad too block-like to be called handsome, resembling a man chiselled from pale marble rather than a being of flesh and bone. His smile, however, was wide and, as far as I could judge, genuine in its warmth, making me realise for the first time that this man was in fact human. He was also taller than me by several inches and a good deal broader too.

Common sense should have dictated that I mumble an apology, bow and move on, but this proved to be one of the many occasions when that particular brand of thinking failed me. Faced with this dread figure at such close remove, the necessary fear failed to rise. Instead, my aching head filled with ugly memories of Moss Mill and the hacked and abused corpses of Deckin's band I had left there. It had been a massacre orchestrated under this man's command, deserved by some, but not by others. Especially not the children.

So, looking Sir Ehlbert in the eye, my own dark with fatigue and the insistent attentions of the throb, I said, "Get out of the fucking way."

A glimmer of bemusement and shock flickered across Sir Ehlbert's brow just for a second before he burst out laughing. His gauntlet landed heavy on my pauldron as he jostled me in appreciation. "I'd heard this scribe was not one for the niceties." Laughter rose from the dozen or so kingsmen standing nearby, making me acutely aware of my vulnerability. There was no love lost between the Covenant Company and this lot, some of whom had once done their best to hang me, and I was now a good distance clear of any allies.

"I'm a captain now," I told the King's Champion, forcing a note of authority into my voice. I doubted rank would count much if this man or his comrades took it into their heads to do me harm, but it was worth a try.

"Really?" Sir Ehlbert raised his brows. "Then please accept my congratulations, good sir. May I also congratulate you on this piece of cleverness." He nodded towards the sprawl of bodies around the fallen duke. "It can't have been easy to orchestrate."

"All my lady's doing." I forced my lips into a strained grin. "She had a vision from the Seraphile, you see."

The warmth on the knight's face dimmed several notches, his smile slipping a little but remaining in place as he turned, keeping his hand on my shoulder and obliging me to do the same. "Princess Leannor requests your presence, Captain," he said, gesturing to a group of mounted figures fifty paces off. "If you would be so kind."

Knowing there was no avoiding this, I walked with him to greet the princess, attempting to force a measure of calculation through the throb. *Where is her brother?* I asked myself. *Where did this army come from?* However, as Sihlda had once told me, asking a question is always easy; the answers are the hard part. At this moment, with the ache in my head jostling for attention alongside recently witnessed horrors, no answers were forthcoming.

By the time we reached her, Princess Leannor had dismounted at the site of Duke Oberharth's demise. Her retinue kept to a respectful distance as she picked her way through the scattered bodies, already part stripped by soldiers and churls keen for loot, before halting beside the duke's body. His helm was gone, probably consigned to a soldier's knapsack, along with his breastplate and weapons.

"A terrible pity," the princess said, sparing me a short glance as I came to a halt nearby and sank to one knee. Her garb was a curious mix of elegant finery and martial accoutrements. A breastplate, edged in gold filigree and engraved with a silver inlaid version of the Algathinet crest, covered her torso and a small, ornamental short sword dangled from the belt about her hips. Her dress was a sombre-hued affair of dark red velvet embroidered with copper thread. Altogether, I estimated the cost of her attire would feed the company for a month or more, despite its uselessness. A dagger could pierce the thin metal of her breastplate and I doubted she had ever drawn the short sword from its scabbard.

She gestured for me to rise, keeping her focus on the slain duke. The body bore no bloodstains, although the cause of his demise was clear in the sharp angle of his neck, snapped by Evadine's blow. I reckoned he had probably been dead by the time he tumbled to the ground. As is the way with corpses, his features were shorn of everything that had marked him in life as the kind of man so many would willingly follow to war, all flaccid, pale flesh and empty eyes.

"He would have been much more valuable alive," Leannor went on. "A hostage to the future loyalty of his family and nobles. Still, I've long come to the conclusion that there is no controlling the outcome of a war. It's like a storm: you ride out its fury then make the best of what remains when calm descends." She angled her head, peering at the duke's slack features. "All you had to do was pay your bloody taxes, Oberharth. Behold the folly of pride married to the persistent delusion of honour." She sighed, shaking her head and shifting her gaze from the duke to me. "A toxic combination, Master Scribe. Wouldn't you agree?"

"It's Captain Scribe now, Your Majesty," Sir Ehlbert put in.

"Really?" The princess gave a very slight bow of her head. "Well done. Did you kill the other one to secure your advancement?"

It was a flippant taunt, but it told me something of import: *This woman thinks she knows me. She doesn't.* "Captain Swain lies wounded in the castle, Majesty," I said. "When he recovers I shall be happy to relinquish my current role. I find the burden of command to be heavy."

"Heavy or not, I'd wager a good deal of our success this day is thanks to you." She raised her hands to the surrounding carnage, a small grimace of distaste marring her features. "Or is it all the Anointed Lady's doing?"

"All the Covenant Company does is at her command and in her name."

"Such devotion." Princess Leannor stepped closer, her eyes narrowing as she scanned my expression. "Yet I see only pain on your face. Not like all those mad folk we met on the road, eh, Sir Ehlbert? Thousands marching the road to Alundia, every countenance shining with divine conviction. Sadly, in the fierceness of their faith, most chose to answer the Anointed Lady's beacon without bothering to pack supplies or even warm clothing. We did our best to succour them, but couldn't have foreseen the need to sustain so many additional mouths during our march, the march my brother solemnly promised to make, as you recall. Sadly, the road to the Alundian border is now marked by a few hundred faithful corpses. Far more than fell here today, I imagine."

I gave no immediate answer, instead casting pointed, searching glances to either side. "Is the king here, Your Majesty? I know my lady would wish to greet him."

"The king is where he should be," she replied without apparent rancour. "At court, seeing to the proper governance of his realm. I am honoured that he saw fit to leave this campaign in my hands. I don't suppose," she went on, moving away from the duke's corpse and striding towards her horse, "you managed to capture Lord Roulgarth? We can't seem to find him anywhere."

"Fled, I assume. If he has any sense, that is."

"Oh, well." Leannor paused to mount her fine white mare while a courtier held the reins. Unlike Blackfoot, this beast was a pure shade of alabaster from nose to tail, seeming to shine in the sun and adding to the throb as I squinted at it. "No matter," the princess said, settling into the saddle. "I'm sure we'll find him at Highsahl, along with the good duchess and her litter of brats. The king is minded to allow her to keep the duchy, let her govern until her eldest comes of age. Lady Celynne's father would take dim view of her removal and the king harbours a lingering affection for her."

"And if she doesn't yield?" I asked, which succeeded in summoning a frown to the princess's brow. "I read that Highsahl is practically impregnable."

"Nowhere is impregnable, Captain Scribe. Especially not when you have expert assistance." She turned and gestured for a member of her retinue to come forwards, a short, grey-haired man of wiry appearance mounted on a sturdy pony. The plain leather jerkin and simple, homespun garb he wore made me think him an odd addition to her entourage, as did the accent he revealed upon speaking.

"Your Majesty," he said in broad Alundian tones, bobbing his head with a servility that seemed at odds with the hard rigidity of his features.

"Captain, I present Master Aurent Vassier," Leannor introduced the Alundian. "The foremost engineer in the entire kingdom. A builder of bridges, houses, cranes and all manner of marvellous novelties. Is that not the case, Master Vassier?"

The grey-haired man bowed again, and I glimpsed a twitch to his features as he fought to conceal dangerous emotions. "My reputation is beyond my control, Your Majesty. But I am a builder, it is true."

"Oh, tosh to your modesty, Vassier." Leannor laughed a little before arching an eyebrow at me. "This man is, in truth, the only soul in Alundia with the knowledge to build an engine capable of bringing down the walls of this . . ." her mouth quirked in amused disdain as her gaze swung to Walvern Castle ". . . stout fortress. Or did you imagine it was pure good fortune that spared your company such an ordeal?"

She walked her mare closer, leaning forwards to address me in a softer tone. "Master Vassier is a man of ambitions, for his son if not himself. Last winter he sent the lad to Couravel for an education, one the king has lately been happy to provide. The builder was so grateful he volunteered his services to the Crown rather than his duke."

A short glance at Vassier's granite-hard features told me his presence here had nothing to do with gratitude. "That was very wise of him," I said. "A man I followed in my outlaw days would certainly have agreed. However, I find it hard to credit that there is but one soul in this duchy with the skills to construct a siege engine."

The princess shrugged her slim shoulders before leaning back in her saddle. "There *were* others. Not all wars are won with battles alone." She gave no further elaboration on this point, not that she needed to. *Spies and assassins*, I concluded. *And I assume her brother leaves control of them in her hands.* The realisation inevitably raised another question, albeit one to which I fancied I already knew the answer.

"I should report a small spot of trouble we encountered during our march, Majesty," I said, causing her to raise an eyebrow in faint curiosity.

"Really? And what, pray, was that?"

"A band of hired cut-throats sent to murder Lady Evadine. They failed, obviously." I stooped to reach for the pocket beneath the greave on my right leg. "However, we did recover a number of these from the bodies."

The sovereign flickered as I tossed it to her, the princess catching it and holding it up before her narrowed eyes. The expression she turned upon me was withering in its disdain. "I had hoped you had gained a more accurate impression of me, Captain."

I knew her to be an accomplished liar but the offence on her face was hard to fake. Killing Evadine before she reached this castle was never part of her plan. Wilhum had been right in calling this place a trap, but it wasn't set for us; we were just the bait. Duke Oberharth, prideful fool that he was, had eagerly come to gobble us up. The beacon, the crusade of beggared churls, were unnecessary. Leannor had kept her army well north of the Alundian border until her spies told her the duke had brought his full might against Evadine. I assumed the princess had also hoped to find us defeated and Evadine slain, providing both a fitting end to the Risen Martyr's tale and a heroic prop to the Algathinet family legend as they went about exacting justice from the Alundians. The threat to Crown authority would thereby be removed and Alundia humbled in one deftly executed move. Therefore, today marked only a partial triumph for Leannor, but still a triumph.

"Keep it, please, Your Majesty," I said when Leannor made ready to toss the sovereign back to me.

"I have no need of coin," she said.

"Consider it a token." I bowed low, finding the throb had lessened a good deal now and wondering if the birth of a new grudge might possess some form of soothing effect. "Of my most profound esteem."

The smallest smile passed over her lips as her fingers turned the coin to and fro. "I'd wager the former owner of this to be possessed of riches but little guile," she said. "One unused to the customs that prevail in the darker corners of society. I'd also judge it an act born of desperation. But . . ." she paused to consign the coin to the pocket ". . . I have little doubt your clever mind had already formed these conclusions, had it not?"

"Suspicions only, Majesty," I told her. "But I am grateful to have them confirmed."

Leannor sniffed and took up the reins of her mare. "Please inform Lady Evadine that King Tomas no longer has need of this castle," she told me in a clipped, commanding tone. "She is to muster her company and march with us to Highsahl, where, as representative of the Covenant, she will witness the submission of Lady Celynne Cohlsair.

In recognition of the Covenant Company's efforts in bringing this matter to a successful conclusion, King Tomas has decreed that all heretical non-orthodox practices in this duchy, and the wider realm, are henceforth prohibited on pain of death."

She kicked her heels and sent her mare into a trot. "I hope to see you in Highsahl, Captain. I hear they have a fine library there too."

PART II

We who call ourselves faithful must always be mindful of the terrible folly in attempting to expand the Covenant through force. An unbeliever who lies slain upon a battlefield cannot learn of the Martyrs' example or know the Seraphile's grace. Nor will those who wielded the sword in such a cause find easy passage through the Divine Portals, as murder stains the soul for eternity.

From *The Testament of Ascendant Sihlda Doisselle*, as recorded by Sir Alwyn Scribe

CHAPTER SEVENTEEN

The engine's timbers creaked and iron bracings groaned as a score of men hauled ropes to draw back its great arm. As was now customary whenever an engine prepared to launch its cargo, a few dozen arrows sailed out from the walls of Highsahl in a vain effort to impede its work. They pattered ineffectually against the roofed wooden stockade erected to protect the men that served the towering contrivance. The range was too great for any accuracy but the Alundian archers, their ranks no doubt swelled by a fair few Vergundians, never failed to try their luck. Occasionally, a soldier or two would fall victim to the arcing iron-heads, but for the most part the dozen engines lined up before the city's eastern wall hurled their stones with impunity.

Master Vassier had arranged them into two groups of six, angling each towards two widely separated sections of the wall on either side of the city's main gate. For three weeks now the engines had continued their work at all hours unless snow or gales forced a halt. Fed by a steady supply of granite from the quarries that were a feature of the Alundian coast, the engines cast the huge boulders higher than I would have thought any device could. The projectiles curved with deceptive slowness through the air, crossing the intervening two hundred paces before plummeting down to wreak yet more destruction on the deepening breaches.

"Stone fell long!" Master Vassier called out from his vantage point at a slot in the stockade. "Lighten the counterweight by one-tenth."

The gang of labourers servicing the engine duly hurried to heave out a portion of mingled rubble and sandbags from the hinged basket at the lowered end of the device's arm. Many days of experience made them well versed in judging the amounts to be added or removed from the counterweight to achieve the required aim. The task done, they set about the chore of hauling another block of granite onto the thick leather sling affixed by ropes to the tip of the raised arm.

Moving to Vassier's side, I peered through the slot at the walls of the great port city. The view was partially occluded by lingering morning mist and the breach itself, the one to the right of the city gate, shrouded in the dust raised by the most recent impact. I could glean little of import from the sight but Vassier possessed an eye more attuned to such matters.

"Just a foot shy of the base," he grunted in satisfaction. Although the past few weeks of overseeing the protection of the engines had left me in no doubt as to this man's scant enthusiasm for his work, there were moments when his professional pride made itself evident. The stitched cut on his forehead was healing well, a souvenir from the night a month ago when a party of Alundian dagger men had sallied forth in the darkest hours past midnight.

The engines had been guarded by a company of Cordwainer men-at-arms then, ill-disciplined drunkards to a man, many of whom paid for their slovenly ways by waking to find their throats cut, if they woke at all. It had been the churlish labourers who saved the day, many of them members of the Common Crusade who had volunteered to join the campaign in the aftermath of the Anointed Lady's salvation. Taking up a variety of tools they set about the Alundians before they could wreak any appreciable damage on the engines. Even so, when it was done a dozen Cordwain soldiers lay dead along with several skilled workers and a handful of churls. Master Vassier had been one of the principal targets of the raid, a dagger man donning the garb of a slain Cordwainer to seek out his tent amid the chaos. Fortunately, Vassier proved as adept with a falchion as he was with a plumb line, fending the would-be assassin off until a party of kingsmen arrived to hack the fellow down. After this ugly incident, Princess Leannor ordered the Covenant Company to undertake the duty of guarding the engines. She also had the captain in charge of the Cordwainers flogged and dismissed in disgrace.

"How much longer?" I asked Vassier as his insightful gaze shifted to the other breach.

"Three days for the one on the right, four for the left," he replied after a pause for deliberation. "But," he added, directing a meaningful nod at the irregular matrix of covered trenches scarring the ground betwixt the engines and the walls, "our miners tell me they need at least another three weeks to place their saps."

"Two breaches won't be enough?"

"A city is not a castle, Captain. Breaches alone won't win this place for your princess. To take Highsahl, the gatehouse bastion needs to fall and it won't until the miners have done their work." His eyes slid towards me, cautious but also intent. "Tell her that."

"You overestimate my importance, good sir."

He snorted and jerked his head at the newly arrived rope stacked in neat coils around the engine. "Got us that didn't you?"

The rope was, admittedly, the result of a representation I had made to Princess Leannor shortly after taking on this duty. Before this, the ropes used by the engine gangs consisted of badly frayed cordage sourced from fishing boats that stank of many years' accumulated salt and guts. They often broke under the strain of working the engines, leading to some crushed limbs and even a few deaths when boulders tumbled loose from their slings at inopportune moments. The Covenant Company's march to Walvern Castle had acquainted me with a merchant with storehouses full of rope lying unsold since the previous year's crisis arising from the loss of Olversahl. My suggestion to Leannor that the fellow would be willing to part with his stocks at a greatly reduced price in return for future royal favour found a receptive ear. Like many a wealthy soul with some experience of the world beyond the sphere of privilege in which she was raised, the princess was parsimonious in the extreme and always open to a bargain. She did, however, take pains to ensure the transaction was carried out by her own clerk despite my offer to handle negotiations.

"Your sword is needed here, Captain," she had told me with a smile. "I wouldn't be much of a general if I allowed all my captains to ride off and haggle on a whim, would I?"

This was, in fact, one of her least waspish comments of recent days, her mood having worsened with each passing day Highsahl remained untaken for the king. The Covenant Company had been on the march from Castle Walvern when the city was first invested by the Crown army. Consequently, I hadn't witnessed the exchange between Princess Leannor and Lady Celynne but the army had been abuzz with it ever since.

The widowed duchess received Leannor beneath the arch of the city's main gate, standing with her captains and principal luminaries of the port in silence while Leannor's page read out the king's proclamation. By all accounts, Celynne had made no comment throughout the recitation, her expression one of rigid indifference as the page listed the various alterations to the arrangements binding Alundia to the realm of Albermaine. Increases in tariffs on both imported goods and wine shipped across the border were endured without comment, as was the forfeiture to the Crown of half the lands held by the Alundian nobility. It was only when the page came to the edict regarding the prohibition of all modes of unorthodox Covenant faith that the duchess's party betrayed some animation. Several nobles were seen to draw their swords and a short uproar was brought to an end by a sharp command from the duchess. Silence resumed as the remaining provisions were read out, the most salient of which being that: "King Tomas, in his compassion and peerless magnanimity, does hereby grant Lady Celynne Cohlsair rights of governance over the Duchy of Alundia in her son's name until such time as he comes of age."

This remarkable generosity succeeded in provoking no more than a raised eyebrow from the duchess who, when the page fell silent, stepped forwards to take the proclamation from his hand. Having done so, she read it for only a short time before beckoning forth a servant with a torch, whereupon she set the document alight. That done, Lady Celynne turned and strode back through the gate without offering so much as a bow or a word to Princess Leannor. The first attempt on the walls came that very night.

Proceeding on the assumption that Duchess Celynne had few soldiers at her disposal, Lord Ehlbert led a full company of kingsmen against the gatehouse bastion. They returned after only a quarter-hour of combat with half their number. Naturally, despite the defeat Lord Ehlbert had managed to further enhance his legend by holding the parapet for a time, cutting down either a dozen or three dozen Alundians depending on who told the tale. His report to Leannor made it plain that, while Lady Celynne had a decent-sized garrison of household men-at-arms, her principal defence lay with the people of the city itself. Apparently, all Alundians of fighting age, men and women, were now in arms and roused to Highsahl's defence. Over a month later, they appeared no more inclined towards surrender than they had been when the siege started, despite the gaps Master Vassier's engines tore in their walls.

"We should shift the engines when these breaches are done," the engineer went on. "Carve a couple more breaches into the north and south walls while the miners do their work."

"I doubt this army has the numbers to assault four breaches at once," I said. The Crown host was large, to be sure, but also dwindling as the winter months wore on. Camp fever and dysentery claimed several lives a week while the ducal levies were prone to desertion. The continuing attentions of Duke Roulgarth and his bands of raiders, dubbed, somewhat grandiosely, the "Grey Wolves of Alundia", also made for frequent interruptions to our supplies, adding occasional hunger to the litany of woes besetting this host.

"The duchess doesn't know that," Vassier pointed out. "Four breaches means four separate divisions to her strength to cover them. This is how sieges are often won, Captain, as much through deceit and distraction as brute strength."

"Keen to conclude this business, eh, Master Vassier?"

"I'm keen for a return to my family above all. That won't happen until this city falls." The caustic tinge to his words bespoke the dislike of his current duty clearly, one I knew he strove to conceal most of the time. For reasons known only to himself, it appeared this master of engines was willing to allow the mask to slip a little in my presence. I felt some sympathy for his plight, one made worse by the fact that the Alundians within the city had contrived to learn of his presence in the Crown army, hence the attempt on his life during that early raid. Since then they had contented themselves with calling out profane insults and threats from the battlements promising dire retribution for the "traitor engineer".

"Not an easy thing," I offered, "to make war on your own people."

The bitterness in his voice deepened as he let out a short laugh. "For the most part my own people shunned me and mine for years, except when they had need of my skills, of course. My wife is a convert to the orthodox Covenant, you see, while I have never held to any faith at all, except when propriety demanded some public mummery." His lean features formed a rueful grimace. "But I have ever been a poor actor. The princess spoke true when she said I sent my son to be schooled in Couravel, but it wasn't for his advancement; it was to spare him the prejudice my family suffered for years. He's a clever lad and deserves a decent chance in life. Still—" he turned back to the city at the crump and hiss of another descending projectile wreaking yet more destruction on the wall "—there are plenty of decent folk in there to go with the bad. The duchess herself is not the fanatic harridan the princess would have us believe, and I doubt every soul within those walls is determined to die defending them. I've seen what happens when a city falls, Captain, and it's never pretty."

"Yet it will fall. You must know that."

A certain guardedness stole over his face and his voice became flat. "I know only the task I am set to by my king."

I let my gaze linger on his unmoving visage until he sighed and pointed to the grey expanse of sea visible beyond the bluffs to the south of the city. "Look there," he said. "What do you see?"

"Just empty water," I replied, shrugging.

"Yes, empty of ships at this hour because of the tide. When it turns there will be ships coming and going, as they always have in this port. When the tide turns the sea will once again become empty." I saw an echo of Sihlda's expression on his brow when he turned to regard me, the sense of one imparting a lesson.

"No Crown ships," I said after a short interval of pondering. "Nothing to stop the flow of trade to Highsahl."

"Exactly. The king, for reasons best known to himself, has chosen not to blockade this port, meaning the people here won't starve as long as their duchess has coin for supplies. I'm sure the storehouses will empty as the ducal treasury runs thin, but that may take months."

"There's no starving them out," I concluded as the lesson sank in. "We either take the city by storm or Princess Leannor's campaign will be a failure."

"Look around." Vassier cast a glance over his shoulder at the sprawl of campfires and tents to the rear of our lines. "How many battles do you think this lot has in them?"

I said nothing, the answer being so obvious. The Crown and Covenant companies would fight as long as they were commanded to it, but they comprised no more than a quarter of this host. With sickness rampant and the miseries of winter sapping the will of all but the hardiest souls, I had little doubt this army would wither away in the aftermath of defeat. We had but one chance to take Highsahl, and if Master Vassier knew it I assumed Leannor did too.

"I'll tell her," I said, turning to trudge through the muddy track to the camp. "About the need for more breaches."

Reasoning that Evadine's voice joined with mine would have the best chance of catching Leannor's ear, I sought her out first. Her tent was the largest among the canvas dwellings, arranged in neat rows that set the Covenant Company apart from most of the encampment. I had chosen a spot on the fringe of the army's southern flank, keen to maintain a distance from the disorderly, mud-spattered confines that characterised the bulk of this temporary town. Soldiers are like all other folk in that instinct leads them to cluster together for warmth when days grow cold. However, such proximity inevitably gives rise to the fevers and myriad other complaints that afflict all armies in the field. It also creates a further danger when tents are pitched too close to fires: it seemed that every night brought a calamitous blaze or two. I was determined that the company avoid such mishaps, enforcing strict observance of the standard camp order where tents were pitched at measured intervals away from the fires. I was also strict in ensuring a level of cleanliness that made Covenant soldiery a stark contrast to their eternally besmirched comrades, save for the Crown Company; kingsmen would be flogged if Sir Ehlbert found even a spot of rust on a single breastplate. I didn't go that far, though the punishments of additional labour and drill I'm sure did little to enhance my popularity.

Despite it all, I was continually surprised by the constancy of the company's respectful obedience. I drew more than a few sullen glances but no outright indiscipline and no soldier had yet questioned an order. The veterans even appeared grateful for such stringent observance of martial routine. "Camp life during winter wears on the soul," Ofihla told me one night when I commanded a pikeman who had fallen asleep on watch be stripped and forced to run around the camp naked for an hour. "It's times like this that soldiers need to be reminded that they're soldiers, Captain, else they'll just turn back into, well, people." She grimaced in disdain. "Can't have that."

As was now customary, I found the Widow standing guard at the entrance to Evadine's tent. She sat beside a small fire running a stone over the spike of her short-staved warhammer, pausing to afford me the full effect of the suspicious glower that now seemed to be her permanent expression. Like many company soldiers she wore a mix of scavenged armour and mail, but only at Evadine's insistence for this woman displayed scant regard for her own protection.

Her expression softened upon seeing me, the hardness slipping into guarded welcome. Among the company entire only myself and Evadine possessed any authority that she deigned to recognise. I suspected her willingness to offer me more than the customary glower arose from the fact that I had gifted her the weapon she cherished. After the relief of Walvern Castle she had been found wandering the battlefield crushing the skulls of any wounded Alundian found still clinging to life. Only Evadine's stern instruction had sufficed to stop her.

"Mistress Juhlina," I greeted her, not expecting a response for she rarely spoke a single word more than she had to. Today, however, she surprised me.

"She's got company," she said, jerking her head at the tent flap. "Said you should go on in if you happened by, though."

"My thanks." She surprised me once again by speaking on as I stepped past her.

"I want to be in it."

"Your pardon?" I enquired, pausing. So terse a statement from any other soldier would have provoked a rebuke but such things were wasted on the Widow.

"The attack," she said. "When the walls come down. I want to be there, at the front, with you and her."

One of the stranger aspects of this woman's disordered character was her unwillingness to afford Evadine any type of honorific. To the Widow she was only ever "she" or "her" never "the Lady," or any of the increasingly elaborate titles Evadine continued to accumulate as her legend grew. Mistress Juhlina was also notably disinterested in observance of Covenant practice. She would stand in rigid and inexpressive silence during Evadine's regular sermons and I never heard mention of either Martyr or Seraphile pass the Widow's lips. Whatever compelled her to follow the Anointed Lady, it wasn't the faith that had set her on the pilgrim's trail.

"We will all be there," I assured her, leaning close to add in a solicitous murmur, "Princess Leannor is not so rich in swords as to spare any the battle to come."

This appeared to satisfy her, for she let out a soft grunt and resumed working the stone along the length of her hammer spike. Never keen to prolong my exchanges with this woman, I stooped to pull aside the tent flap and went inside, the sight that greeted me bringing a swift smile to my lips.

"Captain Swain," I said with a laugh. I briefly entertained the notion of quipping on the strangeness of finding myself pleased to see him, but thought better of it.

Swain appeared gaunter than I remembered, his already scarred forehead marked by a new smear of discoloured flesh. However, he stood straight as ever and returned my greeting with a nod and mildly spoken, "Captain Scribe."

"Captain no longer, now you're here." I turned my expectant grin upon Evadine who, I saw with a plummeting heart, failed to return it.

"Captain Swain is fully recovered," she told me. I could see a faint reluctance in her gaze but it was mostly concealed by stern resolve. She didn't enjoy imparting unwelcome news, but that never prevented her from doing so. "He will resume command of the Covenant Company," she went on, summoning a resurgence of hope to my breast, one that withered and died with her next words, "to be renamed the First Company. You, Captain Scribe, are hereby commanded to raise and ordered the Second."

"Second?" I couldn't keep the weary sigh from my voice, not that I made much effort to do so. "Would that not require permission from the Luminants' Council? Or the Crown?"

"The council are too far away to allow for such niceties, *Captain.*" The emphasis she placed on my unwanted title was hard to miss and did little to leaven my mood. "As for the Crown," Evadine went on, "I recently raised the matter with Princess Leannor who pronounced it an excellent idea. The many good folk who answered our beacon require discipline and training if they are to be of use, and the army's need of soldiers is clear."

"Because those drunken laggards in the ducal levies keep pissing off," I said, voice dulled with impotent frustration. "When they're not dropping dead of fever or the shits."

"Well, quite." Evadine gave a strained smile and turned to Swain. "Excuse us, if you would, Captain. Also, please inform me the moment the Mounted Guard return from their reconnaissance."

"I shall, my lady." Swain nodded to us both and left, heralding a prolonged and potent silence.

"Do you intend to sulk at me, Alwyn?" Evadine asked finally, sinking onto a camp stool while I continued to avoid her gaze. "I thought such things beneath you."

"Then perhaps, my lady, your knowledge of me is not as deep as you imagine." Consenting to meet her gaze, I felt a welling of instant regret at the hurt I saw. It was a sharp reminder that, for all the many who followed her, this woman had few true friends in this world, and only one who could claim responsibility for her continued presence among the living. I have often meditated on the curious paradox that arises from the saving of a life, for I find it burdens the saviour with more obligation than the saved.

"I'll need sergeants," I said, letting out a sigh of resigned submission. "And Ayin to oversee the company books."

"Ayin is a fine scribe now," Evadine pointed out. "I had hoped to keep her."

"Mistress Juhlina reads and writes well enough. Set her to the task. It'll give her something to do besides sharpening her weapons and scaring the shite out of everyone with that balesome look of hers."

Evadine inclined her head. "As you wish. And the sergeants?"

"I'll take Ofihla as Senior Sergeant and let her pick the others from the veterans – those Captain Swain is willing to part with, of course. Also, I'll have Eamond as page. His mind is keen enough to recall a message and it would be good to have someone to watch my back in battle."

"Are you sure? He's hardly the most skilled fighter."

"Then Wilhum won't object to losing him. Besides, Eamond's no coward when the fighting starts. I need someone I can be sure won't run."

"Very well. Have Ayin make the relevant entries and we'll see it done by the end of day." She paused and I felt the weight of an expectant gaze. Apparently, she required more than submission today. "What is it about this that irks you so, Alwyn?" she prompted when I failed to fill the silence. "I can tell it's more than just unwanted responsibility, and certainly not reluctance born of modesty." She gave a short laugh which faded quickly as I moved to rest my rump on the stool opposite hers. The weariness that had afflicted me in recent days was suddenly worse, although mercifully the throb had given me some respite lately. Still, the grimness of my mood must have showed on my face, prompting Evadine to reach out and clasp my hand.

"Speak," she said. "I would know your heart."

"I was never meant to be a soldier," I told her, shrugging in simple honesty. "A thief? Yes. A scribe? Certainly. But a soldier?" I huffed an empty chuckle. "I never wanted it, nor did any of those from whom I learned my principal lessons in life. Deckin wanted a son to take on his mantle, either as Outlaw King or the duke he could never be. Sihlda wanted an emissary, one who would preach her testament and steer the Covenant back to the true path, a path that never strayed to war."

"And you? What did you want?"

"Vengeance, although by the time I crawled free of the Pit Mines most of those I intended to visit it upon were either already dead or, as it transpires, undeserving of my ire. Now I find myself here with you, fighting a war Sihlda would have hated. It would have pained her to see me as I am, steeped in so much blood, the mission she ordained for me long forgotten."

"It needn't be." Evadine's hand squeezed mine. "You must understand that this war is but one step on our journey to something better, something Ascendant Sihlda would have rejoiced to see. The day will come when her testament will be heard throughout this realm and beyond. But to see that day's dawn we must first travel a while in darkness." Her grip on my hand grew tighter still, her eyes staring into mine with an intensity I hadn't seen since her healing. There was a need in those eyes, a hunger in fact, and it captured me, adding another knot to whatever it was that bound us. "Together, Alwyn," she said, voice diminished to a hoarse whisper. "We must walk this road together. Of that I have no doubt."

I realised the space between us had mostly vanished, that she had risen from her stool to huddle at my side, leaning so close that I could feel the heat of her breath upon my lips. There are moments of import in every life, moments when the course of events will shift, and the eventual destination is dependent on the smallest action or, in this case, the Widow's tactless interruption.

"The Guard are back," she said, poking her head through the tent flap. Evadine's gaze swung towards her with an almost predatory swiftness, eyes blazing a harsh command. Mistress Juhlina was unimpressed, her features betraying only vague bemusement before she withdrew.

"On further consideration," Evadine said, releasing my hand and getting to her feet, "I think you had better take her too. I'll find another scribe for the First Company. Now—" she reached for her cloak and fastened it on "—we shall see what intelligence Wilhum has brought us this fine day."

"Three score of the bastards!" Wilhum's was a voice rarely pitched in anger, for he was ever an even-tempered soul. Today, however, it emerged as a viperous rasp, shot through with an added note of pain as he pressed a rag to the bleeding cut on his jawline. I suspected his rage owed much to vanity, piqued by having his handsomeness marred by a wound that would surely scar despite Supplicant Delric's best attentions. "All mounted," he went on, suppressing a groan as Evadine stepped closer and prised the rag away to inspect his cut. "We were lucky to get away with just a few wounds," he added through clenched teeth.

"Where?" Evadine asked, wincing in sympathy as she allowed him to replace the rag.

"No more than eight miles south, near the crossroads."

"Hill country," I said, recalling our march to Highsahl. "Wooded in part too. Fine place for an ambush."

"It wasn't an ambush," Wilhum insisted. "My guess is they just blundered into our path."

"Or you blundered into theirs," I suggested, summoning a scowl to his already peeved brow.

"In either case," he went on with strained patience, turning back to Evadine, "it's my estimation there's a large force gathering in those hills. Not just raiders intent on harrying our supply lines." He jerked his head at Fletchman. "Tell them."

"Found plentiful fresh tracks before the fight began, m'lady," the poacher confirmed. "Foot and horse both, coming from different directions. I'd reckon some had travelled quite a distance too. The tread of a weary soul has a particular depth to it, y'see."

"So," Evadine mused, "the Grey Wolves gather their packs, but for what?"

"Because Lord Roulgarth told them to, I imagine," I put in, casting a glance towards the city. "Their objective is not hard to divine."

"They can't hope to defeat us," Wilhum sniffed. "Not with most of their true soldiers lying dead at Walvern Castle."

"This is a well-populated duchy," I pointed out. "And those that weren't soldiers before can still be willing to take up arms, especially in defence of home and faith." I looked towards the Algathinet banner rising highest among the forest of pennants that fluttered above this camp. "We need to tell her," I said, voice laden with reluctant necessity for the trial awaiting us beneath that banner.

"The duty is mine," Evadine said. "You have a new company to raise."

"I have reports from Master Vassier to relate. Best get that stitched sharpish," I advised Wilhum as I took my first unenthused step towards Princess Leannor's tent. "Don't worry. If it scars I'm sure it'll only add to your rakish charm."

CHAPTER EIGHTEEN

Upon being granted entry to her tent, Evadine and I found Princess Leannor in company with Lord Ehlbert. The princess sat behind a large, ornately carved rosewood desk that had been carted all the way from the royal palace in Couravel. Apparently, it was the one item of furniture from which she refused to be parted and an entire troop of servants had the duty of ensuring it followed her wherever she travelled. Her attention was occupied by the parchment she held, Lord Ehlbert standing by at stiff attention. As required by custom, we both sank to one knee, heads lowered, Leannor not deigning to spare us any notice as she scanned the document in her hand.

"There are fewer names than there were last week," Leannor observed, eyes narrowed as she perused the list. "And only six lashes each. I recall stipulating a minimum of ten for even minor infractions."

"Fewer names means discipline is holding, Your Majesty," Lord Ehlbert said. "And I feel a lessening in the severity of punishment would impart the message that improved behaviour brings reward."

"You feel that, do you?" The princess paused to wave an impatient hand at our kneeling selves, gesturing for us to rise without troubling herself with a greeting. "I don't." Setting the parchment down, she took up a quill and scratched several alterations to the text before adding her signature and handing it to the waiting knight. "Ten lashes apiece, my lord. And be sure that I'll check to confirm my commands have been followed."

"Of course, Majesty." I detected scant emotion in Ehlbert's voice or demeanour as he bowed and turned to go, yet his very blankness told me a great deal. By now I knew him to be a man with but two aspects to his character: hearty good humour or the icy lethality that gripped him in battle. The absence of the former led me to conclude that he was suffering the onset of the latter.

"Forgive me, Your Majesty," Evadine said as the knight stooped to depart via the tent flap, "but I believe Lord Ehlbert should hear my intelligence."

"Very well." Leannor cast a quick, beckoning flick of her hand at Ehlbert, calling him back to her side. The princess sighed and settled back in her tall chair, features assuming the tense weariness of one beset by many troubles. "What assuredly delightful news do you bring me, my lady?"

"My scouts report Alundians gathering in large numbers in the hills to the south," Evadine informed her. "We don't have a full count of their strength but it seems clear they intend to attack us here, hoping to break the siege or at least delay our assault on the city."

Leannor absorbed the news with only a marginal shift in her expression, one that betrayed more irritation than alarm. "Our assault, yes," she said, turning her attention to me, "which raises the subject of our turncoat engineer's progress."

"Master Vassier tells me he expects to pronounce the breaches as fully reduced within three days, Majesty," I reported. "However, we will require three weeks for the miners to place their saps beneath the gatehouse bastion. In the interim, Vassier suggests, and I concur, that the engines be shifted to the north and south walls. Creating further breaches will force the duchess to divide her forces when the assault is made."

Leannor raised a questioning brow at Ehlbert who was swift in voicing his agreement. "A capital notion," he said, directing one of his signature smiles at me, all white teeth and genuine warmth. As ever, I failed to return it and, as ever, the King's Champion didn't seem to care. "It's always preferable to have several lines of attack," he added.

"Preferable or not, the answer is no," Leannor said. "And three weeks to complete placement of the saps is too long." She reached into the stacked papers on her desk and extracted a letter bearing a large wax seal. "King Tomas has been kind enough to forward correspondence recently received from the Duke of Althiene. As you can see—" she wafted the single sheet about "—it isn't very long, but its content is unambiguous. Duke Guhlton wishes for his daughter's safety to be guaranteed by royal decree and she and her children conveyed to his custody as soon as possible. Our sources in Althiene also report mustering of levies by the duke's nobles and much hiring of free swords. The old man, it seems, is greatly distressed by his daughter's plight."

"Distressed enough to go to war?" Evadine asked, which drew a sharp glance from the princess.

"Any true parent would risk all for their child, my lady," Leannor told her. "A lesson you will surely learn should your womb ever find itself blessed with life." She tossed the ducal missive onto her desk. "Make no mistake, this business must be concluded swiftly and we have no leisure for shifting engines or indulging the laziness of our handsomely paid miners."

"The resolve of our foes would surely be diminished if the port could be closed to trade, Majesty," I said. "At present the duchess can import all the supplies she has coin for. Courage is hard to sustain when the belly starts to growl."

The glance Leannor afforded me was withering in its dismissal. "Do you have any notion of what a blockade fleet would cost, Captain? Any ship dragooned into Crown service is one less ship carrying cargo to our own ports, meaning reduced revenue for the royal treasury and empty bellies elsewhere. Besides, keeping the sea lanes open was a way of signalling our good intent: We did not come as conquerors, after all, merely enforcers of the king's justice. If only Celynne would see sense."

Leannor fell to silence, fingers drumming her desk as her brow took on the frown of deep contemplation. I wondered if, like me, this woman had been educated in the ways of calculation or if her various strategies resulted from inherent cunning. I had learned to respect her intellect by now, but also knew it to be far from flawless. She was an accomplished strategist, to be sure, but possessed only a marginal understanding of the tactical minutiae that wins battles.

"Seven days," she said when the drumming of her fingers came to a sudden halt. "Seven days to finish the sap. All hands will be set to the task and those who grumble will face the lash, *ten* strokes each," she added with precise emphasis, casting a sideways glance at Ehlbert. "In the meantime, once the breaches are complete, Master Vassier will make a conspicuous show of shifting his engines to north and south, but the siege lines will not be extended to cover them, we can't spare the labour. Lord Ehlbert, on the morrow you will take command of every knight and mounted soldier in this army and ride south. Find whatever rabble Lord Roulgarth has gathered and destroy it. Five silver crown sovereigns for the one that kills Roulgarth, ten if they capture him alive. Be swift in your mission, my lord, for we'll have need of your sword when the assault begins."

She settled her gaze on Evadine, her lips forming a thin but satisfied curve. "Worry not, Lady Evadine. I shall spare you the indignity of begging the honour of leading the first attack. Rest assured, I would trust the task to no other."

"And I count myself grateful for such trust," Evadine said, bowing low.

The shallow curve of Leannor's lips straightened, an annoyed crease marring her brow before she forced her features back to placidity. It occurred to me that her estimation of Evadine's character was just as faulty as her estimation of mine. The princess looked at me and saw an amoral opportunist and I understood now that her view of Evadine was similarly cynical. *She thinks the Anointed Lady a fraud*, I decided. *Her faith a sham, a ploy to gain power.*

For all the loftiness of her birth, I had plentiful experience of people like Leannor. So mired in their own ambition and deceit they proceed through life possessed of the comforting delusion that all others are cast in the same mould. My amusement at the princess's limited mind and singular misjudgement was muted by the knowledge that, in many ways, I wished her to be right. It is inarguable that my life, and the lives of so many others, would have been far simpler, and in many cases longer, had Evadine Courlain been a liar.

"No harm can come to the duchess or her brood," Leannor went on. "Once the walls are overcome, you will proceed to the palace and take them into custody. If she flees to the harbour, no effort is to be made to prevent her escape. It would be far better if she sailed off and made her way to her father's loving embrace. In fact, I would happily pay her a chest of gold sovereigns to do so this very day. Her absurd stubbornness makes no sense."

"She loved her husband," Evadine said. "Grief will fire a heart to irrational acts. She also loves the people of this duchy and has no desire to abandon them. I very much doubt she will flee when the time comes, Majesty."

"Then it is up to you to ensure she comes before us unharmed, my lady. With his daughter in our grasp, Duke Guhlton will soon find himself of a more agreeable temper, I'm sure. Now then—" she took up her quill again and reached for a sheet of parchment "—I should like to write to my son, if you'll excuse me. I hear he has been inattentive at lessons of lute and a reminder of his duty is in order."

You may imagine, dear reader, that a mere seven days is a completely inadequate interval in which to turn a gaggle of underfed, ill-smelling churls into soldiers. In which regard you are completely correct. The three hundred volunteers for this Second Covenant Company made such a poor impression that I felt compelled to offer Sergeant Ofihla an apology.

"These were the ones I felt might sustain a fight," I told her, wincing in contrition. "For a little while, at any rate."

Ofihla's heavy features remained carefully rigid as she surveyed our recruits, all lined up in ragged order, many clutching blankets about their stooped shoulders and shivering in the drifting sleet that greeted the dawn. I had expected volunteers from the disordered throng of the Common Crusade to be few in number, given their generally degraded state. However, when I climbed atop a cart to read out the Anointed Lady's proclamation the reaction of the beggared mass had been immediate and enthusiastic. I could have raised a force three times the number of those arrayed before us now without difficulty, but the prospect of leading so many unfit if eager fanatics to near certain doom did not appeal. So, sitting at a barrel which served as a makeshift desk, I had them all line up and interviewed each in turn while Ayin took down a list of names and relevant experience. Most had none, of course.

"Liahm Woodsman, m'lord," one fellow replied when asked his name. I suspected he had once been described as brawny but weeks of cold and camp rations had given him a hunched, hollow-cheeked aspect. Yet devotion shone just as bright in his eyes in as all the others'.

"Captain," I corrected before asking, "Woodsman. That's your trade?"

"Aye, sir. Cut timber all my life and have the arms to show for it." He extended his forearms, revealing knotted muscles that remained impressive despite his emaciation.

"Done any soldiering?" I asked. "Before the crusade, that is."

"Can't say as I have, m'captain. Our village was on Crown land, see? We got special permits saying how we didn't have to serve on account of how much timber we cut. Then the flux came a few winters past and there wasn't no village to speak of when it had done its work. Wardens turned up and told us who was left to bugger off so the forest could grow and the king would have somewhere new to hunt deer." A distinct anger grew in his voice, one that he was quick to quell upon noting my scrutiny. "Mean no disrespect to the Crown, o'course, sir." His head bobbed several inches lower. "Such things happen, I s'pose."

"Not to those who follow the Anointed Lady in just battle," I told him before turning to Ayin. "Enter Master Liahm in the company books as a halberdier."

Others were not capable of soldiering in any form and I turned away a good deal more than I took, provoking some argument but no outright trouble. Most of these folk were too underfed to rouse themselves to violence and the presence of Ofihla and the other sergeants served to discourage unwise notions.

With the volunteers chosen, she set about the task of arranging them into troops and apportioning each to their place in the three-rank structure that informed all the company did. Thanks to some industrious scavenging of the corpses littering the plain at Walvern Castle, we were reasonably well supplied with halberds and sundry bladed weapons. Pikes were in shorter supply, so many in the first rank were handed sharpened tree branches which I hoped to be replaced by proper arms once the Crown armourers did their work. The Crown host travelled with its own coterie of artisans, including a moveable smithy. The workshop was overseen by a bladesmith of impressively broad dimensions who clicked his tongue in bored indifference in response to my request for new pikes.

"Lotta work to be done already," he said, offering me a patently false smile of regret. "Orders of Her Majesty take precedence, see? Shoes for her knights' horses. Heads for the bolts her crossbowmen go through like they grow on trees. And those engines of yours are constantly gobbling up ever more nails."

His mood became markedly more cooperative upon sight of the silver crown sovereign I began to play through my fingers. "Are you sure there's no accommodation you can make, master smith?" I asked, taking satisfaction from the greed shining plain in the fellow's gaze. In the end it cost two sovereigns, one in advance, to secure the provision of pikes within seven days. These were the last two coins found on the bodies of the assassins, leaving the company purse in a parlous state. It couldn't be helped, though, and at least the smith was good enough to throw in a dozen new-forged falchions and sundry oddments of armour and mail.

"They won't last a minute, Captain," was Eamond's estimation, standing at my side as we watched the recruits stumble about the field in an unamusing parody of military order. I resisted the impulse to issue a caustic reminder regarding his own lack of experience. His features remained youthful but his scars, small but noticeable, and the hardness to his eyes made a contrast to the fresh-faced novice I had met in the Shavine Woods. He straightened upon seeing the rebuke in my expression, clamping his mouth closed. Ayin felt no such hesitation in adding her own opinion.

"He's right," she said, glancing up from the parchment upon which she was busily scribbling with a charcoal stub. "Even I can see that. You killed loads in the breach back at the castle. They never even got inside. What's to stop the heretics in there doing the same? Especially since this lot can't even march in the same direction."

"Not that long ago," I grated, finding my ire piqued by this unvarnished honesty, "your principal occupation was petting any fluffy beast you could find in between slicing the nuts off rapists, and you—" I shot a glare at Eamond "—didn't even know what end of a sword to hold. Rest assured, when I require your sage counsel on military matters, I shall be sure to ask for it."

In response to this tirade, Eamond's back stiffened yet further while Ayin's face bunched into a frown of hurt. I fought down the welling regret, knowing that a modicum of harshness is a necessary facet of leadership. A good captain is not a friend to his soldiers. Still, I was also aware that my anger amounted to misdirected frustration born from the knowledge that they were both inarguably right: leading my new company into one of those breaches was a death sentence for all concerned.

Calculation, I thought, rubbing my temples as I suffered a brief, aching pulse from the throb. Nevertheless, I struggled through the pain to search out one of Sihlda's favourite aphorisms: *An insoluble problem is not, in truth, a problem; it is an obstacle and therefore best avoided or bypassed. A mind trained in proper calculation will always find a solution to an actual problem.*

"Take yourself off to the forward trenches," I told Ayin. "I want reports on the breadth and height of both breaches, as precise as you can make them. Go with her," I added to Eamond. "Too many wandering hands among the ducal levies and it's best if we don't start littering the place with gelded soldiers."

Ayin arched her chin, avoiding my gaze as she hefted her satchel and strode away with Eamond. "Did you really do . . . that?" he asked.

I caught her reply before they disappeared into the maze of trench lines. "Only a few times." A pause before she raised her voice. "Our stuck-up arse of a captain is given to exaggeration!"

Silently reprimanding myself for expanding her vocabulary, I turned my attention back to the company. Ofihla had paused the march of one troop to deliver hard cuffs to either side of a pikeman's head so as to impart the difference between left and right. The temper of the sergeants overseeing the other troops was revealed in their overly loud shouts, rich in the kind of profanity rarely heard in the Covenant Company.

They won't make it halfway through a breach, I knew with depressing certainty. I recalled the Fool's Gambit assaulting the breach at Walvern Castle only to fall like scythed wheat beneath the hail of bolts and cascading oil. Despite its ugliness, I kept the memory at the forefront of my mind, summoning the calm reflection that allowed for calculation. *The bolts and the oil spelt their doom. Had they made it through they could have engaged our line. Most would still have died but the company soldiers in the courtyard would have been fully occupied with us while Oberharth's men-at-arms followed behind. Surviving the passage through the breach. That's the key.*

Surveying the untidy ranks of my new command, I made note of their scant armour and how many were already sagging from exhaustion despite only a few minutes' drill. Still, they were keen enough. The devotional gleam I had seen in the woodsman's eye was mirrored in his comrades and all suffered the sergeants' fury with stoic forbearance. The crumb of optimism this birthed was short-lived, crushed by the knowledge that a crossbow bolt, arrow or cascade of burning oil cannot be deflected by courage alone. Only sound armour or solid shields would avail us against such torments, and we had neither.

Solid shields. I repeated the thought as something took hold amid my churning calculations. Thoughts of descending projectiles brought to mind the thunk of arrowheads on the timbers of the palisade protecting Vassier's engines. Also, recollections of burning oil raised the memory of the great Alundian ram and its protective frame

226 • ANTHONY RYAN

covered in water-soaked hides. *Shift the engines to north and south,* Princess Leannor had said, *but the siege lines will not be extended.*

As was typical when my calculating mind happened upon a potential solution, fresh notions bubbled up continually, making me only dimly aware of my feet taking me towards the forward lines. By the time I found Vassier, busy overseeing the fixing of a wheel to one of his engines, the notion was almost fully formed. The expression on his face as I explained it was severely sceptical at first, but merely doubtful by the time I finished.

"There's probably a reason why that's never been tried, Captain," he told me. The many creases on his forehead crinkled as he thought further before giving a shrug of agreement. "Still, if you're intent upon it, I'm always happy to build something new."

CHAPTER NINETEEN

The walls of Highsahl presented a far more ominous barrier at close remove, looming ever taller as I led the Second Company through the trenches to the breach. Evadine's command had been allotted the breach to the north of the gatehouse bastion while Sir Ehlbert, never willing to forgo an opportunity for a glorious death, had begged the honour of leading his kingsmen against the southern breach. The King's Champion had returned to camp two days before to report a successful engagement with Lord Roulgarth's growing band of rebels. Wilhum, who had accompanied this expedition with the Mounted Guard, described the fight as "Just a large skirmish, in truth. We cut down about two score before they scattered into the hills. We did find their camps and food caches, however. Burnt what we couldn't carry off. I doubt Roulgarth's Wolves will be in any state to prove more than a nuisance for some time."

With the host's rear flank duly secured, Princess Leannor had no hesitation in ordering what she termed "the final victory in this most excellent campaign" to proceed as planned. While the Covenant and Crown companies assaulted the breaches, the ducal levies and hired free swords that comprised the main body of the king's host would await the firing of the saps beneath the gatehouse bastion. Once that fell and the principal entrance to the city lay open, the fate of Highsahl would be sealed, or so Leannor hoped. Master Vassier, after making careful survey of the saps crafted by the exhausted contingent of miners, was not so sure.

I had accompanied him during his last inspection, my thoughts beset by unpleasant memories of endless days spent below ground in the Pit Mines while we crawled the last dozen yards to the shaft's terminus. "Would've liked them set six feet deeper," Vassier grunted, running a hand over one of the vertical ash beams that formed a small, dense forest between the floor of this artificial cavern and the gatehouse foundations above our heads. We had passed by a long parade of exhausted miners sitting slumped and spent in the trenches, having worked tirelessly to achieve this end, and yet Vassier still thought it inadequate.

"It won't bring down the bastion?" I asked.

"Oh, it'll do that, all right," he told me, squinting as he played the light of his lantern over the far wall of the cavern. "But not so swiftly as we would want." He sighed and turned to me with a sympathetic grimace. "I don't envy you the task ahead, Captain. By my reckoning the breaches will be taken long before the bastion falls." He lowered his voice to a cautious whisper before adding, "If they're taken at all."

"We have your marvellous craftsmanship to aid us," I said, returning his grimace with one of my own. "How can we fail?"

His laugh was short and rang hollow in the confines of the shaft. "Get it packed," he snapped to the waiting labourers as we made our way out. "And don't stint on the fat. I want every inch of timber covered."

By nightfall the saps had been liberally greased with pig fat and the gaps between filled with bundles of dry kindling. Vassier was supposed to wait for Leannor's word before setting it alight but, at my urging, went ahead and tossed in the torch as soon as the work was complete. "If she asks," I said, "tell her it was an accident."

Fortunately, once dusk settled over the camp the princess was more concerned with inflicting a speech upon her assembled troops to concern herself with such trivia. She donned her ornamental breast-plate for the occasion, sitting tall in the saddle of her fine white mare, flanked by torch-bearing knights of the Crown Company. I knew this to be a deliberate attempt to secure a moment of famed posterity. It is therefore with considerable satisfaction that I can report only ever discovering one painting depicting this scene. It wasn't very good, the brushwork clumsy and the figures stilted, which is fitting for it matches the quality of Leannor's speech that evening.

It's true that she was a woman of considerable gifts, but they were of a kind that made her such an expert manipulator, to wit: best displayed in private rather than public. Her voice lacked Evadine's naturally commanding timbre, being somewhat high-pitched and grating when raised. Consequently, when she began what she presumably hoped would be a rousing exhortation to courageous feats in the name of Good King Tomas, she sounded not dissimilar to a wailing cat.

"To arms!" she cried, raising her short sword high, a weapon that had much the same utility as her breastplate. "To battle! To glory!"

The cheers of the Crown Company, no doubt at Lord Ehlbert's urging, were of an appropriately fulsome volume, which served to mask the half-hearted or absent response of the rest of the army. When Evadine addressed the Covenant Company a short while later, drawing a sizeable crowd from the neighbouring ducal levies and churlish labourers, it was a very different scene.

"Have you come for loot?" she asked them, standing atop a platform of piled timber. She spoke on before any answers could be called out, although I did hear a muttered response in a Shavine accent, "Why the fuck else would I be here?"

"Have you come for slaughter?" Evadine demanded, her voice echoing long over the siege lines. "Have you come for vengeance? If so, I command you in the name of the Seraphile to depart this army, for your presence dishonours this blessed crusade. I came here with sword in hand for but one reason: to save the Covenant of Martyrs from utter ruin. Mark these words well and know them as truth, for I have seen what will befall us if we fail this night. I have seen the fruit of our failure and I tell you, friends, it is bitter. It is vile. It is the end of everything."

She paused and I heard no more mutters from the crowd. Again she had managed to snare her audience with but a few words, all unrehearsed and flowing from her lips with fluent honesty. "The people of this city," she said, pointing to Highsahl, "are not our foes. They are the deluded, damned victims of a diseased creed that besmirches their souls from childhood. We come to save them from that, and in their salvation we save ourselves." She drew her sword and raised it above her head, the blade a tall, gleaming contrast to Leannor's pitiful ornament. "For salvation," she repeated, her voice not overly loud but I was sure every ear present heard it. The echo from the Covenant Company was immediate and swiftly taken up by the rest of the audience.

"For salvation!" The fists, swords and halberds of Covenant and common soldier alike rose as the cry continued, growing louder with each shout. "For salvation! FOR SALVATION!"

By happenstance, it was while this acclaim reached its climax that a loud boom sounded from the depths of the sap. The fire had built steadily as night fell, the shaft coughing out a thick pall of greasy smoke that held a faintly appetising tinge thanks to the liberally applied fat that fuelled it. The smoke gusted thicker when the boom sounded, I assumed as the result of one of the beams giving way. The gatehouse bastion, however, remained standing. Some churls opined that they noticed a definite list in the base of the wall but I ascribed this to fanciful optimism. Even so, for Evadine's devotional audience the sound served as a signal, marshalling both Covenant Companies without need of orders. Scanning the ranks of my command, I saw eagerness on the face of every soldier, eyes bright and hungry. I knew battle would inevitably reveal some cowards among this lot but for now didn't doubt all would follow me into the breach when the order came.

"I'm still not best pleased with the structure of our attack," Evadine said, coming to my side as the sergeants toured their troops to impose some final discipline. I had been required to spend a considerable time in persuading her as to the efficacy of my plan. She exhibited complete certainty that Highsahl would fall, but if the manner of its defeat had been revealed to her she chose not to share it. *Sometimes I can change it*, she had said after slaying the duke, *or others change it for me.* I wondered what changes would be wrought upon her vision this night and if they included the demise of her most trusted confidant.

"It's how it has to be if this is going to work," I said, adding a respectful "my lady" for the benefit of the awestruck recruits nearby.

Evadine gave a tight smile before sparing a glance at Eamond and the Widow, both standing to either side of my place in the front rank. "Guard him well," she said, pausing to receive a firmly spoken assurance from Eamond and a nod from the Widow, before striding off towards the First Company.

"Such care she has for you," the Widow observed quietly, tying the leather strap of her warhammer around her wrist. "Must be gratifying to enjoy the Seraphile's protection."

In response to my sharp glare of warning, Mistress Juhlina's features remained the same mostly expressionless mask I had come to expect, a blankness that was at odds with the depth of bitterness that laced her words. "The Seraphile extend their protection to us all this night," I told her, turning and raising my voice to address the whole company arrayed to our rear. "Who do you fight for?"

"We fight for the Lady!" they shouted back with well-drilled and strident uniformity. "We live for the Lady! We die for the Lady!"

Another fortuitous boom sounded from the direction of the sap then faded to allow my ears to detect a clamour from the southern breach. I couldn't see much through the ever thicker smoke emerging from the sap but the noise told the tale: shouts and blaring trumpets amid the tramp of many boots engaged in a rapid march. Lord Ehlbert, apparently, desired to be first to attack. The ceaseless struggle at Walvern Castle had done much to callous my heart against the many fears that arise in anticipation of battle, but I still retained a marked preference for survival over sacrifice. The stratagem I would attempt tonight had as much to do with improving my odds of seeing the morning as it did securing a triumph for the Anointed Lady. Consequently, I considered Lord Ehlbert entirely welcome to the honour of drawing first blood.

"Raise shields!" I called out, hefting the heavy contrivance that sat before me. It consisted of a sturdy, four-foot pole supporting a thick panel of wood a yard square. Nailed to the panel was a fleece that had been soaking in water for a full day. Raising it above my head, I held it still while Juhlina and Eamond lifted their own shields, slotting the edges over mine to create a roof. Behind us the Second Company followed suit with much clattering of timber and grunting of effort.

For the past three days I had eschewed all other drill to practise this one manoeuvre, teaching every soldier the plan and compelling them to repeat it back to me. A week of decent food had done much to fortify them but I still worried over the weakness of many. Simply managing to hold up the shields and march in line wouldn't be enough to withstand what I knew would be hurled upon us. I took comfort from the craftsmanship of the shields' construction, the result of cannibalising the engines' palisades. In accordance with Leannor's instruction, the two divisions of engines had been sent to menace the city's north and south walls. They were to hurl blazing fireballs over the battlements come nightfall in what was probably a vain attempt to divert the Alundians' attention from the main attack. With the engines shifted, it hadn't been hard to persuade Master Vassier to put the now useless palisades to better use.

"At the march," I shouted, "forwards!"

The Alundians on the battlements to either side of the breach were evidently a disciplined lot for they held off unleashing their projectiles until the company tramped up the ramp to bring us free of the trenches. Only when we had fully emerged onto the twenty yards of flat ground separating the siege lines from the breach did they let fly.

"Steady!" I called out as the first arrows and bolts thudded against our moving roof, the reassuring shout echoed by Ofihla and the other sergeants. "Keep to the pace!"

The dull thwack of shaft and bolt impacting the shields rapidly became a constant hail, interspersed by the frequent whoosh of a fire arrow. The Alundian archers quickly realised the pointlessness of loosing their flaming projectiles at this hide-covered roof and soon fire arrows began to career from the hard-packed, frosted earth on our flanks, a few succeeding in bouncing into our midst. They did little damage, since the shafts lost most of their striking power when rebounding from the ground. The flames they birthed on the leggings or boots of the steadily marching soldiers were short-lived, swiftly stamped out or extinguished by the constant and plentiful drip of water from the skins on our shields.

As we covered the last few yards to the breach the rocks began to fall, the hard patter of arrow and bolt joined by the jarring thump of descending boulders. "Close up!" I heard Ofihla shout from the middle of the column, her next words indicating we had suffered our first loss. "Leave him, he's dead! Close it up! Keep to the pace!"

I stiffened my arms as repeated blows from falling rocks threatened to jar the shield's pole from my grip. Next to me, Eamond hissed a curse as his own shield suffered a hefty blow. The wooden square pressed down hard on his helm, dislodging a chunk of rubble twice the size of his head before he grunted and forced it back into place. Further shouts to close up from behind made it plain others hadn't been so lucky, but still the Second Company advanced into the breach in good order at an undaunted pace. As the jagged edges of the breach loomed up on either side, I took heart from the fact that this man-made canyon was only ten yards long at most. It was littered with rubble, forcing us to slow, but I reckoned we would clear it in no more than a minute. Sadly, our enemy once again showed their discipline by not unleashing their most potent weapon until the leading troops marched into the gap.

As boulders continued to rain down I saw a brief curtain of viscous liquid spill over the forward edge of my shield, a good deal more splashing onto the wreckage-strewn ground ahead. A dozen or more torches fell soon after and suddenly the confines of the breach became an inferno. The heat blasted against my unprotected face, the instant haze of smoke birthing tears and a bout of coughing. Feeling a resurgence of the kind of fear that had once beset me at the Traitors' Field, I resisted the impulse to lower my visor in favour of keeping my shield in place. Allowing our formation to falter at this moment meant a fiery end. I also needed my mouth uncovered in order to shout out my next order.

234 • ANTHONY RYAN

"Forward at the run! Keep together!"

This was the second element of my plan and, despite the many hours attempting to drill my troops in maintaining formation while running, I knew it to be the moment of greatest peril. As the Second Company spurred to a run, gaps inevitably appeared in our shield roof, providing opportunities for the eager and keen-eyed archers and oil throwers above. The shouts of the sergeants as they attempted to maintain order were partially smothered by the screams of stricken soldiers, taken by crossbow bolts or flaming oil. Despite the tumult of chaos and pain, I kept my eyes fixed forwards, running in time with Eamond and the Widow until we cleared the breach. It was a certainty that the Alundians would have prepared a welcome for us, and they didn't disappoint.

Arrayed before us a dozen paces from the breach were no less than five ranks of close-packed men-at-arms, their formation bristling with pikes. Beyond the veritable forest of long spears, I saw a great mass of armed folk, standing in looser ranks. These no doubt were the townsfolk who had taken up arms to defend their city, ready to hold the line should this wall of soldiers falter.

"Form crescent!" I called out, the command echoed by the sergeants. "Crossbows up!"

This was the trickiest part of the entire scheme, one about which Ofihla had expressed doubts that even a company of veterans would have difficulty in accomplishing. Still, never one to shirk a duty, she had gone about rehearsing this move for hour after hour, dealing out harsh words and harsher blows until gruffly reporting that it might, just, be possible.

As the Second Company altered formation, I allowed myself a quick survey of the shifting ranks. To my grim surprise, I found that around two-thirds of our strength remained. I had fully expected to lose over half by this juncture. The recruits hurried to form the semicircular, three-rank structure with creditable alacrity if not the expert precision I would have expected from the First Company. The pikemen kept hold of their shields and formed up in front. The halberdiers, denied their usual arms, dropped their own shields, drawing falchions and swords to fall in behind. The dagger men lined out to form the third rank but, like the pikemen, retained their shields and turned about, raising them up to provide protection for the fourth contingent in our company. With Evadine's agreement, I had enlisted every cross-bowman under her command and any willing to volunteer from the ranks of the ducal levies. Their number included Fletchman with his ash bow, who took my quietly spoken suggestion that he tarry at the Lady's side as a personal insult. Altogether, they amounted to just over a hundred bowmen, all veterans with plentiful munitions and a wealth of unprotected targets on the battlements to our rear.

"Loose when ready!" I shouted, a redundant command for the bowmen were already letting fly, a dozen Alundians tumbling from the battlements at the first volley. "Hold in place!"

At first the Alundian men-at-arms standing only a few paces to our front did nothing. One of the principal lessons of war is that confounding expectations will always provide an advantage. These stalwart defenders had expected us to throw ourselves against their well-prepared line, dying by the dozen in the process. Seeing us come to a halt while a host of bowmen rose from our ranks to assail their comrades on the battlements did not conform to their vision of how this battle would unfold. So, for several precious seconds, with ever more Alundians falling to the hail of bolts from below, they did nothing.

Finally, an unseen Alundian captain found the wit to call out an order to attack, although only the left flank of the line did so at first. Our shield-bearing pikemen responded as they had been taught, first lowering their shields as the opposing line closed, then angling them up as the spearpoints touched the upper lip. The result was a clattering, overlapping chaos of raised pikes which inevitably brought the Alundian advance to a halt. The same result played out all along our line as the need to crush our intrusion was communicated through their cohort. Once again the habits of professional soldiers worked to our advantage. The men-at-arms plainly lacked any prearranged drill for this outcome and wasted precious time struggling in a constricted crush as they vainly sought to lower their pikes, many losing their grip in the process. They did succeed in pressing a great weight against the curving wall of our shields, but for now it held.

"Brace!" I shouted repeatedly, putting all my bulk behind the pole holding my shield against the mass of struggling armoured bodies. Incredibly, for the next few moments of strained heaving and shoving, neither side managed to deliver a single blow against the other.

Risking another glance over my shoulder I let out a relieved grunt at the sight of the First Company advancing through the breach at the run, Evadine's tall, helmless form unmistakable at their head. They charged in unimpeded by missiles or oil from above, all the defenders on the battlements having been either slain or forced to take shelter by the continuing volleys of bolts from our crossbows. A keen-eyed commander on the other side of our hard-pressed shield wall must have noticed the danger, for a plethora of fresh exhortations compelled yet greater efforts from the Alundian men-at-arms.

"BRACE!" I called again, hearing the first clang of an edged weapon striking armour somewhere off to my right. A cacophony of clattering wood and metal sounded then as the Alundian pikemen dropped their lances, the pressure on our shields relaxing for the instant required for them to draw their swords or unlimber their axes. Splinters rose in clouds as blades chopped at our wooden barrier, screams pealing out as they found flesh as well as timber.

"Second rank up!" I called out, compelling the halberdiers to join their weight to the effort of holding the shield wall. My own shield was now pressed against my cheek as I leaned my full weight to keeping it in place. A stocky halberdier pushed in next to me, setting his shoulder to the shield. He raised his head a little too high in the process, suffering an instant cut to the forehead as a reward.

"Just a nick, Captain!" he assured me, grinning despite the blood trickling down his face. I recognised Liahm Woodsman's features beneath the grime and red spatter, returning his grin with a surety and confidence that was mostly artifice. More screams and yells rang out to punctuate the constant chopping of the Alundian blades, leaving me in no doubt that this was the moment of greatest danger. However, for all their frenzied desire to break our line, expectation had once again led our foes to the wrong conclusion.

Once the First Company charged into the breach, military logic dictated they would rush to our aid, lending their numbers to our line whereupon this contest became one of brute strength. On this side of the city wall the defenders had a definite advantage in that regard as only so many attacking troops could traverse the breach at once. However, no one in the Alundian ranks had anticipated that, instead of advancing through the breach, the second wave of attackers would climb it.

I craned my neck to see the gratifying sight of ladders being hauled up and propped against the northern shoulder of the breach. I had time to glimpse Evadine swiftly ascending to the battlement before a resurgent bout of shoving compelled me to afford my full attention to more immediate concerns.

"Bowmen about face!" I shouted, the words barely heard above the raucous din of massed folk doing their damnedest to kill each other. I repeated the call several times over before it was taken up by the sergeants. Fletchman was the first bowman to come struggling through the third rank, greeting me with a terse nod before bobbing up to loose one of his bodkin-headed shafts directly into the face of an Alundian soldier. Crossbowmen soon appeared to either side, unleashing their bolts at close and fatal range. For an all-too-brief interlude the pressure eased as the men-at-arms opposing us suffered their first casualties. Then, amid a chorus of exhortations from their sergeants and captains, they surged forwards with renewed fury.

The struggle wore on for several exhausting minutes, we in the first rank desperately holding our wall in place while the bowmen methodically killed the soldiers who sought to pierce it. Recurrent glances at the breach confirmed that most of the First Company had scaled the wall and were fighting their way along the battlement against only meagre opposition. This contest was now a race between the Alundians' desperate efforts to eliminate our foothold and Evadine's ability to bring the First Company down from the battlements to assault their rear.

Inevitably, sheer weight of numbers contrived to force us back. My boots skidded and scraped over bloody cobbles as one Alundian after another fell to the bowmen, yet they pressed on with the courage of those who know that defeat means doom. One axe-bearing man-at-arms clawed his way over the shield wall, apparently heedless of the bolt jutting from his cheekbone. He tumbled over the barrier, hacking the legs from under a crossbowman while thrashing about on his back. Fletchman finished the fellow with a swift slash of his hunting knife before he could wreak further havoc.

More screaming encouragements from the Alundian side saw us pushed back yet further. I chanced a glance above the lip of my shield to see that many of the enraged, wild-eyed faces before me lacked a helm. Some had only swords or hatchets without a scrap of armour. In the direness of their need the Alundians had brought the townsfolk into the fray. They came at us with the same fearlessness, no doubt driven by the terror of what awaited family and loved ones in the event of our victory. Their courage was impressive, but it had been wasted on a fatally mistaken ploy.

The Alundian throng first began to give way off to my right, the shield wall there curving forward with a suddenness that created a small gap in our own line. The Alundians may well have taken advantage of this opening, spelling our doom in the process, if the uproar to their rear hadn't compelled them to turn and face a new threat. Above the milling bodies I saw a long line of bobbing pikes and recognised the formation adopted by the Covenant Company when advancing. The pikes were soon lowered to the horizontal and the surviving men-at-arms and townsfolk found themselves caught between our shields and the First Company. Some reacted with renewed courage, hurling themselves against both us and the oncoming pike hedge; others wavered and some fled. Recognising the moment as the tipping point that arrives in all battles, I shoved my shield forwards into the disordered crowd, letting go of the pole and drawing my sword.

"To me!" I shouted, raising my sword high above my head. "Rally to me! Form spearpoint!"

I slammed my visor in place as the Second Company responded to my call. It would flatter the resultant untidy gaggle to call it a formation, but it did serve to gather us together sufficiently to allow for a charge. I started forwards at a steady run, slashing my sword at the neck of a man-at-arms who raised his halberd to bar our path. He succeeded in parrying the blow with the haft of his weapon only for the Widow to stave in his helm with an overhand blow from her warhammer. A townsman came at me with a levelled spear, a full-throated roar emerging from his snarling features. His bravery and resolve were not matched by any martial skill, however, and it was an easy matter to sweep his spear aside and hack my sword into his shoulder with one swift movement. Thereafter, the struggle dissolved into the chaotic melee that often greets the moment of decision, the ugly chaos of it causing time to take on a peculiar elastic quality. Some of those I killed seemed to die over the course of moments, reeling away from my slashing blade in a slow pirouette, their screams lost to my ears. Others fell in mere seconds, their demise rich in the grating crunch of sundered bone or gurgle of blood.

I suffered several blows in the course of it all, delivered by foes I couldn't see thanks to the constricted view through the slit of my visor. I sustained no injury beyond a resurgence of the throb and a thin seepage of blood from the nose. As the surrounding melee thinned and lessened in ferocity, a volley of crossbow bolts and arrows came sailing out of the close-packed street before us. Wilhum's predic-tion regarding the quality of my armour was borne out when a bolt careened off my breastplate, barely scratching the metal. A handful of my surviving recruits were not so lucky, causing me to bark out orders for the rest to retrieve their shields.

"Got plenty of fighting still to do tonight!" I said, hounding them back into some semblance of order. With the fury of battle temporarily assuaged, my mood soured and my temper shortened by the throb's return. The sight of so many dead and wounded littering the cobbles also denuded any triumphant impulse.

"Are you wounded?" Evadine asked, her tall form striding from a drifting pall of smoke. A fire raged in the northern precinct of the city, presumably the result of a fireball launched by the siege engines. The blaze cast a disorienting flicker over an already night-marish scene along with an acrid haze that further added to the overall confusion.

Evadine halted to peer at my besmirched features, I having raised my visor to reveal the blood trickling from my nose. "It's nothing," I said, wiping it away.

The concern lingered on her face, joined with a certain surprised lift of her brows that made me wonder if one of her visions hadn't included my gruesome death this night. "We need to consolidate before advancing," I told her, looking back at the breach and finding it dismayingly empty of reinforcements.

"The princess must still be awaiting the fall of the bastion," Evadine said. A quick survey of the gatehouse, standing wreathed in smoke but otherwise intact, made me conclude that Leannor was in for a long wait. Also, from the loud tumult of continuing combat rising from the gloom south of the bastion, it appeared Lord Ehlbert hadn't yet succeeded in leading the Crown Company through their breach.

"The King's Champion requires some help, it seems," Evadine said. "I'll take the First Company. Hold here with the Second and send word to Princess Leannor of our success. Mayhap she's missed it in all the excitement."

"The duchess," I reminded Evadine as she turned away. "We're supposed to secure her."

"We can't fight our way through an entire city alone, Alwyn. Besides—" a muted grin of rarely expressed smugness played over her lips as she beckoned to Swain "—seeing Sir Ehlbert's expression when I save him will be well worth the diversion."

"I'd rather you let the bastard die," I muttered, earning a small frown of reproach before she hurried off to muster the First Company into a spearhead formation.

"Eamond!" I called out, scanning the surrounding sprawl of bodies and dazed figures beset by the nausea and confusion that descends post-battle.

"He's over there," the Widow told me. She stood a few paces off, using a rag to scrape accumulated gore from her warhammer and nodding to a small knot of soldiers nearby.

"Eamond," I repeated, striding over. As I drew closer I saw that the group surrounded a kneeling soldier, an Alundian man-at-arms judging by his armour. His plate was streaked in blood and soot, face bearing several wounds. But he retained enough defiance to swing a halberd at the soldiers around him. Lost in the cruelty that arises from survival, they responded with ribald taunts, tormenting the wounded stalwart with jabs of their blades and blows from their staves.

"How's that, you heretic bastard!" one asked, deftly sidestepping a lunge from the Alundian before hacking down with his falchion, dislodging the halberd from the fellow's grip. Several more blows and the Alundian lay senseless on the ground.

"Fetch some oil," another said. "Let's watch this filth burn."

"That's enough!" I said, grabbing the would-be burner by the shoulder and spinning him round. Eamond's features were so transformed by hate-filled malice it took a moment before I recognised him. Also, for the first time I saw defiance in his eyes. *Like Erchel when you got between him and his prey*, I thought, watching Eamond master himself.

"Apologies, Captain," he said, forcing the words out from a dry throat, stepping back with his head lowered. His companion with the falchion was not so cowed.

"Apologies my arse," he spat, moving towards me with a purposeful glare. "This fucker killed my cousin. I'll have justice for it and fuck you if you don't like it, Captain."

A life of reluctant soldiering has taught me that there are many paths to instilling proper discipline in one's troops. Often a solicitous word or kindly spoken compliment will win the hearts of the truculent or disheartened. However, when faced with outright mutiny, there are few methods more effective than a steel gauntlet delivered with full force to the face.

The vengeful recruit's falchion clattered to the cobbles as the blow struck home, birthing a cloud of blood speckled in white from shattered teeth. He tottered about for a time, ruined faced set in a bemused frown, then collapsed. When I turned to regard his fellows, I found them all mimicking Eamond's contrite pose.

"Pick that piece of dung up," I said, pointing my sword at the unconscious soldier. "When he wakes tell him he's dismissed from this company in dishonour. If I ever see him again, I'll flog him to death. The rest of you piss off and find your sergeant. You," I added, turning the full weight of my baleful eye upon Eamond, "get yourself through the wall and find Princess Leannor. Tell her this breach has been secured and Captain Scribe humbly suggests she send all the troops she can to join us."

I watched him scamper off then turned to go, pausing as the wounded Alundian let out a strained gasp, "Please . . ." One look at his face, skin bleached white beneath the soot and gore, told me he had but moments left. "My wife . . ." he sputtered, body jerking. "My children . . . They're at the Duke's Keep . . . You have . . . to stop it . . ." He summoned the strength to crane his head to meet my gaze, eyes bright and pleading. "Stop her . . . You're . . . a good man . . . aren't you . . . ?"

Not especially, no. I left the words unsaid, for they were cruel and in that moment I was too weary for such things. Also, his words stirred my curiosity. "Stop who from doing what?" I asked, crouching at the dying Alundian's side.

"The duchess . . ." he rasped, convulsing as he forced the words out, staining his chin with the dark blood that rises from deep within a body. "She is . . . resolved upon it . . . They all are . . . even my wife. It's madness." He convulsed again, using the last of his strength to flail a hand at me. It fell limply against my vambrace and would have fluttered to the ground if I hadn't caught it. "You'll . . . stop them." His eyes stared into mine, beseeching understanding even as death clouded them. "You're . . . a . . . good . . . man . . ." This emerged as a sibilant whisper that faded into a hiss and then the familiar rattle of a man taking his final breath.

Letting go of his hand, I made my way back to the company line, finding Ofihla had been typically efficient in marshalling the survivors into reasonable order. About half were left, which I knew to be a far better return on the night's fighting than I could have expected, but still the bodies scattered about the breach brought a plummet to my heart. I couldn't claim to have known them well, some hardly at all, but these soldiers had been mine.

A few more bolts and arrows came sailing from the rooftops and windows, creating a nuisance rather than a danger. Even this vexation faded away as the blaze in the northern precinct built, casting a glow on the clouds above and a steady shower of embers. The sight inevitably stirred memories of Olversahl, particularly the inferno that claimed the great library. With the throb raging anew in my skull and ugly memories stirring within, I wanted very badly to be gone from here, having no desire to witness the death of another city.

The duchess . . . She is resolved upon it. I clenched my jaw as the dying soldier's words fought their way through the pain raging in my head. His meaning remained a mystery but his desperation had left me in little doubt as to their dire promise of his words. Also, Leannor had surely been right in trying to orchestrate an avenue of escape for Duchess Celynne. *My children . . . You're a good man.*

Muttering a short but fulsome stream of profanity, I stooped to extract the small bottle from the pouch behind my right greave. "Sergeant Ofihla!" I said, taking a hefty gulp of medicine.

"Captain!" she said, appearing at my side and coming swiftly to attention.

I grunted as I forced the elixir down. "Did we happen to take any captives?"

CHAPTER TWENTY

I took the Widow, Liahm Woodsman and Fletchman along as escorts, leaving the Second Company in Ofihla's hands once reinforcements appeared in the breach and put the actuality of the city's fall beyond any doubt. The assembled knights of the king's host were the first contingent to assault the city proper. They were all mounted and came galloping through at an unwise pace, finding themselves forced to an abrupt halt by the narrow streets. As they milled about in ineffectual confusion, some were lost to the Alundian bowmen prowling the nearby rooftops until the knights consented to dismount and advance on foot. By then the ducal levies were trooping through the breach in a thick stream, led by the Cordwainer companies who lost no time ransacking the nearest houses in search of loot. Most dwellings close to the walls had been abandoned in the weeks preceding our assault and the few townsfolk who remained were mainly those too old, sick or foolish to have left. The treatment suffered by these unfortunates stirred yet more ugly memories of Olversahl and the ravages meted out by the victorious Ascarlians.

"The Covenant Company cannot be besmirched by such crimes," I told Ofihla before setting off in search of the Duke's Keep. "Take them onto the battlements and stay there. Any soldier who breaks ranks will be flogged and dismissed."

I had intended for our lone Alundian captive to lead us to the keep but one glance at this spindly, terrified shade of a man convinced me he was beyond being compelled to anything. He did manage to gabble out directions after a few fortifying gulps of brandy whereupon I ordered Ofihla to set him free when a quiet moment presented itself. Consequently, navigating the smoke-fogged, chaotic streets of Highsahl proved a tedious and frustrating business. At first, the winding cobbled lanes and alleys were largely empty, only becoming thronged with panicked, fleeing folk when the tall masts of the ships at harbour came into view above the rooftops. Knots of townsfolk clustered together in families, their sundry valuables bundled into sacks or chests, faces all wearing the pale, wild-eyed shock that arises from finding oneself amid absolute calamity. For the most part we were taken for Alundian soldiery and ignored by the few who noticed us through their panic, although some felt obliged to cast curses at us for our cowardice or what one well-dressed woman termed "insane loyalty to the duchess that has doomed us all. Yes, run you cravens!" She raised a plump arm to shake a fist as we rounded a corner. "Run and let the orthodox bastards slaughter us, why don't you?"

"She makes a fair point," Fletchman observed, moving with bow unslung and an arrow to his string, eyes constantly roving the alleys and rooftops for trouble. "I'd hazard most folk in this city wanted no part of a war."

"Should've opened the gates then, shouldn't they?" the Widow returned. There was an unusually defensive note to her tone and I saw how her brow had taken on an ever deeper furrow with every burning house or panicked group we passed. I had assumed her capacity for witnessing horror to be inexhaustible, given how much violence she had both seen and partaken in by now. However, something about this unfolding disaster appeared to unnerve her. *Even the mad have limits*, I decided.

The Duke's Keep rose from a rocky promontory extending out into the harbour waters from the northern arm of the bay that formed Highsahl's docks. The building was considerably more impressive in size and sturdiness than Walvern Castle, featuring tall towers and sheer walls no ladder could scale. The causeway connecting it to the dockside was about twelve paces broad and a hundred paces long, a singularly unappetising prospect for any attacking force. Yet, when we came to the guardhouse securing the entrance to this pathway, we found it empty.

"Sent all their soldiers to the breaches or the battlements, most like," Woodsman suggested

"There's one here," Fletchman reported, kicking a pair of boots protruding from the shadowed recess of a doorway. "Stand up, y'sod," he commanded, aiming an arrow at the owner, then lowering his bow as puzzlement creased his forehead. "Fuck me if the bugger ain't already dead, Captain."

A closer inspection revealed him to be right. The man-at-arms slumped in the doorway wore clean, undamaged armour, his halberd lying across his chest with an unstained blade. The man's features were also bloodless, but slack, the mouth open and flecked in vomit.

"Poison," I said, straightening from the body. "Of the quick-acting sort, I'd say." I turned my attention to the keep, my gut plummeting. Torches flickered on its ramparts and light glowed behind many an arrow slit, but I saw no sentries atop the walls. The great doors that should have barred the castle's gate lay open and the portcullis raised.

"Captain," Fletchman warned as I started along the causeway. He crouched in the shadow of the guardhouse, squinting at the keep's battlements. "Even a blind man could drop you at this range."

"Don't worry," I said, striding on. "I've a sense there's no one up there, blind or not."

My loyal band waited until I had covered half the span of the causeway without injury before consenting to follow. We found the twin, conical towers that formed the gatehouse empty save for more corpses: two soldiers, also victims of poison. They lay with arms entwined in an alcove, foreheads touching, making me wonder if these were lovers frozen in the act of sharing their final moment. Fletchman and Liahm grew decidedly twitchy with this discovery, scanning the empty turrets, stairs and walkways looming above with a greater pitch of fear than if they had been packed with determined defenders.

"Something's not right here, Captain," Woodsman said in a clipped murmur. Both he and Fletchman had halted at the edge of the keep's outer courtyard, their feet planted firm on the cobbles with no inclination to take another step. I recognised the fear on their faces as being of a particular type, a chilly caress that sets even faithless souls to muttering pleas for the Martyrs' protection. A sense of wrong permeated this keep, unseen yet thick as any fog. Both these men had seen terrible sights this night, yet instinct warned that what lay within was worse.

"Stay here," I said, feeling more weary annoyance than anger. While a punch to the face is sometimes the correct form of encouragement, I divined it would be of little help now. "Guard the entrance. Anyone comes looking for loot you have my leave to feather their arse. Mistress Juhlina?" I raised an eyebrow at the Widow. "Care to watch your captain's back as he ventures into the den of our enemy?"

She responded with a nod, wordless and curtly delivered. I discerned more than just fear in her expression, seeing the muscles of her jaw bunch beneath the grime, her brow and mouth set in a hard line. For reasons I couldn't fathom, she was forcing herself onwards, determined to see what lay inside this place.

I counted another twelve bodies as we made our way through the innards of the Duke's Keep. At first they consisted of men-at-arms lying close to the doorways or stairwells that I assumed had been their allotted station. Further in, we found servants. These were clustered in larger groupings of three or four and lay in gardens or small courtyards. The means of their demise became apparent when I noticed the goblets lying amid a trio of maids. Pausing to retrieve one, I found it held a few drops of wine, the scent of which was odd and unfamiliar.

"Not one I know," I muttered, holding the goblet out to the Widow. "Do you have a nose for poisons, by any chance?"

She stared at the proffered vessel and shook her head, refusing to take it. I could tell her fear was beginning to overcome her resolve and I half expected her to turn and flee as we traversed the courtyard and mounted the steepest stairwell yet. However, she remained at my side as we crested the steps, bringing us to a broad oval chamber I instantly recognised as the duke's audience room by virtue of the fact that it featured but one chair. A tall, oakwood contrivance of intricate carvings and decoration, it sat in the centre of a space tiled in marble rather than the bare if elegantly dressed stone seen elsewhere in this building. Silken drapes adorned with the rearing black bear of the Cohlsair family cascaded from a vaulted ceiling of impressive height. However, any impression of grandeur was negated by the bodies sprawled about the floor and the sight of none other than Duchess Celynne herself, slumped and still at the base of the chair. Taking a reluctant step or two closer, I felt a dismayed pang when I saw that the bodies closest to her were all considerably smaller than the others.

"Bitch," the Widow said, voice strained to a breathless rasp. Turning, I found her staring at the ugly tableau before us with moistened eyes and a rare tinge of red to her tensed features. "Had to take them with her. Selfish bitch!" Choking to silence, she closed her eyes, lowering her head and refusing to follow as I stepped into the disorderly circle of corpses.

From the finery of their clothes I deduced these to be the duchess's most favoured courtiers and principal functionaries. Goblets and cups littered the tiles between the dead, the air rich with the odour of poison. Predictably, Duchess Celynne was far less pretty in death than she had been in life, lying with sightless eyes staring up at the interlocking arches above, flaccid lips drawn back from teeth that I felt gleamed with unnatural brightness. Her sons lay at her side, their faces mercifully hidden by the folds of their mother's robe. I tried to summon an echo of the Widow's anger but couldn't. Instead, I felt mostly bafflement. I could guess a great deal of what had passed in this chamber before the poisoned cups were raised: the declamations of undiminished loyalty, the willingness to give one's life in service to the true form of Covenant belief. Yet, I couldn't comprehend how a mother, or any other soul with a claim to rationality or compassion, could actually compel herself to this act.

"Did you help them?" I asked Celynne's dead, unseeing face.

"Sweeten the wine so they found it easier to drink? Tell them they were going to meet their father?"

"She said he was waiting for us."

A shout of alarm escaped me as I whirled towards the sound, sword levelled at a small figure rising from beneath the folds of the duchess's cloak. The little girl blinked doleful, drowsy eyes, a line of puzzlement marring her smooth brow. "I only took a sip." She peered up at me, her lingering frown summoning recognition. *The girl from the tent on the banks of the Crowhawl,* I remembered. *Ducinda.*

"It didn't taste nice so I pretended." The Lady Ducinda yawned and pushed her small hands against her mother's leg, huffing in annoyance. "Now they're all sleeping and won't wake up."

She coughed then, the sound possessed of enough wet ugliness to make me kneel and gather her up. "Just a sip?" I asked, shaking her when her head began to loll.

"Mmm . . ." she slurred, small head resting against my breastplate.

"Wake up!" I said, shaking her as I turned and hurried towards the stairs. "Don't fall asleep."

"You're too shouty," the girl groaned. "Like my uncle. He shouts all the time." She gazed blearily around at the passing walls as I descended the stairs and ran through successive courtyards, the Widow following close behind. "Are we going to see him?"

"Perhaps later. First we need to see a friend of mine. He'll make you all better." A frantic journey through the aggravating maze of the keep brought us finally to the gatehouse where Liahm and Fletchman straightened at the sound of my shouted command. "A horse! We need a fucking horse!"

The following day, Duchess Celynne Cohlsair was laid to rest alongside her children in the family mausoleum beneath the Duke's Keep. The funeral rites were conducted by an orthodox cleric in accordance with standard Covenant doctrine, which I felt to be a calculated and final insult to a woman who had died for her faith. However, the fact that she had also obliged her children and a host of soldiers and servants to do the same served to quell my sympathies. *They're mad,* the dying Alundian man-at-arms had told me and surely he had spoken truth. I indulged in the faint hope of finding the fellow's family miraculously alive when the full company returned to search the keep, but we discovered no survivors beyond the Lady Ducinda. The duchess's brood had not been the only youngsters to perish in the tragedy, for we happened upon several families, noble and servant, all huddled together to greet their end. Madness, even when inspired by devotion, remains madness.

The fire raging in Highsahl's northern quarter had been extinguished by a fortuitous snowfall that greeted the dawn. The chill also served to diminish the customary rampage to which soldiers invariably succumb when a city suffers invasion. Several neighbourhoods were thoroughly ransacked during the night and fleeing Alundians cut down with indiscriminate glee before the snow forced a halt to the carnage. When the weather improved later in the day the few bands of ducal soldiers who ventured forth in search of loot were confronted by Lord Ehlbert and the Crown Company. The efficient brutality of the King's Champion normally faded in the aftermath of battle, but not this time. Having lost fully half his kingsmen assaulting the southern breach, the experience had apparently left him with a lingering ill temper. Rumour had it that his darkened mood had much to do with the fact that his attack had faltered so badly it faced utter ruin before Evadine led the First Company against the rear of the Alundians opposing him. Whatever the cause, Lord Ehlbert lost no time in hanging six looters from a hastily raised gallows before the main gate whereupon the criminal impulses of the Crown soldiery evaporated.

By my reckoning, Highsahl was two-thirds emptied by the time order could be said to have returned. A good many townsfolk had been carried away from the harbour by enterprising merchant ships, their captains presumably demanding a hefty price for the privilege. A larger number, lacking coin for a berth, fled the port via the smaller gates in the north- or south-facing walls. Most would trickle back into the city over the course of succeeding days, unable to face the depredations of midwinter in the open. They returned in huddled, miserable groups, fearful and twitchy under the gaze of the northerners who had seized their city. Princess Leannor ordered alms be provided to all and no recriminations taken against any Alundian without her express permission. Her courtiers toured the streets constantly, calling out proclamations regarding the largesse of Good King Tomas and assuring all of his continued protection.

So, when Leannor called her principal captains to council five days after the city's capture, it was with no small amount of self-satisfied preening. "Our messenger will have reached the king with word of our success by now," she said, addressing us while seated on the ornate tallness of the deceased duke's chair. The effluent and spilled wine that had besmirched the fine marble tiles of the audience chamber had been scoured away, the floor gleaming bright in the sunlight streaming through the unshuttered windows.

"Rest assured, my good sirs, and lady," Leannor continued, "I was fulsome in reporting your fine, brave deeds in securing his just victory and have little doubt rewards will be forthcoming in due course."

"Surely reward is due most to you, Your Majesty," one of the captains put in. He was a handsome minor noble from eastern Alberis, commander of a company of free swords raised by his own purse. A rum lot of cut-throats and drunkards, they had been last through the breach and conspicuous among the looters before Lord Ehlbert's intervention.

"For was it not your sage generalship that won this city for the Crown?" the fellow went on, casting an expectant glance at the assembled captains. "We owe you all honour, and know—" he sank to one knee in grave reverence, head bowed low "—my sword is yours forever more, my most esteemed princess."

His obsequiousness quickly spread through the assembly, most of whom lost no time mimicking his gesture. Evadine, myself and, I noted with interest, Sir Ehlbert did not.

"Your kindness is excessive, Lord Elfons," Leannor scoffed, flicking both hands at the kneelers. "Enough of this. Rise, good sirs, for we have important matters to discuss. With this war won, we must now turn our minds to the necessities of peace."

I was obliged to smother a caustic snort at this. With the beloved daughter of the Duke of Althiene slain, albeit by her own hand, and the people of Alundia roused to rebellious fury, peace would not be returning to this realm for many a day.

Leannor paused for a moment of clearly pre-rehearsed reflection, brow set in thoughtful pondering and a finger stroking her chin. "The prospect of governing a rebellious land has always presented a singular set of challenges. We must ask ourselves, how best to govern those who do not wish to be governed?"

"With steel," the verbose Lord Elfons stated, gripping his sword handle for emphasis. "For those that rise in rebellion against a just king deserve no better."

"No, my lord." Leannor shook her head, tilting her chin to a regal aspect. "I have stated many times that we did not come here as conquerors and I will not make myself a liar now. No, my cogitations on this issue led me to but one conclusion . . ."

Her sage pronouncement was temporarily denied us by a loud rumble from beyond the walls of the chamber, the sound accompanied by a faint vibration beneath our feet. "What in the Martyrs' arses was that?" Leannor asked, rising from her chair as composure gave way to surprised alarm.

"The gatehouse bastion, Majesty," I said. "Master Vassier predicted it might well fall today."

"Then," she observed with a bitter sigh, "it seems he's a better prophet than he is an engineer."

This brought forth a laugh from the assembly, the lingering refusal of the bastion to collapse despite the fire still burning beneath its foundations having become a running joke throughout the army. Many soldiers would now be settling wagers placed on the precise moment of its ruin. Princess Leannor, however, was fully aware this was not a moment worth celebrating. Destroying the gatehouse had merit when the city lay in enemy hands; now its destruction left our defences in a parlous state while Lord Roulgarth's Grey Wolves still roved the duchy intent on murderous revenge. A supply caravan from Alberis had been ambushed two days before, every drover and accompanying soldier slaughtered in the process and their precious cargo carried off or put to the torch. Leannor might be content to claim victory, but the reality was that we had taken but one city in a land populated by an uncowed people who now had even greater reason to hate us.

Leannor forced a smile at the merriment, one that froze in place when her eye alighted on something at the base of her purloined chair. It was a mere speck of dark brown matter revealed by a slight altering of the chair's position as she rose, but it captured her full and instant attention.

"I ordered this floor scrubbed!" she said, voice breathless and blazing eyes snapping towards her principal courtier, an austere, plainly attired man bearing the title of Chamberlain Falk. "Scrubbed clean of all marks!" Leannor went on and I saw how her hands clutched at the ermine hem of her cloak, the knuckles white and betraying a poorly controlled tremble. "I believe I was very clear."

"My deepest apologies, Your Majesty," Chamberlain Falk said, bowing low, his tone as bland as his attire. "I shall ensure due punishment is administered . . ."

"Just have it cleaned properly," Leannor snapped, eyes returning to the stain on the floor until she blinked and raised her head. Swallowing, she released the grip on her cloak, flexing her hands before smoothing them over her skirts. "Lord Ehlbert, Lady Evadine and Captain Scribe will remain," she said. "All others have my leave to depart."

As the dismissed captains bowed and trooped out, I caught the brief glare of resentment on the face of Lord Elfons. Clearly, after fawning so conspicuously, finding himself excluded in favour of a former outlaw rankled a great deal. It was therefore my pleasure to afford him a gracious bow and a broad smile, keeping it in place and meeting his eye until he departed the chamber.

"Captain Scribe," Leannor said, her tone now brisk, lacking any trace of the smugness from before. "You will command Master Vassier to commence work on rebuilding the gatehouse bastion forthwith."

"Master Vassier is expectant of receiving leave to depart, Majesty," I replied. "He was charged with securing your entry to this city. Plainly, his task stands complete."

"His task is what I say it is." Leannor's voice took on a grating impatience. "Assuming he ever wants to see that boy of his again. Lord Ehlbert—" she shifted her focus to the King's Champion without pause for further discussion "—what news from your patrols?"

"The Grey Wolves prove elusive," Ehlbert reported. "They scatter after every raid, hide out for a time then re-form their packs when the time is right. Alundia is large and rich in places to hide for hardy soldiers who know the land."

I had noted before that when the number of onlookers thinned, his form of address towards Leannor became markedly less formal. To my surprise, this appeared not to pique her ire one jot. In fact, where Ehlbert was concerned she displayed an ease and familiarity singularly lacking in her discourse with anyone else. Knowing what I knew about this man's true relationship with our king, the favour he enjoyed in royal company was hardly surprising, but it was strange to find it so starkly displayed by the king's sister. *Could it be*, I wondered, eyes shifting from her face to his, *the King's Champion fathered more than one bastard?*

"They're not soldiers," Leannor said. "They deny our king's rightful overlordship of this land and are therefore outlaws. Fortunately—" her attention swung back to me "—there is one among us well versed in the habits of villains. Tell us, Captain Scribe, where best to look for these pestilent Wolves."

I was tempted to profess ignorance of this duchy and its varied landscape, but saw a certain wisdom in the princess's demand. Noble or not, Roulgarth and his rebels were beyond the law now, also shorn of their castles since there were so few soldiers to hold them. Having been reduced to the status of vagabonds, they would need to abide by certain realities of an outlaw's life.

"Scouring mountains and forests will avail us nothing," I said. "We could search for years without finding a single rebel, since they know this country so well."

"Then where, pray tell," Ehlbert said, affording me a quizzical if typically good-humoured smile, "do we look, Captain?"

"In places where they have to be, not where they want to be. Outlaws can hunt for food but will quickly denude a region of game. Nor can they tarry anywhere long enough to grow crops. To continue his rebellion Lord Roulgarth will need supplies, and they will only come from the people of this land. That's where we find them, among the people."

"People who hate us," Evadine pointed out with a sorrowful grimace. "People still clinging to their perversion of the Covenant. People who are hardly likely to betray their countrymen."

"Every land has its traitors," I said. "A truth all outlaws learn eventually." I allowed my expression to sour as I turned to Lord Ehlbert. "Something I'm sure his lordship can attest to, since it was a traitor who led him to Moss Mill and the capture of Deckin Scarl. Is that not the case, my lord?"

"Duchess Lorine would, I'm sure, object to that description," Ehlbert replied with an affable grin, "but it fits well enough."

Lorine wasn't the traitor; that was Todman, you fucking dull-wit, I thought, feeling a clench to my belly at the need to keep such words caged. Instead, I turned back to the princess, keeping my tone clipped and businesslike. "Deckin used to say: someone is always willing to sell you, and the greater your fame the greater the rewards of betrayal. Once the price on an outlaw's head grows enough to make a man rich for life, then his greed starts to outweigh his fear."

Leannor pursed her lips and pondered for a moment. "Five gold crown sovereigns for the death or capture of Lord Roulgarth?" she suggested.

"Ten would be better," I said. "But much depends on word of the reward reaching the right ears. Proclaiming it throughout the duchy will be difficult, since our soldiers can only venture forth in whole companies or face ambush and slaughter. Besides, news flies faster among outlaws than the swiftest messenger."

"My men found a few dozen villains languishing in guardhouses," Ehlbert said. "Some truly vile creatures among them. I was going to hang the lot when time allowed."

"Then, my lord," Leannor said, "it appears you will be spared the chore. Captain Scribe, since I'm sure your voice is best suited to their ears, please visit these outlaws and inform them that Princess Leannor Algathinet has, in her grace and beneficence, seen fit to grant them both clemency and freedom. Set them on the road with food enough for several days and be sure the richness of our reward is known to all."

I bowed low, once again beset by a reluctant admiration for this woman's displays of guile. "I shall, Majesty."

She dismissed us a short while later after hearing reports on various military dispositions, although, feeling I had earned a little indulgence, I lingered a moment. "If I may, Majesty," I said, "I should like to enquire as to the health of Lady Ducinda."

Leannor's expression stiffened, since mention of the only surviving blood heir to the Cohlsair line inevitably returned us to her least favourite subject. I recalled her palpable and unfeigned shock upon hearing the news of Duchess Celynne's suicide and the death of her other children. By now I knew this woman to be both cunning and self-serving. But, unlike those of similar character, her scheming was not accompanied by vindictiveness and she took no pleasure in violence. The destruction of the Cohlsair family had never been part of her plan and it created far more problems than it solved. Lady Ducinda's survival was therefore of considerable importance and Leannor guarded the child closely, even against one who had secured this precious prize.

Upon carrying Ducinda from the Duke's Keep, the Widow had secured me a horse. When its rider, a Cordwainer sergeant-at-arms, voiced foul-tongued reluctance to giving up his mount Mistress Juhlina had simply clubbed him from the saddle with her warhammer. A frenzied ride through the chaotic streets eventually brought me through the breach and onwards to the company encampment. I found Supplicant Delric fully occupied with the wounded streaming back from the battle, but he soon left the work to his assistants upon catching sight of the child in my arms. Saving the girl from the poison in her veins entailed administering a purgative which set her to spewing for much of the night. I sat at her side throughout it all then watched her sleep, mind churning with dark thoughts regarding her likely future. I entertained absurd notions of somehow spiriting her away, perhaps even conveying her into her uncle's arms. Leannor's arrival with a full escort of kingsmen banished such fantasies. The swiftness with which she had learned of Ducinda's survival, despite the fact that I had ordered no word spoken of it, told me Leannor had at least one spy in our ranks. I watched the princess's features turn fully white as I related the news of the terrible scene at the Duke's Keep, after which she quickly gathered the sleeping child into her arms and departed without a word. I hadn't caught sight of Ducinda since.

"She is fully recovered," Leannor stated. "And happy in the many comforts she has been provided."

I wanted to ask more but knew I had already tested the limits of her patience. Fortunately, Evadine, reading my mood with her usual ease, felt no such constraint. "And what are your intentions regarding her future?" she asked with a casual insistence that brought a brief flush to Leannor's face. For all the fawning of her secular captains, the fall of Highsahl was yet another triumphant entry in the ledger of the Anointed Lady. Her soldiers had secured the first breach and her charge saved Lord Ehlbert, thereby sealing the city's fate. Leannor was surely the general of this host, but when the tale of its deeds was told, another name would stand highest in the canon of heroes.

Leannor took a moment to respond. Settling back into her chair to adopt a pose of studied regal elegance, she said, "I find the lady's company charming and will be loath to see her depart this port, but the needs of the realm come first. Soon she will be conveyed by ship to the north and thence to Couravel, where she will enjoy all the protection of the royal household. It is my fervent hope that, when circumstances allow, she be placed in the care of her grandfather. The Duke of Althiene will, I'm sure, find his grieving heart soothed by so loving a child."

"When circumstances allow?" Evadine asked, the words blandly spoken but her expression dark with judgement.

"Lady Ducinda's future is my responsibility now," Leannor replied. "A duty I am resolved to undertake with all due care. Before being conveyed to Althiene she will be betrothed to my son, Lord Alfric. By this act the . . . unfortunate rancour that has arisen between the Crown and the Duke of Althiene will be healed."

And the Algathinet line is forever tied to the dukedom of Alundia, I thought, impressed despite the pall of sadness that descended with her words. I had saved a child's life to see her forced into marriage with the family that had brought about the death of her own. The life of a noble, it seemed, could be as fraught with peril as any churl's.

Sensing Evadine had more to say, much of it likely to cause needless offence, I forestalled her by sinking to one knee and bowing to the princess. "Your kindness and wisdom in this matter is greatly appreciated, Majesty."

There was a pause while Leannor focused an expectant eye on Evadine. The moment stretched to noteworthy length before the Anointed Lady also consented to bend the knee.

"Thank you, Captain Scribe," Leannor said, folding her hands in her lap and favouring me with a serene smile. "Now, begone from here and hunt me some Wolves. I want every one of them dead by spring."

CHAPTER TWENTY-ONE

The Alundian's accent was thick and much of his slang unfamiliar, but I felt I had known him all my life. Outlaws come in varied shapes and sizes, with a similarly disparate range of ill-luck tales describing their path to a lawless life. A small number, however, are not brought to the villain's path by poor choices or misfortune. Rather, like this scarred, wiry villain with his chaotically arranged moustache and whiskers, they are born to it. I have always found it curious that those outlaws most prone to betrayal tend to be of this breed. It was as if avarice had been seeded in the fibre of their being in the womb and would always win out over other concerns when opportunity presented itself. For one such as this, ten gold crown sovereigns proved an irresistible lure. Still, I did catch a small glimmer of shame in the outlaw's eye as he shifted and stuttered out his story, large, bloodshot eyes shifting continually between myself and Lord Ehlbert.

"The old watchtower 'neath Uhlpin's Pass, m'lordships," he said, bobbing his head with every other word. "Got peepers on the trails, though. Scrag-men too." His throat seemed to close of its own volition then, voice faltering and a dry, raspy cough emerging from his cracked lips. The cheeks above his whiskers bore the marks of a man who had lived in the open for weeks, suffering air chilled enough to permanently scar the skin. Although clad in a foul-smelling sheepskin, he shivered continually. *Scared shitless*, I decided, reading the fellow's eyes and finding far more fear than shame.

"Drink, good fellow," Lord Ehlbert told him, sliding a tankard brimming with ale across the table. We were alone in this stone-built hut the locals called an inn. It sat in a huddle of yet smaller huts amid the foothills of the mountains that dominated Alundia's southern border. Getting here required an arduous eight-day journey from the wine country to the east. We had spent weeks among the frosted vineyards in a fruitless search for Lord Roulgarth before a messenger arrived from Highsahl bearing a missive from Princess Leannor. We were directed to venture south where, thanks to a vaguely described source I knew must be one of Leannor's many spies, a man with a useful story could be found. Upon arrival we discovered this lonely, shivering fellow to be the inn's only patron, the village having been denuded of most of its residents as supplies of food diminished due to the chaos of war. The innkeeper had been banished to his shed for the evening and any ears that might be tempted to overhear this conversation warded off by a tight cordon of kingsmen.

"Scrag-men?" I prompted after the Alundian had gulped down a hefty swig of ale.

"Y'know, gutters and knifers," he said, beer froth dangling from his scraggly moustache. "Those that do the killing when need arises."

"Outlaws then," I said. "Like yourself. Seems like strange company for a high-born noble."

"Lord Roulgarth's not a man to judge a fellow for his past." The shame blossomed in his gaze once more and he raised the tankard for another, longer gulp.

"No, don't get drunk," I said, reaching across the table to pull the vessel from his lips. The outlaw's fear shone bright as he shrank from me, shoulders hunching in a manner than told me he was on the verge of bolting for the door. He wouldn't have gotten far had he reached it, but, if what he had to tell us proved true, it would flow easier from a less terrorised soul.

"What do they call you?" I asked, withdrawing my arm. I knew it was pointless asking for his real name, one he probably hadn't used in years.

"Chops," he said, forcing a yellow-toothed grin as he flicked dirty fingers through his whiskers. "On account o'these, see? Not 'cause I'm given to use of a cleaver or such-like, though there's plenty who are in his lordship's band, to be sure."

"You do strike me as a peaceable man," Ehlbert said, causing the fellow's grin to broaden in relief. I could tell he feared me more than he feared the knight at my side. In me he saw one of his own, for the outlaw's mantle is hard to shake and easily discerned by those who share it. In Ehlbert he saw a cheery, oafish noble, one who might be gulled. I concluded, therefore, that this Chops was as lacking in insight as he was rich in greed.

A few weeks previously we had been called to an even less edifying village in the east on promise of sound intelligence regarding Roulgarth's whereabouts. Ehlbert had listened to the informant's plainly invented tale with patient good humour before asking a single but pertinent question: "What colour are Lord Roulgarth's eyes?" As it happens, the informant guessed correctly: blue. However, it was very obviously a guess, one he paid for with a flogging and a sentence of life in the Pit Mines.

Chops, on the other hand, didn't need to guess. "Some calls 'em blue," he replied promptly in answer to Ehlbert's bland enquiry. "But I'd say they're more greyish, like the sea on a cloudy day, m'lord." He paused to burp, peering in disappointment at his mostly empty tankard. "Was a sailor in my time. A trade I'm keen to return to."

"Speak true," Ehlbert told him, taking his tankard and rising to hold it beneath the tap of the barrel in the corner, "and you'll have coin enough to buy your own ship. Captain Chops they'll call you." He sauntered back to the table and set the tankard down, placing a large hand on the villain's shoulder. "Wouldn't that be grand, eh?"

"Grand." Chops bobbed his head again, reaching out to clutch the tankard, hands still shaking more than they should.

"This bastard's lying," I said, getting to my feet, dagger hissing from the sheath on my belt. Chops tried to get up but Ehlbert's suddenly heavy hand kept him in place. "Roulgarth Cohlsair, the Wolf of Alundia," I snarled in derision, "deigning to breathe in the stink of scum like you?" I lunged forward to grip the filthy dampness of his sheepskin. "Do you think me some noble-arse dull-wit?"

"Now, now," Ehlbert chided in easy placation, keeping Chops seated while my dagger-point loomed closer to his eye. "I'm sure Captain Chops can prove the truth of his word." He gave the outlaw's shoulder a friendly shove. "Can't you, Captain?"

"Y-you're the scribe, right?" Chops gabbled, seeking to shrink away from me but finding himself crushed against the unyielding wall of the King's Champion. "The one who held Walvern Castle?"

"What of it?" I asked, halting my dagger a hair's breadth from the pupil of his twitching eye.

"His lordship said he should've killed you at the river. Said, had he known what was to come, he'd've turned the Crowhawl red with your blood that day, and your bitch-martyr."

I quelled the urge to cut him for his insult. The words flowed easily from his mouth and I doubted he possessed the wit to invent them. "Told you that, did he?" I scoffed. "I'd guess he's never even spoken a word to you."

"Not to me; to his nephew, Lord Merick. They talk together some nights, see? I'd get close, find a place where I could listen."

"And what do they talk of most nights?"

"Plans mostly, ambushes and raids and murders." Chops's eyes swivelled from me to Ehlbert and back again. "You two. He badly wants to kill you both but he's all riled up that he can't, not with the worst of winter closing in on the mountains." I eased back a little as the words continued to stream forth, hearing truth in the babble. "Planning to stay there till spring, see? Got nowhere else to go, in truth. There's sympathetic lords and ladies in the south who'll offer refuge but his lordship don't want to risk the journey, the country being so flat and supplies so thin. He'll be there all winter, m'lords. My word on it and I'll swear to all the Martyrs you like that I speak true."

"Like you give a whore's toss for the Martyrs," I grunted, albeit with some satisfaction. I hadn't yet heard an obvious lie from this man, and yet the pitch of his fear gave me pause. It continued to cloud his fevered gaze and I fancied it was born of something deeper than the threat of my blade.

"There's more," I said, shifting my grip from his sheepskin to his neck, holding him in place while I inched the dagger ever closer. "You know my kind," I told him, "and I know yours. No more lies. No more secrets. Cough it up or I'll feed you your fucking eye."

Breath huffed from his mouth in acrid gusts, his spindly chest heaving and eyes blinking sweat. When he spoke, the words emerged in a whisper, the tone tinged with surprise that arose from confessing to a sin he hadn't wanted to acknowledge, "My brother . . ."

I tightened my grip on his neck. "What of him?"

"I killed him." He choked into silence and I felt his throat constrict as he swallowed, his next words issuing forth in a sobbing torrent. "I killed my brother. We were on watch and I said to him, 'Let's go and claim those sovereigns before we freeze our balls off.' But he wouldn't, said we owed his lordship for not hanging us that time we stole those goats, said I was a worthless, shitting coward and it was no surprise Ma never loved me and I killed him . . ." Tears welled in his eyes and he closed them tight, jerking in my grasp, sobs wracking his thin form. "I killed my brother," he gasped as I released my hold and stepped back. "Stuck him through the neck, I did . . . I killed my brother . . ."

I let him weep for a time, inclining my head at Lord Ehlbert in a signal to withdraw his imposing presence. He duly retreated to the stool beside the beer barrel in the corner while Chops mastered himself. It took an irksomely long while but I resisted the urge to bully him back to sensibility. Guilt is a strange toxin, for it can fortify as well as weaken. This man had set himself upon a road he couldn't turn from and sealed his choice in the blood of his kin. In accepting that, his brand of villainy would leave no option but to follow through on his betrayal. So I resumed my seat and waited while the greedy weasel purged his sorrow and returned to a sniffling semblance of reason.

"What did you do with the body?" I asked, keeping my tone flat and businesslike, one outlaw to another.

"Tipped him over a cliff." Chops fought down a recurrence of weeping and palmed snot from his nose. "A tall one a good way from the tower. They won't find it."

"But they will notice you're gone," I pointed out.

"His lordship's band loses folk all the time, especially in the mountains. Some just get fed up and wander off home, others tumble off ledges. Reckon there was four hundred of us when he led us south. When I . . . left there was about fifty."

"Besides your brother, had you told anyone about your intentions?"

"Fuck no." He gasped out a laugh at the absurdity of my question. "Last poor bastard his lordship suspected of turning his coat got tied to a tree and had his tongue cut out. They left him there so's the blood would pool up and freeze in his mouth."

This all rang true to me. Maintaining the loyalty of even the most committed fighters in the midst of winter would be no easy task, especially after the dispiriting loss of Highsahl and the ugly fate of Duchess Celynne. Lord Roulgarth, it appeared, was at a low ebb, spending his days squatting in a tower plotting murders he had little chance of committing. *Perhaps he's gone mad*, I thought, although the notion brought little comfort. *Madness may well make him more dangerous. A cornered wolf can still bite, and its bite is made worse when rabid.*

"Is there means of approaching this tower without being seen?" Lord Ehlbert asked Chops, drawing a nod in response.

"There's a shit channel on the south-facing wall," he said. "Traces all the way to the valley floor. Not an easy climb, nor pleasant, but a man could reach the drain it leads to on a dark night. No more than one, though, else they'll be noticed. I can draw you a map, if it pleases your lordship . . ."

"No maps, Captain Chops." Ehlbert grinned and got to his feet, placing another brimming tankard in front of the outlaw. "You'll be showing us the way, if you want to earn your sovereigns." Chops hunched lower as Ehlbert's hand descended onto his shoulder once again. A faintly sullen frown passed across the villain's brow before he gave a jerky nod. "Excellent!" Chops came close to spilling his ale as Ehlbert clapped him on the back before striding to the door. "We'll set off tomorrow at dawn. Captain Scribe, a moment, if you please."

"When the king sent me to hunt down Deckin Scarl," Lord Ehlbert said, speaking around the pipe clenched between his teeth, tendrils of smoke billowing forth to add a sweet musty tinge to the mountain air, "I heard tell of a lad in his band with an uncanny ear for lies." His eye twinkled as he regarded my inexpressive features and took a hearty puff on his pipe, the sight and the scent raising unpleasant memories of another knight with a fondness for pipe smoke.

Sir Ehlbert rested his back against the stone wall of the hut, features half-lit from the glow through the shuttered windows. The hour was late and the night possessed of a bone-cutting chill unique to mountainous country. A chorus of song rose from the Crown Company encamped at the lower end of the village. The strident voices of the knights and kingsmen made a contrast to the silent camp of the Covenant Riders at the settlement's upper end. After Highsahl's capture, the Mounted Guard of the Covenant Company had been formed into a separate command under Wilhum. He was now Captain Dornmahl of the Covenant Riders, their number having doubled by virtue of some careful recruitment of the mounted free swords who found themselves lacking employment in the aftermath of victory. I had been obliged to leave the unmounted Second Company in Ofihla's hands upon joining Evadine on this Wolf hunt, my presence being insisted upon by Princess Leannor herself.

"A mystery I have often pondered," Lord Ehlbert went on when I failed to respond, "is why that clever lad wasn't able to ferret out the traitor at Deckin's side before my trap was sprung."

"A lie has to be spoken for me to hear it," I said, voice flat. "And Deckin's betrayer was not given to saying much in my presence, beyond the occasional insult."

"Duchess Lorine was not fond you, then?" He came to my side and I turned to face him, finding a frown of shrewd enquiry creasing his brow. "I had heard she was like a mother to you, as Deckin was like a father."

"You could say that. But Ascendant Sihlda Doisselle was more like a mother to me than Lorine ever was."

I saw the barb sink home, a hardness flaring in the knight's gaze before being overtaken by evident regret. He lowered his head and puffed his pipe a few more times before saying in a quiet voice, "I had no part in what befell her. Had I known what Althus planned, I would have stopped it."

"In that case, what prevented you freeing her from the Pit Mines when you did learn of it?"

"Nothing." Smoke blossomed as his brows arched in recollection. "When I discovered what Althus had done I rode to the mines with a full retinue of knights, brooking no refusal from the lord who held sway there." A disdainful grimace passed across Ehlbert's face. "A truly unpleasant man of vicious temperament, as I recall, but also a coward who had the Ascendant brought up from the Pits as soon as I made my demand." His features took on an aspect of recurrent bafflement, as if he had been pondering a singular enigma for years. "She refused to leave. When I asked her why she said freeing her would set the realm on the path to war, for Althus was sure to seek her death and in turn I would seek his. In the chaos of what came next the . . . secret she was privy to would surely become known. She couldn't abide the thought of being the cause of war. Besides, she had a congregation to tend to. In truth, she struck me as a woman who was waiting for something, a promise as yet unfulfilled. In any case, when she told me to go away and never come back, I felt it wasn't my place to argue."

He settled his shrewd, enquiring gaze on me again. "Mayhap you can tell me what it was, Captain, the promised gift she was waiting for. I'd wager you knew her far better than I."

All those years, I thought, mind filled with the image of Sihlda's kind, eternally patient face as she guided me through her lessons. *All those years and she didn't even have to be there.* "She wasn't waiting," I said. "She was working. And the gift was hers to give. One day the

Testament of Martyr Sihlda will stand highest among all Covenant scripture."

"Highest among all?" I heard the faint taunt in his voice as he turned a pointed glance towards the Covenant encampment.

A curt declaration that the Anointed Lady and I were of identical mind when it came to Sihlda's Testament rose then died on my lips. I sensed the King's Champion had an ear for lies that was almost as well tuned as mine. Instead, I took a moment to ease my temper and said, "She gulled you, you know?"

"Sihlda? How so?"

"No, Lorine. She wasn't Deckin's betrayer. That was a man named Todman. She had just done gutting him when she made herself known to you that night at Moss Mill."

Ehlbert huffed out a short laugh, lips pursed in amused appreciation. "But she played the part so well."

"Lorine has played many parts in her time. Duchess is only the most recent."

He laughed again and inclined his head at the inn. "Never trust an outlaw, eh?"

"He's not lying," I assured him. "But neither is he trustworthy. Nor do I think Roulgarth so lacking in vigilance that he would fail to notice the disappearance of two sentries, both brothers of villainous inclinations."

"You think he'll know we're coming?"

"Or suspect it, at least."

"Then he's chosen a poor refuge. Years ago I had occasion to ride past the tower that guards Uhlpin's Pass and it was a ruin then. Some Alundian duke of old built it to guard against incursions from the Caerith, not realising that they have scant desire to cross our borders. It's been out of use for a very long time and I doubt it could be held against a determined assault. Lacking our strength, Roulgarth will either try and slip past us or flee through the pass and into the Wastes. I think I'd prefer he did the latter since it would make it certain we'll never hear from him again."

"There's a third option open to him," I pointed out.

"Glorious death in combat." Ehlbert shrugged and took the pipe from his mouth, tapping the bowl against his palm to dislodge the near-extinguished leaf. "We'll oblige him, if that's his wish. Mayhap he'll challenge me, or you, even?"

I gave an impassive stare in response to his grin and fished in my purse for a single shek. "Head or crown?" I asked, making a fist and perching the coin on my thumb.

"What are we wagering for?" Ehlbert asked, squinting in bemusement.

"Which of us has to order someone to crawl up that shit pipe, for I'm not doing it myself." I flipped the coin, sending it flickering in the air. "Call, my lord, or the laws of chance decree you the loser however it falls."

CHAPTER TWENTY-TWO

"There's no bastard here!" Fletchman's face was a picture of ordure smeared misery as I reined Blackfoot to a halt beneath the tower's half-ruined gate. Having lost the coin toss, the poacher had been my natural choice for this task, one he took to without complaint, although I had a sense he regretted that now. The tower sat at the end of a winding track snaking up from the floor of a constricted valley leading to Uhlpin's Pass. Even viewed from afar it was an unimpressive structure, rising from a cluster of rubble with its walls two-thirds vanished to time and the elements.

"They're not long gone," Fletchman added, wiping something dark and sticky from his brow. "Embers are still warm and they left a good stock of supplies behind. Butchered horses too, lot of salted meat just left hanging. I'd hazard they didn't ride out of here."

Evadine and Wilhum halted alongside us as the Covenant Riders charged on foot into the tumbledown confines of the ancient fortress. I cast my gaze beyond the jagged stones of the tower at the rocky, snow-blanketed slopes rising to ominous majesty on either side of the narrow canyon that formed Uhlpin's Pass. It was the obvious avenue of escape, but very few subjects of Albermaine had willingly traversed it in generations and those that had never returned.

"Even Roulgarth isn't that mad," Wilhum opined, sensing my

thoughts. "If he struck out towards the east we would have caught him before reaching the tower." He raised his eyes to the surrounding peaks, summits lost to the dark and low-hanging cloud that banished the moon. "Mayhap he knows a path across these mountains we do not."

I turned and called over my shoulder to one of the dismounted kingsmen Ehlbert had sent to form the second rank of our attack. "Tell his lordship the Wolf has slipped his trap," I told him. "And get that whiskered villain up here."

"No Wolf, no gold," I informed Chops a short while later, the outlaw whimpering as I pushed him hard against the inner wall of the tower. "Until his neck's in a noose, you get nothing. Now, where the fuck is he?"

"How should I know?" he whined, hunching low in his sheepskin. "Not my fault he took himself off before you got here."

"Perhaps not," Wilhum observed, leaning in to add to the outlaw's trepidation, "but it does make me wonder how he knew we were coming."

"Scouts must've warned him," Chops whimpered, eyes a-bulge above his scraggly whiskers. "I couldn't have told him, could I?"

"Captains, please," Evadine said, resting a hand on Wilhum's shoulder and mine. "Give this poor man some pause to gather his thoughts."

If she expected her intervention to calm the villain's fears, she was quickly disappointed. Like many an Alundian, Chops evidently viewed the Anointed Lady not just as a heretic, but also some manner of arcane-infused witch. Throughout our miserable sojourn across this duchy the sight of Evadine produced a marked reaction wherever we went. Whereas us soldiers would attract a chorus of insults upon entering a new village or town, the sight of Evadine would see these uncowed malcontents fall to pale-faced silence, save for a few hushed murmurs of "Malecite Witch". Some had made the mistake of uttering this blasphemous calumny within earshot of the Covenant Riders leading to violent repudiation, although Evadine could be counted on to ensure things didn't escalate to bloodshed.

So it was with wide-eyed silence that Chops regarded the woman who guided him to a seat beside a hastily lit fire. He shuddered at her touch but, I assume due to the terror-born inability to run, consented to sit and listen while Evadine asked him a series of soft-spoken questions.

"Do you know these mountains well, good sir?"

Melted frost scattered from Chops's whiskers as he shook his head.

"But Lord Roulgarth knows them, does he not?"

A jerky, unblinking nod.

"And I know Lord Roulgarth to be man who would never secure himself in a place with no escape route. A clever and vigilant fellow like yourself must have heard him speak of his plans."

Chops shuddered again, as if trying to resist some form of unseen pressure. I knew him to be suffering the delusion that he was being subjected to unnatural influence, a spell woven by the Malecite Witch. Although nothing more than fruit of his limited imagination, this spell proved useful in finally plucking forth a useful nugget of information.

"The Brandyman's Draw," he said in a voice barely above a whisper.

"And what might that be?" Evadine enquired, staring into his eyes, a kind smile on her lips. I wondered if she was conscious of the fearful compliance she was instilling in this man. Perhaps she imagined it to be a natural product of the Seraphile's blessing, another soul brought to devotion by the mere sound of her words.

"It's a track," Chops said in his near whisper, eyes still wide and face blank, "a smugglers' trail from the days when the duke's excise on brandy was so high only the richest could afford it. The brandymen would haul it on donkeyback over the mountains to the southern ports. It's long been unused and no smuggler ever trod it in winter, but—" his head jerked towards the steep slope beyond the tower's southern shoulder "—it follows the line of that ridge. Heard his lordship speak of it, just once mind."

"And it leads to the southern coast?" Evadine asked, receiving a fervent nod in response. "My thanks," she said, reaching out to clasp Chops's gloved hands, a gesture that sent the most violent shudder through him yet. "Rest assured," she told him, "the Covenant will see you rewarded, even should the king deny you those sovereigns."

She left him by the fire and joined Wilhum and myself in surveying the shadowed, misted heights to the south. "If Roulgarth makes it to the coast he can take ship anywhere," Wilhum said.

"Doing us all a favour in the process," I added with a shrug. "Let him sail far away across the sea if he chooses. His only threat to the Crown arises from his presence in this duchy."

"An exile can always return," Evadine pointed out. "And a living hero's legend poses a greater danger than a slain one, for legends can lead armies whereas corpses cannot." She met my eye and inclined her head at Chops, now sitting staring into the meagre fire with rigid fascination.

"All right, you smelly sod," I said, stomping over to drag him to his feet. "Time to get off your arse and show us this Brandyman's Draw."

"It'll be snowed over," he protested in a reedy whine as I pushed him towards the donkey he had been given as a mount. "And I'll never see it in the dark."

"Be morning soon enough." I shoved him onto the donkey's back, an animal that seemed to share my disdain for its rider for it brayed out a grating objection before twisting its neck and delivering a bite to Chops's foot. The outlaw swore loud and long but fell to abrupt silence when Evadine mounted Ulstan and fell in alongside.

"'S this way," Chops muttered, shrinking low in the saddle and pointing to the track snaking beyond the tower towards the pass.

Our guide's prediction about finding the Brandyman's Draw proved woefully accurate as we spent several hours scouring various gullies without result. Finally, when the sun crested the eastern ridgeline, Chops straightened on his donkey's back and pointed to a jagged notch ascending the slope to the south of the pass.

"No horse can climb that," Wilhum said, eyeing the track, which resembled a sharp-edged scar along the face of the incline.

"Then we proceed on foot," Evadine said, dismounting from Ulstan's back. "Master Chops will be happy to lend us his sturdy beast to carry our supplies, I'm sure."

Chops surprised me by getting down from his donkey and handing over the reins without complaint. He had maintained the same stiff, inexpressive aspect throughout our search, something I ascribed to his deluded fears over having consorted with the Malecite Witch. Outlaws are ever a superstitious lot and Chops was evidently no exception.

"Sooner we find him, the sooner you get your sovereigns," I advised him quietly, heaving a water skin onto his donkey's back. "Then you can take yourself far away from the Anointed Lady."

He replied with a short nod, eyes darting towards Evadine before he started up the rocky confines of the notch. He scaled the slope with a surprisingly purposeful gait I ascribed to a determination to see his betrayal done as speedily as possible, an attitude I understood full well. The journey here had instilled in me a general weariness with this whole enterprise, an impatience to get it done and be gone from this duchy. Our hunt for Roulgarth had left few illusions as to what we had wrought in this land. Everywhere we found recently beggared people facing hard winters, the crops that should have sustained them seized by Leannor's tax-farmers and the next season's harvest destined to be left rotting in the fields for want of hands to reap it. The sorrow and fury I knew Sihlda would have expressed over my part in this was a constant echo in a head already pained by the recurrent attentions of the throb. With Roulgarth captured there would be no more reason to be here and, upon our return to the north, Evadine and I could finally begin planning the promulgation of Sihlda's Testament.

To win peace, you must first spill blood. A quote from Mathis the Third, last Algathinet king of the first Tri-Reign. Sihlda had taught it to me as an example of fallacious thinking, terming it a fine illustration of the absurd contradictions often employed by tyrants seeking to justify their crimes. *Blood, you see, Alwyn,* she had told me in that musty nook where I learned so much, *only ever leads to more blood.*

Lord Ehlbert opted to join us in pursuit of Roulgarth, selecting two score of his most trusted kingsmen to accompany him. The rest of the Crown Company were instructed to skirt the mountains and make their way to the point where Chops claimed the Brandyman's Draw emerged from the peaks. Evadine chose only Fletchman to join herself and me in trekking across the peaks, telling Wilhum to stay with the kingsmen, "Only until you clear the mountains. When you do, feel at liberty to range ahead. I've a sense our quarry has a lead on us. If he's already made it into the southland, try and find his trail. Don't wait for me. Follow and capture him if you can."

"You know he won't permit himself to be captured," Wilhum said.

"No," Evadine agreed with a sigh, "but I would be grateful if you tried. For all his heretical violence, Roulgarth was a good man once. He deserves a trial at the very least."

We were obliged to wait for dawn before setting off, as climbing the ridge at night presented a hazardous prospect. It proved an arduous and perilous ordeal even in daylight. The sheerness of the slope required an ache-inducing effort and the footing, either frosted or loose, caused many a stumble. One unfortunate kingsman contrived to break his ankle when his boots lost purchase on a patch of frost. Lord Ehlbert gave voice to some rare anger in berating the fellow, for leaving him behind required the loss of another kingsman to help him back to the tower.

"I should leave your clumsy arse to freeze on this fucking mountain!" the King's Champion growled. From the way the pale-faced kingsman shrank from his ire, I divined that Ehlbert's temper, although not often roused, was something his soldiers had learned to fear.

We crested the ridge at noon, finding a shallow depression between two peaks. The deep trough scoured through this otherwise pristine blanket of snow made it clear our hunt was not in vain. "No more than a day old," Fletchman judged, crouching to retrieve a pellet of donkey dung from the channel. He sniffed it before tossing it away. "Animals are poorly fed. Reckon they won't last much longer."

We pressed on after a brief rest to recover from the climb, pushing hard while keeping a wary eye on the rocks rising to either side. Aware that Roulgarth might decide to set an ambush, Ehlbert had decided to split our party into four. A small advance group consisting of myself, Fletchman and a now almost entirely silent Chops proceeded ahead. The bulk of the column followed fifty paces behind while crossbowmen moved in smaller cohorts on the flanks. Fortunately, the tracks left by Roulgarth's band maintained a steady and easily followed course through the snow for several miles and we proceeded without incident until twilight. Night seemed to descend with unnatural swiftness in the mountains, the air taking on a lung-paining chill and the sky deepening to star-speckled black before we had time to pause and reflect on the wisdom of making camp.

"Gets narrower a mile or so on," Chops said in his now typical uninflected mutter. "Trail snakes its way around the Sermont. Can't walk that in the dark."

"The Sermont?" I asked, wincing a little as the question drew a gust of icy air into my throat.

Chops pointed to a conical peak to the south, a sheer-sided monolith that towered over its neighbours. "Tallest peak in these mountains," he said. "Never been climbed all the way to the top, so they say."

"Why would you climb a mountain to the top?" Fletchman wondered. "There's sod all there."

Both Evadine and Ehlbert were keen on continuing the pursuit despite the impending dark but grudgingly acceded to making camp after another hour's march brought us to the edge of a plummeting cliff. Here the Brandyman's Draw narrowed to a ledge barely two feet wide, hugging the face of the Sermont to wind around its southern flank. There was some debate about lighting fires but the depth of the cold soon put such concerns to rest; there would be no continuing the hunt if we froze to death before morning. The kingsmen had carried bundles of firewood which were soon stacked and set alight, soldiers clustering around the islands of warmth in tight huddles. Any worries over revealing our presence were obviated by something glimpsed by Fletchman's always keen eye.

"Is he taunting us?" I suggested as Evadine and I peered at the distant yellow-orange speck flickering on the mountainside several miles off. "Luring us on perhaps?"

"Or he's just beyond caring," Ehlbert said, stomping to our side. He had wrapped himself in a bearskin cloak and had his pipe clenched between his teeth despite the cold not allowing an ember to flourish in the bowl. I saw a sombre certainty on the knight's face as he regarded the distant campfire. "I doubt we'll have to chase him much further." His breath steamed as he let out a heavy sigh and turned away. "Come the morrow, he'll be looking for a reckoning. Seems we'll soon find out which one of us he most wants to kill, Captain Scribe."

Our journey the following day remains one of the most alarming and fear-filled memories in a mind rich with competition. Narrow even at the best of times, the route frequently thinned to a ledge no more than a yard across. Never fond of high places, I found the entire experience a prolonged torture of constant trepidation interspersed with moments of terror. Several times I was obliged to flatten myself against the face of the mountain and inch my way left when the wind blustered to a fiercer pitch. Although born to lowland forest, Fletchman proved himself an able and nimble mountaineer as he led the way. Chops was similarly sure of foot, though I took increasing note of his taciturn manner and grim aspect. The previous day his features had betrayed little emotion beyond fear of Evadine, but today I saw in it a worrying despondency mixed with an even more concerning glimmer of resolve. I considered voicing additional threats to keep him in line but a closer look at his sagging features told me this man had reached a point beyond fear. Besides, with Roulgarth so near, what could his betrayer do to impede us now?

Clearing the ledge took all morning, during which one kingsman had, with dire inevitability, contrived to lose his footing and plunge into the misted depths below. His scream was a loud, high-pitched wail that echoed for so long across the mountainside that it seemed the Sermont was voicing a reply. So it was with an unabashed groan of relief that I took the final few steps from the ledge to join Fletchman in surveying the route ahead. Once again, we were left in little doubt as to our course, for a deep trough traced through the snow to the top of a slope a few hundred paces ahead. Our goal was made yet more obvious by the sight of two men standing at the crest of the rise.

"Stay here," I told Chops, who barely seemed to hear the order, his wide, unblinking stare entirely captured by the figures ahead. "Ready your bow," I added to Fletchman, who had already begun to unlimber the ash stave from his pack. I tarried long enough for him to fix the string in place then dumped my pack on the snow and started up the slope. Fletchman followed behind at a short remove while Chops continued to stand and stare at his former leader. I knew it would have been prudent, and expected, to wait for Evadine and Ehlbert to come to my side. However, I had a sense of what Roulgarth intended this day and felt it would be better all round if his last ambition was to be frustrated.

"That's far enough, Scribe!" he called out when Fletchman and I had ascended half the length of the slope. Its angle made for an awkward climb, as it formed the shoulder of a ridge tracing down the western face of the mountain. A glance to my right revealed that it seemed to disappear a few hundred paces off, presumably where it met a cliff. Whatever Roulgarth's intentions, I found the prospect of fighting on ground such as this distinctly unappetising. In the event, it transpired that I was not his object this day.

"Where is she?" he demanded as I came to a halt. I could make out his features clearly now. His cheeks bore dark hollows beneath a beard made white with frost and I noted the tremble in his hands as they gripped his sword. Lack of food and continual cold will sap the strength from even the strongest man, yet his eyes blazed bright. Nearby, the corpses of two donkeys lay partially covered by snow. I guessed that the death of these beasts had been some kind of signal for Roulgarth, a final loss of fortune that compelled him to fulfil Ehlbert's prediction and turn to face his fate.

"Where is the bitch-martyr?" Roulgarth spat. "The Malecite Whore? Bring her to me!"

Hearing a crunch of snow as Fletchman bridled in response to his blasphemy, I shot a warning glare at the poacher before turning back to Roulgarth. I spared him only a cursory glance before focusing on his companion, a youth I had expected to find at his side when the time came.

"It seems madness has robbed this man of his civil tongue, my lord," I observed to Merick Albrisend, Baron of Lumenstor. He was of a similarly reduced state to Roulgarth, youthful face both lean and aged by hunger, yet his gaze was not so fierce. I saw no sling on his arm, indicating he had healed well since our encounter at Walvern Castle, and if he bore me any malice it didn't show on his face. His eyes shifted between his uncle, me and the growing number of kingsmen emerging from the ledge to gather to our rear. Of their own band, I saw no one. The last surviving Cohlsair, it seemed, was shorn of allies.

"Address yourself to me, Scribe!" Roulgarth snarled, stepping in front of his comrade. "And know that I have only rules of combat to parley this day. Go tell the witch you follow that we are destined to fight upon this mountain, and here she will be sent to the eternal torment that is her due."

"I regret, my lord," I replied with a bow, "that I will not be doing your bidding this day. Be so good as to give up your sword and surrender to the custody of the King's Champion, Lord Ehlbert Bauldry. In accordance with Crown law, you will be conveyed to a place of safety pending trial for crimes of treason, murder, thievery and promulgation of heretical falsehoods against the Risen Martyr Evadine Courlain."

"Trial?" A harsh, guttural laugh escaped Roulgarth's lips, his teeth bared in a near-feral snarl. "Trial by combat is my right and my due. Go!" He stabbed a finger at the base of the slope, where I saw Evadine's tall form had now appeared. "Tell her to face me. Unless her malice is matched by cowardice."

"That won't be happening," I told him, drawing my own sword, not without some initial difficulty for the frost had welded the hilt to the scabbard. "If you want to fight, fight me."

"You are not worthy of a knight's steel, Scribe." Roulgarth's face took on a mottled shade as his rage boiled over. He pointed again at Evadine. "Bring her to me."

"Worthy or not," I said, raising my sword before my face and lowering it in the traditional salute of formal combatants, "I'm all you're getting today. You should be grateful. Chops over there told me how you've been intent on my death."

Roulgarth blinked and his gaze switched to his betrayer. Chops had come to a halt halfway up the slope, seemingly frozen in place as he regarded his erstwhile lord with a face drained of both colour and emotion. I expected Roulgarth to rage at him, yell out a stream of condemnation. Instead he merely grunted and called out in a grim voice, "We found your brother's body. Gave him as decent burial as we could. When you see him, please thank him for his faithful service."

Chops gave no reply, but the words evidently had a profound effect for he sank to his knees with a plaintive sob. I spared him a brief, disgusted grimace and turned to Fletchman, finding to my gratification that he had already nocked a shaft to his bowstring. "As soon as you get clear shot," I told him quietly.

He nodded, no trace of recrimination in his gaze. For all his devotion, this man had the vestiges of an outlaw's heart and knightly notions of fair combat were no doubt as absurd to him as they were to me. Roulgarth was clearly in a parlous state, but I well recalled his description of beating the man who had cracked my skull. Ehlbert wouldn't like what I was about to do, and Evadine would surely hate it. But it was my role to protect her.

"And the boy?" Fletchman asked, flicking his eyes at Lord Merick.

"Only if he interferes. Princess Leannor will be disappointed if we don't return with one captive, at least."

Turning about, I started up the slope with a brisk, determined stride, careful to obstruct the Alundian's view of Fletchman and his readied bow. "Now then, my lord," I said, "let's be about it, shall we?"

The Alundian watched me climb the slope towards him without apparent concern, not even deigning to draw his sword. It was only when I closed to a dozen paces that his posture altered, angling his head and frowning at something to my rear. Suspecting a ruse, I at first resisted the urge to turn, only doing so at the sound of a loud, pain-filled exclamation from Fletchman. Spinning about, I found him staggering through snow stained red by a torrent gushing from a wound to his neck. Behind him stood Chops, a small, blood-covered knife in his hand. Where or how he had contrived to hide it I would never know.

I watched Fletchman stagger on for a few more steps before collapsing into the snow, twitching in the manner of fast-approaching death. My fury blazed and I forgot Roulgarth, spitting profane curses and churning snow as I retraced my steps intent on hacking Chops down. The villain paid no heed to my charge. Nor did he make any effort to flee. Instead, he turned to raise his face to the great edifice of the Sermont looming above and opened his mouth wide to voice a scream. It was a grating howl at first, but, as he gathered more air into his lungs, it became a roar, far louder than I would have thought one so thin could produce.

"That's the problem with traitors, Scribe," Roulgarth commented, causing me to halt and whirl to face him, sword levelled and ready. The Alundian, however, still hadn't moved or bothered to bare his steel. I found the sudden change in his expression jarring, the near manic desire for combat replaced by a weary but amused resignation. As Chops continued to roar his maddened sorrow at the mountain, Roulgarth smiled and spoke on, "Betrayal is in their bones, regardless of how much you pay them."

A vast booming came from above, a thunderous crack that had me hunching in instinctive alarm while entertaining the mad idea that the Sermont had decided to voice an answer to the outlaw's roar. In a way, in fact, it had. Staring up at the sheer granite flanks above, I thought at first that an errant gust of wind had caused a bank of cloud to slide down the mountainside. However, as this cloud continued to descend, and thicken in the process, I soon realised my error. Chops was still screaming, though his voice had become a thin, hoarse wail by now, one soon swallowed by the monstrous growl of the roiling white fury sweeping towards us.

Having once dangled from a noose in the full expectation of death, and spent a day in the pillory, I was not a stranger to impotent, helpless fury. Despite the full knowledge that running was pointless, the avalanche bearing down on us was moving faster than horse or man could hope to run, I am ashamed to report that I did not spend the last few seconds left to me engaged in sombre reflection on my many misdeeds in life. Instead, ever a slave to my own vindictiveness, I used those seconds in a vain attempt to kill Chops. This too was a pointless act since we were surely both about to die, and yet I still wanted to carry the satisfaction of ensuring his death to the Divine Portals. Whether the Seraphile would have looked askance at my spite will forever remain a moot point, for the tide of displaced snow and ice bore me away before I could get within sword reach of the whiskered bastard.

CHAPTER TWENTY-THREE

It would, I'm sure, reflect well upon my scholarship, dear reader, if I were at this juncture to shed some light on the experience of finding oneself carried off by an avalanche. Sadly, much of what followed is forever lost to me. It is my theory that there are occasions when mind and body are so overwhelmed with pain and sensation that one's memory simply refuses to accommodate the experience.

I recall running past Fletchman, bloody and twitching in the snow, before closing upon Chops, my sword drawn back for a killing blow. I recall the mountain's roar filling my ears and a sudden icy blast upon my face. I recall seeing Chops, still standing with face upraised, his gaping mouth screaming a sound that could no longer be heard, disappear in a blast of frost-flecked mist. After that all the world turned white and my last clear memory is the sensation of being gathered up and carried off. There was pressure but no pain. That only arrived upon waking. Before then, I was obliged to suffer another visit from Erchel. On reflection, I believe a full awareness of being tumbled down a mountainside amid a cascade of snow and ice would have been a more pleasant experience.

"You've always been a gullible bastard, Alwyn," came his greeting, called out from the depths of a misted field. It seemed his shade had forsaken the Dire Keep for even less picturesque surroundings. Even more bodies lay upon this ground, slumped mounds in the drifting fog transforming into the hacked and mutilated victims of battle when I came closer. Arrows and bolts jutted from carcasses and ground while lifeless eyes stared up from white faces smeared in blood and dirt. Unusually for a dream, I could smell it: the acrid mingling of mud, gore and shit unique to battlefields.

"You weren't here," I told Erchel. "Ayin killed you weeks before the Traitors' Field."

He had perched himself on the body of a knight's charger, its rider crushed beneath the mighty animal's bulk. Erchel busied himself with removing the unfortunate noble's gauntlet, grunting in satisfaction when it came loose to reveal fingers adorned with rings.

"Truc," he said with a shrug, reaching down to pluck a dagger from the ground. "But what makes you think this is the Traitors' Field?"

Despite the fog, as I looked around I discerned several differences between this field and the place where the Pretender's horde had met its doom. There the fighting had raged alongside a river in a shallow dip between two low hills. This ground was flat with no sign of a river anywhere near.

"Did you really think," Erchel muttered, frowning as he worked the blade of his dagger between the knight's fingers, "this realm had seen the end of war?"

"Another warning?" I asked, disliking the need to ask the question. Even as a phantom, I chafed at the notion of being beholden to this wretched soul.

"More like a promise." Erchel grimaced with the effort of sawing the dagger's blade through flesh to find bone. "No need to thank me for my last warning, by the way."

"I may have awoken in time." I shrugged, unwilling to concede anything to this imp. "How am I to know you made any difference?"

"You're not." He spared me an irksomely knowing glance before returning to his work, grunting in satisfaction when the finger came free, allowing him to claim the gold ring it had borne. "Think of me as a signpost, or a marker on a map. I can show you the path, but whether you choose to take it is up to you. The events of this day, however . . ." He squinted and flicked a hand to the surrounding carnage. "Sadly, there's no choice you can make that will prevent all this."

"When?" I asked, grating the question through clenched teeth. "Where?"

"An otherwise unremarkable patch of ground some time from now. Since it's always going to happen, demanding details seems a pointless task."

"Then why bother showing me?"

Erchel's features darkened and he lowered his gaze to contemplate the ring in his palm. "Why d'you think?" he asked in a sullen mutter. "Do you imagine I have any more choice over this than you do?"

I moved closer to him, my hand going to my sword. This dream preserved the garb I had worn on the mountainside, complete with weapons, and the murderous intent I had directed towards Chops lingered like a nagging hunger. "If you are nothing but a slave," I said, "then you must have a master."

"Of course I do." His smile returned, eyes sliding up to regard me with smug malice. "It's one we share. For, if I'm a slave, what the fuck do you think you are?"

It was the smile that did it, the same smile that had rarely failed to stir my anger when we were boys. The blade hissed free of the scabbard, rising and falling with a swiftness and precision that did much credit to Wilhum's tutelage and my hard-won battle sense. Erchel barely flinched as it cleaved his shoulder, biting all the way through his ribs to his sternum. Blood erupted in an ugly geyser as he tumbled from the charger's carcass, sliding to the mud without a sound.

"You never used to delight in it so."

I spun about, finding Erchel standing a few paces to my rear, the same grin on his lips. Snapping my gaze back to his recently dispatched corpse, I found it vanished.

"Killing, I mean to say," Erchel went on. "Always a hardship for Alwyn. A chore Deckin would punish you with. Time has made you vicious, old friend."

"I'd never tire of killing you," I told him, readying the sword for another strike.

Erchel regarded me without apparent concern as I advanced, his voice and face betraying only boredom. "You can't kill what's already dead. I won't even feel it."

I hesitated, torn by the desire to cut him down again, regardless of how little he seemed to care, and the knowledge that he had spoken true: I had delighted in killing him. I also knew that, had he stood just a little closer, I would have taken similar joy in slaying Chops.

Lowering my sword, I fixed Erchel with a hard, demanding glower. "What do you want?"

"To show you the path, as I said." He tossed me the ring he held. "And here it is." Catching it, I turned the golden band over in my fingers, finding it to be a signet ring adorned with a familiar crest. My gaze returned to the fallen charger, uncomfortable realisation rising within.

"You knew she was an agent of change, Alwyn." Erchel's taunt followed me as I approached the horse, skirting its bloody, gape-mouthed head to peer at the face of its rider. "You knew what she would bring, yet you followed her anyway."

The cause of the rider's demise was obvious in the acute angle of his neck, broken when his head collided with the ground. His helm's visor had been jarred loose by the impact, revealing the face in full. King Tomas Algathinet, first of his name, had met a noble end. His armour bore numerous dents and scars and he had died while still clutching his sword, the blade bloody down to the hilt. Neither courage nor his sister's guile, however, had saved him from a falling horse and a snapped spine.

"Not a great king, it must be said," Erchel went on. "But far from the worst. You should have seen what his great-great-grandfather got up to." He laughed and shook his head in rueful disgust. "And you thought I was a monster."

I found I couldn't look away from the dead king's face, my mind locked in feverish calculation. *A kingdom without a king. Who will rule in his stead? And how much blood will spill to decide it?*

"Evadine does this?" I asked, finally tearing my eyes from Tomas to Erchel. He stood idly pushing a toe to the jaw of a slain man-at-arms, taking small amusement from the way the corpse's mouth opened and closed in a parody of speech.

"Alwyn's gone all scared," Erchel said in a high, childish voice, flapping the jaw in concert with his words. "Because Alwyn's a silly, gullible fucker who really thinks his pretend Martyr's going to make Sihlda's Testament the law of the land one day."

My rage boiled anew and I advanced towards him once more, fully intent on hacking his head off this time and not caring whether he felt it. Before I got close, however, a hard chilly wind blasted across the field with sufficient force to bring me to a halt.

"You need to know that this is where it truly starts," Erchel said, his voice serious now, albeit possessed of a reluctant note, a slave compelled to an unwanted duty.

"Where what starts?"

He laughed, the sound filled with as much pity as scorn. "The madwoman you made a Martyr isn't wrong about everything, Alwyn. The Second Scourge is coming, and here—" he jerked his head at Tomas's regal corpse "—is where it's born."

The gale rose with fresh violence then, the implacable, icy grate of it on my skin causing me to hunch low. Snow gusted in thick flurries, swiftly rendering Erchel into a faint shadow. "Her visions are real, Alwyn!" he called to me through the whipping howl of the wind. "But she sees truth when she should see lies! She's lost to those lies now! It's too late for her! In time you'll need to accept that! But . . ."

A blast of air sent me to my knees, the force of it sending an icy wave through my entire body. I shuddered, feeling this dream slip away, but still straining to hear Erchel's parting words.

". . . it's not too late for you . . ."

"Zeiteth dien uhl?"

Voices. Words. Dim, distant. Echoing through a world of gently shifting clouds.

"Eila Tierith."

The voices grew louder. Curious, lilting, high-pitched. I wanted them to go away. I wanted to go back to sleep, lose myself in these soft, billowing clouds, for they were warm, enfolding me like the blanket one of the whores had given me during a frosty night so long ago . . .

"*Ai, Ishlichen!*" Something small and hard jabbed into my back. "*Lihl zeiteth?*"

The jab came again, prodding hard enough to cause pain, ripping away my wonderful blanket and summoning a rush of cold that enclosed me like the frozen fist of a sadistic giant. A yell escaped me as I jerked and spasmed my way into consciousness, feeling snow subside from my head as I blinked clouded eyes at a pair of vertical smudges close by. Rapid blinking transformed the smudges into two small, fur-clad figures staring at me with wide, frightened eyes. I jerked again as another spasm of cold wracked me, whereupon one of the figures dropped the stick it had poked me with.

"Wait . . ." I croaked, seeing the pair exchange a panicked glance. I shuddered with the effort of freeing an arm from the snow and ice that covered it, flailing it at them which, of course, had the effect of causing them to turn and flee. I groaned and sagged in despair as the sound of their small feet pounding snow faded into the distance.

I spent some time face down, grunting in response to various pains which were busily making themselves known as feeling coursed its way through my body. Fiery stings to my forehead and chin told me I had acquired some new scars to add interest to my already disordered visage. The grind and ache of my ribs told of a chest that had suffered through considerable pressure and repeated blows. However, my legs were the most worrying for they remained completely numb.

After some bleary-eyed twisting about, performed to the accompaniment of a good deal of agonised shouting, I found myself to be buried up to the waist in a tall pile of snow and ice. Several trees had also been half consumed by the cascade and some painful craning of my neck revealed the sight of a forest close by. Pines with tiered branches painted white rose tall above dark confines, into which led the footsteps of the two children I had scared off moments before. I could still hear their cries echoing through the trees, cries that would surely summon adult company. Their language, although indecipherable, was familiar. Clearly, the avalanche summoned by the pestilent Chops had carried me to the wrong side of a border no sane soul wished to cross.

Clenching my teeth, I dug my fingers into the snow and tried to drag myself clear of the imprisoning mound. However, denied the aid of my unresponsive legs and beset by pain, I managed only a few inches' progress before collapsing into a slump. Cold mingled with exhaustion has a curious effect, both combining to create a deeply uncomfortable inner welling of heat. For some time, I lay there and actually sweated as the abnormal fever burned in my core. When it faded, it left behind a treacherously enticing afterglow. Once again I found my mind returning to the whore's blanket from long ago, so soft it had been, never did I have a sounder sleep . . .

The steady crunch of trodden snow snapped me back to wakefulness, my head jerking up to regard a pair of fox-fur boots approaching with a purposeful stride. Forcing strength into my arms, I made a last desperate effort to escape, but it seemed no amount of squirming and profanity could free me, for my legs seemed to have become two blocks of useless ice.

"Done?" a voice asked, the word heavily accented and spoken in the gruff tone of an annoyed adult male. I saw that the fox-fur boots had halted only inches from my face and realised this fellow had probably been watching my pointless exertions for some time.

I said nothing, my mind feverishly sifting through every word, fact or morsel of rumour I had ever learned regarding the Caerith. As is often the way when panic takes hold, nothing came and I could only frown in wary annoyance as the man with the fox-fur boots went to his haunches before me. He had broad, heavy-jawed features bearded in black. His skin was light brown and speckled in the red marks that characterised his people. They covered his forehead down to his eyes, which were a bright shade of green. I would have found them pleasing to look upon but for the dark glowering of his brow. I could tell this was a fellow who didn't appreciate visitors, a fact further evidenced by the sight of the curved knife in his hand. I recognised it as a gutting knife, one that had been put to recent use for, even though the blade was clean, the hilt and the hand that held it were liberally spattered in gore.

It was the sight of the blood that finally dislodged something from my head, a single word scribbled down by another idiot who had found himself in similar circumstances. "*Espetha!*" I said, my fear making it a shout. To demonstrate my understanding, I spread the fingers of both hands wide, raising my hands. "Open hands," I added with a hopeful smile.

The green-eyed man's glower softened somewhat at this, though not as much as I would have preferred. If anything, his expression betrayed mostly grim amusement. I wondered if his mirth arose from my pronunciation or the absurd suggestion he abide by this suppos-edly sacred custom. It transpired that this was either a man with little regard for tradition, sacred or otherwise, or Ulfin had been mistaken in describing this aspect of Caerith culture.

"*Ishlichen* hands never open," the green-eyed man told me in broken Albermainish, taking firm hold of my hair and hauling my head up to expose my throat. "Why open mine?"

Another word erupted from my lips as his blade touched my skin, one that finally brought about the intended effect. "*Doenlisch!*"

I felt the sting of the blade's edge as he hesitated, a small trickle of blood beading all-too-brief warmth on my skin. More significant was the tremble I detected in the hand gripping my hair. "*Doenlisch,*" I repeated, speaking softly so the workings of my throat wouldn't cause his blade to cut any deeper. "I am . . . a friend to her. She has . . . blessed me." Not an exactly true nor exactly false description of my association with the Sack Witch, but this unwelcoming fellow couldn't know that. All he knew was that I had spoken a name which possessed obvious power.

The Caerith held me in place for another heartbeat or two, either due to indecision or cruelty, before releasing me with an angry huff. "*Ishlichen* friend with *Doenlisch,*" he growled in disdainful suspicion, although I had a sense he was speaking his own thoughts aloud. He watched me for a time as I feebly wiped the blood from my neck then crouched to take an ungentle hold of my arms and heave. Although plainly a man of considerable strength, it took several attempts to drag me clear of the snow mound. Once freed, he released me and made an impatient gesture with his knife.

"Up!"

I tried to comply but found my legs still unresponsive. I could do no more than rise to all fours, a manoeuvre that sent pulses of agony through my straining muscles, before collapsing into a useless heap. The Caerith assailed me with what I assumed to be some choice profanity in his own tongue before pacing about in evident reluctance. I required no special insight to divine he was considering leaving me here.

"The *Doenlisch*," I said, twisting on the ground to squint up at him, "she'll curse you if you don't help me."

The expression that resulted from this statement brought a crease to his brow and a quirk to his lips, as if I had said something absurd and worrying in equal measure. After another moment's silent contemplation, he sighed and stooped to take hold of my ankles, spinning me about and dragging me through the snow. He wasn't particularly mindful of obstacles throughout the journey that followed and I suffered several bruising encounters with tree trunks, fallen branches and hidden rocks. Fortunately, a resurgent flare of exhaustion soon banished my discomfort and I drifted back into senselessness to the sound of the Caerith calling out something in his own language.

Of course, I had no notion of what his words meant at the time, but my mind contrived to retain them all these years later so I am now able to provide a translation: "Open up the cowshed! I've got some dung for the pile!"

CHAPTER TWENTY-FOUR

The cow was an unfamiliar breed, glancing over its shoulder to regard me with dolorous, barely interested eyes from behind a thick fringe of brown hair as thick as fox fur. It gave a faint, inquisitive moo, then, receiving no response, flicked its tongue into a nostril, snorted and returned to the more important business of chewing hay. Its three sisters were tethered alongside, shaggy, horned heads dipping and rising from the fodder pile in between assailing me with a steady barrage of noxious farts. It had been the stink of their effusions that woke me, the stench soon swamped by the wave of agony that swept through my legs. I flailed about on the floor of the shed as they spasmed, the numbness from before replaced by the burn of life returning to benumbed muscle and sinew. Despite the pain, I took some comfort from the way they jerked about of their own volition for it meant I hadn't suffered any broken bones. When my wayward limbs finally settled into an aching twitch, I took full stock of my surroundings.

I had only dim recollections of being dumped here by the Caerith, such had been the state of my exhaustion. I remembered that it had been daylight then, as it was now, but the rumbling void of my belly and parched state of my throat made it plain this was not the same day. To my surprise, I found the shed door latched but not secured with either chain or rope. Perhaps my reluctant saviour harboured a wish that I would remove my complicated presence and trouble him no more. However, although feeling had returned to my legs I knew I wouldn't be walking again for some time. Even if I had the strength to rise from this chilly floor of hay-strewn clay, the chances of surviving the wilds beyond this shed without food or aid were slim.

Eventually, the discomfort in my legs subsided to a throbbing ache and I embarked upon a quest to get them to obey me. At first they merely flopped about, my feet performing strange circular gyrations that would have been comical but for the pain they caused. An hour or more of effort resulted in the ability to draw them up to my chest and back again without excessive twitching. No great achievement but it at least alleviated the growing suspicion that I might have suffered some permanently disabling injury.

The door finally opened when the angle of the shafting sunlight indicated it to be close on noon. The green-eyed man was the first to enter, followed by an older fellow of slightly smaller dimensions. The third figure was a diminutive old woman moving with a stooped back and the aid of a gnarled stick. Despite being the least physically imposing person in this shed, the obvious deference of her two companions left me in little doubt as to which of them enjoyed the most authority. Her long white hair swayed as she made laborious progress towards me, her stick drawing a rhythmic tap from the floor which I felt to be unnaturally loud. Coming to a halt before me, she leaned closer, a face that was all creases and age spots looming from between dangling white braids. Her eyes were green, like those of my rescuer, though I was surprised to find them even brighter than his, like two glittering emeralds in a leather mask.

I returned her stare, sensing that to look away would be a mistake at this juncture. The notion of once again making mention of the *Doenlisch* rose then faded from my mind. There was a rare but obvious pitch of insight in this woman's gaze that warned me against speaking until required by necessity. Her eyes narrowed as she reached out a hand, trembling with age rather than trepidation. Her fingers hovered close to the cut on my forehead just for a second, then she snatched it back.

I saw both anger and concern flicker across her brow before she calmed herself and spoke in clear, barely accented Albermainish, "So, you weren't lying." Her words possessed a contemplative note and I knew they were only half directed at me. A decisive grimace flattened her cracked lips and she turned to her companions, grunting out a short sentence in the Caerith tongue that sent both hurrying from the shed.

"Did she send you?" the old woman asked, groaning as she sank to her haunches before me. Of course, I had no doubt as to the object of her question but worried over the consequences of revealing all I knew of the Sack Witch. Clearly, she had considerable importance among these people, else the mere mention of her name wouldn't have saved me. But importance didn't necessarily equate to respect or regard. For all I knew, the Sack Witch was as much an outlaw here as I had once been.

"You know her?" I asked. Answering a question with a question was an old ploy, but one this ancient soul proved too clever to fall for.

"No games!" she snapped, hefting her stick to deliver a painful blow to the top of my head. "And don't lie, boy. I've no patience for it and my grandson has a very sharp axe."

I rubbed my head and gave her a frown of recrimination which signally failed to arouse the slightest indication of sympathy or compassion. Instead, her frown deepened in insistence and she raised her stick again.

"No, she didn't send me," I said, raising my hands. "But I am a friend to her and she to me, as I think you can tell."

"Friend." Her lips twisted in disdain. "Silly word, one of many used by your silly people. She is not your *friend*, boy." She settled back into a squat, stick clutched between two hands as she studied me in obvious consternation. I let the silence persist, my attention drawn to the trinkets dangling from a corded bracelet on her wrist. Most were meaningless pieces of abstract metal, but one was a crow skull, very much like the one that adorned Raith's bracelet all those years ago.

"Seen this before?" the old woman asked, noting my interest.

"An . . . acquaintance had something like it," I said, seeing no reason to lie. "He was Caerith too. A charm worker, or so he claimed."

These words brought forth an unexpected laugh, albeit one tinged with disgust. "Charm worker," she repeated, shaking her head. "And what became of him, this Caerith acquaintance?"

"He was murdered, by another Caerith in fact." I fixed the old woman's gaze, keen to gauge her reaction. "A man cursed with the ability to hear the voices of the dead. Perhaps you've heard of him."

I had hoped for some sign of fear, but instead the aged Caerith's features took on a grim, knowing aspect. "I've heard of him. I assume he's dead too?"

"Yes."

"You kill him?"

"I wish I had. Another acquaintance did it, by way of settling a debt she owed me."

She huffed and muttered something in her own tongue, another phrase my memory has seen fit to retain and permit a translation. "So, you took too long in the dying. But a fitting end, at least, to die at the hands of those you wished to emulate."

"I always wondered," I ventured as the woman lapsed into a silence of disconcerting length, "what led to his curse? And how it came to be that he roamed the lands of my people as a chainsman."

"Chainsman?" she asked with a squint. I could tell she understood the meaning of the word, though her voice was coloured by doubt. "That was how he spent his years?"

"It was. And quite horribly good at it he was too. His . . . curse made him amply suited to the role. Not easy to slip a chain when the shades of those you wronged linger to whisper a warning in your gaoler's ear."

A muted but discernible scorn shone in her overly bright eyes then, reminding me of Sihlda in those moments when my mouth ran ahead of my knowledge. "You are a child," she murmured, her voice once again more reflective than disparaging. "Lost in a world of mysteries you barely comprehend. I should pity you, but I don't."

She gave a brisk grunt and used her stick to lever herself upright. Her head stood barely an inch above my own but my well-attuned instincts could sense the palpable threat she posed. If she wished it, I would die here. Of that I had no doubt whatsoever.

"The *Doenlisch* has put her mark on you," she said, "and I am just a bundle of tired old bones with little interest in her games. But still, her mark is nothing to take lightly. You'll be fed and your wounds tended. In time the *Eithlisch* will come and then we'll know what to do with you."

"*Eithlisch*?" I asked but my interrogator had evidently had enough of this exchange. "What does that mean?" I called after her as she tic-tapped her way to the door.

"It means my grandson probably won't need to sully his axe," she said. Her parting words were rendered faint as she exited the shed but still I caught them: "Or you could just piss off and perish in the snow, spare us all this trouble."

True to the old woman's word, food was duly provided, together with a foul-smelling but effective balm for my various cuts. I was also given some form of bitter-tasting cordial that served to alleviate my aches. A day or so of sustenance and medicine allowed me to stand, albeit with a great deal of strained groaning. With the passage of two more days I actually managed to hobble to the door of my unsecured prison. Pushing the door ajar revealed a frosted treeline a dozen paces off, but some careful peering to either side brought glimpses of buildings. They were difficult to make out due to the snow, but I gained an impression of unfamiliar architecture from the broad, slanted roofs and low walls. A few people walked between the structures, most sparing me a short, inquisitive glance. The absence of a guard outside my shed door indicated the old woman had been entirely sincere when expressing her desire for me to simply go away.

Days wore on with what I found to be increasing tedium and an aggravating indifference from my hosts. The only Caerith I met with any regularity was the well-built fellow who had rescued me. It appeared his role as saviour meant he also enjoyed the dubious chore of feeding me, a task he performed every three days with few words despite my attempts to elicit conversation.

"She's your grandmother, isn't she?" I asked one day as he appeared at the door with a sack of onions and bread. "The old woman with the stick," I added when he replied with only a suspicious frown. "I can see it in your face. Same nose, same jaw. I assume she has a name? So must you, for that matter. Mine's Alwyn, by the way."

"Eat," my visitor instructed, dumping the sack at my feet. "And shit . . ." he fumbled for the right word as he waved an arm at the woods ". . . further from here. You stink worse than cows."

"That, good sir, is impossible." I smiled. He didn't, instead turning and stomping off without consenting to offer another word.

As is often the way when the body heals, the next day saw a sudden improvement in my condition. My breath was no longer laboured and my various aches were all dimmed or even vanished. My lightened mood was darkened somewhat by the accompanying realisation that the throb had returned, or rather I was more aware of it in the absence of competing distractions. The fact that I no longer had any elixir to banish what I knew would soon grow to be much more than an annoyance served as an additional worry.

Pushing my fears away and in need of a diversion, I embarked upon my first foray from the vicinity of the shed. It was still early and there were only a few folk about as I wandered through what I discovered to be a sizeable village. The Caerith, it seemed, felt no compulsion to clear a forest to make way for their dwellings. All these one-storey houses with their broad, shallow-angled roofs had been built amid the trees or, in a few cases, around them. The larger structures were all constructed to form circular buildings around the thick trunks of ancient oaks or yews. I counted thirty separate houses before a resurgence of the throb compelled me to less demanding tasks. The pain was severe enough to bring me to a halt, my vision dimming and pulse pounding as I rested against the trunk of a pine near the forest's edge.

When the throb eventually abated after some deep breathing and pained wincing, my vision cleared to afford me a view of what lay beyond the western edge of the village. A near-vertical cliff rose from a wide stretch of broken, boulder-strewn ground, forming the flank of a tall peak that rivalled the Sermont in height. As my gaze tracked over the snow-covered boulders I discerned a certain regularity in their arrangement, finding it all a trifle too neat to be the work of nature. Leaving the forest behind to venture closer, I made out hard edges and sharp corners on the fallen stone that could only be the work of human hands. These were ruins, not boulders.

Further exploration revealed lanes between the dense clusters of rubble. I divined that this had once been a town, perhaps even a city judging by the way the sprawl of disordered, crenellated snow swept around the base of the mountain. Also, following one of the lanes, I found that it connected to several others in a junction from which a larger, broader path proceeded towards the mountain. My newly acquired strength began to flag as I started along this road, coming to a halt several times as my legs weakened and the throb resumed its irksome nagging. Unwilling to surrender to these ailments, I forged on, keen to discover the destination of this thoroughfare since it seemed odd for a road to lead to a sheer cliff.

Soon enough, my efforts were rewarded by the sight of an opening in the base of the cliff. From a distance of a few hundred paces, it appeared as just a narrow, jagged-edged cave mouth, sure to grow to impressive dimensions as I ventured closer. More intriguing still was the fact that the road I followed didn't end at the cave, but instead proceeded directly into the dark confines of the mountain itself.

My battle-won instincts had been dulled by recent experience, but they were not so faded as to miss the creak of a drawn bow an instant before it loosed. Jerking to the side, I felt the rush of air and heard the fluttering buzz of an arrow passing within a foot of my head. It careened off a nearby chunk of masonry with the high-pitched ping of steel on stone as I sought cover behind the largest boulder I could find. By now, however, my strength had reached its lowest ebb and I could only stumble against a plinth before sliding down its side with a sigh of mingled defeat and relief.

"*Kulihr zeiten oethir ohgael!*"

The voice was strident in its command, the words as always unknown even if the meaning was clear. Blinking rapidly to assuage the fatigue-induced fog, I saw a young woman advancing towards me from the ruins on the opposite side of the thoroughfare. She wore deerskin trews and jerkin, her shoulders covered by a short cloak fashioned from beaver pelts. In her hands she gripped a half-drawn flat-staved bow. Dangling from her belt were the carcasses of two recently caught rabbits, white fur stained in red. Her face was dark skinned with red marks encircling her eyes and, while I found the expression worn by the old woman's hefty grandson to be perennially unfriendly, this one was striking in its naked hostility.

"*Ihsa uthir lihl!*" she barked, pointing her arrow at me before gesturing with it to indicate the way I had come. "*Kulihr zeiten, Ishlichen!*"

"*Ishlichen,*" I repeated, voice dull. "I keep hearing that. What does it mean?"

The young woman had apparently exhausted her willingness to converse, raising her bow with purposeful intent, the stave creaking as she drew it further. I noted the way in which she positioned herself between me and the jagged opening at the base of the cliff.

"Something in there I'm not allowed to see?" I ventured, which served only to enrage her further.

"*Zeit!*" she grated, the bowstring now kissing her lips, features set in the hard focus of one about to kill. I had seen faces like this many times and therefore knew this to be no bluff.

"Just," I sighed, raising a hand and attempting to rise, "give me a moment."

Apparently not a patient soul, the huntress bared her teeth and stepped closer, too close in fact for it's never a good idea to approach stricken prey before you're sure it's dead. Summoning what strength I could, I twisted, delivering a kick to the huntress's legs which sent her into a disordered fall. Her bowstring thrummed, launching her arrow high into the sky. She was quick, snatching a knife from her belt and turning it towards me. But, quick or not, I could tell she was no fighter. A fighter would have scrambled clear before I pounced on top of her. I caught her wrist before she could strike, twisting it at the angle that pinches a nerve and robs the fingers of strength. Catching the knife as it fell, I placed the point under her chin, whereupon she wisely fell still.

"Killing a man," I told her, "is not like killing a rabbit."

Her nostrils flared and eyes flashed as I held the knife in place. Infused by the excitement of the moment I realised my aches had vanished. However, the liberating flush of relief was dimmed by the awareness that I was a fairly large man lying on top of a far smaller woman while holding a knife to her throat. *Erchel would've been proud,* I thought, grimacing in shame before raising myself up. I slashed once with the knife, severing the cord securing one of the rabbits to her belt.

"I'm tired of onions," I told her, wincing as I regained my feet, rabbit in hand. "My apologies for any offence caused," I added, tossing the knife on the ground and turning to walk back the way I had come.

I expected some form of punishment but the night and much of the following day passed without incident. Lacking a cooking pot, I skinned and spitted my stolen game using the broken tip of an old sickle blade I found beneath some piled hay in the darkest corner of the shed. Come noon, the beast was fully roasted and ready to be gobbled down by my eager, salivating mouth. So it was with considerable annoyance that I heard a sudden commotion from the direction of the village followed by the sound of running feet. The old woman's grandson duly appeared just as my makeshift blade was poised to slice the first morsel from the carcass. He wore a flushed urgent expression and carried a thick stave, the purpose of which I was quick to guess.

"You couldn't have come to beat me last night?" I enquired. He regarded me with a short glare of puzzled annoyance before pointing his stave at the village.

"You come!" he instructed. "Now!"

I hope they don't have a pillory, I thought, slicing off a large chunk of meat and cramming it into my mouth before rising to comply. It seemed strange that the huntress had waited a full day before reporting my transgression, but, as something of an expert in grudges, I knew well that vengeful souls will often let their grievance fester a while before acting on it.

I found the village busy with more people than I previously suspected it housed, well over a hundred Caerith gathered in the central clearing near the largest building. Never having seen so many of their kind in one place before I was struck by the disparateness of them all. Some had skin as white as marble while others were bronzed or dark like the folk who lived across the southern seas. Hair colour was similarly varied, featuring rich lustrous red alongside jet black and silver grey. Their stature was also far more varied than seemed natural, six-footers standing alongside stocky types barely five feet tall, or others possessed of a lissom slenderness. The only obviously shared characteristic came in the form of their marks. They all had them, red flecks that discoloured faces and the exposed skin of hands and forearms. The patterns changed from face to face, as did the density, but no Caerith I saw, then or later, ever lacked a mark of some kind.

I sensed a palpable tension as I approached the crowd, although no voices were raised. The air seemed to hum with mingled anger and fear. The crowd was formed into a dense circle, all eyes turned to regard whatever lay at its centre. My escort barked out something in Caerith that caused the throng to part before us, revealing the object of their attentions.

The old woman stood there, hunched as before, features set in grim resolve as she cast her bright eyes over a pair of bound kneeling men. Seeing their faces, still recognisable despite the thickened beards, bruises and haggardness born of cold and hunger, I couldn't contain the laugh that escaped my lips.

"My lords," I said, making my way through the parted crowd to offer a bow. "I bid you welcome."

Lord Roulgarth was plainly close to collapse and could only reply with a snarl and a weak jostle that barely strained the rope coiled about his chest and arms. His eyes, however, were fully alive with a bright and shining hate. Next to him, Merick Albrisend was in a less parlous state and demonstrated a previously unsuspected wisdom by providing no response at all.

"My great-niece found these two hiding in a cave a few miles north," the old woman said, gesturing for a third figure to come forwards. The young huntress from the day before afforded me a tense glare that was more guarded than angry. If she had told her aunt of what had transpired between us, the old woman gave no sign of it.

"These are known to you, I see," she went on. "Are they enemies?"

I saw then that standing behind the two captive lords were five Caerith, all bearing axes. The group consisted of two women and three men, all of hardy appearance, holding their weapons with the firm grip that told of familiarity. Their clothing was similar to that of the young huntress, but augmented by wrist and shoulder guards fashioned from hardened leather. Their faces were as mismatched in colour as the rest of the crowd, but far richer in scars. The huntress might not know how to fight, but this lot certainly did. Although I couldn't sense any obvious bloodlust in them, neither did I find reluctance in those firm hands and they all looked to the old woman with expectant eyes.

I owe you nothing, my lord, I thought, staring hard into Roulgarth's hating gaze. I knew that, had Walvern Castle fallen to this man, there would have been no mercy shown to me or any of those I commanded. Strangely, despite a lifetime of frequent indulgence in the drug of vindictive spite, I found I had none for this man, or his nephew. The Grey Wolves had spilt innocent blood, to be sure, simple drovers and cartmen butchered for the crime of bringing supplies to the Crown army. But in war, was killing truly murder? And had I not also done my share?

"Are they enemies?" the old woman repeated with an impatient snap.

Why does she feel compelled to ask? I wondered, my eyes sliding from the unfortunate lords to the aged Caerith. *Why not just kill these two interlopers and have done?* A certain realisation came to me then, something that should have dawned at our first meeting but my reduced state had denied to me.

"It occurs to me," I said, turning to face her, "that I've yet to learn your name. Or the name of anyone else in this village. I should like to hear it now."

The already unnatural shine of her eyes seemed to glow even brighter as her gaze narrowed. "You were not called here to bandy words, *Ishlichen.*"

"There," I said, jabbing a finger at her, "a name. Your name for me. I imagine it's what you name all my people. I'd also wager that it's far from complimentary."

"A wager you would win," the old woman grated. "It means a thing of little or no value. Worthless refuse to be discarded."

"Yet you didn't." I moved towards her, my approach stirring the five axe-bearing warriors into tensed readiness until the old woman held up a hand to calm them. "You kept me," I went on, voice low as I halted barely a footstep from her, looking down into her resentful squint. "I think I know why." Leaning closer so that only she could hear, I spoke in a murmur. "You pretend indifference to the *Doenlisch*. In truth, you're terrified of her. Which makes you also terrified of me." I paused to glance at the two Alundians. "Else, why would you need my permission to kill these two?" Looking back, I found her gaze steady but her mouth tightened, one crinkled corner of it twitching.

"These men are vital to the *Doenlisch*'s plans," I told her. "Plans you profess not to care about. You will spare them, and you will tell me your name. If I'm wrong, have your warriors cut us all down here and now."

Although, but for her squint and the fractional twitch of her mouth, she betrayed no clear sign of contemplation, I feel certain she considered it. One short word from her and the irksome annoyance of our intrusion would be over. But one so old is fully aware of the inconvenient fact that all actions have consequences, some far more severe than others.

"Uhlla," she said, voice as dry and arid as a desert. "My name is Uhlla."

"Alwyn Scribe." I bowed. "At your service." I straightened and gestured to the prisoners. "May I present Lords Merick Albrisend and Roulgarth Cohlsair, late of the Duchy of Alundia. These fine noble persons find themselves lacking a home at present and would, I'm sure, greatly appreciate your hospitality."

The smile slipped from my lips as I fixed her with a glare of my own, voice hardening. "We shall require a house. I'm sick of those fucking cows."

CHAPTER TWENTY-FIVE

From what I could gather, the house they gave us had been the abode of a recently deceased old man. It nestled in its tilted, moss-covered glory against the old, gnarled trunk of a yew that was more round than it was tall. Tree and house were positioned at a predictable remove from the rest of the village, although it put us in fortuitous proximity to a fast-flowing stream. Upon dislodging the unhinged, part-rotted door I found myself confronted by a musty aroma, plentiful cobwebs and, judging by the chorus of panicked skittering, a not-inconsequential number of small prior occupants.

"It's still an improvement on the cowshed," I told Lord Merick as we carried his barely conscious uncle inside. Spying the remains of a cot in the centre of the gloomy space, we manoeuvred the noble's sagging bulk onto a mattress of piled sackcloth and furs, producing an explosion of dust in the process. Roulgarth made a weak effort at protest, mumbling words lacking all intelligibility save one which brought a plethora of unwanted images to mind, "Celynne . . ."

"Fever." I put a gruff note to my voice as I pressed a hand to Roulgarth's forehead. "How long has he been like this?"

Lord Merick didn't answer immediately, instead staring at me with hollow eyes that were too spent to show more than faint bafflement. "Why did you save us?" he asked, his voice as vacant as his expression.

"Because I thought you might be useful." It was a bald lie, for I had no expectation these two would cause me anything but grief. This young, half-starved noble, however, would have assumed the truth to be an attempt to gull him. "How long?" I prompted.

"Days now," he said, blinking and turning a sombre gaze on his uncle. "We would have pushed on after falling from the mountain, but he sickened too quickly. I found a stock of nuts in the forest that fed me for a time, but I couldn't get him to eat more than a few mouthfuls. I searched for more food but found nothing. My tracks must have led that Caerith bitch to our cave."

"Then that Caerith bitch probably saved you both."

I shot a glance at the door where Uhlla's grandson lingered. I had extracted his name during our short journey to this house: Kuhlin. He had surrendered it without argument despite the increased suspicion and heightened fear I saw on his face. Seeing his grandmother humbled evidently made a deep impression. "We need a healer," I told him, fixing him with a commanding glare when he didn't respond right away. "You know this word?"

Kuhlin frowned then nodded before disappearing from the doorway, offering no response to the instruction I called after him. "And be quick!"

"Why do they obey you?" Merick asked, his own features partially mirroring the Caerith's suspicion.

"The blessing of the Anointed Lady reaches even into the hearts of the worst heretics." I reached for Roulgarth's legs. "Help me get his boots off."

Kuhlin's return with the Caerith healer was creditably swift. He was one of the stocky types found in this village, possessed of impressively muscular arms revealed when, after a brief examination of Roulgarth's delirious person, he discarded his cloak to roll up the sleeves of his wool shirt. Wiping a hand across the lord's face, he sniffed the sweat on his palm before grunting out a few words.

"Water," Kuhlin translated. "Much water, and hot."

With Merick too weak for labour, I unearthed a large, bronze pot from the piled detritus of the house and filled it with water from the stream. Kuhlin obligingly built a fire near the door and fetched an iron tripod from which to suspend the pot. I suspected this chore to be a distraction tactic on the part of the healer. I knew those of their craft prefer to work without the annoyance of concerned friends or relatives, not that I was either. Merick had been banished from the house when he became alarmed by the sight of the healer liberally painting his uncle's naked body with some form of foul-smelling paste.

"I don't suppose," I said to Merick as we sat outside, shrouded in steam as the unused water cooled over the dwindling fire, "you encountered Chops on your travels? I'm very keen to meet him again."

"I'm sure you'll meet him soon enough," the young noble responded. Warmth and a bowl of gruel had apparently restored his spirits enough to add some acid to his tongue. "We found him wrapped around a tree with a shard of ice stuck in his neck. He'll be waiting outside the Portals for you with all the other sinners denied the reward of the Eternal Realm."

I replied with a regretful frown, affording Merick a short glance of appraisal. "Your arm healed, I see. Though I'd guess it still aches something fierce in the cold, eh?"

"It does." He fixed me with a steady eye. "Another grievance to settle between us, Scribe. And I'll see them all settled in time, have no doubt of it."

I grimaced in mock trepidation, raising my eyebrows at a puzzled Kuhlin. "He's peeved because I broke his arm," I explained.

"You did far more than that." Merick's voice dropped to a dangerous murmur. "My aunt and cousins now lie dead because of you and your mad Malecite bitch."

My humour leached away as the memory of what I had found in the Duke's Keep that night rose with unpleasant clarity. Also, his mention of Evadine, albeit in insulting terms, raised worries that had been simmering ever since I woke in the cowshed. Although I was sure she had avoided the avalanche that carried me away, what concerned me more was the course my apparent demise might set her on. She could feel compelled to come in search of my body, which would not bode well for her or any Caerith she encountered. But there was a deeper worry, an ominous sense that losing her principal confidant would rouse her to an anger she had so far resisted. Strangely, I feared her anger more than the prospect of her putting herself in danger.

"Your aunt was offered fair terms of surrender," I told Merick, tone hardened by the uncomfortable pondering he had sparked. "Instead she chose to die by her own hand, murdering her children as she did so. That makes her the mad bitch in my book, so spare me your outrage."

His face flushed red, lips parting to emit more temper-shortening words that may well have seen us come to blows if not for the healer's interruption.

He emerged from the house to wash his hands in the water we had warmed, speaking a few clipped sentences at Kuhlin. "Says the fever is . . ." the Caerith paused to search his memory for the right word to convey the healer's gruff pronouncement ". . . deep. Says sickness is from too much cold and eating bad food. He give something to make sleep." The healer went to a leather bag he left near the door and extracted a small earthenware bottle. "One drink in mornings if fever breaks," Kuhlin said when the healer handed the bottle to me.

"If it doesn't?" I asked.

The healer gave an affable shrug when Kuhlin relayed my question, speaking a word which, by now, I could comprehend without benefit of translation: "*Zeiteth.*" *Dead.*

I would be the basest of liars, cherished reader, if I failed to confess spending much of that first night entertaining some hope that Lord Roulgarth Cohlsair would fail to greet the dawn. I busied myself with clearing the various bits of rubbish from the house while Merick sat at his uncle's side. The stricken noble lay insensible for much of the time, only stirring to mumble incoherent nonsense or flap his hands in a near-comic parody of wielding an invisible sword. It seemed Roulgarth was still fighting battles, albeit in his dreams. I doubted they were pleasant.

It appeared that the house's previous owner had been one of those folk given to accruing things of little practical use. He had a particular fondness for oddly shaped rocks, animal skulls and, for reasons I was never able to discover, pine cones. They filled an entire corner of this single-room dwelling from floor to ceiling, all neatly stacked. Knowing them to burn well, I let them be and tossed the rest of the stuff out. It was as I began throwing the animal skulls into nearby foliage that the huntress reappeared.

She stepped from behind the trunk of a large willow dipping its frost-laden branches into the stream only a dozen paces off. I was impressed and a little anxious that I hadn't detected her approach. My fears were quelled a notch when I saw that she had her bow slung and her knife remained sheathed. Her features betrayed a good deal of caution as she came closer, but also a stern determination. Given that she hadn't come to kill me I couldn't divine the purpose of her visit and so said nothing as she halted a few feet away.

"*Lilat*," she said after some awkward matching of stares, pointing to the skull in my hands. It was that of a fox, its dimensions indicating a beast somewhat smaller but bigger of ear than its northern cousins.

"Fox," I said, holding up the skull. "You want it?"

She frowned in consternation then pointed at the skull once more, repeating, "*Lilat*," before pressing the hand to her chest. "*Lilat*."

"Ah," I said in understanding. "Your name. You share it with this." I turned the skull about, gaze slipping from it to the huntress. "It's a good fit, I must say."

She spent a moment chewing her lip in indecision, then, much to my alarm, reached for the knife on her belt. Holding up a hand in placation as I took a wary backwards step, she held up the knife then gripped her wrist with her free hand, shaking it until the knife fell free. After a moment of puzzlement, I realised she was mimicking the trick I had used to disarm her the day before.

Crouching to retrieve the knife she repeated the performance, then once again gathered it up before offering it to me. "*Eilicha*," she said.

"Want me to show you how I did it, eh?" I asked.

She frowned in muted annoyance and held the knife out again, voice hardening in insistence. "*Eilicha*."

"Payment in kind, my dear," I told her, not taking the knife. Instead, I tossed the fox skull into the brush then raised my hands up to my chest. "Rabbit," I said, making a short hopping motion. Just for a second, I fancied I saw a bemused smile play over her lips before she resumed her frown. Pointing to her bow, I mimed the drawing and loosing of an arrow. "You bring rabbit. I teach." I took hold of my own wrist and shook it. "You bring rabbit then *eilicha*."

The aptness of the woman's name became yet more apparent as she afforded me a final glare of predatory resentment before turning and walking away. I expected not to see her again, but when she returned the following morning it was with a freshly killed deer. After that, I never had another hungry day while living among the Caerith which, with the advantage offered by an old man's insight, I can now adjudge to have been all too brief.

As a student of the fighting arts, Lilat proved to be far better suited than Eamond, or in fact anyone else I had taught. Possessed of a natural strength and litheness augmented by instincts honed through a life spent on the hunt, she absorbed my every lesson like a sponge, mastering the wrist-numbing nerve pinch with barely a few minutes' tuition. It transpired that, like her cousin Kuhlin, she possessed some understanding of Albermainish. Although far less accomplished, she was sufficiently well versed to make it plain that she wanted to learn every knife trick I could teach her.

"You fight . . . much?" she asked after successfully shaking my own knife free of my grip. "You . . . kill much? You *taolisch* . . . warrior?"

This brought a frown to my brow. While I knew myself to be a soldier, ever since being compelled to join the Covenant Company I had felt it to be merely an adjunct to my true calling as both scribe and appointed herald of Sihlda's Testament. Yet, now I was a veteran captain with battles aplenty to my name, and a lengthy trail of bodies to show for it. Warrior, however, felt like too grandiose a title for a raised-up outlaw lacking a drop of noble blood.

"Of a sort, I suppose," I said, adding "yes," in response to her evident incomprehension.

"You *eilicha* . . . teach me." She nodded to the gutted and skinned deer carcass hanging from a nearby branch. "You teach, I bring."

I wanted to ask why she was so keen to learn such skills but knew the level of understanding between us would not allow for a meaningful explanation. "You teach too," I said, bending to retrieve the fallen knife. "Knife," I said, holding it up and raising a questioning eyebrow.

She once again proved the quickness of her mind by replying promptly. "*Tuhska.*"

"*Tuhska,*" I repeated then pointed to the hanging carcass. "Deer."

"*Pehlith.*" A smile appeared on her lips, one that turned to a guarded scowl when she spied Kuhlin approaching with the daily ration of onions. "I come . . . tomorrow," Lilat muttered before performing her trick of disappearing into the undergrowth with barely a sound.

I found Roulgarth both awake and absent of fever when I returned to the house, though his weakness was such that he could only lash me with insults rather than the whip he would have preferred.

"Outlaw filth!" he rasped, the undernourished but still impressive muscles of his naked frame straining as he attempted to drag himself from the cot. Fortunately, his weakness was such that he succeeded only in tipping himself onto the floor.

"And a pleasant morning to you, my lord," I replied.

"Calm yourself, Uncle," Merick said, helping the flailing noble up and easing him back onto the soft confines of the cot.

"You'd best kill me, Scribe," Roulgarth panted, trembling and eyes blazing. "Now, while you still can."

I ignored him and went about the business of feeding pine cones into the fire pit in the centre of the room before constructing the spit that would hold the deer. Roulgarth continued to assail me with varied and sometimes inventive insults, none of which raised more than a faint sense of pity in my breast. I might be the outward focus of his hate but one look at his ashen features, stripped of all artifice by sickness and pain, revealed a man beset by a terrible burden of guilt.

"Venison tonight," I said when a bout of coughing finally brought an interruption to his diatribe. "The meat of kings and lords. You'd like that, wouldn't you?"

Spittle flecked his lips as he girded himself to respond. "I want nothing from you but your death."

"Then you'd best eat. Else, how will you have the strength to kill me?"

Although I now recall this interlude as a peaceful lull in a life beset by storms, at the time I felt myself to be enduring a tedious form of genteel imprisonment. Roulgarth continued to recover and his habit of assailing me with hateful invective abated as his strength returned. Still, I saw little in the way of a softened attitude in his hard, promise-filled gaze, one that grew ever steadier as his health returned. He continued to cry out in his sleep sometimes, usually in the dead of night, his plaintive, distressed utterances often loud enough to rouse Merick and I. Always he called the same name in a voice so riven by guilt and regret that I found it pained me.

"Celynne . . . why?" he asked a shadowed corner of the dwelling one night. "Why did I never tell you? Why did I never tell him . . . ?" I usually endured his outbursts with stoic silence, but tonight he had roused me from a pleasantly dreamless slumber.

"Oh, shut your yap, you noble arse!" I snapped, causing Merick to rise from his bed. The young Alundian fixed me with a warning glare as he moved to Roulgarth's side, easing him back onto the furs. "Rest, Uncle," he murmured. "All is well."

"Uncle, eh?" I muttered. Still annoyed at my waking and knowing it would be a while before I could reclaim my untroubled rest, I got up and went to the piss-barrel, lifting my shirt. "Does that put you somewhere in line for the Alundian dukedom, my lord?" I enquired, sighing in relief as I released a fulsome torrent. "Or are you just a bastard like me? Some acknowledged, wrong-side-of-the-bedchamber whelp afforded a title to keep him happy? A common practice among nobility, I've learned."

"Watch your tongue, you ignorant wretch," he hissed back. "I am the true-born son of Lady Ehlissa Albrisend, sister to Lady Verissa, the late wife of this most honoured and brave man, whose feet you are not fit to grovel beneath."

"So, Lord Roulgarth had a wife." Bladder emptied, I shook the last drops from my cock and returned to sit on my bed. "No children of his own?"

Merick's face tightened, aggrieved, I assumed, by the very notion of relating personal matters to a mere churl. So his answer came as a surprise, one I suspected to be driven by a need to voice something he had never actually spoken before. "Lady Verissa died in childbirth," he said in a low whisper, as if worried his uncle might hear. "And her infant daughter with her. Lord Roulgarth accepted me into his household as a boy, my father having been slain in battle and my mother lost to the madness of grief." He reached out a tentative hand to Roulgarth's but didn't touch it. "By any measure, this man has always been my father, and I his son."

I felt a faint urge towards mockery, a taunting jibe or two, but they withered before reaching my lips. It was the nature of war to destroy families, rend them apart and scatter them wide. These two at least still had each other. It made me slightly envious, but mostly sad. When a churl's lord is banished or slain they will simply acquire a new master or move on to lands in need of labour. What use did the world have for nobles stripped of land and station?

I sighed and lay down on my makeshift bed, turning away and leaving Merick to his silent vigil.

By the time Roulgarth recovered enough to walk, I was spending much of my days with Lilat. Our explorations of the surrounding forest spared me the Alundian's dire countenance and alleviated the growing certainty that I would soon have to kill him. My knowledge of the Caerith tongue increased to the point where I could form sentences, albeit with a measure of clumsy mispronunciation that often set her laughing. Her facility with Albermainish also improved sufficiently for her to provide partial answers to some of my more searching questions.

"Uhlla teach me," she said when I asked how she had acquired her knowledge of the *Ishlichen* language. "She . . . learn from . . ." Lilat frowned, rummaging in her mind for the correct term ". . . grandmother."

"Uhlla's grandmother travelled the *Ishlichen* lands?"

This brought a guarded look to Lilat's brow, as if I had intruded upon some manner of private business. "Caerith sometimes . . . travel your lands." I detected a certain evasiveness in the way she looked away, pointing to the distant bulk of the mountains rising above the treetops to the east. "They go. Come back long time later."

"Why?"

Her expression became yet more guarded. "Sent . . . to learn," she said then gathered up her bow. "We hunt now. You teach after."

"Sent by who?" I pressed, which earned me only a scowl and prolonged silence for the hour it took her to track and bring down a white-pelted hare. It was as she worked the arrow loose from the twitching corpse that she grunted a short, reluctant reply. "*Eithlisch*, he send them."

"The *Eithlisch*?" I recalled Uhlla's mention of this name at her first meeting, and her refusal to elaborate on what it meant. Seeing Lilat's tension now, I divined it to be a person of considerable importance, also one to be feared. "Who is that?"

She avoided my gaze and scooped up some snow to wipe her arrowhead clean before returning it to her quiver. "He come soon."

"And that's bad?" I asked.

Lilat hesitated then turned to face me, her features drawn in a sympathetic grimace, rich in uncertainty. "Not know . . . yet. Come." She rose, hefting the hare. "You teach knife now."

"I think you've mastered most of what I can teach you about that." Looking around, I picked out a fallen branch amid the surrounding, snow-laden foliage. "Tell me," I said, walking over to retrieve the branch which I felt would provide two lengths of suitable wood, "what do the Caerith know of swords?"

"Not like that!" Merick's voice was filled with the scorn of the expert for the amateur and I found his accompanying sneer piqued my resentment no small measure. "Who taught you the sword, Scribe? A dance master?"

I lowered my branch, stripped of bark and crudely fashioned into a sword-like shape, and straightened from the on-guard posture Wilhum had taught me. I had just demonstrated the basics of the parry to Lilat, sweeping aside her clumsy thrusts by means of the flowing arcs it had taken me so long to master. Turning to fix the snobbish youth with a baleful eye, I said, "I was taught, my lord, by a knight of excellent reputation who learned his skills from one of the finest swordsmen of his age."

"The disinherited Lord Dornmahl, you mean," Merick returned. "As I recall, his reputation consisted chiefly of losing nigh-on every tourney he entered and forsaking his oath to the king to take up with the Pretender. He would have lost his head after the Traitors' Field if your Malecite bitch hadn't taken him for a pet."

"A tourney is not a battle." My rising temper made my words short. "And I'll thank you to watch your tongue."

Merick's face flushed in the face of my clipped instruction, his indignation roused by the disrespect of an outlaw churl. "Why don't I show you?" he said, shifting from the house doorway where he had loitered to cast his scorn on my lesson. "If I may, my lady?" he asked, affording Lilat a short bow before extending a hand to her wooden blade. The huntress appeared both amused and puzzled by his gesture, but duly handed her weapon to him on receiving a nod from me.

"We did this before," I pointed out as Merick turned to face me. "You lost and suffered for it."

"Much can happen in the chaos of battle." He gave a thin, anticipatory smile and adopted an *en garde* stance of his own. It was less rigid than the one Wilhum had drummed into me, his knees only slightly bent and sword held flat and level with his waist. He began to advance then stopped at the sound of his uncle's voice.

"Merick."

Lord Roulgarth stood in the doorway, back stooped with one hand resting on the frame. I judged his face to be less ashen than usual and his tall, lean frame was clad only in shirt and trews despite the chill. His gaze was steady and fixed upon his nephew.

"Uncle, I . . ." Merick began only to fall silent when Roulgarth shook his head.

"You want a lesson, Scribe?" he asked, emerging from the house. Moving to Merick's side he held out his hand, the youth filling it with the stave after a slight hesitation. Roulgarth twirled the length of ash briefly then raised and lowered it to me in a sketchy parody of a knightly salute. "Try me."

I let out a short, pitying laugh. "Hardly a fair contest, my lord. Given your current state."

"Yes," he agreed, the thinnest of smiles ghosting across his lips. "I should really hang some rocks about my neck to give you a chance."

He settled his gaze upon me and raised his stave until, sighing, I consented to match him. It happened far too quickly for my eye to catch, just a fractional lowering of his wooden blade as he took a half-step closer, then a blur followed by the uncomfortable rush of foreboding as my own stave was batted out of my hand. Pain erupted in my belly and I found myself on my rump, alternately retching and gasping for breath. It was only then that my treacherous memory consented to recall Evadine's words that day at the ford after my first encounter with Roulgarth: *You have learned much, but that man is of a different order.*

Still, I had never been immune to the perils of injured pride and, when the pain in my gut subsided and a modicum of breath returned to my lungs, I scrambled to retrieve my fallen stave. Rounding on Roulgarth, I found him regarding me with barely a change to his previous posture. His expression was mostly bland save for a weary but expectant arch to his brows. Had he taunted me, I feel my anger might actually have cooled. But this near indifferent certainty set a flame to my temper and I attacked without pause, gripping the stave in two hands and attempting an overhead swipe aimed at Roulgarth's crown. He barely consented to move at all, instead angling his body so the descending length of ash met only the ground as it completed its arc, whereupon Roulgarth was presented with my unprotected side.

Another eruption of pain, this time to my ribs. Over the course of the next painful few minutes I knew the kind of humiliation I thought I had left behind in the whorehouse or the outlaw-ridden forest of my childhood. I tried every sword trick taught to me by Wilhum, every additional tactic learned on the battlefield, and all I earned were yet more blows to different parts of the body. I had thought Althus Levalle to be the most lethal fighter I would ever face, but now I knew him to have been little more than a clumsy brute in comparison to this man.

As I stumbled away from yet another bruising encounter with his stave, I knew with infuriating certainty that I was being toyed with. It served only to raise me to greater heights of unreason of a sort that can rob a man of his pains and, if he's lucky, transform a duel into a brawl. Ignoring a strike to my sword arm, I let it fall and surged in close, attempting to drive a punch at Roulgarth's nose. Once suitably stunned, I would enclose him in as tight a bear hug as I could manage, whereupon this dance would descend into a wrestling match. This kind of rough and tumble had partially worked with Sir Althus but proved fruitless with Roulgarth.

Sidestepping my punch, he flicked the tip of his stave to my own nose, drawing an instant stream of blood, then brought it down to connect with my knee. It was as I fell that I contrived to land my only blow of the contest, blindly flailing my stave and, purely by chance, landing a solid thwack to his hip.

Roulgarth's own anger finally made itself known then, taking the form of a hard kick to my belly and a blow to my wrist that sent my stave tumbling away. "A true knight, Scribe," he told me in a ragged, cracking rasp, driving another kick into my midriff, "spends his every spare waking hour in the study of combat. A true knight knows the meaning of honour. A true knight—" the point of his stave pressed into my temple as I attempted to rise, pushing me down and adding a growing red cloud to my vision "—is not a puffed-up churlish scribbler who imagines he has the right to bandy words with his betters . . ."

"*Ascha!*"

The pressure in my temple stopped, then faded as Roulgarth withdrew the stave. Blinking, I looked up to see Lilat standing a few paces off, flat-bow drawn and arrow aimed at the Alundian's neck. The hard, narrow focus of her features made it clear that her willingness to loose was real, something Roulgarth evidently recognised.

"So," he said, a tired groan colouring his voice as he stepped back from me, "I kill you and these savages kill us. As if life had not tormented me enough."

He walked stiffly to my fallen stave, groaning as he bent his back to retrieve it. "My nephew has the right of it, good woman," he told Lilat, now glaring at him in suspicious reproach, her bow only partially lowered. Roulgarth gave a hollow laugh and tossed his stave to her feet before throwing the other to Merick. "I suggest you look to him for instruction. This villain—" he inclined his head to me "—knows only the cutting of throats and the stealing of purses."

Laughing again, he returned to the house, his mirth surprisingly long and loud for one so weakened by illness.

There was a time when such a thorough beating would have set my mind roiling with all manner of vindictive schemes. Yet, as I lay abed that night nursing my numerous bruises, none of which hurt as much as my injured pride, my lifelong addiction to vengeance failed to exert its usual grip. While various retributive cruelties came to mind, none managed to gain purchase on my soul. Resentful and sullen though I was, it was odd to discover that my main attitude towards Roulgarth remained one of pity. I wondered if I had finally grown beyond the lure of the grudge, at least where defeated, landless nobles were concerned.

Upon slipping from the pile of furs that formed my bed to approach Roulgarth's cot, I found him awake. His eyes were dull and face mostly expressionless save for an echo of the same weary expectation from before. "No knife?" he asked, arcing an eyebrow at my empty hands. The fact that he had expected me to come armed made me ponder the possibility that his actions had been designed to compel me to revenge. Perhaps he wanted me to wield the blade that would end his life since he lacked the fortitude to do so himself.

"No knife," I said, dragging a stool across the clay floor and perching my posterior upon it, wincing at my aches in the process. "Sorry to disappoint, my lord." I sat regarding him in silence until he consented to speak, his voice a fatigued sigh in the gloom.

"Then what do you want, Scribe?"

"Another lesson," I said. "In fact, I want many lessons. I wish to learn all the skills you can teach me."

Roulgarth raised his forearm and rested it over his eyes. "Why?"

"You're right, I'm not a knight and never will be. I can fight well enough when it comes to a man-at-arms or an unskilled noble, but not when it comes to one such as you. And I know when I return to the realm I won't find it peaceful."

"That's true, at least. It's only a matter of time before your Malecite Martyr and the king get to fighting. Keen to do slaughter in her name, are you?"

"She deserves my service, and my protection."

"But not mine. So, Scribe, can you please tell me, in the name of the Martyrs, the Seraphile and all that is good in this world, why I would ever consent to teach you one fraction of the skills it has taken me a lifetime to acquire?"

"Firstly, do you currently have anything else to do?"

A very faint snort emerged from beneath his arm. "And secondly?"

"You get to beat me every day."

Roulgarth didn't respond for some time, although I could see an increased swell to his chest and a new tension to his jaw that told of a man girding himself for something. Suspecting he was about to lunge at me, I inched back on the stool, preparing to dive clear of his grasp. Instead, he lowered his forearm to reveal a hard, intent gaze. "If I'm to do this, I require payment in advance."

"Payment?" I asked, brow furrowed. "You want coin?"

"No, you fool." Roulgarth grimaced and heaved himself up so that he half sat, leaning towards me. "I require answers to a few questions. *Honest* answers, Scribe."

I relaxed somewhat, though the implacable need I saw in his eyes kept me on edge. Whatever he wanted to know, I felt certain he knew he wouldn't like what I had to tell him. "Then ask," I said.

"After Highsahl fell," he began, eyes barely blinking as they searched my face, "all manner of wild rumour spread through the duchy. One story has it that you were the first to reach the Duke's Keep. That you led your band of cut-throat heretics into the duke's chamber where . . ." He paused, throat constricting before he forced himself to continue. "Where the duchess in her piety drank poison rather than submit to your vile advances."

"That's the story, is it?"

"It's one story. There are many others."

"If you thought it to be true, I suspect you would have killed me today regardless of the consequences."

His features twitched, body trembling with the effort of keeping himself upright. "But you were there? At the keep . . . at the end? What did you see?"

I considered lying, concocting some fanciful tale that would offer him a measure of comfort. But, as I had an instinct for detecting lies, I also had an instinct for those who couldn't abide them. Besides, I doubted Roulgarth was in search of comfort at that moment. His hatred for me was as nothing to the hatred he nurtured for himself, and hate can be as potent a drug as the finest poppy milk.

"They were all dead when we got to the keep," I said. "Every soldier, every servant, every noble. Dead by their own hand. I assume they drank the poison when they received word the walls had fallen."

"The duchess?" he demanded. "The children?"

"The same, apart from Lady Ducinda. Her mother gave her the cup but she drank only a sip. We managed to get her to our healer in time. I daresay you know Princess Leannor had her shipped off to Couravel where she's to be betrothed to young Lord Alfric."

Roulgarth's mouth twisted, his trembles becoming a violent shake. "A marriage that will never happen while there's still blood in my veins." He convulsed, back arching as he let out a series of coughs, which had the unfortunate effect of rousing Merick from slumber.

"What are you about?" he demanded, scrambling free of his own makeshift bed. I saw that he had secured himself a small knife, presumably dug out from beneath the general mess of the house. He levelled the blade at me, hurrying to put himself between me and his uncle. "Back, you villain!"

"It's all right," Roulgarth rasped, his coughing subsided. He slumped into the bundled sackcloth that formed his mattress, closing his eyes. "Tomorrow, Scribe," he muttered, "find some better wood. It's beneath my dignity to spar with such misshapen twigs."

CHAPTER TWENTY-SIX

My second lesson was a more prolonged and only marginally less painful repeat of the first. On this occasion Roulgarth administered his beating with one of the two wooden swords I had spent much of the morning carving. For the better part of an hour he stood in the centre of the circular patch of flat ground outside our dilapidated home and commanded me to attack him. This time I attempted a mixture of Wilhum's tricks augmented by my own, putting the same energy into my strokes and thrusts as I would in a real fight. Despite this, I enjoyed no greater success than I had the day before, acquiring another crop of bruises in the process. However, I took some small satisfaction from forcing Roulgarth to move a trifle more.

"That'll do for today," he said, having sidestepped an upward swipe before slashing his wooden blade to my overextended arms.

"I am bound to observe, my lord," I grunted, teeth gritted against the freshly acquired aches as I bent to retrieve my once again fallen sword, "that I am yet to hear a word of instruction from you lips."

He seemed about to ignore me but paused in the doorway. "As my own tutor once told me, Scribe," he said, glancing over his shoulder, "fighting is of the body, and words do not make purchase on the body the way action does. You learn to fight by fighting." He gave me a mirthless smile and disappeared into the house. "Now, bring me my supper."

Thus our daily routine was set, a morning of chores or hunting with Lilat, then an afternoon of beatings. Merick and Lilat followed much the same routine, albeit with less painful results. At my urging she had taken up Roulgarth's suggestion that she learn the sword from his nephew and the young lord proved an enviably less harsh teacher than his uncle. Curiously, as the days passed I noted how Merick's speech began to be peppered with Caerith words while the huntress's command of Albermainish increased to a point of near-fluency. In time, her version of our tongue became a strange melange of flowing noble inflection and clipped, churlish vowels, although I take credit for her impressively wide vocabulary.

"Inelegant," she said, frowning in disapproval when Merick contrived to trip her to the ground with a kick to the ankles.

"But effective," he said, offering her his hand. "An ugly *pehlith* is still worth eating."

The next week or so revealed the wisdom of Roulgarth's words, for I noticed a growing improvement in my skills. I began to discern patterns in his movements, the angle of his blade when he parried my inexpert thrusts and the way he would twist his torso to deliver the counterstroke. It allowed me to parry his blows for the first time, our wooden swords clattering together as I succeeded in deflecting a slash that would have surely opened a cut on my forehead. I saw a small shift in Roulgarth's features as he stepped back, a narrowing of the eyes that might have signalled satisfaction. If so, it didn't earn me any largesse, for, as quickly as I adapted to his tricks, he would unveil more. Still, I knew I was getting better, evidenced by the fact that my tutor's previous stillness increasingly transformed into measured mobility. This was partially due to Roulgarth recovering more of his strength, but not entirely. By the third week I even came close to landing a blow of my own and had the pleasure of seeing him draw a laboured breath when the bout ended.

In time our antics began to attract an audience. Some villagers would find reason to wander by and gawp at us in puzzlement or ridicule, often both. However, the most persistent and lingering spectators were the *taolisch*, the half-dozen warriors who appeared to be in permanent residence in this village. Unlike the other Caerith, they watched with a distinct lack of amusement, their eyes narrowed in shrewd appraisal. Their continued presence, and silence, eventually began to grate on me, not least because they were witness to my repeated failures.

One day, my mood darkened by Roulgarth introducing a previously unseen feint that had succeeded in putting me on my arse, I looked up to find this leather-armoured group exchanging murmured comments. Although absent of obvious scorn, I felt them certain to be uncomplimentary.

"If you're not going to join in, piss off!" I called to them, climbing to my feet.

This earned a parade of puzzled glances in Lilat's direction until, with some measure of relish, she consented to translate. I had noticed before how she rarely spoke to the *taolisch*, or they to her, and the huntress's expression when in their proximity was never welcoming.

One of the *taolisch*, a woman a few years older than the others, afforded Lilat a short, expressionless glance before she rose from the log she had perched on and came towards me, hefting her weapon. I had heard Lilat refer to this as a *tahlik*, which translated as "spear". I found the resemblance vague at best, the *tahlik* consisting of a yard-and-a-half-long, double-curved stave of oak with an elongated sickle-shaped blade sprouting from one end.

Upon drawing close, the woman spared me only the shortest glance before moving on to halt a few feet from Roulgarth. "*Elthtao*," she said, raising her weapon to her chest.

"It means 'fight', my lord," I told a bemused Roulgarth. "Apparently, she feels you to be the more worthy opponent."

For the first time since his recovery, the knight's features betrayed some amusement. It was just a small curving to the corners of his mouth, but it did signal the return of emotion I thought may have been stripped from him. "A judgement I find it hard to argue with," he said, stepping back and raising his wooden sword in a salute. "Then lay on, good woman, but know the risks . . ."

The *taolisch* struck before the last word escaped his lips, whirling, her sickle-bladed weapon flashing in an arc towards Roulgarth's neck. He ducked in time, albeit barely, shifting into a crouch, sword drawn back for a thrust at the woman's chest. However, she had already launched her second attack, leaping with her weapon raised high, spinning as she descended, forcing Roulgarth to roll clear of the plummeting blade.

They circled each other then, their faces set in concentration. I could tell Roulgarth had instantly learned to afford this opponent far more respect than he showed me, biding his time before launching an attack of his own. It came in the form of a feinted thrust of his sword point at her face followed by a broad but swift slash intended to sweep her legs from under her. The *taolisch* whirled again, leaping the arc of Roulgarth's blade and lashing out with her *tahlik*, the blade slicing the air a whisker from the knight's nose. It was an impressive display from the *taolisch*, but I quickly discerned that Roulgarth's previous move had in fact all been a feint, intended to lure her into a riposte, placing her within reach of his principal attack.

Lowering himself into a crouch, Roulgarth launched himself forward while the woman was still recovering from her spin. Instead of striking with his wooden sword, he drove his shoulder into her flank, sending her sprawling. The *taolisch* attempted to regain her feet, rolling away and rising to a half-crouch, but the knight didn't allow her the respite. His sword came down in a blur, trapping her *tahlik* beneath the blade, whereupon he backhanded her across the face. The blow was hard enough to draw blood and should have left the woman stunned. Instead her counter was quick and near instantaneous. It seemed as if her body convulsed, coiling snake-like to deliver a kick to the back of Roulgarth's head. The knight staggered from the blow, head lolling and sword hanging limp in his grasp as he staggered clear.

"Uncle," Merick said, starting forwards as the *taolisch* sprang to her feet, twirling her *tahlik* for a final blow.

"No," Lilat said, stepping into the young noble's path, face and voice stern.

Apparently, intervening in this spectacle went severely against custom. Merick began to object, trying to edge around the huntress, which only provoked her into shoving him back. Things may have escalated further if I hadn't moved to Merick's side, speaking quietly into his ear.

"Interfere and they'll kill us," I said, casting pointed glances at the nearby *taolisch*. They had all straightened, practised hands gripping their axes and *tahliks*, all regarding Merick with fiercely disapproving expressions. "This is more than just a bout of sparring. Besides—" I inclined my head at Roulgarth "—you should have more faith in your uncle."

Although the kick had been hard, I had experienced enough of Roulgarth's vitality by now to know he was not as stunned as he appeared. He waited until he heard the whoosh of the *taolisch*'s weapon then dropped to one knee, allowing it to whistle overhead. Reversing his grip on his sword, he thrust it underarm at the woman's face. She caught the point on her jaw, head snapping back and blood trailing from her already damaged nose. Roulgarth spun before she could recover, the flat of his sword striking the *taolisch* on the side of the head. The blow was delivered with expert care, not hard enough to kill but weighted with enough force to render the woman unconscious. Watching her fall, I understood that, for all his cruelty, Roulgarth had in fact been sparing me the worst of his abilities. I wondered why.

I cast a tense eye over the other *taolisch*, unsure how they would react to so sound a defeat of one of their own. Fortunately, I saw a fair amount of disappointment but no anger as they came forward to gather up the woman's limp body. I even caught glimmers of grim satisfaction on several faces, as if they had witnessed confirmation of a long-held suspicion. They carried her off in the direction of the village after casting a few words at Lilat.

"They say they'll come back tomorrow," she said, voice coloured by a sullen disappointment. "They want to learn the sword too."

And so that was how Lord Roulgarth Cohlsair, renowned knight of Albermaine and once Warden of Alundia, began his journey as educator to the Caerith people in the ways of *Ishlichen* warfare. In time he would, as the more educated among you will know, become far more to the Caerith than a mere teacher, but that is a tale for the more distant reaches of this narrative.

To my lasting regret, I failed to keep an accurate count of the days I spent among the Caerith. However, I was increasingly aware that weeks were becoming months, and that the snows of winter were gradually giving way to the sludge and dripping ice of impending spring. My Caerith improved enough to facilitate basic conversation, so much so that I managed to convey to the stocky healer my need for an elixir to banish the throb. For reasons I couldn't fathom, it had abated since taking up residence in the decrepit house and beginning my lessons with Roulgarth. I began to ascribe its absence to the possibility that my dented skull had finally healed itself. But, with the change of seasons, a series of awakenings to find my head gripped by an invisible vice made it clear I had merely been granted a temporary reprieve.

"Mmm," the healer mused, stubby but nimble fingers probing the uneven surface of my scalp with keen interest. His pronouncement after much subsequent prodding and pressing was short and easily translated. "You should be dead."

"Never was a more eternal truism spoken, good sir," I told him. Receiving only a crinkled brow in response, I added in Caerith, "Pain." I pointed to my head. "You make go away. Yes?"

His brow remained crinkled, but the matrix of creases altered as bafflement gave way to a worrying mix of agreement and regret. "For a time," he said, reaching for one of the many stoneware jars on a nearby shelf. Removing the lid, he revealed a granular paste of greyish hue, speaking in Caerith that was too fast and rich in unfamiliar words.

"Put here," he said slowly in response to my uncomprehending frown, miming dipping his fingers into the jar and smearing the paste over his upper brow and temples. "Morning and night."

"My thanks." I hesitated for an awkward moment, unsure of what payment he expected. So far my lessons with Lilat hadn't extended to the Caerith form of commerce and I realised I was yet to see a single coin change hands in this village. "I have . . ." I began, fumbling for the correct phrase and finding it absent ". . . owings to you."

This brought another set of crinkles to his brow, this time more amused than puzzled. "Owings?" he asked.

"You give." I held up the jar. "So I give."

"I am a healer," he said, which appeared to be the only explanation he felt necessary. I was ushered from his dwelling shortly after, his parting words mostly beyond my ken but I understood enough to grasp that he had a good deal to do and no more time to waste on my *Ishlichen* arse.

The paste had a potent, dung-like smell to it and a gritty texture that made me pause before applying it to my brow that night. However, a sudden flare from the throb soon banished my hesitation. The efficacy of the concoction became apparent the instant it touched my skin, birthing a chilly, not unpleasant sensation that increased into pain-banishing numbness as I spread it about. The throb faded quickly, bringing a sigh of relief to my lips, although my appreciation was not shared by my housemates.

"Martyrs' balls, that stinks!" Merick griped. "At least open the shutters."

The next day I awoke from the soundest sleep I had enjoyed for weeks, rising to find the throb attempting to reassert its viperous grip and taking great satisfaction from once again quelling it with another application of paste. Such a marvellous remedy would surely have commanded a fortune in Albermaine and I found it baffling the healer would part with it without expectation of payment.

"Payment?" Lilat asked when I posed the question during our morning hunt. "What is payment?"

We were ascending a wooded slope to the south of the village, Lilat leading me towards a ridge that overlooked the valley. I assumed she wished to explore fresh hunting grounds since we had taken a fair amount of game from the hills close to the village in recent days. The climb was steep and the footing often slippery on the recently thawed ground, not that the huntress seemed to notice. Although no stranger to traversing rough country, I was still obliged to labour in her nimble, sure-footed wake.

"Your people have no coin?" I asked when we paused for rest.

"Coin?"

"Yes." I fished in my boot to extract one of the few coins left to me, a single shek piece that had survived the avalanche. "Here." I tossed it to her. "This is coin."

Lilat turned the copper disc about in her fingers. The stamped head of King Tomas's father brought a glimmer of interest to her brow but it was plain she had no notion of what it might be for. "What does it do?"

"You buy things with it."

"Buy?"

It was then that I first understood the true gulf betwixt the Caerith and the peoples beyond their borders. The endless, all-consuming cycle of labour, trade and greed that characterised much of the outside world was unknown here. Explaining it all to one who had no concept of money would, I realised, require more than a hurried conversation during a paused hunt.

"Tihlun," I said, trying a different tack. "The healer. He gave me something but wanted nothing in return."

"He is a healer," she said simply, rising to resume the climb.

"So he works but expects nothing for his labour?" I persisted, once again struggling to match her fluid pace.

"Healers like to heal. As hunters like to hunt." She spared me a short backward glance, grinning. "And warriors like to fight."

"I'm not really a warrior . . ." I trailed off when she abruptly disappeared into a dense patch of undergrowth. This was a common occurrence during our hunts. Mostly she would reappear a few seconds later, but on occasion she might vanish for hours leaving me to make my way back to the village alone. I waited a while then concluded she had probably opted to pursue her prey without the impediment of my clumsy presence. "I'm a scribe," I muttered, turning about to begin the descent.

"What's that?" Lilat asked, stepping into view from the opposite side of the trail. She had demonstrated this apparently impossible ability several times and, although I suspected she did it as a jape, never displayed any particular smugness or pride over it.

"I write," I said, which brought forth only a blank uncomprehending stare. Sighing, I gestured for her to continue the climb and followed as best I could. "Writing," I began, "is the act of inscribing words . . ."

An hour later it became clear that, if Lilat found the concept of money difficult to comprehend, writing proved a far deeper mystery. "How can words be captured?" she asked when we finally crested the ridge. "Just with this . . . ink and paper?"

Drawing in a few laboured breaths, I perched myself on a nearby boulder and began to search for a stick to scratch a few letters in the ground by way of a demonstration. I stopped when my gaze happened upon what I at first took to be a tree of unusual size and thickness but, upon closer inspection, I realised to be a man-made structure of some kind. Vines and branches entwined curved walls forming a tower.

"What is that?" I asked, turning to find Lilat regarding me with a small, secretive grin.

"Something I wanted to show you," she said, starting forward.

Upon nearing the base of the tower, I judged that it was somewhat larger and taller than I had first assumed, rising to at least forty feet. The stonework visible through the covering of vegetation was aged and cracked but also possessed much the same precision I had seen in the ruins in the valley below. I made out the dim shapes of windows in the upper portions of the tower but could see no way in through the dense mass of bushes and tree roots enveloping its base.

"I found this when I was small," Lilat said. "When I told Uhlla about it she told me to stay away, which only made me come back again and again. I needed to get inside. It felt . . . necessary. Three winters I spent scouring every inch of this ground until I find it." She turned, gesturing for me to follow as she made her way towards a shallow depression on the ridge's northern slope. Like the rest of the ground here it was heavily overgrown and at first glance seemed impassable to me, but not to Lilat.

"Old buildings are like aged carcasses," she said, slipping into Caerith speech as she went to her hands and knees and crawled into a narrow opening in the foliage my eyes had failed to spot. "The flesh slips from the bones leaving gaps. It took a long time to find one wide enough to let me in."

"You've been inside this?"

She nodded. "I come when the seasons change."

"Why?"

"You'll see."

The damp earth soon gave way to the thick stones of ancient foundations, Lilat leading me through a narrow crack between two monolithic granite slabs. The space beyond was almost pitch-black save for a few narrow shafts of light slanting down from above. "Here," Lilat said, taking my hand as I groped around. She led me to the curving barrier of the tower's interior wall, my feet stumbling over an intact set of steps. As we climbed, the gloom receded somewhat but not enough to make me confident in my footing, despite the rapidity of my companion's ascent. Given the evident age of this place, I climbed in the expectation that my feet would soon meet empty space leading to a bone-shattering fall. Luckily, the moment of catastrophe never came and we eventually emerged into a broad circular chamber. It was lit by a tall window only partially overgrown by vines, so at least I could step upon its flat, dust-covered floor with some measure of confidence.

"I don't see much of interest here," I said, causing Lilat to nudge me and point upwards.

"Wait, it's nearly time."

I spent a prolonged interval staring in expectation at the empty void above until boredom caused my eyes to drift to the window. I had climbed several hills near the village during our daily hunts, but never so high as this and had therefore been denied a clear view of the lands my people referred to as the Caerith Wastes.

Even though spring had not yet dawned in full, the muted colours of the rolling hills, deep valleys and undulating forest combined to convey a sense of verdant richness. More mountains rose to the south-west, not so tall as those I had traversed to get here but still impressive. Ulfin's *Travels* had contained no descriptions that matched this, his depiction of the Caerith homeland mainly consisting of allusions to vile weather and treacherous peaks. It occurred to me that Ulfin's actual experience of this place and its people had been far more meagre than he pretended. Either that or he had simply been a very poor scholar, for what scribe would omit mention of a view like this? I had grown up amid nature but something about this land stirred a sense of unfamiliarity, the cause of which I arrived at after a moment's pondering. *It's wild*, I decided, eyes roving over the untamed beauty of it all, unscarred by hedge, wall or road. *It's truly wild.*

"All this—" I gestured to the vast wildness beyond the window "—is Caerith land?"

"All Caerith," she confirmed, eyes still raised to the gloomy loft.

"How many are there? How many Caerith?"

She appeared to find the question irrelevant or meaningless, simply shrugging and saying, "Many." She straightened suddenly, her hand gripping my forearm. "Now it happens. Look."

I raised my eyes once more then started in shock as a bright flare of light bloomed in the blackness above. Cursing and blinking wet eyes, I staggered back. When my vision cleared I saw a single beam of light describing a perfectly vertical line from the tower's roof to the centre of the chamber floor. It was too bright to be sunlight peeking through a crack. This was a beam that exuded both heat and light as I ventured closer. It wasn't so fierce as to prevent me playing a hand through it, but I knew allowing my skin to linger beneath its touch would soon result in a burn.

"How?" I asked, peering upwards once more.

"I could never climb high enough to find out," Lilat said. "But it must be some kind of glass. But that's not the interesting thing." She crouched, smoothing a hand through the dust to reveal a faded image on the stone beneath. I deduced that it was painted and not inscribed, though the colours remained sufficiently vivid to make it out: a sun wreathed in flame.

"Always at the start of spring," Lilat said, "this is where it points. When winter falls, it points here." She moved to scrape away another portion of dust a yard to the right of the revealed sun. This time its wreath of flame had vanished and it was shrouded by cloud.

"A sundial that tracks the seasons instead of the hours," I mused. Crouching, I ran my hand over the floor, revealing yet more painted images, mountains and beasts arranged in a circle around the symbols that signified winter and spring. Also, closer inspection revealed some familiar lettering between the pictograms.

"This," I said, pointing to the script. "This is writing."

Her brow furrowed as she peered closer. "You know the meaning of it?"

"No. The language is not my own." I felt a pang for the book and its accompanying guide to translation of Caerith script, gifted to me by a soon-to-be-bereft librarian and later surrendered to the woman these people called the *Doenlisch*. I had carried it for days without learning even a morsel of its secrets, and now I most likely never would.

"I need paper," I told her, moving in a crouch from one image to another, my gaze hungry. "And ink. This must be recorded."

Lilat's features took on a reluctant cast. "I don't think Uhlla would like that."

Fuck what she likes. I wisely caged the words, instead forcing a patient smile. "This is important," I said, gesturing to the revealed script and symbols. "It's history. Your history. One day this tower will be dust and all this lost. Don't you think it should be preserved?"

Lilat, however, was patently unconvinced, her reluctance hardening into suspicion as she rose to her feet. "The ruins below the mountain, what lies within the mountain, this." She pointed to the floor. "Uhlla says they are warnings, not treasures. Also—" her eyes shaded in worry "—the *Eithlisch* says so too."

"Why? Warnings of what?"

She spoke a short phrase, one I had heard from the Sack Witch. "The Fall." She turned away, moving to the steps. "We should go now."

My plea for her to wait died as she began a rapid descent, clearly in no mood to listen. Realising that I was entirely reliant on her to escape this place, I decided my scholarly curiosity would have to wait. Hopefully, I could persuade her to make another visit in future, whereupon I fully intended to bring some manner of writing materials with me.

After emerging from the tower, Lilat maintained an unbroken silence for much of the journey. From the way she avoided my gaze I discerned her annoyance was directed inwardly rather than at me. I waited upon breaking the silence until we neared the village and her hunter's instinct caused her to crouch and inspect what looked to my eyes like a few minor scrapes to the earth.

"Rabbit?" I ventured, earning a glance of muted if amused disparagement.

"Boar," she said, straightening with a disappointed sigh. "Running now. He must have smelt us."

"He? How can you tell?"

"Tracks are deep and wide apart. He's big and old, wise enough to run when his nose tells him to."

"You have impressive skills. I would have thought the *taolisch* would welcome you."

Her face took on a closed, guarded look and she turned away. Keen to maintain the conversation, I persisted. "You want to learn to fight, why not get them to teach you?"

"Not allowed," she said, voice soft but also bitter. She let out a thin sigh and turned back to me. "To be *taolisch* you must be . . ." She paused, frowning as the correct term in Albermainish eluded her. "*Ohlat*," she said in Caerith which, fortunately, was a word I knew.

"Judged?" I asked, adding, "Tested?" when her furrowed brow indicated I was a little wide of the mark.

"Tested, yes," she confirmed.

"And you . . . failed the test?"

"Tests," she corrected. "There are many." Her features took on a sorrowful cast. "But not for me."

"You weren't even allowed to try?"

She nodded, gesturing to the mountain range rising above the western horizon. "Years ago I travelled to the *Taowild*, the home of the *taolisch*. Every year young people go there for *Ohlat*. The *Ohlisch*, the one who has care of the *Taowild*, met me at the foot of the mountain. I had never seen him before but he knew me. He told me, 'You are *veilisch* – hunter – not *taolisch*.' But always I wanted to be *taolisch*. I grew up listening to their stories." The sadness on her face deepened further. "They liked me then. So, I came back here and asked them to teach me. They said no and wouldn't talk to me after. I asked Uhlla why. She said they are forbidden by the *Ohlisch*. She said I should follow his word, for he is wise. I said he is a stupid old man." Lilat gave a rueful shrug. "Uhlla only ever hit me once. That was when I understood that it was she who told the *Ohlisch* to send me away. She did not want me to be *taolisch*. I was angry for a long time, then you came, but you have the mark of the *Doenlisch* and are not bound by Caerith ways. Uhlla cannot stop you teaching me."

"War," I said, "*tao*, is nothing to be relished. I hope you never see it. Uhlla was trying to protect you."

"I know. But she knows my—" she placed a hand on her chest "—*mielah* is *taolisch*. To deny another's *mielah* is wrong." *Mielah* was also a word I knew but one with a meaning that was difficult to grasp. I had heard it in reference to the heart or the soul, but also in relation to mention of purpose or path. Apparently, the Caerith saw their purpose in life as indistinguishable from their nature. One was what one did, and, if Lilat was to be believed, obstructing this was akin to blasphemy.

I thought back to that day on the flanks of the Sermont, how I had instructed Fletchman to put an arrow in Roulgarth when the chance arose despite the fact that I had issued a challenge to fair combat. I also recalled knowing that Evadine's anger would be fierce. Perhaps she would even find my actions unforgivable. For her, nobility was more than just a word, whereas for me it had always been a convenient fiction, a mask for the likes of Althus Levalle or Deckin's hated father to do and take as they pleased. Therefore, Evadine's *mielah* was in many ways akin to Roulgarth's, but neither were mine.

"Sometimes," I said, "we do wrong to protect those we love. Don't judge your aunt too harshly."

Lilat gave a tight smile of a sort that indicated the acceptance of a point but not agreement. Her smile faded quickly when a fresh breeze from the south swept the ridge. She straightened, taking on the alert readiness that told of a newly caught scent.

"The boar?" I asked.

"Smoke," she said, shaking her head.

I searched the vastness below but saw no sign of fire. "Trouble?"

"Campfire. Still far off, but he'll be here tomorrow."

"He?"

Lilat turned to me with an expression that mingled regret with foreboding. "The *Eithlisch*. He has come for you."

CHAPTER TWENTY-SEVEN

I n fact, despite Lilat's prediction, the *Eithlisch* didn't appear for another two days and when he did it was in a most unexpected manner.

I spent the following day beset by tense expectation, struggling through Roulgarth's lesson with distracted clumsiness. Recently, he had consented to add some instruction to the daily bout of punishment. The words were snapped out with a terse lack of inflection, usually punctuated by a painful jab of his sword by way of demonstration.

"Always be ready to move," he said, wooden sword point delivering a hard prod to my shoulder. "Don't just stand there like a prickless groom on his wedding night."

I gave a vague nod in response, allowing my gaze to stray towards the village. Even though I had heard no mention of the *Eithlisch* since returning from the visit to the tower, I noticed how my tension had become mirrored by the Caerith. Conversations grew short and expressions guarded, the villagers going about their business with hurried, mostly silent efficiency. The *taolisch* were also on edge. Always a taciturn lot, their daily sparring under Roulgarth's guidance was marked by an uncharacteristic fractiousness. Usually they assailed each other with controlled aggression that was forgotten as soon as the contest ended. Today, however, they demonstrated a peevish absence of control, their sparring escalating into unrestrained combat that was impressive to witness but jarring in the blood they spilled. A few suffered cuts and severe bruises before Roulgarth ordered a halt and sent them on their way.

"Wake up, Scribe!" Annoyed by my lack of attentiveness, the knight brought the flat of his sword down on to the top of my head. The blow was light by his standards, and I would usually have shrugged it off, but today his casual sadism lit a rare flame of anger, compelling me to respond before I could quell the impulse. This would be the second of only two blows I ever landed on the person of Roulgarth Cohlsair. The strike to his leg during our first bout had aroused his ire; this hard slash across his midriff brought a different reaction.

Instead of an angry snarl, Roulgarth's features shifted into narrow-eyed appraisal. A very faint grunt of satisfaction escaped his lips before, with no pause or warning, he launched an attack. His sword rose and fell in blurring arcs, forcing me back, wooden swords clacking as I desperately parried each strike. The Alundian was relentless and fluid in his ferocity, allowing no time or space to dodge clear and find room to riposte. I could only keep fending him off in the certain knowledge that he would inevitably find an opening and inflict his agonising revenge. Yet, as the contest wore on, I realised that I was actually managing to hold my own against this peerless knight. Thrusts and strokes that would once have put me on my arse or left me reeling I now parried or deflected with much the same speed as he delivered them. Also his myriad repertoire of tricks failed to gull me into dropping my guard or luring me into a fatal misstep, and I fancy he tried them all.

I doubt it was a pretty thing for Merick and Lilat to watch, but the contest betwixt myself and Roulgarth that day stands in my memory as a moment of accomplished art the equal of any manuscript I ever penned. For, in surviving this, the most determined and unstinting assault he ever launched against me, I knew that I had finally absorbed his lessons. Thanks to a combination of reflex and muscle honed through arduous repetition I was, at last, truly a swordsman.

In the end it was simple exhaustion that brought this milestone event to a close. Although mostly recovered from his illness, Roulgarth's impressive frame would still tire after prolonged exertion. He was also nigh fifteen years my senior, not that I would ever have dared point it out. I saw his fortitude reach its limit when he made a small, near imperceptible retreat. An uneducated spectator would have taken it for a slight repositioning of the feet in preparation for his next thrust, but I knew its meaning clear enough. I also knew he would probably keep on until he collapsed. Allowing my sword to drop just a fraction, I made a botch of deflecting his jab at my midriff, taking the sword point just below the sternum.

Air fled my lungs in a rush and I slipped to my knees, head lowered and gasping. Lilat came to my side and helped me up while Merick bowed to his uncle, expressing a reverential admiration which the knight waved away with an irritable hand. Whereas I hadn't succeeded in angering him before, I had now.

"Don't ever do that again, Scribe!" he growled, levelling his sword at me. Evidently my charitable subterfuge had been noticed, and not appreciated. "I am not some infirm dotard deserving of pity."

I found my temper piqued by his resentment, causing me to summon a caustic rejoinder. *No, you are a landless pauper deserving of pity.* However, the words withered on my tongue as I beheld his furious visage. Pride, after all, was all he had left.

"My apologies, my lord," I said with a bow, my tone and bearing blandly respectful.

Roulgarth's face flushed and he spent a moment in unaccustomed dithering until his gaze swung to Lilat. "Tell your people if they are going to keep bothering me for instruction they'll have to observe some rules in future. If I'm compelled to be a sword-master to heretics it won't be as an overseer for wanton bloodletting."

Lilat's features bunched in preparation for a retort of her own, but she paused when I reached out to grasp her arm. "I tell them," she said in a sullen mutter, lowering her head.

"See that you do." Roulgarth sniffed, straightening and gesturing for all three of us to line up. "Now, demonstrate the scales I showed

you yesterday. Yes, you too, Merick. Even learned skills must be practised."

It was the voice that woke me. It wasn't loud; in fact it was soft and
evenly modulated. Yet it held an unfamiliar, compelling resonance
that contrived to pierce both the aged walls of the house and my
slumbering mind.

" . . . a slave to hate is most wretched of captives," it said. "For his
chains are of his own making . . . "

Raising my head from my rabbit-fur pillow, I found the interior of
the house shadowed and still. Merick lay sleeping but Roulgarth's cot
was empty. A narrow, jagged rectangle of moonlight was splayed
across the floor, cast by the door which stood slightly ajar. But for
Roulgarth's absence, I would have ascribed the voice to a mysterious
conjuring of my dreaming mind and fallen back into the soft embrace
of sleep. I spent a confused interval blinking at shadows until the
voice came again.

"You ask for certainty in a world of chaos. All I can offer is truth,
and my truth may differ from yours."

Rising, I reached for the wooden sword at the foot of my bed before
moving cautiously to the door. Peering through the crack I could
make out Roulgarth, head lowered and tall form perched on the tree
stump that served as a welcome resting place betwixt practices. I knew
instinctively that the voice I had heard had not come from the
Alundian's mouth, it being so different to his own broad vowels.

Lifting his head, I saw the knight's throat constrict before he
responded in a tone that was jarring in its tremulous quietude, "And
you know this without doubt?"

"I do, *Vahlisch*," the unseen speaker replied. "Her heart was a mirror
to yours. But like you, duty commanded her above all. I know it must
have been hard, to see the woman you loved married to your brother
and never in all those years speak a word of your heart's truth."

A shudder ran through Roulgarth and I saw to my alarm that he
held a sword. Not the wooden stave I had spent so much time carving
for him, but an actual longsword of the pattern typically carried by

knights. The blade was sheathed and Roulgarth held the scabbard with a surprisingly tentative grip. I watched him contain his sorrow before he raised his sight to the sword, eyes tracing the handle to linger upon the gleaming brass of the pommel. "Why would you give me this?" he asked.

The voice's reply was prompt and coloured by a small chuckle. "What, pray, is the *Vahlisch* without a blade to call his own?"

"*Vahlisch?*"

"In your tongue the term would mean 'master of blades', or sword-master if you prefer. It has been quite some time since the title was used, but I think it suits you well." There was a short pause as Roulgarth continued to look upon his gifted sword in silence, then the voice spoke again, louder with an amused note of command. "Are you going to join us, Master Scribe, or do you intend to eavesdrop a trifle longer?"

Roulgarth stiffened and his gaze snapped to the door, narrowing in suspicious reproach as I levered it open. The clearing was dappled in moonlight and rich in complex shadows. My experienced eye soon discerned one concordance of shadow and light to be a hunched figure seated on the fallen oak branch where the *taolisch* usually rested. He was big, I could tell that much, his features concealed within the cowled robe that covered him from head to foot.

"The *Eithlisch*, I presume?" I said.

"Aye." A grunt sounded from the depths of the cowl as he got to his feet, although he remained hunched as he approached me. I saw how the robe he wore sat strangely on his form, like a curtain draped over a mound of misshapen rock that swayed ponderously when he halted, too far off to make out his face within the cowl. Still, I could sense his gaze upon me and found it uncomfortably weighty. As the moment stretched I knew instinctively he was appraising me with more than just his eyes.

"Yes," I said when the pause lengthened yet further, "the *Doenlisch* put her mark upon me. Can we dispense with the formalities now?"

Another chuckle sounded from the depths of his hood. "Formality," he said, "is one of the few things about your people I actually recall with some fondness. The rituals, the etiquette, the forms of address. Endless lists of pointless rules, constantly changing according to the whims of the wealthy or the powerful. I found the emptiness of it all strangely beautiful, in its way. The Caerith have little to match such vacuous enticements."

He seemed to swell then, though he came no closer, the robe swaying anew as the form beneath expanded. He was already a match for Roulgarth in height and it quickly became apparent that he outdid us both in sheer bulk. I found I had to quell the impulse to step back and raise my wooden sword. When he spoke again the *Eithlisch's* voice had acquired a decided edge.

"And yet, even we know the value of putting a civil tongue in your head, especially when addressing an elder representative of a people who could have left your rude, ungrateful carcass to freeze in the snow."

A breeze stirred the edge of his cowl then, an instant of moonlight playing over a bulge of veined, disfigured flesh before the shadow veiled his features once more. Possessed since childhood of a finely honed instinct for danger, I had no illusions about the potency of the threat this malformed person represented. Yet, even then my truculent resentment of authority made it impossible for me to offer the contrition that was evidently expected.

"I'm alive only because she wants me that way," I returned, staring hard into the depths of his hood. "Gratitude is, therefore, irrelevant."

A sound that was pitched somewhere between a growl and a sigh came from the *Eithlisch*, the unnatural throatiness of it making me wonder if the man standing before me was fully human. However, something in my defiance appeared to satisfy rather than enrage him, for his inflated bulk receded to its former hunched lumpiness.

"I bid you sound sleep and pleasant dreams, *Vahlisch*," he said to Roulgarth who had sat in silent, distracted witness to our exchange. "Tomorrow I make my way westwards and would be gratified if you would journey at my side. You," he went on, the edge returning to his voice as the cowl swung back to me. A large hand, the flesh pale and mottled with a dark matrix of veins, emerged from his robe to

342 · Anthony Ryan

beckon me as he turned and began to walk away. "Come with me. We have much to discuss."

Despite his statement, the *Eithlisch* remained silent as, after hurriedly dressing and donning my boots and jerkin, I followed him from the house. He led me through the village outskirts and on to the expanse of ruins occupying the flat ground before the mountain. Now bare of snow, the nature of the city this had once been became even more obvious. Despite many years of weathering, the stonework had a precision that told of greatly skilled masons raising once impressive architecture. My busy mind couldn't help but imagine the great houses that lined these streets, the columns that must have ascended from broad plazas and squares, perhaps crowned with statuary to the great and the good of this place.

"Did it have a name?" I asked the *Eithlisch*. "The city that stood here."

He maintained the same steady, unhurried pace for a time before consenting to utter a quiet response: "*Tier Uthir Oleith.*"

The last word was unknown to me but I recognised "*tier uthir*" as referring to a door or a gateway, meaning this city had been dubbed the gateway to somewhere. I required no special insight to divine that something of importance lay within the jagged crack in the base of the mountain ahead. It now seemed to loom considerably larger than it had at my first sight of it and I recalled how far Lilat had gone to prevent me venturing inside.

"You're right to be afraid," the *Eithlisch* told me. "My people avoid this place with good reason."

"Then why are we going there?" Another round of silence, the hunched form of the *Eithlisch* plodding on without deigning to reply. "What happens if I don't go with you?" I asked, coming to an annoyed halt.

He kept walking and didn't turn, although this time his reply was prompt and spoken with bland, inarguable assurance. "I'll kill you."

"*She* wouldn't like that," I said, hating my voice for suddenly acquiring a treacherously higher pitch.

"No," the reply came in a reflective mutter, "I don't suppose she would."

I watched him plod on a few more steps before consenting to follow, quelling the urge to hurry my pace. "You were sent for before Lilat discovered Roulgarth and his nephew," I said, in need of distraction and beset by a reasoning desire to delay reaching our destination. Curiosity had ever been one of my principal vices but always tempered with my keen instinct for danger. "How would you know to bring him a sword?"

"Don't pretend to naivety," the *Eithlisch* told me. "One who has felt the *Doenlisch*'s touch as deeply as you cannot be so ignorant." He stopped then, the crack in the mountain now looming above, its depths as anonymous as ever. "Plainly, you are given to asking a great many questions. I caution you, Alwyn Scribe, be careful what questions you ask within this shadow. I bring you here to impart understanding, that is all. If you are wise, and I know you are not, you will accept only the insight I offer and be on your way. Anything else you learn within is of your own choosing and I will bear no responsibility for it."

Before stepping into the gloom, his frame swelled again, though not as impressively as before and I realised he was drawing a fortifying breath. He started forward without further delay, disappearing into the seemingly absolute shadow and leaving me to dither in his absence. *I'll kill you*, he had said, a promise I had heard often enough to know when it was truly spoken. Still, I couldn't help the growing suspicion that experiencing whatever lay beneath this mountain might be worse.

"I am Captain Alwyn Scribe of the Covenant Company," I whispered to myself. "I have fought the worst battles, faced the worst foes." Still, it took some effort to take that first step into the dark, and only marginally less to take the second.

CHAPTER TWENTY-EIGHT

I soon found myself fully enveloped in darkness. As I moved on tentative feet into the guts of the mountain, I formed the panicked conclusion that so dark a place must be unnatural in origin. My years in the Pit Mines had left me with an ingrained tolerance for the sunless tracts beneath the earth, and an understanding that a portal so close to the surface would not be so lacking in illumination. This was so completely devoid of light that I felt myself to be lost, denied even the echo of my own feet upon the bare rock. I fought the severe temptation to turn back, flee this arcane trap. I would return to the house, gather what supplies I could and take my chance on the mountains. I knew that, even with the coming of spring, many of the passes were still closed. However, thanks to Lilat, I also knew there to be a pathway to the south that might be navigable. She had also made it clear that traversing said path was treacherous in the extreme and probably impossible for one so lacking in experience as I. At this juncture, however, I found it preferable to continuing this faltering totter into the dark.

I was on the verge of coming to a halt when a glimmer finally appeared in the gloom. It was just a slight variation in the all-encompassing wall of darkness at first, but, after a few more hesitant steps, resolved into the flickering glow of a torch recently set to flame.

As I approached the torch another flared to life off to my left and I caught the bulky shadow of the *Eithlisch* silhouetted by the light before he shifted into the shadow once more. There came the faint scrape of metal on flint then a third torch guttered to life, the blazing trio creating a circle of luminescence upon a floor of stone. It had the uneven, cracked nature of a cave surface rather than the creation of human hands. Looking at the iron stanchion supporting the closest torch, I saw how old and rusted it was, its three legs flaked in red that dusted the stone beneath. At first glance, the gloom beyond the torches' glow appeared absolute, another void a man might wander into never to return. Then my eyes discerned faint specks in the wall of shadow, the flickering flame catching some manner of irregular surface.

What is this place? I swallowed the words before they could escape my lips, recalling the *Eithlisch's* warning regarding the speaking of questions within the mountain. Instead I sifted through my knowledge of Caerith lore, trying to summon a clue as to his intent in bringing me to this featureless, subterranean refuge. Most of what I knew came from the mostly fanciful scribblings of the fraudulent Ulfin, and a few allusions to matters spiritual uttered by Lilat. Of course, I once possessed a very singular book that I felt sure would have provided no end of insight into this place, if I still owned it. My mind had crafted various notions of arcane treasures or threats this mountain might harbour. To find it empty was, therefore, both a disappointment and a relief, although my curious mind tended towards the former rather than the latter.

"The more ordered your thoughts," the *Eithlisch* advised, concealing his flint and striker somewhere within the curtain of his robe, "the easier you'll find this."

Without further preamble he shrugged off his covering. The body beneath wore a sleeveless jerkin of loose, thin material that clung to a frame I could only describe as both grotesque and magnificent. What I had taken for some form of deformity I now understood to be composed mostly of enlarged muscle. It bulged in pale, veined slabs from the *Eithlisch's* shoulders to his wrists. His head appeared almost comically small in comparison, a hairless, marbled ball sitting atop a neck of thick, corded sinew. It seemed as if he grew at least a foot in height by the time the robe fell to the ground, all artifice of malformed weakness falling away to reveal a being of considerable power.

"Come, Alwyn Scribe," he said, reaching out to lift the nearest torch from its stand. "It's time for you to choose."

Choose what? Another question trapped behind hastily clenched teeth. *Be careful what questions you ask within this shadow.* I had a strong sense of being lured by his cryptic allusions. A test perhaps? Or just a minor venting of his evident disdain? Nevertheless, I followed as he stepped into the wall of shadow surrounding us, the torchlight revealing what lay in the blackness.

At first I thought the ancient Caerith had, for reasons unknown, chosen to fill this mountain with piles of old firewood. However, my folly was soon laid bare when the flickering torchlight played over the cracked but still intact dome of an age-blackened skull. "Bones," I said aloud, my eyes shifting over the pile which stretched away into the occluded recesses of this vast cavern. I saw ribs, arms, spines all jumbled up like an obscene thicket. Not all were human – bear skulls sat alongside those of birds and wolves while teeth of all shapes and sizes littered the stone beneath.

"You have brought me to a tomb," I observed which drew a dismissive huff from the *Eithlisch*.

"Your word and your custom," he said. "You see only death here, for your limitations prevent you seeing anything else." He crouched, extending the torch to illuminate a human skeleton. Through either chance or design the way it lay amid the piled bones kept it mostly intact, creating the illusion of a fleshless body in relaxed, idle repose.

"This was once a life of great power," the *Eithlisch* said. Reaching out with his free hand, he placed his palm upon the skull, his touch absurdly gentle for one so strong. He closed his eyes, voice softening as he spoke on. "Possibly great wisdom, who can know? She lived for many years, survived days of darkness and rejoiced in days of light. Once she joined her strength to the *taolisch* to turn back a great raid upon the southern coast, so fierce was she that the raiders did not come again for many years."

Sighing, he withdrew his hand and straightened. "Choose," he said, gesturing to the pile. From the shortness of his tone and stern glint in his eyes I understood that no further explanation would be forthcoming.

Still mystified, I turned my gaze upon the chaotic assemblage of bones, searching vainly for meaning and wary of demanding guidance. A few moments of fruitless scrutiny and, still unenlightened, I began to turn away, deciding I had had enough of this giant's enigmatic torments. It was as my gaze slipped to the edge of the pile that it happened upon something that gave me pause: a crow skull.

The memory returned in a rush, that day on the road in the chainsman's wagon. The worst day in that monster's clutches, for that was the day he had killed Raith. "*Caihr teasla?*" he had asked before crushing his fellow Caerith's head with those terrible hands of his. When he posed the question he had taunted Raith with a bronze crow skull torn from his charm necklace. I recalled how, after the murder, the chainsman had kept hold of the trinket for a brief moment before tossing it away, as if pondering some hidden value it possessed.

"*Caihr teasla,*" I repeated the words now, stooping to retrieve the skull. I knew the word *teasla* by now, it meant "here" or "present", but could also allude to something contained within a vessel. The meaning of *caihr*, however, remained a mystery.

The crow skull felt like any other aged piece of bone in my hand, a light and fragile thing of no value, its empty eyes regarding me with blank indifference. Then it screamed at me. The sound filled my mind but not my ears, an enraged squawk of repugnance that caused me to yelp and drop the thing, retreating from it and rubbing my hand on my shirt.

"It doesn't like you," the *Eithlisch* observed. "Don't be offended. Most who come here receive the same response. Only very few of us ever receive the blessing of the *Oleith*." He put an emphasis on this word that signalled it as bait, the lure for another question I shouldn't ask.

"*Caihr*," I said once the alarmed thumping in my chest had abated enough to allow for speech. "It means . . . power. There is arcane power in these bones."

"Arcane." The *Eithlisch* gave an amused chuckle. "Your people and their foolish words. But you show some insight. *Caihr* is the power that resides here in these vestiges of those that once lived. *Vaerith* is the power that flowed into them in life. Among some of us, the flow is strong. In life we come here to receive their blessing. In death we join with them." He raised his arms, turning to encompass the whole chamber. "The *Oleith*, the great joining of those whose *Caihr* lingers after death to provide guidance, when they want to."

"Among some of us," I repeated, a realisation coming to mind. "The *Doenlisch*. *Vaerith* flows strongly in her. She would have come here too. She received the blessing."

I could see the *Eithlisch*'s features clearly in the light of the torch he held, finding them a curious parody of handsomeness, as if they had been carved by a sculptor with a skewed sense of proportion. His lips, full and shapely, seemed to pout as he pursed them. "She chose a clever one, at least," he reflected softly before speaking on in more strident tones. "How fares she in your lands?"

"That is a question," I pointed out, which caused his pout to transform into a bland smile.

"Yes. Not all are dangerous here. It's just a matter of knowing which ones to ask." His eyes narrowed and voice hardened. "The *Doenlisch*. I would have you tell me how she fares."

I shrugged. "Well enough, last I saw her. Though she feels it necessary to walk our lands with a sack on her head."

"As she should. Your people are beasts, savages driven by base greed and uncontrolled lust." He spoke in a mild tone but I heard the barb in it, also the expectation of a heated retort, one I took satisfaction in denying him. The smile faded from his lips as he continued. "I have long argued the wisdom of allowing your kind to wither. Leave you to your endless wars and recurrent famines. The *Doenlisch* . . ." He trailed off, the stark veins lacing his forehead forming a tight web as he frowned. When he continued it was in a tone that mingled disdain with puzzlement. "Some time ago she came here and asked a question of the *Oleith*. The exact particulars of the answer she received are unknown to me, but they led her to conclude that your people are in fact worth saving, yet she chose you to be the agent of her grand design. I can only ascribe this to a want of better candidates."

"She didn't choose me, exactly," I replied, still failing to rise to his taunts and indulging in the smug pleasure of realising I actually knew more than he did. "My life, you see, was prophesied, in a Caerith book written long ago."

The *Eithlisch*'s features froze, the planes of his strange mockery of a face flickering in the torchlight. "Book?" he repeated. His voice had taken on a hoarse aspect and all trace of humour had vanished from his expression. Seeing the fierceness of his gaze, I wondered if the only true danger here lay in him and his monstrous thews. It made me painfully aware that I possessed no weapon of any kind, save my wits. Yet, as I couldn't hope to match this man in strength, I also had severe doubts I could match him in intellect.

"You have it?" he asked, the corded mass of his neck writhing. I could tell he was engaged in a strenuous effort to keep himself from expressing his desire for knowledge in more physical terms. I remembered the chainsman's face just before Lorine killed him, how mention of the book had instilled much the same sense of shock. Clearly, the thing was of far greater importance than even I had realised.

"I had it," I said. "For a time. She gave it to me as part of a bargain we struck. I couldn't read it, of course, but I eventually found one who possessed the means of translating the text. It was the story of my life, written down centuries ago in Caerith script. Sadly, before I could . . . make proper use of it, I was obliged to return it to the *Doenlisch* as part of our agreement. As far as I know, she has it now." I paused before adding another nugget of information, sensing it might in fact be the most valuable one I possessed. "And the means to translate other books. I gave that to her too."

Sadly, as I had taken pleasure in denying the *Eithlisch* the response he wanted, he now refused to display either the anger or the fear I expected. Instead, he regarded me with unblinking eyes that told of considerable inner turmoil kept caged through sheer effort of will. Eventually, he blinked and turned his gaze from me.

"As you have surely deduced by now," he said, "not all Caerith remain within our borders for the entirety of their lives. Some are exiled, driven out due to their malice. We have no laws as you do, nor do we kill our own kind. But even among us there are those we cannot tolerate. Others, those for whom *Vaerith* flows strongest, go forth willingly to learn new languages and customs. Long have we known that our survival depends not only on the skills of the *taolisch*, but also knowledge. To counter a threat, you must first understand it."

"That's how you know Albermainish so well," I said. "You walked our realm."

"I did, many years ago. At first I was shunned, driven away from every hovel and village by folk who saw only a malformed thing sure to bring destruction or disease. In time I met a clever man who fed me, and tended the wounds inflicted upon me by the churls I had unwittingly terrorised. It was clear this man had judged me to be a simpleton, huge of body but small of mind, and therefore easily controlled. When I awoke in the morning I found he had put a collar and chain around my neck. I could have freed myself, of course, for he was not a strong man, but I was curious and so I continued to play the peaceable dullard and allowed my captivity to continue. He put a cloak over me and led me from village to town, following the trail of the travelling fairs. People would gather to gawp at the monster for a shek apiece. If they paid more, he would permit them to poke me with sticks. Ten sheks and he would let them beat me with clubs on promise he would return the fee should they succeed in knocking me over. They never did. I bore it all for the passage of four full seasons, learning your language and your ways in the process. I will not say that I witnessed only cruelty and greed. There was kindness too, but it was fleeting.

"I began to understand that the people who paid to torment me did not do so out of hatred, but the viciousness that arises from a concordance of fear and powerlessness. These ragged, famished wretches had nothing and lived their lives at the whims of the finely clothed nobles I caught only rare glimpses of, until one day a lord took it into his mind to take me for his own. My gaoler demanded a high price which the lord bargained down to a single shek by the expedient of having his men beat the fellow to a pulp for his insolence. I was duly taken to a strange stone building that I learned was called a castle and consigned to the dungeons. My only companion was a somewhat emaciated fellow with a florid way of speaking, and it was from him that I acquired my eloquent Albermainish. It transpired he had been tutor to one of the lord's daughters, a comely girl with charms that had proven dangerously tempting. This man knew a great deal about the history of your land and, most interestingly for me, the strange form of belief that dominates your lives."

He paused to grin and shake his head in parlous wonder. "Martyrs," he said. "Seraphile. Malecite. The Covenant. A fascinating concoction of fable, myth and, I must admit, even a morsel or two of wisdom."

I detected an arch superiority to his tone. Although, despite my present occupation, I could never claim to be a devout soul, I still found it grated on my sensibilities. "From what I can gather," I said, "your people have no beliefs. Or at least no faith that is worthy of the name."

"Faith?" He raised his hairless brows in blatant mockery. "Is that what you possess, Alwyn Scribe? Have you submitted that ball of cynical self-interest you call a heart to service of the Seraphile?" He held my gaze for a second. "I think not. As for faith," he sighed, looking away, "the Caerith have no use for the vagaries of belief. We are certainly prone to introspection, it is true, but for us belief arises only from that which can be experienced or observed. Still, this Covenant of yours bears an unusual distinction, in that it is a faith that in some ways reflects reality. But we'll get to that." He frowned. "Where was I?"

"In a dungeon," I said, possessed of the fervent wish he had stayed there.

"Oh yes. My time with the tutor was sadly short-lived, although I did acquire a considerable amount of knowledge before the lord took him away. I overheard the guards talking about his fate. Apparently the lord had set him loose in the nearby forest then hunted him down with a pack of starved dogs. I wondered if he had a similar amusement in store for me but it transpired my end was intended to be far more elaborate.

"It was during some manner of midwinter feast that they led me from the dungeons. The lord and all his noble friends sat at a table in the courtyard, happily gorging themselves on roasted meats of varying description, apart from his daughter, of course. She ate nothing and, in truth, presented such a picture of abject misery I found it hurt my heart to look upon her. I was stripped naked and my chains removed whereupon another prisoner was led forth."

The *Eithlisch* paused again, the faintly amused reminiscence that had coloured his tone before giving way to genuine sorrow. "How terrible it was to see so magnificent a creature in such a pitiable state. Brown bears grow large but he was a giant of his kind, twice my height when he reared. However, the torments they had subjected him to made him monstrous, fur mangy and matted, his snout scarred by the whip. I could tell he wished only for death and resolved to make him a gift of it, but not his own." He let out a soft laugh. "It is monumental folly for a collector of interesting creatures not to fully understand the nature of his captives. In the case of the bear, my lordly host saw no more than a cowed beast that could be roused to provide a gory spectacle. In me, he saw something barely human that might last a little longer than a common outlaw or unfortunate churl. I don't normally revel in acts of violence or destruction, but I must confess I was very happy to prove him wrong that day."

The *Eithlisch* came towards me, halting a few paces away with hands now balled into fists. As I watched, he swelled again, his already impressive frame expanding, muscles and veins bulging to the extent that I wondered they didn't split his skin open.

"*Vaerith* is well named," the *Eithlisch* said, his voice now possessed of a far deeper and more commanding resonance. "For the word is an echo of what we name a river. But it flows differently in all of us, as is the way with rivers. They find their own course, one that can never be denied, not by steel, or arrows, or fire." Bones and muscles made an ugly grinding sound as he grew yet further until I beheld a true giant. "Or," he added, a smile that was more a snarl ghosting across his lips, "the pleas of cruel lords who piss themselves and beg like any other coward when death comes to their castle."

Until this point I had been staring in appalled fascination, struck silent and still by the impossibility of what I witnessed. The strange things I had seen in the north and all I had experienced at the hands of the Sack Witch had left me no recourse but to accept the existence of arcane forces, but never had I expected to witness so stark and terrible a demonstration.

"*Vaerith* courses through the fabric of this world," the *Eithlisch* told me, "like blood racing through the veins of the body. Once tapped, it can be released, and controlled." His smile took on a decidedly cruel aspect as he moved closer, looming over me, a monolith of inhuman strength. "Would you care to taste it, Alwyn Scribe? The bear was certainly appreciative that day. Once I shattered his chains, he set about ravaging his way through the lord's guests with great enthusiasm."

"No." The word emerged in a clipped stutter, escaping lips made rigid with terror. It gripped me from head to toe and I found I had to force my legs to retreat as he took another step closer. "Get . . . get away from me!" I gabbled, shrinking back like a child quailing in the face of a parent's vicious temper.

"Hold still, you fool!" His voice became an irritable mutter as, moving with blurring speed, he clamped his hands to my head. The resultant sensation was a vibrant and far more painful echo of what had occurred during the Sack Witch's healing of Evadine. Then I had felt the shift of forces within me, the passage of strength from one body to another. This time the current of strength had been reversed. My vision became swamped by light, a deep, throbbing warmth flooding my body but burning hottest at the temples where the *Eithlisch*'s hands gripped me like tongs drawn from the heart of the forge. I flailed at him in my panic, raining blows against his arms, his shoulders, his head, my efforts akin to beating my fists against unyielding rock.

"Enough!" the *Eithlisch* commanded in an impatient grunt, shaking me hard enough to rob my flailing limbs of strength. "Don't you know you're dying, you stupid little man? The crack in your skull has healed poorly and whatever foul concoction you've been drinking to dull the pain is rotting your insides. If that doesn't end you, the bones in your skull are knitting together to create a growth that will kill you within the space of a year. And, as you say, *she* wouldn't like that."

The burn suddenly transformed into an all-consuming blaze, filling my head and dispelling all thought. Through my fear and panic I could feel the grinding of my skull, hear the sibilant, fibrous scrape of bone being reordered. The throb returned, just for an instant, a last dreadful eruption of agony so absolute I felt sure it heralded my departure from this world. When it faded, I found myself on my hands and knees, sobbing out ragged gasps as a thick cascade of drool issued from my mouth.

"The bear didn't kill them all," the *Eithlisch* was saying, his tone once again one of convivial conversation. My bleary eyes made out his diminishing bulk as he retreated from me. "It spared most of the servants, and the lord's comely daughter. I must say, in all my extensive years, I have never seen a child more delighted to watch a parent's demise. She and the bear became steadfast friends that day and, at my suggestion, chose to come home with me. She prospered here, finding a happiness that would surely have eluded her in your kingdom of horrors. I fancy I can still see an echo of her face in Uhlla's features. She was her great-grandmother, you see? Knowledge of Albermainish is something of a family tradition in these parts."

My drooling and shuddering abated as he talked, the pain of his touch fading away to leave a jarring sense of well-being. Also, all trace of the throb had vanished.

"You . . ." I gasped, craning my neck to look up at him ". . . you healed me."

His response came in the form of a sour, resigned mutter. "Yes. You have many more years ahead, Alwyn Scribe. Or, depending on your choices in the fraught days to come, you don't. Only time will tell . . ." He trailed off, his eyes snapping to the far side of the cavern. He stared into the gloom for a long time, a slow hiss escaping his lips. I couldn't tell if it was an expression of disappointment or surprise. "It appears you have been granted a question after all."

Following his gaze, I saw only the dull flicker of torchlight on more bones, but I felt something. The sensation held an echo of the aggrieved squawk of the crow skull, but far more welcoming. It felt like being called to from a far distance.

Stumbling to my feet, I made a wayward progress across the bare stone, standing in bleary regard of the bones piled there. At first, the notion of finding the right one seemed impossible, but then the call sounded again in my head and I swear I heard my name spoken by another voice. "*Alwyn . . . Old ghost. So, you've come again.*"

The skull lay deep in the pile, forcing me to wade through the thicket of bones until I found it. Empty eye sockets stared up at me from the remains of a part-shattered ribcage, the sound in my head welling as I stooped to retrieve it.

"Your question," the *Eithlisch* instructed with hard insistence. "Ask it now. I doubt you'll get another chance."

Staring into the black caves of the skull's eyes, I found the question came easily to my lips, as if it were the only one worth asking. "Who wrote the book?"

CHAPTER TWENTY-NINE

For a time, I was blind. I shuddered as the skull exploded into a blossom of light that invaded my eyes then poured through to flood my entire being. The chill of the vast cave vanished, creating a sense of being cast adrift in an endless white sea. I groped about in my insensate fear, feeling nothing. I have no doubt the absence of sensation would have robbed me of reason had it continued for long, for it is a singular but potent form of torment to know oneself to be, essentially, nothing.

So, when sight returned to my eyes, it was with a suddenness that had me reeling in confusion. A rush of images assailed me all at once: a bright clear sky, a distant sprawl of tall buildings beneath a mountain, all accompanied by a stiff, cutting wind alleviated only slightly by the warm caress of a noonday sun. The wind carried with it a palpable tinge of smoke and, beneath its gusty whistle, I fancied I could hear a great many voices raised in distress. I staggered under the assault, my midriff colliding hard with some kind of solid barrier.

"So, you've come again, old ghost."

The voice came from behind, unfamiliar and curiously accented. Whirling about, I found myself regarding a dim figure standing in a shadowed arch. A glance to either side confirmed that I stood upon a balcony, while further inspection revealed that it was positioned close to the top of a tower.

"So much younger now," the figure said, stepping forwards into the light. I blinked wary, confused eyes at a tall, dark-skinned man, his hair thinned on top but his strong jaw covered by a neat beard of steely grey. He wore a fine robe of pale blue silk and deep red velvet, embroidered in elegant, abstract lines of gold thread.

"Are you the king of this land?" I asked him. He wore no crown but I found it hard to credit that one so obviously wealthy, domiciled in a tower no less, could be anything less than a prince of some description.

The bearded man's brow furrowed as he scanned my face, recognition clear in his searching eyes. "So, it's finally come," he mused, a flicker of a smile passing across his face. I saw now how lined it was, how marked by sadness. The sorrow was etched into his features, deep lines surrounding hollowed eyes; the face of a man who hadn't known joy in a long time.

I shook my head as a wave of confusion swept through me. The shock of the *Eithlisch*'s healing lingered and now I found myself in an impossible place conversing with a man who offered only bafflement. "What has come?" I asked, shifting to regard the world below the tower. It sat upon a hill at a remove of over a mile from a view both familiar and alien. The mountain was the same, although it lacked the crack in its base. The city surrounding it stretched away for many miles in each direction, a far greater and more pleasing conurbation than any I had seen before, or expected to see ever again. Towers yet taller than this rose everywhere, casting thin shadows over great halls and squares below. The pattern of streets seemed jumbled: neat, straight grids abutting more chaotic, curving labyrinths. Rather than diminish my growing awe, this only served to enhance it for I realised it signified growth. This was a very old city, one that had blossomed and prospered over the course of centuries. The impressiveness of it all would have been more overwhelming if not for the many columns of smoke I saw rising wherever I looked, and the ever-thicker clusters of people filling the streets and parks. Their

358 • Anthony Ryan

voices rose in an accumulation so discordant it could best be described as a collective howl. It was clear I had arrived in a moment of crisis.

Despite the differences, the sense of looking upon something already seen was strong, the reason coming to me in a rush of realisation. Shifting my gaze to the tower itself, I saw fine, smooth stone free of vines and branches, but there was no doubt that this was the old tower Lilat had led me to days ago.

"Our first and last meeting," the bearded man said. Looking to him, I saw the same faint smile ghost across his lips before he turned away. "Come," he beckoned to me before the shadow beyond the arch swallowed him. "Time is short."

Beset by uncertainty, I hesitated, casting another befuddled glance at the city as a very loud boom echoed in the distance. My eyes flicked to the sight of a huge blossom of smoke ascending from an eruption of flame that had consumed one of the fine halls. The building was gone in seconds, the flames searing through stone as easily as wood, the sounds of its destruction merging with the great wailing of accumulated voices. Perversely, it sounded more like wild cheers of celebration rather than panic or distress.

"Quickly, old ghost!" The bearded man's voice, strident with urgency, broke through my morbid fascination and I followed him through the arch. I found the interior lost to gloom until my eyes blinked away the glare from outside. I recognised the room immediately. The floor, now free of dust with its pictograms symbolising spring and winter. It was also plainly a scribe's domain; books lined the curving walls and it featured three separate lecterns where pinned sheets of parchment waited, each only partially filled with text. My attention was inevitably drawn to the closest, and I peered at the page in the hope of enlightenment. A hiss of disappointment escaped me as I beheld script I could recognise but not read.

"Caerith . . ." I said, moving from one lectern to another. "You are a Caerith scribe."

"No," the bearded man said, voice flat with impatience. He was busy sifting through a mound of parchment atop a rosewood desk in the centre of the room. "I am a historian, as I've told you before . . ."

His voiced faded and he paused in his task to let out a flat, humour-less laugh. "Which, of course, you would not know."

"You have no marks," I said, approaching the desk to squint at his face. His dark skin was wrinkled but lacked any trace of the discol-ouration borne by all his people.

His reply was softly spoken and riven by poorly controlled fear, his eyes shining bright as he stared into mine. "No. But I wager I will before long. Now—" he hastily finished tidying the piled documents on his desk and reached for a blank sheet of parchment "—I'm reason-ably sure I have it all in order. When last we spoke you finished relating your capture at Castle Duhbos. Deckin was dead and you had almost been hanged . . ."

"Stop!" I held up a hand, then swayed as another wave of confusion coursed through me. I found I had to grip his desk to prevent myself from falling over. As my hands grasped the hard, polished wood, a thought occurred to me. "If I'm a ghost here, how can I touch things?"

"We've been through all of this . . ." The bearded man's voice dwin-dled to a sigh and he closed his eyes in self-reproach. "You're not really touching it," he said with forced patience. "But your mind thinks you are. Your consciousness is present in this moment, but your body is not."

Finding his tone somewhat condescending and my temper short-ened by the absolute strangeness of it all, I lashed out at the papers on his desk, intending to scatter them. I felt the coarse weave of the parchment, soft then sharp as my fingers slipped through the stack without making any impression.

"You see?" my host asked, reaching for a quill and dipping it into an inkpot. He sat, smoothing a hand across the parchment before looking up at me in anticipation. "Deckin died and you were captured. I have all that happened next, but not what led you there."

I watched a minute drop of ink fall from the tip of his quill, dislodged by the tremble of the hand that held it. "How can you know that?" I said.

Another drop of ink spattered the page. "Because you told me," the historian grated. "How else?"

"I have never seen you before. I have never been here before . . ." I trailed off as a singular and highly significant notion occurred. "You know what will happen to me. You know the course of my life from this point on . . ."

"We have no time, old ghost!" His gaze snapped momentarily to the balcony as another boom sounded from the city. "Tell me the beginning of your tale so I can be gone from here. So much depends upon it."

I looked into his eyes. They held a light I had seen many times, the desperate, near feverish gleam of a man who didn't know if he would live out the day. Yet, instead of fleeing he stayed merely to scribble down the words of a ghost.

"If you want my story," I said, "then I want answers first."

The historian's nostrils flared, the hollows beneath his cheekbones deepening as he ground his jaws. "You always did warn me your younger self would prove the most trying company," he muttered. "Ask then and be quick."

I inclined my head to the balcony. "What's happening in the city?"

"What you told me would happen. What I am powerless to prevent."

"Riddles are no use to me. Speak plainly."

He sighed again, then winced as another boom sent a tremor through the floor. "The Fall," he said. "Your people will call it the Scourge. It has started, finally. When you first appeared all those years ago, you told me, warned me of the Fall. I didn't believe . . ." He fell silent, eyes closed, head shaking. "It is the inevitable fate of those who think themselves wise to suffer the starkest evidence of their folly."

I barely heard him, my head filled with the sheer import of what he had told me. I found myself returning to the balcony to gaze upon the distant scene of burgeoning chaos. More buildings lay in flaming ruin now, tree-lined avenues burned, the mass of voices raised even louder in either panic or madness. It was too far for me to make out the people thronging the streets as anything other than a seething mass, but I could tell that this surging throng was the author of all of this chaos for flame and destruction followed in its wake.

All will be fire! Words from years ago, spoken by a man I had taken for a deluded fool. *All will be pain! As it was before, so shall it be again when the Seraphile's grace is denied us once more . . .*

"It truly happened," I whispered, mind suddenly full of those many discussions with Sihlda in the Pits. She had always regarded the Scourge as little more than a useful metaphor. *Most probably it wasn't just one event,* she had told me. *I tend towards the theory that what the scrolls refer to as the Scourge was a conglomeration of dire events from ages past. An era of war, pestilence, flood and famine that tumbled forgotten kingdoms over the course of decades or even centuries. What it was doesn't truly matter, young Alwyn. What matters is what it means.*

"You were wrong, dear teacher," I murmured. The city was dark now, the sky so laden with smoke it rendered the whole scene a shadowy nightmare of red flame and screaming souls. "You were so wrong."

"Please." I turned to see the historian at my side, eyes wide with entreaty. "Your testament. We need it. In time you will know why, but for now you must complete the tale."

I gazed at him with dazed eyes before surveying the carnage once more. "Who wrote the book?" A shrill laugh escaped me, one that blossomed into something more full throated, hearty and prolonged.

"You wrote your own book, Alwyn Scribe!" The historian's eyes blazed at me now, bright with anger. If he could have struck me he would. "I merely set down the tale that you dictated. Now we must complete it. For a story to have meaning, it must have a beginning."

My mirth subsided into a disparaging grunt. "Why?" I gestured to the raging nightmare below. "Will it stop any of this?"

"No. But it will be the seed that will one day allow my people to regain what they lost, and will be the key that stops it happening again. That is the bargain I struck with a ghost years hence. I know you have no memory of giving your word, but nonetheless I demand that you keep it."

Hearing an upsurge in the tumult, I looked down to see a seething mass of people had spread into the outskirts of the city. Their collective howl was even louder now, reaching across the distance to pain my ears. There was a ferocity to it, a violent hunger that served to dispel my shock. I may have been only a ghost in this tower born of a lost age, but this was all undeniably real. My host was right: time was short.

"I need to know what caused this," I said. "My people have a . . . belief, a faith . . ."

"The Covenant." He nodded. "You told me. It's absurd in many respects, despicable in others, but there is truth in it. What you call the Seraphile and the Malecite, their unending war brought this upon us. That much is true."

"The Seraphile and the Malecite. They truly exist?"

"They aren't what your Covenant imagines them to be, but yes, they are all too real. I can't explain further." He raised a hand to forestall my torrent of questions. "Suffice to say that the world you see is but one aspect of something far more . . . complicated. As to the exact chain of events that led to this . . ." he paused to cast a sorrowful eye towards the dying city below the mountain ". . . I cannot say, except that discord and suffering are as meat to the Malecite. If I had time I could relate what will bring the people of your time to the same fate, but I do not."

"The Second Scourge," I said, an unpleasant knot of realisation forming in my gut. "I told you of the Second Scourge. Evadine was right . . ."

"Evadine . . ." His eyes blazed again, but whatever he had been about to tell me faded as the loudest boom yet sounded from outside. Turning, I saw the last of the tall towers fall into streets that were now rivers of fire. It sufficed to convince me I had seen more than enough of the past.

"How do I get out of here?" I enquired of the historian. The expression he offered in response was a picture of aggrieved bafflement.

"You appear," he said, "you tell me a fragment of your story, not in any easily recognisable chronological order I might add, then you disappear." He raised trembling hands and gave the most helpless of shrugs. "That is all I know."

"Then let's get it done." I hurried through the arch, gesturing for him to follow. Watching him clumsily scrabble about his desk for quill, ink and parchment, I wondered if this might be the first day of true peril he had known in his life.

"You survive this," I said, hoping to ease his distress.

"How could you know?"

"The book." I pointed to the piled papers. "My . . . testament. I've seen it. You must live, otherwise it wouldn't exist in my time."

He nodded, taking a deep, ragged breath before, with deliberate care, he perched himself on his seat. Smoothing the parchment with the sleeve of his fine but now besmirched robe, he dipped his quill and looked up at me with tense expectation.

"I assume you don't require the unpleasant details of my years in the whorehouse," I said.

The historian bit down on another impatient outburst. "I think that can be merely alluded to in passing."

"Very well. I suppose it began the day we ambushed the royal messenger. Deckin wanted what he carried and, to get it, I had to kill a man. I'd always found it calming to regard the trees . . ."

CHAPTER THIRTY

"LIAR!" I returned to the world with a shout, breath pluming before my lungs took in a cold gasp of air. I had expected to find myself confronted by the *Eithlisch*'s distorted visage so blinked in surprise at finding Lilat peering at my features with a worried frown.

"You are . . . back?" she asked, voice hesitant with uncertainty.

"Where is . . . ?" I began, only to trail off as the words misted my breath again and I suffered a full appreciation for the depth of cold that surrounded us. Looking away from Lilat, I beheld the broad spectacle of mountains stretching away to either side. Judging by the fact that I was looking upon their summits, it was clear we were now at a considerable height.

I spent a short time squinting at the view in confusion, distracted by the last few words I had exchanged with the Caerith historian, words that had left me enraged by his deceit. Even though I hadn't known him for more than the space of an hour, it was clear by then that my older self had looked upon him as a friend. Consequently, the lies he attempted to gull me with when I had completed my narrative felt like a betrayal. The moment was made all the more jarring by the confidence with which he spoke his lies, almost as if he had told me something I already knew. My facility for detecting deception was never faultless, for some have the gift of speaking falsehood as if it's absolute truth. Yet, I had never before encountered a more accomplished deceiver than this ancient, long-dead scribbler.

Feeling Lilat poke an inquisitive finger to my chest, I shook away the memory. "How did I get here?" I asked her.

"You walked." The doubt faded from her brow and she withdrew to tend a small fire blazing in the lee of a wide boulder. She sprinkled herbs into an iron pot casting appetising steam into the thin mountain air. "He said you wouldn't remember."

"The *Eithlisch*? He said that?"

"Yes." Lilat dipped a wooden spoon into the pot and tasted the contents, pursing her lips in appreciation. "We eat now."

"How long?" I asked when she handed me a bowl of rabbit stew.

"Three days." She swallowed a spoonful of her concoction and pointed at my bowl. "You should be hungry. You didn't eat all that time, or talk."

More questions rose but were forgotten as my nose took a fulsome sniff of her offering, stirring my belly into an instant and demanding growl. I consumed the stew in a minute or two of unsightly slurping before helping myself to the remainder in the pot.

"Roulgarth?" I asked after scraping the last dregs into my mouth. "Merick?"

"Gone with the *Eithlisch*. I go with you."

"Go where?"

Her mouth quirked in amusement and she nodded to my rear. "Where else?"

Following the direction of her nod I saw little familiar in the swath of snow-covered peaks but I did divine that we were headed east. "Home," I concluded. "He told you to guide me home."

"And other things." Her voice held a certain purposeful note and, as her gaze lingered on the eastern peaks, I saw a troubled but determined cast to her features that told of a hefty weight of responsibility.

"He's sent you to my homeland to hunt for something," I said. "Or someone. May I know what it is?"

Lilat just smiled and set about cleaning the stewpot. "Dark soon," she said when all the accoutrements had been consigned to her bundle. "We climb. Get over the mountain before then or—" she gave a shrug before starting off up the slope at a brisk stride "—we freeze and die."

"I can only think of one person he would send you to look for," I said, inching my way along the narrow ridge and trying not to let my gaze wander to the apparently bottomless abyss on either side. Lilat didn't respond, remaining intent upon her own far more sure-footed advance across this perilous bridge. We had arrived at this place a short while after breaking camp that morning, a jagged knife blade of frosted granite spanning the gap between two mountains. Apparently this was the pass she had told me about when I had been plotting my escape. One look at its steep flanks and the cloud-misted depths below made me glad I hadn't followed my usual instinct to flee captivity. Attempting this course in winter, even if I had managed to find it without a guide, would have been suicidal.

"The *Doenlisch* is not a deer to be tracked," I went on, voice echoing down the razor-sharp flanks of the ridge. "You won't find her unless she wills it."

"You know her well?" Lilat asked, hopping nimbly across a short gap between boulders. "You are . . . friends?"

This raised a question I hadn't pondered much before. What exactly was I to the Sack Witch? For that matter what was she to me? For all their import, our actual meetings had been few and brief in nature. Still, I couldn't deny a fundamental sense of connection whenever I thought of her, an instinctive knowledge I had felt from the start but couldn't describe until now: *our fates are entwined.*

"I suppose we are," I said, pausing at the gap she had just traversed. It was only a couple of feet wide and, had I been at a lower altitude, I wouldn't have thought twice about leaping it. Now, however, I opted to laboriously clamber into the dip between the boulders. "Do you know her?" I asked, hauling myself up the other side to find Lilat paused, features set in weary patience as she accommodated my craven slowness.

"All Caerith know of the *Doenlisch*," she said, resuming her progress. "But I have never met her. Uhlla did once, many summers ago when she was but a girl. She speaks of it little."

I frowned as the implications of her words sank home. *Many summers ago* . . . "How many summers does Uhlla have?"

Although Lilat's Albermainish had improved considerably thanks to my tutelage, my attempts to teach her basic numeracy had been markedly less successful. "Many," she said, slowing a little to ponder before halting and raising her hands to me, fingers splayed to indicate the number ten. "I have this many." She clenched her fists four times then held up three fingers. "Uhlla has many more."

Her brows furrowed as I stared at her in naked disbelief. "What? You are forty-three years old?"

"Years are four seasons together, yes?"

I nodded.

"Then yes. Forty-three."

I had reckoned this young woman's age at only a few years shy of my own. Now it transpired she was my senior by well over a decade. *They don't age as we do*, I thought, mind racing through a parade of all the Caerith I had met. Uhlla appeared old but was clearly far more aged than I could have guessed. Yet she had met the Sack Witch when only a girl, and when I had finally looked upon the face beneath the sack she seemed to be scarcely older than I.

"How many summers for the *Doenlisch*?" I asked Lilat.

"Who can say? Time is different for her, and the *Eithlisch*. *Vaerith* makes it so."

Vaerith, the power that courses through the fabric of the world. The power that had torn my mind free of my body and cast it into the past. Clearly its gifts were many and, I now knew, suffused throughout the bloodline of the Caerith people, giving them longer lives but more so in some than others. *How many years has she walked the realm?* I wondered. *And was it all just to find me?*

"What did he tell you to do when you find the *Doenlisch*?" I asked. I met Lilat's eyes with a hard focus that told her I expected an answer regardless of what instructions she might have to the contrary.

Fortunately, she was willing to share this portion of her mission, albeit with a reluctant curtness.

"I will give her a message," she said, turning away to recommence her nimble passage across the ridge.

"What message?" I called after her, but this time she plainly had no intention of waiting for me and we traversed the ridge in silence that continued until the next morning.

Two more days of occasionally perilous climbing and inching along ledges of alarmingly narrow proportions brought the welcome sight of the valleys of south-western Alundia. Spring added a pleasing aspect to the gentle curving fields, sparse and uncultivated in the foothills but taking on the walled and stepped regularity of vineyard and farm where they faded into the distant horizon.

"What happened to this land?" Lilat asked. We stood atop a steep cliff below one of the lesser peaks. Off to the north I could see the sheer majesty of the Stermont, the great peak's summit scraping a furrow through the clouds. I therefore judged our position as several miles from the spot where the avalanche summoned by the treacherous Chops dragged me across the border.

"People," I said, starting along the cliff. It descended to the foothills in a wide arc and I wanted to be off these slopes before nightfall.

"Will we meet them soon?" she enquired, following. "Your people." I divined her to be enlivened by the prospect of practising her Albermainish with someone other than me.

"If there's any left nearby to meet," I murmured, casting a cautious glance at the valley ahead. "When we do, say nothing, and keep your bow handy."

"People here are your enemies?"

"Some. There was war here. Mayhap there still is."

"War about what?"

"Faith, land . . . greed. The usual things."

"So, bad people came here and you fought them? Did you win?"

I paused, glancing back at her with what I imagined to be a mirror of the sullen reticence as when I had quizzed her on her mission. I should have been flattered that she had cast me in a heroic role, but instead it stirred an irrational resentment. Even when I lived as a true villain I had never liked the mantle. "My people . . . my company came to fight the people of these lands. And yes, we won."

We camped that night on a wooded rise several miles from the foot of the mountains, having encountered not another soul during the day's journey. The only building I saw was a tumbledown shed filled with rotted turnips. The damage looked old so it may have been abandoned, but the contents spoke of a crop harvested but uneaten. All day I had nursed a rising tension that gripped me the moment we descended the mountain. It was irksome in the way it stiffened the shoulders and sharpened the eyes to imagined threats, but also comforting in its familiarity. I realised this had been how I had lived most of my life, either as an outlaw or a soldier. I also knew it had faded during my days among the Caerith and wondered why.

Those lands were at peace, I reminded myself during a fretful vigil when I took the first watch and Lilat slept. *These are not.*

We found the hanged man the next day. He swung in gentle circles above a broad stretch of the trail we had followed much of the day. His body, bound hand and foot, was suspended from the thick branch of a tall pine, the rope around his neck creaking as he swayed. From the bloat of his features and the pallor of his skin I judged him about three days dead. I could discern little from his face or bearing, since death tends to rob one of identity, but his plain but well-made clothing bespoke a member of the Alundian peasantry. More interesting was the wooden sign about his neck, the letters scorched into the wood with a burning taper.

"What do these words mean?" Lilat asked after I spent some time in silent regard of the dead man and the sign.

"It says, 'I denied the Rising of the Anointed Lady.' "

"Anointed Lady? She is . . . queen here?" My attempts to educate Lilat in the complexities of Albermainish society had been only marginally successful, since she apparently found it impossible to comprehend the entire notion of separate noble and churlish classes.

The concept of kings and queens, however, was easier to grasp since they featured in the older Caerith legends.

"No," I said. "But she is the woman I serve." I cast around the trail, spying a sizeable fallen tree trunk a short way off. "Help me with this."

"The woman you serve did this?" Lilat enquired as we dragged the heavy chunk of timber beneath the body.

"She wouldn't." I hopped onto the trunk and, taking tentative hold of the ill-smelling corpse, drew my knife to saw at the rope about his neck. "But I'd guess someone thought she wanted them to."

We buried the fellow as best we could, piling rocks and loose dirt over him, much to Lilat's bemusement. "The Caerith don't bury their dead?" I asked her, realising that throughout the winter at her village I hadn't witnessed a single funeral.

"The dead are our gift to the forest," she said, shaking her head. "From the forest we take game and wood and other things. We give our dead as nourishment in gratitude. It is a sad thing and a happy thing."

I spared a final glance at the hanged man's swollen, grey features, noting the deep wrinkles about his eyes. An old man then, left alone and defenceless with all the younger folk slain or fled. "Fare you well through the Portals, Grandfather," I sighed, kicking sod over his lifeless face.

I entertained some small optimism that his would be the last corpse we would find, but was inevitably soon disappointed. Before noon we encountered another four hanged souls, three men and a woman, all adorned with the same sign proclaiming their blasphemy against the Anointed Lady. We cut them down and opted to follow the Caerith custom of simply laying them to rest in the trees. When every other mile of the succeeding journey became marked by another victim, I told Lilat to just leave them be, except for the last one we happened upon just before nightfall.

His killers had strung him high in the branches of an old oak, small body dangling amid the shadowed branches. I would have missed it but Lilat had keener eyes. She tossed me her bow and swiftly climbed the oak's broad trunk, scrambling into the limbs with fluent ease to cut the boy down. Unwilling to let his corpse thud to the ground, I caught it. He wasn't long dead but his small face was swollen by the manner of his death, eyes bulging in pale, black-veined flesh. Whoever had done this had evidently run out of signs for the word "heretic" was carved into his forehead. The amount of dried blood indicated it had been done before the hanging. I judged the boy's age to be ten years at most.

"Tracks," I told Lilat when she descended the oak, my voice hoarse. She set about the task with no need for further urging, her peerless eyes finding the trail of our prey in moments.

"We'll bury him first," I said, carrying the boy into the trees.

"Have you ever killed a man or a woman?"

For the duration of the hunt Lilat's face had been fixed in the narrow concentration of the hunter at work, her eyes also gleaming with a roiling anger I hadn't seen in her before. Now, as we crouched in the bushes fringing the village ahead, the gleam was not so bright. We had sparred many times and I didn't doubt her courage, but both she and I were keenly aware this would be her first taste of actual combat.

Voices rose loud in the village, the silhouettes of perhaps a half-dozen men flitting across the large fire that blazed in the centre of the clustered cottages. Six men was a lot but I took comfort from the familiar, raucous pitch of those voices. *Drunkards are always easier to kill.*

The oval of Lilat's face caught a faint glowing outline from the fire which thinned and swelled as she shook her head. "It's not the same as a deer, or a bear, or anything else you've killed," I told her, slipping into my halting Caerith. It was important she understood me. "If we are to do this, I need to know you can."

By way of reply she turned from me, gripping the stave of her bow and running her fingers through the fletching of the arrow she had already notched to the string.

"Stay here," I said, rising from the bushes. "You'll know when."

I considered adding a parting comment about not sinking an arrow in my arse by mistake, but my mood this night was too raw for humour. Besides, I knew she would never miss anything she loosed at.

It may strike you, cherished reader, as a moment of singular bravery for me to walk into a camp of murderous men armed only with a hunting knife. However, an outlaw learns at an early age to weigh advantages. Most are small, often missed by the uneducated, but taken together they can tip seemingly impossible odds in your favour. For a start, these men were drunk. I also knew they would be infused by a sense of their own power having spent days visiting it upon those unable to resist. Such things inevitably lead to overconfidence, as evidenced by the fact that they hadn't bothered to post a sentry. Finally, as far these soon-to-be-dead men knew, I was on their side.

"Hello to the camp!" I called out upon reaching the southern end of the village. Naturally, my approach caused a stir, the drunkards' revels falling silent. I heard the tinkle and smash of dropped bottles as they scrambled to gather up weapons. Casting my eye over the cottages, I saw doors smashed and household items strewn about. A pair of lifeless legs protruded from one doorway; a woman's legs, bare and bloodied around the thighs. Drawing closer to the men at the fire, I was reassured to find that none held a crossbow. However, my confidence slipped a little when it became clear that my count had been off; there were eight of them, not six. Still, they all appeared to be gratifyingly inebriated, the ground surrounding their bonfire of piled furniture liberally covered in discarded wine bottles. Those closest to me formed a loose line, peering at the approaching stranger with swaying, dull-eyed suspicion rather than overt wariness.

"'S far enough," one of them slurred, a hefty fellow with an impressive mane of shaggy hair. He had a somewhat soldierly appearance, holding a hatchet and his broad torso clad in an ill-kept and heavily stained brigandine. "Who the fuck are you?" he demanded, brandishing his hatchet when I came fully into the light.

"Captain Alwyn Scribe of the Covenant Company," I told him, continuing my unhurried approach. "Who the fuck are you?"

"Captain Scribe is dead," one of the hefty fellow's companions said. He was of markedly smaller stature with sharp features and a recently healed scar tracing from his brow to his chin. He carried a billhook that stood considerably taller than he did. My soldierly disdain was piqued to find he hadn't bothered to clean the gore from the blade of his weapon. "Slain in glorious single combat with the heretic Roulgarth Cohlsair," he went on. "We heard the Anointed Lady's sermon on it with our own ears. She wept and everything."

This brought a murmur of agreement from the rest, firelight flickering on the swords and axes they held as the urge towards violence began to rise.

"No," another voice said from the far side of the fire, "that's him all right."

At first I assumed the man who stepped into view to be wearing some form of mask, so misaligned were his features. His nose had been flattened to the extent that it appeared to have melted into his face and his upper lip was the smear of scarred flesh that results from being poorly stitched after a grievous injury. When he spoke he revealed a set of jagged teeth that resembled those of a fish, the words emerging in a nasal, spittle-flecked rasp.

"Had the honour of serving under him at Highsahl," he said, arranging his malformed lips into a ghastly parody of a smile. "Or don't you remember, Captain?"

So here was the would-be mutineer with an incautious mouth, the one whom Eamond had joined in tormenting the maimed Alundian. Like the hatchet-bearing brute, he wore a brigandine of studded quilt besmirched by both wine and blood. Clearly, a gauntlet to the face hadn't done much to alleviate this man's vicious tendencies. He was also considerably less drunk than his friends, which drew me towards him.

"I remember," I said, sparing a short glance at the others. "I also remember dismissing you from Covenant service. Which begs the question: who do you serve now?"

"The Anointed Lady, of course." Flat-nose broadened his smile to reveal more jagged teeth, raising a clenched fist and turning to his companions. "Do we not, lads?"

They all responded with fervent if drunken alacrity, voicing a strident cry I knew well. "We fight for the Lady! We live for the Lady! We die for the Lady!"

"And yet I see no banner," I observed, coming to a halt a carefully judged distance from Flat-nose.

"Those who march in the Lady's cause need no banner," he replied, smile slipping from his malformed lips and a decided caution creeping into his gaze. "I heard her say so myself. You may have dismissed me, Captain, but she did not. All are welcome at her sermons and the truth of her mission is not to be denied."

"Her mission?" I turned, my gaze tracking from one ransacked cottage to another. "She set you to this, did she?"

"She did!" There was a fierceness to the fellow's nasal affirmation that told me he at least hadn't been compelled to murder and thievery by base motives alone. "By her truth! By her word!"

"Her truth! Her word!" the others repeated with discordant but enthusiastic volume. This one I hadn't heard before but a dispiriting instinct warned me this wouldn't be the last time. Dogmatic exhortations are like a plague, easily spread and hard to extinguish.

"Where did you last hear her speak?" I asked, making a careful and hopefully unnoticed survey of Flat-nose's armaments. He had a dagger on the right side of his belt and a longsword in a scabbard on the other. The sword's brass pommel gleamed bright, marking it as a knight's weapon, probably looted at Highsahl.

"The Anointed Lady journeys to all corners of this land," Flat-nose said, his voice a good deal softer now and the narrow caution in his eyes shifting to outright suspicion. I've often observed how the inherently cruel always have a keen sense of danger. "Spreading her word to heretic ears in the hope they'll hear the truth of it. Some do, most don't." He cast a hand at the pillaged cottages, no doubt home to more corpses. "Those who deny her word can expect no better, for in doing so they succour the Malecite and bring the Second Scourge ever closer."

"Every evil act does that." I conducted a brief, final survey of this band, fixing the position of each in my mind before once again focusing on Flat-nose. I thought about asking his name but decided I had no desire to remember it. "That's a nice blade," I said, nodding to the longsword at his belt and putting a commanding edge to my voice. "You'll notice I lack one at present. So give me yours."

Had Flat-nose been an outlaw he would have known this to be the moment for violence. A direct challenge demanding compliance required a brutal and unhesitant response. But, for all his recent spree of looting and murder, this man had not been a villain for long and so reacted exactly how I expected him to, raising his left hand to grip the sword's pommel with possessive refusal instead of drawing it. Outlaws only bandy words before the blades start flying to gain advantage, and by allowing me to get so close he had given me mine.

He opened his mouth to utter some form of retort, one that would be forever lost to posterity, for I had been closing distance with men I needed to kill since boyhood. Also, the many hours of punishment at Roulgarth's expert hands had made me faster than ever. So I never got to hear Flat-nose's last, assuredly impolite utterance. His eyes widened in shock and, to his credit, he managed to get his right hand to the sword before my knife slashed across the apple of his neck. I gripped his shoulder, keeping him upright long enough to bat his twitching hands away and drag the longsword from its scabbard. By the time I whirled to confront the others, I heard two arrows cut the air.

Lilat chose her targets wisely, sinking one shaft into the eye of the brute with the axe and the second into another tall shape on the opposite side of the bonfire. The tall man fell instantly but the axeman kept his feet, staggering about, drool-covered lips squirming as he tried to speak. His companions stood staring, eyes uniformly wide in shock. The bizarre ugliness of his demise was apparently so fascinating that they continued to stare rather than raise arms against the murderous captain who had just acquired a sword.

I cut down the sharp-faced man with the billhook next. He wore no brigandine or other form of protection and the longsword cleaved easily into his shoulder. I drove it deep enough to ensure a mortal blow before I kicked his body away. The remaining villains finally began to react, their drunkenness rousing them to resistance rather than the more sensible course of simply running off into the night.

A stocky man with a flushed, ruddy face made darker still by rage came at me with a levelled falchion. I sidestepped and parried the thrust in the same motion, then slashed the longsword across his legs. He fell thrashing while another fellow with long knives clutched in both hands threw himself forwards in a frenzy. I swayed clear of his flashing blades and shifted to the left, causing the knifer to follow, still snarling and stabbing at thin air. As he did so he silhouetted himself against the raging fire and presented a fine target for Lilat's next arrow. His frenzied assault ended abruptly as the shaft took him in the left buttock. He stumbled to a halt, dropping his knives to clutch at the arrow, a pointless exercise since all it earned him was another through the mouth. His head snapped forwards then back and he toppled into the fire, sending a cloud of embers into the night sky.

Besides the still tottering and gibbering brute, only two remained standing, the youngest of the group judging by their beardless, terror-stricken faces. I might have felt a pang of pity for them if I hadn't been sure their reaction to the ravaging of this village had been very different. One of these gaping youths was clearly smarter than the other, for he ran, albeit not very far before Lilat's arrow streaked from the gloom to skewer him through the back. The other one dropped his weapon, a rusted wood axe with a chipped blade, and fell to his knees, staring at me with naked entreaty.

"Craven . . . fucking dolt!" the ruddy-faced fellow rasped from the ground, trying and failing to rise on his maimed and bleeding legs. "Bastard's gonna kill you anyway!" He flailed about, managing to get a hand to his fallen falchion. "Might as well die fight—"

I stamped down on his back and finished him with a thrust to the base of the skull. Hearing a sibilant voice, I looked up to find the hulking axe man was staggering towards me with Lilat's arrow jutting from his eye. "Portalsss . . ." he said in a wet slur, blood now staining the drool dribbling down his chin. "Lady promisssed . . ."

"I'm sure she did," I told him, moving to deliver a merciful thrust to his neck. However, he consented to topple face first to the ground before I could strike, the fall driving the arrow all the way through his skull whereupon he lay thankfully silent.

"Please, Captain," the kneeling lad said, face imploring and eyes wet. He held his hands above his head as he wept and begged. "Wasn't my doing. Came in answer to the Lady's beacon, I did. We all did. When the war in the north ended we followed her, but she didn't need no more soldiers . . ."

"Shut your yap," I told him, which he did, continuing to stare up at me with his begging eyes until Lilat's appearance drew forth a fearful whimper. She appeared out of the shadows on the far side of the fire, moving from one body to the other. Any doubts I might have harboured about her suitability for the warrior's life faded at the sight of her sinking her knife into every one, each blow delivered with a precise absence of hesitation.

"The Anointed Lady," I said to the kneeling youth. "Where is she now?"

"Last saw her heading north, Captain. Back to her castle, so we heard."

"You mean Walvern Castle?"

He bobbed his head. "It's called the Martyr's Reach now. The king gave it to her as a reward, and all the lands around."

I nodded. This made sense and I heard no lie on his lips. "Did she really set you to this?" I asked, causing him to shudder. He might have fled if Lilat hadn't appeared at his back, bloody knife in hand.

"Didn't order it, or us, exactly," the lad gabbled. "But her sermons . . . they'd gotten so angry. You've heard her, you know how they fire folk up something terrible. And what she did to those other rebels . . ."

"What other rebels?"

"There was a town in the south, near the coast. Mersvel I think they called it. When the Lady led the company to their gates they barred them and stuck heads of true-faithers on the walls. The Lady burned the whole place down, so they say. None were spared."

I stepped closer, fixing his tear-streaked gaze. "You saw this?"

"No . . ." His voice slipped to a whisper and he shook his head.

"Saw the ashes after, though. Nothing was left. That's why, y'see? Why they thought it was all allowed . . ."

"They but not you, right? We found a boy no more than ten summers old hanging in a tree not far from here. That was just them too, I suppose?"

His head shakes became frantic. "Had no hand in that, I swear! On my fucking mother I swear!"

This time I heard the lie, albeit one coloured by a hefty dose of despairing guilt. He had a full share of the horrors this lot had wrought in this valley. However, I also didn't doubt his claim that his friends would have killed him if he hadn't joined in. Regarding his unblinking, desperate eyes, I recalled my boyhood devotion to Deckin, something born as much of terror as respect or gratitude. Had he set me to massacring churls, I would surely have done it. Then again, Deckin would never have issued such an order; you couldn't thieve from murdered villagers.

"Get yourself gone," I said, stepping back and jerking my head at the darkness beyond the cottages. "Spread the word of what happened here to any other scum you meet. And, boy—" my hand came down on his shoulder, gripping hard and stilling the tearful babble of thanks tumbling from his lips "—it'd be best if I never saw your worthless carcass again."

Lilat watched the youth flee into the gloom with a quizzical expression. "Why these and not him?" she asked, kicking the feet of the fallen axe man.

"Those who serve the Anointed Lady know the value of mercy." The words sounded empty even to my own ears, a man muttering an old joke he had long since decided wasn't funny after all. I moved away, my boots scattering some empty wine bottles. "I need a drink. These bastards must've left me something."

CHAPTER THIRTY-ONE

The wine, I'm sure, was a fine vintage. So fine its recently slain owners had felt the need to hide it beneath a trapdoor in their woodshed. Yet, it tasted like vinegar on my tongue as I sat watching the villains' bodies burn in their own bonfire. I hadn't lost myself in drink for many months and now found its tempting oblivion beyond reach. After the first few gulps failed to produce the sought-after numbness I passed the bottle to Lilat.

"Fruits of the Duchy of Alundia," I said, watching her give the contents a suspicious sniff. "Enjoy."

She frowned at the first taste but apparently found it pleasing enough to keep hold of the bottle. She had betrayed little outward concern over what we had just done, but the loud crack of a collapsing timber from the corpse-laden fire provoked a shudder.

"You were right," she said, eyes lingering on the flame-licked bodies. "Not like a deer."

"You did well," I told her, forcing a tight smile. "A true *taolisch*."

The compliment did nothing to smooth her increasingly creased brow, gaze still fixed on the burning villains. "War is like this all the time?"

"More or less. Not pretty is it?"

She shook her head, taking another swallow from the bottle.

"The Caerith must fight wars," I said, realising it was a question that hadn't arisen before. "Else why have warriors?"

"There are . . ." She paused, fumbling for the right word and, not finding it, settled for a clumsy translation. "Bad people in ships. They come in the south where Caerith lands meet the sea. *Taolisch* fight them and they not come again for many seasons. But always come back when memory fades."

"So you fight raiders but not each other?"

This question seemed to be so puzzling that Lilat clearly had trouble comprehending the entire notion of strife between the Caerith. "No," she said simply after a long, bemused interval. She drank again, a faintly woozy smile appearing on her lips. "This is good fruit."

"Many of my countrymen would agree."

I lapsed into silence, contemplating the fire and its grisly fuel. In time, the flames ate away their clothes and stained the air with a familiar, meaty stench that had me covering my nose with my cloak. I found my eyes straying to the west where the shadowy bulk of the Stermont rose into a starlit sky. I had only had a taste of the land beyond, as Lilat had only partaken of a meagre amount of wine. But, like her, I couldn't deny I wanted more.

"This was all supposed to end, you know," I said, gesturing to the ruined village. "We ended one war, winning a victory that assuredly meant peace for decades to come. Instead, we were sent off to the north to fight a second." I gave a humourless chuckle. "We lost and when we came back they sent us here to fight yet another. The Anointed Lady preaches peace wherever she goes, but war is never far behind."

"You can go back." I turned to find Lilat regarding me with both sincerity and sympathy. "Caerith know you now. Won't kill you."

"Perhaps not. But I doubt Uhlla or the *Eithlisch* would appreciate my presence. Besides—" I hefted my newly acquired sword and got to my feet, nausea rising at the stink from the fire "—I have a book to write. Come on, we'll camp further along the road."

*

Upon climbing the ridge south of Walvern Castle I found the old pile of stones barely recognisable. The walls and tower were all encased in a dense web of scaffolding from which arose the continual cacophony of many masons and carpenters at work. The entire site was ringed by a tall wooden stockade that extended for at least a quarter-mile. Wagons arrived and departed via the track that had been improved into a true road since my last visit.

"The Martyr's Reach," I said softly, eyes tracking from the toiling workers to the surrounding hills where yet more artisans laboured. The ridgeline to the east featured a tall tower, recently completed judging by the absence of scaffolding, while three more were under construction at opposite points of the compass. Whoever had been given charge of transforming this once-vulnerable place clearly had no intention of allowing an enemy force to approach unde-tected in future.

"This is a castle?" Lilat asked, brow furrowed in doubt as she surveyed the scene. The Caerith possessed little in the way of forti-fications and our journey north had been lacking in examples. I had been at pains to keep clear of any place where we might encounter people in large numbers. The borderlands were rich in evidence of a troubled land; ravaged villages became a common sight and corpses plentiful, including that of the youth I had spared that first night. Three days on we found him nailed to the floor of a ruined Martyr shrine, split from groin to chops. Whether he had been caught by vengeful Alundians or other devotional brigands I couldn't say. Nor did I surrender to the temptation to have Lilat hunt down the lad's killers. It was plain that if we paused to admin-ister justice for every atrocity we encountered, our journey through this land would be long indeed.

Signs of discord grew less evident as we moved north, staying off the roads and relying on Lilat's skills to keep us fed. We even passed by a small number of once-destroyed Martyr shrines under recon-struction. Each one featured a sizeable guard I assumed must be of the Covenant Company, although I resisted the impulse to make myself known. When I looked upon Evadine's face I wanted her to have no warning of my arrival. I had questions, and lies were harder to speak in moments of surprise.

"It was old," I told Lilat. "Now it is . . . reborn."

Hearing a chorus of alarm from the nearest half-built tower, I watched a half-dozen soldiers quickly gather weapons and make their way towards us at the run. The burly fellow at their head came to a sudden halt upon catching sight of my face. Only a couple of the soldiers at his back were veterans and displayed a similar pitch of shock, while their comrades squinted at them in puzzled indecision until one levelled his halberd at me.

"This is not free land!" he growled, advancing. "State your business . . ."

His challenge ended when the burly man delivered a hard cuff to his head. "Curb your tongue, dung-wit!" He turned to me, bowing in apology. "Captain . . . I . . . We thought . . ."

"Sergeant Castellan Estrik," I cut in, sparing him more stuttered formality. "Good to see you." I nodded to the castle. "You've been busy, I see."

He raised his head, smiling in relief since talk of building was always his most comfortable subject. "The Lady gave me free rein to plan it all," he said. "Walvern Castle will be but a shadow to the Martyr's Reach. With all the coin the king's given over, reckon we'll have it mostly done before winter. It's my honour to raise for her a castle that'll never be taken."

"I've no doubt of it. Is the Lady in residence?"

"Aye." Estrik's eyes flicked towards Lilat in obvious curiosity but, ever a circumspect soul, he asked no questions. "We'll escort you . . ."

"No need." I started down the slope, jerking my head at Lilat to follow. "I'm sure you have work to do. I look forward to hearing a full account of your plans."

I heard the soldiers mutter among themselves as we descended the ridge. "He's s'posed to be dead . . . The Lady said she'd see they made him a Martyr . . . Does that mean he's Risen too?"

Such talk brought a darkening of my mood as we tracked across the plain to the stockade. It appeared my supposed demise had become the stuff of unlikely legend, which was understandable. Talk of being made a martyr was decidedly not something I either comprehended or welcomed.

"You recall what I told you about lying?" I asked Lilat as we drew near the gate to the stockade.

"Your people do it all the time," she replied. Dishonesty wasn't unknown among the Caerith but it did carry a far greater stigma than it did here.

"Yes," I said. "And I'm about to do a good deal more of it. For both our sakes, it's best if you say, well, nothing."

"Nothing?"

"Indeed. Nothing at all. As far they'll know, you don't speak their tongue. It's for your own protection." I didn't add that I suspected it might also prove advantageous, for folk will happily gabble out all manner of interesting things in front of one they think incapable of comprehension.

Fortunately, the gate was manned mostly by veterans who let us pass without hindrance beyond a few irksomely awed comments. "The Seraphile truly bless our company, Captain!" called one earnest young woman I recalled leading through the breach at Highsahl. "To return you to us for the battles ahead!"

The reception we received upon entering the castle itself was both overwhelming and aggravating, making me wish I had contrived some manner of approaching the place by stealth. Soldiers downed tools or paused in their duties to stare at the resurrected captain who strolled through the gate, with a Caerith in tow no less. Hearty greetings soon filled the air and many came to offer salutes and bows, some breaching custom by clapping me on the shoulder.

"I hoped . . ." Eamond was among the first to throng around me, shaking his head in wonder, voice choked. "But they said you were beyond hope now. It's a miracle—"

"No," I cut in, moving to put a firm hand on his neck. "Just blind luck, and," I added, casting a glance at Lilat who stood nearby regarding the scene with tense uncertainty, "kind assistance."

I huffed out a sharp breath as a slight figure slipped through the throng to enfold my waist in a fierce hug. Ayin buried her head in my chest for a time, eyes closed tight, then drew back to thump a fist into my shoulder. "Don't die again!" she instructed, delivering another, harder punch that was sure to leave a bruise. "I didn't like it."

"It wasn't a parcel of laughs for me either." I returned her embrace before easing her away as a strident and familiar voice rang out.

"Give the captain some room." The surrounding knot drawing back as a tall figure in full armour pushed his way through. Wilhum surprised me with a warm smile as he surveyed my ragged garb, eyes coming to rest on the longsword at my belt. "That's new. Lost your own, did you?"

"Hard to keep hold of a sword when you're tumbling down a mountain."

He gave a short laugh before voicing a more serious and expected question. "Roulgarth. Did you kill him?"

I shook my head. "A whole mountainside's worth of snow and ice did that. Saw the body. Wasn't much left, I'm afraid."

"Good. Might put paid to all the dung the Alundians spout about the return of the Righteous Sword, but I doubt it."

"Righteous Sword?"

"It's what they've taken to calling Roulgarth now. To hear the tales, you'd think he'd actually won the war and then graciously decided to take himself on an excursion. Legend has it he'll return one day to slaughter all of us heretic interlopers."

"No. He won't be doing that." I didn't feel this to be a lie at the time. Although I had been denied a farewell with Roulgarth, my last glimpse of him contemplating the sword gifted to him by the *Eithlisch* had made a deep impression. Intuition told me that the once-vengeful man I had left behind on the far side of the mountains was gone, or at least transformed. *Vahlisch*, the Eithlisch had called him. Master of Blades, a title that I felt sure had set him on a new path, one I doubted would lead him back to this duchy anytime soon.

"Aren't you going to introduce me to your interesting companion?" Wilhum asked, offering Lilat a florid bow.

"She calls herself Lilat," I said. "I won't bother telling her your name since she doesn't speak a word of the civilised tongue." I paused, raising my voice so that all the gathered soldiery could hear. "I'll tolerate no insult or injury to this woman, for it's thanks to her that I still draw breath. She found me, you see," I added in a softer tone, turning back to Wilhum. "Broken and bleeding at the foot of the Stermont. Hid me in a cave and fed me for months. When I was well again she followed me over the mountains." I lowered my voice to a whisper, stepping close to him. "I think she's a tad smitten with me, truth be told. I suspect, according to some bizarre Caerith custom, she thinks we're married."

Lilat had very keen ears and it was to her credit that she endured this nonsense while maintaining a determinedly baffled expression.

"Poor woman," Wilhum sighed. "To be afflicted with both blindness and bad judgement." He shook his head in a manner that made it clear he believed either very little or nothing at all of my story. Still, I was thankful that he played along.

"Company to attention! Stand aside!"

The rasping authority of this new voice brought a smile to my lips and I turned to greet Swain with a respectful bow. His features, however, were hard and yielded no response save a stiff nod. Around us the soldiers all adopted the customary straight-backed posture, eyes snapping forwards, even Wilhum, whom I would have expected to enjoy some largesse. There was a shuffling of feet on cobbles as they made way for the Anointed Lady.

She wore no armour today, clad in the simple dark cotton trews and shirt she favoured, a thin cloak about her shoulders. Still, I felt her aura of command, that inescapable feeling of presence, had actually increased in my absence. Her soldiers had always been respectful but rarely had I seen them rendered so utterly still and silent by her proximity. I caught a twitch or two on more than a few faces as they stood awaiting her word, eyes blinking in the manner that told of as much fear as it did regard.

Evadine herself seemed serene to my eyes, as close as she would come in reality to the many images painted of the Risen Martyr since.

She looked upon me with a steady gaze, one I might have read as hostility in another soul.

"My lady," I said, sinking to one knee and lowered my head. "I humbly crave your pardon for my lengthy absence . . ."

I fell silent as her hand, cool and soft, fluttered across my brow before resting on my chin. "Rise," she said, her voice a whisper, and when I did, she stared into my eyes, blinking tears before throwing her arms around my neck and crushing herself against me. And there in that courtyard, as her soldiers stood like statues and pretended not to see, the Risen Martyr Lady Evadine Courlain wept.

"How could you think that of me?"

The fury in Evadine's eyes matched the flames blazing in the fire-place of her quarters. She was the tower's sole occupant now, save for the small watch party on the roof and even they were obliged to ascend to their perch via ladders propped against the exterior wall. The Anointed Lady, it transpired, would no longer tolerate any intru-sion upon her privacy, except mine, apparently.

"You consider me a murderer now, Alwyn?" she asked, her voice possessed of a quiet put palpable anger. "You think me a slaughterer of innocents?"

"I don't think anything," I replied, maintaining an even tone shorn of either accusation or servility. "I merely relate a tale I heard and ask about its veracity."

After the strange interlude in the courtyard she had retreated from me with an order to follow her to the tower, turning and striding off without another word. In her wake the collection of soldiers continued to stand at attention until Swain barked out a curt dismissal. I asked Ayin to find a suitable lodging for Lilat then paused as Wilhum put a hand on my arm.

"Craft your story with care," he said softly, eyes flicking towards Evadine's receding back. "She is not . . . as she was."

He walked away before I could ask after his meaning. I found the tower's main chamber largely unchanged except for the banners that lined the walls. The emblems they bore were mostly unfamiliar and

I concluded they must be trophies, captured sigils of Alundian noble houses. This meant that the company's campaign in this duchy hadn't ended at Highsahl, leading me to enquire as to the fate of Mersvel. Although I hadn't heard of the place before it babbled from the lips of the doomed youth, it had sat festering in my mind throughout the journey north.

"And who told this tale?" Evadine demanded. "Am I to be denied the name of my accuser?"

"He was a renegade miscreant who now lies dead," I replied. "But I didn't judge him a liar. In fact, he and the band of scum he ran with believed that what happened at Mersvel gave them licence to visit whatever atrocity they pleased upon the folk of this duchy."

"I cannot be held accountable for the actions of the wretched and the mad." She stared at me with her fiery gaze for a heartbeat longer then looked away, moving to rest her hand on the fireplace mantle, head lowered. "Things were done at Mersvel, vile things, but not by my hand. I came to take a town in the name of the king and to secure the lives of true adherents to the Covenant, taken as hostages by diehard heretics. And die they did, taking their homes and families with them. The fire that consumed that place was not set by my order, and I gave succour to any who survived it." She let out a long, ragged sigh. "Not that there were many. Had you been there, perhaps we could have contrived some stratagem, some trick to take the place without those fanatics setting it to the torch. But you know such things are not my province and there are no others in this company with your gifts."

I endured the implied reproach in silence which seemed to anger her further. "Does this account meet with your approval, Alwyn?" she demanded, gaze flashing at me. "Do I stand free of sin in your eyes?"

I couldn't tell if she had told the entire story of Mersvel's demise, but I didn't see or hear a lie in her bearing or her voice. It was clear that the event pained her, yet I divined that she at least considered herself blameless for the town's fate. I remembered the historian's final words before our parting, the lie he told made starker and absurd as

I beheld Evadine's face. She, I knew, had suffered a great deal in her devotion, and was willing to suffer yet more.

"Long did I hope," she went on, looking away once more. "At night, alone in the dark and suffering the torments of doubt and guilt, I hoped that the Seraphile in their mercy had seen fit to spare you. They granted me no visions, no dreams of you, where you might be. And yet, a small part of me knew you still drew breath and, if you could, you would return to me. And now, here you are, returned not with love but condemnation."

Lacking an answer, I moved to stand at the fireplace, regarding her in silence. Her perfect profile, painted a soft shade of red by the glow, would have been a placid mask but for the way her eyes danced. They seemed to be searching the flames, as if trying to discern some meaning in the chaos.

"On the road I saw many ugly sights," I said. "You and I had no small part in bringing this duchy to ruin. So, if there's condemnation to be had I'll suffer my share, so long as I know the end we strive for is worth the blood we spill."

"Do you doubt it?" Much of the anger had leached from her voice, but it still held a drop or two of acid. "Or did your time among the savage heathen turn your heart away from the Covenant? Legend speaks of how . . . seductive their ways can be."

I considered maintaining my lie about skulking in a cave for months, but an instinctive certainty warned me she would hear the falsehood. In her own way, she had as keen an ear for lies as I did, especially when born of my tongue.

"Heathens they are," I said. "But they are not savage. They could have killed me but didn't. Nor did they try to entice me into their heretic customs, of which I saw scant evidence. Mostly, they just wanted me to heal and go away." I felt there to be enough truth in this to mollify her, but still a suspicion clouded her eyes.

"Except for the girl who followed you here," she said and I couldn't deny the clear note of jealousy that coloured her tone. "What is her purpose in this realm, exactly?"

"She's very far from being a girl," I replied, my own voice hardened by a protective urge. I had never seen Evadine jealous before and it rendered her normally pleasing features into something decidedly off-putting. "And her purpose is her own. Given the debt I owe her, I'll not abide any obstruction to it, or her."

"What is this regard you have for them? First, you consort with that *witch* after the Traitors' Field, now this."

That witch saved your life. There are times when allowing anger to spill truth from one's lips will have dire consequences, and this would surely have been such an occasion. Gritting my teeth, I turned away, speaking in as even and controlled a manner as I could. "Ascendant Sihlda taught me to accept all souls I meet in this world, until their actions prove them unworthy of such acceptance. I'll not shun an entire people merely because they were not born into the Covenant."

Evadine gave no response but a sideways glance revealed her still contemplating the fire, although now her eyes no longer searched the flames. Letting out a small sigh of regret, I ventured a softly spoken entreaty. "I recall what you said to your father back in the Shavine Forest. About how your visions tormented you as a girl, about the Caerith charm worker . . ."

"I'll hear no more on that, or this," she snapped, moving away, arms crossed and showing me her back. After a lengthy pause and several slow breaths, she said, "I made Ofihla captain of the Second Company. She has done very well and I am loath to replace her. Also, Wilhum now commands near four hundred armoured horse who would be better employed in battle than reconnaissance. Therefore, you will undertake a new role, that of captain of scouts. You may have your pick of recruits, within reason. Wilhum will not be best pleased if you take his best riders. You will also choose a select few with skills beyond riding and tracking. Those with keen ears and eyes who know how to pass unnoticed in a crowd. One thing this campaign has taught me is that a single morsel of sound intelligence is worth more than a thousand soldiers."

So, you've learned the value of guile at last, I thought, saying, "If I'm to be your spymaster it would help if I knew the current state of the realm."

Evadine moved to her tall chair, resting a hand on the back which I noticed had acquired some leather padding since last I saw it. "Princess Leannor held court in Highsahl throughout the winter," she said, "but departed for Couravel a month ago. It seems she's keen to oversee the betrothal ceremony for her son and Lady Ducinda. Lord Elfons Raphine has been appointed Protector Royal of Alundia and exercises Crown authority in this duchy. Before she left the princess was kind enough to communicate her brother's grant of this castle and surrounding lands to me. The Luminants' Council have also seen fit to elevate me to the rank of Ascendant."

"No less than you deserve, my lady."

She responded with an irritated shrug. "Titles and lands are meaningless now. I presume the king and the council intended them as rewards, an attempt to keep me quiescent in this forgotten corner of the realm while they pursue their endless intrigues."

"Speaking of which, what of the Duke of Althiene? Last I heard the death of his daughter had roused him to gather troops."

"Reports are sketchy but Duke Guhlton remains behind his borders. The fact that his only surviving grandchild now resides in Algathinet hands may well prove sufficient to keep him at bay, for now at least. Still—" she consented to meet my eye, speaking with carefully phrased intent "—it would be to our benefit if we had a better understanding of the situation in the north, especially in regard to the actions of the council. Rumours have reached us of a new Covenant Company being raised on council coin."

"A company that will not march under the banner of the Anointed Lady, I take it?" Receiving another shrug in response, I grunted a laugh. "Free swords, beggars and villains is all they're likely to recruit. Those with a sincere desire to fight for the Covenant will flock to only one banner."

"Nevertheless, I would know more of it."

I nodded, seeing the wisdom of her course. Recent victor and duly recognised Risen Martyr or not, the Luminants' Council could never truly accept this woman's rise. She made their irrelevance far too stark. "I'll set out once I've picked my choice for the Scout Company..."

"No!" Her eyes flashed again, this time in alarm rather than anger. "No, henceforth your place is at my side. This I have seen. This I know." I watched her fingers twitch before she closed them into a fist, moving to settle herself into the chair. Speaking with measured deliberation, she said, "I regret speaking to you in harsh terms, Alwyn. Know that I do so only out of concern. I have seen clearly that I cannot do what the Seraphile demand of me without your . . . guidance, your insight. You try to hide it, but I can see your doubts. Sihlda was a fine teacher, I'm sure, but when you were . . . absent, in my grief I finally read her testament. There is much wisdom in those pages, and great compassion, but her judgement regarding the Scourge—"

"She was wrong," I cut in, closing my eyes against the memory of the great city in the past, all those countless souls beset by insanity. "I know. The Scourge was real, as real as anything in this world. Be assured I no longer have any doubts as to the rightness of our cause."

Evadine angled her head a little, eyes narrowing in a scrutiny that was intense enough to make me shift in discomfort. "What happened on the other side of those mountains, Alwyn?" she asked. "What did you see?"

Acutely aware that her long-standing antipathy to the Caerith and their heretical customs made a full telling of my story unwise, I opted instead for obfuscated truth. "The Caerith write nothing down but they do have legends, old tales of an event they call the Fall, a time when madness seized the souls of all and tumbled great cities to rubble. I have walked among the sundered stones of a once-great empire. Only the worst calamity could have destroyed such greatness."

Evadine sat back, her previous anger all but replaced by cautious acceptance. "So, we are of like mind at last. It is well that it comes now at the beginning of what I'm sure will be our hardest trial."

I detected a particular weight to her words, one I had heard often enough to recognise. "You had another vision," I said.

"I did. Last night in fact, which I refuse to count as a coincidence."

"What did you see?"

A heavy sigh escaped her lips and she looked back at the fire, eyes dancing once again. "A wonderful and terrible opportunity," she said in a tone that made it clear no further elaboration would be forthcoming.

Reclining further, she drew her legs up to her chest, wrapping her arms around them. Suddenly she was no longer the Anointed Lady; now I looked upon a young woman facing awesome responsibilities. "Will you sit with me a while, Alwyn?" she asked, voice faint. Her lips pressed tight and she blinked rapidly, still contemplating the fire. "We can talk about Sihlda's Testament if you would like. It is my opinion that it's past time for the council to formally name her a Martyr."

Her chamber was lacking in chairs save for a single stool in a shadowed corner. "I should like that very much, my lady," I said, fetching the stool to sit opposite her. "What passage would you like to discuss first?"

I saw the corners of her mouth curl as she said, "I leave the choice to you, Captain." Evadine didn't look away from the fire as I began a short recitation of Sihlda's commentary on the value of charity. To this day I wonder what Evadine saw in those twisting flames.

PART III

Scholars will often wax poetic on the terrors and depredations of war, but in doing so they blind themselves to an awful truth: war is as alluring and seductive as it is destructive and terrible. True peace will only come when we close our hearts to its promises, for always they are proven to be lies.

From *The Testament of Ascendant Sihlda Doisselle,*
as recorded by Sir Alwyn Scribe.

CHAPTER THIRTY-TWO

Deckin once told me: *If I only ran with thieves I liked, I'd never run at all.* Never was this particular jewel of wisdom more apposite than when contemplating the distasteful person of Tiler. I didn't merely dislike this wiry, pinch-faced cur; I detested him, fully and without reservation. My loathing had first been piqued when I scared him away from Lord Eldurm Gulatte's body when it was dragged from the river after the Traitors' Field. The mercifully infrequent encounters with him since had done much to deepen that initial, odious impression. The aftermath of every battle since had revealed Tiler as an enthusiastic looter of the dead or not-yet-dead, for he would happily speed the mortally stricken on their way, especially if he espied gold in the teeth they bared in their agony.

Yet, vile as he was, a detestable man can still be useful, and Tiler was a fellow of undeniable skills. Despite many months in the company he had no reputation for cowardice, meaning he could fight, or at least hold his place in line without pissing himself. More useful for my purposes, however, were the thieving skills that had landed him in the sanctuary town of Callintor. In truth, I never met a better pickpocket. Even the skills of lovely, light-fingered Gerthe paled in comparison to Tiler's gift for transferring the valuables of others into his own hands. The order of his skill naturally caused me to question how he had managed to end up in Callintor at all.

"Base treachery, Captain," he said, not quite managing to keep the sullen cast from his face. He did contrive to keep his tone respectful, albeit with some effort. It is the nature of the detested to hate their detesters, after all. "Beat a prideful man at cards and he'll find a way to settle the debt. So it was with me. Woke up one morn in the brothel to find a brace of sheriff's bastards standing over me with noose in hand. Cost me all my riches to bribe the fuckers to turn their backs long enough for me to make it to Callintor. This was all before I heard the Lady speak, o'course. Such villainy is behind me now, my soul being filled with the Seraphile's light . . ."

"All right, shut it," I said wearily, which added a resentful gleam to his surly eye. Like many a former outlaw in this company, Tiler could perform the curious mental trick of combining genuine devotion to the Anointed Lady with mostly unchanged criminal habits. "I'm told you can read," I said, handing him a scrap of parchment. "What's this say?"

He peered at the text before stumbling through a halting but accurate recitation of the opening passage to the Scroll of Martyr Lemeshill. "And great . . . was the . . . g-grief and the . . . guilt of m-mighty . . . Lemeshill. Sh-shunning his . . . palace and his . . . wives, he went forth . . . into the desert where . . . holy Stevanos once trod . . ."

"Good enough," I said, taking the parchment from him before subjecting him to a lengthy glare of unstinting scrutiny. He bore it in discomfited but wise silence. I had taken over the completed watchtower on the south-facing ridge to serve as the home for my new company, thinking it best that training and instruction occur away from curious eyes and ears. The weeks since my return had produced fifty-three recruits besides Ayin, Eamond and the Widow, all chosen as much for familiarity as anything else. Most were the more skilled riders Wilhum was willing to part with, lacking the muscle or aggression for mounted warfare but capable of swiftly traversing many miles on horseback. There were no hunters or skilled trackers among them, making me miss Fletchman, but I had Lilat for that if need be. Of the company entire, I found only a half-dozen with the necessary skills suited to the more subtle aspect of my new commission, all but one former outlaws. It should come as scant surprise that honest folk rarely make good spies.

"You've a Shavine accent," I observed to Tiler eventually. "But it speaks of the coast rather than the forest. Am I right?"

"Partly, Captain. Mam was a smuggler from the northern ports. Da was a thief, ran with one of the old bands in the forest. One of those bands that mostly got their throats slit when Deckin Scarl made himself King of Outlaws." The steadiness of his gaze told me he knew well whom I had once run with, but it was a commonly known story and Deckin was long dead.

"Yes," I said. "I heard that happened a lot. You ever hear the name Shilva Sahken?"

His thin brows quirked. "O'course. Every cutpurse who ventured near the sea had to pay her tribute, and there's plenty of sailor's coin to be had in the ports. Mam was kin with her. Distant, mind, but blood is blood."

"So you could find her, if I set you to it?"

"Reckon so. There's bound to be a few villains in the ports who remember the Tiler." His expression became suddenly cautious. "Iffen that's the Lady's wish."

The small but perceptible doubt in his voice caused me to fix him with an unblinking stare. "It is," I said in a murmur, holding his gaze until he consented to lower it.

"You will read and memorise this," I told him, handing over a second document. "When I'm satisfied that you've committed it to memory you will travel north to the Shavine Marches, find Shilva Sahken and repeat every word exactly as written. When she gives her reply, you will bring it to me."

"Way I hear it," Tiler said, unfolding the parchment to squint at the contents, "in recent years she's become a woman of notoriously changeable temper. What if she takes it into her mind to kill me?"

"Then I'll regard that as her reply."

A humourless snort came from his narrow nose but he uttered no argument. "I'll need coin for the journey."

"You'll have it. And company on the road, to keep you safe." I beckoned to the hefty figure standing in the lee of the tower. "Master Liahm will go with you."

The thief and the woodsman exchanged wary glances of appraisal that told of instant and mutual dislike. Devoted he might be, but Tiler remained a villain at heart. Liahm I had chosen for his keen mind and undistinguished appearance, strong of body but not so tall as to attract attention. Also, he had the churls' gift for obsequious artifice if need arose. Even observant nobles tend to pass by those who bow lowest.

"Take yourself off to Ayin," I instructed Tiler. "She'll school you in any words you don't know. And have a care around her," I added as he started towards the tower. "They don't call her the Ball-cutter without reason."

I took satisfaction from the dark glower on the woodsman's face as he watched Tiler disappear into the tower. It suited my purposes for them not to be friends. "He's cunning and distrustful by nature," I said. "But he's never wavered in following the Lady. Still, when surrounded once again by his villainous associates he may find temptation hard to resist. If you suspect for one instant he might prove disloyal, don't hesitate."

Liahm lowered his head in agreement, although I discerned a reluctance in his bearing. "Do you have an issue with this errand, Master Woodsman?" I asked.

"It's just . . ." He straightened, wincing in discomfort. I remembered that this man had lived most of his life without ever being asked for an opinion on anything save perhaps the weather or the seasoning of felled timber.

"Speak your mind," I told him. A spy given to blind obedience was little use.

He phrased his question with a creditable care which did much to buttress my faith in my own judgement. "Would I be wrong in thinking you're sending us to find this Sahken woman with a view to agreeing some form of alliance?"

"You would," I said. "I am sending you to open negotiations regarding trade, to wit: information in return for coin."

"Forgive me, Captain," he coughed and shifted his feet, "but to sully the Lady's renown by associating with, well, the scum of the realm seems . . . wrong."

"Scum of the realm?" I asked, enjoying the sight of him squirming. "What does that make me? Or half the soldiers in this company? The Lady has never shunned an outlaw. Why should I?" I let him fidget some more while fumbling for a response before putting an end to his torment. Liahm Woodsman was certainly uneducated, but he was no fool and I sensed his pragmatic soul would respond best to simple honesty.

"There are now three powers in this realm," I said. "The Crown, the Covenant and the Anointed Lady. The balance between them is precarious and it's only a matter of time before it tips. It falls to me to ensure it tips in the Lady's favour, yet I have but a pittance of scouts to work with. Princess Leannor has spies in every corner of this realm. The Luminants' Council can call upon the eyes and ears of every cleric in shrines scattered throughout every duchy. Shilva Sahken, however, sits at the head of a vast web of smugglers, thieves and whores, and trust my villainous word when I say that there is no better well of knowledge to draw from, scummed or not."

I raised my eyebrows, smiling tightly until he bowed his head again. "We live for the Lady—"

"That we do!" I broke in, clapping him on the shoulder and steering him towards the watchtower. "Come, we'll see if Master Eamond has managed to cook a supper worth eating for once. Wouldn't do to send you off with a growling belly, would it?"

After Tiler and Liahm departed on the northward adventure, the better part of another month passed before the royal messenger arrived at the Martyr's Reach. I tend to look upon those days as a pleasing interlude, perhaps because they offer such a contrast to those that followed. I made Eamond a sergeant and left the mounted scouts mostly in his hands, sending them off on extended patrols through the surrounding country. It was largely empty now, the few villages that once dotted the nearby vales now charred and abandoned ruins that harboured little danger. I sent Lilat with them to serve as a tracker. She was keen on learning to ride despite the art being apparently unknown in her corner of the Caerith dominion. I made great play of pretending to teach her Albermainish in a remarkably short time, enhancing my stature in the eyes of my mostly youthful recruits. The Widow was a singular exception, seeing through the pantomime in short order.

"She appears to know words many of us do not, Captain," Mistress Juhlina observed one day. "Words I can't recall you saying in her presence."

"The heathen have a remarkable gift for languages," I replied, somewhat tartly since her perception grated on my pride a little. Still, it would certainly serve the company well if this woman could be taught to curb her violent instincts.

Having begun to school my small cadre of spies in the finer points of the outlaw's craft, it became quickly apparent that Juhlina was my most adept student. However, the swiftness with which she acquired new skills was matched by the shortness of her temper. A basic lesson in how to win at Sevens erupted into a fist fight when one of the other recruits succeeded in switching an honest die for a weighted copy without Juhlina noticing.

"Of course he cheated," I said, dragging her off the bloody-nosed unfortunate. "He's supposed to."

Under the guise of punishment, I gave her time to cool off by giving her a double watch on guard that night. When the sky was fully dark, I left the tower with a brandy bottle in hand. Juhlina had perched herself on an outcrop that jutted from the ridge's crest to create a useful vantage point. She stared in morose stillness at the view, stirring only a little at the sound of my approach. "Here," I said, handing her the bottle. "Something to keep the chill off."

"It's a balmy night," she said, but still raised the bottle to her lips. Taking a swig of unwise volume, she blinked and coughed. "That's quite a brew, Captain."

"You're not used to liquor, are you?" I said, seeing the telltale scrunch of her features.

"Hardly tasted a drop before I joined you lot." She smiled and put the bottle to her lips again, taking an even longer pull. "Not sure I like it, in truth," she said, working her tongue around her mouth before drinking again. I watched her gulp down half the contents, seeing the tension leach from her as anger dissolved into drunkenness. "Frowned upon it was, y'see," she slurred finally, "in the Favoured."

"The Favoured?"

"It's what we called ourselves, the Favoured." She staggered a little and I gestured for her sit, the pair of us perched together on the edge of the outcrop. "The Seraphile's Favoured, we were. So Mother and Father told me and my sisters, anyhow." She leaned closer, brows drawn in a conspiratorial frown. "Not s'posed to tell any of you filthy un-Favoured this, but why not?" She paused to let out a small burp before adding in a bitter sigh, "Why the fuck not, eh?"

"Tell me what?" I prompted, which transformed her sigh into a chuckle.

"Why, the undeniable truth that you and every other un-Favoured are going to be denied the Portals when you die, of course. No blessed eternity for you benighted sinners. It's only for us, 'cause only the Favoured could bother their holy arses to traipse around every single fucking pilgrim trail in this miserable fucking realm."

I winced. Although hardly a stranger to profanity, I felt it sat ill on her tongue, like a child speaking forbidden words for the first time.

"Thass the key, see?" She wiggled her eyebrows at me. "That's how you make it through the Portals. 'Course you have to do a lot of other stuff too. Not drink . . ." she paused to grin at the bottle in her hand ". . . .not fuck unless it's with your husband, who the elders choose for you. Hardly knew the bastard the night he bedded me. Isn't that funny?"

I didn't think it funny at all. In fact, it sounded very sad. "Perhaps they were right," I suggested. "Maybe such devotion earned them the eternity they wanted."

She laughed again, the sound taking on a harsh note. "Balls it did. Devotion doesn't undo sin, no matter how many miles you walk or how many Martyr bones you bow to. And there was sin aplenty among the Favoured. The Most Favoured, that's what we called our pious leader, who must've fucked half the congregation, all in secret even though we all knew but pretended not to. And it wasn't just that. They were a mean bunch, Captain. Every day was all nasty gossip and jealousy, everyone vying for the Most Favoured's approval." She fell quiet, taking a more measured sip of brandy, a distant cast dimming in her eyes. "Won't claim I was the best of them, for that's what it is to be part of something you think greater than you. You lose yourself in it, become part of it, just another mean, gossipy bitch among all the others, then . . ."

She lapsed into silence once more and I let it play out, sensing it would be a mistake to prompt her. "Then I had a baby," she said finally. "Lyssotte I called her. The Favoured rarely stayed in one place for long, life was just one endless trek between shrines, so I carried her until she was old enough to walk, a child born to a life of pilgrimage. Life among such company should have made her a sad child, but she wasn't. She was so . . . happy, all the time, rarely a tear or a tantrum. In my devotion I imagined her to be a reward, a gift from the Seraphile for this life of trudging among folk I increasingly despised. She saved me, or my soul at least, long before you turned up to rescue me, an act for which I realise I've never thanked you."

I shrugged. "I think you've demonstrated enough thanks since."

"No." She shook her head. "I've just killed a lot of people, and it wasn't born of gratitude. I killed because I was angry. I still am. Lyssotte was four years old when I watched them cut her throat. I'm not sure it's a kind of rage that ever fades."

"It could, in time. If you stop feeding it. You don't have to do this any more. You could leave. I won't stop you."

"Where would I go? What else am I fit for now?" She raised the brandy bottle once more, then paused. "No offence, Captain," she said, tossing the bottle away, "but I don't think I'm fond of liquor after all."

I tracked the falling receptacle until it was lost to the gloom, hearing the faint tinkle of it shattering on the rocks below the ridge. "You owe me ten sheks," I said with a regretful sigh. "That was good stuff . . ." I trailed off as my eyes detected something else on the shadowed plain.

"Rider?" Juhlina asked, peering at the pale plume of rising dust.

"Just one," I confirmed. "Pushing hard, whoever it is."

I watched the galloping form make for the narrow dip between the hills enclosing the Martyr's Reach. Hurrying to the opposite side of the ridge I saw horse and rider come to a halt at the stockade. This was evidently a person of some import for they were permitted entry after only the briefest delay.

"Go stick your head in the horse trough," I told Juhlina, starting towards the track that led down the ridge's western slope. "It'll sober you up. Then get the others out of bed. I've a feeling we'll either be marching or fighting soon."

I judged the royal messenger to be a former man-at-arms, having the blunt, scarred features and sturdy frame common to soldiers. His appearance was in fact at odds with his voice, a pleasant, lilting Dulsian brogue better suited to a balladeer. Yet for all its pleasing tones, his voice couldn't obviate the darkness of his tidings.

"Duke Guhlton of Althiene has made common cause with the Pretender Magnis Lochlain," he informed Evadine and her assembled captains. We had all gathered in the tower without benefit of a summons from the Anointed Lady, all of us by now attuned to the portents that signal a sudden change in fortune. "Duke Guhlton has issued a proclamation denying the paternity of King Tomas," the messenger went on, "and hailing the Pretender as the true monarch of Albermaine. They crossed the border into the northern counties of Alberis three weeks ago leading a host reckoned at three thousand horse and twenty thousand foot. Acting with the peerless courage for which he is famed, King Tomas gathered his entire host and set forth to crush the rebellion. Through treachery and subterfuge, the king was taken unawares on the road north and his forces scattered." The messenger hesitated, maintaining the formal composure expected of his office but allowing himself a small cough before continuing. "The king's whereabouts and current disposition are unknown. Princess

Leannor was journeying north when this news reached her. She has called all true and loyal servants of the realm to muster at Couravel with utmost speed, bringing with them as many retainers and churls as can be gathered and armed. You, my lady, are also hereby so commanded."

This is where it truly starts. I contained a shudder as the voice of Erchel's dream-haunting phantom sang loud in my head, summoning memories of King Tomas's lifeless face. I had tried to push the vision from my thoughts ever since, suppressing it with the hope, albeit faint, that it had all been the concoction of a mind confused by trauma. Sadly, it was now terribly clear that, although Erchel's ghost was a dreadfully accurate reflection of his living self, he didn't lie.

Heart beating a good deal faster, I watched the messenger bow and proffer a letter to Evadine, sealed with a hastily applied spatter of wax embossed with the royal seal. Evadine accepted the letter without demur, offering the messenger a gracious smile. "A command duly acknowledged and accepted, good sir. Your performance of your role does the Crown honour. Go now, refresh yourself and rest."

"I can pause only briefly, my lady," the messenger replied, "for I am charged with carrying word to Lord Elfons in Highsahl. If I could trouble you for a fresh horse, however?"

"Of course. Tell the stable master to provide his swiftest mount, on my authority."

As the messenger strode from the tower, Evadine broke the seal on the letter. She began to issue orders after only the most cursory glance at the contents. "Captain Swain, Captain Dornmahl, muster your companies to march at first light. Captain Ofihla, you will have command of the Reach in my absence . . ."

"If I might interject, my lady," I said, speaking with a volume and forcefulness that brought the flow of commands to a halt. The interruption also caused every other person present to stiffen and stare in abject shock. "I would crave a moment in private," I added, meeting Evadine's narrowed eyes. "For I feel there are matters to discuss."

*

Evadine ordered the others to begin preparations to march before curtly instructing me to follow her to the top of the tower. The sentries were commanded to report to their companies, leaving us alone to endure a short but tense silence before she consented to speak.

"I know what you're about to counsel. And I prefer not to hear it."

"And yet," I replied, "I will counsel it nonetheless." She could, of course, have told me to be silent and concern myself with mustering the Scout Company for the march, but she didn't. Instead, she turned her back, resting her hands on the stone balustrade to cast her gaze northwards. Dawn had smeared a deeper than usual shade of red over the clouds above the eastern horizon, bespeaking ill weather for the days ahead.

"Kings and queens rise and fall," I said to Evadine's back. "You made accommodation with one king, why not another?"

"Because," she said, still looking north, "I gave my word to one king and not the other."

"Words are just that, words. They have power but it is a power easily moulded. What was once a solemn promise can become an unavoidable expedient, when presented in the right context."

"And who better than the skilled hand of Alwyn Scribe to craft that context, eh? Would you make a liar of me?"

I quelled a sudden and unwise impulse to share the contents of my dream with her. How exactly a dead man had come to haunt my dreams with visions of the future was not something I understood or relished explaining. All I knew with certainty was that King Tomas was most likely dead and Evadine should avoid entangling herself in the chaos that would surely follow. *The Second Scourge is coming, and here is where it is born.*

"I would make you what you need to be," I said. "And what do you owe the Algathinets? Had their scheme gone how they wished you would be dead along with every soldier who followed you. With Tomas a prisoner or slain, the Pretender may seize the throne through force of arms, but he won't hold it without the blessing of either the Covenant or the Anointed Lady. It's my guess he'll put more value on your blessing than that of the Luminants, since they were always so

406 • ANTHONY RYAN

ardent in condemning his claims. He can sit the throne if he wishes, call himself all the titles that please him, but the reins of power will sit in your hands. You spoke of a great and terrible opportunity. Here it lies before us."

Evadine maintained her silence for a time, still apparently lost in her scrutiny of the lands north of the Crowhawl River. "The opportunity I spoke of," she said finally in a tone of soft reflection, "came to me via the Seraphile's grace, and it won't be seized through treachery. That much I know. The Anointed Lady cannot become the Pretender's Whore, for that is what they will surely call me."

She turned, regarding me with an expression that was not at all stern, but neither was it lacking in conviction. "The Covenant Company will march to Couravel and join our strength to Princess Leannor's host. Thence we will meet the Pretender's new horde in battle and defeat him for once and all."

She moved to me, reaching out to clasp my hands in hers. "I continue to cherish your counsel above all, Alwyn, you know that. But this course is set and cannot be altered." Her eyes were fixed upon mine, rich in a need for understanding, and something more. I had seen glimmers of it before, most clearly when she awoke from her healing at the hands of the Sack Witch. Now it shone bright and stark as ever. Evadine Courlain, Risen Martyr, saw more in me than just a trusted confidant and adviser. It is a strange and intoxicating brew to find yourself wanted by a woman such as this, as potent and addictive as any I ever drank. I will not lie, for succumb I did, though it surely damned me more than any other act in a life rich in theft, lies and murder.

From the courtyard came the loud clamour of Swain marshalling his troops into ranks, the tumult of sergeants shouting and boots tramping enough to break this moment and remind Evadine of who and where she was. She lowered her face, now possessed of a girlish shyness that I found jarring in its unfamiliarity.

"I shall," she began, clearing her throat and moving to the stairs, "require your insight more than ever in the days ahead, Captain Scribe. I leave you to take your company north in what manner suits best the swift gathering of sound intelligence."

This is where it truly starts. Erchel's voice rose to taunt me again as I watched her descend the stairs, but I was too lost in my new-born obsession to listen. I had been gifted my first taste of her affection and, like any addict, all I wanted was more.

CHAPTER THIRTY-THREE

"I told them to piss off," the Widow said, casting a sour glance at the gaggle of churls following her horse. "Rode off and left them several times, but they kept catching up."

The Scout Company was encamped at a crossroads some twenty miles north of the Crowhawl, half a day's march in advance of the main body of what was now referred to as the Covenant host. In my absence, the ranks of Evadine's soldiers had swelled to such an extent that the mere term "company" no longer sufficed. It was, in effect, now a small army and, I concluded as I surveyed the Widow's unwanted clutch of followers, about to grow yet larger.

"Come to fight for the Lady, m'lord," the apparent leader of this group said in response to my enquiry. He was a sturdy enough man with shoulders that bespoke many years' toil with plough and scythe. Like the dozen or more people at his back, he was clad in cloth made dark and ragged through excessive wear. None could be described as overfed and I picked out a few with the hollowed cheeks and sunken eyes that told of sustained hunger.

"Hard winter, was it?" I asked, causing the ploughman to blink in surprise. I deduced he had expected an instruction to recite some scripture as proof of his devotion.

"King's tax-farmers took more than usual, m'lord," he said, head bobbing. "And the frost was worse this year."

"The Seraphile took their grace from us," the woman at his side stated. She had a far wilder look to her gaze than he did and her voice quavered despite its apparent conviction. "The king sent the Lady away so we were denied her blessing."

This brought a murmur of agreement from the other churls, one that had a decidedly ugly growl to it. These people were angry, and not without reason. In more settled times I might have enquired if they knew that the Lady whose banner they wished to follow intended to fight for the very king they blamed for their ills. But I didn't. Angry people were valuable now.

"Are there others in this county who feel the same?" I asked, to which many heads nodded in gratifying agreement.

"Hundreds, m'lord," the wild-eyed woman said. "'Cepting those cowards up in Gallsbreck. Had it too easy, they have. Rather sit on their arses and sup ale than fight for the Lady." Her overly wide eyes narrowed a little in calculation. "Reckon you should stop by there, y'lordship, burn the place down."

"I'm a captain, not a lord," I stated, raising my voice to cut through the rising babble of agreement. "And the Lady does not set her soldiers to wanton destruction." I pointed to the verge fringing the crossroads. "Sit there and await the Covenant host. They'll be along by nightfall. Make yourselves known to Captain Swain."

I had Ayin and Eamond hand out bread to the churls while also gathering names and directions to every village or farmstead within a day's ride. Breaking camp before nightfall, I mustered the scouts into pairs, giving each a list of places to visit and proclaim the Lady's northward march.

"Some will be willing, many will not," I cautioned before sending them off. "Don't tarry to persuade, just spread the word. Tell any who have the heart to fight for the Lady to head for Gildtren." I glanced at the churls on the verge, all busily eating with nary an axe or a billhook to their name. "And bring whatever weapons and supplies they can."

*

Eight days later, I reined Blackfoot to a halt atop a rise a few miles from the mill town of Gildtren. The warhorse was not best suited to scout service, being bred for the charge and the melee. In the Reach he had reacted to my reappearance with a surprising excitement, tossing his head and consenting to allow me to scratch his nose in welcome. Now, after days spent carrying me along tracks made soggy by intermittent rain, his old aloofness had re-emerged and he uttered a disdainful snort as I smoothed a hand over his neck.

"So, it seems we built her an army," Juhlina observed. Gildtren was formed of a sprawl of water mills, cottages and storehouses that followed the line of the Mergild River to create a decent-sized town. Viewed from this distance, it appeared to have been deformed by some form of swelling disease. A disordered camp of tents and makeshift shelters clustered around the town and the riverbank, the lanes and fields all crowded with people. A soldier's life had taught me the folly of attempting to count a mass of folk with any accuracy, but I felt an estimate of close to eight thousand wouldn't be far from the mark.

Our journey through the southern marches of Alberis had been met with plentiful enthusiasm. People, most in a state that mirrored the angry degradation of the mob that followed Juhlina to the cross-roads, listened to word of the Lady's northwards march with rapt attention. The culmination of every speech featured the same question: "Who has the courage and faith to fight for the Lady?" Despite the many eager hands raised in agreement, the numbers gathered here bespoke a far greater response than I expected. Many will display considerable enthusiasm for a fiery speech delivered to a receptive crowd only to slink away when the cheers fade to leave them contemplating the prospect of actual battle. The lure of the Lady's blessing, however, sufficed to fortify even the faintest hearts.

"Feeding so many will not be easy," I griped, prompting the Widow to take some relish in pointing out the obvious.

"This was your idea."

She met my reproachful scowl with an open smile, something I noticed she was more wont to do these days. It appeared life on the move leavened her mood, providing a distraction from the depthless rage that was her lot.

"Return to the host," I told her, taking firmer hold of Blackfoot's reins and kicking him into motion. "Tell Lady Evadine what she'll find when she gets here. In the meantime, I'll endeavour to make some order out of this chaos."

It is the nature of newly formed groups to produce leaders, some worthy of the role by dint of prior experience or well-earned respect. Others, like the tall bearded man in a pilgrim's garb who emerged from the throng to bar my path, ascend through a facility for winning over the easily fooled. Not all outlaws accrue their spoils through thievery or violence. Some, those Deckin referred to as "gullers", possess the uncanny gift of accomplishing larceny by words alone. Lorine had certainly possessed such a gift, employing the careful combination of performance and lies to great effect and, I felt, far more subtlety and skill than this deceitful beard-face.

"Who is this that comes to speak in the Lady's name?" he demanded in a voice practised in addressing crowds, raising a staff above his head. From the mostly hushed expectancy of the onlooking throng I concluded they had been hearing a good deal of this fellow's well-honed sermons over the course of several days. "We who gather to fight for the Covenant will hear no voice but hers!"

I marked the pilgrim as a guller at first glance. It was clear in the way his eyes shone with the unblinking, fervent glare of the fanatic but would occasionally flick to the crowd to judge the effect of his words. True believers are lost in a world of their own certainty and don't care if their preaching finds purchase on other souls. When I failed to offer any manner of response beyond a placid angling of my head, I saw his composure slip for an instant. A smart thief is one who knows when to run. This one displayed his dearth of intelligence by lingering to brazen his way through the impending confrontation, presumably fortified by the sizeable crowd at his back.

"Visions have I had," he intoned, clasping his staff in both hands. He closed his eyes as he added volume to his voice, putting a tremble in his arms to buttress the impression of a divine inspiration. "Of the Scourge that was and will be. Of the Lady leading us through darkness and despair to salvation. It is only to her that we will bow! If you truly be her messenger, soldier, then get you gone and tell her." He opened his eyes, spreading his arms wide, quivering with pious rectitude. "Tell her we congregants await her word!"

The trick is not to play the part you are cast in, Lorine told me one night at the campfire long ago. *That's how you avoid the guller's snare.* So, instead of responding with a blustering statement of my identity, I sat in the saddle and fixed the bearded man with a steady, decidedly unfriendly stare. The crowd had greeted his pronouncement with a hearty cheer, but the accumulation of voices dwindled as the moment stretched. The supposed visionary further confirmed my judgement by allowing a frown of confusion to pass over his face. I had been supposed to stridently proclaim my authority only to be shouted down by this devotional and surely self-appointed voice of the Lady's Crusade. My protestations would then be smothered by the roused tumult of the crowd, probably stoked to a dangerous pitch by the guller, thereby forcing me to retreat and allow him another day or two of lucrative fleecing.

Watching him fix his actor's mask in place after a moment's uncertain lip-licking, I felt a sore temptation to simply tug on Blackfoot's reins, causing the beast to lash out with his forehooves. *Just trample the bastard and have done.* I pushed the notion away, knowing it to be born of anger. Ever since the moment atop the tower, thoughts of Evadine had crowded my addict's brain, thoughts that grew dark whenever confronted by anything or anyone that might do her harm. I didn't doubt Evadine's ability to capture the hearts and souls of this lot with a single sermon, but it wouldn't do to allow one such as this to continue lurking amid her newly acquired army. However, simply killing him would create a poor impression on folk who felt themselves called to a higher purpose.

So, putting a smile on my lips, I climbed down from the saddle to approach the false pilgrim with arms wide. "Will you embrace me?" I said, taking satisfaction from the rapid blinking of his eyes. "For I know a brother in the Covenant when I see one."

I closed my arms around him before he could step away, hugging him tight and turning him a little so the crowd couldn't see me whisper in his ear. "You've no more faith in you than a turd in a puddle, my friend." He flinched, trying to draw away, then froze as I tightened my arms. He was a well-built man, but plainly unused to violence, as those who talk for a living often are. "When I let you go, you will proclaim me the herald of the Lady's host," I instructed in a hiss. "Then you will kindly disappear. If I find you in this camp come morning, I'll slice your cock off and feed it to you."

I gave him a final, crushing squeeze then released him. A greedy liar he certainly was, but idiocy was not among his vices for he was very quick to raise his staff, voice booming loud: "Behold the Anointed Lady's blessed herald!"

"Nine thousand, three hundred and eighty-two," Ayin said with precise enunciation. "Those that have made their mark and taken the oath, that is." She appeared almost comical holding the voluminous company ledger, as if she had stolen it from a giant's library. However, all present knew better than to laugh at her. We were gathered in Evadine's tent, she having arrived to a near-frenzied welcome the day after I sent the false pilgrim packing. I had been gratified to find no sign of the fellow since, and I hadn't been stinting in my search.

"How many have marched with the banners before?" Swain asked.

It was a standard question asked of all company recruits and Ayin's answer brought a dispirited sigh from most present. "Eight hundred and nine."

"You'd think there would be more," Wilhum said. "What with all the recent wars."

"Those that go off to join the banners rarely come back," I pointed out. "These people are keen enough. Even better, they're angry and—" I allowed my gaze to slip towards Evadine "—their love for the Anointed Lady is sincere. Nine thousand willing fighters is not to be sniffed at, however lacking in skill they may be."

"Numbers aren't the only thing that makes an army," Swain said. "And we've no time for training." He straightened, addressing his next words to Evadine. "My lady, I must submit that burdening ourselves with such an ill-disciplined mob may well act against our purposes. Marshalling them into order and sustaining it all the way to Couravel is well-nigh impossible. Not to mention the fact that we've scarcely enough supplies to feed our own soldiers. All the storehouses in this place stand near empty already. I suggest we enlist only the veterans and march on come the morrow."

Evadine had maintained a preoccupied silence until now, features drawn in thought and paying only partial attention to Ayin's numbers. Now she stirred herself, fixing Swain with an expression that was only a little shy of a full glare. "You talk as if this were merely another campaign, good captain," she said. "It is not. None of us should have the slightest doubt as to the import of what we do now. Support for the Pretender's cause was always most prevalent among the commons of Althiene and northern Alberis. Now he has won a victory, which means the small folk will once again be flocking to him, perhaps in numbers even greater than before. To match him we need the entire strength of those who call themselves true adherents to the Covenant. Many called our mission to Alundia a crusade but they were wrong. This is where the true crusade begins and I will not deny the people of this realm their place in its ranks. Disordered, ill trained, starved or no, any who wish to march with me to secure their future are welcome. These are the words I will speak today when I address them. These are the words I will speak every day until we meet the Pretender's horde and battle is joined."

The tempo of my heart doubled as her gaze swung to me, eager for every morsel of attention she saw fit to bestow. I am sure, dear reader, you will be conversant with much of what followed, and I'll claim no innocence of the crimes laid at our door. Yes, I was her captive now, just as poor, deluded Lord Eldurm Gulatte had been when I transcribed the clumsy, heart-sore letters he dictated. How I pitied him then, the same pity that roils in me now as I view my younger self from atop the precipice of age. But Gulatte had been an ill-matched suitor to a woman who afforded him the same fondness as she would a favoured pup. Evadine and I were entwined; her need matched mine which, I now understand with terrible clarity, made all that came next so much worse. Our crimes were many, and they began that day with what her chroniclers have chosen to call the Sacrifice March.

It is strange how the mind accommodates itself to horrors. Sights that would once render a soul to shocked and pale-faced silence fail to arouse more than a grimace when they become one of many. So it was from the very first day of the Sacrifice March. It began with the old and infirm, those who would never have attempted so arduous a journey but for the inspiring light of the Anointed Lady.

Her sermon that morning had been briefer than usual and lacking in fine or flowing oratory. Evadine's ability to capture the hearts of a multitude had always been more than a matter of concocting the right words. It was her, the sight of her: tall, beautiful, black-enamelled armour gleaming in the burgeoning sun. She was everything their devoted imaginings wanted her to be, and her voice . . .

"I come before you as a penitent." It echoed across the assembled mass that morning, clearer and truer than I ever heard it, made more so by the strained note of guilt with which she imbued every word. She spoke from a grain platform jutting from the roof of the tallest mill in Gildtren, the rapt audience thronging the lanes and paddocks below. "I come to beseech not your loyalty but your forgiveness. For it is my duty to tell you that we have reached this pass because of my failure."

Shouts of denial rose from the multitude, all quelled when she raised her hands. "The burden of failure should never be shirked," she told them. "For in accepting it we confront the truth. Long have I striven to keep the Second Scourge at bay, but I did not strive with the vigour or courage equal to the task, and so I failed. I allowed my heart to soften when it should have been as steel. I stayed my hand when it should have struck. My weakness, my failure, my truth. That is my burden and it pains me to have you share it."

More unbidden shouts, declarations from tearful faces. "We will share all your burdens, my lady! Command us!"

This time she let the acclaim build to a peak whereupon she pointed an unwavering arm north. "Today I march to confront the Scions of the Scourge. The corrupted Duke of Althiene and the vile wretch we know as the Pretender, both revealed to me by the Seraphile's grace as servants of the Malecite." The crowd's cheers built, mixing with an ugly growl of rage. Instead of smothering Evadine's voice, she seemed to be buoyed by the tumult, her words carried aloft by the upsurge of adulation.

"March!" she cried out, drawing her sword and pointing it at the northern sky. "March in the name of the Martyrs!"

It occurred to me later that she had intended this to be the battle cry of her crusade, a chant to be taken up and echoed throughout the hard days ahead. The crowd, however, had an exhortation of their own, one they had heard from the Covenant soldiers in their midst.

"We live for the Lady!" The shout was ragged at first, but acquired concordance and strident volume as it spread. "We fight for the Lady! We die for the Lady!"

Evadine maintained the pose for only a short while before sheathing her sword and returning to the mill loft where I waited for her. The smile of beneficent acceptance she wore quickly shifted into a doubtful frown as she met my eyes. "This is not for me," she said in a murmur. "You know that, don't you?" Her moments of doubt were rare and thus unsettling when they occurred.

"I know," I said, grasping her gauntleted hand, only briefly so the gesture didn't attract undue notice. "But we should welcome any words that keep them on the road, for it will be long."

And to the road they went, a long snaking column of churls and townsfolk tramping its way north with scant sign of military order. The crusaders carried sacks laden with whatever scant provisions they could gather, their weapons a swaying forest of pitchfork and improvised spear. All ages were present, save for children. Some mothers had attempted to drag broods of screaming infants along, but here at least Evadine drew the line and issued firm commands to go home. Otherwise, any and all who wished to march behind the Anointed Lady's banner were welcomed, but not succoured. Those who marched did so on their own devices, for the Covenant host had no rations or arms to spare. This should have dissuaded all but the hardiest from embarking upon this course, but it didn't.

I spent a good portion of the first day watching an old man die. His thin frame, once that of a brawny forge master he assured me, was propped against a milestone as he gasped his last few breaths. He was the sixth old soul I had seen in a similar state that day, fallen out of the column to totter to the verge and sit down, never to rise. For reasons I have still not fathomed, I stopped for him and not the others.

"Here, Grandfather," I said, putting my canteen to his lips.

He drank a decent swallow then spluttered and choked, the stark muscles of his scrawny throat working feebly. "Always . . . too fond . . . of the pipe," he muttered in a halting whisper. "Makes a ruin . . . of the gizzard." He waved a tremulous finger at me. "You remember that . . . young lord."

"I'm not a lord . . ." I let the correction die and settled at his side, accepting the canteen as he weakly attempted to pass it back. I watched him labour his way through several more breaths, his head lolling to regard the many folk traipsing past.

"So many," he murmured, mouth curling a little in a smile. "All marching . . . for something good . . . for once."

"Is that why you came?" I asked, receiving a slow nod in response.

"All the other wars . . ." He managed to shake his head. "Not ours . . . nobles fighting for land . . . not our land . . . Never ours."

Knowing there was little else to be done, I sat with him, watching the crusade pass by until the sun began to fade. He spoke in halting and increasingly faint tones of his life in the forge, of the first wife he had loved and buried and the second wife he had hated and endured. He avowed shame over the son who had fled his temper to join the banners, never to return. He confessed to the murder of a man who had wronged him in a business matter, a crime overlooked and never punished by the sheriff for the victim was widely detested in the county.

"Mayhap . . . he waits for me," the old man said when the first stars began to bead the evening sky, his voice just a shallow gasp now. I could tell he saw none of the stooped, exhausted stragglers still attempting to follow the Lady north. "At the Portals . . . mayhap he waits . . . to tell the Seraphile . . . what I did." His head lolled towards me, his previously dull eyes suddenly lit by desperation as he expended the last dregs of strength to force the words from his lips. "This will . . . save me . . . won't it, my lord? I . . . marched with the Anointed . . . Lady . . . They'll judge me well . . . They'll forgive me, won't they?"

"The Seraphile judge all with unending compassion," I told him. "The Lady assures me of this."

"Thank the Martyrs . . ." He settled his head against the milestone, eyes closing for the last time as I watched his chest rise, fall and stop. I left him where he lay, for there was no time for rites and burials. Mounting Blackfoot and setting off at a steady canter, I chided myself for not learning the old forge master's name. Later, I would take comfort from the manner of his passing. Compared to many destined to expire during the Sacrifice March it was a gentle, even enviable fate.

"Ninety-two today." Ayin's brows bunched in concentration as she scribbled in the company ledger. "Better than yesterday. That was a two-hundreder."

"Must you do that?" the Widow asked, casting a disapproving eye over the neat entries adorning the revealed page. Ayin, ever a scrupulous bookkeeper, had drawn up a chart detailing the daily losses suffered by the crusade since setting out from Gildtren eight days before.

"The Lady wants a proper accounting," Ayin retorted, sparing Juhlina a sharp glance before returning to her work.

The Scout Company occupied a hill overlooking the chosen campsite of the main host. The Covenant soldiery had covered the daily allotment of twenty miles well before sunset. As had become typical, the bulk of the crusade would continue to straggle in to construct their untidy sprawl of camps until well after sunset. Also typical were the bodies, dead or spent, that littered the road in our wake. After the first day's march, I had set the scouts the task of scouring the country ahead for supplies. I presented it to Evadine, and myself, as a compassionate mission, since even a parlous amount of scavenged food would diminish the daily toll. However, I knew it mostly arose from base cowardice. I had no desire to watch another old man or limping cripple die on the side of the road. Ayin appeared to have no such qualms, trotting her pony up and down the column as she went about the task of counting the dead with cheery dedication.

Her toll might have been less grievous if our foraging expeditions had enjoyed more success. Sadly, this land yielded little. Wise merchants and farmers, well versed in the habits of passing armies, will be quick to cart away harvested produce and drive their livestock to more distant pastures. Some of those I had dealt with during the company's southward march were now vanished, their steads and storehouses mostly empty save for what little they hadn't been able to carry off.

It was a different story with the various villages and towns we passed through, for the Anointed Lady's allure had lost none of its potency. They heard her sermons and flocked in their dozens and then hundreds to follow her banner, swelling our ranks but also increasing the price paid in sacrifice. Still, the march never faltered. Some, wiser or less devout than others, deserted when dreams of glory gave way to a daily trial of hunger and fatigue. Yet most who answered the Lady's call stayed to the end. It is strange, even depressing to report that when Ayin's final accounting was done on the eve of battle, she found more living souls in the ranks of the Commons Crusade than when it started.

The rapid drum of hooves on sod drew my gaze to the sight of Eamond galloping hard from the north. He was a rider of some skill these days and had proven himself one of my better scouts, being keen of both eye and mind, despite the latter being somewhat addled by his undiminished faith.

"There's a mounted company five miles ahead, Captain," he

reported, reining his long-legged hunter to a halt. "I'd say about a hundred. Knights and men-at-arms, all armed and armoured."

"Banners?" I asked.

"Saw one, but it was too distant to make out the sigil and I thought it best not to linger. They're keeping to the road in tight order. No flank guards or scouts."

"Mount up!" I called to the rest of the scouts, hurrying to haul the saddle onto Blackfoot's back. I thought it unlikely that the Pretender could have pushed so far south of Couravel but, since he was a man of famous energy, it was best to be cautious. Climbing into the saddle, I issued orders sending scouting parties east and west before galloping to the main camp, knowing Evadine would be keen to meet our visitors.

CHAPTER THIRTY-FOUR

"Father." Evadine's greeting was spoken without inflection, nor did she feel obliged to bow. For his part, Sir Altheric Courlain's demeanour was marginally more solicitous, affording his daughter a tight smile.

"Evadine," he said, his eyes searching her face in a manner very different to the guarded disapproval I had seen in the Shavine Forest.

Surveying the knight's armour, I found the breastplate, enamelled with the white and black rose of the Courlain family crest, scratched and stained with dried mud and the brownish flecks of recently spattered blood. I also noted that the helm at his side was similarly besmirched and dented in several places. Shifting my gaze to his men, I picked out many bandaged heads and faces both bruised and scarred. The retinue of so renowned a noble would normally number at least a hundred men-at-arms, yet here I counted just over fifty.

A hard and perhaps lost battle, I concluded, eyes returning to Altheric's searching visage. *A man who survives a near-fatal encounter will often get to pondering his mistakes.*

"I take it you had occasion to meet the Pretender's horde recently, my lord," I observed, feeling that the times were too fraught for circumspection.

His reply was prompt and lacking offence. "A nasty skirmish with the Duke of Althiene's personal guard, in point of fact, Master Scribe. They call themselves the Silver Lances, apparently. Blundered into them a rain-sodden eve two days ago. Came within a few paces of the duke himself, but the bugger slipped the noose and rode off."

"A great pity," Evadine said. "With Duke Guhlton slain or taken, this business could be settled without bloodshed."

"Sadly, I doubt that would be the case," her father told her. "The Pretender's horde has doubled since he crossed the border, so the duke's contingent barely makes up a quarter of his strength. It transpires there were a great many dissatisfied churls awaiting the day the usurping swine raised his banner once more."

"The promise of hope is always tempting to the hopeless," Evadine replied. "Even when patently false. More than ten thousand true Covenanters march at my back, Father. Tell me where the usurper is and we'll finish this in short order."

The ardency in her voice brought a frown to Altheric's brow, reminding me how many years parent and child had been estranged. He might crave his daughter's forgiveness but it occurred to me he didn't truly know her. To him she was a deluded girl he once castigated and shunned to his shame, a shame I felt sure would only deepen when he understood the nature of the Risen Martyr she had become.

"Princess Leannor has done me the honour of naming me knight marshal of the royal host," Sir Altheric said, voice taking on a cautious note. "Our patrols relate that the Pretender paused his march on Couravel two days ago. He has encamped only a mile from the city while Princess Leannor has mustered eight thousand foot and a thousand horse to the west. Loyal contingents from the Cordwain and the Shavine Marches are hurrying to her side, but it will take them days to arrive. However . . ." he paused and shifted in his saddle, watching Evadine's face closely ". . . there is more afoot than just the march of armies. This crisis has another complication."

"The king," I said.

The Knight Marshal inclined his head. "Quite so, Master Scribe."

"Captain Scribe," Evadine said, speaking with soft precision. "Please address my most trusted companion with his correct title, Father."

Altheric's eyes narrowed as they shifted between the two of us, a dark and uncomfortable comprehension creeping into his expression. "My compliments, Captain," he told me in a flat tone at odds with the sudden glint of anger in his previously conciliatory gaze.

I accepted his forced civility with a nod before returning to more important matters. "The king is a prisoner?"

"So it seems. Yesterday a herald arrived at the royal encampment under a truce pennant, bearing an invitation to parley. Princess Leannor is especially keen for your attendance, Captain. I am to escort you to her presence with all dispatch. You, my lady," he added, turning to Evadine, "are ordered to bring your full strength to muster beneath the royal banner. One of my men will guide you to the encampment."

Evadine and I exchanged only a brief glance at this, our facility for wordless communication blossoming once again. *Go,* her eyes said, *and tell me all that transpires.*

Turning in unison, we both bowed to Sir Altheric, Evadine speaking in grave acceptance. "As the princess commands, my lord."

"She's had another of her visions, hasn't she?"

Sir Altheric had maintained a rigid silence for much of the journey to the encampment of the royal host. Only when we passed through the picket line into the grand accumulation of tents, carts and paddocks did he deign to address me. The disapproval in his bearing was plain, but I sensed a deeper well of concern beneath his noble disdain.

"During the time I have had the honour to serve her," I replied, "the Anointed Lady has been blessed by several visions, my lord."

"And yet she failed to foresee all of this." He jerked his chin at the surrounding assembly of soldiery, grunting out a humourless laugh. "Always the way with her . . . special insight. By the time she speaks up it's all too late."

"The timing of her visions rests in the hands of the Seraphile," I said.

"Really?" The question had a definite, curious weight to it, one that matched the depth of scrutiny I saw in his face as he reined in his charger, obliging me to bring Blackfoot to a halt. "Is that what you believe?"

"I believe she is an anointed servant to the Covenant of Martyrs, risen from death by virtue of the Seraphile's grace to save this world from the ravages of the Second Scourge." I was surprised by the heat with which I spoke, unable to stem a rising but ill-judged anger. Who was this man to question the daughter he had failed? This man who hadn't even believed the truth of her blessed insight, thereby subjecting her to years of torment?

"Then you're a fool," he stated and I found my anger stoked yet further by the fact that I heard more pity in his voice than ridicule. "When next you have the chance, ask her about her first vision. Ask her about how her mother died . . ."

"Master Scribe!" The call came from a voice rendered unrecognisable by strain and worry. It was only when I turned to see Sir Ehlbert hurrying towards us that I realised it had come from his lips. His features were as much a contrast to the man I knew as his voice, pale and unshaven, his normally close-cropped hair a matted, thorny mess. He regarded me with eyes dark and sunken from lack of sleep, beckoning urgently.

"You're here, good," he said. "Come, you're needed."

Upon my first sight of the herald standing in Princess Leannor's tent, I was forced to the instant suspicion that the Pretender had ordained her appearance as a deliberate contrast to Evadine's. Her honey-blonde hair was bobbed so that it reached just below her ears, framing an oval face of undeniable comeliness, albeit set in a hostile frown that bordered on naked distaste for all that she saw. Her armour was polished to a silver sheen, the breastplate and pauldrons inlaid with swirls of sky-blue enamel. She kept a hand on the ornate hilt of her longsword, the gauntleted fist tightening as Ehlbert led Sir Altheric and I into the tent.

Her gaze flicked over Lord Courlain briefly before settling on me, whereupon her hostility faded a little as she bared white teeth in a wolfish smile. "The scribe but not the Martyr, eh?" she asked, her voice so smooth and imbued with the noble accent that she made even Sir Ehlbert sound like a commoner.

"Do I know you, my lady?" I asked, which caused her smile to broaden.

"Not yet," she said, inclining her head. "But you will, just not for very long."

"This . . . person," Princess Leannor said, rising from behind her ever-present desk, "is not a lady, Captain, but a dispossessed traitor despised by both family and Crown."

"The True King named me Countess Desmena Lehville," the herald said, ignoring Leannor to afford me a bow of surprising depth. "The only title I will ever accept, it being afforded by the only worthy monarch ever to rule this realm . . ."

"Enough!" Sir Ehlbert's curt instruction featured a good deal of his former authority, although his pensiveness was plain in the way he moved to the princess's side, fists clenching. I noted how Leannor attempted to calm him with a gentle touch to his forearm, but he scarcely seemed to feel it. "Your tidings," he said, nodding to me. "Repeat them for Captain Scribe."

"I have already stated the True King's terms," the countess replied with a sniff, raising her head to an angle of dismissive disdain. "Now I suffer your company only as long as it requires for you to answer . . ."

"Repeat!" Sir Ehlbert cut in, teeth clenched and speaking with slow deliberation that told of barely contained fury. "Your. Tidings."

Fortunately for the herald's immediate well-being, her haughtiness allowed for at least a small measure of good sense. Her face took on a pinkish hue as she ground her jaw and fixed her gaze upon me. She delivered her message in clipped tones that betrayed little, though, the pitch of anger was useful. Evidently, I had been called here to listen to this woman's words and judge their veracity. Listening to her speak, I doubted she knew that if I proclaimed her a liar she was unlikely to leave this tent alive.

"Be it known," Countess Desmena began, "that the person of Tomas Algathinet, false king of Albermaine, resides under the protection of the True King Magnis Lochlain, having been taken in just battle.

While the crimes committed by the false king are many, King Magnis is both wise and merciful. He feels this realm has suffered far too much discord, thanks to the endless feuds and greed born of the Algathinet family's years of misrule. Therefore, he is prepared to spare his prisoner the trial and execution that are his due. Accordingly, Lady Leannor Algathinet is hereby instructed to disband her host and dismiss her retainers, all of whom are commanded to pay due homage and tribute to King Magnis at a future place and time of his choosing. In return, Tomas Algathinet will be returned to his family on condition that both he and his sister depart all lands within the borders of Albermaine on solemn promise that they will never return."

When she fell silent I saw the inevitable question rise to Ehlbert's lips, only for him to keep it caged when Leannor gripped his hand. "Your words have been heard," she told the countess. "The guards outside will escort you to a place where you will await an answer."

"If I may, my lady," I said, holding up a hand when the herald made to leave. "You have seen the king?" I asked, keeping my tone light and the scrutiny from my gaze, even though I watched her reaction closely. "With your own eyes, I mean to say?"

"I have seen the false king resting comfortably in my liege's hospitality," she stated. It was just a small twitch to her mouth and easily missed by the inexperienced eye, marking her an accomplished liar. The Pretender had chosen his herald well, and her lies might have succeeded but for the hatred and anger she so clearly bore towards the occupants of this tent. Strong emotion has a way of stripping artifice from expression, easily missed by the uneducated eye, but not mine.

"So you can vouch for his health?" I pressed.

She snorted. "The True King does not indulge in falsehood, Master Scribe." She turned to offer a thin smile to Leannor. "He leaves that for his enemies."

"The king was taken in battle," I persisted. "Did he suffer any wounds?"

"None bar a few scratches," she said with pointed disparagement. "Had he fought harder perhaps it would be different."

"Shut your mouth, you traitorous bitch!" Leannor hissed, starting forward with a murderous glint in her eye. This time it was Ehlbert's turn to extend a restraining hand.

"My thanks, my lady," I said, sweeping aside the canvas and bowing low as she made her exit.

"Your courtesy is appreciated, Master Scribe," she told me with another white-toothed smile. "But it pains me too, when I contemplate your impending fate."

I responded with a laugh and watched her step outside, the two kingsmen falling in on either side to escort her away. I waited until they had proceeded beyond earshot before letting the flap fall into place.

"Well?" Ehlbert demanded, uncaring of the shrill note of desperation that coloured his tone.

"I can't vouch for the truth of the Pretender's offer, my lord," I said. "Nor do I believe that woman has set eyes on the king, unharmed or no. Of course, that doesn't mean he isn't alive and currently captive in the enemy camp. Only that, for whatever reason, her beloved True King chose not to show him to her."

"Meaning my brother may be wounded," Leannor concluded.

"Why conceal that?" Sir Altheric asked. "As long as the king draws breath they have the advantage, regardless of his wounds."

"The Pretender knows that a wounded king is less of a prize than a healthy one," the princess replied, once again squeezing Ehlbert's hand. "He doesn't think we'll treat with him if we suspect Tomas is likely to succumb to his wounds. A singular misjudgement, of course, but it's in the nature of schemers to think the worst of those they wish to gull."

"Your Majesty, my lord champion." Altheric stepped forwards to offer them both a bow of grave assurance. "Give me all the knights in this camp and I will ride into that den of traitors and wrest the king from their clutches. You have my most solemn word upon it."

Ehlbert stiffened in response, and I knew he would have wished nothing more than to mount his own charger and do the same. However, in this moment he was no longer a champion but a father desperate to secure his son's safe return. "They'll cut his throat the moment their pickets catch sight of you," he sighed, shoulders sagging and shaking his head.

"If we strike at dusk we have a chance," Altheric insisted. "I will divide the force, charge from two directions to confuse them."

"We don't even know where in the camp Tomas is being held," Leannor pointed out with an air of strained patience that told me she had already endured a prior version of this discussion. Sir Altheric, undaunted, continued to argue, adding a company of crossbowmen to his proposed attack.

As the argument wore on, I pondered, Erchel's gift of foreknowledge looming large in my mind. *Tomas Algathinet's corpse, trapped beneath his fallen horse, neck snapped like a twig. "This is where it truly starts . . ."* Countess Desmena had lied; I had no doubt of that. Yet, to trust everything to ugly sights glimpsed in a dream would have seemed like folly if I hadn't known it to be far more than a dream. Sir Altheric might charge into the heart of the Pretender's encampment but all he would find would be a kingly corpse. But I also knew confirming the king's demise at this juncture would be a mistake, for a stratagem had taken seed in my ever-busy head, one that required my own not inconsiderable facility for deception.

"All of this is moot," I said, quelling the increasingly heated exchange between princess and knight marshal.

"Mind your place, Scribe," Sir Altheric snapped, eyes flashing a rebuke.

I grimaced with the appropriate pitch of contrition, bowing low before making for the exit. "I crave your pardon, my lords, Your Majesty. I shall leave you to your . . ."

"Wait," Leannor instructed. "Why do you say that?"

I halted and straightened, allowing a short, uncomfortable pause before speaking with the appropriate air of reluctance. "Your Majesty, it is my belief that the Pretender has no intention of returning the king to you in any circumstance. Nor will he allow you both to go into peaceable exile. To seize and hold this realm he needs the Algathinet line to end." I hesitated, then added with careful emphasis,

"*All* members of the Algathinet line." From the rapid blinking of her eyes I divined she took my meaning clearly, and in fact had probably already reached the same conclusion: her son's life depended on the Pretender's defeat.

"Then why offer to return King Tomas at all?" Altheric asked. "Why not just kill him, assuming he still lives, and bring us to battle? The numbers are in his favour."

"I've seen enough war by now to know that there's more to a victory than just the size of an army," I said. "Skill at arms matters a great deal too. It's my guess that the only true soldiers in the Pretender's horde are Duke Guhlton's levies and whatever free swords they've hired. The rest are untrained and ill-armed churls, much as it was at the Traitors' Field, and we all saw what happened there. I feel Lochlain is not a man given to repeating his mistakes."

"He seeks to paralyse us," Leannor said. "Gathering yet more supporters to his banner while we dither and doubt thanks to his false bargain."

"We have reinforcements arriving by the day," Altheric put in. "The ducal levies from the Shavine Marches will be here by the morrow, the Cordwainers only a day or so behind . . ."

"Not enough." Leannor shook her head. "And the host we have gathered could well lose heart if news of Tomas's capture spreads, worse if he's . . ." She trailed off, turning to Ehlbert with a stricken glance.

The King's Champion lowered his head, fingers twitching as they played over his heavy brow. "Had I but been at his side . . ." he murmured before straightening, fixing Leannor with an implacable stare. "Whether this bargain be false or no," he grated, "we must know. *I* must know."

I will not claim a pause for reflection before speaking my next words, for my stratagem had coalesced into a firm course by this juncture. The risks were great, but that is so in all wars. Still, when I think of it now, the alacrity with which I wove this snare brings a sharp pain to my aged heart. The crimes I shared with Evadine were many, as I said, but this one was all mine.

"If I were to hear it from the Pretender's own lips," I said, "then I feel sure I could discern the lie, if lie it is. It's certain he'll never agree to produce the king until the bargain is struck. However, we could send the countess on her way with a counter, a statement that the Pretender's offer will only be considered if he speaks it to you personally, Princess. You could frame it as a demand for his word, bring along a cleric so that he must swear it before the Covenant."

"He'll suspect a trap," Altheric said. "Martyrs know he's slipped free of plenty in his time."

"Then tell him to bring his host." I addressed my words to both Leannor and Ehlbert, knowing real authority lay with them. "And you will bring yours. Insist the parley is held some miles south of here two days hence. Lord Altheric will choose ground that favours us. It will allow Lady Evadine to bring up the Covenant Crusade and bear witness to the parley. The most revered cleric in the realm come to hear the truth of the Pretender's word. If he refuses then all will know him a liar. If nothing else it buys us time, for have no doubt the Covenant Crusade will more than match his strength, in zeal if nothing else."

I had seen Leannor ill at ease before, for despite her guile she was not skilled at concealing emotion. The pitch of her distress now was so acute it almost stirred my pity, but not quite. She had never been an easy woman to like. "Lord Altheric," she said, a quaver in her voice as she turned to the knight marshal. "Your counsel?"

Altheric flicked a hand through his beard, settling a steady gaze on me for a time. He was a much harder personage to read than Leannor, but I could perceive a keen mind hard at work. "I see some merit in this," he said finally. "Though we must agree our contingency beforehand."

"Contingency?" Leannor asked.

"If Captain Scribe hears truth or lie, what then? If it's truth, how do we respond since the Pretender can't be trusted in any case? If it's all a lie, then do we resort instantly to battle?"

"It's truth," Ehlbert said, his fearful gaze distant now. "I feel it. If my . . . If the king is dead I would know. When his survival is confirmed we will be bound to consider another bargain. I will offer myself in exchange for the king, along with all treasure it is within my power to provide, for fortune has made me wealthy these past years. The Pretender is ever greedy for gold, is he not?"

He's greedy for power above all else. The words rose then faded from my lips at a warning glance from Leannor. A quick appraisal of Sir Ehlbert confirmed that I looked upon a man teetering on the edge of reason. The fact that I took grim satisfaction from this adds further to the shame I feel now. I summoned grim memories of Moss Mill and the many slain at Walvern Castle to buttress my resolve, channelling the long-suppressed anger and resentment into a bitter conclusion: *I owe these noble wretches nothing.*

"Free swords must be paid, it's true," I said, keeping my tone one of mild agreement. "And, like any canny merchant, the Pretender's first offer will surely be a mask for something else."

"Lady Ducinda," Ehlbert said with the air of a sea-tossed man clutching at a rope. "Duke Guhlton will greatly desire her return. She will be our offer."

"Perhaps, my lord," Leannor said, moving to clasp both hands to Sir Ehlbert's clenching fist. Turning to me, she stiffened her back, speaking with brisk authority. "In any case, my brother's champion speaks true: we must know the king's fate. Only then can we truly plan this war. Captain, you will deliver our counter to that bilesome woman. I've suffered her company enough for one day. Besides, I think she likes you."

CHAPTER THIRTY-FIVE

"Parley after parley," Countess Desmena grumbled, reaching for her sword. "Had my fill of them when the True King struck his alliance with Duke Guhlton."

"Better parley than battle," I returned, which earned me a disparaging chuckle.

"Are you a coward then, Master Scribe?" She reached for the reins of her fine grey destrier. "All I had heard of you would seem to indicate otherwise. How disappointing."

"Cowardice is an accusation often laid at the door of those who prefer reason to violence. For example, it was entirely reasonable for the man you call the True King to flee the Traitors' Field after barely exchanging a cut or two with the Anointed Lady. Yet, there are many who still term him a coward for doing so."

I expected rage but she merely shot me an amused grin. "I do like you," she sighed, putting her foot to the stirrup. "It's a shame. Tell me," she grunted, climbing into the saddle, "does Wilhum Dornmahl still ride with your false Martyr?"

I let the jibe at Evadine pass, phrasing my response in an easy tone. "He does, and his service is greatly appreciated by the Anointed Lady. They were childhood friends, you know."

"I know." I heard a deep well of resentment in the hardened grate of her voice as she stared down at me. "Tell the traitor I'll look for him on the field. He was unworthy of the love given unto him by a far better man, and it will be my honour to take recompense for it, in blood."

"He still speaks well of the Pretender on occasion. Although, of course he now recognises the folly of his prior allegiance."

"I speak not of the True King. I speak of Aldric Redmaine." She fixed me with a hard glare, the innate cynicism I had marked in her shifting into something far more dire in its promise. "He was my brother."

With that she put the spurs to the destrier's flanks and rode away in a cloud of raised sod, scattering a good many kingsmen from her path as she galloped through the camp with uncaring haste. Feeling a spot of rain, I looked up to find the sky had taken on the hue of an angry bruise, the sun hidden by shifting cloud. I chose not to take the distant rumble of thunder as an ill omen.

"So, Desmena's still alive." Wilhum's expression mingled disappointment with the grim humour of hearing news both dreaded but expected. "That makes sense. If there was ever a soul destined to survive any circumstance, it was her."

"Her family name is Lehville," I said. "But she claims Aldric Redmaine as her brother."

We sat alone at a campfire positioned a good distance from the Mounted and Scout Companies, mingled now in anticipation of battle. The leading elements of the Covenant host were only ten miles shy of reaching the newly repositioned royal encampment. Sir Altheric had chosen a range of broad hills as the site where we would await the Pretender's answer. My estimation of the knight marshal's abilities increased upon viewing the spot, finding it afforded clear views of the surrounding country without conveying an overt impression of advantage. A brownish grey smudge on the horizon drew my curious eye, whereupon Wilhum explained it as the smoke rising from the many chimneys of Couravel. We were less than a day's march from the capital, the city's fate likely to be decided by the impending confrontation. Come nightfall my scouts returned with tales of many folk fleeing the city with all they could carry, bespeaking a considerable lack of faith in their current rulers.

Evadine and Swain were still with the main body of the crusade, attempting to keep those that had survived the trek on their feet just a day longer. I was grateful for their absence, since bringing my stratagem to fruition would require a mind more attuned to moral compromise than theirs, a mind like Wilhum's in fact.

"I told you about Aldric Redmaine before, did I not?" he said, poking at the fire with a stick.

"You said his father taught you the knightly arts," I said, pausing before adding, "He sounded like a man of harsh temperament."

Wilhum huffed a mirthless laugh, eyes lost in the fire. "That he was. A miserable, prideful, selfish soul to be sure, but for reasons best left to mysteries of the female mind, women of all stations were drawn to him as moths to a flame. Aldric would joke about the number of bastards his father had sired in far-flung castles throughout the realm. Of them all, it was only Desmena who Aldric regarded as a true sibling."

"She and Aldric were raised together?"

"If raised be the right word. Whether through her father's influence or natural inclination, Desmena showed more interest in matters martial than she did dolls or dresses. Redmaine was a famously hard tutor, but, as Aldric had it, not so when it came to her. If his son stumbled during a sword scale he could expect a beating, while all Desmena earned for the same offence was a laugh and a few words of kind instruction. She was, to put it bluntly, a spoiled little bitch, a despoilment of character that persisted into adulthood. Aldric always loved her, though, for his big, guileless heart could do no less, despite she and I detesting each other at first sight. I had hoped that when we ran off to ally ourselves with the True King she would stay behind, but sadly it wasn't to be. Desmena wanted blood for her murdered father, blood for her disgraced mother, blood for all the petty insults and humiliations suffered as a bastard. But, I suspect her wanting blood arose mainly because she just likes the sight of it, and in Magnis

Lochlain she found herself someone who would let her spill as much as she wanted. In time she grew to love the True King more than she did her brother, but I doubt the affection was ever returned in the manner she wished."

He fell silent, frowning as he regarded the dancing flames, head no doubt crowding with memories. I allowed him a short pause before venturing a softly spoken question: "So, you'll have no compunction in killing her, should you have to?"

Wilhum's eyes slid to meet mine, brows knitting in familiar suspicion. "Do I detect a scheme stewing in that clever brain pot of yours, Alwyn?"

"This war can end tomorrow," I said, "with a few hundred dead, maybe more, maybe less. Or it can drag on for years claiming Martyrs know how many thousands of lives. And if that happens we'll be no closer to raising Evadine to the status she requires for true peace to reign in this land. You know this."

A sour grin played over Wilhum's lips. "I've thought on it a great deal, though evidently not with your facility for cunning."

"Call it cunning or call it good sense. Call it base treachery if you want. I couldn't give a rat's turd. We acted to preserve her life before, perhaps to the damnation of our souls, but act we did. Now we must act again, but I need to know you are willing to raise your hand against the man you once called king and the woman your lover called sister."

The humour faded from his face, replaced by the grim acceptance that is often the lot of a dutiful soldier. Swallowing a sigh, he asked, "What do you intend?"

I sought out Lilat after leaving Wilhum, finding her with the horses. She had developed a marked fondness for the beasts, taking to riding with an enviably swift aptitude. She had named the long-legged, black stallion she rode *Kaelihr*, the Caerith word for a gale or storm depending on the inflection. The animal let out an appreciative snort as she smoothed a fine-haired brush over his hide, shifting his head to nuzzle at her in a way that stirred a small pulse of jealousy in my breast. All I ever received from Blackfoot as thanks for performing the same chore was a stamping hoof and an impatient shudder.

"They're skittish," she told me, glancing up from her task. "I think they can smell the other people, sense what's coming."

Despite my attempts at explanation, Lilat had given up trying to understand the various causes of the conflict in which she found herself embroiled. She knew she travelled with one force soon to engage in battle with another, but the who and why of it all eluded her, as well it might. The Pretender's horde were simply "the other people" while the Covenant host she termed only as "your friends, so they are my friends".

For the most part the Scout Company, rightly fearing my reaction to any disrespect, treated her with deferential and mostly unspoken curiosity. Ayin was a predictable exception, bedevilling Lilat with a constant barrage of questions, scribbling the answers down to add more words to the growing bundles of parchment stuffed into her saddlebags.

"Where did you get that?" I asked, nodding to the falchion I noticed propped against a nearby water cask.

"Eamond," Lilat said, an unsurprising response. He was another who paid Lilat notable attention, albeit of the blushing, stuttering variety. "He said I would need it tomorrow. He also gave me this to wear." She set aside her brush to heft an iron-studded brigandine. "It's heavy," she added with a grimace of dislike. "I don't have to wear it, do I?"

"No," I said, reaching out to take the garment from her. "You won't need it, or the weapon."

I set the brigandine down, exchanging it for her saddle. "It's time," I said, hauling it onto Kaelihr's back.

"Time?" Lilat asked, squinting at me in puzzlement.

"For you to fulfil the task set you." I settled the saddle in place then reached for the girth. "Time to hunt for the *Doenlisch*."

"But the battle . . ."

"Is not your battle." I cinched the strap and pulled it tight, straightening to meet her gaze. "Nor is this your war. You have to go now, and I'll hear no argument upon it."

"The *Eithlisch* told me to preserve you . . ."

"And you did, in the mountains. That was your place. This is mine and I can't keep you safe, not tomorrow or any of the days that follow. Things are different here; you've seen that. You've seen what we do to each other, the children murdered, the villages burnt. You've seen folk starve themselves for the chance to die in a cause they understand only little better than you do. You've seen what my people are, and I am no different."

Hearing the increasingly raw and ragged tones of my voice, I faltered to silence. When I looked at Lilat again I saw the hurt and reluctance stark in her unguarded gaze. Coughing, I strapped the falchion Eamond had given her to the saddle's back skirt, avoiding her gaze as I spoke on.

"Once I had another friend I forced into a battle," I said. "And she hated me for it. That's what battle does, it changes us, moulds us into something new and it's rarely an improvement. The next time I see your face, I would rather it was without hate. Finding the *Doenlisch* is the more important task, in any case. Besides, Uhlla was right. I can see it if you can't. You are not *taolisch*; you are *veilisch*, a hunter, and that is by far the better thing to be."

She argued further, our exchange becoming ever more heated until I threatened to have her bound, thrown into a cart and carried twenty miles away before being set loose. It was not an idle threat. I was determined she wouldn't see what occurred on the morrow, not just because I wished to spare her the horrors of pitched battle. No, it was baser and more selfish than that. I didn't want her to see my crime. Even though she might never understand the nature of it, still I was resolved to damn my soul beyond her sight.

"Where?" she muttered having finally consented to mount up. "Where am I to look? This land is vast."

"You're a hunter," I reminded her, offering a smile she failed to return. "Besides, I've a sense that the *Doenlisch* will find you when the time is right." I stepped back, maintaining my smile and fighting a catch in my throat. "Be wary of those you meet on the road. Trust no one and take every word for a lie."

Lilat looked away, hand tightening on the reins, and I thought she was about to ride off into the dark without a farewell. Yet she paused, the reproach still lingering on her brow, but her gaze had softened. "The *Eithlisch* said the same about you," she said. "'All his kind are liars and he is one of the worst.' That's what he told me."

"Can't say I cared for him either," I replied, forcing a laugh. "But neither can I doubt his wisdom."

She nodded, the anger fading as she straightened. "Don't die tomorrow," she said before kicking her heels, sending Kaelihr into a fast trot. The night sky was darkened by cloud and I tracked her for only a short time before horse and rider were lost to the dark.

CHAPTER THIRTY-SIX

The Pretender arranged his horde with care that day, placing Duke Guhlton's seasoned Althienes on his right flank with the assembly of free swords and the remnant of his own loyal followers in the centre. This neatly appointed line shifted into a swollen, stretched mob of churls as it proceeded west to form the left flank of the rebel army. Despite their lack of cohesion, the commoners who had flocked to the Pretender's banner still created a formidable impression. Ayin's superior eye for numbers gauged them at over ten thousand, a figure matched by the rest of the host. By contrast, Princess Leannor's forces could be estimated at somewhere between fifteen and eighteen thousand, since reinforcements were arriving even as the drums and trumpets summoned the soldiers into ranks. Evadine had arrived with the Covenant host just before dawn with perhaps another six thousand crusaders at her back. The rest of the Commons Crusade was spread out on the road to southern Alberis, a plodding, ragged snake that continued to feed tired but keen churls into the royal host throughout the morning.

I spent the hours before the parley helping Swain marshal the crusaders into something that passed for a formation, placing the least malnourished and better armed in the first rank. They had benefited from a few hours' rest and some decent food, but fatigue and the depredations of the Sacrifice March were plain on every face. I saw the signature distant expression that bespeaks recent bereavement on many faces. *Grieving for family and friends lost on the road*, I concluded. Yet, despite all they had suffered, I took guilty comfort in the fact that I saw no doubt among the grief and weariness. Their faith in the Lady burned bright as ever, stoked by her daily sermons, which I had come to understand matched the arcane power of anything I had seen from the Sack Witch or the *Eithlisch*.

However, if my stratagem worked there would be no sermon today, no last-minute oratory from the Risen Martyr to fire them up so that they might stand against the Malecite Horde. I credited her sermon before the Traitors' Field with securing the Covenant Company's victory that day, or at least its survival. Now I had to trust that the crusaders' devotion would stir them to swift action when the time came.

Deciding a little exhortation wouldn't hurt, I mounted Blackfoot and rode about for a bit in front of the ragged ranks. Having captured their attention, I brought the stallion to a halt and raised myself up, calling out in as loud a voice as I could muster: "Who do you fight for?"

The response was immediate, and fierce in its strident concordance. "The Lady!"

"Who do you live for?"

"The Lady!"

"Who do you die for?"

"THE LADY!"

Unbidden, they began to stamp their feet and pound the staves of their varied weapons against the ground, taking up a rhythmic chant. "We fight for the Lady! We live for the Lady! We die for the LADY!"

I expected the chorus to be confined to the crusaders alone but it was soon taken up by the Covenant host arrayed in neat ranks to their front. Nor did it end there, the chant spreading to the ducal levies to our right and left, the Covenant troops having been placed alongside the Crown Companies in the centre of the line. Soon the entire royal army were crying it out, the sound echoing across the shallow vale to the Pretender's horde.

"THE LADY! THE LADY! THE LADY!"

Evadine herself sat atop Ulstan to the front of the battle line, positioned on the periphery of the cluster of royalty and nobles beneath the Algathinet banner. I saw Leannor stir at the continuing chant, but the distance was too great to make out her expression. I wondered if worries over her brother's fate would allow for any jealousy, but concluded that the princess's heart was more than capable of accommodating both fear and envious resentment. For her part Evadine gave no response to the chant, continuing to sit in stoic regard of the opposing host. Her apparent indifference, of course, only added to the impression of selfless resolve and rectitude.

"It would be best to bring this lot closer to the rear of the company," I told Swain. He remained on foot as was his preference in battle, obliging me to lean low in the saddle, shouting to make myself heard over the ongoing tumult. "Station sergeants to relay swift orders, should the need arise."

Swain squinted up at me, an echo of his old, habitual suspicion showing in his face. "You expect the parley to fail, then?" As the most experienced soldier in the Anointed Lady's service, he knew that parleys before battle were uncertain affairs. It wasn't uncommon for agreement to be reached as one or both parties found the courage of their convictions challenged by the very real prospect of ugly and violent death. From Sihlda's lessons I knew of several wars that had ended in just such a manner, but I had chosen not to enlighten Swain to the certain fact that this would not be among them.

"For all his claims to kingship," I said, leaning lower and lowering my voice a notch, "the Pretender is a thief at heart and not to be trusted. And I should know, should I not? Keep a close watch on proceedings and be ready to act with all haste, Captain."

I saw his suspicion deepen as I drew back and angled Blackfoot's head towards the royal banner. However, he consented to afford me a grave, wordless nod before I cantered away. I hadn't gone far when a familiar voice hailed me, one I had thought it unlikely to ever hear again.

"I never took you for a speech maker."

Lorine Blousset, Duchess of the Shavine Marches, regarded me from atop a tall white mare, flanked on either side by armoured men-at-arms in ducal livery. My last view of her had been of a face half lit by the chainsman's campfire, flecked in blood from when she drew the dagger free of his spine. I found it to have acquired much in the way of noble authority, her beauty enhanced rather than dimmed by the passage of years. The ermine-trimmed cloak of blue velvet she wore complemented her colouring perfectly, creating the very image of a woman born to her station, which, like much else about her, made it a lie. Her expression was friendly but I saw the careful scrutiny beneath the affable facade. Of all the clever minds I encountered, Lorine occupies a position near the summit of the list and I knew recent events would have given her a great deal to ponder.

"My lady duchess," I said, bowing in the saddle. "You will forgive me for not dismounting, but the royal party expects my presence."

Lorine gave a short laugh. "How far you've risen," she said. "Perhaps higher than I, eh?"

"An impossibility, my lady." I glanced to either side of her, seeing guards but no duke. "Your husband isn't present?"

"You didn't hear?" Lorine's features slipped effortlessly into the sorrowful mask of a grieving widow. "Duke Rouphon, my cherished husband, passed from this world some weeks ago. An ailment of the stomach no physician or entreaty to the Martyrs could cure."

"A terrible loss," I stated, not troubling myself to colour the words with any pretence of regret. What little I had seen of Duke Rouphon left me with the impression of a small man attempting to fit himself into a role he could never fill, unlike his wife. "Your . . . child?" I ventured.

"Well and healthy under the care of trusted servants in Castle Ambris, though it pained me greatly to be parted from him. His name is Bouldin."

We shared a smile of mutual understanding: Bouldin had been the name of Deckin's grandfather, on his mother's side. The infant heir might not share any blood with the fallen Outlaw King, but Lorine had surely cast Deckin in the role of father nevertheless. I knew then that Duchess Lorine Blousset would never marry again, that she had only loved one man, once and forever. The thought summoned memories of that old band of villains and our days in the forest, memories that were an indulgent distraction now, for I had a crime to orchestrate.

"You should ensure your troops are well ordered today, my lady," I said, meeting her eye to ensure she took my meaning.

Lorine's gaze slipped briefly to the royal party before she trotted her mare closer, voice pitched in low and carefully expressionless tones. "Does the Pretender truly have the king, Alwyn? Or is this all just farce?"

Despite the lack of inflection in her question, I could hear the true query beneath the words. *She's wondering whether to turn her coat.* I bit down on a laugh, finding I couldn't fault Lorine for pondering treason. It would have been akin to castigating a she-wolf for biting anything that might threaten her cub.

"Ensure your troops are well ordered," I repeated. "Have especial care for their left flank and all will be well."

She frowned in puzzlement. "My captains tell me Lochlain's best troops are in the centre."

"Their left flank." I smiled, taking up Blackfoot's reins and turning him towards the Algathinet banner. "Trust me." I hesitated, turning back to her. "I am glad to see you again."

Her frown lingered though she inclined her head with duchess-like grace as I kicked my heels, compelling Blackfoot into a trot. The three ranks of kingsmen parted to allow me to approach the royal party whereupon I slowed my mount to a walk, making a careful inspection of the far right of our line. To my satisfaction, I saw Wilhum had positioned the mounted scouts and Covenant Riders slightly forwards of the Covenant host infantry, allowing for a rapid charge when the time came.

I must confess to a certain queasiness upon reaching the cluster of nobles beneath the Algathinet banner. Although I harboured no doubts as to the rightness of my course, it was not something to be done lightly. Nor did I entertain any surety that it would work, such a thing being so unprecedented. In fact, I remain unaware of any parallel in history, not that my stratagem that day has been recorded before I set my quill upon these pages. My worst crime has always been my most long-lived lie, revealed only unto you, cherished reader, for I know your judgement will be fair.

"The bastard's late," Sir Altheric grunted as I reined Blackfoot to a halt. The knight marshal's gaze scanned the opposing host with predatory focus, one that shifted into a disapproving scowl when he turned to me. "But then, so are you, Captain."

"Merely seeing to the proper disposition of my company, my lord," I told him, fighting to contain an uneasy roil from my belly. I didn't quite succeed but fortunately my armour contained the treacherous growl. Unlike all others present, my armour remained a mix of scavenged plate and accoutrements of varying hue and age. However, my lack of chivalric glamour was more than matched by Sir Ehlbert that day. He sat atop his mighty destrier clad in finely crafted but unpolished steel, unshaven features constant in their animation as his eyes searched the Pretender's horde. Once again a mote of pity swirled within me, for seeing such a man so reduced can raise a pang in even the iciest heart. But, once again I crushed the impulse. *What do I owe these noble wretches?*

"When the Pretender comes," Princess Leannor told me, speaking with stern command, "the parley will take place in accordance with established custom. You will listen only. Nothing will be decided in this moment. Our next course will be determined once we have retired to hear your judgement." Her expression darkened into one of dire warning. "You understand me, Captain Scribe?"

I bowed low, curling an armoured finger and putting it to my forehead, every bit the cowed churl she wanted to see. "I do, Your Majesty."

The distant sound of trumpets snapped all eyes towards the enemy host. The neat centre ranks rippled and parted as a tall banner made its way to the fore. Cheers rang out when a figure in resplendent bronze-hued armour rode through, the rebel army calling out its acclaim for the Pretender. I noted how the most fervent cheers came from the massed commons on the left rather than the Althienes. The soldiers and free swords cheered along with gusto, but not the same animation or volume. Once clear of the line, the tall man wheeled his charger about, raising his banner high while the warhorse reared. It was an assuredly impressive sight, one that stirred the Pretender's adoring churls to yet louder cheering.

Wheeling about once more, he struck out towards the royal party at a steady gallop, silken banner trailing. For a moment I thought the Pretender might intend to conduct this parley alone, which could well work to my advantage, then saw another group of riders emerge from the enemy line. Duke Guhlton rode beneath his own banner, a full retinue of a dozen armoured knights at his back. These were surely the Silver Lances Sir Altheric spoke of, the points of their upraised spears catching a brief gleam from the sun before a bank of cloud swept in to cast the shallow vale in shadow.

Magnis Lochlain, claimant to the throne of Albermaine, reined in a dozen yards short of the royal party. He wore no helm and, seeing his features for the first time, I was struck by the absence of any similarity to King Tomas or Princess Leannor. His was a handsome face, to be sure, strong jawed and narrow of nose, long dark hair twisting in the burgeoning wind to create a creditable image of a warrior king. However, I saw scant sign of any Algathinet blood, buttressing my conviction that this man was the greatest of liars. All his claims were as false as any lie I had ever spoken, worsened by the fact that they enjoyed so much more success. I saw a keen intelligence in that face, but also a hungry ambition in the way he surveyed the assembled nobles. It was therefore surprising when he shifted his gaze from the royal party to Evadine, walking his charger towards her.

"Lady Evadine Courlain," he said, bowing low. His voice held another surprise in that it lacked any attempt at a noble accent. It was measured and presumably well practised in speech making, but it was also coarse, the voice of an educated churl or well-read townsman. "We have met before, of course, but never have we been introduced. Seeing you now, I consider this a terrible oversight on my part."

He spoke with an air of honest solicitation and an unquestionable charm, very much like a suitor greeting a prospective bride. However, instead of jealousy, it stirred only amusement in my breast for I knew this woman, and he plainly did not.

In response to his greeting Evadine said and did nothing, although her features were far from lacking in expression. She stared at Lochlain with the unwavering, icy focus I had seen in battle; her killing face.

I saw the Pretender's mouth quirk in amused offence as Evadine's silence persisted. Reclining in the saddle, he asked, "Have you no words for me, my lady? To act in so . . . uncivil a manner beneath the protection of a truce pennant ill befits one of such devotional renown."

Evadine's gaze narrowed. "Yes, I have words for you," she said, voice clipped with restrained fury. "Conclude this pointless charade so I can proceed to the business of sending your corrupted soul back to your Malecite masters."

The humour slipped quickly from Lochlain's face. Having fought this woman before, albeit briefly, he would have no doubt as to her skills, so her deadly antipathy was clearly sobering. "I am no servant of the Malecite," he stated with a tone of seemingly genuine grievance. "Always I have honoured the Covenant." He pointed to the host at his back. "There are clerics standing in the ranks of yonder army as we speak."

"'Beware the voice of the corrupted,'" Evadine replied, a quote from the scroll of Martyr Stevanos, "'for the Malecite tongue will weave a cage of lies around any heart.'"

"'Guard your soul against the lure of prideful ambition,'" Lochlain shot back, a rejoinder from the sayings of Martyr Melliah. Plainly, the man was no stranger to scripture, although I found his choice of passage so ironic as to constitute rank hypocrisy. "'Ascend only by the just acclaim of honest men. All else is vanity.'"

The exchange of scriptural barbs might have continued if the thunder of hooves on earth hadn't announced the arrival of Duke Guhlton's party. "Lochlain!" he called out, hauling his destrier to a halt in a shower of sod. "Enough dalliance with that holy wench. We've a war to win."

Duke Guhlton was nearly equal in height to Sir Ehlbert, although his girth was several inches wider. He wore a suit of mostly undecorated armour save for the breastplate, emblazoned with a silver and enamel motif representing the spread-winged osprey of the Pendroke family crest. Unlike the Pretender, he wore a helm, the visor raised to reveal a heavily bearded visage, deeply lined across the forehead and about the eyes. Also in contrast to Lochlain, his attention was fixed entirely on the principal members of the royal party.

Guhlton Pendroke sat in silent, baleful regard of Leannor and Ehlbert, offering no greeting while his retinue fanned out on either side. The silence persisted and thickened as Lochlain favoured Evadine with a parting bow then walked his steed to Duke Guhlton's side. The tension was such that it brought another churn to my guts and set my heart to increased labour. *What do I owe these noble wretches?* The question echoed with increasing hollowness every time I asked it, stirring a welter of doubt.

Finally, Leannor turned and nodded to Altheric who raised his voice to utter the required formalities. "Be it known that all who gather under this pennant are agreed no blood will be spilled beneath its shadow. We gather in peace and depart in peace. Affirm your oaths to this or depart now to battle."

The princess was the first to speak, straightening her back and raising her hand. "I so affirm, in the name of the Crown, the Algathinet family and in the sight of the Martyrs and the Seraphile."

Ehlbert spoke next, his face still twitching with contained distress, his hand actually trembling as he raised it. "I so affirm."

Lochlain's affirmation was phrased with a gracious smoothness, although the way his eyes constantly slid towards Evadine told of simmering pique. "For my people and the realm, I so affirm."

"I so affirm," Duke Guhlton snapped, his voice an impatient growl. "Get on with it, Courlain."

Sir Altheric exchanged glances with Leannor and, receiving a nod, spoke on: "The terms conveyed unto Princess Leannor by the herald of Magnis Lochlain are hereby rejected as being without merit. No further discussion as to these terms will be entertained. However, the princess's love for her brother and fervent desire not to mire this realm in yet more needless bloodshed compels her to at least seek some form of accommodation."

The knight marshal paused only briefly to gather breath, but Duke Guhlton saw little reason not to state his own terms. "My granddaughter," he said with gruff implacability. "Give her to me, if you haven't killed her already."

"Lady Ducinda is unharmed," Leannor said, heat rising in her cheeks, "and resides in all safety and comfort in my family's care."

"So you can shackle her to your Algathinet whelp." Guhlton's growl grew ominous. "I think not. My family's blood will never be soiled by yours, woman. Give me my granddaughter and . . ." he paused to grind his teeth ". . . we'll give you your brother."

It is in the small things that lies are seen. The hesitations, the slight moistening of a lip or overly rapid blinking of an eye. In this case it was Guhlton's mix of anger and self-recrimination as he set his jaw. I almost laughed as the realisation dawned, the knowledge that altered my careful scheme, in detail if not effect. I had come expecting to point the accusing finger in one direction, guilty or not. Now I had a genuine culprit to point to.

Most present missed my fractional start of surprise, but not Sir Ehlbert, his reddened eyes fixing on me with frantic need. "What did you see?" he said, voice pitched low so that the others failed to notice as Sir Altheric began speaking once again.

"Any agreement reached here," the knight marshal said, "is dependent on sureties given regarding the health and well-being of King Tomas. Accordingly, Princess Leannor requires your oaths that the king remains alive and unharmed."

"What did you see, Scribe?" Ehlbert demanded, this time loud enough to draw the eyes of the rest of the parley.

I looked from the King's Champion to the Duke of Althiene, now shifting in the saddle as his destrier stirred, perhaps sensing his rider's alarm. The duke regarded me with bafflement but also naked suspicion, as any guilty man might.

"Give me my granddaughter," he told Leannor again, forcing his gaze away from mine, "and we'll give you your brother."

"Scribe?" Ehlbert asked again, although his voice was now filled with a terrible certainty.

On this occasion I will lay claim to a moment of hesitation, weighed as I was by the sheer import of the task, not to mention the annoying and undiminished roiling in my guts. Looking into Ehlbert's forlorn, sagging face, I knew I was about to wreak terrible destruction upon this man. But it was only a short interval of doubt, for there was more at stake here than just a father's heart.

"I believe King Tomas lies dead," I stated, speaking with both volume and clarity, returning my gaze to the Duke of Althiene, "slain in battle by the hand of Duke Guhlton some days ago."

I've little doubt that Guhlton Pendroke was a fearless man for most of his life, that he rode to war many a time with resolve and fortitude the equal of the most renowned knights in all history. In that moment, however, when Ehlbert turned to him, I saw the curious sight of a hero instantly transformed into a craven.

"I tried to spare him," he said, voice thin, eyes wide and fixed on Ehlbert whose features had suddenly taken on a horribly familiar calmness. "It . . ." Guhlton faltered as the King's Champion, moving without particular haste, drew his sword. "It was an accident . . . His horse fell. I never intended . . ."

Whether his cowardly pleading would have spared him Ehlbert's wrath seems doubtful but will forever remain a point of conjecture, for he was not the only vengeful soul present. Princess Leannor moved with a speed and ferocity I would never have suspected of her, an ugly screech emerging from lips drawn in a feral snarl. Spurring her mare into a forward leap, Leannor launched herself from the saddle, the dagger she held raised high. If he hadn't been so preoccupied with the dread intent of the King's Champion, Duke Guhlton might have saved himself. Unfortunately for him, he barely managed to half raise an arm before Leannor's dagger came down to skewer him through the right eye. It was a blow delivered with lethal strength, the dagger sinking in all the way to the hilt. Guhlton's armour-clad form flailed as he and Leannor tumbled to the ground in an untidy tangle, but I knew it to be his death throes.

It is impossible to accurately relate all of what happened over the span of the next few moments, much of which I failed to witness since my attention was so fixed upon the slain duke and the reaction of his escort. Having accrued a good deal of detail since, what is striking is that all the most salient events of that day took place before the much-studied battle itself actually began.

For the space of perhaps two heartbeats the Silver Lances simply sat and stared at their fallen duke while Leannor struggled to disentangle herself from the corpse. Drawing the dagger clear of Guhlton's twitching eye socket, she knelt atop his armoured chest and began to repeatedly drive it into his neck, spitting barely comprehensible obscenities all the while. This proved sufficient for the duke's escort to stir themselves. Appalled, vengeful shouts rang out as they began to lower their lance points, horses rearing in anticipation of combat. I feel sure the princess would have met her end beneath the trampling hooves of many warhorses if Sir Ehlbert hadn't charged headlong into the midst of the Silver Lances. His longsword arced left and right in a blur, cutting down two men before they had chance to avoid the strokes. Their comrades attempted to wheel their mounts to meet the assault but Ehlbert moved through them like a shark amid schooling fish, killing with the skill and precision for which he was famed. Even so, one against so many was a hopeless prospect even for him and I've no doubt he too would have met his end that day but for Sir Altheric's quick thinking.

The knight marshal had reacted to Duke Guhlton's murder with much the same wide-eyed, open-mouthed shock as all others. Fortunately, his soldierly instincts quickly overcame any attachment to chivalric custom. "Kingsmen forward!" he barked, drawing his sword and snapping his visor into place before spurring his charger into a gallop. The twenty or so mounted men-at-arms of the Crown Company followed him into the fray with unquestioning haste and the scene soon descended into a chaotic melee. Lances shattered and maces whirled amid screaming horses and tumbling knights while I watched it all with a curious detachment, one apparently felt by the armies facing each other across this vale.

Perhaps the strangest aspect of what has been dubbed "The Battle of the Vale" is the passive inactivity of most of the assembled troops at this most critical juncture. Like me, the long ranks of soldier and churl simply stood and watched nobles kill each other in an increasingly vicious frenzy, with one most important exception. In accordance with my disrupted but still extant plan, Wilhum sounded the charge to the Covenant Mounted Company the moment violence erupted among the parley. The distance from the extreme right flank of the royal host to the scene of combat was perhaps two hundred yards, not great for a horse and rider at full gallop. Yet, it seemed to take a very long time, not least because Magnis Lochlain finally decided to stir himself to action.

It appeared to me that he charged across my line of sight as if through thickened air, my mind consenting to slow time in response to so much frenzied activity. Lochlain hadn't paused to don his helm, his long black hair streamed as he raised his sword above his head. It would have been a more impressive sight if his target hadn't been a defenceless young woman kneeling and sobbing atop the chest of the man she had just killed. There are many who will claim great things of the Pretender, some of them true, many the delusions of those prone to miring themselves in the folly of hero worship. In time I would come to know him as not truly a bad man, but in his attempt to kill Leannor it was clear that neither was he a particularly good one. The Pretender had been presented with a chance to remove one more obstacle on his path to power and he took it, although I'm sure he would have had the decency to feel bad about it later, had I given him the chance.

I had reached for my own helm when Ehlbert began his murderous assault on the Silver Lances, but not yet donned it. The gap betwixt myself and Lochlain was too great to cover before he reached Leannor but I had always been something of a dab hand at throwing things. The helm sailed through the air and caught Lochlain on the side of his unprotected head, dealing a blow of sufficient force to leave him reeling in the saddle. He hung on for a few more yards, dragging his charger's reins so that the beast veered away from Leannor, stumbled then fell in a gout of churned sod.

Seeing my chance, I hauled my longsword from its scabbard and kicked Blackfoot's flanks, spurring him to an instant gallop. As I bore down on him, Lochlain scrambled free of his flailing horse, turning towards me with features set in the blank stare of one confronting an inescapable demise. Sadly, before I could ride him down, his irksomely faithful mount regained his footing. Letting out an aggrieved whinny, the charger thrust its bulk into Blackfoot's flank, the force of the collision sending us veering wide of our target. Blackfoot made a creditable attempt to keep upright but the blow had been too great. He stumbled and skidded, his forelegs giving way to send me sprawling from the saddle. I had enough practice in leaping clear of a falling horse by now to suffer no injury beyond a few bruises, pulling my feet from the stirrups and rolling away at the moment of impact. I also contrived to keep a hold of my sword, a greatly fortuitous outcome for it enabled me to parry the overhead swing of the Pretender's blade as he brought it down towards my head.

Our steel ground and scraped together as he loomed over me, the abject realisation of seconds before replaced by a grimace of fury. "The scribe, is it?" he asked, teeth gritted, his weight pressing down. "Pity, I was hoping to spare you."

"Really?" I slipped my weight to the side, angling my sword as I did so then jerking the pommel forward to deliver a sharp blow to his nose. "I was never going to spare you."

He drew back from me with a grunt of pain, allowing me space to fully regain my feet. But it was the briefest of respites. Lochlain came at me like a storm, sword describing a series of swift arcs as he slashed blow after blow at my helmless head. One salient lesson from all those many hours of punishment at Roulgarth's hands was never to parry when you can dodge. Deflecting a blade can require just as much energy as thrusting it, and in a sword fight victory usually went to the one who could conserve his strength the longest. So, as the Pretender assailed me, I swayed and ducked rather than clashed my steel against his, waiting for the inevitable pause for breath. When it came, I launched an attack of my own, feinting a thrust at Lochlain's face then sweeping the blade up and down in a strike at his sword arm. I knew the blade wouldn't penetrate his well-crafted armour, but the force might suffice to break the bone beneath. He drew back in time to avoid the worst of the blow, although it did succeed in catching his gauntlet at the wrist. Cursing, Lochlain drew back another step, trying to switch his grip from one hand to the other. I didn't allow him the leisure to complete the task, surging forwards to deliver a series of slashes at his legs and midriff. He backed away quickly, wincing in pain as he worked his injured wrist to parry my blows. While driving him back a profound realisation rang in my mind, clear as a bell: *I'm better than him.*

Lochlain was no slouch with a blade, it was true, but nor was he especially skilled. A sturdy fighter, and assuredly an inspiring leader, but nothing more. I doubt he could have held me off for much longer, even if Evadine hadn't come galloping free of the melee at his back. She leaned low in the saddle, her sword, already bloodied from an encounter with an unfortunate foe, drawn back for a decapitating slice to the Pretender's neck. Lochlain's famous luck failed to desert him then, however. Warned by the drumbeat of pounding hooves, he jerked aside in an effort to escape. Luck may have favoured him, but his judgement didn't, for he shifted in the wrong direction, saving himself from Evadine's blade but also placing himself in the path of her horse.

Lochlain rebounded from Ulstan's flank like a rag doll, his sword tumbling away and limbs flailing. He sailed a short distance through the air before landing face down, scraping a muddy rut in the earth then coming to rest at my feet. Brown and red mixed in a pool around his mouth as he sputtered, trying and failing to raise himself up.

"Kill him, Alwyn!" Evadine called to me, dragging Ulstan to a halt and wheeling about. "End this for once and all!"

I would later ascribe my failure to follow her command to distraction, for at that moment the Pretender's horde gave voice to a shout of collective rage and finally stirring itself to advance. However, that was another of my not infrequent lies. Looking down, I saw the man who claimed himself a king spit blood and mud onto my steel-shod feet, a final act of defiance that stirred a crumb of mercy in my heart. I had killed helpless men before, most deserving of the act. But, as Lochlain strained himself to regard me with baleful eyes, his gaze lacking all fear, I felt this was one that deserved a more salutary end.

"Rest a-while, Your Majesty," I said, placing a foot on his shoulder and pushing him down. "We'll attend to you shortly."

Looking about, I gained a swift and alarming appreciation for the unfolding battle. Duke Guhlton's Silver Lances were all slain or fled, Wilhum busy mustering the Covenant Riders back into order. Beyond them I could see the entire rebel line advancing. The Althienes in the centre began their march with a semblance of discipline, but their ranks soon grew ragged, many of them spurring to a run in their rage. The murder of their duke had evidently riled them up, but anger makes a poor general. Off to the left the mass of rebel churls came on in a mob, screaming and brandishing their varied weaponry, desperate to preserve the man they called the True King. To their front was but one opponent, a knight on horseback pelting headlong towards the heart of the charging throng. Sir Ehlbert, it appeared, was not done killing for the day.

"Alwyn!" Evadine repeated, face stern as she reined Ulstan to a halt nearby. She pointed her sword at Lochlain's recumbent form, face set in an impatient scowl.

"We have a battle to attend to, my lady," I said, inclining my head at the oncoming horde. "Besides, this man has yielded. You wouldn't wish me to dishonour myself, I hope."

"Fucking liar!" Lochlain gasped. With a groan, he strained against my foot to twist his neck and shout at Evadine. "I have not yielded! Kill me if you have the heart, you Malecite-worshipping bitch!"

"Now, now," I said, shifting my weight to press harder, his words sputtering into the mud. "That's enough of that, oh foolish king." I kept my attention on Evadine as I spoke, seeing her face bunch in frustration before she closed her eyes and summoned a calming breath.

"If it seems they're going to reclaim him," she said, spurring Ulstan to motion once more, "don't hesitate."

With that she rode off, calling out commands to Wilhum to see to Leannor's safety. I took the precaution of delivering a sharp blow to the base of Lochlain's skull before dragging his limp bulk towards the security of the royal host. A perturbed glance over my shoulder revealed the rebel host no more than a hundred paces off and closing fast, albeit in a state that had little recourse to military order. I briefly considered following Evadine's instruction, thinking it unlikely that I could drag this man the required distance in time. Fortunately, Captain Swain had clearly taken my warning to heart and the Covenant host was already advancing. They came on at a measured run, moving around me and the Mounted Company then forming the standard three-rank defensive line. Not to be outdone, the Crown Company soon followed suit while, off to their left, the ducal levies of the Shavine Marches were also in motion. I would learn later that Duchess Lorine overrode her principal captain's objections to order the advance. The duchy men marched with markedly less speed than the Crown and Covenant soldiers, forming a line at a diagonal to the kingsmen just in time to meet the great mob of charging churls.

When this mass collided with the wall of defenders it birthed an explosion of voices crying out in pain and rage merged with the hard thuds of flesh impacting armour and bladed weaponry. The slight incline of the hill gave me a decent view of the Pretender's horde breaking upon the royal host like waves rebounding from rocky shore. The line bowed where the tide met the ducal levies, but didn't break. It spread to the left as more enterprising churls attempted to work their way around the flanks. Luckily the Cordwainer companies had come up by then, hemming the rebels in while a hundred or more mounted knights rode out to harry their flanks.

In the centre the Althienes were throwing themselves against the Crown and Covenant Companies in undaunted fury, without avail. Had their advance possessed a modicum of discipline their numbers might have forced a breakthrough, but with the momentum of their charge spent, all they could do was hack and stab at the hedge of pikes and halberds. I saw a large party of mounted rebels attempting to charge around the royal host's right flank only to find themselves embroiled in a chaotic melee with the great seething throng of the Covenant Crusade. The riders hacked at the enclosing mob with impressive resolve, but inevitably most were overwhelmed and dragged down in short order. Shifting my gaze to the slope beyond the Althienes, I was gratified to see a large number of figures disappearing over the crest; hired swords have little reason to linger when their paymaster lies slain.

Although I felt confident in how the battle would end, it was plainly still far from over. Sighing, I let go of Lochlain's breastplate and quickly scanned the ranks of the Covenant Riders drawn up nearby. "Eamond! Mistress Juhlina!" I called out, seeing them both still mounted and apparently uninjured.

"Captain?" Eamond asked as he and the Widow trotted their mounts towards me. Both their faces bore the signature smearing of blood and mud unique to battle. Eamond had acquired a vicious cut to the face, tracing from his left cheek to the side of his skull where the top of his ear had been sliced away. He didn't appear overly pained by it.

"Bind him and get him to the rear," I said, driving a kick into the Pretender's armoured side. "Keep him under guard and," I added, addressing the words to Juhlina, "I had better find him alive when this is done."

"And you, Captain?" Eamond asked as he dismounted, reaching for the rope on his saddle.

I looked around, spotting Blackfoot stamping his hooves not far off. "I still have work to do here," I muttered, keenly feeling the absence of my helm. Walking to the horse, I paused to crouch and remove a replacement from a slain member of the Silver Lances. It was a poor fit, but I was still glad of it by the day's end. The Pretender's horde took a long time dying that day, but die it did.

CHAPTER THIRTY-SEVEN

I found Sir Ehlbert sitting atop the corpse of his destrier, encircled by a carpet of churl bodies. Some, I assumed, were his victims, but most were feathered by a forest of crossbow bolts. Sir Altheric had brought up his bowmen while the elongated melee raged on. The blizzard of bolts they unleashed, poking their weapons between the shoulders of the kingsmen and Covenant soldiery, had been enough to finally communicate the imminence of defeat to the rebel army. As is often the way, the bulk of the killing in this battle came in the rout rather than the fight. Loyal knights and mounted men-at-arms reaped a terrible harvest among the fleeing soldiers and churls. In response, many clustered together for protection thereby providing the crossbowmen with bountiful targets. I witnessed some making wagers on how many they could bring down before sunset.

The rain eventually put paid to the slaughter, a hard, driving deluge unleashed from a bank of dark grey cloud that had lingered above for most of the day. The chilly discomfort of it seemed to cool the murderous joy that often seizes the hearts of victorious soldiers. The scenes of unleashed cruelty abated and dwindled from the field, leaving the bodies behind to be looted by those whose greed outweighed their dislike of inclement weather.

I watched Sir Ehlbert tip his head back, features momentarily occluded by the rain, washing much of the gore away in the process. When he lowered his face to regard me I found it mostly empty of emotion, lacking the madness I thought might be his due. Yet, there was a knowledge in the stare he fixed upon me, although his voice was flat when he spoke.

"You knew, didn't you, Scribe?" he asked me. "You knew they'd killed my son."

"A suspicion only," I said. I felt this to be only a marginal untruth, my stratagem having been based on a vision afforded me by a leering ghost in a dream, after all. "But, I knew if it proved true it would come out at the parley. I'll not claim any regret for it, my lord. This war had to end today else this realm would have known nothing but blood for a decade." I paused to swallow. An hour or more of fighting should have inured me to fear. Yet despite my fatigue and a head full of recently witnessed horrors, this man still never failed to make me afraid. "Nor will I run from the consequences," I went on, "if you've a mind to seek recompense."

"How very brave of you." Such previously unseen cynicism from so earnest a soul might have stoked my fear even higher, but I could tell he was too spent and mired in grief to allow for more violence. "Tomas wasn't supposed to be king," he said, eyes growing distant. "I assume you know that. If Mathis had reigned a little longer and that dim-witted sot Arthin had managed to avoid breaking his neck . . ." Ehlbert trailed off into a humourless laugh, shaking his head as it bowed low in the rain. I thought he might be done, that I would walk off and leave him here to drown in his grief, perhaps never to rise. But, it transpired he had a tale for me.

"Two princes, both dead by the same misfortune," he said, raising his head with a bitter sigh. "I would suspect a curse if I weren't a rational man. I remember the day they came to tell us. Queen Laudine, Leannor, Tomas and I were in the private garden at the palace where they played most days. It was a fine summer morning, the sun bright and the scent of roses was strong. Tomas's mother loved roses, you see? She planted them all herself. Laudine loved things that grew. It always pained me so that she never got to see her son grow, for I believe he was a good man. But her face that day when the herald came with news of Arthin's death . . . To see the heart of the woman you love break in an instant is a terrible thing. She knew what lay in store for Tomas then. Mathis would claim him, make Tomas the prince he wanted him to be, the mirror to his cold, unyielding tyranny. It broke her, in body and spirit. She only lived another two years, wasted away by her own sorrow. But before she passed she found the strength to make me swear. She demanded an oath in the name of the love we shared that I would preserve our son. And so, that is what I have striven to do for all these years. All the blood I spilled, all the crimes committed in service to a promise given to a dead woman."

His eyes hardened, both in warning and judgement. "A love like that can be a terribly dangerous thing, Scribe. I see the way you look at your Anointed Lady, and I know it's not the adoration of a devout soul for a Risen Martyr. And I see the way she looks at you, which makes you doubly cursed, the same manner of curse that I shared with Tomas's mother." Ehlbert raised his gauntlets, still flecked with blood despite the rain, gesturing to the surrounding carnage. "And see where it has brought us. Where will yours bring you?"

I regarded him in silence for quite some time, heedless of the rain pounding my skull. I found my fear of him had faded, replaced by the anger one feels for another when they voice unwanted truths. Yet, that old, years-long resentment had gone too, for his judgement was undeniable. If this man was a murderer, then what was I? This bloody day was the fruit of my scheme, not his, nor anyone else's.

"Princess Leannor lives," I said. "She travels to Couravel to proclaim her son King of Albermaine. I'm sure she would appreciate your presence, my lord." I bowed low and turned away, sloshing through the mud towards Blackfoot, the horse busy nuzzling the foot of a man who lay dead with a broken lance jutting from his back.

"I should have known, Scribe," Ehlbert called after me. Although his voice held no trace of a taunt I refused to turn, keen to get myself clear of his irksome honesty. "Sihlda tried to warn me, all those years ago in her marsh-bound shrine. 'Your best course is to flee these lands with your child and the woman you love,' she told me. 'Nothing but heartbreak and torment will result if you stay.' Why didn't I listen?"

I mounted Blackfoot and spurred him to a trot, though his pace was slowed by the rain, allowing me to hear the forlorn call of the King's Champion as I rode away. "Why didn't I listen?"

"Be it known that on this day we proclaim Arthin Algathinet, fifth of his name, monarch and liege lord of all the lands, duchies and holdings of this realm of Albermaine."

The ceiling of the cathedral in Couravel was a dizzyingly high, vaulted chamber that added a long echo to the voice of Luminant Durehl Vearist. I recall the air being heavy with incense, a useful mask to the accumulated sweat of so numerous a congregation. The storm that had deluged the aftermath of the Battle of the Vale heralded two days of rain before subsiding into clear skies and a bright sun of unseasonal warmth. It made for an uncomfortable hour of kneeling, standing and kneeling again as the Luminant proceeded through the varied rituals of the coronation. Having engaged in some research regarding this curious obligation of the Luminant's role, it is strange to report that much of Durehl's performative devotions that day had no precedent. What I, and I assume many of my fellow congregants, took for ancient, long-required prayers and incantations beseeching favour from Seraphile and Martyr, the old bastard had simply made up for the day. Faith may be real, but I am forced to the conclusion that ritual is, and always has been, mere farce.

The throne sat atop a raised dais, positioned in front of the reliquary, a wall of gold-encased Martyr bones and tokens that formed the principal objects of worship for this most monumental example of Covenant architecture. King Arthin the Fifth was dwarfed by the gilded, red velvet contrivance he perched upon, a small figure managing not to squirm as Durehl held the crown above his head. I assumed it had been Leannor's decision to cast aside Alfric's name for the more kingly Arthin, a common practice throughout the many decades of the Algathinet dynasty. The tactful disappearance of his father's family name, Keville, was another signal intended to stamp dynastic authority on his ascension. Most Arthins had a decent, only occasionally ugly reputation among scholars. Their reigns tended to provide a peaceable contrast to the more fractious or despotic Mathis's and Jardins. Watching this pale-faced boy dart a glance at his mother, I found it hard to credit him either war-maker or tyrant, but time would tell.

"All here present will now kneel," Durehl intoned, crown still hovering over the boy king's head, "and swear their loyalty to King Arthin." The Luminant gave a brief pause and I saw his throat work before he continued. "As witnessed by the Luminants' Council and the Risen Martyr Evadine Courlain."

Evadine stood alongside Leannor to the right of the throne, the assembled Luminants positioned to the left, a stark and unsubtle signifier of the shift in clerical influence. I had argued for something more circumspect but Evadine maintained an uncompromising mood since the Vale. "The time for intrigues and petty manoeuvrings is over, Alwyn," she told me. "To fulfil our mission I must grasp power where I can."

"I so swear," I said after dropping to one knee, head lowered, the cathedral thrumming with the same words repeated in various tones of reverence by the entire assembly. They represented as much of the nobility of Albermaine as could be gathered in short order. Lorine was there, as was Duke Ayerik Tahlsier of the Cordwain, a tall man of cadaverous aspect and a perennially suspicious cast to his eye. Ambassadors from Dulsian and Rhianvel had also been summoned to swear fealty on their dukes' behalf along with a smattering of refugee merchants from the Fjord Geld despite its recent loss to the Sister Queens of Ascarlia. Of course, there were no nobles from Alundia present and the only drop of noble blood from Althiene lay in the person of Lady Ducinda. Unlike her betrothed, the girl felt no compunction about squirming or fidgeting during the ceremony. She held Sir Ehlbert's hand willingly enough but her eyes often rolled and cheeks bulged as she let out a series of bored exhalations, her lack of manners bringing a covert smile to my lips.

"And so," Durehl proclaimed, voiced pitched in a gratefully received tone of finality, "here marks the first day of a long and glorious reign. All hail King Arthin!"

"All hail King Arthin!"

When the chorus of acclaim died away, Leannor stepped forwards while the Luminant retreated. I found the princess's demeanour off-putting in its lack of artifice. Her gown was almost entirely black save for a few silver embroidered motifs and her face lacked all paint apart from a light dusting of powder. Her expression was the most concerning, however, for she scanned the gathered notables with dark eyes beneath a lowering brow. It was a gaze rich in blame and admonition, one I'm sure that set a few noble arses itching. Still, when she spoke she contrived to do so with an even tone, albeit possessed of a slight, authoritative snap.

"By right of law and motherhood," she began, "the burden of regent falls upon my shoulders. Until my son comes of age, the governance of this realm lies in my hands. Rest assured that my cherished brother's gifts of compassion and justice reside as much in my heart as they did in his. The vile architects of rebellion now lie dead or consigned to our dungeon awaiting trial. Before us lie the twin gifts of peace and prosperity if we can but grasp them. Let all prior grievances be forgotten, all ill-chosen words or misplaced sentiment forgiven. So speak I, Princess Regent Leannor Algathinet, in the king's name."

She paused, gaze shifting to the front row of pews where the principal captains of the royal host sat with the more prominent courtiers. "Now," Leannor continued, "we must turn our attentions to recognition for the selfless courage and service of our soldiers. Captains Swain, Dornmahl and Scribe, please come forwards."

I noted how Leannor's features gave the smallest twitch as she said this, just a slight shifting of her eyes in Evadine's direction, but it told me the true author of this unexpected turn. Swain, Wilhum and I exchanged puzzled glances as we rose and moved to stand at the base of the dais whereupon Leannor favoured us with a patently forced smile.

"Kneel, good sirs," she said, "and receive your king's reward."

Arthin had difficulty holding the sword his mother placed in his hands as he carefully navigated the dais steps. Fortunately, the blade was purely ornament with a blunted edge so it failed to draw any blood as it scraped my ear before landing on my shoulder.

"I name thee Sir Alwyn Scribe," the boy said in the overly precise manner adopted by children when reciting rehearsed speech. He proceeded to perform the same clumsy ritual for Swain and Wilhum, stumbling somewhat over the latter's dubbing which required some additional words.

"Thine honour is . . ." the boy king began then faltered to a frowning stop until his mother provided a whispered prompt ". . . hereby restored. Know that I am a . . . monarch who forgives all crimes when due . . . contrition and penance are performed."

Evidently pleased with himself, the newly renamed Arthin chose to engage in some impromptu theatrics. "Arise my fine knights!" he called out, raising the sword above his head. "And smite my enemies! Let all who witness this know that King Arthin will strike down all rebels just like the Pretender and the Traitor Duke!"

"Well spoken, Your Majesty," Leannor said, moving quickly to relieve the boy of the sword. Beckoning a courtier to escort the diminutive monarch back to his overlarge throne, she turned to the three newly ennobled men standing before her. "It is customary to award grants of land and moneys at this juncture," she said, "but I'm assured the only reward you three gentlemen require is to continue to serve the Covenant and follow the Anointed Lady."

"It is, Your Majesty," Swain stated with a stiff bow, one that Wilhum and I were obliged to copy, somewhat to my annoyance. Given the chance, I might have bargained for a chest or two of royal coin to bolster the company coffers.

"However, my son's generous heart is one not easily denied." Leannor raised a beckoning hand to summon a trio of courtiers from the shadowed recess beyond the reliquary. They moved with ponderous, stiff-backed formality, each bearing a longsword. "Wield these blades well, good sirs," Leannor told us, the courtiers kneeling before us to proffer the swords. "In the king's name and to the glory of the Covenant."

I took up my sword right away, while Wilhum and Swain were

more hesitant. I assumed it was the finery that gave them pause, somewhat ostentatious for those sworn to devotional service. Looking at mine, I found the locket and chape of the scabbard were formed of embossed silver, the motif composed of a sword flanked by two quills. The same motif featured on the silver of the hilt and the pommel, which had also been inset with a large, gleaming garnet.

Looking up I found Leannor regarding me with a raised eyebrow and a faint smile, the first sign of humour I had seen in her since the Vale. "This is very fine, Your Majesty," I said, bowing low. "My sincerest thanks to the king for his bountiful heart."

"Thank you, Sir Alwyn," she replied, the smile slipping away as a harder note crept into her voice. "And always remember that a king's gift demands a knight's loyalty."

She turned away, gathering her skirts to ascend the dais once more where she accepted a scroll from another bowing courtier. "Now," she went on, voice once again raised to fill the cathedral as she unfurled the scroll. "We must turn to matters of justice. Those named hereafter are traitors to the realm and subject to immediate arrest. All current rights and titles held by these most faithless, undeserving villains are hereby nullified and all lands and property held in their name forfeit to the Crown." That said, she began to read out a list of names. It was a long list but, fortunately, none of those present were included so at least the whole affair concluded without the embarrassing sight of panicked nobles running for the exits.

I squinted as I peered through the slot in the cell door. The scene beyond was gloomy, a lone candle fluttering in the draught, casting a flickering glow over the broad back of a well-built man seated at a table. A stack of parchment sat to his left, an inkpot to the right. The man stooped as he wrote, the scrape of his quill slow and laboured to my scribe's ear.

"He truly asked for me?" I said, turning to the master gaoler.

"You and no other, my lord," he said. "Various clerics have turned up over the past few weeks, even an Ascendant or two. He told them all to piss right off, the king's chamberlains too. Said, 'Get me the scribe or leave me in peace.' Hasn't said much else of note, truth be told. Just sits scribbling all day, though his penmanship is fairly poor." He paused to let out a short, disparaging chuckle. "Could do better m'self, and I can barely write my own name."

It's my experience that those charged with the confinement of lawbreakers are often worse than their prisoners, a viciousness of temperament and suspicion bordering on mania being necessary for their trade. Although this one had much of the brutish aspect I had come to expect, he was also possessed of a surprising affability, not that I doubted for one moment his willingness to use the brass-studded cudgel that dangled from his belt.

I had been summoned to the palace dungeons by a royal herald, one given to more superior manners and disdainful glances than the hardy fellow who had ridden to the Martyr's Reach. The Covenant host had been given a row of riverside warehouses to serve as a barracks, all empty thanks to the disruptions of war and hasty buying of sundries. In the five days since the coronation of King Arthin, the host had swelled in number. The losses suffered at the Vale were more than made good by willing volunteers from the crusade. A surprisingly large number of these emaciated and beggared folk had survived the battle, their taste of it apparently not so off-putting as I would have expected. Consequently, the number of soldiers now marching under the Anointed Lady's banner was so large it couldn't be accommodated at the palace or any Covenant building.

My time had become filled with weeding out unsuitable recruits while surreptitiously sending my more circumspect scouts into the city to garner what intelligence they could regarding the mood of the populace. So, I looked upon this interruption as an irksome distraction, but a royal summons was not something to ignore. It had been written in Leannor's own hand and was fairly terse in tone: "Proceed to the Royal Dungeons and record the Pretender's Testament. Apparently, he refuses to talk to anyone else. Signed, Princess Regent Leannor Algathinet."

I wondered why she found recording the arch-rebel's final words to be of such import, ascribing it to the appearance of propriety. All condemned souls were offered the chance to make testament so denying it to the Pretender would tarnish the appearance of fairly administered justice. I also suspected Leannor hoped Lochlain might spill a few more names for her traitors' list in the course of telling his tale. The royal coffers had been swollen by so many recent forfeitures and I didn't doubt Leannor was keen for more, the Crown's debts being reputedly huge.

"All right," I said. "Open it."

Magnis Lochlain spared me a short glance as the door squealed open, observing, "So, you've come after all," with a faint note of surprise before returning to his scribbles. The gaoler had been considerate enough to provide me a chair, which I dragged to the opposite side of the table. The door swung closed with the echoing boom that I have often suspected to be a deliberate feature of dungeons, leaving me to watch in silence as the captive's quill continued its scratching. My gaze tracked from the heavy chain tracing from an iron bracket in the wall to the manacle on Lochlain's ankle before proceeding to the contents of his stacked pages. I found the gaoler hadn't been wrong in his estimation of his prisoner's skill with a pen. The words were clumsily formed, rich in misspellings and frequently marred by blotched ink and erasing squiggles.

"My mother taught me," he said and I saw that he had abandoned his labour to regard me with a steady gaze. "She learned from a maid at the lord's castle who learned from a groom the lord's son liked to bugger of an evening. He wanted to bugger me too when I grew old enough to catch his eye. I broke his vile, grasping fingers and ran away that very night. I still like to recall the sounds of his screams. The first noble I ever humbled. It keeps me warm on cold nights."

"Is that what you're writing?" I asked, nodding to the pages. "A list of all the nobles you've humbled?"

"In part, though I find I must resist being too fulsome in my accounts, for it smacks of self-indulgence." He set his quill aside and reclined in his chair, the wood creaking in a manner that reminded me of his size and strength. Lochlain groaned and worked his head from side to side, rubbing at the muscles of his neck. "This is worse than sword practice. I don't know how you scribes do it all day."

"Linseed oil mixed with cloves helps the aches," I said. "And it's important to piss regularly."

He gave a short laugh before settling his gaze upon me. "Thank you for coming, Master Scribe." He paused, eyebrows raised in expectation of a heated correction, for he had surely heard of my ennoblement. When I simply sat and stared he laughed again. "No great attachment to titles, then? No, me neither, but I doled them out liberally enough. Cravens sometimes become heroes when you put a 'sir' in front of their name, don't you find?"

"I find that the distinction between craven and hero is meaningless," I replied. "All depends on circumstance. A man who runs from a tavern brawl may fight to the death to defend his family. A knight who performs great feats in battle will bow and weep to win back the favour of a disapproving liege lord. A surfeit of courage can often be a deadly affliction."

He accepted the pointed barb with ruefully raised eyebrow before reaching for the clay bottle sitting alongside his inkpot. "Just water, sadly," he said, pouring some into a cup. "I offered the master gaoler a map to buried treasure in exchange for some decent wine, but to no avail."

"I expect he's heard that one before."

"So," Lochlain paused to drink, "how do you find Couravel?"

"It stinks of too many people and the houses are too close together. Even on a clear day you can barely see the sky through the smoke."

"Yes." The Pretender let out a wistful sigh. "I had such grand plans for the place, you know? Plazas, statues, bridges and the like. Under my guiding hand it would have become a true capital of a great realm, rather than just a mass of disease-wracked hovels. Tell me, Scribe, have you ever seen the cities of the eastern kingdoms? The tall spires of Ishtakar, elegant curving walls of pure white marble crowned with bronze burnished minarets. Streets lined with cherry blossom so that the air is always sweetened by their scent. Now that is a capital worthy of the name."

"Also the scene of the worst massacre in recent history," I pointed out, recalling one of Sihlda's history lessons.

"Saluhtan Alkad's famous purge, you mean? Yes, a messy business. Luckily, I contrived to absent myself shortly before all that."

"You were there?"

"I was. In my youth I travelled widely. I'd been tutored in the arts martial from an early age so it wasn't too difficult to find work as a free sword. In time, I fetched up in Ishtakar, which became my home for several years. It's a long-standing tradition for the Saluhtan to hire foreign mercenaries into his personal guard. Less likely to stick a knife in his back on account of some ancient family grudge, you see? It was his hired swords who did much of the initial throat slitting when the purge began, a business I wanted no part of. It's all here." He rested a hand on the stacked parchment, his gaze taking on a certain expectant weight. "If you'd care to take a look."

"If you've already written it down, why do you have need of me?"

"Read it and find out."

Sighing, I reached for the top page. My perusal of the barely legible script was brief but told me a great deal about Lochlain's gifts as a writer.

"Terrible, isn't it?" he asked, reading my expression. "That, my lord Scribe, is why I need you."

The best scribes are always also scholars, for to properly inscribe a text one must understand it. In that moment I couldn't deny the depth of my scholarly curiosity. Whatever this man had to say would be of undeniable historical importance, no matter how dishonest or self-serving. Despite my initial reluctance, in the end my scribe's heart found it irresistible.

"I will not lie for you," I warned him. "And, as I think you will know better than most, I have a very keen ear for untruth."

"I don't want you to lie, Scribe." His expression became yet more intent, a suddenly darkened mood drawing his features into a grim frown. "Lies will not serve my purpose. That can only be served if my story is told in full, with all my crimes laid bare, all my scars opened though it pains me so. I want all to know how I lived for then they will understand what I died for." He suddenly appeared much older than I had thought, a man confronting the end of a life rich in hardship but also unquestionable significance.

I reached into the satchel I had brought, extracting my writing implements and setting them out on the table. "If that's the case," I said, "there is one question that demands an answer before we start."

"And what is that?"

"Are you truly a royal bastard?"

He laughed again, longer and louder than before. When it faded I expected some manner of obfuscation, an arch witticism or allusion to the malleability of truth. Instead, his reply was very succinct and, it is my sad duty to report, I did not hear a trace of a lie. Nor did I hear one throughout the entirety of the tale that followed. Magnis Lochlain was many things, some good, even admirable, some undoubtedly villainous and worthy of damnation. But, at the end at least, he was no liar.

CHAPTER THIRTY-EIGHT

I got drunk the day they executed the Pretender, although the word "drunk" seems markedly insufficient for the welter of inebriation into which I cast myself. In the sleepless hours since concluding that final interview with Lochlain I hungered for oblivion. I wanted the day of his death to be a day that I had never lived, or at least rendered into some vague, best forgotten nightmare. But it was real. Lochlain died and I watched it happen. Then I drank yet more. It didn't help.

"You stink like a slop bucket," Ayin told me, wrinkling her nose as I took my place in the first rank of the Covenant host. Fully a third of the Anointed Lady's soldiers were paraded upon the broad, cobbled square that separated the cathedral from the royal palace. They faced a yet greater number of kingsmen standing in neat ranks on the opposite side of the square. Occupying the ground between was a hastily erected pavilion where Leannor sat, flanked by the tallest of her guards. Even in my befuddled state I couldn't help but discern a good deal of significance in the absence of both the king and Sir Ehlbert.

"Spares them the spectacle but not us," I grumbled, fervently wishing I was back in the wine shop. "Lucky bastards."

At my side, Ayin put a hand to her mouth to smother a giggle, the sound drawing Evadine's eye. Looking down from atop Ulstan's back she favoured Ayin with a short glance of reproach before turning to me. Her disapproving frown held a suggestion that was just shy of a command, one our connection enabled me to read with the usual ease: *If you're going to embarrass me, then leave.*

Martyrs forbid I should embarrass you, my lady, I replied inwardly. *For surely that is the worst crime to be committed here this day.* A good deal of defiance must have shown on my face for she gave an exasperated grimace before returning her attention to the scaffold.

Charge of the proceedings had been given to a spindle-limbed lord constable, one I realised with sour dismay I had seen before. His voice hadn't changed since the day of Deckin Scarl's execution, overly loud for one so thin, shrill in its strident condemnation.

"Who will come forward to bear arms in this traitor's defence?"

The ritual question cast out to the crowd at all such occasions, except there was no crowd today. The audience for this fatal spectacle was composed entirely of kingsmen, Covenant soldiery and royal courtiers. Those townsfolk that had begun to gather in the small hours had been swiftly harried from the square and cordons of guards stationed at select junctions to prevent all but the invited from witnessing the Pretender's end. I couldn't fault Leannor's reasoning in this; allowing Lochlain an audience for his last words would have been an invitation to riot. The slaughter at the Vale had been comprehensive but far from complete. A good number of diehard rebels had escaped north thanks to the storm, Lady Desmena Lehville among them. My spies brought me numerous rumours of rebels infiltrating the city in hopes of rescuing their beloved True King. However, deeper investigation revealed no firm evidence of anything beyond truculent sedition whispered by disaffected churls, sentiments easily cured with a back alley beating or two.

It may have been the absence of an audience that caused Lochlain to forgo a speech. When Luminant Durehl came forward to hear his testament the Pretender shook his head. His reply was muted by distance, but I heard it. "I have already made testament, your Luminance," he said in a clear and unwavering voice. "Though, I thank you for the consideration."

Manacles encased his wrists and ankles, but he was not so constrained as to prevent him raising his arms towards the awning-shaded platform where Leannor sat. "Will you not embrace me, cousin?" he called out. "Should family not succour one another with small comforts at times like these?" I heard a curious absence of mockery in his tone, as if this was the genuine entreaty of a condemned man. Yet, sincere or not, Leannor did not deign to reply. Her features were dimmed by the awning's shadow, but I had little doubt the expression she wore was one of grim satisfaction. I knew her well enough by now to feel sure she wouldn't relish the grisly sights that lay ahead, but neither would she turn from them. Her brother's death demanded a reckoning, one she felt had not been paid in full despite all the blood-letting at the Vale.

Switching my gaze back to the scaffold, I squinted, hoping to make out the telltale bulge in Lochlain's cheek as he worked loose the small wax-covered capsule I had given him the night before. "Bite hard and spill the contents on your tongue," I had said. "I'm assured it's very fast in its . . . effect."

"Would you have me face the Seraphile a craven?" he asked, lips pursed as he considered the bean-sized gift.

"You know the list of torments prescribed for an arch-traitor, I'm sure," I replied. "You are deserving of death; I'd not spare you that. But the rest . . ."

"If I deserve death, then what do you deserve? For would our crimes not balance if they were set upon a scale? Don't forget, I know your tale, Alwyn Scribe."

"You've a dozen years' or more sin to account for than I."

"Can a king be called a sinner if all he has ever done is in service to his people? If so, would not your Anointed Lady also be counted as such?"

I turned away from him then, jaw clenched to prevent a shout that would draw guards to the cell door. Often during our meetings this man had roused me to anger. I suspect he found it his principal amusement. "Take it or don't," I said, moving to the door. "I've done all I can for you."

"Not quite all."

My hand paused as I raised it to hammer for the turnkey's attention.

"You can be there," Lochlain went on. "Tomorrow. I should like you to bear witness and write what you see, the epilogue to this testament to which we have afforded so much labour. That is all I ask of you, my lord."

So I had come, drunk and angry and wishing to be very far away, but still I had come because he asked it of me. I knew at the first slice of the torturer's blade that he hadn't swallowed the capsule's contents. The way his bared chest spasmed at the blade's kiss, the grit of his teeth, stoic and resolute in the refusal to scream. This was a man fully awake to the pain he suffered. The list of torments suffered by the Pretender is famed for its length and inventiveness, from the flaying of his chest that exposed his ribs to the white-hot iron pressed into his thighs. You will, cherished reader, I'm sure appreciate being spared every detail. However, the blinding demands mention in these pages, for that was the only time he screamed. It was just one word, erupting like a battle cry from his gaping mouth as the nails were hammered home into the sockets.

"MOTHER!"

It echoed for some time, even as Lochlain slumped into the widening slick of his own blood and effluent and the hangman came forwards to finally loop the noose about his neck. In years to come many would ponder that word, seeking to parse meaning from a supposed mystery. Why that and not something more salutary? Something for the ages? A line of scripture or an exhortation to further rebellion? Of course, having taken his testament I knew why. For all his professed love for the commons of Albermaine, Magnis Lochlain had loved but one soul his entire life. It is my belief he went to his unmarked grave filled with the desperate hope that he would find her awaiting him on the far side of the Divine Portals.

I hope you will not judge me too harshly for my ultimate cowardice, dearest reader, for I did not linger to witness the Pretender's last, twitching demise at the end of the rope. When the noose tightened about Lochlain's neck I turned and shouldered my

way through the ranks of the Covenant host and went in search of
the oblivion I craved. I didn't find it, of course, because all you will
ever find at the bottom of a bottle is glass. If it's well polished you
might even experience the misfortune of finding your drunken self
peering back at you, as I did in a dingy, ill-smelling liquor den at
some Martyr-forsaken hour.

"More!" I recall bellowing to the barkeep, casting away the bottle
and its ugly reflection to shatter on the soot-stained brickwork. "More
brandy for this king of liars! And I'd best not find it watered, you
miserly dungheap! I'm a fucking lord, y'know!"

In the dream Lochlain's voice was as it had been in life: steady, measured, absent of fear. "The cleric told me it was always the greatest
gamble," he said, the same words spoken only days before his execution. "He told me that the chances of success were no more than a
sliver of light in an ocean of darkness. But, he also told me the stakes,
so what choice did I have?"

On the whole, I found I preferred Erchel's nocturnal visits to this
achingly lucid visitation by the Pretender. There was no strangeness
to it, no unexplained shifts in location or appearances by long-dead
compatriots. The cell, the table, the parchment and quills, all as real
and tactile as they had been in the waking world.

"The cleric?" I asked, the word spoken with an additional emphasis
that compelled interest.

"A visiting Supplicant from the Cordwain, so he claimed," Lochlain
replied. "Though I couldn't hear a trace of that duchy in his voice.
He stayed but one night at the lord's private shrine, a pilgrim pausing
for rest as he followed the Martyrs' trail. I'd been given the task of
serving him his meals that night, the only night I ever met him.
Strange it is that so much can weigh upon a single meeting, but that
is how it was. Such things he told me, things in my boyish ignorance
I didn't realise no man could or should know. Yet he did."

"Can you describe him . . . ?"

At this point the dream's absence of strangeness abruptly ended
when the cell's wall disappeared, blasted into rubble by a wave of

surging white water. It swallowed Lochlain's unperturbed features before gripping me in its chill embrace, flooding my mouth, invading my lungs . . .

I came awake sputtering, the grassy taste of trough water on my tongue, wincing as my head throbbed for the first time in months. The pain sharpened at the sound of a bucket being dumped onto flagstones, my watery vision swimming then clearing to reveal Ayin's smiling face.

"Did you have to?" I asked in a groan, collapsing onto my sodden bedroll.

"You wouldn't wake up," she said, shrugging. "Oi!" she added, jabbing an insistent finger to my shoulder as I allowed my eyes to close. "Time to rise, your slovenly lordship. Tiler and Woodsman are back and awful keen to talk to you."

Muttering curses, I heaved myself upright, feeling a sudden lurch in the belly. "Best leave that," I told Ayin as she hefted the bucket. Letting out a disgusted sigh, she dumped it at my feet and fled the room.

From their demeanour I quickly divined that Tiler and Woodsman had failed to form much in the way of a bond during their mission. Both stood at a decent remove from one another in the former warehouse clerk's room that served as my private quarters, faces set in the signature blankness of mutual dislike. Still, the fact that they had both turned up alive was a sign of professional tolerance; it also boded well for their mission.

"Shilva Sahken says yes, Captain," Tiler informed me. "But with a good deal of conditions attached. Mostly to do with coin, as you'd expect." He tapped his temple. "It's all up here, o'course. Thought it best not to write anything down."

I pushed parchment and pen across the desk. "Do so now. Also, anything else of note you remember, especially regarding her current location and the strength of her band."

"I will." Tiler hesitated and exchanged a brief glance with Woodsman. "Turns out there's another matter to discuss, Captain. Something she told us before she sent us on our way."

I smothered an irritated sigh, reaching for the jug of clean water on my desk and wishing I still had some of Tihlun's ache-banishing balm. "What something?"

"Something she said. 'Tell the scribe he could do worse than take a stroll past the Dire Keep someday soon.'"

I paused in the act of pouring water into my cup, a host of boyhood memories bubbling to the fore of my befuddled mind. "She say anything else?" I asked.

"Just that," Woodsman confirmed. "Gave the impression she was offering something of import, though. Gesture of goodwill sort of thing."

"I've heard of the Dire Keep," Tiler ventured. "Old story filled with ghosts and such, I seem to recall. Sits on the eastern edge of the Shavine Forest, not far from the coast. Reckon I could track my way there if I had to."

"I know the way," I said, nodding to the door. "Go write your account then get some rest. I'll have another task for you both soon."

"No." Evadine's voice was a hard snap of refusal, her gaze no less sharp than her tone.

"It shouldn't take very long," I persisted. "A month at most."

"Thereby denying me my most valued counsellor while our regent sits in her palace plotting away. Last week she set my father to plan a campaign to retake the Fjord Geld, with the Covenant host in the vanguard of the fleet, no doubt." Evadine shook her head. "This is not a time to sanction some foray into the woods on the basis of an outlaw's word."

"I won't be alone. And you know it's not my way to be incautious."

"Really? I seem to recall your famous caution sending you tumbling down a mountainside to what I thought certain to be your death."

She took a deep breath, resting her hands on the pommel of Ulstan's saddle. I sat mounted atop Blackfoot alongside her as we watched the Covenant host engage in their daily drill. The flat fields fringing the upper stretches of the Alber River north of the city walls had become our practice ground. Every morning the full host would march forth from the city for manoeuvres. Losses at the Vale meant that veteran troops had been filled out with recruits from the crusade. To my experienced eye, the ranks were still somewhat ragged in comparison to the Crown Company or more experienced ducal levies. However, they improved rapidly thanks to Swain's tireless efforts and there were a great many of them, over nine thousand by Ayin's most recent count. Feeding and arming so many was an expensive business, made only a little easier by a recent stipend from the Crown. I found it highly significant that no funds at all had yet been paid by the Luminants' Council, despite repeated promises while I had accumulated many reports of a second Covenant host being raised in the vicinity of Athiltor. Clearly, my duties as spymaster were far from over, yet the lure of the Dire Keep kept tugging at my mind.

"You set me to this role," I reminded Evadine. "And Shilva Sahken wouldn't point me towards this place without reason."

"You trust her, this smuggler queen?"

"Deckin trusted her, and she him. Also, she knew his fondness for me. I doubt she'd wish me harm."

"Making her a somewhat unusual soul in this realm." This was a point I couldn't argue. Recently I had become ever more aware of the dark looks cast my way by all manner of folk. I saw clear resentment on the faces of clerics with Luminant sympathies, also in the lowered brows of nobles and courtiers piqued by the elevation of a one-time outlaw. More worryingly, I also saw it in the bright, unblinking stares of some among the ranks of the Anointed Lady's own followers. This lot were mainly men, those who would stare longest at Evadine during her sermons, also shout the loudest when she roused them to voice their devotion. Those lured to her side by a conflation of lust and faith, although they surely denied the former while proclaiming the latter, were bound to view our evident closeness with a jealous eye. I'll not deny that my desire to investigate Shilva's cryptic words arose partly from a desire for respite from so much open detestation.

"So what is it exactly?" Evadine asked with a note of grudging resignation. "This Dire Keep?"

"A ruin," I said. "Once a castle of impressive size tumbled decades ago. The lord who held it had some manner of falling out with the then Duke of the Shavine Marches. Mayhem and bloody revenge resulted and the castle was torn down at the duke's command. As is the way with old places it's said to be haunted, the unjustly slain lord and his banner men roaming the ruins in search of living souls to devour and so forth."

"It sounds like a place best avoided."

"Thereby making it useful for those who might wish to hide something. Those who might wish harm to our cause, for example."

Evadine lapsed into silence, brow drawn in a frown of consideration. As usual I was able to read her thoughts. "You are needed here," I said in a tone of flat refusal that matched hers.

Her jaw clenched in a manner that told of a contained rebuke. "You will take the entire Scout Company," she said. "And will be escorted at all times. I will hear no argument on this."

"As my lady wishes."

Her features softened a little as she did some thought-reading of her own. "You've already formed a suspicion as to what you'll find, haven't you?"

"Our regent plots, as you said. So does the council. If there's anything to be found in the Dire Keep it's a fair bet it involves one, or both." I allowed an uncertain pause, unsure if I wanted to hear her response to my next words. "Which raises the question of what is to be done should it prove a danger to us."

Evadine's reply was softly spoken but unhesitant: "End it. Without mercy. And bring me firm evidence of villainy, the kind that cannot be denied. I can tolerate the Crown as an uncertain ally, or the council. But not both at once. For our cause to prevail the balance in the realm cannot remain so . . . precarious." She gave a tight, regretful smile. "And have the greatest care, Sir Alwyn Scribe. Our enemies know now that I am as nothing without you."

CHAPTER THIRTY-NINE

I missed Fletchman's senses in the forest. Lilat's too. Traversing the green maze of gully and foliage that seemed to have thickened in my absence brought more unease than it did familiarity. It should have felt like a homecoming, so many remembered sights and smells, the chorus of birdsong and creaking branches forming a welcoming tune. But it didn't. Riding beneath the thick overlapping canopy once again I realised the stark and uncomfortable sensation it awoke within me had always been there: a justified awareness of hidden but constant danger.

In accordance with Evadine's wishes I rode with the Scout Company, but contrived to divest myself of most of them a few days after entering the forest. I had led them to Leffold Glade, drawn more by curiosity than a desire for a secure encampment. I knew these woods had been largely scoured of outlaws in the aftermath of Deckin's fall, but it stood to reason that some bands must have formed in the years since. Yet I found no evidence of their existence among the old stones of the glade. There was little sign anyone had lit a fire within the cracked, moss-covered circle of the amphitheatre for a long time. The caches of hidden supplies were mostly empty and those that weren't were rotted or cobwebbed to uselessness. It was dispiriting to find this place now shorn of its purpose as truce site and outlaw forum, just another ruin waiting for the forest to claim it. My companions, however, found it fascinating, especially Ayin who scampered about peering into every nook and cranny, finding much fuel for her inexhaustible capacity for new songs. The tunes were wordless at first, as was her wont, but soon acquired the lyrics that would shape them into yet another verse for her library.

"In times of old they came . . ." she hummed in a quiet murmur, plucking on the strings of the mandolin she had acquired somewhere on the road from Alundia. We were encamped in the centre of the amphitheatre, our fires casting smoke into the evening sky. "For frolics and blood 'neath the sheltering trees—"

"I don't think that's what this place was for," I interrupted. Seeing the ruins again after so long had presented me with the inescapable sense of recognition. I had seen more than an echo of these forms in the abandoned Caerith city beneath the mountain. *Tier Uthir Oleith*, the *Eithlisch* had called it. A city that was also a gateway, fallen countless years ago, as had this place, though now I felt certain that the people who had built that city had some hand in raising this oval of stone. Nor did I doubt that their demise had arisen from the same cause: the Scourge.

"Then what was it for?" Ayin asked, slender fingers still strumming.

"Oh, a great many things, I suspect." I cast a glance at the vine-encrusted stone, recalling the ancient letters I had seen etched there, now mostly hidden. "I think the folk who built it came to talk, as outlaws did not so long ago. They also came to play their songs, as you do, perhaps watch players caper in their comedies, but I doubt they came for blood."

"Clear all around for a mile or more, Captain," Eamond reported. Like the rest of the scouts he observed my injunction against referring to me as "my lord". I found I didn't like it, at least not from their lips. With the Pretender's execution still so fresh in my mind it felt like a lie, even mockery.

"Post pickets atop the walls and get something to eat," I told him. "In the morning, I'll make for the keep with the Widow, Tiler and Woodsman. You'll stay here with the rest of the company, patrol the woods for sign of troops passing through. If you find any I want to know where they're from and where they're going. Don't reveal your presence unless you have to. The same goes for any clerics you might encounter. It's not clear who we can trust these days."

"Beg pardon, Captain," Tiler piped up, "but what iffen we find trouble at the keep? More trouble than four of us can handle, I mean to say."

I could have rebuked him but I had learned by now not to discourage sensible questions, even when they came from Tiler's unpleasant mouth. A captain who deafened himself to his soldiers' concerns didn't deserve the title. "I don't intend to make our presence known to whoever we might find there," I said. "Approaching in strength will attract too much notice. If there's business needs doing at the keep, we'll return here for the whole company. It may be that we have to send to the host for reinforcements. We won't know until we've scouted the place."

At first glance, the Dire Keep appeared much as I remembered it: a half-ruined tower some thirty feet high rising from the only intact corner of the castle that once stood here. The hour was late when we approached, dismounted and moving low and slow through the undergrowth. Woodsman had been left with the horses half a mile back. Although no stranger to the wilds, he was a little too heavy of foot compared to Tiler and Juhlina. The keep tower jutted up from the gently swaying silhouette of the treeline a few hundred paces ahead. I knew that a bubbling stream traced through the ground between us and the keep, useful in masking any noise we made moving closer.

"Can't see bugger all," Tiler said in a barely audible whisper. "And we're close enough to make out the glow of a fire."

"No scent of smoke either," Juhlina commented. "Mayhap we've come a long way on a fool's errand."

"We need to make sure," I said, unbuckling my sword belt. I slung it across my chest, positioning the long blade on my back to make for easier passage when moving at a crouch through undergrowth. I allowed Tiler to take the lead, the wiry thief having the better eye for concealing ground. Juhlina was not so stealthy of foot as the two of us, but her natural litheness worked to her advantage. Consequently, we made a mostly silent approach to the keep, the tower's shaded outline looming ever taller through the trees. Still the air lacked any trace of woodsmoke and the walls of the Dire Keep remained blank of flickering flames. I flared my nostrils continually for the telltale odours of people, detecting nothing, that is until we crossed the stream.

I had followed Tiler onto the far bank, Juhlina still struggling through the churning water behind, when it came to me: the smallest whiff of sweat-dampened leather. The first slingshot whistled just as I began to voice my warning to Tiler. The stone, fast and invisible in the gloom, struck him smack on the temple, felling him instantly. I dropped flat to the earth, the air just above my head hissing as more slings cast their missiles, then the sound of many feet pounding the forest floor as the ambushers broke cover.

"Run!" I shouted to Juhlina only to find her face down in the stream, arms limp and flailing in the current. It would have been wise to follow my own advice, but a soldier's instincts had long supplanted the outlaw within and I lunged for the Widow instead. Catching hold of her jerkin, I hauled her onto the bank. She slumped onto her back with a distressed moan, blood matting her hair where the stone had struck.

Slings but not bows, I realised, drawing the longsword free of its scabbard. *Want to take us alive.* I crouched, listening to the fast-approaching feet, sword handle gripped in both hands, not too tight as Roulgarth had taught me. *More fool them.*

I waited until I saw the legs of the closest assailant, allowed him one more step then surged to my feet, sweeping the sword up in the same motion. The first man I killed that night had features blackened by soot so that his eyes stood out stark and bright as the blade sliced across his chest. He reeled away, spattering me in blood, the heavy club he bore spinning from his twitching grip.

Hearing a footfall to my right I swayed back, bringing the sword level with my chest then driving it into the throat of the oncoming club-man. More running feet and the whoosh of clubs as I kicked my victim away, suffering blows to the shoulders and back before whirling clear, the sword sweeping deadly arcs left and right. Screams pealed out among a chorus of obscene exclamations, the voices harsh but familiar in their profane cadence; these were outlaws, not soldiers.

I ducked a swipe at my head, punishing the swiper with a slash to his rump. Backing away, I parried an overhead blow to the shoulder, the longsword splintering the ash club before hacking deep into the face of its owner whereupon a lull descended. They had formed a circle around me now, about a dozen in all, crouched in wary aggression, eyes glimmering with ugly intent in their blackened, tense faces.

Words are of no use in a fight, I recalled Roulgarth saying. *Except as distraction.*

Drawing a breath, I let out a taunting laugh. "You fuckers going to stand there all ni—?" I struck before the last word escaped my mouth, lunging to stab the closest in the belly, then lowering my shoulder to force my way between him and the man alongside. I turned as the rest of the mob came for me, sword hacking and slicing, felling another club-man and creating a sufficient gap for me to turn and run if I chose. *Tiler*, I thought with sour indecision. Then, with an upsurge of guilt: *Juhlina.*

It was only a momentary hesitation but it lasted just long enough for an unseen slinger to take aim and let fly with a stone. It sent stars blazing through my head when it struck home, smacking into the bone behind my ear. I recall managing to keep my feet despite the blow, still swinging the sword, albeit to such scant effect that the club-men had little difficulty beating me down. They were enthusiastic in their labour, though my stunned senses fortunately shielded me from the worst of it. I've little doubt I would have met my end under their clubs if a gruff, irritated voice hadn't intervened.

"Enough, you stupid fucks! Remember your orders!"

I rolled onto my back, looking through recurrently blurred eyes at the strangely pleasing sight of a cloudless night sky speckled with stars, only partly occluded by the dark veins of tree branches. *I always liked to contemplate the trees*, I thought, surprising myself when the notion brought a laugh to my lips. It faded when a bulky silhouette invaded my pleasing view to peer down at me with dully glimmering eyes.

"A thief but not a scrapper," the same gruff voice said with a faint note of amused admiration. "That's what Deckin once said of you. Looks like he had that wrong, eh, lad?"

"He got a lot . . . of things . . . wrong," I muttered back as my mind finally lost purchase on consciousness. "But then . . . so have I . . ."

CHAPTER FORTY

I slipped in and out of awareness for a time, jerking in the grip of the ungentle hands that carried me. My befuddled eyes caught the flare of torches and stacked fires blazing to life. Also the accumulated grumble and growl that told of a busy camp. Between bouts of head-lolling stupor I took in the sight of a good many tents pitched among the stunted, ragged walls and pillars of the Dire Keep. Despite my confusion, the shame of having blundered into a trap became a potent jab at my pride. Maintaining strict silence spoke of a disciplined group rather than a mob. The glimpses I caught of passing figures confirmed that these were soldiers, complete with arms and armour. Many were of slovenly appearance but all shared a uniform frown of ugly promise as I was ported through their ranks.

"Give the heretic bastards to us, Captain," I heard one coarse voice call out. "We'll get 'em singing soon enough."

The subsequent laughter and jeers rose then faded from my ears as a fresh wave of fatigue swept through me, taking away all sensation save an impression of falling into a chilly maw of shadows.

It was the echoing splash that woke me, distant but reverberating from the depths with uncanny clarity. My slumber, if it could be termed such, had been mercifully dreamless, a blank void of thought and sensation I instantly yearned for when the pain made itself known. Fiery agony erupted in my shoulders and arms, quickly spreading to my chest. Gasping, I jerked with the instinctive need for escape, my body swaying with the motion, kicking feet chilled by the absence of boots finding no purchase on hard ground. A period of ineffectual struggling made it plain that I was suspended by the wrists from a rope. Blinking, I craned my neck to look up, finding the knots encasing my wrists had been fashioned by expert hands. It would be impossible to work myself loose without many hours of skin-chafing labour.

"Up and about finally," a voice observed in a clipped grunt, the same voice I had heard before the void claimed me. I jerked afresh at the sound, fogged eyes peering into a melange of shadow. "Go and tell him," the voice added.

"Do I have to?" The reply was formed of far less imposing tones shot through with a reluctant whine. That whine told me much, for there was a depth of genuine fear to it rather than laziness. The first speaker gave no answer and a short silence reigned before I heard the shuffle of feet on stone.

"It would be best if you were fully awake, Master Scribe," the first voice advised, my eyes discerning a shift in the confusion of shadows. A figure resolved out of the blur, a powerfully built man about my own height, his face difficult to make out through my veil of pain. "You don't want to face him with dulled wits."

"It's . . . 'my lord' . . . to you," I replied in a strained groan, repeatedly closing and opening my eyes. I had cause to regret this when the man's face swam into focus. At first I thought he must be wearing some manner of mask, so misaligned and scarred were his features. It would be impossible to list every disfigurement I beheld, for his malformations overlapped in several places. Suffice to say his face appeared to have been ripped off then poorly stitched back together before being reattached to his skull. Curiously, his lips were the least damaged portion of his visage, allowing for clear if baffling speech.

"You don't recognise me?" he asked in a tone of faux offence. He angled his head, peering at me with his multiply scarred brows raised to what looked vaguely like a questioning angle. "No? Not a glimmer, eh? Understandable. We only met once. And, to be fair, I looked a little different then."

"I trust," I grunted, shifting my gaze to survey my surroundings in more detail, "this isn't all on account of some long-forgotten debt or petty feud." Peering to either side of the fellow's distracting features I made out faint light slanting over damp, stone brick walls and an age-cracked floor. I found no sign of other occupants, meaning Tiler and Juhlina, if they still lived, were being kept elsewhere. The sight of a circular opening in the floor brought a flood of remembrance and a realisation as to the identity of my prison, if not my captor. The bowels of the Dire Keep, where Erchel had seen fit to visit me in that first dream. I supposed it made a doleful, if mystifying, kind of sense.

"Debt?" the scarred man asked. "No, my lord, you don't owe me a single shek. Feud, however, is closer to the mark, even if it isn't with you. Not personally, at least. Although, please don't permit yourself the delusion that will make any difference."

"So—" I shifted my focus back to him, forcing a smile that I'm sure was more in the vein of a rictus grin "—a genuine promise of enough gold to let you live out your days in luxury would be pointless, then?"

"Quite. As would any assurances as to royal pardons or merciful treatment. So please don't insult me with such." Although his tone was light, or at least as light as his granulated voice would allow, I saw the hard warning in his eyes and knew this was not a man given to threats but promises.

"Wouldn't dream of it," I said. "I would, however, prevail upon you for your name, since you seem to have the advantage of me."

He retreated a step, straightening his back to adopt a soldierly bearing. "Danick Thessil, my lord. And may I say it is an honour to meet one of such renown, albeit earned in a malevolent cause. I think it would be beyond contradiction for me to say that Deckin Scarl would have taken a good deal of pride in how you turned out."

"Danick Thessil," I repeated, squinting doubtfully at his ruined face. The grisly fate of the Thessil brothers was one of the most oft-told tales to emerge from the massacre at Moss Mill. "You look well for a man who died dangling by his guts from the sails of a windmill years ago."

He shook his head, his eyes growing distant and his scars shifting into something I took for reluctant remembrance. "That was some other poor bastard with a burnt, hacked-up face they dragged from the pile of wounded that night. A man's fate often turns on such strangeness, don't you find? The mere fall of a die will make him rich or a pauper. Meeting the right woman will see him happy while the wrong one will herald a life of misery. In my case, it was finding myself tossed onto the pile next to a fellow outlaw who had suffered much the same injuries as I had. It was him they dragged out and forced to watch as they desecrated my brother's corpse, him they slit open and hung from the mill so they could wager on how long he would last. All the while I lay there among the dead and the dying, quelling my screams. Come the dawn, I strangled the guard they had set on the dead and fled. Much as you did, eh?"

Not quite, I thought. *I murdered one of my own to get away.* "You spoke of a feud," I reminded him.

"Indeed. It transpires there's something about lying in abject agony among corpses that changes a man." The stiffness slipped from his stance and he moved to sit, letting out a groan as he perched his bulk on the raised step that encircled the well. "Not to besmirch your mentor's memory, my lord, but my brother and I never had much truck with Deckin's talk of seizing the duchy. It was the gold and the arms we wanted, the true prize to be had when we stormed Castle Duhbos. With decent coin and weapons we could strike out for the east, form our own free company far beyond the reach of the kings and dukes of Albermaine. No more sullying our honour with common thievery and consorting with the dregs of the Marches. Such things were beneath us, so we thought, something we had been driven to by ill luck and noble injustice. We longed to be soldiers again, you see, the only trade we had ever excelled at. Beyond the eastern frontier there are wars unending, and a great many princes and chieftains willing to pay foreigners to fight them."

Danick paused, letting out a bitter sigh. "It shames me to think of it now, Scribe. Such base greed, such disregard for the suffering that arises from war. Lying there among all that twitching, maimed flesh I came to a certain realisation: Deckin's dream of seizing the duchy had always been hopeless, for how could one so base ever hope to rise so high? That can only happen when there's no one else to rise above. In that moment I resolved that I had but one war to fight henceforth, one grudge to settle." His voice took on a fervent cadence then, in the manner of one reciting a creed. "I would avenge my brother and tear down the rotten facade of corruption that has turned this realm into what it is. The Covenant, the Crown, the grasping, venal dukes and their lickspittle nobles. All of it will fall."

As a man well attuned to the dangerous moods of fanatics, I thought it best to say nothing at that juncture. Instead, I hung limp in my bonds, letting the slow twist of the rope traverse my gaze as I sought more information about my surroundings. My eyes had adjusted to the gloom by now, allowing me to make out the numerous barrels that lined the walls. I also caught the faint glint of light playing over a goodly amount of stacked weaponry: halberds and billhooks – newly forged judging by the gleam.

"You've got your armoury, then," I observed, wincing as a fresh wave of agony swept from my wrists to my dangling ankles. "Must've cost a bit. Rebellion pays, does it?"

"Still as keen-eyed as ever then?" Danick replied, evading my question. "Deckin said you were his best spy."

"Tell me, did you pay Shilva Sahken to lure me here?"

"As it happens, she doesn't even know I'm still alive. Baiting this snare required only a few whispers in the right ears. I was assured you'd be quick to quash any threat to your beloved Anointed Lady." It was difficult to tell but I thought his ruined face took on what might have been a judgemental cast. "Deckin would've taken pride in your strength, lad, but not your sympathies. The nobles and the Covenant are rotten branches of the same diseased tree."

I considered arguing the point, enumerating the many ways in which Evadine was set apart from both Covenant and nobility, but I had the measure of this man now. For him, argument was redundant.

His hatred and his mission had been carved too deeply into his bones the day his brother died.

"I must say I'm surprised I didn't find you slain at the Vale," I observed instead. "Given your sympathies, I mean to say. The Pretender could've used a man like you."

Danick let out a disdainful snort. "That prideful fop was always going to fail. I'll confess to marching with him for a while, but it's not an easy thing to be led by one less worthy than yourself. After the Traitors' Field I knew I had to forge my own path, build my own host, or," he added, voice lowering to a murmur as the sound of footfalls descending stone steps echoed in the gloom, "at least persuade others to let me build one for them."

I found the appearance of the trim man who stepped from the shadows so unsurprising I greeted him with just a short, grunting laugh. Ascendant Arnabus wore the same plain grey cloak of a humble Supplicant. His cowl was drawn back to reveal features that were very different from the mostly amiable and occasionally taunting expression I remembered so well from our meeting in the Covenant Library of Athiltor. Now his face was tensed in a hard, enquiring frown, also possessed of a very slight twitch around the eyes and mouth. I knew fear when I saw it and, upon squinting further at him, concluded this man was in fact bordering on being terrified. He returned my stare readily enough, albeit with a good deal of blinking, offering no greeting. Our glare of mutual antipathy was interrupted by the arrival of a second figure. This one also wore a cleric's garb, but kept his cowl in place, not moving from the gloomy recess of the chamber.

I thought of voicing many a caustic witticism as the silence stretched, but found my dislike of Arnabus was such that I didn't care to afford him even the meagre gift of humour. Eventually, weary of the delay, I groaned out an impatient sigh and grunted, "What the fuck do you want?"

Arnabus's narrow features flushed and his frown deepened to a scowl. "Has he said anything?" he snapped at Danick.

"Merely some shared reminiscence about the old days," Danick replied, shrugging.

Arnabus turned back to me, eyes tracing over my suspended form in careful appraisal, lingering in particular on the knots binding my wrists. Apparently satisfied, he came closer, skirting the black orifice of the well at a wide berth. I saw a near-desperate scrutiny in the way he peered into my glowering eyes. "Is she close?" he asked, keeping his voice to a whisper which failed to conceal the quaver it held.

I said nothing, affording him a slow blink before lolling my head to the side to regard his shadowed companion. "Why don't you come out, Your Luminance?" I asked, the question echoing to the depths of the well and back again. "I'm not one to stand on ceremony, but failing to offer greeting to a knight of this realm is a trifle rude, don't you think?"

Luminant Durehl Vearist hesitated only a moment before stepping forwards, brawny arms emerging from the sleeves of his robe to draw back his cowl. In contrast to Arnabus, his features were composed, brows drawn in conviction rather than fear. I felt it to be mostly artifice. Why would a man so sure of his course hide his face?

"Lord Scribe," he said. "I would like you to know that I regret this . . . necessity."

"Oh," I let out another laugh, "piss off, you old hypocrite."

Hearing Danick Thessil smother a laugh of his own, I shifted my focus to him. "So, now I know who bought all your shiny new weapons. I assume I have the honour of addressing the Marshal of the Council Host, do I not?"

Danick inclined his head, scars shifting to form something that resembled a smile. "What else can I say other than that faith came to me later in life?"

"Any dog that doesn't bite is a friend, eh?" It was an old outlaw saying, one that lessened his smile a notch or two.

"I told you, lad," he said, his expression lacking both Arnabus's fear and the Luminant's artifice, "all of it will fall. And I don't much care how."

"Enough," Arnabus said, affording Danick a sharp glance before jerking his head at the shadows. "See to your company, Captain."

From the way Danick let his eyes linger on the cleric's face, blank of expression but narrow of eye, I divined his liking for Arnabus was of much the same pitch as my own. Wordlessly, he got to his feet and stomped off into the gloom, the sound of feet ascending steps echoing shortly after.

"His Luminance has questions," Arnabus told me. "I advise you to be both prompt and honest in your answers."

He moved aside as Durehl came forwards, his face still set in the same mix of rectitude and forbearance, a man unwilling to shirk a distasteful act. "Aspirant Viera was kind enough to show me the accounts you gifted to the Covenant Library in Athiltor," he said. "Exceptional work, young man. Labour of such accomplishment demands admiration, regardless of the hand that crafted it."

"Your admiration means no more to me than a maggoty turd, you old fart," I told him. I had little doubt my circumstances were about to become markedly less comfortable and wanted to convey as many insults as possible while time allowed.

Luminant Durehl, however, disappointed me by accepting the barb with only a faint curl to his lips. "As you may imagine," he went on in the same measured tone, "I found your account of Martyr Evadine's resurrection in Farinsahl to be of particular interest. I don't think I've ever encountered a more impressively structured and poetically phrased concoction of lies."

I offered him an empty smile, annoyed that the pain in my arms was such that it transformed my reply into a spittle-flecked grunt. "I've little doubt you've had plenty of practice writing your own."

"So you admit to your falsehood?" He stepped closer, looking up at me with a fierce scrutiny. "You confess to penning a fabrication?"

I bared my teeth, speaking through the increasing pain. "Martyr Evadine rose from death thanks to the divine intervention of the Seraphile. I cherish the memory and consider myself blessed for eternity to have witnessed it."

Durehl's features bunched in regret as he shook his head. "So much talent," he mused. "To waste it upon one so undeserving. Tell me, Scribe. Does she know it's all farce or is she mad enough to think herself truly Risen?"

"Martyr Evadine is the true voice of the Seraphile." The rope creaked and swayed as I attempted to spit my words at him. "The champion of the Covenant. Through her it will become what it was meant to be, not some clutch of money-grubbing, power-hoarding bastards."

I saw anger join with determination on Durehl's face. "For centuries it has been the council that has stood between this realm and chaos," he said. "Kings rise and fall but the council and the Covenant endure, so that all may endure. It is the council that brings order to this land, gives its people hope, makes wrong into right."

"Chaos is it?" I attempted a caustic laugh that emerged as a snarl. "Have you been sleeping for the past decade, old man? This land is nothing but chaos and I see scant evidence your precious council has done shit-all to prevent it. And if we're talking rights and wrongs, perhaps you can explain how an innocent Ascendant of your own faith came to rot in the Pit Mines for the crime of learning the truth."

"There are times when the necessities of the moment outweigh all other concerns. Ascendant Sihlda understood this, even if you do not. Sadly, your actions have brought another such moment upon us." Durehl lowered his gaze, drawing breath in a manner that told me he was steeling himself for something. "I will offer no more chances for willing confession, Scribe," he said, raising his eyes to mine and speaking with a steady, almost solicitous tone. "If it must be wrung from you, then I will see it done. But I implore you: don't force me to this. Confess the lies you have told. Proclaim in your own words that Evadine Courlain is a false Martyr." He paused, and I saw him swallow as he spared a brief glance at Arnabus. "Confess that you did bring a Caerith witch to Lady Evadine's bedside and it was through her foul magics that the false Martyr was raised."

I bit down on a groan of realisation, my eyes slipping towards Arnabus. Clearly, it was through his agency that the Sack Witch's presence in Farinsahl had been discovered. He knew of the *Doenlisch*. He knew the Caerith tongue and he had Leannor's network of spies to draw upon for all manner of useful gossip and rumour. Although

I expected to find him smiling in triumphant malice, instead I saw a man still mired in barely controlled fear. Like Durehl, I could tell he was forcing himself to an unwanted action. However, I knew he had a far better understanding of the consequences than did the Luminant. In truth, I suspected his comprehension of this entire episode was deeper even than mine. Still, I had a few more cards to play. I had no illusions as to the outcome of all this, but a man facing torment and death will seek any means to delay the first kiss of blade or whip.

I convulsed in my bonds, body trembling with the combination of strain and fear. "Talk of absurd and unnatural things brings to mind a recent conversation," I said. "You will recall it was I who took the Pretender's Testament, Your Luminance." Although the words were addressed to Durehl, I kept my eyes focused on Arnabus. "Such things he had to say . . . "

"Quiet!" Arnabus snapped, the twitch of his features suddenly more animated.

I ignored him and swung back to Durehl. "Tell me, Your Luminance, just how much do you know about this man? What manner of man he is, I mean to say. Think back to the first time you met him. How old did he appear?"

"Be quiet!" Arnabus hissed, stepping closer then coming to an abrupt halt when I addressed him in Caerith.

"*Vaerith courses through your veins.*" I grinned as I looked upon his now-quivering features. "*Were you born with it or did you steal it somehow?*"

"What is he saying?" Durehl demanded but Arnabus didn't appear to hear him. Instead he launched himself at me in a flapping, arm-flailing rage that I would have seen as comical if I hadn't been the object of his fury. His blows were unpractised and poorly delivered, but also plentiful and considerably energetic. Even an amateurish beating will have an effect if it's allowed to continue for a time and, while I heard the Luminant voice some more baffled questions, he didn't feel compelled to intervene.

"Where is she?!" Arnabus screamed as he flailed at me. "Is she close?! Tell me, you worthless cur!"

I felt my nose break with a dispiritingly familiar crack, the rush of blood filling my throat and denying me breath. I slipped back into the void to the sound of Arnabus's shrill demands. "Why did she vanish? Where did she go? Where is the fucking *Doenlisch*?!"

CHAPTER FORTY-ONE

O nce again I was summoned from the void by the echoing splash of something cast into the well. This time my awakening was greeted by the feel of cold stones on my side and the absence of agony in my arms and shoulders. Still they ached, drawing a groan from my lips as I slowly levered myself upright. Night had fallen during my slumber, banishing the slanting patches of light from the rough-hewn walls. Instead there was the dim glow of a lantern playing over a slightly built form in a cleric's robe.

Arnabus was seated on the floor on the far side of the well, back propped against the step, one arm rested atop a raised knee. I caught the glitter of his eyes as he noticed my rousing before he flicked his wrist, a small pebble arcing through the air to plunge into the well. The muted splash seemed to take a long time.

"What did Lochlain tell you?" Arnabus asked. I could tell much of his fear had abated, along with his anger. Now the impression I gained was one of dejection, almost defeat. It was obvious to me that something he expected to happen had failed to occur, leaving him forlorn.

"A good many things," I said, wincing as I manoeuvred myself into a sitting position, coarse rope scraping my wrists and ankles. Both had been bound in thick cordage covered with pitch, since cooled to form a binding as secure as any chain. One glance sufficed to convince me there was no working these bonds loose and any attempt to gnaw through them would likely result in lost teeth. Being bound hand and foot also precluded any notion of reaching Arnabus, except in the form of a slow, comedic hop. I felt a surprising lack of animus towards him, despite the beating he had given me. If anything, my sense of the moment was that he was the injured party. I still intended to kill him the moment opportunity arose, of course, but I fancied I wouldn't take my time over it.

"Which did you have in mind?" I went on. Resting my back against the step, I raised my bound hands to prod the more sensitive portions of my face. His assault hadn't been professional but it had been thorough.

"Stop playing games," Arnabus told me, his voice a weary sigh. "It's tiresome. Not to mention pointless now."

Casting my gaze around at the blank gloom beyond the lantern's glow, I asked, "His Luminance isn't joining us?"

"He was persuaded that a private interview would extract his precious confession."

"Something you have scant interest in, I assume?"

The cleric's robe shifted as he shrugged. "Answers to mysteries already solved do not concern me. But your newly acquired depth of knowledge does, and I'll have it from you, Scribe."

I raised my eyebrows, mouth quirking in a taunting grin. "Information of value normally attracts a price, and I've yet to hear you offer a reward."

"A delay in torture and death is not a reward?"

"Not one I'm willing to bargain for, since you mention a delay and not a reprieve. Do better."

The lantern flickered over Arnabus's narrow, grim features before he plucked another small stone from the flagstones and pitched it into the well. "You've been here before," he said when the faint splash echoed from below. "As a boy. You and that gelded wretch, daring to risk the wrath of ghosts in your childish pride."

My bruises took on a deeper ache as I frowned. "How could you know that?"

"You wanted a bargain, here it is. Tell me what Lochlain said of me and I'll tell you how I know of your guttersnipe exploits." It was his turn to taunt, a feat accomplished with only a raised eyebrow. "And a little more besides, because I think it might amuse me."

Perhaps I'll take my time over it, after all, I decided. Disguising my annoyance with a sniff, suffering a harsh pang from my re-broken nose in the process, I said, "Lochlain spoke of a cleric who paused for rest at the castle where he was raised. A cleric who told him the tale of his true parentage. He told him of a maid raped by a drunken prince come to visit the castle's lord, a rape unwitnessed by other eyes and that she had never spoken of, yet this cleric knew the tale in every ugly detail. Even before he went to his mother and demanded her story, Lochlain knew it as truth. He didn't need to see the fear in her eyes, nor hear the horrid tale from her own sobbing lips. He had grown up believing himself sired by a passing minstrel with a winning smile and a fine repertoire of songs, the kind of man a girl in bloom will be drawn to when the ale flows free. He liked to think of his minstrel father out there somewhere beyond the castle walls, happily wandering the realm with his gift of song. Discovering his father was, in fact, none other than Prince Arthin, heir to the throne of Albermaine, came as a great disappointment to Lochlain, for what man of worth wants to know himself at the product of so vile an act?

"He never saw that cleric again, but he remembered him very well. And not just his face, but his manner of speaking. So well in fact that, when he told his tale, I had little difficulty recognising you, Ascendant Arnabus. Is that your real name, by the way?"

Arnabus's lips formed a slight, indifferent grimace. "After a while names begin to mean little. Names are for kings and princes, or Martyrs. They're not for the likes of us. Therein lies your great mistake, Sir Alwyn Scribe. Becoming a man of renown has weakened you, made you a target for His Luminance and others. You would have been better off keeping to the shadows, as I prefer to do."

"Our bargain," I said, unwilling to concede the point, despite the undoubted fact that he was right. "You knew I'd been here before, which I can't help but suspect may have something to do with why I find myself here again."

He regarded me for a short interval of immobile silence, then tilted his head, his features forming a leer that was uncanny in its familiarity. The voice that emerged from his mouth was not his own, but I had heard it many times before. "Come to see, have you, Alwyn?"

My many pains should have smothered all other feeling, but there was no denying the icy caress that gripped me from crown to foot. *Erchel!* He spoke in Erchel's voice.

"Don't you want to see what you made?" Arnabus continued in the same dead man's voice, his leer becoming yet more exaggerated as he leaned towards me, much as Erchel had in the dream version of this very place.

I said nothing, finding all I could do in the moment was stare in shocked horror. Letting out a short laugh, Arnabus resumed his former expression and reclined once again. "*Vaerith* is a word that encompasses many things," he said. "Many skills, great and minor. Some of us can choose those skills, but only a few. Most, like me, must make the best of what crumbs are thrown to them."

"I . . . dreamt . . . " I stuttered, finally managing to summon some words.

"Yes," Arnabus said, smiling an empty smile, "you dreamt the dream I made for you. It's what the Caerith called me when I lived among them, *Oleith Ethaleha*, the Dream Crafter. Finding the right character to cast as your harbinger of peril wasn't easy, but thanks to the beating Lord Althus gave you I had plenty of time to rummage around in your memories while you lay senseless."

"Erchel warned me," I said. "On the road south. The assassins . . ."

"A necessary episode to build trust in your dream companion. It wasn't hard to persuade the Luminants to hand over some sovereigns for assassins of impressive skill. Your precious lady Martyr's display at Athiltor put them in quite a tizzy, I must say. I had little doubt the attempt would fail, of course, but Durehl and the rest are somewhat uneducated in such things. Or did you think it was Leannor's doing?" His brow creased in consideration. "No, you wouldn't be so foolish."

"Erchel knew things," I insisted, experiencing a perverse difficulty in accepting the notion that my nocturnal visitations had all been born of arcane subterfuge. "He showed me things before they happened. King Tomas's death . . ."

"Because they had been shown to me." The knowing humour faded from the cleric's face, the grimness from before returning in full. "Shown to me by the *Doenlisch*, who remains so conspicuously absent from this reunion despite my best efforts to invite her."

I bridled, angered by the absurdity of the Sack Witch associating with this man. "She would have no truck with the likes of you."

"Why? She seems happy to sully herself consorting with the very dregs of this realm. Or do you consider yourself my better, Alwyn Scribe? You have been dancing to her tune for mere months, while she and I have shared lifetimes."

"She works for the good. She heals. She brings life . . ."

"And what do you think I do?!" Arnabus's voice rose to a shout as he lunged forwards, teeth bared in a near-feral snarl. "What do you think I have been doing for fucking centuries, you upstart fool? Everything I have done was done for her."

I met his fury with anger of my own, staring into his tensed, aggrieved gaze. "You are a schemer," I said. "An intriguer. A liar. A man who would orchestrate the unjust execution of an innocent woman . . ."

"Oh, don't speak to me of your Martyr, Scribe." Arnabus gave a disgusted laugh. "I have seen her before so many times. Different face, different gender, but always the same story. A hero risen high by the sheer power of their goodness. A saviour of the beggared and oppressed somehow touched by a divine hand. It's all shit and it always ends in blood." His features settled into a bland grin. "I did try to warn you, remember? Erchel showed you what she's going to do."

"The *Doenlisch* saved her," I said. "She wouldn't have done that without a reason."

The tension seeped out of Arnabus then, and he slumped back, repeating the word with soft despair. "Reason . . ." I watched a parade of emotions pass over his features, from self-pity to sorrow then anger before finally subsiding into puzzled reflection. "I gave up asking her for reasons, oh, a century ago or more," he said. "It was enough to know that she needed my help. It was enough to be permitted to be near her. She saved me, you see, long ago, when the mob came to hang the wicked orphan boy they all detested but didn't know why. I knew why: they feared me. Somehow they knew it was me who put those bad things in their heads when they slept. Fear will drive us to the worst of crimes, even the murder of a child. But, for all their fear of me, they feared the Sack Witch more. 'Come, little brother,' she said, taking me by the hand and leading me away. 'I have many things to show you.'"

Some of the sorrow fell from his face as his gaze took on the distant cast of memory. "And show me she did. I suppose you could say she became my mother, for a time. I travelled with her to all corners of this realm, and beyond when the need arose, for the *Doenlisch*'s task is not limited to these duchies. I learned as she tended to the sick. I listened to her Caerith songs. When manhood dawned she guided me across the mountains to live among her people. That was the first time she left me. I didn't like the Caerith, nor they me, but they tolerated my presence because she willed it. In time I returned to Albermaine, where she waited for me. 'This new faith, little brother,' she said. 'This Covenant that grows ever stronger. I should like to know more of it.' And so, the Covenant became my task. For so many years have I watched it build into this decadent monolith, like some great diseased beast that doesn't know its every plodding step takes it closer to the grave. I'll not deny helping it along here and there, once again because she willed it, but, in truth, it was always going to end this way. Your Risen Martyr is just the last cut of the butcher's knife that puts an old beast out of its misery. But when the crows come to feast upon the carrion," he grunted a humourless laugh, "now that will be something to see. Mayhap the *Doenlisch* will want to witness that, since she seems so indifferent to your fate."

Sighing, he got to his feet, hefting the lantern. "Tomorrow will be a very difficult day. My advice is to shorten your pains and give Durehl what he wants. That brute Thessil captured three of your companions alive and his pet torturer will flay them before your eyes before he starts on you. Confess your vile perfidy. Write it down in that pleasing script of yours. The Luminant would like that, I think. After all, it's not as if it matters, is it?"

"You said she left you," I said, making him pause. "What did you mean?"

He had turned his back and the lantern's glow caught only a portion of his face as he spared me a final glance. "It means that for many years now she has not spared me a single thought. Nor do I feel her . . . regard, as I once did. I stood but a few hundred paces from her at the encampment of the royal host the day before the Traitors' Field, and yet it was as if she stood on the other side of the world. She wouldn't let me come near, but *you*." His features twisted in a concordance of envy and revulsion. "You she welcomed. Twenty years has it been. Twenty years of carving my own path through the history of this realm, hoping that I was following her course, fulfilling her wishes, but never knowing for certain. I sought to summon her by executing your Martyr, since I had learned of the *Doenlisch*'s intervention at Farinsahl. If she had saved the Courlain bitch once I hoped she might appear to save her again. Instead, once again it was *you*, an outlaw scribe in ill-fitting armour, that stepped from the crowd, and I could sense her touch upon you." He hesitated and I saw how his hand gripped the lantern's handle, tight enough to make the brass squeal. "I thought you might be some form of message, a signal of her renewed interest, or at least a fresh amusement. Now I understand that she has forsaken us both. I had hoped at least she would come to tell me why."

The lantern swayed as he stalked off, denying me his face, but he did offer a parting comment. "By the way, the rumours are true. There are ghosts haunting this keep, though they're a sullen lot and rarely consent to appear. Still, you might have some company during your final hours. Sleep well, Alwyn Scribe."

As you may imagine, cherished reader, sleep did not come easily that night. It is in the nature of the captive soul to ponder its fate and the curse of imagination to make such pondering a form of torture in itself. Yet, simple exhaustion will exert its inevitable grip on even the most fearful mind and, incredible as it may seem, I did indeed sleep for a time. In such circumstances, dreams of the darkest hue were a certainty and they came to plague me as soon as my drooping eyes consented to close.

I have often pondered if these night terrors were the work of Arnabus's peculiar form of arcane ability, but feel them to have been both too strange and too inventive to be of his design. For all his age and undeniable acumen, he was a very limited man in most respects. It was King Tomas who arrived first on the field of nightmare, tottering about a misty, ashen plain in full armour with his head still crooked at an impossible angle. It might have been comical but for the utter despair and pain I saw on his tilted features. He spoke to me but his words were nonsense, sibilant mumbles from drooling lips that had the inflection of a question, but not one I could comprehend.

"I'm sorry, Your Majesty," I told him. Although I bore no responsibility for his demise, the sight of him still stirred my guilt. I hadn't killed him but I had used his death to orchestrate the Pretender's fall. These thoughts, of course, summoned Lochlain to this field of ash, appearing stripped to the waist, his flesh bearing full testimony to the torments suffered on the scaffold. Unlike Tomas, I found I could understand his words.

"What a useless bastard, eh?" he observed, nodding to the tottering, broken-necked king. "You can't deny I would've been better, can you, Scribe? Not least because I had some Algathinet blood in my veins, unlike this puffed-up turd."

Grunting in anger, he lunged to shove Tomas over, the king scattering black dust as he scrabbled about on the ground, putting me in mind of a malformed crab spilled from a fisherman's pot. "Look at him!" Lochlain taunted, bared red muscle leaking blood as he pointed, his voice a pitiful parody of the man I had spent so many hours with. "Look at King Crook Neck, Shite Monarch of Albermaine!"

"Leave him alone!" I snapped, stepping towards Lochlain, too disgusted by his wounds to push him away.

"Or what?" Lochlain enquired in a snarl, rounding on me. "Going to write another lying testament about me, are you?"

"I wrote the truth!" I insisted.

"There is no truth, you fucking dullard. You wrote what I told you, that's all, and I'm as big a liar as any bastard who ever trod this earth."

He laughed again, but it was a shrill, desperate thing that soon dwindled into a faltering sob. "Why did you do it, Scribe?" he asked, face stricken by a combination of defeat and accusation. "Why did you stop me taking what was mine? Why did you fight for these worthless lords? But for chance, I'd wager your life would have ended in a muddy gutter years ago. What did the Crown ever offer you beyond hunger and injustice?'"

"I didn't fight for lords or Crown," I said. "I fought for something better." The words were soft from my lips, bland and unconvincing even to my own ears.

"No," Lochlain stated. "You wanted to, that's why. You wanted to clear the road for that insane woman and her mad visions. Did you think she'd fuck you as a reward? Was that it?" His voice rose in volume with every word, fury and delusional pride swelling his flayed, bleeding chest to absurd proportions. "I was the True King!" he raged, skinless flesh squelching as he batted a fist to his chest. "And my reign would have been a golden age. To me there are no churls, no lords and no venal Covenant. Just the worthy and the worthless, and the worthy would have risen high in my kingdom. You would have been my chamberlain, Scribe. Wilhum the commander of my guard. Swain my knight marshal. I'd even have found a place for that gelding wench you're so fond of. Now, thanks to you, they'll all be corpses within a year."

"This is a dream." I closed my eyes, striving for calm. "A dream I made from my fears. You know only what I know. And I cannot see the future."

"Perhaps not." Lochlain's laughter was cruel this time. "But you can see the past. Open your eyes. Take a good look."

As is often the way with dreams, I was denied control over my own actions and I found myself staring at the many horrors now littering the black ash surrounding us. Some staggered, dripping blood from gaping wounds. Others crawled upon the ground, many of them limbless and squirming like worms. There were hundreds of them, growing to thousands when I raised my gaze to peer into the distance, beholding an army of shamblers and crawlers. Every face I beheld was that of a corpse, fresh and oozing or old and desiccated.

"So busy have you been," Lochlain observed. "Far busier than Deckin ever was."

"I have killed," I muttered back, eyes flicking from one dead face to another. "But never so many . . ."

"My army stumbles before you," he countered. "All the dead from Walvern Castle too. The fall of Highsahl, the Sacrifice March, all those skirmishes in between. That's a long trail of death, Scribe. When the time comes to write your own testament, be sure to pen it in red."

"Wars I didn't start." I felt an upsurge of panic as the lifeless horde came closer. They made no sound save the scrape and shuffle of their dead flesh upon the ash, yet I felt the weight of their accusation like a scream from a thousand throats. "Battles I never wanted." Desperation coloured my tone now, panic swollen to terror by the certainty that there was no escape from my victims' revenge. I clamped my eyes shut once more when they closed in, those with arms reaching out, dripping or rotting fingers grasping in need. "I'm sorry . . ." The plea emerged from my lips in a whimper, transforming into a gasp at the first icy touch of the dead . . .

"Why are you doing this?"

The chilly caress against my cheek vanished at the sound of this new voice. It was mostly calm but shot through with a sharp note of reproach. It was also familiar in its faint Caerith accent.

When I opened my eyes the dead were gone. Lochlain and gibbering, broken-necked Tomas had also vanished from the black plain. In their absence there stood a woman of youthful appearance, blonde hair trailing in the breeze, her brow, marked with a single red birthmark, drawn in a frown of recrimination.

"Why torment yourself like this?" the Sack Witch, the *Doenlisch*, asked. The annoyance in her voice had taken on an angry, judgemental edge. Clearly, finding me in such straits had been both unexpected and aggravating. I knew instantly that she was not the conjuration of my memory. She was here by her own arcane agency, an uninvited but very welcome intruder.

"I don't choose my dreams," I told her.

"You don't?" The notion appeared to cause her some genuine puzzlement before an expression of irritated realisation flickered across her face. "Oh, yes. Sometimes I forget how young you are."

The lightness of her tone set my own anger simmering. She had found me on the eve of torture and spoke as if we had just happened across one another on market day. "In point of fact," I went on, "Arnabus has been choosing my dreams for me of late. They weren't pleasant."

"I don't doubt it. My little brother always did prefer crafting night-mares."

"You might have told me you and he were acquainted."

"Why? Would it have changed your opinion of him?"

"It might. Knowing he followed your wishes would certainly have helped."

"He hasn't done that for a long time, despite what he might claim." Her face took on a sombre cast, mouth forming a hard line. "It's no easy thing to face your failures, Alwyn. Nor have I always possessed the will required to put them right. The twisted, cruelty-prone man he became was so very different from the scared, mischievous but sweet boy I raised. When my failure became plain I would, night after night, mix the herbs that would see him from this life in the midst of a peaceful slumber, but never could I bring myself to hand him the cup."

"He has done terrible things just to gain your notice. And I've little doubt he'll do more."

"Then I will prevail upon you to do what I couldn't." She gave a tight smile, coming closer, raising a hand to stroke my cheek then wincing as I flinched from it. "I understand your anger," she said. "But nothing I have done was intended to hurt you."

"I stand to be flayed to death tomorrow," I said. "Something you could prevent quite easily. You know where I am, do you not?"

"I do." She raised a faintly amused eyebrow. "Do you know where I am?"

Abruptly the surrounding plain of black ash swirled into dust, briefly enveloping us both in a maelstrom that shifted in hue from black and grey to blue and white. Soon it settled, solidifying into a mountain range. I had thought the tall peaks that bordered the Caerith dominion would be the most impressive landscape I would ever see, but they were dwarfed by the sheer scale of what unfolded now. Cliffs of snow-speckled granite rose high above, the summits of the many mountains mostly swallowed by cloud. Forests covered the lower slopes in a thick blanket that also filled the narrow valleys, the dark green sprawl broken here and there by winding rivers.

"My task requires me to walk far," the Sack Witch told me. "These mountains rise in lands that few of your people have ever seen. I have walked sun-blasted deserts and sailed storm-riven seas. I have seen islands of both fire and ice. I have been blessed by delight and cursed by danger. All of it in service to my task, as are you, Alwyn."

"Whether I wish it or not?"

"Why do you assume either of us ever had a choice? You wrote the book, don't forget."

"So you know I met the *Eithlisch*."

"Of course. The historian wrote down an account of the meeting centuries ago, because you told him of it."

"So you also know that the *Eithlisch* is very desirous of your return to Caerith lands. He sent a *veilisch* to hunt for you."

"Yes. Charming, isn't she? But I feel her talents would be better used at your side, as you still have so much to do."

"All of which is in the book, I assume?"

She inclined her head, a faintly apologetic smile curving her lips that drew a bitter sigh from mine, but also put a nugget of hope in my breast.

"I still have much to do," I said. "Much that was written down. So it must be that I survive this."

"Mmm." Her smile shifted into a muted grimace. "Here things become . . . confusing."

"Confusing how?"

"At first glance time often appears as a circle – certainly so in your case. To have written so fulsome an account of your life you must have lived a long time in order to relate it to the historian. Yet, the more I learn of time the more I find it resembles a river rather than a wheel. It flows ever onwards, changing course frequently, sometimes turning back on itself and sometimes splitting apart, unexpectedly forking in myriad different directions. It always comes back together, but some of its tributaries are lost, regardless of prophesy or vision."

"You mean I could very well die tomorrow."

"You could very well die any day, Alwyn. Why is tomorrow so important?"

I ground my teeth. "The imminence of torment and death would appear to make it so."

"Haven't you been listening? Nothing is imminent. Nothing is inevitable. Yet, I suspect that you have many more days ahead, or it could be that I am victim to hope, for your end would pain me so. The river will change course come the morn, but I think it will carry you onwards. Others, however, may be lost to the current." Her gaze took on a hard glint. "*She* may be lost."

I had no doubt whom she meant; the sharpness of her emphasis made it clear. "Evadine? She doesn't even know what's happened."

"To heal her I had to take from you, the core of you. You were joined, bound together with a knot that can never be broken. She sensed your danger not long after you set out, probably thinking it another vision. Rest assured she comes for you and when she arrives it may spell her end, for it's in the nature of love to strip away caution."

Heart suddenly pounding, I stepped towards her, voice flat and commanding. "How do I stop it? How do I escape this?" I reached for her, hands gripping her shoulders, shouting my demands into her face, all the while her expression betraying only scant concern. "You know! It's in the book. Tell me!"

"You wrote many things in the book, Alwyn," she said, voice mild with sorrow. "Only some of them happened. This life, the life that led you to this place at this time, was not in those pages. The river

turned, and you turned with it. All I know, I have already told you."
Her hand came up to stroke my cheek again, and I saw a small glimmer
of tears in her eyes. "Please survive this and save her if you can. A
great deal depends upon it. Now—" she gave a brisk sniff and drew
her hand back "—it's time you woke up." Her hand slammed into my
jaw like a hammer, shattering the dream like glass. The mountains
fell into shards, tumbling in the void while my body jerked in response
to its many bruises, a soft, rhythmic scraping invading my ears with
irksome insistence.

I came awake with a shudder, tasting the gritty dampness of the
stone beneath my face. I had been energetic in my slumber, my
struggles having brought me close to the edge of the well. As I lay
panting in alarm, I realised that the rhythmic scraping came from
this gloomy orifice. *Rats*, was my immediate assumption, although
my time here had been notable for the absence of any rodent visitors.
Then another, darker thought occurred, stirred by the parting jibe
Arnabus had cast my way: *The ghosts of the Dire Keep. They're real.*

My bonds allowed for only an ineffectual squirming as I attempted
to put distance between myself and the well, soon finding any progress
hindered by the single stone step that encircled it. Consequently, I
could only lie fearful and trembling while the scraping continued
until, finally, it ended in the clumping rattle of a very heavy stone
falling free of a wall. The splash came after the now-expected
prolonged interval, birthing a loud echo I thought might bring guards
running. The gauge of my fear was such by then that I would probably have welcomed their appearance. Yet, no guards came. Instead,
from the well there rose the grunts and muted slaps that told of
something climbing.

Tales of the Dire Keep and its spectral denizens inevitably rose to
mind as I stared at the lip of the well, the lurid accounts of souls
claimed by the vengeful murdered lord and his cohort of phantom
knights. *They drag you down, deep into the dark places beneath the
earth. They make you one of them, a soul cursed to linger forever,
always denied the Portals . . .*

I feel I should, therefore, be forgiven for the whimper that escaped my throat when the hand appeared. To my fearful gaze it was the blackened, skeletal claw of a risen corpse, rising to clamp down on the edge of the well with unnatural strength. More inhuman grunts echoed forth as its owner began to heave themself up. The face that appeared shortly after was everything my terror-infused imagination expected: black with rot, eyes glowing white with the arcane fire of hate that had sustained it for centuries of undeath.

I could only stare in frozen horror as it fixed its burning sight upon me and spoke: "Are you alone?"

The nature of my shock was abruptly shifted from fear to abject mystification, for this spectre had not only spoken in a cautious whisper, but also in Caerith. The ghost's darkened brows knitted in annoyance as it continued to haul itself free of the well, revealing a form that was athletic and fully alive despite the grime that covered it. Relieved recognition finally flooded me when Lilat approached in a crouch to inspect my bonds with a vexed hiss.

"This will take a while," she muttered, drawing her knife and setting to work on the pitch-encrusted knot binding my ankles.

CHAPTER FORTY-TWO

"Old buildings are like aged carcasses," Lilat said, crouching in predatory readiness near the thick oaken door that guarded the entrance to this subterranean prison. "The flesh slips from the bones leaving gaps. It took a long time to find one wide enough to let me in."

I swallowed a groan as I worked my fingers into the flesh of my ankles, flexing my toes and fighting the pain of blood rushing to constricted veins and muscles. "I seem to recall sending you on your mission," I said.

"And now you're glad I didn't go." I couldn't see her face in the gloom but could hear the satisfied grin in her voice.

"You've been tracking me all this while?"

"It wasn't hard. Besides, I couldn't find any scent of the *Doenlisch*."

"No." I got to my feet, wincing at the overlapping plethora of aches. "And I don't think you will until she wants you to."

Lilat shifted from the door, moving to the well and hefting the rope she had brought. "I can tie this off on that," she said, nodding to a pillar. "You go first . . ."

"I can't leave," I said. "They have friends of mine. And . . ." I trailed off before voicing the rest of it, the Sack Witch's warning ringing loud in my head. *She may be lost.*

"The company," I said. "The woman I follow. Did you see them close by?"

Lilat shook her head and shrugged. "It took a day to crawl through the drain to the well. They may have come, but I saw no sign."

"They'll be here," I said, moving to the racks of weapons lining the wall. I chose a dagger and a hatchet, both plain but well made with a honed edge to their blades.

"We are two; those above are many," Lilat pointed out as I crouched to inspect the lock.

"I don't intend to kill them all." I grunted in disappointment at finding the lock both heavy and well crafted. Toria would surely have made short work of it but I didn't have her skills and Lilat had no notion of what a lock was. "Hide yourself," I told her. "And you may want to cover your ears."

Once she had secluded herself in a nearby confluence of shadows, I took a deep breath, threw my head back and began to scream.

"Martyrs' arses," the man who came to investigate my wailing muttered as he heaved the door open. "Shut yer yapping, y'fucker! There's soldiers of the council needs their sleep, y'know."

Luring him in had required near a half-hour of the most throat-paining, desperate screams, interspersed with bellowing assurances that I was about to pound my own head into bloody mush. The guard was a large man, though fortunately his size wasn't matched by intelligence. Otherwise he wouldn't have come alone.

He hesitated upon swinging the door open, lantern clanking as he cast the glow about the vaulted chamber then starting in surprise at finding my bound form absent. His start became a rigid, arch-backed rictus when I stepped from the shadow of the door, driving the dagger deep into the base of his spine, then delivering an ear-to-ear slash across the throat to cage his screams as he fell. Some skills never fade.

I was quick to relieve him of his boots, finding they fit reasonably well. His body also yielded a quarter-filled purse and another knife before we dragged him into the shadows.

Beyond the door lay a winding, narrow spiral of stone steps, mostly dark but with a faint flicker of candlelight playing over its upper reaches. I crouched and listened for a time, hearing muted voices. A little more listening and my practised ears concluded there were only two men above. Their voices were bored at first but took on a reluctant note of concern as the seconds ticked by. Soon they would come to investigate the fate of their comrade. Lilat and I could retire to the vaults once again and await them, but time was against us and there was no telling how long their dithering would last.

"We have to make it quick," I whispered to Lilat then started up the steps, hatchet in one hand and dagger in the other. I allowed only the briefest pause upon reaching the top, taking in the sight of two brawny men, one with a smoking pipe in his mouth, the other pausing in the act of lifting a tankard for a final swig. I killed the tankard bearer first, since he was the first to react, dropping the vessel and reaching for the falchion at his belt. The hatchet cleaved into his forehead before he had chance to draw his blade. Blinking against the red vapour that misted my eyes I drew the hatchet free, my victim sliding down the wall behind with a torrent of red and grey leaking from his sundered skull. Turning to the pipe smoker I found he had been seized by the immobility that often grips those unaccustomed to sudden and unexpected violence. He stood with features frozen in shock, teeth clamped hard on his pipe stem as the bowl continued to leak tendrils of sweet-smelling leaf.

"Soldiering isn't your trade, is it?" I asked him, holding up a hand as Lilat rose behind the frozen guard, knife poised for a thrust.

"I-I'm . . ." the pipe smoker stuttered in an Althiene accent, his pipe finally falling from his lips. "A-a cattle drover . . . sir. Lost me herd in the wars . . ."

He fell silent as I stepped closer, taking hold of his sword belt and slicing through it with the knife. "The folk I was brought in with. Where are they?"

His reply was astute in its promptness: "The old cells in the base of the tower, sir."

"How many soldiers does Thessil have here?"

He blinked in panicked bafflement. "Thessil, sir?"

"Your captain," I said, realising Danick would probably have forsaken his real name years ago. "Danick Thessil, once a renowned outlaw in these parts. Didn't you know?"

From the rapid shake of his head and increasingly sweat-covered face, I deduced this fellow neither knew nor cared about his captain's origins. "There's seventy of us here, all told, sir," he said, wisely choosing not to make me repeat myself. "All those who can ride. Rest of the council host is up in Athiltor." He revealed his quick mind yet again by offering up information I hadn't yet asked for. "I heard the captain tell the Luminant there's near five thousand of us now."

"That won't be enough." I pointed to the stairs. "Wait down there until it's over. Then go home and be a drover again. This life isn't for you."

The drover's head bobbed in eager agreement as he backed away. "Thank you very much, sir," he said before descending the steps fast enough to make him stumble. I often wonder if he broke his neck before he reached the bottom.

The drover's sword was an old length of iron with an uneven look to the blade that nevertheless seemed well forged. Buckling on the slain guard's belt, I replaced the falchion with the sword then tucked the hatchet into the belt on the opposite side. The dead guard's knife I slid into my boot for good measure.

"He's the last one we spare," I told Lilat. "From here on, kill quickly and quietly."

The chamber's only light was a candle stub guttering in an alcove. Snuffing it, I then moved to the rickety door set into the wall of this constricted guardhouse, easing it open an inch. Outside I found a roofless corridor, the walls tumbled with many gaps revealing the council host camp, still mercifully undisturbed. Careful glances left and right revealed no guards nearby so I pushed the door open just wide enough to allow me to pass through, emerging into the corridor in a low crouch. The tower lay some twenty yards to the left of the guardhouse, its base lost to the shadows, but I caught the gleam of firelight on the blades of two halberds.

Lilat and I approached in a crawl, keeping to the darkest stretches of the passage. It ended in a short stretch of grass separating the tower from this portion of ruins. Fortunately, the grass was long and the dim outline of the guards told of a pair slumped against the tower wall, exchanging bored conversation. As I crept towards them I reflected on Danick's parlous standards of recruitment. Cowardly former drovers and men who couldn't keep alert for a few hours' watch made for a poor army.

The guards were better armoured than those we had left in the vaults, clad in helms and mail with stout halberds. Killing both with any attempt at stealth should have presented a difficult prospect, but their inattentiveness proved a fatal weakness. Lilat and I were able to approach to within three yards without drawing notice, and when we surged from cover with knives in hand the laggardly pair failed to even shout a warning. The one I killed at least tried to bring his halberd to bear, but with the kind of slowness that would have earned him some of Swain's worst punishments. The knife slipped past the haft of his halberd to take the fellow in the throat, aimed for the point where he had failed to fasten the topmost catch of his mail shirt. I pushed the knife in deep, covering his mouth with my free hand to cage the sound. To my right, Lilat jerked her own blade free of the eye socket of the other guard, pressing the body to the wall and easing it down so his armour wouldn't jangle as he fell.

The tower door was unlocked, leaking the bright glow of a well-lit interior as I cracked it open. Fortunately, the sliver of light failed to arouse any notice from the rest of the camp and we made our way inside without incident. The first assault to greet me came in the form of a stench, sweet and sickly with an acrid tinge that caught the throat. However, I was not permitted the chance to cough for the second assault followed immediately, this time in the form of a lean, bare-chested man wielding a glowing poker.

I had taken the precaution of drawing my looted sword before entering the tower, one that proved wise for it parried the overhead swing of the poker with a loud clang and a flurry of sparks. The bare-chested man let out a barely comprehensible string of obscenities and backed away a few steps, throwing his head back with the obvious intention of crying out an alarm. I lunged, sword aimed for his throat, but Lilat was quicker, letting fly with her knife which flickered past my head to bury itself in the poker-man's neck.

He still contrived to make a decent amount of noise as he staggered back, clutching at the blade embedded in his flesh, guttural shrieks joining with the gurgle of blood erupting from his mouth and nose. I finished him with a thrust to the hollow just below the centre of his ribcage, driving the blade deep enough to sever the spine. He fell to the flagstones, shuddering and leaving this world with a swiftness I was soon to regret when I beheld his handiwork.

The interior of the tower was a shell of fallen stairwells and tumbled stone, cleared into piles around a bare floor, in the centre of which there stood a brazier piled with glowing coals. Beside the brazier a steaming pot of melted pitch hung from a tripod above a well-stoked fire. Woodsman, Tiler and Juhlina lay around the brazier, bound in the same manner I had been, except their mouths were gagged. They were also all naked. The Widow's flesh appeared to be unmarked but Tiler and Woodsman had not been so fortunate. Moving to them I saw a dozen or more black marks on their upper arms and faces, the stench of burnt flesh mingling with their copious sweat. My mind was quick to connect the lean man's red-hot poker with the torment inflicted here, each burn mark covered over in black pitch. I had heard of this form of torment but never seen it; the pitch would increase the pain while also sealing the wound to prevent split skin from bleeding.

"Told . . ." Woodsman gasped as I severed the twine securing the peg clamped into his mouth. "Told the bastard nothing, Captain." He shuddered as I got to work on his bonds. "None of us did."

"I know," I said. Having sawed my knife blade through his knots I moved to Tiler while Lilat freed Juhlina. I had expected her to exhibit the most rage upon being freed, but it was Tiler who gave fullest vent to his feelings.

"Fucking shit-eating whoreson bastard!" he screeched, snatching up the fallen poker and hurling himself upon the torturer's corpse. I considered cautioning him against raising too much noise but he went about his subsequent mutilations with wordless dedication so I thought it best to leave him to it.

Some rummaging amid the rubble unearthed a pile of part-ripped clothes and boots which I handed out to Woodsman and Juhlina. Despite Woodsman's shuddering pains and Tiler's fury, I found the Widow's demeanour the most worrying, for she barely exhibited any concern at all.

"Saving me for tomorrow, he said," she told me, seeing the notice I took of her unmarked skin. "Said it would make the best impression on you." Shrugging on her jerkin she donned her trews before pointing to the hatchet in my belt. "May I?"

"Please do." I handed her the weapon and took stock of our surroundings, dismayed to find there was but one point of ingress and egress to this tower.

"Any old bare bones to dig through?" I asked, raising a questioning eyebrow at Lilat and receiving an apologetic shake of the head in response.

"We could go up," she offered, glancing at the gloomy heights of the tower's upper portions. "Then down the other side."

"Beg pardon, Captain," Woodsman said, the muscles of his face and neck stark with subdued agony, "but I couldn't climb an inch just now."

"It'll be dawn soon, in any case," I said, moving to the door. "No time for anything but sneaking our way clear of here. You done?" I asked Tiler as he paused in his exertions. He straightened from the torturer's body, scraping his wrist across his nose and flicking the accumulated skull fragments and brains from the poker.

"For now," he sniffed, then turned to me with a steady, gleaming eye beneath burnt, blackened brows. Never the most appealing of men, he now possessed a face that made even me handsome by comparison. "I want Thessil, though," he said. "When I'm done he'll wish to all the Martyrs he'd stayed dead."

"You'll have him if he's to be had," I promised. "Put some clothes on and let's be on our way."

Had our party consisted of just myself, Tiler and Lilat, I feel sure we could have escaped the Dire Keep that night without incident. Sadly, neither Juhlina nor Woodsman possessed the accustomed stealth or outlaw's instinct for self-preservation required for such a task. We did make a fair stab at it, however, slipping through the tower door into the grass and pausing only for Woodsman to take up a halberd from one of the slain guards. It is a point of lasting regret to me that I didn't tell him to leave it be, for it was the weapon's blade that undid us. Its former owner had been an indolent guard but irksomely diligent in caring for his arms. It was as we attempted to scale a low wall near the keep's southern edge, tantalisingly close to the dark, welcoming embrace of the forest, that the blade caught a gleam from the first glimmer of dawn cresting the treetops. The nearby sentry, sadly, failed to share his comrades' laggardly approach to soldiering and began bellowing the alarm with instant and full-throated enthusiasm.

Tiler and I, spurred by outlaws' instincts, immediately vaulted the tumbled wall into the field beyond and began to run for the trees, Lilat following swiftly. Woodsman and Juhlina, sadly, did not. Hearing the abrupt end of the sentry's cry, I came to a halt and turned to see Woodsman hacking at the sentry with enraged abandon. Beyond him, another dozen guards were hurrying towards the scene. I watched with a plummeting heart as Juhlina hefted the hatchet and hurled herself at the oncoming knot of soldiers. *The kind of rage that never fades*, I thought, recalling her words that night on the ridge. She had been too calm when we freed her, a bottle of pent-up fury waiting for the chance to explode. Now she had it.

"You can go if you want," I told Tiler, starting back towards the keep at the run.

I had covered a few yards when I heard his running feet at my back, following not fleeing. "Oh, shit on it," he muttered, echoing that poor sod I had hacked from the ladder at Walvern Castle. This time the absurd lack of poetry in the face of death brought a grin to my lips, but it soon faded when I hurled myself into the fray at Juhlina's side.

CHAPTER FORTY-THREE

Further evidence of the council host's lack of soldiering skill was revealed by the fact that, several moments after cutting down my first victim, all of us were still alive. By the time I reached Juhlina she was squatting above a fallen council-man, her hatchet rising and falling to further disarrange his already shattered features. The man I killed was a youthful halberdier who lunged towards her with an inexpert thrust, arms overextended and feet off balance in a manner that made it easy for me to hack my sword deep into his exposed neck.

The Widow, of course, wasn't yet done. Rising from the inert form of the man with the mashed face, she sidestepped the sword thrust of another and shattered his knee with a swift chop of the hatchet. A resolute soul, he attempted to reverse his sword and stab at her back, only to fall dead when Lilat darted forwards to slice his throat open. Hearing a grunt and clatter to my right, I turned to see Tiler driving the point of his poker into the gaping mouth of a council-man, bearing the fellow down with both knees on his chest, then putting all his weight on the poker to push through.

"This lot could've done with some of Captain Swain's teachings," he observed, snatching up the fallen man's axe.

An upsurge of bellowing drew my gaze to where Woodsman was

sweeping his halberd to and fro in an effort to force back the increasingly dense throng of assailants. The air was filled with discordant shouts of fear and anger, shot through with voices attempting to impose some order on this untidy scrum.

"Move around them, you stupid fucks!" Thessil boomed. I caught a glimpse of him above the enclosing mob, mounted and shouting orders, his ruined face a dark, mottled mask of thunderous anger.

My ears also detected a voice from an unseen source, though I was able to discern Luminant Durehl's strident and practised tones: "The scribe! Spare the scribe!"

There was a brief interlude of frenzied combat during which the world slipped into the now-familiar haze of action and counteraction. My sense of time and pain dimmed amid the red fog of it all, narrowing to the faces of the men I killed or maimed over the course of what may have been a moment or an hour. When the fog thinned the council-men had formed a wary cordon around the five of us, the ground in between littered by still or flailing bodies. We stood back to back, chests heaving, though I felt no sense of fatigue. Nor did I appear to be injured save for a shallow cut on my forearm. Woodsman hadn't been so fortunate, his stocky frame shuddering as he propped himself up on his halberd, blood leaking from numerous wounds to his legs and back. I knew it wouldn't be much longer before his strength gave out.

"You're done, Scribe!" Danick Thessil called to me, kicking his horse to force passage through the ranks of his men. "Give it up and I'll spare these others."

"Oh, get fucked," I replied, annoyed by his obvious lie and also finding myself possessed of a perverse impatience. "Your gaggle of cravens isn't up to the job, and you know it." I fixed a hard glare upon him, speaking in clear tones to ensure his men heard me. "How's about we settle it, just you and me? Or perhaps you'd prefer to piss yourself and run off like you did at Moss Mill?"

It was a calculated, cruel and unfair taunt, but it served its purpose. Snarling, Danick drew a broad-bladed axe from the scabbard on his saddle, tensing himself to spur the beast towards me. I harboured a faint hope of hobbling his mount with a slash to the legs and escaping in the ensuing carnage. Whether it would have worked is doubtful but will forever remain unknown, for Danick never made his charge.

A familiar whipping noise, followed by a brief cacophony that resembled a hail storm of unfeasible weight, caused me to duck, reaching out to drag Lilat and Tiler down with me. Around us a dozen soldiers tumbled to the ground, crossbow bolts jutting from faces and helms. Then came the drumbeat of many hooves before the thud and clang of a mounted charge meeting a close-packed body of men. A loud whinny drew my gaze upwards to behold the sight of a large black destrier vaulting the ruined wall. As was her habit in battle, Evadine wore no helm, the dawn light playing on her trailing hair and upraised sword as she and Ulstan seemed to hang in the air for a heartbeat before plunging into the disturbed ranks of the council-men.

Screams abounded as she began to hack her way through the convulsing mob of soldiers, terror spreading like the worst fever as they beheld the sight of the Anointed Lady giving full vent to her rage. Her sword rose and fell like a blurring scythe, reaping a harvest of blood with every sweep of the long blade. The milling confusion of the council soldiers transformed swiftly into a rout when more mounted figures charged in from several directions, swords and maces reaping bloody havoc. I saw Wilhum slash his way clean through the panicking throng, wheel about then charge again, his sword red from point to hilt.

In their fright, a few soldiers attempted to fight their way past our small band, meeting undaunted foes in the shape of both Juhlina and Woodsman. Despite his wounds, the brawny churl cut down two men before a third succeeded in driving his falchion deep into his chest. For the first time that morn I felt a true kindling of rage at the sight of Woodsman falling lifeless to the earth. The falchion-bearer displayed impressive courage by lingering to raise his blade against mine as I barrelled towards him, but it didn't save him. Batting the falchion's parry aside, I hammered the hilt of my sword into his face then kicked his legs out from under him, pinning his prone form down with a boot on his breastplate. I allowed him a moment of terror as I reared, staring into his wide, desperate eyes before bringing the sword down. It was good steel, piercing his skull between his eyes to a depth of several inches.

Glancing at Woodsman's unmoving bulk, Tiler, Lilat and Juhlina crouched around him, I felt my rage diminish. They were all bloodied, Lilat by a bad cut to the forehead, Tiler by a dozen more to his arms and face. Juhlina's condition was harder to judge, given the amount of gore that covered her. I would later discover that she barely suffered a single injury beyond a collection of bruises. But not all wounds are of the body and, seeing the unblinking cast to her eye, I worried this woman may finally have tipped over the precipice into outright madness.

A chorus of pleas for mercy drew my gaze to the ruins where those council-men not slain or fled were on their knees, weapons cast aside and hands pressed together. I watched Wilhum issue orders to start rounding them up and spied Eamond among those dismounting to see to the task. Noting a flurry of activity off to the eastern edge of the ruins, I glimpsed the sight of a half-dozen horses galloping into the trees. At their head was Danick's hefty form and among those riders following I espied the grey of a cleric's robe. *Arnabus, or perhaps Durehl?*

Before the group disappeared into the dark wall of the forest I saw one figure galloping in pursuit: Evadine, spurring Ulstan to his fullest speed.

Jerking my sword free of the corpse at my feet, I ran towards Eamond, ignoring his greeting and hurrying to mount his horse. "Tell Captain Dornmahl to gather riders and follow me," I snapped before wheeling the hunter about and striking out towards the trees, shouting over my shoulder, "And scour this place for a cleric. If he runs, feel at liberty to kill the bastard."

Light was meagre beneath the trees but I wouldn't allow the hunter to slow, forcing him on despite the complex and treacherous shadows painting the forest floor. I followed the sounds of combat, mostly shouts and the occasional clash of steel, passing three riderless horses in quick succession. Evadine was clearly intent on claiming her prize today. I found that the forest's deceptive way with sound frustrated my attempts to close with her, the increasingly infrequent song of conflict becoming ever more distant until I was forced to stop. Straining my ears for a signal, I was soon rewarded by the dim sound of voices off to my right. Spurring the hunter forward, I emerged into a clearing where I beheld the satisfying sight of a dismounted Danick attempting to haul a man in a cleric's robe from beneath the struggling bulk of a crippled horse.

The beast had evidently snapped a leg, probably thanks to the less than expert handling of its rider. It whinnied and thrashed in alarm while Danick cursed and hauled at the trapped cleric. The sound of my approach, however, caused him to leave off his labour. For all his pretensions to a soldierly character, I saw only the outlaw in the brief, fearful glance he shot at me before turning and sprinting for his horse. He was mounted and gone in a trice and, for the moment at least, I was content to let him go.

I trotted the hunter forward a few yards before dismounting, drawing the sword from my belt. The cleric let out a series of energetic grunts as I came closer, finally succeeding in freeing himself and getting to his feet. From the way he hobbled, I deduced that his leg had suffered the same fate as that of his horse.

My intent was apparently plain in my expression for he straightened, scowling in severe admonition. "Would you do murder in the name of your false martyr, Scribe?" he asked, voice stern in its demand, lacking the expected quaver of a man about to meet his end.

"I've done worse, Your Luminance." My fist closed on Durehl's robe, dragging him away from the stricken horse. To his credit, he made no effort to beg as I forced him against the broad trunk of a nearby yew. "I regret," I said, raising the sword level with his chest for a quick clean thrust through the ribs, "I have no time to hear your testament. But I'll allow a few words, if you're so minded."

"You serve a woman of evil intent," he stated, glaring defiance into my eyes. "Those are my words. If you have a care for your soul, you'll heed them."

"Save your cares for your own soul," I replied, drawing the sword back.

"Alwyn!"

Evadine's voice froze me, the fierce implacable command dispelling my rage in an instant. With jarring suddenness, I saw this tableau as if through other eyes: a raised-up churl about to murder the principal Luminant of the Covenant of Martyrs. I had been made a knight, gained the favour of the Crown and won fame throughout the realm, but none of it would save me from the consequences of a sin so great.

Turning, I found her climbing down from Ulstan's back, bloodied sword in hand. She came to me with concern shining in dampened eyes, her fingers tracing over the bruises on my face. "I saw," she murmured. "The Seraphile saw fit to let me save you."

"You saw nothing but your own delusions, woman!" Durehl said, causing Evadine's gaze to slowly veer towards him. "Can't you see that?" he demanded. "Don't you know you are no more than a madwoman bringing this realm, this Covenant, to ruin."

"I forgive you your own delusions, Luminant," Evadine replied, her voice placid. "For I know it must be hard for a soul so blinded by greed and power to accept their own misdeeds."

Durehl's voice became a growl. "All I have done I did for the Covenant, and the people of this land. I am the only true servant of the Seraphile here."

"Hiring assassins was the Seraphile's wish, was it?" I asked, causing Evadine to turn to me a with a questioning brow. "That lot with the sovereigns on the road south," I explained, staring hard at the Luminant. "Arnabus was kind enough to enlighten me. You should have more care over your choice of accomplice, Your Luminance."

"I'll make no claim to a pure soul," Durehl shot back. "But I sullied it for the good of all."

"No," Evadine said, shaking her head. She took her hand from me and set her palm upon his head, the Luminant flinching at her touch as if burned. "No, brother, you did not," Evadine told him, her voice soft with regret rather than condemnation. "But I thank you for your sin, nonetheless, for now I perceive my path with more clarity than ever before. I see now that the only way for peace to reign in this realm is for Crown and Covenant to unite. Yet both are corrupt beyond salvation. Therefore the union must be forged by other means, in me. This is my mission; this is what I have been guided to: I must become the Ascendant Queen."

She smoothed a kind hand over Durehl's brow, stepped back from him and opened his throat with a single slash of her sword. The Luminant's blood sprayed in a torrent as he fell, bathing us both. I should have been shocked, even terrified at the enormity of her crime. Yet, in those few seconds it seemed right, an act of inevitable necessity rather than murder. So, when Evadine spared his twitching corpse a short glance before moving to me, her arms encircling my neck, drawing me close, I'll not pretend any reluctance in returning the kiss she pressed to my lips. In that moment I could resist her no more than the avalanche that had once borne me down a mountain. Despite what she had done, despite the blood I tasted as our mouths joined, I was hers now. Yet even then, even as we stumbled away from our victim, she stripping off her armour and I the ragged garments I wore, even as we lay upon the earth and coiled together in both blood and sweat, I found my memory to be a traitor.

You're a liar, I had spat at the historian in his tower, yet I'd heard no falsehood when he'd repeated what he had told me. Although I knew I would see him again to relate more of my testament to his younger self, for him this was our last meeting. I could discern a need in him to impart a final truth, one I refused to believe then, and refused to believe even as it nagged at me now: "Evadine serves the Malecite."

The story continues in...

THE TRAITOR

Book Three of The Covenant of Steel

ACKNOWLEDGEMENTS

Many thanks to everyone who helped bring the second part of Alwyn's journey to a conclusion, especially my editors, James Long and Bradley Englert; my agent, Paul Lucas; and my ever-vigilant second set of eyes, Paul Field.

extras

orbit

meet the author

Photo Credit: Ellie Grace Photography

ANTHONY RYAN lives in London and is the *New York Times* best-selling author of the Raven's Shadow and Draconis Memoria series. He previously worked in a variety of roles for the UK government, but now writes full time. His interests include art, science and the unending quest for the perfect pint of real ale.

Find out more about Anthony Ryan and other Orbit authors by registering for the Orbit newsletter at orbitbooks.net.

if you enjoyed
THE MARTYR

look out for

THE JUSTICE OF KINGS

Book One of the
Empire of the Wolf

by

Richard Swan

From a major new debut author in epic fantasy comes the first book in a trilogy where action, intrigue, and magic collide. The Justice of Kings introduces an unforgettable protagonist destined to become a fantasy icon: Sir Konrad Vonvalt, an Emperor's Justice, who is a detective, judge, and executioner all in one. But these are dangerous times to be a Justice....

The Empire of the Wolf simmers with unrest. Rebels, heretics, and powerful patricians all challenge the power of the Imperial throne.

Only the Order of Justices stands in the way of chaos. Sir Konrad Vonvalt is the most feared Justice of all, upholding the law by way of his sharp mind, arcane powers, and skill as a swordsman. At his side stands Helena Sedanka, his talented protégé, orphaned by the wars that forged the Empire.

When the pair investigates the murder of a provincial aristocrat, they unearth a conspiracy that stretches to the very top of Imperial society. As the stakes rise and become ever more personal, Vonvalt and Helena must make a choice: Will they abandon the laws they've sworn to uphold in order to protect the Empire?

I

The Witch of Rill

"Beware the idiot, the zealot and the tyrant; each clothes himself in the armour of ignorance."

FROM CATERHAUSER'S THE SOVAN CRIMINAL CODE:
ADVICE TO PRACTITIONERS

It is a strange thing to think that the end of the Empire of the Wolf, and all the death and devastation that came with it, traced its long roots back to the tiny and insignificant village of Rill. That as we drew closer to it, we were not just plodding through a rainy, cold country twenty miles east of the Tolsburg Marches; we were approaching the precipice of the Great Decline, its steep and treacherous slope falling away from us like a cliff face of glassy obsidian.

Rill. How to describe it? The birthplace of our misfortune was so plain. For its isolation, it was typical for the Northmark of Tolsburg. It was formed of a large communal square of churned mud and straw, and a ring of twenty buildings with wattle-and-daub walls and thatched roofs. The manor was distinguishable only by its size, being perhaps twice as big as the biggest cottage, but there the differences ended. It was as tumbledown as the rest of them. An inn lay off to one side, and livestock and peasants moved haphazardly through the public space. One benefit of the cold was that the smell wasn't so bad, but Vonvalt still held a kerchief filled with dried lavender to his nose. He could be fussy like that.

I should have been in a good mood. Rill was the first village we had come across since we had left the Imperial wayfort on the Jägeland border, and it marked the beginning of a crescent of settlements that ended in the Hauner fortress of Seaguard fifty miles to the north-east. Our arrival here meant we were probably only a few weeks away from turning south again to complete the eastern half of our circuit – and that meant better weather, larger towns and something approaching civilisation.

Instead, anxiety gnawed at me. My attention was fixed on the vast, ancient forest that bordered the village and stretched for a hundred miles north and west of us, all the way to the coast. It was home, according to the rumours we had been fed along the way, to an old Draedist witch.

"You think she is in there?" Patria Bartholomew Claver asked from next to me. Claver was one of four people who made up our caravan, a Neman priest who had imposed himself on us at the Jägeland border. Ostensibly it was for protection against bandits, though the Northmark was infamously desolate – and by his own account, he travelled almost everywhere alone.

"Who?" I asked.

Claver smiled without warmth. "The witch," he said.

"No," I said curtly. I found Claver very irritating – everyone did. Our itinerant lives were difficult enough, but Claver's incessant questioning over the last few weeks of every aspect of Vonvalt's practice and powers had worn us all down to the nub.

"I do."

I turned. Dubine Bressinger – Vonvalt's taskman – was approaching, cheerfully eating an onion. He winked at me as his horse trotted past. Behind him was our employer, Sir Konrad Vonvalt, and at the very back was our donkey, disrespectfully named the Duke of Brondsey, which pulled a cart loaded with all our accoutrements.

We had come to Rill for the same reason we went anywhere: to ensure that the Emperor's justice was done, even out here on the fringes of the Sovan Empire. For all their faults, the Sovans were great believers in justice for all, and they dispatched Imperial Magistrates like Vonvalt to tour the distant villages and towns of the Empire as itinerant courts.

"I'm looking for Sir Otmar Frost," I heard Vonvalt call out from the rear of our caravan. Bressinger had already dismounted and was summoning a local boy to make arrangements for our horses.

One of the peasants pointed wordlessly at the manor. Vonvalt grunted and dismounted. Patria Claver and I did the same. The mud was iron-hard beneath my feet.

"Helena," Vonvalt called to me. "The ledger."

I nodded and retrieved the ledger from the cart. It was a heavy tome, with a thick leather jacket clad in iron and with a lockable clasp. It would be used to record any legal issues which arose, and Vonvalt's considered judgments. Once it was full, it would be sent back to the Law Library in distant Sova, where clerks would review the judgments and make sure that the common law was being applied consistently.

I brought the ledger to Vonvalt, who bade me keep hold of it with an irritated wave, and all four of us made for the manor. I could see now that it had a heraldic device hanging over the door, a plain blue shield overlaid by a boar's head mounted on a broken lance. The manor was otherwise unremarkable, and a far cry from the sprawling town houses and country fortresses of the Imperial aristocracy in Sova.

Vonvalt hammered a gloved fist against the door. It opened quickly. A maid, perhaps a year or two younger than me, stood in the doorway. She looked frightened.

"I am Justice Sir Konrad Vonvalt of the Imperial Magistratum," Vonvalt said in what I knew to be an affected Sovan accent. His native Jägeland inflection marked him out as an upstart, notwithstanding his station, and embarrassed him.

The maid curtseyed clumsily. "I—"

"Who is it?" Sir Otmar Frost called from somewhere inside. It was dark beyond the threshold and smelled like woodsmoke and livestock. I could see Vonvalt's hand absently reach for his lavender kerchief.

"Justice Sir Konrad Vonvalt of the Imperial Magistratum," he announced again, impatiently.

"Bloody faith," Sir Otmar muttered, and appeared in the doorway a few moments later. He thrust the maid aside without ceremony. "My lord, come in, come in; come out of the damp and warm yourselves at the fire."

We entered. Inside it was dingy. At one end of the room was a bed covered in furs and woollen blankets, as well as personal effects which suggested an absent wife. In the centre was an open log fire, surrounded by charred and muddy rugs that were also mouldering thanks to the rain that dripped down from the open smoke hole. At the other end was a long trestle table with seating for ten, and a door that led to a separate kitchen. The walls were draped with mildewed tapestries that were faded and smoked near-black, and the floor was piled thick with rugs and skins. A pair of big, wolf-like dogs warmed themselves next to the fire.

"I was told that a Justice was moving north through the Tolsburg Marches," Sir Otmar said as he fussed. As a Tollish knight and lord, he had been elevated to the Imperial aristocracy – "taking the Highmark", as it was known, for the payoffs they had all received in exchange for submitting to the Legions – but he was a far cry from the powdered and pampered lords of Sova. He was an old man, clad in a grubby tunic bearing his device and a pair of homespun trousers. His face was grimy and careworn and framed by white hair and a white beard. A large dent marred his forehead, probably earned as a younger man when the Reichskrieg had swept through and the Sovan armies had vassalised Tolsburg twenty-five years before. Both Vonvalt and Bressinger, too, bore the scars of the Imperial expansion.

"The last visit was from Justice August?" Vonvalt asked.

Sir Otmar nodded. "Aye. A long time ago. Used to be that we

saw a Justice a few times a year. Please, all of you, sit. Food, ale? Wine? I was just about to eat."

"Yes, thank you," Vonvalt said, sitting at the table. We followed suit.

"My predecessor left a logbook?" Vonvalt asked.

"Yes, yes," Sir Otmar replied, and sent the maid scurrying off again. I heard the sounds of a strongbox being raided.

"Any trouble from the north?"

Sir Otmar shook his head. "No; we have a sliver of the Westmark of Haunersheim between us and the sea. Maybe ten or twenty miles' worth, enough to absorb a raiding party. Though I daresay the sea is too rough this time of year anyway to tempt the northerners down."

"Quite right," Vonvalt said. I could tell he was annoyed for having forgotten his geography. Still, one could be forgiven the occasional slip of the mind. The Empire, now over fifty years old, had absorbed so many nations so quickly the cartographers redrew the maps yearly. "And I suppose with Seaguard rebuilt," he added.

"Aye, that the Autun did. A new curtain wall, a new garrison and enough money and provender to allow for daily ranges during fighting season. Weekly, in winter, by order of the margrave."

The Autun. The Two-Headed Wolf. It was evens on whether the man had meant the term as a pejorative. It was one of those strange monikers for the Sovan Empire that the conquered used either in deference or as an insult. Either way, Vonvalt ignored it.

"The man has a reputation," Vonvalt remarked.

"Margrave Westenholtz?" the priest, Claver, chipped in. "A good man. A pious man. The northerners are a godless folk who cleave to the old Draedist ways." He shrugged. "You should not mourn them, Justice."

Vonvalt smiled thinly. "I do not mourn dead northern raiders, Patria," he said with more restraint than the man was due. Claver was a young man, too young to bear the authority of a priest. Over the course of our short time together we had all had grown to dislike him immensely. He was zealous and a bore, quick to anger and judge. He spoke at great length about his cause – that of recruiting Templars for the southern Frontier – and his lordly contacts. Bressinger generally refused to talk to him, but Vonvalt, out of professional courtesy, had been engaging with the man for weeks.

Sir Otmar cleared his throat. He was about to make the error of engaging with Claver when the food arrived, and instead he ate. It was hearty, simple fare of meat, bread and thick gravy, but then in these circumstances we rarely went hungry. Vonvalt's power and authority tended to inspire generosity in his hosts.

"You said the last Justice passed through a while ago?" Vonvalt asked.

"Aye," Sir Otmar replied.

"You have been following the Imperial statutes in the interim?"

Sir Otmar nodded vigorously, but he was almost certainly lying. These far-flung villages and towns, months' worth of travel from distant Sova even by the fastest means, rarely practised Imperial law. It was a shame. The Reichskrieg had brought death and misery to thousands, but the system of common law was one of the few rubies to come out of an otherwise enormous shit.

"Good. Then I shouldn't imagine there will be much to do. Except investigate the woods," Vonvalt said. Sir Otmar looked confused by the addendum. Vonvalt drained the last of his ale. "On our way here," he explained, "we were told a number of times about a witch, living in the woods just to the north of Rill. I don't suppose you know anything about it?"

Sir Otmar delayed with a long draw of wine and then ostensibly to pick something out of his teeth. "Not that I have heard of, sire. No."

Vonvalt nodded thoughtfully. *Who is she?*

Bressinger swore in Grozodan. Sir Otmar and I leapt halfway out of our skin. The table and all the platters and cutlery on it were jolted as three pairs of thighs hit it. Goblets and tankards were spilled. Sir Otmar clutched his heart, his eyes wide, his mouth working to expel the words that Vonvalt had commanded him to.

The Emperor's Voice: the arcane power of a Justice to compel a person to speak the truth. It had its limitations – it did not work on other Justices, for example, and a strong-willed person could frustrate it if on their guard – but Sir Otmar was old and meek and not well-versed in the ways of the Order. The power hit him like a psychic thunderclap and turned his mind inside out.

"A priestess . . . a member of the Draeda," Sir Otmar gasped. He looked horrified as his mouth spoke against his mind's will.

"*Is she from Rill?*" Vonvalt pressed.

"Yes!"

"*Are there others who practise Draedism?*"

Sir Otmar writhed in his chair. He gripped the table to steady himself.

"Many . . . of the villagers!"

"Sir Konrad," Bressinger murmured. He was watching Sir Otmar with a slight wince. I saw that Claver was relishing the man's torment.

"All right, Sir Otmar," Vonvalt said. "All right. Calm yourself. Here, take some ale. I'll not press you any further."

We sat in silence as Sir Otmar summoned the terrified maid with a trembling hand and wheezed for some ale. She left and reappeared a moment later, handing him a tankard. Sir Otmar drained it greedily.

"The practice of Draedism is illegal," Vonvalt remarked.

Sir Otmar looked at his plate. His expression was somewhere between anger, horror and shame, and was a common look for those who had been hit by the Voice.

"The laws are new. The religion is old," he said hoarsely.

"The laws have been in place for two and a half decades."

"The religion has been in place for two and a half millennia," Sir Otmar snapped.

There was an uncomfortable pause. "Is there anyone in Rill that is not a practising member of Draedism?" Vonvalt asked.

Sir Otmar inspected his drink. "I couldn't say," he mumbled.

"Justice." There was genuine disgust in Claver's voice. "At the very least they will have to renounce it. The official religion of the Empire is the holy Nema Creed." He practically spat as he looked the old baron up and down. "If I had my way they'd all burn."

"These are good folk here," Sir Otmar said, alarmed. "Good, law-abiding folk. They work the land and they pay their tithes. We've never been a burden on the Autun."

Vonvalt shot Claver an irritated look. "With respect, Sir Otmar, if these people are practising Draedists, then they cannot, by definition, be law-abiding. I am sorry to say that Patria Claver is right – at least in part. They will have to renounce it. You have a list of those who practise?"

"I do not."

The logs smoked and crackled and spat. Ale and wine dripped and pattered through the cracks in the table planks.

"The charge is minor," Vonvalt said. "A small fine, a penny per head, if they recant. As their lord you may even shoulder it on their behalf. Do you have a shrine to any of the Imperial gods? Nema? Savare?"

"No." Sir Otmar all but spat out the word. It was becoming increasingly difficult to ignore the fact that Sir Otmar was a practising Draedist himself.

"The official religion of the Sovan Empire is the Nema Creed. Enshrined in scripture and in both the common and canon law. Come now, there are parallels. The Book of Lorn is essentially Draedism, no? It has the same parables, mandates the same holy days. You could adopt it without difficulty."

It was true, the Book of Lorn did bear remarkable parallels to Draedism. That was because the Book of Lorn *was* Draedism. The Sovan religion was remarkably flexible, and rather than replacing the many religious practices it encountered during the Reichskrieg, it simply subsumed them, like a wave engulfing an island. It was why the Nema Creed was simultaneously the most widely practised and least respected religion in the known world.

I looked over to Claver. The man's face was aghast at Vonvalt's easy equivocation. Of course, Vonvalt was no more a believer in the Nema Creed than Sir Otmar. Like the old baron, he had had the religion forced on him. But he went to temple, and he put himself through the motions like most of the Imperial aristocracy. Claver, on the other hand, was young enough to have known no other religion. A true believer. Such men had their uses, but more often than not their inflexibility made them dangerous.

"The Empire requires that you practise the teachings of the Nema Creed. The law allows for nothing else," Vonvalt said.

"If I refuse?"

Vonvalt drew himself up. "If you refuse you become a heretic. If you refuse to *me* you become an avowed heretic. But you won't do something as silly and wasteful as that."

"And what is the punishment for avowed heresy?" Sir Otmar asked, though he knew the answer.

"You will be burned." It was Claver who spoke. There was savage glee in his voice.

"No one will be burned," Vonvalt said irritably, "because no one is an avowed heretic. Yet."

I looked back and forth between Vonvalt and Sir Otmar. I had sympathy for Sir Otmar's position. He was right to say that Draedism was harmless, and right to disrespect the Nema Creed as worthless. Furthermore, he was an old man, being lectured and threatened with death. But the fact of the matter was, the Sovan Empire ruled the Tolsburg Marches. Their laws applied, and, actually, their laws were robust and fairly applied. Most everyone else got on with it, so why couldn't he?

Sir Otmar seemed to sag slightly.

"There is an old watchtower on Gabler's Mount, a few hours' ride north-east of here. The Draedists gather there to worship. You will find your witch there."

Vonvalt paused for a moment. He took a long draw of ale. Then he carefully set the tankard down.

"Thank you," he said, and stood. "We'll go there now, while there is an hour or two of daylight left."

if you enjoyed
THE MARTYR

look out for

ENGINES OF EMPIRE

Book One of
The Age of Uprising

by

R. S. Ford

From an unmissable voice in epic fantasy comes a sweeping tale of clashing guilds, magic-fueled machines, and revolution.

The nation of Torwyn is run on the power of industry, and industry is run by the Guilds. Chief among them are the Hawkspurs, whose responsibility it is to keep the gears of the empire turning. That's exactly why matriarch Rosomon Hawkspur sends each of her heirs to the far reaches of the nation.

Conall, the eldest son, is dispatched to the distant frontier to earn his stripes in the military. It is here that he faces a threat he could never have seen coming: the first rumblings of revolution.

Tyreta is a sorceress with the ability to channel the power of pyrestone, the magical resource that fuels the empire's machines.

She is sent to the mines to learn more about how pyrestone is harvested—but instead, she finds the dark horrors of industry that the empire would prefer to keep hidden.

The youngest, Fulren, is a talented artificer and finds himself acting as a guide to a mysterious foreign emissary. Soon after, he is framed for a crime he never committed. A crime that could start a war.

As the Hawkspurs grapple with the many threats that face the nation within and without, they must finally prove themselves worthy—or their empire will fall apart.

PROLOGUE

Courage. That ever-elusive virtue. Willet had once been told a man could never possess true courage without first knowing true fear. If that was so, he must be the bravest man in all Torwyn, as fear gnawed at him like a starving hound, cracking his bones and licking at the marrow.

He knew this was not courage. More likely it was madness, but then only the mad would have walked so readily into the Drift. It was a thousand miles of wasteland cut through the midst of an entire continent, leaving a scar from the Dolur Peaks in the north to the Ungulf Sea on the southern coast. A scar that would never heal. The remnant of an ancient war, and a stark reminder that sorcery was the unholiest of sins.

Willet glanced over his shoulder, squinting against the midday sun toward Fort Karvan as it loomed on the distant ridge like a grim sentinel. Had there ever been built a more forbidding bastion of stone and iron?

Five vast fortresses lined the border between Torwyn and the

Drift, each one garrisoned by a different Armiger Battalion, the last line of defence against the raiding tribes and twisted beasts of the wasteland. Fort Karvan was home to the grim and proud Mantid Battalion, and though Willet hated it with every fibre, he would have given anything to be safe within its walls right now. Instead he was traipsing through the blasted landscape, and the only things to protect him were a drab grey robe and his faith in the Great Wyrms. Well, perhaps not the only things.

"Pick up your feet, Legate Kinloth," Captain Jarrell hissed from the head of the patrol. "If you fall behind, you'll be left behind." The captain scowled from within the open visor of his mantis helm, greying beard reaching over the gorget of his armour.

Willet quickened his pace, sandals padding along the dusty ground. Captain Jarrell was a man whose bite was most definitely worse than his bark, and Willet wasn't sure whether he was more afraid of him or of the denizens of the Drift. The only person he'd ever known with sharper teeth was his own mother, though it was a close-run thing.

By the time he caught up, Willet was short of breath, but he felt some relief as he continued his trek within the sizeable shadow of Jarrell's lieutenant, Terrick. The big man was the only inhabitant of Fort Karvan who'd ever offered Willet so much as the time of day. He was quick to laugh and generous with his mirth, but not today. Terrick's eyes were fixed on the trail ahead, his expression stern as he gripped tight to sword and shield, wary of any danger.

At the head of their patrol, Lethann scouted the way. In contrast to Terrick she was the very definition of mirthless. She wore the tan leather garb of a Talon scout, travelling cloak rendering her almost invisible against the dusty landscape. A splintbow was strapped to her back, a clip of bolts on her hip alongside the long hunting knife. Every now and then she would kneel, searching for sign, following the trail like a hunting dog.

Three other troopers of the Mantid Battalion marched with them but, to his shame, Willet had no idea what they were called. In fairness, each of their faces was concealed beneath the visor of a mantis helm, but even so they were still part of his brood, and he their stalwart priest. Willet was charged with enforcing their faith in the Great Wyrms, and when would they need that more than now, out here in the deadly wilds? How was he to provide sacrament without even knowing their names? It reminded him once again of the impossibility of the task he'd been given.

Since his first day at Fort Karvan, Willet had been ignored and disrespected. The Draconate Ministry had sent him to instil faith in the fort's stout defenders, and Willet had gone about that role with all the zeal his position demanded. It soon became clear no one was going to take him seriously. Over the days and weeks his sermons had been met with indifference at best. At worst outright derision. The disrespect had worsened, rising to a tumult, until the occasion when he had drunk deeply from a waterskin only to find it had been filled with tepid piss when he wasn't looking.

Had Willet been posted at another fort in another part of the Drift, perhaps he would have been received with more enthusiasm. The Corvus at Ravenscrag or the Ursus Battalion at Fort Arbelus would have provided him a much warmer welcome. For the Mantid Battalion, it seemed faith in the Guilds of Torwyn far outweighed faith in the Ministry. But what had he truly expected? It was not the Draconate Ministry that fuelled the nation's commerce. It was not the legates who built artifice and supplied the military with its arms and armour. It was not Willet Kinloth who had brought about the greatest technological advancements in Torwyn's history.

His sudden despondency provoked a groundswell of guilt. As Saphenodon decreed, those who suffer the greatest hardship are due the highest reward. And who was Willet Kinloth to question the wisdom of the Draconate?

"That lookout can't be much farther ahead," Terrick grumbled, to himself as much as to anyone else. It was enough to shake Willet from his malaise, forcing him to concentrate on the job at hand.

They had first spied their quarry four days ago from the battlements of Fort Karvan. The figure had been distant and indistinct, and at first the lookouts had dismissed it as a wanderer, lost in the

Drift. When they spotted the lone figure again a second and third day there was only one conclusion—the fort was being watched, which could herald a raid from one of the many marauding bands that dogged the border of Torwyn.

Raiding parties had been harrying the forts along the Drift for centuries. Mostly they were small warbands grown so hungry and desperate they risked their lives to pillage Torwyn's abundant fields and forests. But some were vast armies, disparate tribes gathered together by a warlord powerful enough to threaten the might of the Armiger Battalions. No such armies had risen for over a decade, the last having been quelled with merciless violence by a united front of Guild, Armiger and Ministry. But it still paid to be cautious. If this scout was part of a larger force, it was imperative they be captured and questioned.

The ground sloped ever downward as they followed the trail, and the grim sight of Fort Karvan was soon lost beyond the ridge behind them. Willet stuck close to Terrick, but the hulking trooper provided less and less reassurance the deeper they ventured into the Drift.

Willet's hand toyed with the medallions about his neck, the five charms bringing him little comfort. The sapphire of Vermitrix imparted no peace, the jade of Saphenodon no keen insight. The jet pendant of Ravenothrax did not grant him solace in the face of imminent death, and neither did the solid steel of Ammenodus Rex give him the strength to face this battle. His hand finally caressed the red ruby pendant of Undometh. The Great Wyrm of Vengeance. That was the most useless of all—for who would avenge Willet if he was slain out here? Would Undometh himself come to take vengeance on behalf of a lowly legate? Not likely.

Lethann waved from up ahead. Her hand flashed in a sequence of swift signals before she gestured ahead into a steep valley. Willet had no idea how to decipher the silent message, but the rest of the patrol adopted a tight formation, Captain Jarrell leading his men with an added sense of urgency.

Their route funnelled into a narrow path, bare red rock rising on both sides as they descended into a shallow valley. Here lay the remnants of a civilisation that had died a thousand years before. Relics from the age of the Archmages, before their war and their magics had blasted the continent apart.

Willet stared at the broken and derelict buildings scattered about the valley floor. Alien architecture clawed its way from the earth, the tops of ancient spires lying alongside the weathered corpses of vast statues. He trod carefully in his sandals, as here and there lay broken and rusted weapons, evidence of the battle fought here centuries before. Cadaverous remnants of plate and mail lay half-reclaimed in the dirt, the remains of their wearers long since rotted to dust.

Up ahead, Lethann paused at the threshold of a ruined archway. It was the entrance to a dead temple, its remaining walls standing askew on the valley floor, blocking the way ahead. She knelt, and her hand traced the outline of something in the dust before she turned to Jarrell and nodded.

Terrick and the three other troopers moved up beside their captain as Willet hung back, listening to Jarrell's whispered orders. As one, the troopers spread out, Jarrell leading the way as they moved toward the arch. Lethann unstrapped her splintbow and checked the breech before slotting a clip of bolts into the stock, and the patrol entered the brooding archway.

Willet followed them across the threshold into what had once been the vast atrium of a temple. Jarrell and his men spread out, swords drawn, shields braced in front of them. Lethann lurked at the periphery, aiming her splintbow across the wide-open space. At first Willet didn't notice what had made them so skittish. Then his eyes fell on the lone figure perched on a broken altar at the opposite end of the temple.

She knelt as though in prayer. Her left hand rested on a sheathed greatsword almost as tall as she was, and the other covered her right eye. The left eye was closed as though she were deep in meditation. She wore no armour, but a tight-fitting leather jerkin and leggings covered her from neck to bare feet. Her arms were exposed, and Willet could make out faint traces of the tattoos that wheeled about her bare flesh.

"There's nowhere to run," Jarrell pronounced, voice echoing across the open ground of the temple. "Surrender to us, and we'll see you're treated fairly."

Willet doubted the truth of that, but he still hoped this would end without violence. This woman stood little chance against six opponents.

Slowly she opened her left eye, hand still pressed over the right, and regarded them without emotion. If she was intimidated by the odds against her, she didn't show it.

"You should turn back to your fort," she answered in a thick Maladoran accent. "And run."

Lethann released the safety catch on her splintbow, sighting across the open ground at the kneeling woman. With a sweep of his hand, Jarrell ordered his men to advance.

Terrick was the first to step forward, the brittle earth crunching beneath his boots. Two of the troopers approached from the flanks, closing on the woman's position. Lethann moved along the side of the atrium, barely visible in the shadow of the temple wall.

"I tried," the woman breathed, slowly lowering the hand that covered her eye.

Willet stifled a gasp as he saw a baleful red light where her right eye should have been. Stories of demons and foul sorceries flooded his memory, and his hand shook as it moved to grasp the pendants about his neck.

Terrick was unperturbed, closing on her position with his sword braced atop his shield. When he advanced to within five feet, the woman moved.

With shocking speed she wrenched the greatsword from its sheath and leapt to her feet, blade sweeping the air faster than the eye could comprehend. Terrick halted his advance before toppling back like a statue and landing on his back in the dirt.

Willet let out a gasp as blood pooled from Terrick's neck, turning the sand black. The other two troopers charged in, the first yelling in rage from within his mantis helm, sword raised high. The woman leapt from atop her rocky perch, sword sweeping that mantis helm from the trooper's shoulders. Her dance continued, bare feet sending clouds of dust into the air as she sidestepped a crushing sweep of the next trooper's blade before thrusting the tip of her greatsword into his stomach beneath the breastplate. Willet saw it sprout from his back in a crimson bloom before she wrenched it free, never slowing her momentum, swift as an eagle in flight.

The clacking report of bolts echoed across the temple as Lethann unleashed a salvo from her splintbow. Willet's lips mouthed a litany to Ammenodus Rex as the woman sprinted around the edge of the temple wall, closing the gap on Lethann. Every bolt missed, ricocheting off the decayed rocks as the woman ate up the distance between them at a frightening rate. Lethann fumbled at her belt for a second clip, desperate to reload, but the woman was on her. A brutal hack of the greatsword, and Lethann's body collapsed to the dirt.

"Ammenodus, grant me salvation that I might be delivered from your enemies," Willet whispered, pressing the steel pendant to his lips as he did so. He found himself backing away, sandals scuffing across the dusty floor, as the woman casually strode toward the centre of the atrium. Captain Jarrell and his one remaining trooper moved to flank her, crouching defensively behind their shields.

They circled as she stood impassively between them. For the first time Willet noted the white jewel glowing at the centre of her greatsword's cross-guard. It throbbed with sickly light, mimicking the pulsing red orb sunk within her right eye socket.

This truly was a demon of the most corrupt kind, and Willet's hand fumbled at the pendants about his neck, fingers closing around the one made of jet. "O great Ravenothrax," he mumbled. "The Unvanquished. Convey me to your lair that I might be spared the evil propagated by mine enemies."

In the centre of the atrium, the three fighters paid little heed to Willet's prayers. The last trooper's patience gave out, and with a grunt he darted to attack. Captain Jarrell bellowed at him to

"Hold!" but it was too late. The woman's greatsword seemed to move of its own accord, the white jewel flashing hungrily as the blade skewered the eye socket of the trooper's helmet.

Jarrell took the initiative as his last ally died, charging desperately, hacking at the woman before she ducked, spun, twisted in the air and kicked him full in the chest. Willet held his breath, all thought of prayer forgotten as he saw Jarrell lose his footing and fall on his back.

The woman leapt in the air, impossibly high, that greatsword lancing down to impale the centre of Jarrell's prone body, driving through his breastplate like a hammered nail.

It was only then that Willet's knees gave out. He collapsed to the dirt, feeling a tear roll from his eye. The pendants in his fist felt useless as the woman slowly stood and turned toward him.

"Vermitrix, Great Wyrm of Peace, bring me a painless end," he whispered as she drew closer, leaving her demon sword still skewered through Jarrell's chest. "And may Undometh grant me vengeance against this wicked foe."

She stood over him, hand covering that sinister red eye once more. The jewel that sat in the centre of the greatsword's crossguard had dulled to nothing but clear glass, but Willet could still feel its evil from across the atrium.

"Your dragon gods will not save you, little priest," the woman said. Her voice was calm and gentle, as though she were coaxing a child to sleep.

Willet tried to look at her face but couldn't. He tried to speak, but all that came out was a whimper, a mumbled cry for his mother. He could almost have laughed at the irony. Here he was at the end, and for all his pious observance he was crying for a woman who had made his life a misery with her spiteful and poisonous tongue.

"Your mother is not coming either," the woman said. "But the voice is quiet, for now. So you should run, little priest. Before it speaks again."

Somehow Willet rose to his feet, legs trembling like a newborn foal's. He took a tentative step away from the woman, who kept her hand clamped tight over her eye. The white jewel in her sword, still skewered through Jarrell's chest, shone with sudden malevolence. It was enough to set Willet to flight.

He ran, losing a sandal on the rough ground, ignoring the sudden pain in his foot. He would not stop until he was back at the gates of Fort Karvan. Would not slow no matter the ache in his legs nor lack of breath in his lungs. He could not stop. If he did, there would be nothing left for him but the Five Lairs. And he was not ready for them yet.

TYRETA

The journey from Wyke to the Anvil was over five hundred miles of undulating land. It would have taken longer than two weeks by wagon, with regular stops and changes of horse. Tyreta Hawkspur would complete the journey in less than three days.

From the viewing deck of the landship she could already see the rising minarets of the Anvil in the distance, growing ever larger as the open fields and rivers glided by. The vessel was elevated on rails, engines growling, the sound bellowing over the wind as it rushed into her face. It was an ingenious feat of engineering. The Hawkspur Guild had established a network of such lines across the length and breadth of Torwyn, on which the long trains of steel and iron snaked. Tyreta was heir to this legacy, one that had seen the Hawkspurs rise from simple couriers to one of the most powerful Guilds in the land. It should have made her proud. All she felt was bored.

"Try to look more enthused. Your uncle will have gone to a great deal of trouble to greet us. I'd rather you didn't look like you've just eaten a bag of lemons when we arrive."

There it was.

Tyreta's mother, Rosomon, stood at the rail beside her. A constant reminder of what Tyreta was to inherit. Of her responsibilities.

"Oh, there's a big smile on the inside, Mother," Tyreta replied.

She said it under her breath, but as usual Lady Rosomon's hearing was almost preternatural.

"Well, when we arrive, see if you can conjure one on your face."

Her mother moved away, off to prepare herself to greet the emperor. It wouldn't do for Rosomon Hawkspur to look anything less than resplendent when she was met by her brother, the great Sullivar Archwind.

As she left, Tyreta contorted her face into a twisted semblance of a smile. It was a pointless act of defiance but at least one she could get away with—Rosomon's hearing might have been keen as a bat's, but she certainly didn't have eyes in the back of her head. As her mother left the viewing deck, Tyreta saw she'd not been quite as discreet as she'd anticipated.

Her elder brother Conall was watching her from across the deck, wearing a mocking grin. He was tall, handsome, sharp-witted, impeccably dressed in his blue uniform—all the things an heir to the Hawkspur Guild should be. Conall never put a foot wrong, in contrast to Tyreta's constant missteps. He was the future of their line and a captain in the Talon, the military arm of the Guild. All her life she'd been trying to live up to his example and failing miserably. He was the last person she would want to catch her acting like an infant. Well, if her mother and brother thought her so feckless, maybe she'd demonstrate just how talented she was.

Ignoring her brother's smugness, she moved from the deck and made her way below into the cloying confines of the metal carriage. If the sound was deafening on the viewing deck, it was much worse inside. The roar of the engines resonated throughout the length of the landship, the walls of the carriages trembling with the power of it. Tyreta could feel the energy coursing through the vessel, propelling it along the rails. For everyone else on board, she guessed it was just about bearable. For Tyreta it was a drug to the senses.

They were almost at their destination now, the Anvil no more than a few miles away. Surely this was the time to indulge? If her mother chided her, what was the difference? What was the worst that could happen?

Tyreta made her way forward through the carriages. Past the soldiers of the Talon, busy polishing their hawk helms and ceremonial blades, past the servants and staff, to the engine room, the head of the snake.

The steel door was shut, a wheel at its centre keeping the engine room locked away from the rest of the landship. Tyreta turned the wheel, hearing the clamps unlock, and swung open the door. She was greeted by the growl of the engine and the hum of the power core within, feeling it nourishing her, energising her.

When she entered, the drivers immediately stood to one side and bowed their heads. There were some advantages to being heir to a Guild.

The men were masked to protect them from the smoke and dust of the engine, but Tyreta ignored the cloying atmosphere as she approached the power core. She could feel its hum, a sweet lamenting tune sung only to her. Reaching out, she placed a hand on it, sensing the energy emanating from the pyrestones within—those precious crystals pulsating with life.

This was her gift. As a webwainer she could control the pyrestones, imbuing them with life, and at her touch they responded, glowing hotter, agitated by her presence. The drivers gave one another a worried look, though neither dared offer a word of complaint.

"Is this the fastest this crate can go?" Tyreta shouted above the din.

One of the drivers pulled down his mask. "It is, my lady. Any faster and we risk—"

"I think we can do better," she replied.

She pressed her palm to the core and closed her eyes. A smile crossed her lips as she felt the pyrestones respond to her will, the core growing hotter against her palm. The engine whined in protest as the stones urged the pistons and hydraulics to greater effort.

"My lady, this is against regulations," shouted one of the drivers, but Tyreta ignored him.

The landship began to accelerate. She opened her eyes, seeing through the viewing port that the landscape was beginning to shoot past at an alarming rate. Still she did not yield. Tyreta wanted more.

She pressed the core further, communing with it, talking to it in a silent whisper, urging it to greater and greater effort. This was what her webwainer gift was for, and for too long she had been forbidden to use it. What did her mother know anyway? Lady Rosomon had never experienced the privilege of the webwainer talent. This was Tyreta's right—and besides, what harm could she do?

The landship bucked, the wheels momentarily sliding on the rails. She glanced across the cab, seeing abject terror on the drivers' faces. Before she could release her hand, there was a yell behind her.

"Tyreta!"

She snatched her hand from the core as though she'd been bitten, turning to see her mother's furious face in the doorway. The train immediately slowed, the rattling and bucking relenting as the landship slowed to its former speed.

Lady Rosomon didn't have to say a word. Tyreta removed herself from the engine room, moving back through the carriages and past the chaos she'd caused. Baggage had fallen from the securing rigs, garments and trinkets were scattered about the floor. The Talon soldiers were picking themselves up from where they lay, their arms and armour strewn all about.

Tyreta reached her cabin and closed the door, resting her back against it and breathing heavily. There might be a price to pay for this later. Lady Rosomon had never been a tolerant woman. Whatever that price was, Tyreta thought as a smile played across her lips, it had been worth it.

orbit

Follow us:

/orbitbooksUS

/orbitbooks

/orbitbooks

Join our mailing list
to receive alerts on our
latest releases and deals.

orbitbooks.net

Enter our monthly
giveaway for the chance
to win some epic prizes.

orbitloot.com